ZOMBIES:
THE RECENT DEAD

Other Books Edited by Paula Guran

Embraces
Best New Paranormal Romance
Best New Romantic Fantasy
Year's Best Dark Fantasy & Horror 2010

ZOMBIES:
THE RECENT DEAD

Edited by Paula Guran

PRIME BOOKS

ZOMBIES: THE RECENT DEAD

Prime Books
www.prime-books.com

For more information, contact Prime Books:
prime@prime-books.com

ISBN: 978-1-60701-234-4

For Linda and Laura—
who have kept me from becoming
one of the living dead myself lately,
and who I trust will know when
to hit me in the head with a baseball bat.

Table of Contents

Preshamble

I've never thought of them as zombies; I never called them zombies. When I made *Night of the Living Dead*, I called them flesh-eaters. To me, zombies were those boys in the Caribbean doing Bela Lugosi's wet work for him [in *White Zombie* (1932)]. I never thought of them as zombies. It was only when people started to write about them and said these are zombies that I thought maybe they are. All I did was make them the neighbors; take the voodoo and mysterioso out of it and make them the neighbors, and I don't know what happened after that. The neighbors are scary enough when they're not dead. Maybe that's what made it click.

—George Romero

As David J. Schow correctly points out in the following introduction, the modern zombie archetype is derived from cinematic rather than literary roots.* But we'd be remiss if we did not note the *other* zombie mythos—and the roots of an earlier round of zombie popularity.

Haitian Voudou is not an easily explained belief system. For our purposes we will only mention that the idea of the "voodoo zombie" arises from a mixture of African folklore—the *dodo* of Ghana, for example, shambles, hides in trees, and eats unwary travelers—and the Afro-Caribbean religion of Voudou. Essentially the "traditional" zombie is a dead or living person stripped of their own will and/or soul who is under the control of a sorcerer.

American and European understanding of Haitian Voudou is steeped in racism, racial and cultural stereotyping, and a complex socio-political history. For our purposes, let us state only a few overly simplistic facts:

---

* Yes, there is a grand literary and folkloric tradition of the undead. Some posit Mary Wollstonecraft Shelley's *Frankenstein*, Bram Stoker's *Dracula*, some of Edgar Allan Poe's stories and H.P. Lovecraft's tales, etc. are the roots of the modern zombie. Romero himself has often acknowledged the Richard Matheson novel *I Am Legend* as his direct influence. But just read David J. Schow's introduction, okay?

• A slave rebellion beginning in 1791 ended with the establishment of an independent Haiti in 1804, a black republic composed of former slaves.

• This successful rebellion by black slaves inspired American slaves, but it terrified white slave-owning Americans. As black, white, and multi-racial Haitian refugees arrived in American port cities, slave owners fears of a black revolution spreading to the to the United States were further exacerbated.

• After the American Civil War Haiti was still generally held in disdain by the U.S. In the nineteenth century, fiction (and "nonfiction" that was just as imaginative) concerning "voodoo" gained popularity. (Zombies— albeit not by that name—appeared in some of it. An 1882 novel, for example, by "Captain" Mayne Reid, *The Maroon: A Tale of Voodoo and Obeah*, features a voodoo practitioner who resurrects himself from the dead.)

• Fear that Germany might establish a military base in Haiti— dangerous close to the Panama Canal—and imperialist motivations led to the United States' occupation and rule of Haiti by means of a military government between 1915 and 1934.

• Although the occupation had some positive aspects (such as infrastructure improvement), Haiti was still ruled by white foreigners with profound racial prejudices and contempt for its inhabitants.

• Both fiction and nonfiction fed on and imbued the predominant racism and ethnocentricity concerning "voodoo" and its supposed sorcery and black magic.

• The American public, which had already developed an appetite for entertainment based on such fallacies and prejudices, was further misinformed by a hugely popular book: *The Magic Island*, a 1929 "travelogue" on Haiti by William Seabrook.

Seabrook—in dramatic style—reinforced current and earlier American and European thought about "voodoo" while introducing new innuendo and "facts" about zombiism. " . . . Dead Men Working in the Cane Fields," a twelve-page chapter in *The Magic Island* featured the first widely read English language account of Haiti's "walking dead" that referred to them specifically as "zombies":

> It seemed . . . that while the zombie came from the grave, it was neither a
> ghost, nor yet a person who had been raised like Lazarus from the dead.
> The zombie, they say, is a soulless human corpse, still dead, but taken from
> the grave and endowed by sorcery with a mechanical semblance of life—it
> is a dead body which is made to walk and act and move as if it were alive.
> [Seabrook, W.B. *The Magic Island.* New York: Harcourt, 1929.]

Kenneth Webb, inspired by Seabrook, wrote a dud of a Broadway play, *Zombie.* Opening on February 10, 1932 at the Biltmore Theatre in New York City, it lasted only twenty-one performances.

Now-forgotten fiction written for *Weird Tales* and other pulp magazines by writers like Hugh Cave, Seabury Quinn, Robert E. Howard, Jane Rice, Henry S. Whitehead, and others was at least partly inspired by Seabrook's book. But such stories were relatively rare, of no great literary merit, and made little impact on popular culture as a whole.

The first feature-length zombie movie, *White Zombie* (1932), and later films provided a far more lasting cultural influence.

Ultimately much of what Western culture *thinks* it understands about Voudou is still based on Seabrooks' depiction, films like *White Zombie* and *I Walked With a Zombie* (1943), and consequent pop-culture fantasies.

Voudou/voodoo also played a role in more recent Haitian politics during the oppressive regimes of Francois "Papa Doc" Duvalier (1957-1971) and his son Jean Claude "Baby Doc" Duvalier (1971-1986). Papa Doc exploited Haitian belief in Voudou, reputedly practiced sorcery, and even claimed to be a loa (spirit) himself.

Canadian anthropologist and ethnobotanist Wade Davis theorized in his 1985 book *The Serpent and the Rainbow* that tetrodotoxin (TTX) is used in Haiti to place people in a pharmacologically induced trance by use of "zombie powder" containing TTX. (A horror movie directed by Wes Craven, *The Serpent and the Rainbow,* very loosely based on the Wade's book, was released in 1988.) Wade's ideas have been both challenged and defended. Most recently, Terrence Hines ["Zombies and Tetrodotoxin," *Skeptical*

Inquirer, Volume 32, Issue 3: May/June 2008] refuted Wade's claims on a physiological basis writing that TTX does not produce the trance-like "zombie" state.

We still have fiction and based on the "traditional zombie"—some fine examples are contained in this volume. But the currently prevalent "Romero" archetype assumed the name "zombie," become disassociated from Voudou, and has taken on an undeath of its own.

The "new zombies" have little in common with the controlled, non-cannibalistic "old zombies." Traditional zombies were enslaved victims; contemporary zombies are uncontrollable flesh-eating monsters.

Not that the stories about either variety are *really* about zombies . . .

Paula Guran
June 2010

Introduction:
The Meat of the Matter

When the film opened, it was met by outraged attacks against its motives, its competence of execution, and the unabashed saturation of gore. It was dismissed by critics, flagellated by concerned commentators who viewed it as a prime example of the pornography of violence, and cited as a contributing factor to everything from crime in the streets to the corruption of the morals of American youth.

—George A. Romero, from the Introduction to
Night of the Living Dead by John Russo (1974)

Once upon a time, an independent Pittsburgh filmmaker and commercial cinematographer named George A. Romero conceived of a low-budget movie about corpses that reanimate and attempt to eat everyone still alive. Supposedly activated by a space virus (possibly the product of governmental experimentation gone horribly wrong), these walking dead laid siege to the living, killing and infecting them with the virus so they, in turn, became new walking, flesh-hungry zombies.

Romero originally wrote out his concept as a prose piece titled "Anubis" (after the Egyptian god of the dead) and presented it to his partners in his company, Image Ten. The topic of an independently financed movie had been tabled and hashed around by others in the company, becoming a sort of community casserole of gags, ideas, and set-pieces which one the partners, John Russo, eventually completed as a feature screenplay.

Miles of copy have been written about the Romero "zombie trilogy" in the years since 1968, when *Night of the Living Dead*—originally titled *Night of the Flesh Eaters*—first became notorious for depicting naked corpses on the hoof, greedily devouring, on camera, "stunt guts" (animal entrails standing in for human tripe). This poverty-budgeted black-and-white quickie offended nearly everybody and established what was then an important new foothold for graphic special effects in film: no movie since *Psycho* and *Peeping Tom* had demonstrated such an ability to grab its audience by the genitals and honk. It also kicked off Romero's career as a "real" moviemaker and, in due course, between other projects, he presented the world with the second and third acts of his zombie saga, *Dawn of the Dead* (1979) and *Day of the Dead* (1985).[1]

Where *Night* laid down the rules of game play, *Dawn* eagerly exploited them to become *the* exploding head movie of the seventies. By deftly setting its action in an iconographic (and characteristically characterless) suburban shopping mall, its theme of identity loss through the consumer ethic resonated heavily with another basic American fear: victimization by the masses, the Wad. Thus, *Dawn* became not only an ass-kicking zombie movie splashed out in lurid anatomical primary colors, but also an incisive observation on the burial of the individual by the herd.

"When there's no more room in Hell, the dead will walk the Earth," intones Ken Foree in *Dawn*. The grand joke of the film is that most of the zombies he must battle were "dead" even before they died—they were dead inside, finding solace only as a consumer mob. He points out why the zombies are magnetized tropistically back to the mall: "This place was important in their lives." It is a conclusion not only simple but elemental: Now they only exist to consume, the shifted priority being now they only exist to consume you. Instead of being swallowed up by a mercantile culture, they now do the swallowing. Being dead gives them a more unified purpose; they exist to do what viruses do—perpetuate themselves (even as that pointedly nonspecific virus from Out There that started it all did).

Dawn also depicted its zombies as a nascent new class, below peons, below derelicts (who were at least nominally human), below even the brain-dead (who at least didn't try to gobble you up). Yet it is clear that by the timeframe of the second movie, the walking dead are slowly learning basic tool use and retaining some functional memory.

---

1   For in-depth background, please consult *The Complete Night of the Living Dead Filmbook* by John Russo (Harmony Books, 1985), *The Zombies That Ate Pittsburgh: The Films of George A. Romero* by Paul R. Gagne (Dodd, Mead & Co., 1987), *Night of the Living Dead* by John Russo (novelization based on the screenplay by Romero and John Russo, Warner, 1974), *Dawn of the Dead* by George A. Romero and Susanna Sparrow (novelization based on the screenplay by Romero, St Martin's Press, 1978), and *Day of the Dead*, by George A. Romero and John Russo (novelization based on the screenplay by Romero, Simon & Schuster, 1988). Watching the movies might help you along, too.

Then came "Anubis," Phase Three.

Romero conceived a spectacular conclusion for his zombie trilogy, set in a terminal environment in which the living dead have actually become part of a New World Order. In *Night*, the phenomenon was freshly rooted; by *Dawn*, this dark new "race" was clearly giving humankind stiff competition, so to speak. By the final third of this triathlon, the seesaw has definitely tipped in favor of the virus and its constituents. As Paul R. Gagne summed it up in *The Zombies That Ate Pittsburgh*:

> In the third and final stage of "Anubis," Romero's original story on which the trilogy was based, an army of the living dead chases a solitary human figure over a hill . . . [this] treatment took the zombie "revolution" to the point where the living dead have basically replaced humanity and have gained enough of a rudimentary intelligence to be able to perform a few basic tasks. At the same time, an elite, dictatorial politburo of humans has found that the zombies can be *trained*, and are exploiting them as slaves. (Prior to the film being made, it was often facetiously referred to as *Zombies in the White House*.)[2] The hitch, of course, is that they have to be *fed* in order to be controlled (something alluded to in *Dawn*), and we all know what zombies like to eat.

Prior to filming, *Day of the Dead* hit a speed bump of surpassing mundanity—United Film Distributors, Romero's backers, refused to pony up the $6.5 million required for this biggest of the filmed trio unless an "R" rating could be guaranteed. Since *Dawn* had been a success arguably because of its lack of a rating rather than in spite of one, *Day* had to hew to a similar graphic, gory mark *just for starters*.

"For me, the Grand Guignol is part of these films, part of their character," Romero remarked to *Fangoria Magazine* in 1985. Accordingly, *Day of the Dead* was scaled down to accommodate a $3.5 million budget, and as a result was not quite the vast final curtain Romero had hoped for. On its own terms, however, it is quite stark, bleak, and depressing in its chronicle of a tiny band of surviving humans fighting legions of zombies (as well as each other) within

---

2   The White House / *Living Dead* connection was explicated by Robert Bloch in one of the last short stories written before his death, "Maternal Instinct," which depicts a President who proposes Nazi-like mass cremations to control the exponentially swelling numbers of unruly "necros," while revealing himself to be a much better class of zombie—one killed with a fast-acting poison in order to reanimate with nearly all of his mental faculties intact, and thus remain in power in a world full of intellectually-dead cannibal corpses.

the confines of an underground missile facility. The film successfully conveys the impression that these characters are perhaps the only "real" humans left *in the whole world* . . . and for that reason alone it remains essential viewing for the zombie enthusiast.

Originally, Romero's zombies were the product of white pancake and dark eye shadow, deriving from such cinematic precedents as the ghosts in the black-and-white cult classic *Carnival of Souls* (1962) and the titular walking corpses in Hammer Films' *Plague of the Zombies* (1966), in which the dead are resurrected as slave workers for a tin mine via more time-honored Voudou methods, hence "zombis." Once the zombie archetype had been revitalized by *Night of the Living Dead*, it crashed face-first into the prosthetic innovations of *Dawn of the Dead* . . . and a new zombie mythology had grabbed hold of popular consciousness. Horror writers new and old were taken with this retrofit of the traditional—the first "new" monster since that nice Norman Bates proved that even the boy-next-door could kill you without preamble. Romero's zombies are both a logical extension of Norman and a trump on him, upping his ante.

They are also one of the first monster archetypes to spring from cinematic rather than literary roots, along with the giant Japanese city-stompers and the *Creature from the Black Lagoon*. Living dinosaurs had been a staple of literary horror since Arthur Conan Doyle's *The Lost World* (and later became just as fundamental to the science fiction juveniles of the 1950s); *King Kong* was just another dinosaur in spirit, and anyway, Bela Lugosi in *White Zombie* had beat Kong into the movie houses by one year.

As Hugh Lamb pointed out:

> The zombie . . . embodies aspects of most of the stock horror types—the use of magic and witchcraft, the dead revived (*Dracula*), the lurching monster (*Frankenstein*), and mastery over the soul that goes even beyond death. Yet for all this, the zombie has no literary roots whatsoever . . . it lacks any basic work of fiction to draw from. Voodoo zombie tales are rare. One fairly successful story is "Ballet Negre" (1965) by Charles Birkin, in which a troupe of Haitian dancers turn out to be zombies.

Romero's science-fictional rationale for the revivification of corpses—never meant to bear intensive scrutiny, but merely provided as a neat one-liner to kick off the entire phenomenon—has its antecedent in a zombie tale written by Richard Matheson in 1955, "Dance of the Dead," in which a biowar germ takes the blame for making stiffs jump up and jitterbug. One of the most unusual zombies in all of literature is found in Gordon Honeycombe's 1969 novel *Neither the Sea Nor the Sand*, in which love is the motivational power that keeps the dead moving (the film version followed in 1972). To travel even further back along the timeline, there's Tiffany Thayer's *Dr. Arnoldi*, a 1934 novel in which death just plain stops; nobody dies anymore for any reason, and the world begins to choke on the living. It includes one scene where a condemned man is electrocuted numerous times before his executioners give up and shove him into a giant meat grinder . . . and when the burger plops out, it's still squirming around![3]

But it was the "Romero zombies"—scoffed at by purists as more properly ghouls or ghosts or cannibals or some weird potpourri of all three—that captivated idle young minds aplenty, and the influence on writers of Romero's zombie triptych was seen in its most concentrated form in the late 1980s to early 90s. In the U.S., Bantam Books issued *Book of the Dead*, an anthology of original zombie stories edited by John Skipp and Craig Spector in 1989. Its sequel, *Still Dead*, was published in 1991. *The Mammoth Book of Zombies*, edited by Stephen Jones, followed in 1993. Byron Preiss and John Betancourt's *The Ultimate Zombie* (Byron Priess Visual Publications) was also published that year. Clearly, everyone from Stephen King to Clive Barker to Anne Rice had something to say about the walking dead, and when they said it, they influenced other writers. This zombie "virus," it was clear, could infect in more ways than one.

"Zombie fiction" had become a subgenre.

So, how does one introduce the topic of social-archetype walking cadavers in the midst of the biggest carnevale ever? Ira Beaudine's best buddy summed it up one way in *Midnight Graffiti #2* (Fall 1988):

According to Romero, twilight brought the virus Earthward, and afore decent folks coulds switch from wrestlin to news, dead people wa sup and walkin almost as good as their survivin relatives. Problem was, what they call "peaceful co-existance" was out from the git. Y'see, we liked shootin 'em almost as much as they liked eatin us. Ira Beaudine said it best: "Why, hell, what you got here is your ee-volution inaction. These dead peckerwoods is like new, improved human beans. They're sposta replace us, see? 'Cos this ole world just ain't fit for old puds like you 'n me no more."

---

3   Bloch in fact cites Dr. Arnoldi in the text of "Maternal Instinct."

Now, personally, I think the only way Ira would ever git stiff was by liquorin up. Bu the fact was, dead folks was marchin and eatin and marchin some more, and pretty soon they began to outnumber the rest of us. So just incase we hafta wave bye-bye altogether, somebody should set down a chronicle . . . .in case some 'o them space aliens land and want to find out what the fuck transpired here, pardon my Frog.

Or, throw caution to the winds, as Karl Edward Wagner did, when he cued the entire apocalypse this way: "It seems that the world has been overrun by flesh-eating zombies, see—and then . . . "

Better (Dead) Homes and (Dead) Gardens

George Romero pooh-poohs the popular notion that his Living Dead films hew to a grandly incisive, sardonic, and preplanned evisceration of American cultural mores. He is not responsible for much of the import read into his work by eager fans. One critical specification overlooked by rabid *Dawn of the Dead* acolytes—whose first exposure to the Zombie Apocalypse probably came on videotape or laserdisc—is the sheer impact this material had when it was new. If you weren't there, you don't have any idea.

In a lot of ways, my own zombie fiction began when *Dawn of the Dead* hit the Holly Cinema on Hollywood Boulevard. Don't look for the theatre today because you won't find it; not even the address, 6523 Hollywood Boulevard, technically exists in the wake of retrofitting the Walk of the Stars and the ravagement brought to the real estate by the Hollywood-sized folly of MetroRail. There's a shoe store there now, in the space.

I recently spoke to an out-of-town guest who had been warned not to go near the Boulevard after dark; to me, a ridiculous and cowardly notion, the kind upon which fearsome urban paranoia is built. Before *Dawn of the Dead* struck Hollywood, I was living in a two-bedroom apartment on Normandie Avenue, south of Santa Monica Boulevard—not a neighborhood wimps would bid you to explore, even today. It's different when you live in the center of a "bad neighborhood," so-called by people who never go there.

I missed *Night of the Living Dead* in its original release; nearly all of my contemporaries did, catching up with it in second-run houses, cult or grind house theatres, or the deep-South "werewolf circuit" of drive-ins (then they lied about when they'd first seen it, in a kind of endless slapjack of geek credibility). *Night*'s underground popularity far exceeded its visibility in the days before the term "independent film" had become comfortably co-opted. The first time I saw *Night* was at a midnight show in Chicago, across the street from the Biograph Theatre, site of John Dillinger's assassination (the Biograph was then hosting weekly conclaves of *Rocky Horror Picture Show* fanatics). The print of *Night* was a grainy, abused 16-millimeter dupe, which only added to the documentary look and surreal experience.

But for *Dawn*, I was there on the first day. The Holly was then owned by a chain called SRO Theatres, which also owned the Paramount (refurbished in recent years into the Disney-centric El Capitan, its original name). In 1979, you could still find movie theatres on Hollywood Boulevard; from west to east: The Chinese, the Hollywood, the Vogue, the Egyptian, the Pussycat, the Holly, the Fox, the Pacific, the Vine, the Pix, and the World. Usually, new or premium features started on the west end, and worked their way east through second runs and bargain double bills. It was possible to work your way theatre-to-theatre and watch movies for more than twenty-four hours straight with no repeats, which our crew did on more than one occasion. It was also possible to do this even though most of us were normally dead-ass broke, because virtually everyone worked as an usher or assistant manager at one or another of the cinemas, and favors were exchanged often and eagerly.

My Los Angeles flop was with a gang of budding graphic artists who had holed up in a threadbare one-bedroom apartment on Harold Way, one door north of the house where Bela Lugosi died. (The apartment house is still there in 2010, and looks more threateningly downscale than ever; we were in #7.) All of these guys and gals held jobs at Boulevard theatres, most for SRO (even Frank Darabont worked as an usher and ticket-taker at the Paramount, and had to wear one of those poop-brown jackets)—Ramon Mahan, Grant Christian, Peggy Sniderman, Alex Kent, Michael Takamoto, Marcus Nickerson. At any given time there were no fewer than five people living at what we called the Harold Way Station, not counting sofa and floor sleepovers—on average, two extra people per night—plus girlfriend cameo appearances. I, an out-of-towner, generally slept directly beneath a long table fashioned from a door scavenged from the Paramount. There was a single rotary phone and chuddering refrigerator that got murdered one night when one of our roomies sought to hack away accumulated ice with a meat cleaver and hit the Freon line. The fridge actually screamed as it died . . . and for the next six weeks, we hiked to the 7-Eleven whenever we wanted a cold beverage. To do this entailed a sortie around the backside of a Jaguar dealership on

Hollywood Boulevard that butted up on the freeway. It was a good idea to venture forth in groups, because Morlocks waited back there.

We watched every movie playing at every theatre on the Boulevard even though we were broke most of the time. Assorted under-the-table deals with the ushers at competing theatres meant perpetual free admission. This was in addition to the free flow of ticket scams and back-door discounts.

The furniture at Harold Way didn't last long, either, the eighth-hand coffee table and sofa getting quickly destroyed by impromptu "wrestling practice" in the living room. The stereo components were kept imprisoned in a padlocked closet, and the carpeting had so much stuff spilled on it that we thought to file claims with the *Guinness Book*. One night, two guys climbed through the bedroom window to burglarize the joint. Boy, were they surprised when the light clicked on. Six of us braced them with ball bats, pipes, buck knives, and bare knucks . . . all in our underwear or in the buff. They practically shit themselves getting out the window, and we were laughing so hard we wound up not chasing them.

About now, you are probably wondering what all this seedy autobiography has to do with *Dawn of the Dead*, so I'll spare you the story of the bottle rockets, the two fifths of scotch, the freeway off ramp, and the police cars.

Dawn of the Dead, bearing all the stigma of an unrated movie, landed at the Holly Cinema and played there for weeks. Our practice, once we had exhausted all auxiliary movie-going activities on the Boulevard, was to safe-house it at the Holly, since one of our own, Ramon Mahan, was then the manager. Hence, when there were no more movies to watch, we watched *Dawn of the Dead* again and again and again. And we witnessed the singular phenomenon of audiences literally staggering out of the theatre, glassy-eyed, disoriented, stunned, not much different from zombies on the lurch, looking like they'd been whacked in the head with one of those rubber things you use to separate your groceries on the supermarket conveyor.

We also noticed the audiences got *bigger* the longer the movie played. Word of mouth was getting out. Now, for us, seeing *Dawn of the Dead* twenty or thirty times on the Holly screen would seem to be a saturation point, yes? We had no idea. There was more submersion yet to come.

During *Dawn*'s run at the Holly, our Harold Way crew began to break up, courtesy of Michael Takamoto scoring an entry-level job in animation at Hanna-Barbera (Mike's dad, Iwo Takamoto, was VP of the studio at the time). Mike vetted several others into newbie positions, but remember that nearly all of these guys were artists, and they rose quickly through the company ranks. They weren't washing cels for long. Suddenly, unexpectedly, and for the first time ever, they were making real money.

Inevitably, people started getting their own apartments, with bedrooms all to themselves, an unprecedented notion for us at the time, and it came to pass that the Harold Way contingent dwindled to a skeleton crew. Further new digs were procured and Harold Way had to be vacated. Due to the exigencies of leases, firsts-and-lasts, and delays, there was a period during which several of us would be technically homeless for a few days.

Unless we stayed in the basement at the Holly Cinema. With the rats and the substantial roach population.

Moreover, available monies were sunk in apartment deposits, rendering our already-Spartan food budget nil. For three days, we subsisted on all-you-can eat popcorn from the snack bar, leftover hot dogs, and all the fountain Coke we could stomach. Candy bars were off-limits, as these were inventoried, same as the soft drink cups and popcorn containers. So, providing our own cups, scarfing surplus popcorn, we eagerly awaited the close of business each evening to divide up the unpurchased snack bar hot dogs, if any. In keeping with the zombie theme that had overrun our lives, these refugee wieners—if any —had been doing the "rotisserie roll" for hours, and by the end of the day they had decomposed into a sort of greenish hue, a color that doesn't exist in nature and one which you can only see today if you watch an extremely faded trailer for the drive-in snackbar goodies of yesteryear. They also had next to no structural integrity whatsoever; if you picked one up by the end, it would fall apart. Thus we had to procure a loaf of 35¢ Wonder Bread to hold the dogs together long enough for consumption, since, yes, the buns were inventoried too, and off-limits.

And *Dawn* played on. Five-to-seven shows per day; extra screenings on weekends. And somewhere in mid-process, that movie ingrained itself indelibly on our malleable widdle brains. Holed up in the Holly, rarely seeing daylight, we absorbed each beat of the Goblin score and every line of dialogue until we felt we were actually there, stranded inside the drama along with Peter and Roger and Steven and Fran. Hearing that music or seeing any footage from *Dawn* has a visceral effect to this day, and I'm thankful it's not the reaction caused by the living dead hotdogs.

In 1990, *Night of the Living Dead* was subjected to a revisionist remake directed by Romero protégé Tom Savini, the makeup artist responsible for the ground-

breaking splatter effects of *Dawn of the Dead*. The re-make did not spark a
zombie renaissance, but it did prove that some things can rise from the grave
no matter how many times they are pronounced dead. In 1998, John Russo's
thirty-years-after spin on Romero's original footage (with "added scenes" shot
contemporaneously) revisionist version was released to VHS and DVD as an
"anniversary" edition that cheesed off a lot of true believers. In 2001, Beacon
Films announced a remake, of all things, of *Dawn of the Dead*.

And George Romero himself has been endlessly pressured to return to the
realm of his own *Living Dead*, despite dozens of rip-offs and retrofits of his
ground breaking work. The world, it seems, can't get enough of zombies—the
Romero kind—and the durability of this new icon was further demonstrated
when documentarians Jason Bareford, William Schiff, and Christian Stavrakis
focused their efforts on *Dawn2K*, a reminiscence of *Dawn of the Dead* by all its
principals and many interested observers.

The plain fact is that the aptly-christened "Romero zombies" have infiltrated
the culture to the extent that even people who have never experienced the
movies "know" what zombies are in short form: *They're dead, they walk, they
want to eat you, and they usually outnumber you.* The codicil, courtesy of Dan
O'Bannon's *Return of the Living Dead* (1985), is that they want to eat your
brains, in particular, and this specification has percolated down through
subsequent zombie movies from all cultures in all parts of the world. In sum,
people know zombies, now, the way everybody knew what a vampire was,
thirty years ago.

Zombie fiction, like it or not, for better or worse, has arrived . . . and this
probably isn't the last you'll see of it.

BONE appetit!

Addendum 2010: Not only was *Dawn of the Dead* subjected to a revisionist
reboot (in 2004), but *Day of the Dead* was, too (in 2008) and *28 Days Later*
begat *28 Weeks Later*. George Romero self-resurrected and begat a second
zombie trilogy: *Land of the Dead* (2005), *Diary of the Dead* (2007), and
Survival of the Dead (2009).

—*David J. Schow*
New Year's, 2003/Revised May 2010

[Originally from the *Introduction* and *Afterword* of *Zombie Jam*,
Subterranean Press, 2003]

Deaditorial Note:
The World Has Been Overrun By Flesh-Eating Zombies, See——And Then . . .

Mr. Schow was, in fact, not only correct about not seeing the last of zombie fiction, 2003 turned out to be the dawn of yet another era in the popularity of the walking dead.

Despite the early 1990s boomlet in short zombie fiction, the icon's popularity was confined primarily to diehard horror fans. By the mid-1990s horror itself, as a commercially viable marketing category, dwindled. New York publishers produced less horror while specialized presses published for what was evidently a niche market.

From 1993 through 2003, zombies still lurked in horror literature—popping up in the occasional short story or novella here and there. Zombies also shambled into a few novels. Outside of Eric Powell's droll *The Goon* series (2003) and *The Walking Dead* written by Robert Kirkman with art by (originally) Tony Moore (series began in 2003) zombies weren't notably present in comics. James Lowder teamed up with Eden Studios and their zombie-related role-playing game to produce three anthologies: *The Book of All Flesh* (2001), *The Book of More Flesh* (2002), and *The Book of Final Flesh* (2003).

Gaming, in fact, provided the prime conduit for zombies to continue eating our brains during those earliest years of the twenty-first century. The immensely popular video game *Resident Evil* debuted in 1996 and, by 2003, had been followed by three sequels, a remake of the original and a prequel. S.D. Perry wrote novelizations of the games and the first of the *Resident Evil* movies was released in 2002.

Further film success came in 2002 with Danny Boyle's Romero-inspired film *28 Days Later* (2002).

But the true resurgence of zombie literature began in September 2003 when *The Zombie Survival Guide: Complete Protection from the Living*

Dead, authored by Max Brooks, was released by Crown. With his parody of a survival guide, Brooks defined, detailed, documented "historical" encounters, and supplied handy tips and tactics for humans to survive— evidently inevitable—attacks by hordes of the walking dead. Zombies had escaped the confines of the horror genre and invaded the mainstream.

As Stefan Dziemianowicz summed it up in a *Publishers Weekly* article of July 13, 2009:

> Three years and hundreds of thousands of units [of *The Zombie Survival Guide*] sold later, Brooks's publisher . . . released *World War Z*, a no-bones- about-it serious horror novel chronicling a global zombie pandemic enabled by contemporary social and political intrigues . . . The success of Brooks's books awakened the mainstream reading audience to the relevance of zombies. The same year that World War Z hit the bestseller list, David Wellington saw *Monster Island*, a zombie holocaust tale, published under the Thunder's Mouth imprint. The book had begun as a novel serialized for free at the author's blog site, and its instant notoriety netted him a print contract for the trilogy that ultimately came to comprise *Monster Nation* (2006) and *Monster Planet* (2007). By the time Scribner published Stephen King's *Cell* (2006), which tells of all but a fraction of the world's populace being turned into rampaging zombies by a sinisterly manipulated cellphone pulse, the zombie was well established in publishing culture . . .
>
> Then came Quirk Books' *Pride and Prejudice and Zombies*, a tongue- in-(festering)-cheek splice of Jane Austen gentility with zombie cannibal shenanigans coauthored by Seth Grahame-Smith. With his outrageous riffing on Jane Austen's painfully proper prose . . . [which] cut the velvet ropes keeping zombie genre fiction away from the literary classics . . . With more than 600,000 copies in print, *Pride and Prejudice and Zombies* is a bestseller that has already inspired its share of genre splices and revisionist zombie literature.
>
> Between *The Zombie Survival Guide* and the Austin/zombie mash-up (released in March 2009) the zombie icon has again risen from its (shallow) grave, infected the world, and attained unparalleled popularity.

The Dead Walk Among Us . . . Again!

During the first decade of the twenty-first century, zombie fiction became a force to contend with in both novel form and short stories. In the short form the walking dead started filling anthologies. The two most notable: John Joseph Adams selected some of the best zom-themed short fiction published 1975-2008 with *The Living Dead* (Night Shade Books, 2008). Stephen Jones complemented his 1993 *The Mammoth Book of Zombies* (Carroll & Graf) with *The Dead that Walk* (Ulysses Press, 2009).

The hefty and stylish *Zombies: Encounters With the Hungry Dead*, edited by John Skipp (Black Dog & Leventhal Publishers, 2009) was another notable compilation. Skipp had earlier found specialty press publication for *Mondo Zombie* (Cemetery Dance, 2006), an anthology that had originally been planned as a third *Book of the Dead* in 1991.

Minuscule press zombie anthologies were numerous and the quality of most was, at best, mediocre. Three exceptions were Kim Paffenroth's *The World is Dead* and *History Is Dead*, as well as *The Best of All Flesh*, a compilation of stories from the three earlier *Books of Flesh* by editor James Lowder. All three were somewhat uneven, but still stood above their competition.

Bentley Little published an "old school zombie" horror novel featuring mindless, walking dead zombies: *The Walking* (2002). Tim Waggoner and Brain Keene overcame a primary problem of developing novels based on zombies—mindless, empty husks, with no personality make for poor protagonists or antagonists—and introduced intelligent zombies in their novels.

In Keene's post-apocalyptic world of *The Rising* [Delirium, limited editions: 2003; Leisure, mass market paperback (2004)] and its sequel, *City of the Dead*, a government-experiment-run-amok results in an opening to The Void which allows demons through who then possess the dead. The resultant zombies are swift, crafty, and prone to cracking morbid jokes.

Nekropolis, which was underpublished in 2004 (by Five Star, which caters to libraries with no trade distribution) was, to quote its author "as much a mystery as . . . fantasy and horror (with a little science fiction, and romance sprinkled in here and there)." In the underground city of Nekropolis, the supernatural inhabitants include zombies. Most are enslaved and have no free will, but the hard-boiled, wisecracking private eye protagonist is an unmastered zombie. (A new and expanded version of *Nekropolis* was published in 2009 in the UK and Australia, and 2010 in the U.S, by angry Robot Books.)

The "modern zombie" literary icon was inspired by film, and film continued to feed the growing frenzy. Romero's *Dawn of the Dead* was remade and released in 2004 as was the horror comedy *Shaun of the Dead*—both an *hommage* and a parody. Romero himself returned with the start of a new zombie trilogy, *Land of the Dead* in 2005 followed by *Diary of the Dead* (2007). The *Resident Evil* franchise was revived in 2007 as was *28 Days Later*, the sequel to Boyle's 2002 hit. Romero's latest zombie movie, *Survival of the Dead*, is, at this writing, playing in select cities.

Meanwhile, literary zombiemania—both good and bad—continued to grow, proliferating in fiction of all lengths, not only for adults but for teens and younger readers, cross-pollinating with romance, science fiction, mystery, steampunk, and other fantasy subgenres.

By the summer of 2010, zombies—in any and all media—were so prodigious that merely keeping track would be a full time occupation.

So, here we (and zombies) are now, more than a decade into the twenty-first century. As for zombie *literature*:

The "traditional zombie" is still with us—as social commentary; as a metaphor for individual emptiness; in some new configuration or with some innovative twist; or simply an aspect of the eternal story of good vs. evil.

We have Romero zombies—in general, a condemnation of late-twentieth-century values (or lack thereof) that project a bleak apocalyptic ending (probably deserved) for humankind—and post-Romero zombies that still focus on humanity's flaws, but offer hope of our survival/redemption, usually through some embodiment of community.

There are also variations on both Romero and post-Romero zombies: zombies that are not mindless or do not shamble or have feelings or vary in some way from the "codified" zombie—but remain acceptable to modern zombie purists.

There are zombie stories that use the idea of the archetype in original ways that may cause aforementioned zombie purists to foam at the mouth and vent their displeasure that they are not "real zombies"—if they take the time away from their interactive games to read.

As much as I'd like to forget them, we also have zombie stories and books (print and electronic) that are mostly meaningless exercises in gross-out value. You won't find examples here.

We also have zombies that offer comic relief—both tribute and parody to the trope—while still addressing societal concerns. As Simon Pegg (who co-wrote and starred in *Shaun of the Dead*, 2004) said in an interview: "The great thing about zombies is that they're ever-changing—because they're basically us. They can be employed to represent any facet of our development." [Russell, Mike. "Interview with *Shaun of the Dead*'s Simon Pegg and Edgar Wright," *CulturePulp: Writings and Comics by Mike Russell*. September 23, 2004.]

And combinations and variations and evolutions of all of the above. And more.

They Keep Coming Back . . . and Coming Back . . .

By now it's pretty clear that the modern zombie mythos has a nasty habit of auto-cannibalizing itself to puke up new generations of dead, deader, and deadest—with the British being the first to port the phenomenon to commercial television in *Dead Set* (2008), which seems eerily like what might have transpired if Romero's *Dawn* quartet had never left the TV station seen in the beginning of the film. Nothing succeeds like excess—where the concept of a "zombie TV show" was played for laughs in the original *Book of the Dead* (in Brian Hodge's "Dead Giveaway"), now it has become assimilated. Some say zombies are the new vampires. And the new zombies? No doubt there: To quote the original *Dawn* again, they're us. Can a Zombie Channel be far behind?

Like the hardiest viruses, the zombie subgenre has metastasized from trickle to torrent, and like the best phenomena, it has earned its right to historical documentation, starting with the fiction presented in this volume. All the stories included were published in this first decade (2000 through 2009) of what has become (so far) the Zombie Century—some of it influential, some of it overlooked, all of it worthy of your perusal and debate.

Even the dead crave entertainment.

—*Paula Guran*
(with further thanks to David J. Schow)
June 2010

Addendum: Following the author's biography at the end of each story, you'll find comments by the editor. Ignore them, enjoy them, hate them, debate them—just don't peruse them *before* you read the story!

Twisted

Kevin Veale

We were driving past Kalamazoo towards the edge of the desert when the withdrawal began to set in. I remember feeling light-headed for moments before phantom weevils scuttled down my spine. Caustic burblings oozed through my gut. Dogwood, my Minister for Lateral Problem-Solving, looked askance at me under his dust-encrusted ski-goggles.

"We can't stop again, man."

He left it at that, aware I understood the situation. The Minister had insisted on liberating a convertible and driving it with the top down across broken plains that required goggles to shield the eyes. Our holy mission necessitated a certain vibe, he'd argued, and felt this justified grit in the teeth and a car with a dying battery. Besides, it was all right for him: I'd been seeking gastro-intestinal regularity by varying the elements of my drug intake, producing gut-locked stony constipation on one side, and fluid Lovecraftian bowel-horrors on the other.

Our rationing was forcing me towards Accidental Soiling, and the Minister jouncing us at high speed across the dusty hills towards the yellowing bowl of Lake Michigan didn't help.

Dogwood elbowed me then—distracting me from a passing cramp—and pointed out to a ditch ahead of us. It was surrounded by clouds of flies over corpses, like the foaming head on some sun-warmed simmering flesh-beer.

Not a good place to stop, no.

Dogwood pawed one-handed at one of our satchels of Supplies as we crested a cracked rise above the sprawling incline of the desert bowl: "I need amyl nitrite. Popper. Just the one. Keep me focused."

"Our resolve must be strong, Minister," I said, thrusting forward a heroic chin.

"Screw resolve! Gimme!"

I understood the battery situation, and the Minister understood the drug situation. Then again, he'd also insisted on calling me "Horse," since he'd learned we intended to cross the desert, and did nothing but giggle when I demanded explanations. I pulled the bag out of his reach as our car picked up speed and caught sight of movement behind us in the wing-mirror. A zombie clambered out of the flesh-beer like a whale breaching in a thick sea of meat and tried to follow us down the slope. I winced and shook myself—truly, this was a bad scene. I then settled back into my seat just in time for the Minister to guide our descent into an old drier, half-sunk in crusted Michigan mud, the impact smashing us briefly airborne.

"You did that on purpose!" I cried stridently.

"An amyl would help me drive."

I remember bickering as the corpse behind us fell away in the dust, following our movement since it couldn't smell us. Dogwood eventually had his amyl, I made vile assertions about his mother, and peace was restored.

I remember that our mission happened the same year as the infamous Presidential debate between Ozzy Osbourne and Tommy Lee, or would have done if either of them had turned up. Perhaps nobody told them, but it had been a great party nonetheless.

Our essential problem was that our home town of Bad Axe was not a key pharmacopeia to greater Michigan, and as such the supply of drugs available to we survivors was becoming thin. The Minister and I had realized this and begun to spread the word.

It had been a clear morning when we saw Smiley Fletcher staggering down the street, haggard and horrified through the pains of withdrawal. When some of the ubiquitous zombies turned toward him in one movement and began to close in, it had all became clear. The Minister crash-tackled Smiley to the ground and held him down while I squirted wood glue—nice and toxic—into a supermarket fruit-bag, hands thick and nerveless with my own drug song. I handed it to Dogwood, who covered Smiley's face and roared, "You *reckless bastard!*" as Smiley sucked down the fumes and went limp.

I remember waving vaguely—I was deep in a Green Shrieker spiral, beatific, wise and spiritually well-hung as Christ on a stump—and declaiming, "Forgive him, Minister, he knows not what he do. Does . . . ? Whatever."

The Minister had ignored me, but we each took an end of the man and hustled him away from the zombies activated by his sobriety. I took the time to waft glue fumes around to further mask the scent, and we got him to safety. There is, however, a central problem with the Emergency Glue, or Emergency Drugs as a wider class: it is very difficult to interrogate someone high as a kite.

So we'd given up.

Indeed. Ours is an interesting society.

In the days that followed, the scope of the problem became clear. Drugs, however communal, were running low in Bad Axe. All but the cheapest, nastiest grunge was gone, and it is a truly sad state of affairs when a liberated society dependant on illicit pharmaceuticals for its very survival *isn't having fun*. So the Minister and I had scrounged up our supplies along with what anyone else could be persuaded to part with, taking it upon ourselves to quest forth for the common good.

Dogwood was along as Minister for Lateral Problem-Solving due to his greater experience in escaping lock-up situations. The man kept a spare Zippo in one boot for the express purpose of starting distraction fires, and his inclusion seemed a good idea at the time. I, sterner of vision and focus, was the noble leader.

As we careened down Lake Michigan I remember noting that the Minister's horrible hat was still on his greasy head, despite my demands he throw it away. A graying and cracked nacho cowboy hat, serrated at the rim with flaked chips, which the Minister had sprayed with lacquer weeks before as a preservative. The bell of the hat, originally filled with plastic petrochemical cheese, was crusted with dead flies and cigarette ash beneath layers of road dust.

It was an undying affront to gods and men alike. How could he possibly not know the hideousness of the lamentable hat? Perhaps it had been only to spite me, and had I not mentioned my Hate for the thing it would have slipped the Minister's mind and been forgotten. And yet here we were.

I refused to fill our journey with the baboon squeals and high gibbering which would follow a defense of the Hat, so bore its company in silence, hoping it would shake itself apart as Dogwood drove.

Our immediate mission was but part of a larger path that I had been traveling at the time, Minister Dogwood at my side. We were used to each other, and this helped explain what I was doing stuck in a convertible beside a man wearing a scrofulous nacho hat and filthy ski-goggles. We plummeted on bad suspension towards the damp flats of Lake Michigan, with its treacherous patches of sucking mud and sundered machine hulks like the rising rusted fists of days gone by.

Night found us on the far side of Lake Michigan in a scrubby wooded area, dying trees around a fire that was objectively dangerous in the dry conditions. As the Minister had said, "Screw it, it's cold."

And it was cold, night in this new pupating desert. Over-irrigation had salted the earth, which had been survivable till the Feds drained our water-table and routed it to wealthier drought-stricken parts of our fair feral nation. Once they had, the salts settled out and nothing new would grow, leaving us with a savage new landform on our doorstep, waiting to be born.

I had always wondered what it had been like for the Feds when the dead rose. All those DEA guys figuring out that their stockpiles of confiscated drugs could be the key to survival. You'd have straight-laced preppy swine taking precise, measured doses of whatever they had nearby to stave off the hungry dead. Which would have worked great, right until Cookie Monster lunged for them from the dark foot-well of their desk, shrieking in unhallowed tongues.

That's the thing, you see. The levels of drugs required for safety aren't the kinds of demons you can dance with and expect to get away unscathed. They're going to ride you, scar you, write their initials in your skin . . . and occasionally one is going to climb into your skull, grab the wheel and take you for a ride.

The Minister, myself, and those like us have enough experience to respect the demons and know that expecting to keep control is folly, leading only to Bad Craziness. Roll with the punches, embrace the demons and surrender.

The Suits? How they'd have handled it? I wish I could have seen.

Had a friend called Shanks once whose theory was that the zombies tracked brain activity, and so drugs messed you up enough that they couldn't find you.

Then again, this is from a guy who became so monstrously drunk with the technician of his local black-market Augmentation chop-shop that he wound up with a Mister Stun implant where a Mister Stud implant should go, the poor bastard. Heard he found a girl who likes that recently, though. Calls him "Tickler."

But that's beside the point.

What you need will not play nice, will not play fair, but it means you can sleep without being surrounded by groaning fiends come morning. That was how they got you. Sooner or later you have to sleep. The central benefit of our lifestyle was that when I saw the fetid corpse of my first crush reaching out to tear off my face, I could be *practically certain* it wasn't real. It made for an interesting transition period, but after a while the wandering dead fell away into background irrelevance, like parking wardens and homeless people before the world changed.

Such peace was not always two-way. I remember that our evening's ration carried the Minister away on a tide of energy and impulse-control problems. We were still clad in our road clothes, the Minister in the Lamentable Hat and a blue Hawaiian shirt decorated in dirty playing cards, with unclean jeans and army boots. Dust and silt ground into his face except for patches left by the goggles, like some demented reverse-raccoon with mania shining in bright eyes. He'd found three or so zombies lurking nearby our fire-pit, and was gleefully diving and swooping around the lumbering beasts, seeking opportunities to tie their shoelaces together and watch them shuffle and stumble about. I can't recall what I wore myself, just that it was cold so I sought my sleeping-bag early.

In retrospect this was probably for the best. Soon after that, I worked through the lag you get with decent mescaline and suddenly everything mattered less. I was still aware of the Minister gallumphing around in his untied army boots, but was rapidly distracted by drifts of red, juicy butterflies hanging from tree branches like ripe fruit. What were these things, I remember thinking? Thick, fleshy wings, like ham steaks, flaps of foreskin or perhaps thickly sliced tomato, with no bodies to speak of. In a resonant conundrum, perhaps they were all of these *at the same time*. This needed more thought, I decided.

They shivered delicately with every muffled roar or clatter Dogwood produced, the motion echoing in my nervous system like they were under my skin. I understood instantly that his noise offended them, and terror that they might flee thrilled through me. I was considering how best to calm the Minister—couldn't he see how he frightened these poor things?—when a succession of sharp popping cracks, each one electricity flaring down my skull and out my limbs, filled the air and startled the hamforeskintomatoflies. Then someone screamed.

I was already on my feet before I consciously thought, *Christ, what's the Minister doing now?* And found myself heading towards the source of the noise. I located Dogwood, stripped to the waist but still wearing the Hat, wrestling with a dark woman in combat fatigues. Fallen zombies littered the ground around them, all shot in the head, but more silhouettes were grumbling towards us through the trees.

"Glue, Horse!" the Minister roared.

I hiccupped and ran back to the camp on uneven feet as bruised flesh-petals fell in slow flurries, the delicate crimson creatures in the trees coming apart from the stressful vibrations humming all around us. The wood-glue leapt into the plastic bag like an oddly warm, fat voluptuous slug, making me squeal.

How had this happened, I wondered? Confusing beauty swirled into malevolent slugs and screams in the night, leaving me bewildered and undone.

The Minister was hustling the woman towards me through the dry and dying trees in a near headlock, one arm twisted behind her back. I held the gruesome pulsating slug-bag to her face, prompting muffled screams and sharp movements as she tried to get away.

"Take it, you daft cow!" hissed the Minister, for he had grown up a Briton and was prone to slipping into the vernacular of his youth in times of crisis. "Breathe it in."

She went limp, which made it easier for us to drag her away from the pursuing zombies and the eerily silent patient tread they always fell into when following prey. I fell back, waving the glue around to confuse the trail and hoped that would lose them. The dead are dull-witted but canny predators, like some form of flesh-eating math teacher, but once they're agitated and activated by potential food, they'll go for anything in the vicinity whether it's medicated or not.

You're either good and fucked up or a danger to everyone, nothing in between. The Minister was furious. We dropped her, swooning and puking, back at the camp and wordlessly took up our weapons—a crowbar and tire-iron between the two of us—to go clean up her mess. The zombies were disoriented and had lost the trail, but they were still meandering around. Once activated, they'd keep stumbling through the area for a while, and there was always the chance they'd be agitated enough to go for movement if they found any. It was easy enough to sneak up on them and club their heads to slurry for safety's sake, but an unpleasant task indeed. All the more so for its unnecessary nature.

What the hell had she been thinking?

Her rifle and pistol were empty, meaning she'd caught my attention firing the last of her wad. Paranoia and bad-craziness curled through me, as if tiny people were sneaking up on me over my own skin. Who was this woman? Shooting zombies was a mug's game. However many there were, more would follow the noise, as they followed any atypical stimuli.

Why would she be here by herself, intent on riling up zombies near where the Minister and I planned to sleep?

Who had sent her, and what did she *know?*

I remember turning from my dark thoughts to see the Minister caught in what I initially took to be his own paranoid spiral, but then I realized his rage had shifted on him again. He was contemplating the unconscious woman and vaguely fingering a small bag he'd carried for years, filled with what the vendor had sworn was genuine Spanish fly.

Then he saw me watching him. An avalanche of expressions crossed his face as he thrust the bag away, out of sight.

"Didn't! Wasn't! Never would!" the Minister cried sharply, before subsiding with a muttered, "Can't be helped."

There was a moment of peace, and then his hand flashed to the fractal-blade he kept on a thong around his neck with a shriek of "Don't you judge me!"

My eyes locked on the intricate blade, glittering in the dying firelight. It was serrated all the way down, and considering the sickly radioactive gleam in the Minister's eyes, more than capable of making me much less pretty. He'd been carrying the damnable knife ever since his sister had used one to cut herself free from a trapped inverted canoe, although he didn't share an interest in that sport or any other.

You must understand that I'd known Minister Dogwood for many years, since high school in fact, and so I had a firm awareness of just how untrustworthy a fiend I was dealing with.

I pointed the woman's pistol at him, hoping he hadn't seen me check it earlier.

"Back off, you unhinged bastard! I wield *indiscriminate justice!*"

Dogwood's gleaming eyes narrowed, the knifepoint tracing unsteady Moebius strips in the air. Desperate now, I cried, "Go to sleep! What would your mother think?"

A moment of stasis then, before fat tears filled his eyes. He nodded to me once, then climbed sniffling into his sleeping-bag and curled into a ball. I waited for a moment and went for a walk to calm the screaming in my blood, treading on the fallen meaty petals of whatever those poor doomed fantastic things had been.

Something crunched underfoot and I found the shattered remains of the Minister's Lamentable Hat, where it must have been crushed as he wrestled the mysterious woman. I took the loss of the horrible artifact as a good sign for our journey—thankful that the Minister hadn't noticed—and then went to bed myself, suddenly aware of how cold it was and had been for some time.

Morning was a dangerous time for us, full of disorientation and spikes of crystalline suffering into the brain. I felt restrained and lashed out, eventually struggling free of the sleeping bag as from a warmly padded womb. I then made an attempt to remember where I was.

The presence of the woman was very confusing to me.

Who was she?

Had we *done* something?

Her guns and the zombie remnants brought it all back before self-accusation cut too deep, but also raised more questions than were answered. As I considered her, she stirred and woke, clearly with a splitting headache. I sympathized. Our Emergency Glue was not a fun ride, but it did the job.

I poured some water from our rations and set it down where she could get it before drinking some myself. She eyed me warily.

"There were zombies," she said eventually, in an even tone. "Then that maniac attacked me."

"Course they followed you. You sobered up, and were pulling them in from all over."

"*Excuse me?*"

Nonsensical. Perhaps speaking of bad damage. I played along, as patiently as I could.

"They follow you unless you're ripped. Can't shoot them or you attract more. Easy."

I dragged out the breakfast amyls and offered her one. She recoiled.

"What's that?"

"Amyl nitrite. Good for you. Got vitamins."

Nothing in her expression suggested comprehension. I sighed, pondering how a pharmacological virgin could have survived this long. Perhaps she was some Unabomber nutcase only now out of bullets. Since she seemed to be a newbie I took pity and opened one of the bags.

"You're going to have to take something, or the Minister over there is going to wake up and make you take something, maybe the glue again, and the glue is a harsh and caustic mistress."

She blinked in silence. I continued.

"We have amyls . . . Mescaline . . . Some weed, but that's recreational rather than safety related . . . The last of the Green Shrieker . . . Some skinpatches with Mayhem Tweed and Strict Blue . . . Some meth, which will sort you out properly but rots your head and your teeth . . . A decent amount of acid and shrooms . . . Hard liquor and speed—"

"—Booze will save you from zombies?"

Incredulous hostility came from her in waves. It gave me a headache, and even more in need of my own dosage.

"Are you *from the past?*" I yelled, grabbing some gear from the supply bags and leaning over the Minister, punching him on the shoulder a few times. "Hang on," I said to her, before returning to Dogwood. "Come on, Minister, breakfast dosage!"

He mumbled something unhelpful; I cracked an amyl under his nose and held it there.

"Come on, breathe deep . . . Good man."

He went limp, which is always more comfortable when you're already lying down. I grabbed one myself and turned back to her.

"Anything that'll fuck you up properly will work," I said, aiming for patience. "Booze will do, but you need a lot of it. You'd need to be utterly wasted."

She chewed over the idea, then defaulted to the familiar: "I guess I'll go with the booze."

Handing over a bottle of tequila, I cautioned, "You're going to need to be dedicated with this, and if they come after you again it's back to the glue."

Gamely enough she took a big swig and grimaced. Hardly surprising; it wasn't very good tequila. I cracked my own amyl and breathed deep, carried away by the biting chemical scent and a delightful tide of dizziness. Purple haze hung in my vision, suspended in a timeless silence in which the world turned around me.

The main wave passed, leaving me with ongoing light-headedness and a sudden awareness of hunger. Food! Yes! I craved sugar and fat, perhaps caffeine. During a visit to the Minister's sprawling family in the U.K. before the dead rose, I had encountered the deep-fried Mars bar: molten delectable battered money-shots from some chubby god of cardiac arrest. Couple of them, some speed or ecstasy and perhaps a pint or two, and I'd be fuelled for another ten hours of experimental hooliganism.

The Minister maintained the same effect could be achieved with just the speed—with beer to flavor—but the man lacks an artists' soul, any respect for the culinary arts, and a basic knowledge of nutrition.

Alas the issue was moot: there was no access to the pinnacle of Western civilization that was deep-fried chocolate bars. Not without the underlying substrate of Western civilization. That ship had long since sailed, carried away by a rising tide of the walking, hungry dead.

The woman took another swig from the bottle and woke me from my reverie. "If it's just us against the zombies, I'm going to need to know what to call you. I'm Chantal."

"He's the Horse," interjected Dogwood, putting the lie to his apparent coma.

I jerked a thumb at him. "The man who is full of *lies* is Dogwood, my Minister for Lateral Problem-Solving, long term companion and sidekick."

I noticed that the woman had made a healthy dent in the tequila and was looking rather green. Heavy booze on an empty stomach. I saluted her enthusiasm, but she was going to geyser.

"Whoa!" said I. "Slow down or you're going to lose it all!"

It was hard to say whether she heard me. Wordlessly Dogwood began loading our gear into the car and started the long road to actually getting the engine running.

"Why are you two out here?" she asked, clearly bilious. "Where are you going?"

"The Minister and I are on a quest for more Safety Drugs for our community of Bad Axe."

"We're heroes," Dogwood said sagely, fiddling vaguely with the car.

"We head west, seeking population centers which might have a pharmacological bounty for us. But not into central Chicago itself. No, that might be a little too exciting. We seek the outlying regions."

Dogwood added, "Detroit would have been way too exciting."

I saw in that moment that she understood, but in retrospect it was probably somewhere between my experience with the amyl, and hers with rising bile. She took another swig and shuddered.

"So that's your plan? Survivors just taking drugs forever?"

The Minister and I exchanged a glance and started to laugh. It was not an unreasonable question. Hell, I'm the first to admit that we had not hit upon an ideal long-term solution. Kids, for example. Kids could not be expected to be as Resilient as the Minister or myself, and yet the situation remained. Any given babies had the choice of being pulled apart like some struggling, gut-filled jelly-donuts, or growing into dribbling addicts with skulls full of bad cheese.

I'm not saying we had the answers then, but this was a bridge to cross another day. However, Chantal had inadvertently stumbled onto the larger path that the Minister and I walked, a noble plan to which our current holy mission was but one small part.

"Nah," Dogwood said. "We're going to get Twisted."

It was a simple statement, perhaps too simple by the blankness in Chantal's eyes, and as Dogwood said it he popped the engine cover. At the time I wasn't paying attention, but in hindsight the signs of the car's doom were all there. But leaving that aside, the Minister was absolutely right. Our larger quest was to get Twisted, like those noble leaders of men, Presidents Ozzy and Tommy Lee. I believe myself to have been more attached to the notion and disciplined in its pursuit than Minister Dogwood, even then.

"Twisted," I said sagely, "is when you take enough different drugs over enough time that you—you—"

"Smell different than people," called Dogwood, from somewhere inside the car.

"—Thank you, Minister—enough that your body-chemistry changes. Then they never find you, even if you're straight."

Dogwood straightened up and mused, "Sounds useful, but I don't see the point of that bit."

As I say, the Minister lacks true vision.

I remember waxing lyrical, but can't remember precise details. To be Twisted is to be truly free in this new benighted world of ours, untouched by the dead. Transcending natural human body-chemistry to become divine acid-casualties walking the world at will, spreading the word. Why do you think Ozzy and Tommy Lee are probably President? Nobody wants a Commander-in-Chief who might get eaten. It's just sense.

I was about to go into my theories about why cocaine doesn't seem to work when the Minister proclaimed, "Car's buggered."

He was right. Upon investigation, the battery reeked of sulfur.

I'm sure that to someone who knows anything about cars, that'd mean something important. As it was, we were instantly reduced to moving by foot.

"Everything out of the car, Minister," I said, knowing he was already working on it. "This will not slow us down, for we are Resilient."

"True," he said, "unless you mean in overland speed."

Manfully, I ignored him, for we did actually have a plan. I went for our supply bags. Moving by foot was going to expose us to more zombies, so we needed something good and nasty, with fundamental endurance of effect. I went for the acid; the Minister went for a skinpatch of the Mayhem Tweed. He slapped the patch onto a forearm, giving himself a temporary tattoo like a piece of living couch or librarian's jacket which sank slowly beneath his skin. Dogwood's face flushed and paled in rapid succession while his irises bloomed darkness.

"That's good Tweed," he breathed. I eyed him sidelong while peeling a decent chunk of blotter free. Under Tweed, he was going to need watching, but that was hardly new. After the amount of acid I was intent on taking, I wasn't going to be up for sainthood myself.

Chantal hid behind her tequila bottle when I offered her the bag, drinking more before vomiting copiously into the bushes. With the wad of blotter tucked into one cheek, I began sizing up westward angles to take—it's always easier to take downhill trends on acid—when she spoke up and wiped her lips.

"You're looking for drugs, right?"

The Minister and I exchanged a glance.

"Why?"

"Jackson. Lots of drugs in Jackson." She straightened up and took another pull from the bottle. "Police station lockup is full of stuff. I just came from there."

Dogwood snorted. "Bollocks you did, not on foot. That's way the hell back east and—"

"—You have a better idea?"

He deflated with a shrug and looked at me.

"She raises a compelling point."

So without a better idea of destination, and a limited timeframe to decide before polysyllabic demons got a vote, Jackson it was.

Retracing the path towards Jackson wasn't hard. The trail of patient zombie steps and sporadic corpses was pretty clear, but six hours of blisters later and the Minister was on the verge of mutiny. A rising column of anger seethed from him and stained the sky above the bleeding footsteps left in his wake.

The Tweed had taken him to a dark place without words or otherwise numbed his tongue. He stalked in silence over the dusty ground while the world throbbed and hummed nameless tunes around us. Chantal obliviously clutched her bottle like a savage cactus-based teddy-bear. She was a metronome vomit-fountain, staining the dust with stinking neon horrors that ate into the ground and sang of vague malevolence.

Me? I just felt kind of mellow.

The air was filled with the scent of dust and dry vegetation, along with crushed parsley and burning insulation rising in waves from the Minister's every bleeding footstep.

It was when the ground stood up and started yelling that I thought I was really freaking out. I can't explain the terror I felt when vaguely humanoid figures the color of dirt were suddenly there, shedding dust and trailing vines, reeking of anger and the cruelty man poured into the very soil.

Several things happened in rapid succession.

The Minister collapsed into a paralyzed crouch, a high keening in his throat, his eyes glistening white with fear as the compost beasts came for us.

I screamed in what I was later assured was an appropriately masculine manner.

Chantal dropped her bottle, raised her hands and said, "They're harmless, sir! Phillips reporting!"

One of the creatures spoke, each word a hideous Darth Vader rasp of Inescapable Doom. It was at that point I believe I dropped to the dirt and began to grovel, but in a clearer mind I remember it said, "Christ, Phillips. You go for bullets and find mouths."

"Civilian drug-fiends, sir. They saved me . . ."

The conversation was ongoing, but I stopped paying attention when I noticed the monsters encircling the Minister as he wailed wordlessly against their dusty existence. The outrage pulled me to my feet.

"You can't have him!" I roared. "He's mine!"

Chantal and the dirt-beast looked around.

"Mother of—" it said, pausing before making a cutting motion. "Fine. We'll sort these two out. You smell of puke."

"They think intoxication keeps them safe, and weren't happy unless I played along . . . I drank enough that I kept throwing up most of it."

Treachery!

The thought thrilled electrically through me, but by now I was already making efforts to dodge the monsters coming after me like they were herding a rabbit. The wrongness of their presence made me shrill and dizzy, but I am no rabbit.

Some fiend threw a sack over my head, the fabric membranous and alive, softly mewling. I crashed to the ground and hauled part of it off in time to see one monster touch the Minister.

The physical contact told him whatever he was seeing was tangible. In an instant he went from paralyzed silence to a gargling howl. One hand flashed to the fractal-blade at his throat and then he waded into the offending monster's leg like a kid into red-spurting birthday cake.

Shouts, then. Noise and bad confusion.

Next thing I remember is finding myself in restraints on a gurney.

A relief. This had happened before.

But where was the Minister?

I shifted as the restraints would allow, and there was no sign of Dogwood. Some medical personnel were dickering nearby, a woman and middle-aged man. I overheard, "—what Phillips says it's a miracle they survived this long, but we'll soon sort them out."

"You can't threaten me!" I shouted, channeling the stern hybrid spirit of Clint Eastwood and Charlton Heston. "I deal with scarier things than you in my shoes every morning, and that's only the stuff that's real!"

He knelt down beside the stretcher then, one of those paternal doctors you just want to dose with something vivid and enduring, then set free in a shopping mall. We'd see who's so smug *then*.

"My poor boy," he said truculently. "What have you been doing to yourself?"

"No negotiation with terrorists, doc! Return my Minister to me immediately, and we'll be on our way."

"In your current state, you'll poison any Reanimates who bite you!" he laughed, rotund and jocular.

"Ha. Ha. Yes. I fucked your daughter."

I could see this statement displeased him as he backed away, so I tried to figure out these restraints now that I lacked his gaze. Curses! The Minister was much more talented than I in this area. I fiddled and tested and pulled, only to overhear:

"—flush their systems and clean out the muck, straighten them out good and proper."

"Wait, what?"

Silence and blankly hostile faces. The Fear began to rise in me from some chill and murky underground well.

They couldn't do that! They mustn't! I was so close to being Twisted I could taste it in the very air. A few more months! That was it! The Minister and I had started on this path long before the zombies provided a reason.

We were *ahead of the game!*

It became obvious that I was thrashing and probably yelling when they came with glinting unfriendly needles to silence my uncomprehending horror.

I howled out, "The drugs are good for meeeeeee!" before icy oblivion climbed up a vein, put the chairs on the tables and turned out the lights.

I woke to the smell of smoke, who knows how long later, under a sense of vague, watery sedation. Unrestrained, which meant they were getting careless or trusting, but confronted with a mutinously solid door. However, I guessed that the smoke meant that the Minister was nearby, and about to teach them Proper Caution.

I dragged myself upright and everything felt wrong. The criminals had leached the drugs from my system and replaced them with weakness—fat and heavy metals, weighing me down. Peering through the door's little window, I banged and hollered as best I could: "Fire! You can't leave me in here with this maniac! *Fire!*"

A disorganized pack of people came and let me out, suspicious but fundamentally uninformed of my basic nature. There was something on the air along with the smoke, some primal trapped terror and confusion. These people had far bigger problems at the moment than even myself and the Minister could provide. It was at that moment I remember thinking that we might get out of this yet.

We'd had a lot of practice dealing with panic and disorder as it all came down, and this felt like a flashback or a sequel. First thing's first, however, I had to locate Dogwood. I harnessed my rescue crew with a cry of "Dear Lord! Smoke!" and ran towards it, leaving nothing more than a startled, "Hey, wait!" in my wake. I figured they'd be keeping the Minister nearby, and that if I could keep these people off-balance enough, they'd forget to be too suspicious.

The smoke coincided with frantic hammering on a heavy door. I turned to the confused pack following me and cried, "What are you waiting for? Get the poor man out!"

Dogwood tumbled to the concrete and linoleum-tile of the corridor through thick smoke as the door opened, half-naked and wheezing, grabbing my leg.

"They tried to kill me, Horse!" he coughed. "Locked me in and left me to burn!"

"No more of that 'Horse' garbage, understand?" I hissed in his ear before straightening to proclaim, "This man is ill and my responsibility—"

But my words were interrupted as the Minister coughed till he was sick on my foot.

"Look," a haggard youth said, unshaven and reeking of The Fear. "We don't care about whatever line of bullshit you're trying to spin. It doesn't matter. And just trust me when I say you'll fight with all the rest of us when the time comes."

I nodded busily, grinning in what I hoped was a manner that spoke of agreement and total comprehension: "Indeed! Fighters, us. Stern repose. All that stuff."

It seemed that we'd been less clever than I'd thought, but they really believed something terrible was coming. It seemed best to trust them on this, and just focus on getting the hell out of Dodge before it arrived. The Minister caught my attention again with another coughing fit, making me pull my foot out of range. His eyes rolled pink like an agitated lab-mouse, wearing nothing but boots and jeans, both legs torn raggedly so that one ended above the knee and the other courted indecency.

"Where are your clothes, Minister?"

"Burned 'em. Had to start somewhere."

Of course he had, but it couldn't be helped. Definitely time to be moving on, away from this foreign place and its aura of doom.

Wait, where *are* we, I thought?

The Minister and I staggered from the concreted area of our incarceration—gray, glass and steel—only to find ourselves on the third story of an incomprehensible madhouse, when we could see the ground. Vast walls and fences surrounded an area of something akin to four blocks, teeming with shanty structures and fetid masses of humanity. Buildings, clearly pre-existing the Reanimates or whatever these guys called zombies, hauled themselves up out of the complicated mass below. Few people were left at ground level, seeming to prefer to get as high as they possibly could.

What kind of lunacy was this?

Why were they all trying to get off the ground? It looked safe. Or were they looking out over the walls, and if that was the case, why were they freaking out so much?

The furled edges of a conclusion touched my mind, but I will admit that Dogwood got there before I did and saved us the trip upstairs to investigate.

"They've got zombies. A scorching case."

Of course. All of Chantal's weird behavior and the incomprehensible drug-theft treachery could fit if these misguided cretins were from the past, and simply hadn't noticed that pattern. Morons.

This was something out of *Mad Max*. Razor-wire and gun-emplacements at the top of the wall, never mind that the repetitive noise would bring them in like nothing else. Well, excepting the smell of legion overheated unwashed humans, or maybe concentrated brain-radiation, or whatever it was they homed in on.

In any case, this place was sun-ripened spam in a can.

It was time to run away.

"You're right, Minister! My god, these people are going to get us both killed!"

"Bad scene, man," he grated on a smoke roughened throat. "Irresponsible."

"Indeed! We need to get to the ground and get out before the zombies arrive."

"What if they're at the gates already?" he clutched my arm. "We might *smell of food!*"

A chill went through me, reminding me of how physically dissolute and watery I felt, sapped of Power and Resilience. A conundrum.

"These people will stockpile gear, Minister. For one thing, they'll have ours. That should be enough to get free of this place. We must find it!"

The two of us slinked and reeled down sets of stairs to reach the ground, passing or jumping barriers across the stairs when we found them. We were straight-sober for the first time in living memory and the experience was ghastly, stripping away all the filters sane humans need to function and setting us loose like panicky rats under snake-eyes. There was nothing on these levels but shoddy hotel-sized units turned apartment shanty-towns.

Not what we needed. I remember peering over banisters and scanning around for a structure that would predate the Big Zs. It'd be run down and blocky. Utilitarian. Just *scream* "police."

In the end, the Minister found it by falling down the stairs. He came to rest and, when the swearing died down, reported that there were low windows at the street, containing a six inch view of what looked like cells. And the Minister knew cells.

Breaking into police stations turned out to be surprisingly easy when all the police are AWOL for fear of flesh-rending horrors. I was bent on getting the lock picked or finding something to chisel the hinges when the Minister kicked in one of the ground windows and climbed inside.

"Minister!" I said, scrambling down to the window. "We want to avoid jail cells, and you don't like them. Been very clear on that in the past . . . "

"Door's open, Horse . . . " came the muffled response.

I dislike crawling over even the most tidily broken glass, but truly these were Desperate Times. Dogwood was missing, as happened frequently in times of stress and confusion, but would not stray far. I could hear him scuffling around somewhere beyond the cells, which were indeed open.

I called, "Find anything?"

"Cops stop filing when the world starts to end. Guess it's been ending here for a while."

The man can be a poet when he wants, when the demons aren't soiling that part of his mind, or riding him around the city like a radioactive jet-propelled scooter bent on mass destruction.

The real question was, where would they have put our stuff? Or failing that, where would they have been keeping other people's stuff, which we could then get into and abscond with? The search took some time, from memory, leading two increasingly desperate men—both of whom were in the early depths of different flavored DTs as the sedation wore off—through a plethora of pathologically dull police rooms. By a process of elimination we found an evidence lock-up, and it was there that the dark gods smiled upon us with their blackened grimy teeth and decided we'd suffered enough. If the cops had still been in a filing mood we might never have found it, but getting into all the lockers and drawers meant that we located bags that looked suspiciously like our supplies. The Minister was even reunited with his fractal-blade, still rusty with monster juice or—in retrospect—soldier blood. He returned it to its thong, and to the gap it left in the tan around his neck. All of the Safety Drugs were there, tagged and dated in little plastic bags.

And then we noticed all the other stuff in the locker. In little plastic bags. And in the lockers next to ours.

They say when it rains it pours, and *howling crackbaby CHRIST* but it was beautiful. My mouth went dry as the Minister began to laugh a low, dirty chuckle.

It was more than we could carry by a significant margin, such riches that to take all of it would have been lamentable greed. The Minister and I were and are pillars of the global community and would not dream of it.

"We have to try some of this . . . " the Minister said.

"Indeed! It's medicinal! Choose your weapons and see what you can find by way of a wheel-barrow or box mover, something wheeled." I grabbed a decent chunk of acid and some speed. "Take what you want, Minister; we're making up for lost time and need to be safely wasted by the time the zombies get in."

He rooted in the bins and suddenly looked up. "They'll be agitated when they arrive. Won't matter if we're wasted so long as we're moving!"

A relevant, alarming point. "True. Drugs, a barrow and a stolen car, Minister. We have our mission."

We didn't find anything so useful as a wheeled box conveyance, but I did find some decent back-packs and a roll of carpet from the adjoining office, which I figured might be useful for getting over any barbed wire. However, in the time it took me to return, the Minister had chosen to plunge us forward once again into Interesting Times.

Different shades of upholstery fabric crawled detectably up each arm and stained his torso, with a third mounting one leg. His eyes were intense and manic, shining with an unwholesome inner light.

I shudder thinking about it, even now. Little will make a grown man more foolhardy, unstable and depraved than mixed, conflicting Tweed. And from the way the cloth pattern stain was spreading, all were unusually high doses.

The plan had changed, although the overall mission remained the same: complete all objectives before Minister Dogwood became a portal for horror and bad confusion to enter this benighted world.

How long could I keep control of my own demons, I wondered? The gust-front of the acid was curling through my brain like a serpent returning to a comfortable lair, and pretty soon it was going to take the wheel.

Here I was, responsible for Minister Dogwood, currently the human equivalent of a dirty suitcase-nuke with a low timer and nothing but red wires. The two of us trying to get out of an armed compound before an unspecified number of the undead—an unknown distance away—broke inside, and all before the acid-snake took me for a joyride.

It is challenges which make us grow.

A susurrus of voices and the sharp taps of gunfire carried in the air when we managed to get out of the police station. The cell windows were much too high to escape from the inside, so we had to use the door. Far above, I could see the arms and gestures of the milling throngs as they surveyed their impending doom arriving on implacable rotting legs. No idea how long we had, so safest to assume not much time at all and then work from there.

"Minister," I declared, trying to keep him focused. "Look for vehicles."

I was aware myself of the incipient dust melting into an iridescent sheen and climbing slowly up our legs.

Dogwood's gaze was fixed on the balconies above, apparently on a once-fat woman with sagging bundles of flesh holding onto a malnourished Pomeranian.

"Dogsa darkmeat, yeh?"

Sinking feeling, or was that the melting dirt? Our downward spiral begun so soon? Had to keep him focused, and that would be increasingly difficult.

"No good, Dogwood. Too many bones."

"Can't trust the bones, no."

"Cars, Minister! Focus."

We were attracting attention and shouts from the people above, but that wasn't the real concern. I had to think. Cars would be outside the camp to give them space and since zombies wouldn't damage them, so we had to seek a way out of these hideous walls. The Minister was following me and I wasn't worried about anyone here interfering with him. Mostly naked except for lopsided torn pants, clashing upholstery patterns crawling under his skin and mixing in his torso, brightly maniacal eyes and a fixed grin . . . He was obviously far too crazy a person to mess with. The Tweed patterns were a biological warning to predators, part of how the world declares Do Not Disturb. He was like some feral fusion-powered couch-based Frankenstein lurching around this little settlement in defiance of God's laws, and daring polite society to form a mob. Fortunately, polite society had bigger concerns.

Our wanderings lead us to a change from concrete to hurricane fencing, beyond which the horizon could be seen behind indistinct humanoid figures in the distance. Progress at last! I climbed up enough to throw our carpet over the sharp wire, then hurled the gear bags I was carrying over the fence to the other side. I hoped the Minister would follow my lead, but I was beset by traitorous whispers. Setting him loose here would be like throwing a sack of weasels into a kindergarten; it would definitely afford time for my own escape, but I couldn't do that! He was my Minister, and the crazy bastard for all his faults didn't deserve that. And these poor misguided swine didn't deserve him, not in this state.

I climbed the fence, the wire under my hands throbbing with a giant, slow heartbeat and singing in a phantom wind. I was aware of hostile attention from the crowds above and hurried, aiming to cajole Dogwood across once I was on the other side. As I reached the dirt I saw him throw his arms wide and look up at the crowds before booming, "Don't worry, citizens! We're not the undead!"

Thank you, Minister. I remember thinking. *Succinctly put.*

"Come on, throw me the gear and climb over," I yelled. I could see Chantal moving our way through a growing crowd daring the balconies of the lower levels, but ignored her. Dogwood, however, was confused by my interruption.

"What? Why are we leaving? Have you caved in to these people?"

"Over the fence, you animal! We don't have time for games!"

Dogwood glared intensely and began to climb, still carrying all his bags. He fought his way up to the carpet, his underskin patterns growing out behind him as membranous fabric wings while my pulse roared and sang in my ears.

Hold it together, I thought. *Maintain!* I thought.

Lose control now and the two of you will be lost in the storm.

When the Minister came down, the carpet came with him. Shrieking, he rolled in its embrace, punching and biting. I hauled it away and Dogwood looked up at me with huge, mad eyes.

I dragged him bodily away from the fence and looked for vehicles. As I did, the community's situation became clearer. They were in a box-canyon, so the gunshot echoes would summon zombies for miles. The initial forerunners of the undead horde dropped like ripe rupturing fruit as they reached the range of the guns, but that was a finite solution at best—particularly given their thickening crowds. Despite the pace they were being cut down, the mob was still making visible if very slow progress towards the walls. And then they'd start to climb each other.

The two of us had seen this before.

Well, not with the whole *Mad Max* walls and gun-emplacement thing, but otherwise we'd seen it.

The car-pool was dusty and some of the vehicles looked dilapidated, but that'd never stopped us before. I unleashed the Minister and directed him to the nearest jeep. He was always better with hotwiring than me, even while chemically unbalanced.

I watched the man plunge beneath the dashboard and rip into the wires there with a high, tearing scream of laughter. Perhaps, I thought, this time he was too far gone. Yet this was negative thinking and of no purpose. The jeep had some big water tanks strapped to the side which sounded full, and a pile of silver-wrapped food packs in the back. Food and water would be useful if we wanted not to have to drink our piss before we reached civilization.

Never fun.

The engine turned over with a zapping scream, matched with a cry from Dogwood, who began punching the dashboard and swearing. He seemed to have the situation in hand, and my attention was drawn back to the walls of the bleak settlement that was doing everything wrong.

Poor, misguided, uncomprehending wretches. Trapped in a new world they didn't understand, and much of which wanted to consume their living flesh. A very bad scene today, fear in the air, yet another apocalypse the Minister and I had to witness. The acid hummed, spat and whispered that perhaps this was no accident. Were we the karmically-invested sin eaters of an entire way of life?

Troubling thought, but I doubted it. We didn't really know these people, not even Chantal.

Chantal.

My eyes narrowed as a conclusion formed, even if I wasn't completely conscious of it at the time. Chantal was a crystalline example of this community. Misguided, unheeding, desperately human, and seeking a means to continue that state. She had a face, particularly in comparison to everyone else the Minister and I had dealt with here, all of whom realistically had been total dicks.

She had a face and a name even if we didn't know her, and she deserved another chance. By extension, so did the rest of them.

I clambered around to the back of the jeep and rooted around for tools, spooking the Minister. He brandished a pair of pliers at me from the floor and weaved dangerous, eerie patterns in the air with the shining points, like a crab signaling territory over lake mud.

These people were organized. There were two sorts of tire-iron, and right where they should be, rather than under the seats or taped to the bodywork. I grabbed the longer one that was unimpeded by a cross-piece, and set out at an angle that would bring me towards the thickening tide of zombies while keeping me visible to the watchers above.

The chattering of the idiot guns was still keeping them far enough back that it was a long walk in the afternoon sun, any moment expecting a stray round. The acid wave hit and broke over me en route, melting the ground into a thick stodgy soup and staining the sky with strobing neon torment. An endless staticky hiss filled the world, like a bad recording of surf on a stony eternal shore. The zombies seemed to join the soup, reminding me of the ghastly visions which beset me when Chantal lead us into that trap.

For a moment I contemplated going back and ceasing my rebellion against The Fear, soured by memory of that betrayal. But no! I would be holy Teflon to that ugliness, and refuse to soften my resolve.

The lecherous, biting gunfire laughter stopped altogether as I neared and singled out one particular zombie, which at least suggested they'd noticed me and cared. I was touched. Then they started up again, to chew away at the fringes some distance from me.

I focused on my target as the viscous world lurched, bubbled and sang.

You can't trust the dead. For every staggering Romero-brand which saps your caution, you'll find another one fresh enough to run screaming or throw something. Or one dried by desert winds into staggering carnivorous cordwood, seemingly harmless till they get close enough to release the crossbow tension in twisted tendons like steel cables and rip you in half. And then occasionally you find a zombie with activated Augments and implants. If you're wary you have a very bad day. If you're not wary you probably don't get a chance to have a bad day.

Even if you're ripped or Twisted, there are few guarantees. Not when you're up close and personal, and particularly not when they can smell flesh on the wind.

The one I'd singled out was dry and old, but lively enough. His stiffened leathery skin—all in patches—creased into a frown as he neared me, aware I was there but not what I was. I steeled myself and held out an arm before the creature, watching its rotting nostrils flex in and out, wuffling around and searching for this weird thing I was. Those horrible nostrils! They unfurled slowly like miniature elephant trunks on the hunt, or seemed to, sparking thrills of nauseous horror. I didn't move except to turn back to the walls and balconies where binoculars winked.

Backing a safe distance away from the hideous, duel-elephant thing, I pointed and roared, "See? No bitey!"

At the noise, all the zombies recalibrated to me, until the settlement fired again and refocused them on the walls. With luck, the villagers finally noticed that part of the pattern. I moved back to the zombie I'd initially targeted and smacked it in the skull with the tire-iron till it stopped moving. The body smelled like opening a bag of jerky which has started to turn—dry, salty and corrupt. It took me back to that god-awful bar in Terra Haute, with gleaming soiled gems of teeth and enamel fragments in the urinal, but I forced the memory down and decided to drive the point home to these people. After all, they were woefully behind the times.

I spent five or ten minutes running through this forest of corpses and played the Minister's games. I pushed them over like tipping humanoid cows, danced around before them, safe in their confusion, and even tied one's shoelaces together to leave it stumbling and crawling. Nothing without risk, but I was high on superiority.

Puffed by my Heroic Exertions, I moved back toward the settlement to see results. People with rifles were watching me, one with binoculars. Chantal was also in evidence with that group. As I watched, one of the armed figures turned to the man with the binoculars and spoke.

Instantly, I knew what was said, like a voice from over my shoulder stating in a reasonable tone, "Maybe we should shoot him?"

Paranoia gripped me in a cold, thorny fist. A finger lanced out at Chantal.

"Her!" I screamed. It took a second or two for the sound to hit the balconies. "Indeed! She's seen it! Ask her!"

Already she was engaged in conversation with Official Looking People, perhaps to deny knowing me. It was hard to say. But it can be very hard to stop talking when acid is at the wheel, words tumbling out despite my terror that I was only making things worse.

"The police station! Full of glorious drugs to keep you safe! More than you need! And *stop shooting at them!*"

People on the move, either towards their miraculous drug cache or to come get us.

It was Time to Leave.

I ran back towards the jeep, finding the engine running and the Minister strapped securely into the passenger seat, grinning alarmingly and showing bright teeth. His eyes held mine, inhuman intensity and mirth unblinking in shining white orbs. I'd seen that stare. Hell, I've stared that stare, and it is a noted harbinger of nothing good. No matter, I thought. A problem for another time, and we had many miles to travel yet.

Climbing into the driver's seat, I made sure that the supplies were actually in the car. Dumping the soiled tire-iron in the back, I floored it, sending us towards more comprehensible climes in a cloud of dust—or would do, as soon as I figured out where we were. Chantal had mentioned Jackson, but was this another Unfortunate Lie?

I considered the situation as we drove into the golden heat of the late afternoon sun. The growl of the engine thrummed through the very ground until the sky itself coruscated to its tone before the two of us, a pair of Chemical Saints, mission accomplished and returning home—as soon as we found it.

Warily, I also kept an eye on the Minister as he savaged open the packaging on a Meal Ready-to-Eat with his fractal blade.

It was serrated, you see.

All the way down.

Kevin Veale has had fiction published in Andromeda Spaceways Inflight Magazine. *He is a Ph.D. student in media studies at the University of Auckland, and lives in New Zealand.*

Welcome to the gonzo zombie story. To me, this *Fear and Loathing in Las Vegas*-style zombie defense is highly (pun intended) appealing and makes perfect sense: transcend human body chemistry and melt your cerebrum to avoid the mindless brain-eating walking dead. Beats barbed-wire, dwindling ammo, and imposed militaristic discipline any day.

But hey, that's me. You might feel differently. Of course, I lived through the seventies and even remember some of it.

The Things He Said

Michael Marshall Smith

My father said something to me this one time. In fact he said a lot of things to me, over the years, and many of them weren't what you'd call helpful, or polite—or loving, come to that. But in the last couple months I've found myself thinking back over a lot of them, and often find they had a grain of truth. I consider what he said in the new light of things and move on, and then they're done. This one thing, though, has kept coming back to me. It's not very original, but I can't help that. He was not an especially original man.

What he said was, you had to take care of yourself, first and foremost and always, because there wasn't no one else in the world who was going to do it for you. Look after Number One, was how he put it.

About this he was absolutely right. Of that I have no doubt.

I start every day to a schedule. Live the whole day by it, actually. I don't know if it makes much difference in the wider scheme of things, but having a set of tasks certainly helps the day kick off more positively. It gets you over that hump.

I wake around 6:00 PM, or a little earlier. So far that has meant the dawn has either been here, or coming. As the weeks go by it will mean a period of darkness after waking, a time spent waiting in the cabin. It will not make a great deal of difference apart from that.

I wash with the can of water I set aside the night before, and eat whatever I put next to it. The washing is not strictly necessary but, again, I have always found it a good way to greet the day. You wash after a period of work, after all, and what else is a night of sleep, if not work, or a journey at least?

You wash, and the day starts, a day marked off from what has gone before. In the meantime I have another can of water heating over a fire. The chimney is blocked up and the doors and windows are sealed overnight against the cold, so the fire must of necessity be small. That's fine all I need is to make enough water for a cup of coffee.

I take this with me when I open the cabin and step outside, which will generally be at about 6:20 AM. I live within an area that is in the shade of mountains, and largely forested. Though the cabin itself is obscured by trees, from my door I have a good view down over the ten or so acres between it and the next thicker stretch of woods. I tend to sit there on the stoop a couple minutes, sipping my coffee, looking around. You can't always see what you're looking for, though, which is why I do what I do next.

I leave the door open behind me and walk a distance which is about three hundred yards in length—I measured it with strides when I set it up—made of four unequal sides. This contains the cabin and my shed, and a few trees, and is bounded by wires. I call them wires, but really they're lengths of fishing line, connected between a series of trees. The fact that I'm there checking them, on schedule, means they're very likely to be in place, but I check them anyway. First, to make sure none of them need re-fixing because of wind—but also that there's no sign something came close without actually tripping them.

I walk them all slowly, looking carefully at where they're attached to the trees, and checking the ground on the other side for signs anything got that far, and then stopped—either by accident or because they saw the wires. This is a good, slow, task for that time in the morning, wakes you up nice and easy. I once met a woman who'd been in therapy—hired a vacation cottage over near Elum for half a summer, a long time ago this was—and it seemed like the big thing she'd learned was to ignore everything she thought in the first hour of the day. That's when the negative stuff will try to bring you down, she said, and she was right about that, if not much else. You come back from the night with your head and soul empty, and bad things try to fill you up. There's a lot to get exercised about, if you let it. But if you've got a task, something to fill your head and move your limbs, by the time you've finished it the day has begun and you're onto the next thing. You're over that hump, like I said.

When that job's finished, I go back to the cabin and have the second cup of coffee, which I keep kind-of warm by laying my breakfast plate over the top of the mug while I'm outside. I'll have put the fire out before checking the wires, so there's no more hot water for the moment. I used to have one of those vacuum flasks and that was great, but it got broken. I'm on the lookout for a replacement. No luck yet. The colder it gets, the more that's going to become a real priority.

I'll drink this second cup planning what I'm going to do that day. I could do this the night before, but usually I don't. It's what I do between 7:30 and 8:00 AM. It's in the schedule.

Most days, the next thing is going into the woods. I used to have a vegetable patch behind the cabin, but the soil here isn't that great and it was always kind of hit-and-miss. After the thing, it would also be too much of a clue that someone is living here.

There's plenty to find out in the woods, if you know what to look for. Wild versions of the vegetables in stores, other plants that don't actually taste so good but give you some of the green stuff you need. Sometimes you'll even see something you can kill to eat—a rabbit or a deer, that kind of thing—but not often. With time I assume I may see more, but for now stocks are low. With winter coming on, it's going to get a little harder for all this stuff. Maybe a lot harder.

We'll see. No point in worrying about it now. Worry don't get nothing but worry, as my father also used to say.

Maybe a couple hours spent out in the woods, then I carry back what I've found and store it in the shed. I'll check on the things already waiting, see what stage they're at when it comes to eating. The hanging process is very important. While I'm there I'll check the walls and roof are still sound and the canvas I've layered around the inside is still water-tight. As close to air-tight as possible, too.

I don't know if there are bears in these parts any more—I've lived here forty years, man and boy, and I haven't seen one in a long time, nor wolves either—but you may as well be sure. One of them catches a scent of food, and they're bound to come have a look-see, blundering through the wires and screwing up all that stuff. Fixing it would throw the schedule right out. I'm joking, mainly, but you know, it really would be kind of a pain, and my stock of fishing wire is not inexhaustible.

It's important to live within your means, within what you know you can replace. A long game way of life, as my father used to say. I had someone living here with me for a while, and it was kind of nice, but she found it hard to understand the importance of these things, of playing that long game. Her name was Ramona, and she came from over Noqualmi way. The arrangement didn't last long. Less then ten days, in fact. Even so, I did miss her a little after she walked out the door. But things are simpler again now she's gone.

Time'll be about 10:30 AM by then, maybe 11:00, and I'm ready for a third cup of coffee. So I go back to the cabin, shut and seal up all the doors and windows again, and light the fire. Do the same as when I get up, is make two cups, cover one to keep it semi-warm for later. I'll check around the inside of the cabin while the water's heating, making sure everything's in good shape. It's a simple house. No electricity—lines don't come out this far—and no running water.

I got a septic tank under the house I put in ten years back, and I get drinking and washing water from the well. There's not much to go wrong and it doesn't need checking every day. But if something's on the schedule then it gets done, and if it gets done, then you know it's done, and it's not something you have to worry about.

I go back outside, leaving the door open behind me again, and check the exterior of the house. That does need an eye kept on it. The worse the weather gets, the more there'll be a little of this or that needs doing. That's okay. I've got tools, and I know how to use them. I was a handyman before the thing and I am, therefore, kind of handy. I'm glad about that now. Probably a lot of people thought being computer programmers or bankers or TV stars was a better deal, the real cool beans. It's likely by now they may have changed their minds. I'll check the shingles on the roof, make sure the joints between the logs are still tight. I do not mess with any of the grasses or bushes that lie in the area within the wires, or outside either. I like them the way they are.

Now, it's about mid-day. I'll fill half an hour with my sculpturing, then. There's a patch of ground about a hundred yards the other side of the wires on the eastside of the house, where I'm arranging rocks. There's a central area where they're piled up higher, and around that they're just strewn to look natural. You might think this is a weird thing to do for someone who won't have a vegetable patch in case someone sees it, but I'm very careful with the rocks. Spent a long time studying on how the natural formations look around here. Spent even longer walking back from distant points with just the right kind of rocks. I was born right on this hillside. I know the area better'n probably anyone. The way I'm working it, the central area is going to look like just another outcrop, and the stuff around, like it just fell off and has been laying there for years.

It passes the time, anyway.

I eat my meal around 1:00 PM. Kind of late, but otherwise the afternoon can feel a little long. I eat what I left over from supper the night before. Saves a fire. Although leaving the door open when I'm around the property disperses most of the smoke, letting it out slowly, a portion is always going to linger in the cabin, I guess. If it's been a still day, then when I wake up the next morning my chest can feel kind of clotted. Better than having it all shoot up the chimney, but it's still not a perfect system. It could be improved. I'm thinking about it, in my spare time, which occurs between 1:30 and 2:00 PM.

The afternoons are where the schedule becomes a tad more freeform. It depends on what my needs are. At first, after the thing, I would walk out to stock up on whatever I could find in the local towns. There's two within reasonable foot distance—Elum, which is about six miles away, and Noqualmi, a little further in the other direction. But those were both real small towns, and there's really nothing left there now. Stores, houses, they're all empty and stripped even if not actually burned down. This left me in a bit of a spot for a while, but then, when I was walking back through the woods from Noqualmi empty-handed one afternoon, I spied a little gully I didn't think I knew. Walked up it, and realized there might be other sources I hadn't yet found. Felt dumb for not thinking of it before, in fact.

So that's what I do some afternoons. This area wasn't ever home to that many vacation cabins or cottages, on account of the skiing never really took off and the winter here is really just kind of cold, instead of picturesque cold-but there are a few. I've found nine, so far. First half-dozen were ones where I'd done some handy work at some point—like for the therapy woman—so they were easier to find. Others I've come upon while out wandering. They've kept me going on tinned vegetables, extra blankets. I even had a little gas stove for a while, which was great. Got right around the whole smoke problem, and so I had hot coffee all day long. Ran out of gas after a while, of course. Finding some more is a way up my wish list, I'll tell you, just below a new vacuum flask.

Problem is, those places were never year-round dwellings, and the owners didn't leave much stuff on site, and I haven't even found a new one in a couple weeks. But I live in hope. I'm searching in a semi-organized grid pattern. Could be more rigorous about it, but something tells me it's a good idea to leave open the possibility you might have missed a place earlier, that when you're finished you're not actually finished—that's it and it's all done and so what now?

Living in hope takes work, and thinking ahead. A schedule does no harm, either, of course.

Those lessons you learn at a parent's knee or bent over it-have a way of coming back, even if you thought you weren't listening.

What I'm concentrating on most of all right now, though, is building my stocks of food. The winter is upon us, there is no doubt, and the sky and the trees and the way the wind's coming down off the mountain says it's going to land hard and bed itself down for the duration. This area is going to be very isolated. It was that way before the thing, and sure as hell no one's going to be going out of their way to head out here now.

There's not a whole lot you can do to increase the chance of finding stuff. At first I would go to the towns, and had some success there. It made sense that they'd come to sniff around the houses and bins. Towns were a draw, however small. But that doesn't seem to happen so much now. Stocks have got depleted in general and—like I say—it's cold and getting colder and that's not the time of year when you think hey, I'll head into the mountains.

So what I mainly do now is head out back into the woods. From the back of the cabin there's about three roads you can get to in an hour or so's walking, in various directions. One used to be the main route down to Oregon, past Yakima and such. Wasn't ever like it was a constant stream of traffic on it, but that was where I got lucky the last two times, and so you tend to get superstitious, and head back to the same place until you realize it's just not working any more.

The first time was just a single, middle-aged guy, staggering down the middle of the road. I don't even know where he'd come from, or where he thought he was going. This was not a man who knew how to forage or find stuff, and he was thin and half-delirious. Cheered right up when he met me. The last time was better. A young guy and girl, in a car. They hadn't been an item before the thing, but they were now. He believed so, anyway. He was pretty on the button, or thought he was.

They had guns and a trunk full of cans and clothes, back seat packed with plastic containers of gasoline. I stopped them by standing in the middle of the road. He was wary as hell and kept his hand on his gun the whole time, but the girl was worn out and lonely and some folks have just not yet got out of the habit of wanting to see people, to mix with other humans once in a while.

I told them Noqualmi still had some houses worth holing up in, and that there'd been no trouble there in a while on account of it had been empty in months, and so the tide had drifted on. I know he thought I was going to ask to come in the car with them, but after I'd talked with them a while I just stepped back and wished them luck. I watched them drive on up the road, then walked off in a different direction.

Middle of that evening—in a marked diversion from the usual schedule, but I judged it worth it—I went down through the woods and came into Noqualmi via a back way. Didn't take too long to find their car, parked up behind one of the houses. They weren't ever going to last that long, I'm afraid. They had a candle burning, for heaven's sake. You could see it from out in the back yard, and that is the one thing that you really can't do. Three nights out of five I could have got there and been too late already. I got lucky, I guess. I waited until they put the light out, and then a little longer.

The guy looked like he'd have just enough wits about him to trick the doors, so I went in by one of the windows. They were asleep. Worse things could have happened to them, to be honest, much worse. There should have been one of them keeping watch. He should have known that. He could have done better by her, I think.

Getting them back to the cabin took most of the next day, one trip for each. I left the car right where it was. I don't need a car, and they're too conspicuous. He was kind of skinny, but she has a little bulk. Right now they're the reason why the winter isn't worrying me quite as much as it probably should. Them, plus a few others I've been lucky enough to come across—and yes, I do thank my luck. Sure, there's method in what I've done, and most people wouldn't have enjoyed the success rate I've had. But in the end, like my father used to say, any time you're out looking for deer, it's luck that's driving the day. A string of chances and decisions that are out of your hands, that will put you in the right place at the right time, and brings what you're looking for rambling your way.

If I don't go out hunting in the afternoon, then either I'll nap a while or go do a little more sculpting. It only occurred to me to start that project a few weeks ago, and I'd like to get some more done before it starts to snow.

At first, after the thing, it looked like everything just fell apart at once, that the change was done and dusted. Then it started to become clear it didn't work that way, that there were waves. So, if you'd started to assume maybe something wasn't going to happen, that wasn't necessarily correct. Further precautions seemed like a good idea.

Either way, by 5:00 PM the light's starting to go and it's time to close up the day. I'll go out to the shed and cut a portion of something down for dinner, grab something of a plant or vegetable nature to go with it, or—every third day—open a can of corn. Got a whole lot of corn still, which figures, because I don't really like it that much.

I'll cook the meat over the day's third fire, straight away, before it gets dark, next to a final can of water—I really need to find myself another of those vacuum flasks, because not having warm coffee in the evening is what gets me closest to feeling down—and have that whole process finished as quick as I can.

I've gotten used to the regime as a whole, but that portion of the day is where you can still find your heart beating, just a little. I grew up used to the idea that the dark wasn't anything to fear, that nothing was going to come and do anything bad to you—from outside your house, anyway. Night meant quietness outside and nothing but forest sounds which—if you understood what was causing them—were no real cause for alarm. It's not that way now, after the thing, and so that point in the schedule where you seal up the property and trust that your preparations, and the wires, are going to do their job, is where it all comes home. You recall the situation.

Otherwise, apart from a few things like the nature of the food I eat, it's really not so different to the way life was before. I understand the food thing might seem like a big deal, but really it isn't. Waste not, want that—and yes, he said that too. Plenty other animals do it, and now isn't the time for beggars to be choosers. That's what we're become, bottom line—animals, doing what's required to get by, and there isn't any shame in that at all. It's all we ever were, if we'd stopped to think about it. We believed we had the whole deal nailed out pretty good, were shooting up in some pre-ordained arc to the sky. Then someone, somewhere, fucked up. I never heard an explanation that made much sense to me. People talked a lot about a variety of things, but then people always talked a lot, didn't they? Either way, you go past Noqualmi cemetery now, or the one in Elum, and the ground there looks like Swiss cheese. A lot of empty holes, though there are some sites yet to burst out, later waves in waiting.

Few of them didn't get far past the gates, of course. I took down a handful myself, in the early days.

I remember the first one I saw up here, too, a couple weeks after the thing. It came by itself, blundering slowly up the rise. It was night-time, of course, so I heard it coming rather than seeing anything. First I thought it was someone real, was even dumb enough to go outside, shine a light, try to see who it was. I soon realized my error, I can tell you that. It was warmer then, and the smell coming off up the hill was what gave it away. I went back indoors, got the gun. Only thing I use it for now, as shells are at a premium. Everything else, I use a knife.

Afterwards I had a good look, though I didn't touch it. Poked it with a stick, turned it over. It really did smell awful bad, and they're not, something you're going to consider eating—even if there wasn't a possibility you could catch something off the flesh. I don't know if there's some disease to be caught, if that's how it even works, but it's a risk I'm not taking now or likely ever. I wrapped the body up in a sheet and dragged it a long, long way from the property. Do the same with any others that make it up here from time to time. Dump them in different directions, too, just in case. I don't know what level of intelligence is at work, but they're going to have to try harder at it if they ever hope to get to me—especially since I put in the wires.

I have never seen any of them abroad during the day, but that doesn't mean they aren't, or won't in the future. So wherever I go, I'm very careful. I don't let smoke come out of my chimney, instead dispersing it out the doors and window—and only during the day. The wires go through to trips with bells inside the cabin. Not loud bells—no sense in broadcasting to one of them that they just shambled through something significant. The biggest danger is the shed, naturally—hence trying to make it air-tight. Unlike just about everything else, however, that problem's going to get easier as it gets colder. There's going to come a point where I'll be chipping dinner off with a chisel, but at least the danger of smell leaking out the cracks will drop right down to nothing.

Once everything's secured for the night, I eat my meal in the last of the daylight, with the last hot cup of coffee of the day. I set aside a little food for the morning. I do not stay up late.

The windows are all covered with blackout material, naturally, but I still don't like to take the risk. So I sit there in the dark for a spell, thinking things over. I get some of my best ideas under those conditions, in fact-there's something about the lack of distraction that makes it like a waking dream, lets you think laterally. My latest notion is a sign. I'm considering putting one up, somewhere along one of the roads, that just says THIS WAY, and points. I'm thinking if someone came along and saw a sign like that, they'd hope maybe there was a little group of people along there, some folks getting organized, safety in numbers and that, and so they'd go along to see what's what.

And find me, waiting for them, a little way into the woods.

I'll not catch all of them—the smart guy in the car would have driven straight by, for example, though his girl might have had something to say on the subject—but a few would find my web. I have to think the idea through properly—don't know for sure that the others can't read, for example, though at night they wouldn't be able to see the sign anyway, if I carve it the right way—but I have hopes for it as a plan. We'll see.

It's hard not to listen out, when you've climbed in bed, but I've been doing that all my life. Listening for the wind, or for bears snuffling around, back when you saw them up here. Listening for the sound of footsteps coming slowly toward the door of the room I used to sleep in when I was a kid. I know the wires will warn me, though, and you can bet I've got my response to such a thing rigorously worked out.

I generally do not have much trouble getting off to sleep, and that's on account of the schedule as much as anything. It keeps me active, so the body's ready for some rest come the end of day. It also gives me a structure, stops me getting het up about the general situation.

Sure, it is not ideal. But, you know, it's not that different on the day-to-day. I don't miss the television because I never had one. Listening to the radio these days would only freak you out. Don't hanker after company because there was never much of that after my father died. Might have been nice if the Ramona thing had worked out, but she didn't understand the importance of the schedule, of thinking things through, of sticking to a set of rules that have been proven to work.

She was kind of husky and lasted a good long time, though, so it's not like there wasn't advantages to the way things panned out. I caught her halfway down the hill, making a big noise about what she found in the shed. She was not an athletic person. Wasn't any real possibility she was going to get away, or that she would have lasted long out there without me to guide her. What happened was for the best, except I broke the vacuum flask on the back of her head, which I have since come to regret.

Otherwise I'm at peace with what occurred, and most other things. The real important thing is when you wake up, you know what's what—that you've got something to do, a task to get you over the hump of remembering, yet again, what the world's come to. I'm lucky that way.

The sculpting's the one area I'd like to get ahead of. The central part is pretty much done—it's coming up for three feet high, and I believe it would be hard to get up through that. But sometimes, when I'm lying in the dark waiting for sleep to come, I wonder if I shouldn't extend that higher portion; just in case there's a degree of tunneling possible, sideways and then up. I want to be sure there's enough weight, and that it's spread widely enough over the grave.

I owe my father a lot, when I think over it. In his way, through the things he said, he taught me a great deal of what it turned out I needed to know. I am grateful to him for that, I guess.

But I still don't want to see him again.

Michael Marshall Smith *is a novelist and screenwriter. Under this name he has published over seventy short stories and three novels—*Only Forward, Spares, *and* One of Us—*winning the Philip K. Dick, HWA, August Derleth and British Fantasy Awards, as well as the Prix Morane. Writing as Michael Marshall, he has published six internationally-bestselling thrillers, including* The Straw Men, The Intruders, *and* Bad Things, *and 2009 saw the publication of* The Servants, *under the name M.M. Smith. His new Michael Marshall novel* The Breakers *will be published in 2011. He lives in North London with his wife, son, and two cats. His Web site is: www.michaelmarshallsmith.com*

Elsewhere, the author has said this story "came about from a very simple idea . . . that the end of the world as we know it might not come as either a big change to some people or even seen as a bad thing." Encouraged by the media we focus too often on "the Next Big Thing, the Oncoming Big Disaster. But the truth of the matter is that in our heart if hearts, where we really live, the biggest and most destructive events of our lives may already have happened."

Naming of Parts

Tim Lebbon

"A child grows up when they realize that they will die."—Proverb

That night, something tried to break into the house. Jack heard the noises as he lay awake staring at the ceiling, attempting to see sense in the shadowy cracks that scarred the paintwork. The sounds were insistent and intelligent, and before long they were fingering not only at window latches and handles, but also at the doorways of his mind.

He liked listening to the night before he went to sleep, and out here in the country there was much to hear. Sometimes he was afraid, but then he would name all the different parts that went to make up that fear and it would go away. *A sound I cannot identify. A shape I cannot see. Footsteps that may be human, but which are most likely animal. There's nothing to be afraid of, there are no monsters. Dad and Mum both say so; there are no such things as monsters.*

So he would lie there and listen to the hoots and rustles and groans and cries, content in the knowledge that there was nothing to fear. All the while the blankets would be his shield, the bedside light his protector, and the gentle grumble of the television from downstairs his guarantee.

But that night—the night all guarantees were voided—there were few noises beyond his bedroom window, and with less to hear, there was more to be afraid of. Against the silence every snapped twig sounded louder, each rustle of fur across masonry was singled out for particular attention by his galloping imagination. It meant that there was something out there to frighten everything else into muteness.

And then the careful caress of fingertips across cold glass.

Jack sat up in bed and held his breath. Weak moonlight filtered through the curtains, but other than that his room was filled with darkness. He clutched at his blankets to retain the heat. Something hooted in the distance, but the call was cut off sharply, leaving the following moments painfully empty.

Click click click. Fingernails picking at old, dried glazing putty, perhaps? It sounded like it was coming from outside and below, but it could just as easily have originated within his room, behind the flowing curtains, something frantically trying to get out rather than break in.

He tried naming his fears, this time unsuccessfully; he was not entirely sure what was scaring him.

A floorboard creaked on the landing, the one just outside the bathroom door. Three creaks down, three back up. Jack's heart beat faster and louder and he let out a gasp, waiting for more movement, listening for the subtle scratch of fingernails at his bedroom door. He could not see the handle, it was too dark, it may even be turning now—

Another creak from outside, and then he heard his mother's voice and his father hissing back at her.

"Dad!" Jack croaked. There were other sounds now: the soft thud of something tapping windows; a whispering sound, like a breeze flowing through the ivy on the side of the house, though the air was dead calm tonight.

"Dad!" He called louder this time, fear giving his voice a sharp edge to cut through the dark.

The door opened and a shadow entered, silhouetted against the landing light. It moved towards him, unseen feet creaking more boards. "It's okay, son," his father whispered, "just stay in bed. Mum will be in with you now. Won't you, Janey?"

Jack's mother edged into the room and crossed to the bed, cursing as she stumbled on something he'd left on the floor. There was always stuff on the floor in Jack's room. His dad called it *Jack debris*.

"What's going on, Dad?" he asked. "What's outside?"

"There's nothing outside," his father said. His voice was a monotone that Jack recognized, the one he used to tell fatherly untruths. And then Jack noticed, for the first time, that he was carrying his shotgun.

"Dad?" Jack said uncertainly. Cool fingers seemed to touch his neck, and they were not his mother's.

She hugged him to her. "Gray, you're scaring him."

"Janey—"

"Whatever . . . just be careful. Be calm."

Jack did not understand any of this. His mother hugged him and in her warmth he found the familiar comfort, though tonight it felt like a lie. He did not want this comfort, this warmth, not when there was something outside trying to get in, not when his father stood in his pyjamas, shotgun closed and aimed at the wall, not broken open over his elbow as he carried it in the woods.

The woods. Thinking of them aimed Jack's attention, and he finally noticed just how utterly silent it was out there. No voices or night-calls, true, but no trees swishing and swaying in sleep, no sounds of life, no hint of anything existing beyond the house at all.

His father moved to the window and reached out for the curtains. Jack knew what he would find when he pulled them back—nothing. Blankness, void, or infinity . . . and infinity scared Jack more than anything. How could something go on forever? What was there after it ended? Occasionally he thought he had some bright idea, but then sleep would come and steal it away by morning.

"Dad, don't, there's nothing out there!" he said, his voice betraying barely controlled panic.

"Shhh, shhh," his mother said, rocking him.

"I know," his father said without turning to offer him a smile. He grabbed a curtain and drew it aside.

Moonlight. The smell of night, a spicy dampness that seemed always to hide from the sun. And the noises again, tapping and scraping, tapping and scraping.

"Mum, don't let Dad open the window," Jack said, but his mother ignored him because she was hugging him, and that was usually enough. He would forget his bad dreams and go back to sleep, Mum would smile at the foolishness he'd spouted, but didn't she know? Didn't she see that they were all awake, and that what he was thinking was not foolishness because his dad really was standing in his room with a shotgun, opening the window, leaning out now, aiming the weapon before him like a torch—

There was an explosion. Like an unexpected scream in the depths of night it tore through Jack's nerves, shred his childish sense of valour and set him screaming and squirming in his mother's lap. Her arms tightened around him and she screamed too, he could smell the sudden tang of her fear, could feel the dampness between her breasts as he pressed his face to her chest.

"Gray, what the fuck—"

Her words shocked Jack but he could not lift his face to see.

"What the hell? What are you doing, what are you shooting at?"

Somewhere in the blind confusion his father came across and offered soothing words, but they were edged with his own brand of fear. Jack could not see him but he could imagine him standing there in silence, staring at a wall and avoiding his mother's eyes. It was his way of thinking about what to say next.

He said nothing. Instead, Jack felt his dad's strong hands under his arms, lifting him up out of the warmth of his mother's fear and letting the dark kiss his sweaty skin cool.

"Dad," Jack sobbed, "I'm scared!"

His dad rocked him back and forth and whispered into his ear, but Jack could barely hear what he was saying. Instead he tried to do what he had once been told, name the parts of his fear in an attempt to identify them and set them open to view, to consideration, to understanding.

Something, outside in the dark. Dad, he saw it and shot it. The sounds, they've gone, no more picking, no more prodding at our house. Monsters, there are none of course. But if there are . . . Dad scared them off.

"Gray," his mother said, and Jack looked up sharply.

"They weren't monsters, were they, Dad?" His father did not say a word. He was shaking.

"Gray," his mum said again, standing and wrapping them both in her arms. "We should try the police again."

"You know the phone's dodgy, Janey."

"You shot at someone. We should try the police."

"*Someone*? But you saw, you—"

"Someone," Jack's Mum whispered softly. "Robbers, I expect, come to steal our Jackie's things." She ruffled his hair but Jack could not find a smile to give her.

"I heard them picking at the putty," he said. "Robbers would just smash the window. Least, they do in *The Bill*. And there's nothing else making a noise, like the fox in the woods. I always hear the fox before I go to sleep, but I haven't heard it tonight. Dad!"

His father turned and stared at him, his face unreadable.

"Did you shoot someone, Dad?"

His father shook his head. He began to smile as he pulled Jack's face into his neck, but the expression was grotesque, like one of those old gargoyles Jack had seen on churches when they were in France last year. "Of course not, Jack. I fired into the air."

But he had not fired into the air, Jack knew. He had leaned out and aimed down. Jack could not help but imagine something squirming on the ground even now, its blood running into the gravel alongside the house, screams of pain impossible because it had no jaw left to open—

"Come on," his dad said, "our room for now, son."

"Didn't you try the mobile?" Jack asked suddenly, but the look on his mother's face made him wish he hadn't.

"That's not working at all."

"I expect the batteries have run out," he said wisely.

"I expect."

His father carried him across the creaking landing and into their bedroom, a place of comfort. He dropped him gently onto the bed, and as he stood the telephone on the bedside table rang.

"I'll get it!" Jack shouted, leaping across the bed.

"Son—"

He answered in the polite manner he had been taught: "Hello, Jack Haines, how may I help you?" *It's the middle of the night*, he thought. *Who rings in the middle of the night? What am I going to hear? Do I really want to hear it, whatever it is?*

"Hey, Jackie," a voice said, masked with crackles and pauses and strange, electronic groans. "Jackie . . . the town . . . dangerous . . . get to Tewton . . . Jackie? Jackie? Ja . . . ?"

"Mandy," he said, talking both to her and his parents. "It's Mandy!"

His mother took the receiver from his hand. "Mandy? You there?" She held it to her ear for a few seconds, then glanced at Jack. "No one there," she said. "Line's dead. It did that earlier." She turned to his dad and offered the receiver, but he moved to the window and shaded his eyes so he could see out.

"She said we should go to Tewton," Jack said, trying to recall her exact words, afraid that if he did he would also remember the strange way she had spoken. Mandy never called him Jackie. "She said it was safe there."

"It's safe here," his dad said without turning around. He was holding the shotgun again and Jack wanted to believe him, wanted to feel secure.

His mum stood and moved to the window. "What's that?" Jack heard her mutter.

"Fire."

"A fire?"

His father turned and tried to smile, but it seemed to hurt. "A bonfire," he said, "over on the other side of the valley."

"At night? A bonfire in the middle of the night?" Jack asked.

His parents said nothing. His mother came back to the bed and held him, and his father remained at the window.

"It *was* Mandy," Jack said.

His mother shrugged. "I didn't hear anyone."

He tried to move away from her but she held him tight, and he thought it was for her own comfort as much as his. He didn't like how his mum and dad sometimes talked about Mandy. He liked even less the way they often seemed to forget about her. He was old enough to know some stuff had happened—he could remember the shouting, the screaming, the punching on the last day Mandy had been with them—but he was not really old enough to realize exactly what.

It was so quiet, Jack could hear his father's throat clicking as he breathed.

They stayed that way until morning.

"There are secrets in the night," Mandy once told him. She was sitting next to his bed, looking after him because he'd been lost in the woods. He usually liked it when Mandy talked to him, told him things, but today even she could not cheer him up. She and his parents were hardly speaking, and when they did it was to exchange nothing but nastiness.

"What do you mean?"

She smiled. *"You know, Jack. Secrets. You lie awake sometimes, listening for them. Don't you? I know I do."*

"I just like listening," he said, but he guessed she was right. He guessed there was more going on than most people knew, and he wanted to find out what.

"If you find a secret, sometimes it's best to keep it to yourself. Not to tell Mum and Dad."

Jack was subtly shocked at her words. Why keep something from Mum and Dad? Wasn't that lying? But Mandy answered for him.

"Sometimes, grown-ups don't understand their kid's secret. And I'll tell you one now."

He sat up in bed, all wide-eyed and snotty-nosed. He wondered why Mandy was crying.

"I'm leaving home. At the weekend. Going to live in Tewton. But Jack, please, don't tell Mum and Dad until I'm gone."

Jack blinked as tears stung his eyes. Mandy hugged him and kissed his cheeks.

He didn't want his sister to go. But he listened to what she said, and he did not tell their parents the secret.

Three days later, Mandy left home.

In the morning Jack went to fetch the milk, but the milkman hadn't been. His father appeared behind him in the doorway, scowling out at the sunlight and the dew steaming slowly from the ground, hands resting lightly on his son's shoulders.

Something had been playing on Jack's mind all night, ever since it happened. An image had seeded there, grown and expanded and, in the silence of his parent's bedroom where none of them had slept, it had blossomed into an all-too-plausible truth. Now, with morning providing an air of normality—though it remained quieter than usual, and stiller—he was certain of what he would find. He did not *want* to find it, that was for sure, yet he had to see.

He darted away from the back door and was already at the corner of the house before his dad called after him. The shout almost stopped him in his tracks because there was an unbridled panic there, a desperation . . . but then he was looking around the side of the cottage at something he had least expected.

There was no body, no blood, no disturbed flower bed where someone had thrashed around in pain. He crunched along the gravel path, his father with him now, standing guard above and behind.

"You *didn't* shoot anyone," Jack said, and the sense of relief was vast.

Then he saw the rosebush.

The petals had been stripped, and they lay scattered on the ground alongside other things. There were bits of clothing there, and grimy white shards of harder stuff, and clumps of something else. There was also a watch.

"Dad, whose watch is that?" Jack could not figure out what he was seeing. If that was bone, where was the blood? Why was there a watch lying in their garden, its face shattered, hands frozen at some cataclysmic hour? And those dried things, tattered and ragged around the edges, like shriveled steak . . .

"Gray!" his mother called from the back door, "where are you? Gray! There's someone coming down the hill."

"Come on," Jack's dad said, grabbing his arm and pulling him to the back door.

Jack twisted around to stare up the hillside, trying to see who his mother was talking about, wondering whether it was the Judes from Berry Hill Farm. He liked Mr. Jude, he had a huge Mexican moustache and he did a great impression of a *bandito*.

"We should stay in the house," his mum said as they reached the back door. "There's nothing on the radio."

If there's nothing on the radio, what is there to be worried about? Jack wondered.

"Nothing at all?" his dad said quietly.

His mother shook her head, and suddenly she looked older and grayer than Jack had ever noticed. It shocked him, frightened him. Death was something he sometimes thought about on the darkest of nights, but his mother's death . . . its possibility was unbearable, and it made him feel black and unreal and sick inside.

"I thought there may be some news . . . "

And then Jack realized what his mum had really meant . . . no radio, no radio *at all* . . . and he saw three people clambering over a fence higher up the hill.

"Look!" he shouted. "Is that Mr. Jude?"

His father darted into the cottage and emerged seconds later with the shotgun—locked and held ready in both hands—and a pair of binoculars hanging around his neck. He handed his mother the shotgun and she held it as if it were a living snake. Then he lifted the binoculars to his eyes and froze, standing there for a full thirty seconds while Jack squinted and tried to see what his dad was seeing. He pretended he had a bionic eye, but it didn't do any good.

His dad lowered the glasses, and slowly and carefully took the gun from his wife.

"Oh no," she said, "oh no, Gray, no, no, no . . . "

"They did warn us," he murmured.

"But why the Judes? Why not us as well?" his mum whispered.

Jack's father looked down at him, and suddenly Jack was very afraid. "What, Dad?"

"We'll be leaving now, son," he said. "Go down to the car with your mum, there's a good boy."

"Can I take my books?"

"No, we can't take anything. We have to go now, because Mr. Jude's coming."

"But I like Mr. Jude!" A tear had spilled down his dad's cheek, that was terrible, that was a leak in the dam holding back chaos and true terror, because while his dad was here—firm and strong and unflinching—there was always someone to protect him.

His father knelt in front of him "Listen, Jackie. Mr. Jude and his family have a . . . a disease. If we're still here when they arrive they may try to hurt us, or we may catch the disease. I don't know which, if either. So we have to go—"

"Why don't we just not let them in? We can give them tablets and water through the window, and . . . " He trailed off, feeling cold and unreal.

"Because they're not the only ones who have the disease. Lots of other people will have it too, by now. We may have to wait a long time for help."

Jack turned and glanced up the hill at the three people coming down. They didn't look ill. They looked odd, it was true, they looked *different*. But not ill. They were moving too quickly for that.

"Okay." Jack nodded wisely, and he wondered who else had been infected. He guessed it may be something to do with what had been on the telly yesterday, the thing his mum and dad had been all quiet and tense and pale about. An explosion, he remembered, an accident, in a place so far away he didn't even recognize the name. "Mandy said we should go to Tewton, she said it was safe there."

"We will," his father nodded, but Jack knew it was not because Mandy had said so. His parents rarely listened to her any more.

"That big bonfire's still burning," Jack said, looking out across the valley for the first time. A plume of smoke hung in the sky like a frozen tornado, spreading out at the top and dispersing in high air currents. And then he saw it was not a bonfire, not really. It was the white farm on the opposite hillside; the whole white farm, burning. He'd never met the people who lived there but he had often seen the farmer in his fields, chugging silently across the landscape in his tractor.

Jack knew where the word *bonfire* came from, and he could not help wondering whether today this was literally that.

His dad said nothing but looked down at Jack, seeing that he knew what it really was, already reaching out to pick up his son and carry him to their car.

"Dad, I'm scared!"

"I've got you, Jackie. Come on Janey. Grab the keys, the shotgun cartridges are on the worktop."

"Dad, what's happening?"

"It's okay."

"Dad . . . "

As they reached the car they could hear the Jude family swishing their feet through the sheen of bluebells covering the hillside. There were no voices, there was no talking or laughing. No inane *bandito* impressions this morning from Mr. Jude.

His parents locked the car doors from the inside and faced forward.

Jack took a final look back at their cottage. The car left the gravelled driveway, and just before the hedge cut off the house from view, he saw Mr. Jude walk around the corner. From this distance, it looked like he was in black and white.

Jack kept staring from the back window so he did not have to look at his parents. Their silence scared him, and his mum's hair was all messed up.

Trees passed overhead, hedges flashed by on both sides, and seeing where they had been instead of where they were going presented so much more for his consideration.

Like the fox, standing next to a tree where the woods edged down to the road. Its coat was muddied, its eyes stared straight ahead. It did not turn to watch them pass. Jack thought it may be *his* fox—the creature he had listened to each night for what seemed like ages—and as he mourned its voice he heard its cry, faint and weak, like a baby being dragged from its mother's breast and slaughtered.

They had left the back door open. His mum had dashed inside to grab the shotgun cartridges, his dad already had the car keys in his pocket, they'd left the back door open and he was sure—he was *certain*—that his mum had put some toast under the grille before they ran away. Maybe Mr. Jude was eating it now, Jack thought, but at the same time he realized that this was most unlikely. Mr. Jude was sick, and from what Jack had seen of him as he peered around the corner of their cottage, toast was the last thing on his mind.

Living, perhaps, was the first thing. Surviving. Pulling through.

Jack wondered whether the rest of Mr. Jude's family looked as bad.

The sense of invasion, of having his own space trespassed upon, was immense. They had left the back door open, and anyone or anything could wander into their house and root through their belongings. Not only the books and cupboards and food and fridge and dirty washing, but the private stuff.

Jack had a lot of private stuff in his room, like letters from Mandy which he kept under a loose corner of carpet, his diary shoved into the tear in his mattress along with the page of a magazine he had found in the woods, a weathered flash of pink displaying what a woman *really* had between her legs.

But that sense of loss was tempered by a thought Jack was suddenly proud of, an idea that burst through the fears and the doubts and the awful possibilities this strange morning presented: that he actually had his whole life with him now. They may have left their home open to whatever chose to abuse it, but home was really with his family, wherever they may be. He was with them now.

All except Mandy.

He named his fears:

Loss, his parents disappearing into memory. Loneliness, the threat of being unloved and unloving. Death . . . that great black death . . . stealing away the ones he loved.

Stealing *him* away.

For once, the naming did not comfort him as much as usual. If anything it made him muse upon things more, and Mandy was on his mind and why she had run away, and what had happened to start all the bad stuff between the people he loved the most.

Jack had come home from school early that day, driven by the headteacher because he was feeling sick. He was only eight years old. The teacher really should have seen him into the house, but instead she dropped him at the gate and drove on.

As he entered the front door he was not purposely quiet, but he made sure he did not make any unnecessary noise, either. He liked to frighten Mandy— jump out on her, or creep up from behind and smack her bum—because he loved the startled look on her face when he did so. And to be truthful, he loved the playful fight they would always have afterwards even more.

He slipped off his shoes in the hallway, glanced in the fridge to see if there were any goodies, ate half a jam tart . . . and then he heard the sound from the living room.

His father had only ever smacked him three times, the last time more than a year before. What Jack remembered more than the pain was the loud noise as his dad's hand connected with him. It was a sound that signified a brief failure in their relationship; it meant an early trip to bed, no supper, and a dreadful look on his mother's face which he hated even more, a sort of dried up mix of shame and guilt.

Jack despised that sound. He heard it now, not only once, not even three times. Again, and again, and again—smacking. And even worse than that, the little cries that came between each smack. And it was Mandy, he knew that, it was Mandy being hit over and over.

Their mum and dad were in work. So who was hitting Mandy?

Jack rushed to the living room door and flung it open.

His sister was kneeling on the floor in front of the settee. She had no clothes on and her face was pressed into the cushions, and the man from the bakery was kneeling behind her, grasping her bum, and he looked like he was hurting, too. Jack saw the man's willy—at least he thought that's what it was, except this was as big as one of the French bread sticks he sold—sliding in and out of his sister, and it was all wet and shiny like she was bleeding, but it wasn't red.

"Mandy?" Jack said, and in that word was everything: *Mandy what are you doing? Is he hurting you? What should I do?* "Mandy?"

Mandy turned and stared at him red-faced, and then her mouth fell open and she shouted: "What the fuck are you doing here?"

Jack turned and ran along the hallway, forgetting his shoes, feet slapping on quarry tiles. He sprinted across the lawn, stumbling a couple of times. And then he heard Mandy call after him. He did not turn around. He did not want to see her standing at the door with the baker bouncing at her from behind. And he didn't want her to swear at him again, when he had only come home because he felt sick.

All he wished for was to un-see what he had seen.

Jack spent that night lost in the woods. He could never remember any of it, and when he was found and taken home the next day he started to whoop, coughing up clots of mucus and struggling to breathe. He was ill for two weeks, and Mandy sat with him for a couple of hours every evening to read him the fantastic tales of Narnia, or sometimes just to talk. She would always kiss him goodnight and tell him she was sorry, and Jack would tell her it was okay, he sometimes said *fuck* too, but only when he was on his own.

It seemed that as Jack got better, so everything else in their family got worse.

It was a little over two miles to the nearest village, Tall Stennington. Jack once asked his father why they lived where they did, why didn't they live in a village or a town where there were other people, and shops, and gas in pipes under the ground instead of oil in a big green tank. His dad's reply had confused him at the time, and it still did to an extent.

You've got to go a long way nowadays before you can't hear anything of Man.

Jack thought of that now as they twisted and turned through lanes that still had grass clumps along their spines. There was no radio, his mum had said, and he wondered exactly what they would hear outside were they to stop the car now. He would talk if they did, sing, shout, just to make sure there was a sound other than the silence of last night.

The deathly silence.

"Whose watch was that in the garden, Dad?"

"I expect it belonged to one of the robbers."

Jack thought about this for a while, staring from his window at the hedges rolling by. He glanced up at the trees forming a green tunnel over the road, and he knew they were only minutes from the village. "So, what was the other stuff lying around it? The dried stuff, like meat you've left in the fridge too long?"

His dad was driving so he had an excuse, but his mum didn't turn around either. It was she who spoke, however.

"There's been some stuff on the news—"

"Janey!" his dad cut in. "Don't be so bloody stupid!"

"Gray, if it's really happening he has to know . . . he will know. We'll see them, lots of them, and—"

"All the trees are pale," Jack said, the watch and dried meat suddenly forgotten. He was looking from the back window at the avenue of trees they had just passed, and he had figured what had been nagging him about the hedges and the fields since they'd left the cottage: their color; or rather, their lack of it. The springtime flush of growth had been flowering across the valley for the last several weeks, great explosions of rich greens, electric blues and splashes of colors which, as his dad was fond of saying, would put a Monet to shame. Jack didn't know what a Monet was, but he was sure there was no chance in a billion it could ever match the slow-burning firework display nature put on at the beginning of every year. Spring was his favorite season, followed by autumn. They were both times of change, beautiful in their own way, and Jack loved to watch stuff happen.

Now, something *had* happened. It was as though autumn had crept up without anyone or anything noticing, casting its pastel influence secretly across the landscape.

"See?" he said. "Mum? You see?"

His mum turned in her seat and stared past Jack. She was trying to hide the fact she had been crying; she looked embarrassed and uncertain.

"Maybe they're dusty," she said.

He knew she was lying; she didn't really think that at all. "So what was on the news?" he asked.

"We're at the village." His dad slowed the car at the humpback bridge, which marked the outskirts of Tall Stennington.

Jack leaned on the backs of his parents' seats and strained forward to see through the windscreen. The place looked as it always had: the church dominated with a recently sandblasted tower; stone cottages stood huddled beneath centuries-old trees; a few birds flitted here and there. A fat old Alsation trundled along the street and raised its leg in front of the Dog and Whistle, but it seemed unable to piss.

The grocer's was closed. It opened at six every morning, without fail, even Sundays. In fact, Jack could hardly recall ever seeing it closed, as if old Mrs. Haswell had nothing else to do but stock shelves, serve locals and natter away about the terrible cost of running a village business.

"The shop's shut," he said.

His dad nodded. "And there's no one about."

"Yes there is," his mum burst out. "Look, over there, isn't that Gerald?"

"Gerald the Geriatric!" Jack giggled, because that's what they called him at school. He'd usually be told off for that, he knew, on any normal day. After the first couple of seconds he no longer found it all that funny himself. There was something wrong with Gerald the Geriatric.

He leaned against a wall, dragging his left shoulder along the stonework with jerky, infrequent movements of his legs. He was too far away to see his expression in full, but his jowls and the saggy bags beneath his eyes seemed that much larger and darker this morning. He also seemed to have mislaid his trademark walking stick. There were legends that he had once beaten a rat to death with that stick in the kitchen of the Dog and Whistle, and the fact that he had not frequented that pub' for a decade seemed to hint at its truth. Jack used to imagine him striking out at the darting rodent with the knotted length of oak, spittle flying from his mouth, false teeth chattering with each impact. Now, the image seemed grotesque rather than comical.

His mother reached for the door handle.

"Wait, Mum!" Jack said.

"But he's hurt!"

"Jack's right. Wait." His dad rested his hand on the stock of the shotgun wedged down beneath their seats.

Gerald paused and stood shakily away from the wall, turning his head to stare at them. He raised his hands, his mouth falling open into a toothless grin or grimace. Jack could not even begin to tell which.

"He's in pain!" Jack's mum said, and this time she actually clicked the handle and pushed her shoulder to the door, letting in cool morning air.

"Janey, remember what they said—"

"What's that?" Jack said quietly. It was the sound a big spider's legs made on his posters in the middle of the night. The fear was the same, too—unseen things.

His mum had heard it as well, and she *snicked* the door shut.

There was something under the car. Jack felt the subtle tickle of soft impacts beneath him, insistent scrapings and pickings, reminiscent of the window fumblers of last night.

"Maybe it's a dog," his mum said.

His dad slammed the car into reverse and burnt rubber. The skid was tremendous, the stench and reverberation overpowering. As soon as the tyres caught Jack knew that they were out of control. The car leapt back, throwing Jack forward so that he banged his head on his mother's headrest. As he looked up he saw what had been beneath the car . . . Mrs. Haswell, still flipping and rolling where the chassis had scraped her along the road, her hair wild, her skirts torn to reveal pasty, pitted thighs . . .

His father swore as the brakes failed and the car dipped sickeningly into the ditch. Jack fell back, cracking his head on the rear window and tasting the sudden salty tang of blood as he bit his tongue. His mum screeched, his dad shouted and cursed again, the engine rose and sang and screamed until, finally, it cut out.

The sudden silence was huge. The wrecked engine ticked and dripped, Jack groaned, and through the tilted windscreen he could see Mrs. Haswell hauling herself to her feet.

Steadying her tattered limbs.

Setting out for their car with slow, broken steps.

"Okay, Jackie?" his mum said. She twisted in her seat and reached back, the look in her eyes betraying her thoughts: *My son, my son!*

Jack opened his mouth to speak but only blood came out. He shuddered a huge breath and realized he'd been winded, things had receded, and only the blood on his chin felt and smelled real.

"What's wrong with her?" his dad said, holding the steering wheel and staring through the windscreen. "That's Mrs. Haswell. Under our car. Did I run her over? I didn't hit her, did you see me hit her?"

"Gray, Jackie's bleeding."

Jack tried to talk again, to say he was all right, but everything went fluid. He felt queasy and sleepy, as if he'd woken up suddenly in the middle of the night.

"Gray!"

"Jack? You okay, son? Come on, out of the car. Janey, grab the binoculars. And the shells. Wait on your side, I'll get Jack out." He paused and looked along the road again. Mrs. Haswell was sauntering between the fresh skidmarks, and now Gerald the Geriatric was moving their way as well. "Let's hurry up."

Jack took deep, heavy breaths, feeling blood bubble in his throat. The door beside him opened and his dad lifted him out, and as the sun touched his face he began to feel better. His mum wiped at his bloody chin with the sleeve of her jumper.

There was a sound now, a long, slow scraping, and Jack realized it was Mrs. Haswell dragging her feet. She'd never done that before. She was eighty, but she'd always been active and forceful, like a wind-up toy that never ran out. She hurried through the village at lunchtime, darted around her shop as if she had wheels for feet . . . she had never, in all the times Jack had seen her or spoken to her, been slow.

Her arms were draped by her sides, not exactly swinging as she walked, but moving as if they were really no part of her at all. Her mouth hung open, but she did not drool.

"What's wrong with her, Dad?"

"She's got the disease," his dad said quickly, dismissively, and Jack felt a pang of annoyance.

"Dad," he said, "I think I'm old enough for you to tell me the truth." It was a childish thing to say, Jack understood that straight away at some deeper level; petulant and prideful, unmindful of the panic his parents so obviously felt. But Jack was nearly a teenager—he felt he deserved some trust. "Anyway," he said, "she looks like she's dead." He'd seen lots of films where people died, but hardly any of them looked like the old woman. She seemed lessened somehow, shrunken into herself, drained. She had lost what little color she once possessed. In his mind's eye, this was how a true, real-life dead person should look.

His dad aimed the shotgun at Mrs. Haswell.

Jack gasped. For the second time in as many minutes, he found himself unable to talk.

"Gray," his mother said cautiously, quietly, hands raised in a warding-off gesture, "we should go across the fields."

Jack saw his dad's face then—tears stinging the corners of his eyes; lips pressed together tight and bloodless, the way they'd been on the day Mandy left home for the last time—and he realized what a dire situation they were in.

His dad had no idea of what to do.

"Across the fields to the motorway," his mum continued, "if there's any help, we may find it there. And I'm sure they couldn't drive." She nodded at Mrs. Haswell as she spoke. "Could they? You don't think they could, do you?"

His dad was breathing heavily, just as Jack did whenever he was trying not to cry. He grabbed Jack's hand.

Jack felt the cool sweat of his father's palms . . . like touching a hunk of raw meat before it was cooked.

They walked quickly back the way they had come, then hopped over a stile into the field.

Jack glanced back at their car, canted at a crazy angle in the ditch, and saw that the two old people had stopped in their tracks. They stood as still as statues, and just as lifeless. This was more disturbing than ever—at least before, they had seemed to possess some purpose.

She was under our car, Jack thought. *What purpose in that?*

And then his own words sprang back at him: *She looks like she's dead.*

"You know what an open mind is, Jack?" Mandy said. She had crept into his room in the middle of the night after hearing him whooping and crying. Sometimes she would sit on the edge of the bed until daybreak, just talking. Much of what she said confused him—she read all the time, and occasionally she even confused their mum and dad—but he remembered it all . . . and later, some of it began to make sense.

Jack had a grotesque vision of someone with a trapdoor in their skull, their brain pulsing and glowing underneath. He smiled uncertainly at this bloody train of thought.

"It's the ability to believe in the unbelievable," she continued, apparently unconcerned at his silence. "It's a free mind. Imagination. Growing up closes off so many doors. The modern world doesn't allow for miracles, so we don't see them. It's a very precious gift, an open mind, but it's not passive. You've got to nurture it like a bed of roses, otherwise it will wither and die. Make sure you don't close off your mind to things you find strange, Jack. Sometimes they may be the only truth."

They sat silently for a while, Jack croaking as he breathed past the phlegm in his throat, Mandy twirling strands of her long black hair between her fingers.

"It's something you have," she said suddenly, "and you always will. And that's another secret, to keep and tend."

"How do you know I have it?" he asked.

Mandy smiled at him and he saw a sadness behind her eyes. Maybe she still blamed herself for him being lost in the woods. Maybe she could already see how different their family was going to be.

"Hey," she said, "you're my brother." As if that was an answer.

The further they moved away, the more Tall Stennington appeared normal. Halfway across the field they lost sight of the shuffling shapes in the road, the empty streets beyond, the pigeons sitting silently on the church tower. Jack found himself wishing for any sign of life. He almost called out, wanting to see windows thrust open and people he knew by name or sight lean out, wave to him, comment on what a lovely brisk spring morning it was. But his tongue hurt from the car wreck. His dad had crashed because a busy old lady had cut or torn the brake cables. And she had done that because . . . because . . .

There was nothing normal this morning. Not with Tall Stennington, not with Mr. Jude, not with the fox at the edge of the woods. Not even with his parents, because they were tense and worried and hurrying across a newly-planted field, and his mum still had on her slippers. His dad carried a shotgun. His mum had her arms crossed, perhaps against the cold but more likely, Jack thought, against something else entirely.

No, nothing was normal today.

They followed the furrows ploughed into the field, stepping on green shoots and crushing them back into the earth whence they came. Jack glanced behind at his footprints, his identity stamped into the landscape only to be brushed away by the next storm. When he was younger he wanted to be an astronaut, purely for the excitement of zero-G, piloting experimental spacecraft and dodging asteroids on the way out of the Solar system. The idea still appealed to him, but his main reason now would be to walk on the moon and leave his footprints behind. He'd heard that they would be there forever, or at least near enough. When he was dead—perhaps when *everyone* was dead—some aliens might land on the moon, and see his footprints, and think, *Here was a guy willing to explore. Here was a guy with no closed doors in his head, with an open mind. Here was a guy who might have believed in us.*

Jack looked up at the ghost of the moon where it still hung in the clear morning sky. He wondered if his exact centre-line of sight were extended, would he be looking at Neil Armstrong's footprints right now?

He looked down at his feet and one of those doors in his mind flapped wide open.

Falling to his knees, he plucked at a green shoot. It felt dry and brittle between his fingers, not cool and damp as it should have. He rubbed at it and it came apart, shedding its faded outer skin and exposing powdery insides.

He picked another shoot and it was the same. The third bled a smear of greenish fluid across his fingertips, but the next was as dry as the first, and the next.

"Jack, what's up son? What are you doing?" His dad had stopped and turned, glancing nervously past Jack at the stile as if constantly expecting Mrs. Haswell and Gerald the Geriatric to come stumbling after them.

Jack shook his head, not *unable* to understand—he understood perfectly well, even for a twelve year old —but *unwilling*. The doors were open but he was stubbornly grasping the frames, not wanting to enter the strange rooms presenting themselves to him now.

"This crop's dead," he said. "It looks fresh, Dad. Mum? Doesn't it all look so fresh?" His mum nodded, cupping her elbows in her hands and shivering. Jack held up a palm full of crushed shoot. "But look. It's all dead. It's still green, but it's not growing any more."

He looked back at the village. Their footprints stood out in the young crop, three wavering lines of bent and snapped shoots. And the hedge containing the stile they had hopped over . . . its colors like those of a faded photograph, not lush and vibrant with the new growth of spring . . . He'd once read a book called *The Death of Grass*. Now, he might be living it.

To his left the hillsides, speckled with sheep so still they looked like pustules on the face of the land.

To his right the edge of a stretch of woodland, at the other end of which stood their house, doors open, toast burnt in the grille, perhaps still burning.

"Everything's dying."

His dad sighed. "Not everything," he said.

Jack began to shake, his stomach twisted into a knot and he was sure he was going to puke. Another terrible admission from his father, another fearful idea implanted when really, he should be saying, *There, there, Jackie boy, nothing's changed, it's all in your imagination.*

What could he name? How could he lay all this out to understanding, to comprehension, to acceptance, all as he had been told? He tried, even though he thought it was useless: *The villagers, like walking dead, perhaps they are. The plants, dry and brittle even though it's springtime. Mum and dad, scared to death* . . . He thought at first there was nothing there that would work, but then he named another part of this terrible day and a sliver of hope kept the light shining: *Mandy, in the town, saying it's safe.*

"Not everything, Jack," his dad said again, perhaps trying to jolt his son back to reality.

"Let's go," his mum said. "Come on, Jack, we'll tell you while we're walking . . . it's only two or three fields away . . . and there'll be help there." She smiled but it could not reach her eyes.

The motorway was not three fields away, it was six. His parents told Jack all they knew by the time they'd reached the end of the second field. He believed what they said because he could smell death in the third field, and he mentioned it, but his mum and dad lied to themselves by not even answering. Jack was sure as hell he knew what death smelled like; he'd found a dead badger in the woods a year ago, after all, and turned it over with a stick, and run home puking. This was similar only richer, stronger, as if coming from a lot more bodies. Some of them smelled cooked.

They saw the stationary cars on the motorway from two fields away. Wisps of smoke still rose here and there. Several vehicles were twisted on their backs like dead beetles.

From the edge of the field abutting the motorway they saw the shapes sitting around the ruined cars—the gray people in their colorful clothes—and although they could not tell for sure what they were eating, it was mostly red.

Jack's dad raised his binoculars. Then he turned, grabbed Jack's and his mother's hand and ran back they way they had come.

"Were they eating the people from the cars?" Jack asked, disgusted but fascinated.

His father—white-faced, frowning, shaking his head slightly as if trying to dislodge a memory—did not answer.

They walked quickly across another field, their path taking them away from the woods and between Tall Stennington and the motorway. Neither was in view any longer—the landscape here dipped and rose, and all they could see around them was countryside. Nothing to give any indication of humankind's presence; no chimney smoke or aircraft trails; no skyscrapers or whitewashed farm buildings.

No traffic noise. None at all.

Jack realized that he only noticed noise when it was no longer there.

"Dad, tell me!" Jack said. "The dead people—were they eating the people from the cars?"

"No," his father said.

Jack saw straight through the lie.

He had taken it all in, everything his parents had told him, every snippet of information gleaned from the panicked newscasts yesterday, the confused reports from overseas. He had listened and taken it all in, but he did not really understand. He had already seen it for himself—Mr. Jude and the people in the village did not have a disease at all, and the young crop really was dead—but he could not believe. It was too terrifying, too unreal. Too crazy.

He whispered as they walked, naming the parts that scared him the most: *Dead people, dead things, still moving and walking. Dumb and aimless, but dangerous just the same.*

Those fingers last night had not sounded aimless, those probings and proddings at their locked up, safe cottage. They had sounded anything *but* aimless.

He carried on naming. *Those of you who are immune, stay at home.* The broadcasts his parents had listen to had told of certain blood groups succumbing slower than others, and some being completely immune. In a way, these positive elements to the broadcasts—the mentions of immunity—scared Jack more. They made him feel increasingly isolated, one of the few survivors, and what was left? What was there that they could use now, where would they go when dead people could cut your brake cables (and that sure as shit wasn't aimless, either), when they caused crashes on the motorway so they could . . . they could . . .

Jack stumbled, dug his toes into a furrow and hit the dirt. His face pressed into the ground and he felt dry dead things scurrying across his cheeks. He wanted to cry but he could not, neither could he shout nor scream, and then he realized that what he wanted most was comfort. His mother's arms around him, his father sitting on the side of his bed stroking his brow as he did when Jack had the occasional nightmare, a cup of tea before bed, half an hour reading before he turned out his light and lay back to listen to the night.

Hands did touch him, voices did try to soothe, but all Jack could hear was the silence. All he could smell was the undercurrent of death in the motionless spring air.

Before the world receded into a strange flat brightness, Jack saw in sharp detail a line of ants marching along a furrow. They were moving strangely—too slowly, much slower than he'd ever seen one moving before, as if they were in water—and he passed out wondering how aimless these red ants really were.

He was not unconscious for long. He opened his eyes to sunlight and sky and fluffy clouds, and he suddenly knew that his parents had left him. They'd walked on, leaving him behind like an injured commando on a raid into enemy territory, afraid that he would slow them down and give the dead things a chance—

And then his mother's face appeared above his and her tears dropped onto his cheeks. "Jackie," she said, smiling, and Jack could hear the love in her voice. He did not know how—it did not sound any different from usual—but out here, lost in a dying landscape, he knew that she loved him totally. She would never leave him behind. She would rather die.

"I want to go home," Jack said, his own tears mixing with his mother's on his face. He thought of the cottage and all the good times he had spent there. It would be cold inside by now, maybe there were birds . . . dead birds, arrogantly roosting on plate racks and picture frames. "Mum, I want to go home, I want none of this to happen." He held up his arms and she grabbed him, hugging him so tightly that his face was pressed into her hair, his breath squeezed out. He could smell her, a warm musk of sweat and stale perfume, and he took solace in the familiar.

"We can't stay here too long," his father said, but he sat down in the dirt next to his wife and son. "We've got to get on to Tewton."

"To find Mandy?"

"To find safety," his dad said. He saw Jack's crestfallen expression and averted his eyes. "And to find Mandy."

"She never hurt me, you know," Jack muttered.

"She scared you, made you run away!"

"I ran away myself! Mandy didn't make me, she only ever hurt herself!" Once more, he tried to recall his time in the woods, but the effort conjured only sensations of cold, damp and dark. Ironically, he could remember what happened afterwards with ease—the coughing, the fevers, the nightmares, Mandy by his bed, his shouting parents, Mandy running down their driveway, leaving her home behind—but still a day and a night were missing from his life.

It was a pointless argument, a dead topic, an aimless one. So nothing more was said.

They were silent for a while, catching their breath and all thinking their own thoughts. His mother continued to rock him in her lap but Jack knew she was elsewhere, thinking other things. His dad had broken open the shotgun and was making sure the two cartridges in there were new.

"How do you kill a dead thing, Dad?" Jack asked. A perfectly simple question, he thought. Logical. Reasonable.

His dad looked across the fields. "Tewton should be a few miles that way," he said. He looked at his watch, then up at the sun where it hung low over the hills. "We could make it by tonight if we really push it."

Jack's mum began to cry. She pulled a great clod of mud from one of her slippers and threw it at the ground. "We can't go that far alone," she said. "Not on foot. Gray, we don't know what's happened, not really. They'll come and help us, cure everyone, send us home."

"'They'?"

"You know what I mean."

"There was a film called *Them* once," Jack said. "About giant ants, and nuclear bombs. It was nothing like this, though." Even as he spoke it, he thought maybe he was mistaken. He thought maybe the film was *very much* like this, a monstrous horror of humankind's abuse of nature, and the harvest of grief it reaps.

"It's all so sudden," his dad said then. Jack actually saw his shoulders droop, his head dip down, as if he was being shrunken and reduced by what had happened. "I don't think there's much help around, not out here. Not yet."

"It'll be all right in Tewton," Jack said quietly. "Mandy said it was safe there, she phoned us because she was worried, so we've got to go. I don't want to stay out in the dark. Not after last night, Mum. Remember the noises?"

His mother nodded and tightened her lips.

"I don't want to know what made those noises." Jack felt close to tears once more but he could not let them come, he would not.

A breeze came up and rustled through the dead young crop.

Jack jerked upright, eyes wide, mouth hanging open.

There was something around the corner of the L-shaped field, out of sight behind a clump of trees. He could not hear it, nor smell it exactly, but he knew it was dead, and he knew it was moving this way.

"Mum," he said, "Dad. There's something coming."

They looked around and listened hard, his dad tightening his grip on the shotgun. "I can't—"

"There!" Jack said, pointing across the field a second before something walked into view.

His mother gasped. "Oh, no."

His dad stood and looked behind them, judging how far it was to the hedge.

Eight people emerged from the hidden leg of the field, one after another. There were men and women, and one child. All of them moved strangely, as if they only just learnt how to walk, and most of them wore nightclothes. The exceptions were a policeman—his uniform torn and muddied—and someone dressed in thick sweater, ripped jeans and a bobble hat. He had something dangling from his left hand; it could have been a leash, but there was no dog.

One of the women had fresh blood splattered across the front of her nightgown.

The child was chewing something bloody. Flies buzzed his head, but none seemed to be landing.

Perhaps, Jack thought, the flies were dead as well.

The people did not pause. They walked straight at Jack and his parents, arms swinging by their sides from simple motion, not habit.

"I doubt they can run that fast," Jack's dad said.

"I'm scared," his mother whispered.

"But can they get through the hedge, Dad? Once we're through, will they follow us?"

Jack looked from the people to the hedge, and back again. He knew what was wrong with them—they were dead and they craved live food, his parents had learned all that from the news yesterday—but still he did not want to *believe*.

Their nostrils did not flare, their mouths hung open but did not drool, their feet plodded insistently . . . but not aimlessly. These dead things had a purpose, it seemed, and that purpose would be in their eyes, were they moist enough to throw back reflections.

"They're looking at us," Jack said quietly.

They walked slowly, coming on like wind-up toys with broken innards; no life in their movements at all.

Seconds later, they charged.

Whatever preconceptions Jack had about the ability of dead things to move were slaughtered here and now. The dead folk did not run, they rampaged, churning up the earth with heavy footfalls, shattering the strange peace with the suddenness of their movement. Yet their faces barely changed, other than the slack movement of their jaws snapping shut each time their feet struck mud. They did not shout or pant because, Jack guessed, they had no breath.

His dad fired the shotgun and then they all ran towards the hedge. Jack did not see what effect the shot had, he did not want to. He could sense the distance rapidly closing between them. The hedge seemed a hundred steps away, a thousands miles, and then he saw his father slowly dropping behind.

"Dad, come one!"

"Run Jackie!"

"Dad!" He was fumbling with the shotgun, Jack saw, plucking out the spent cartridges and trying to load fresh ones. "Dad, don't bother, just run!"

"Gray, Gray," he heard his mother panting under her breath, but she did not turn around. She reached the hedge first and launched herself at what she thought was an easy gap to squeeze through. She squealed, and then screamed, when she became impaled on barbed wire and sharp sticks.

Jack was seconds from the hedge but his dad was now out of sight, behind him and to the left. Jack was watching his feet so he did not trip, but in his mind's eye he saw something else: his father caught, then trampled, then gnawed into, eaten alive while he lay there broken-backed and defenseless . . .

He reached the hedge but did not slow down. Instead he jumped, scrabbling with his hands and feet even before he struck the tangled growth, hauling himself up and through the sharp thorns, the biting branches, the crisp spring foliage. Bloody tears sprang from cuts on his hands and arms.

"Mum!" he shouted as he tumbled over the other side. The breath was knocked from him as he landed, and he crawled back to the hedge in a kind of silent, airless void.

As he found his breath, he heard the blast of the shotgun once more. Something hit the ground.

His mum was struggling in the heart of the hedge and Jack went to her aid. She was already cut and bleeding, the splashes of blood vivid against withered leaves and rotting buds. "Stop struggling!" he shouted.

The shotgun again.

"Dad!"

He could see glimpses of frantic movement through the hedge—

And then he knew it was going to be all right. Not forever—in the long term everything was dark and lonely and different—but for now they would all pull through. He saw his bloodied parents hugging each other, felt the coolness of blood on his neck, smelled the scent of death receding as they left the mindless dead behind to feed on other things. He also saw a place where everything would be fine, but he had no idea how to get there.

"Jack, help me!" his mother shouted, and everything rushed back. He reached out and grabbed her arms, and although she screamed, still he pulled.

The hedge moved and shuddered as bodies crashed into it on the other side. He could not see his dad but he did not worry, there was nothing to worry about (*yet*, nothing to worry about *yet*) and then he came scrambling over, throwing the shotgun to the ground and following close behind.

His mother came free with a final harsh scream. Jack saw the wounds on her arms and shoulders where the barbed wire had slashed in and torn out, and he began to cry.

"Oh Janey," his dad said, hugging his wife and letting his tears dilute her blood. Jack closed his eyes because his mum was bleeding . . . she was hurt and she was bleeding . . . But then she was hugging him and her blood cooled on his skin.

"Come on, I don't want to stay here a minute longer," his father said. "And maybe they'll find a way through. Maybe."

They hurried along the perimeter of the new field, keeping a wary look out in case this place, too, had occupants ready to chase them into the ground.

Jack looked back only once. Shapes were silhouetted on and in the hedge like grotesque fruits, their arms twitching uselessly, clothes and skin stretched and torn on barbed wire and dead wood

He did not look again, but he heard their struggles for a long while. By the time he and his family reached the gate that led out into a little country lane, their stench had been carried away on the breeze.

The lane looked unused, but at least it was a sign of humanity.

Jack was so glad to see it.

They turned east. Jack wondered at his conviction that there was something dangerous approaching, moments before the crowd had rounded the corner in the field. He had smelled them, of course, that was it. Or perhaps he had heard them, he had a good sense of hearing, his mother always said so.

Or perhaps he had simply known that they were there.

His mother and father were walking close together behind him, almost rubbing shoulders. Almost, but not quite, because his mum's arm was a mess, there was blood dripping from her fingertips as they walked, and Jack had seen her shoulder where a flap of skin hung down across her armpit, and he'd seen the *meat* of her there where the barbed wire had torn her open.

It didn't hurt, she said, it was numb but it didn't hurt. Jack knew from the way she talked it that the numbness would not last. Once the shock had worn off and the adrenaline drained from her system, the slow fire would ignite and the pain would come in surges. For his mother, the future was a terrifying place promising nothing but worse to come.

Total silence surrounded them. The landscape had taken on an eerie appearance, one normally reserved for the strangest of autumn evenings, when the sun was sinking behind wispy clouds and the moon had already revealed itself. The hills in the distance were smothered in mist, only occasional smudges of green showing through like old bruises. Nearer by, clumps of trees sprouted on ancient hillocks. The trees were all old, Jack knew, otherwise the farmers would have cut them down; but today they looked positively ancient. Today they looked fossilized, petrified like the wood his friend Jamie had brought back from his holiday in the Dominican Republic the year before, wood so old it was like stone.

What would those trees feel like now, Jack wondered? Would their trunks be cold and dry as rock, or was there still that electric dampness of something alive? Were their leaves as green and fresh and vibrant as they should be in the spring . . . or were they as dead inside as the young harvest across the fields?

If I cut them, Jack thought, *will they bleed?*

"Hang on," his mum said, and he knew that the pain had begun. He turned back and saw her sink slowly to her knees in the lane, his dad standing over her, one hand reaching out but not touching her shoulder because he did not know what to do. It was always Jack's mum who did the comforting, the molly-coddling when Dad had a cold, the reassuring when Jack woke from nightmares and became frustrated when he just could not explain exactly what they were about. And now that she needed comforting, his dad was standing there like he was balancing a teacup on the back of his hand, unable to help his wife where she knelt bleeding and crying into the muck.

"Mum," Jack said, "my teacher said that pain is transitory."

"Big words, Jackie," she said, trying to smile for him.

"It's what he said, though. He was telling us because Jamie was going to the dentist for a filling, and he was scared of the needle. Mr. Travis said pain is transitory, you feel it when it happens but afterwards you can't remember exactly what it was like. You can't recreate pain in your memories because your body won't let you, otherwise it'll only hurt again."

His dad handed her a handkerchief and she lifted her sleeve slowly, revealing some of the smaller cuts and dabbing at them as if that would take her attention from the gaping wound in her shoulder. "The point being?" she said, sharply but not unkindly. Jack could see that she was grateful for the distraction.

"Well, if you're hurting just cast your mind into the future. When you're all better, you won't even remember what the hurting was like. And pain doesn't actually *hurt* you, anyway. It's only in your head. Your cuts will heal, Mum. In a few days it won't matter."

"In a few days . . . " she said, smiling and sighing and opening her mouth as if to finish the sentence. But she left it at that.

"It's almost midday," his dad said.

"I should be in school."

"School's off, kiddo!" Tears were cascading past his mum's smiling mouth.

"We should get moving, if we can. Janey, you think you can move, honey? If we're going to get to Tewton—"

"Where are we now?" Jack's mum asked suddenly.

His dad frowned but did not answer.

"Gray? Don't tell me that. Don't say we're lost."

"Well," he said, "Tall Stennington is maybe three miles back thataway." He turned and pointed the way they had come, though Jack thought he was probably off by about a sixth of a circle anyway. "So we must be nearing the river by now. You think, Jackie?"

You think, Jackie? His dad, asking him for advice in something so important. He tried to see himself from his father's eyes. Short, skinny, into books instead of his dad's beloved football, intelligent in his own right but academically average . . . a kid. Just a kid. However much Jack thought about things, used big words, had a hard-on when he watched bikini-clad women on holiday programmes . . . he was just a kid to his dad.

"No," Jack said. "I think you're a bit out there, Dad. I reckon we're closer to Peter's Acre than anything, so we really need to head more that way, if we can." He pointed off across the fields to where the landscape rose in the distance, lifting towards a heavily wooded hillside. "Tewton is over that hill, through the woods. If you drive you go that way, yes," he said, indicating the direction his father had suggested. "But if I was a crow, I'd go there."

"So by the time we get that far," his mum said, "what I'm feeling now I'd have forgotten."

Jack nodded, but he was frowning.

"Okay, Jackie. Let's hit it." And up she stood, careful not to look down at the strip of her husband's T-shirt wrapped around her shoulder, already stained a deep, wet red.

They left the lane and moved off across the fields towards the tree-covered hillside in the distance. Between them and the woods lay several fields, a veiny network of hedges, hints of other lanes snaking from here to there and a farmstead. It looked quiet and deserted; no smoke rose from its chimneys; its yard seemed, from this distance, empty and still. Yet for the first time, Jack was glad that his dad was carrying the gun.

Something had changed, Jack thought, since before their flight from the dead people and his mother being tangled and wounded in the hedge. It was her attitude to things—the nervousness had been swept aside by the pain, so that now she seemed to accept things more as they came than as she expected them to be. But this change in his mother had also moved down the line to his father and himself, altering the subtle hierarchy of the family, shifting emphases around so that none of them were quite the people they had been that morning.

Jack suddenly wanted to see Mandy. In the four years since her leaving home she had become something of a stranger. They still saw her on occasion—though it was always she who came to visit them—but she changed so much every time that Jack would see a different person walking in the door. She and Jack were still very close and there was an easy atmosphere between them that his parents seemed to resent, but she was not the Mandy he remembered.

Sometimes Jack would imagine that his sister was still living at home. He would go into her bedroom, and although it had been cleared out by his parents and left sterile and bland—forever awaiting a visitor to abuse its neatness—he could sense her and hear her and smell her. Only his memories placed her there, of course, but he would sit and chat with her for hours.

Sometimes, when he next spoke to her on the phone, they would carry on their conversation.

"When can we go to see Mandy?" he asked, realizing as he spoke that he sounded like a whiner. They were going, that was that, and they certainly could not move any faster.

"We'll be there by tonight, Jackie," his mother said comfortingly.

"You do love her, don't you?" he asked.

"Of course we do! She's our daughter—your sister—so of course we love her!"

"So why don't we go to see her any more?"

His mother was silent for a while, his father offering no help. There was only the crunch of their feet crushing new grass into crisp green fragments in the dirt. It sounded to Jack as though they were walking on thin ice.

"Sometimes people fall out," his mother said. "There was that time she made you run away—"

"She didn't make me, I told you, I did it myself!"

His mother winced in pain as she turned to him and Jack felt ashamed, ashamed that he was putting her through this soon after she had been dragged through a wire fence and torn to shreds. But then, he thought, maybe there was no better time. Her defences were down, the pain was filtering her thoughts and letting only essential ones through, holding back the ballast and, maybe, discarding it altogether.

"Mandy scared you," she said. "She was doing something she shouldn't have been doing and she scared you and you ran away. We didn't find you until the next day, and you don't . . . " She looked up at the sky, but Jack could still see the tears. "You don't know what that night did to your Dad and me."

"But you still love her?"

His mother nodded. "Of course we do."

Jack thought about this for a while, wondering whether easy talk and being together were really the most important things there were. "That's okay then," he said finally. "I'm hungry."

Mum dying, because she's hurt, he thought, naming his fears automatically. *Things changing, it's all still changing. Dead people. I'm afraid of the dead people.*

"We'll eat when we get to Tewton," his dad said from up ahead.

"And I'm thirsty." *No food, no drink . . . no people at all. Death; we could die out here.*

"When we get to Tewton, Jackie," his dad said, more forcefully than before. He turned around and Jack could see how much he had changed, even over the last hour. The extraordinary had been presented to him, thrust in his face in the form of a gang of dead people, denying disbelief. Unimaginable, impossible, true.

"I expect those people just wanted help, Dad." He knew it was crazy even as he said it—he *knew* they'd wanted more than that; he had seen the fresh blood—but maybe the idea would drain some of the strain from his dad's face. And maybe a lie could hide the truth, and help hold back his mother's pain, and bring Mandy back to them where she belonged, and perhaps they were only on a quiet walk in the country . . .

"Come on, son," his father said, and Jack did not know whether he meant *move along*, or *give me a break*. Whatever, he hated the air of defeat in his voice.

My dad, failing, he thought. *Pulling away from things already, falling down into himself. What about Mum? What about me?*

Who's going to protect us?

They had crossed one field and were nearing the edge of another when Jack suddenly recognized with their surroundings. To the left stood an old barn, doors rotted away and ivy making its home between the stones. The ivy was dead now, but still it clotted the building's openings, as if holding something precious inside. To the right, at the far corner of the field, an old metal plough rusted down into the ground. He remembered playing war here, diving behind the plough while Jamie threw mud grenades his way, *ack-ack-acking* a stream of machine gun fire across the field, crawling through the rape crop and plowing their own paths towards and away from each other. Good times, and lost times, never to be revisited; he felt that now more than ever. Lost times.

"I know this place!" he said. "There's a pond over there behind that hedge, with an island in the middle and everything!" He ran to the edge of the field, aiming for the gate where it stood half-open.

"Jack, wait!" his dad shouted, but Jack was away, cool breeze ruffling his hair and lifting some of the nervous sweat from his skin. The crinkle of shoots beneath his feet suddenly seemed louder and Jack wanted nothing more than to get out onto the road, leave these dead things behind, find a car or thumb a lift into Tewton where there would be help, where there had to be help, because if there wasn't then where the hell *would* there be help?

Nowhere. There's no help anywhere. The thought chilled him but he knew it was true, just as he had known that there were dead people around the corner of the field—

—just as he knew that there was something very, very wrong here as well. He could smell it already, a rich, warm tang to the air instead of the musty smell of death they had been living with all morning. A *fresh* smell. But he kept on running because he could not do anything else, even though he knew he should stay in the field, knew he *had* to stay in the field for his own good. He had played here with Jamie, they had shared good times here so it must be a good place.

Jack darted through the gate and out onto the pitted road.

The colors struck him first. Bright colors in a landscape so dull with death.

The car was a blazing yellow, a metal banana his mum would have called it, never lose that in a car park she would say. Inside the car sat a woman in a red dress, and inside the woman moved something else, a squirrel, its tail limp and heavy with her blood. The dress was not all red, he could see a white sleeve and a torn white flap hanging from the open door, touching the road.

Her face had been ripped off, her eyes torn out, her throat chewed away.

There was something else on the road next to the car, a mass of meat torn apart and spread across the tarmac. Jack saw the flash of bone and an eyeless head and a leg, still attached to the bulky torso by strands of stuff, but they did not truly register. What he did see and understand were the dozen small rodents chewing at the remnants of whatever it had been. Their tails were long and hairless, their bodies black and slick with the blood they wallowed in. They chewed slowly, but not thoughtfully, because there could not have been a single thought in their little dead minds.

"Dad," Jack gasped, trying to shout but unable to find a breath.

More things lay further towards the pond, and for a terrible moment Jack thought it was another body that had been taken apart (because that's what he saw, he knew that now, his mind had permitted understanding on the strict proviso that he—)

He turned and puked and fell to his knees in his own vomit, looking up to see his father standing at the gate and staring past him at the car.

Jack looked again, and he realized that although the thing further along the road had once been a person—he could see their head, like a shop dummy's that had been stepped on and covered in shit and set on fire so the eyes melted and rolled out to leave black pits—there was no blood at all, no wetness there. Nothing chewed on these sad remains.

Dead already when the car ran them over. Standing there in the road, dead already, letting themselves be hit so that the driver—he had been tall, good looking, the girl in his passenger seat small and mouse-like and scared into a gibbering, snotty wreck—would get out and go to see what he had done. Opening himself up to attack from the side, things darting from the ditches and downing him and falling on him quickly . . . and quietly. No sound apart from the girl's screams as she saw what was happening, and then her scream had changed in tone.

When they'd had their fill, they dragged themselves away to leave the remains to smaller dead things.

"Oh God, Dad!" Jack said, because he did not want to know any more. Why the hell should he? How the hell did he know what he knew already?

His dad reached down and scooped him up into his arms, pressing his son's face into his shoulder so he did not have to look any more. Jack raised his eyes and saw his mother walk slowly from the field, and she was trying not to look as well. She stared straight at Jack's face, her gaze unwavering, her lips tensed with the effort of not succumbing to human curiosity and subjecting herself to a sight that would live with her forever.

But of course she looked, and her liquid scream hurt Jack as much as anything ever had. He loved his mum because she loved him, he knew how much she loved him. His parents had bought him a microscope for Christmas and she'd pricked her finger with a needle so that he could look at her blood, that's how much she loved him. He hated to hear her scared, hated to see her in pain. Her fear and agony were all his own.

His father turned and ushered his mum down the road, away from the open banana car with its bright red mess, away from the bloody dead things eating up what was left. Jack, facing back over his dad's shoulder, watched the scene until it disappeared around a bend in the road. He listened to his father's labored breathing and his mother's panicked gasps. He looked at the pale green hedges, where even now hints of rot were showing through. And he wanted to go home.

"Are you scared, Jack?" Mandy had asked.

"No," he said truthfully.

"Not of me," she smiled. "Not of Mum and Dad and what's happening, that'll sort itself out. I mean ever. Are you ever scared, of things. The dark, spiders, death, war, clowns? Ever, ever, ever?"

Jack went to shake his head, but then he thought of things that did frighten him a little. Not outright petrified, just disturbed, that's how he sometimes felt. Maybe that's what Mandy meant.

"Well," he said, "there's this thing on telly. It's Planet of the Apes, *the TV show, not the film. There's a bit at the beginning with the gorilla army man, Urko, his face is on the screen and sometimes it looks so big that it's* bigger *than the screen, it's really in the room, you know? Well . . . I hide behind my hands."*

"But do you peek?"

"No!"

"I've seen that program," Mandy said, even though Jack was pretty sure she had not. "I've seen it, and you know what? There's nothing at all to be scared of. I'll tell you why: the bit that scares you is made up of a whole bunch of bits that won't. A man in a suit; a camera trick; an actor; a nasty voice. And that man in the suit goes home at night, has a cup of tea, picks his nose and goes to the toilet. Now that's not very scary, is it?"

Even though he felt ill Jack giggled and shook his head. "No!" He wondered whether the next time he watched that opening sequence, he'd be as scared as before. He figured maybe he would, but in a subtly different way. A grown-up way.

"Fear's made up of a load of things," she said, "and if you know those things . . . if you can name *them . . . you're most of the way to accepting your fear."*

"But what if you don't know what it is? What if you can't say what's scaring you?"

His sister looked up at the ceiling and tried to smile, but she could not. "I've tried it, over the last few days," she whispered. "I've named you, and Mum, and

Dad, and the woods, and what happened, and you . . . out there in the woods, alone . . . and loneliness itself. But it doesn't work." She looked down at Jack again, looked straight into his eyes. *"If that happens then it* should *be scaring you. Real fear is like intense pain. It's there to warn you something's truly wrong."*

I hope I always know, *Jack thought.* I hope I always know what I'm afraid of. *Mandy began singing softly. Jack slept.*

"Oh no! Dad, it's on fire!"

They had left the scene of devastation and towards the farm they'd spotted earlier, intending to find something to eat. It went unspoken that they did not expect to discover anyone alive at the farm. Jack only hoped they would not find anyone dead, either.

They paused in the lane, which was so infrequently used that grass and dock leaves grew in profusion along its central hump. Insipid green grass and yellowed dock now, though here and there tufts of rebellious life still poked through. The puddled wheel ruts held the occasional dead thing swimming feebly.

Jack's dad raised his binoculars, took a long look at the farm and lowered them again. "It's not burning. Something is, but it's not the farm. A bonfire, I think. I think the farmer's there, and he's started a bonfire in his yard."

"I wonder what he could be burning," Jack's mother said. She was pale and tired, her left arm tucked between the buttons of her shirt to try to ease the blood loss. Jack wanted to cry every time he looked at her, but he could see tears in her eyes as well, and he did not want to give her cause to shed any more.

"We'll go and find out."

"Dad, it might be dangerous. There might be . . . those people there. Those things." *Dead things*, Jack thought, but the idea of dead things walking still seemed too ridiculous to voice.

"We need food, Jack," his dad said, glancing at his mother as he said it. "And a drink. And some bandages for your mum, if we can find some. We need help."

"I'm scared, why can't we just go on to Tewton?"

"And when we get there, and there are people moving around in the streets, will you want to hold back then? In case they're the dead things we've seen?"

Jack did not answer but he shook his head, because he knew his dad was right.

"I'll go on ahead slightly," his dad said, "I've got the gun. That'll stop anything that comes at us. Jack, you help your mum."

Didn't stop the other people, Jack thought. *And you couldn't shoot at Mrs. Haswell, could you Dad? Couldn't shoot at someone you knew.*

"Don't go too fast," his mum said quietly. "Gray, I can't walk too fast. I feel faint, but if I walk slowly I can keep my head clear."

He nodded then started off, holding the shotgun across his stomach now instead of dipped over his elbow. Jack and his mother held back for a while and watched him go, Jack thinking how small and scared he looked against the frightening landscape.

"You all right, Mum?"

She nodded but did not turn her head. "Come on, let's follow your Dad. In ten minutes we'll be having a nice warm cup of tea and some bread in the farmer's kitchen."

"But what's he burning? Why the bonfire?"

His mother did not answer, or could not. Perhaps she was using all her energy to walk. Jack did the only thing he could and stayed along beside her.

The lane crossed a B-road and then curved around to the farmyard, bounded on both sides by high hedges. There was no sign of any traffic, no hint that anyone had come this way recently. Jack looked to his left where the road rose slowly up out of the valley. In the distance he saw something walk from one side to the other, slowly, as if unafraid of being run down. It may have been a deer, but Jack could not be sure.

"Look," his mum said quietly. "Oh Jackie, look."

There was an area of tended plants at the entrance to the farm lane, rose bushes pointing skeletal thorns skyward and clematis smothered in pink buds turning brown. But it was not this his mother was pointing at with a finger covered in blood; it was the birds. There were maybe thirty of them, sparrows from what Jack could make out, though they could just as easily have been siskins that had lost their color. They flapped uselessly at the air, heads jerking with the effort, eyes like small black stones. They did not make a sound, and that is perhaps why his father had not seen them as he walked by. Or maybe he had seen them and chosen to ignore the sight. Their wings were obviously weak, their muscles wasting. They did not give in. Even as Jack and his mother passed by they continued to flap uselessly at air that no longer wished to support them.

Jack kept his eyes on them in case they followed.

They could smell the bonfire now, and tendrils of smoke wafted across the lane and into the fields on either side. "That's not a bonfire," Jack said. "I can't smell any wood." His mother began to sob as she walked. Jack did not know whether it was from her pain, or something else entirely.

A gunshot coughed at the silence. Jack's father crouched down low, twenty paces ahead of them. He brought his gun up but there was no smoke coming from the barrel. "Wait—!" he shouted, and another shot rang out. Jack actually saw the hedge next to his dad flicker as pellets tore through.

"Get away!" a voice said from a distance. "Get out of here! Get away!"

His dad backed down the lane, still in a crouch, signaling for Jack and his mum to back up as well. "Wait, we're all right, we're normal, we just want some help."

There was silence for a few seconds, then another two aimless shots in quick succession. "I'll kill you!" the voice shouted again, and Jack could tell its owner was crying. "You killed my Janice, you made me kill her again, and I'll kill you!"

Jack's dad turned and ran to them, keeping his head tucked down as if his shoulders would protect it against a shotgun blast. "Back to the road," he said.

"But we could reason with him."

"Janey, back to the road. The guy's burning his own cattle and some of them are still moving. Back to the road."

"Some of them are still moving," Jack repeated, fascination and disgust—two emotions which, as a young boy, he was used to experiencing in tandem—blurring his words.

"Left here," his father said as they reached the B-road. "We'll skirt around the farm and head up towards the woods. Tewton is on the other side of the forest."

"There's a big hill first, isn't there?" his mum said. "A steep hill?"

"It's not that steep."

"However steep it is . . . " But his mum trailed off, and when Jack looked at her he saw tears on her cheeks. A second glance revealed the moisture to be sweat, not tears. It was not hot, hardly even warm. He wished she was crying instead of sweating.

His father hurried them along the road until the farm was out of sight. The smell of the fire faded into the background scent of the countryside, passing over from lush and alive, to wan and dead. Jack could still not come to terms with what he was seeing. It was as if his eyes were slowly losing their ability to discern colors and vitality in things, the whole of his vision turning into one of those sepia-tinted photographs he'd seen in his grandmother's house, where people never smiled and the edges were eaten away by time and too many thumbs and fingers. Except the bright red of his mother's blood was still there, even though the hedges were pastel instead of vibrant. His dad's face was pale, yes, but the burning spots on his cheeks—they flared when he was angry or upset, or both—were as bright as ever. Some colors, it seemed, could not be subsumed so easily.

"We won't all fade away, will we Dad? You won't let me and Mum and Mandy fade away, will you?"

His dad frowned, then ruffled his hair and squeezed the back of his neck. "Don't worry son. We'll get to Tewton and everything will be all right. They'll be doing something to help, they're bound to. They have to."

"Who are 'they,' Dad?" Jack said, echoing his mum's question from that morning.

His dad shook his head. "Well, the government. The services, you know, the police and fire brigade."

Maybe they've faded away too, Jack thought. He did not say anything. It seemed he was keeping a lot of his thoughts to himself lately, making secrets. Instead, he tried naming some of his fears—they seemed more expansive and numerous every time he thought about them—but there was far too much he did not know. Fear is like pain, Mandy had told him. Maybe that's why his mum was hurting so much now. Maybe that's why *he* felt so much like crying. Underneath all the running around and the weirdness of today, perhaps he was truly in pain.

They followed the twisting road for ten minutes before hearing the sound of approaching vehicles.

"Stand back," Jack's dad said, stretching out and ushering Jack and his mum up against the hedge. Jack hated the feel of the dead leaves and buds against the back of his neck. They felt like long fingernails, and if he felt them move . . . if he felt them twitch and begin to scratch . . .

The hedges were high and overgrown here, though stark and sharp in death, and they did not see the cars until they were almost upon them. They were both battered almost beyond recognition, paint scoured off to reveal rusting metal beneath. *It's as if even the cars are dying*, Jack thought, and though it was a foolish notion it chilled him and made him hug his dad.

His dad brought up the gun. Jack could feel him shaking. He could feel the fear there, the tension in his legs, the effort it was taking for him to breathe.

"Dad?" he said, and he was going to ask what was wrong. He was going to ask why was he pointing a gun at people who could help them, maybe give them a lift to Tewton.

"Oh dear God," his mum said, and Jack heard the crackle as she leant back against the hedge.

There were bodies tied across the bonnets of each car. He'd seen pictures of hunters in America, returning to town with deer strapped across the front of their cars, parading through the streets with kills they had made. This was not the same, because these bodies were not kills. They were dead, yes, but not kills, because their heads rolled on their necks, their hands twisted at the wrist, their legs shook and their heels banged on the hot metal beneath them.

Jack's father kept his gun raised. The cars slowed and Jack saw the faces inside, young for the most part, eyes wide and mouths open in sneers of rage or fear or mockery, whatever it was Jack could not tell. Living faces, but mad as well.

"Wanna lift?" one of the youths shouted through the Ital's smashed windscreen.

"I think we'll walk," Jack's dad said.

"It's not safe." The cars drifted to a standstill. "These fuckers are everywhere. Saw them eating a fucking bunch of people on the motorway. Ran them over." He leaned through the windscreen and patted the dead woman's head. She stirred, her eyes blank and black, skin ripped in so many places it looked to Jack like she was shedding. "So, you wanna lift?"

"Where are you going?" Jack asked.

The boy shrugged. He had a bleeding cut on his face; Jack was glad. The dead don't bleed. "Dunno. Somewhere where they can figure out what these fuckers are about."

"Who are 'they'?" Jack's dad asked.

The youth shrugged again, his bravado diluted by doubt. His eyes glittered and Jack thought he was going to cry, and suddenly he wished the youth would curse again, shout and be big and brave and defiant.

"We'll walk. We're going to Tewton."

"Yes, Mandy rang and said it's safe there!" Jack said excitedly.

"Best of luck to you then, little man," the driver said. Then he accelerated away. The second car followed, frightened faces staring out. The cars—the dead and the living—soon passed out of sight along the road.

"Into the fields again," Jack's dad said. "Up the hill to the woods. It's safer there."

Safer among dead things than among the living, Jack thought. Again, he kept his thought to himself. Again, they started across the fields.

They saw several cows standing very still in the distance, not chewing, not snorting, not flicking their tails. Their udders hung slack and empty, teats already black. They seemed to be looking in their direction. None of them moved. They looked like photos Jack had seen of the concrete cows in Milton Keynes, though those looked more lifelike.

It took an hour to reach the edge of the woods. Flies buzzed them but did not bite, the skies were empty of birds, things crawled along at the edges of fields, where dead crops met dead hedges.

The thought of entering the woods terrified Jack, though he could not say why. Perhaps it was a subconscious memory of the time he had been lost in the woods. That time had been followed by a mountain of heartache. Maybe he was anticipating the same now.

Instead, as they passed under the first stretch of dipping trees, they found a house, and a garden, and more bright colors than Jack had names for.

"Look at that! Janey, look at that! Jack, see, I told you, it's not all bad!"

The cottage was small, its roof slumped in the middle and its woodwork was painted a bright, cheery yellow. The garden was a blazing attack of color, and for a while Jack thought he was seeing something from a fairy tale. Roses were only this red in stories, beans this green, grass so pure, ivy so darkly gorgeous across two sides of the house. Only in fairy tales did potted plants stand in windowsill ranks so perfectly, their petals kissing each other but never stealing or leeching color from their neighbor. Greens and reds and blues and violets and yellows, all stood out against the backdrop of the house and the limp, dying woods behind it. In the woods there were still colors, true, vague echoes of past glories clinging to branches or leaves or fronds. But this garden, Jack thought, must be where all the color in the world had fled, a Noah's Ark for every known shade and tint and perhaps a few still to be discovered. There was magic in this place.

"Oh, wow," his mum said. She was smiling, and Jack was glad. But his father, who had walked to the garden gate and pulled an overhanging rose stem to his nose, was no longer smiling. His expression was as far away from a smile as could be.

"It's not real," his dad said.

"What?"

"This rose isn't real. It's . . . synthetic. It's silk, or something."

"But the grass, Dad . . . "

Jack ran to the gate as his father pushed through it, and they hit the lawns together.

"Astroturf. Like they use on football pitches, sometimes. Looks pretty real, doesn't it, son?"

"The beans. The fruit trees, over there next to the cottage."

"Beans and fruit? In spring?"

Jack's mum was through the gate now, using her one good hand to caress the plants, squeeze them and watch them spring back into shape, bend them and hear the tiny *snap* as a plastic stem broke. Against the fake colors of the fake plants, she looked very pale indeed.

Jack ran to the fruit bushes and tried to pluck one of the red berries hanging there in abundance. It was difficult parting it from its stem, but it eventually popped free and he threw it straight into his mouth. He was not really expecting a burst of fruity flesh, and he was not proved wrong. It tasted like the inside of a yogurt carton: plastic and false.

"It's not fair!" Jack ran to the front door of the cottage and hammered on the old wood, ignoring his father's hissed words of caution from behind him. His mum was poorly, they needed some food and drink, there were dead things—*dead* things, for fucking hell's sake—walking around and chasing them and eating people. Saw them eating a fucking bunch of people on the motorway, the man in the car had said.

All that, and now this, and none of it was fair.

The door drifted open. There were good smells from within, but old smells as well: the echoes of fresh bread; the memory of pastries; a vague idea that chicken had been roasted here recently, though surely not today, and probably not yesterday.

"There's no one here!" Jack called over his shoulder.

"They might be upstairs."

Jack shook his head. No, he knew this place was empty. He'd known the people in the field were coming and he'd seen what the dead folk in the banana car were like before . . . before he saw them for real. And he knew that this cottage was empty.

He went inside.

His parents dashed in after him, even his poorly mum. He felt bad about making her rush, but once they were inside and his dad had looked around, they knew they had the place to themselves.

"It's just not fair," Jack said once again, elbows resting on a windowsill in the kitchen, chin cradled in cupped hands. "All those colors . . . "

There was a little bird in the garden, another survivor drawn by the colors. It was darting here and there, working at the fruit, pecking at invisible insects, fluttering from branch to plastic branch in a state of increasing agitation.

"Why would someone do this?" his mum asked. She was sitting at the pitted wooden table with a glass of orange juice and a slice of cake. Real juice, real cake. "Why construct a garden so false?"

"I feel bad about just eating their stuff," his dad said. "I mean, who knows who lives here? Maybe it's a little old lady and she has her garden like this because she's too frail to tend it herself. We'll leave some money when we go." He tapped his pockets, sighed. "You got any cash, Janey?"

She shook her head. "I didn't think to bring any when we left this morning. It was all so . . . rushed."

"Maybe everything's turning plastic and this is just where it begins," Jack mused. Neither of his parents replied. "I read a book once where everything turned to glass."

"I'll try the TV," his dad said after a long pause.

Jack followed him through the stuffy hallway and into the living room, a small room adorned with faded tapestries, brass ornaments and family portraits of what seemed like a hundred children. Faces smiled from the walls, hair shone in forgotten summer sunshine, and Jack wondered where all these people were now. If they were still children, were they in school? If they were grown up, were they doing what he and his parents were doing, stumbling their way through something so strange and *unexpected* that it forbore comprehension?

Or perhaps they were all dead. Sitting at home. Staring at their own photographs on their own walls, seeing how things used to be.

"There it is," his dad said. "Christ, what a relic." He never swore in front of Jack, not even damn or Christ or shit. He did not seem to notice his own standards slipping.

The television was an old wooden cabinet type, buttons and dials running down one side of the screen, no remote control, years of mugs and plates having left their ghostly impressions on the veneered top. His dad plugged it in and switched it on, and they heard an electrical buzz as it wound itself up. As the picture coalesced from the soupy screen Jack's dad glanced at his watch. "Almost six o'clock, news should be on any time now."

"I expect they'll have a news flash, anyway," Jack said confidently.

His dad did something then that both warmed his heart and disconcerted him. He laughed gently and gave him a hug, and Jack felt tears cool and shameless on his cheek. "Of course they will, son," he said, "I'm sure they will."

"Anything?" called his mum.

"Nearly," Jack shouted back.

There was no sound. The screen was stark and bland, and the bottom half stated: "This is a Government Announcement." The top half of the screen contained scrolling words: "Stay calm . . . Remain indoors . . . Help is at hand . . . Please await further news."

And that was it.

"What's on the other side, Dad?"

Buttons clicked in, the picture fizzled and changed, BBC1, BBC2, ITV, Channel 4, Channel 5, there were no others. But if there were, they would probably have all contained the same image. The government notice, the scrolling words that should have brought comfort but which, in actual fact, terrified Jack. "I wonder how long it's been like that," he said, unable to prevent a shiver in his voice. "Dad, what if it isn't changing?"

"It says 'Please await further news.' They wouldn't say that unless they were going to put something else up soon. Information on where to go, or something."

"Yeah, but that's like a sign on a shop door saying 'Be back soon.' It could have been there for months."

His dad looked down at him, frowning, chewing his lower lip. "There's bound to be something on the radio. Come on, I think I saw one in the kitchen."

His mum glanced up as they entered and Jack told her what they had seen. The radio was on a shelf above the cooker. It looked like the sort of antique people spent lots of money to own nowadays, but it was battered and yellowed, and its back cover was taped on. It crackled into instant life. A somber brass band sprang from the speakers.

"Try 1215 medium wave," Jack said. "Virgin."

His dad tuned; the same brass band.

In six more places across the wavelengths, the same brass band.

"I'll leave it on. Maybe there'll be some news after this bit of music. I'll leave it on."

They tried the telephone as well, but every number was engaged: 999, the operator, the local police station, family and friends, random numbers. It was as if everyone in the world was trying to talk to someone else.

Twenty minutes later Jack's dad turned the radio off. They went to check the television and he switched that off as well. His mum laid down on the settee and Jack washed the cuts on her arms and the horrible wound on her shoulder, crying and gagging at the same time. He was brave, he kept it down. His mum was braver.

Later, after they had eaten some more food from the fridge and shared a huge pot of tea, his dad suggested they go to bed. No point trying to travel at night, he said, they'd only get lost. Besides, better to rest now and do the final part of the trip tomorrow than to travel all night, exhausted.

And there were those things out there as well, Jack thought, though his dad did not mention them. Dead things. *These fuckers are everywhere.* Dead cows, dead birds, dead insects, dead grass, dead crops, dead trees, dead hedges . . . dead people. Dead things everywhere with one thing in mind—to keep on moving. To find life.

How long before they rot away?

Or maybe the bugs that make things rot are dead as well.

There were two bedrooms. Jack said he was happy sleeping alone in one, so long as both doors were kept open. He heard his mother groan as she lowered herself onto their bed, his father bustling in the bathroom, the toilet flushing . . . and it was all so normal.

Then he saw a spider in the corner of his room and there was no way of telling whether it was alive or dead—even when it moved—and he realized that "normal" was going to have to change its coat.

Night fell unnaturally quickly, but when he glanced at his watch in the moonlight he saw that several hours had passed. Maybe he had been drifting in and out of sleep, daydreaming, though he could not recall what these fancies were about. He could hear his father's light snoring, his mother's breathing pained and uncomfortable. What if something tries to get in now? he thought. What if I hear fingers picking at window latches and tapping at the glass, nails scratching wood to dig out the frames? He looked up at the misshapen ceiling and thought he saw tiny dark things scurrying in and out of cracks, but it may have been fluid shapes on the surfaces of his eyes.

Then he heard the noises beginning outside. They may be the sounds of dead things crawling through undergrowth, but so long as he did not hear them shoving between plastic stems and false flowers, everything would be fine. The dark seemed to allow sounds to travel further, ring clearer, as if light could dampen noise. Perhaps it could; perhaps it would lessen the sound of dead things walking.

The night was full of furtive movements, clawed feet on hard ground, sagging bellies dragging through stiff grasses. There were no grunts or cries or shouts, no hooting owls or barking foxes screaming like tortured babies, because dead things can't talk. Dead things, Jack discovered that night, can only wander from one pointless place to another, taking other dead things with them and perhaps leaving parts of themselves behind. Whether he closed his eyes or kept them open he saw the same image, his own idea of what the scene was like out there tonight: no rhyme; no reason; no competition to survive; no feeding (unless there were a few unlucky living things still abroad); no point, no use, no ultimate aim . . .

. . . aimless.

He opened and closed his eyes, opened and closed them, stood and walked quietly to the window. The moon was almost full and it cast its silvery glare across a sickly landscape. He thought there was movement here and there, but when he looked he saw nothing. It was his poor night vision, he knew that, but it was also possible that the things didn't want to be seen moving. There was something secretive in that. Something intentional.

He went back to bed. When he was much younger it had always felt safe, and the feeling persisted now in some small measure. He pulled the stale blankets up over his nose.

His parents slept on. Jack remained awake. Perhaps he was seeking another secret in the night, and that thought conjured Mandy again. All those nights she had sat next to his bed talking to him, telling him adult things she'd never spoken of before, things about fear and imagination and how growing up closes doors in your mind. He had thought she'd been talking about herself, but she'd really been talking about him as well. She'd been talking about both of them because they were so alike, even if she was twice his age. And because they loved each other just as a brother and sister always should, and whatever had happened in the past could never, ever change that.

Because of Mandy he could name his fears, dissect and identify them, come to know them if not actually come to terms with them. He would never have figured that for himself, he was sure.

What she said had always seemed so right.

He closed his eyes to rest, and the dead had their hands on him.

They were grabbing at his arms, moving to his legs, pinching and piercing with rotten nails. One of them slapped his face and it was Mandy, she was standing at the bedside smiling down at him, her eyes shrivelled prunes in her gray face, and you should always name your fears.

Jack opened his mouth to scream but realized he was not breathing. It's safe here, he heard Mandy say. She was still smiling, welcoming, but there was a sadness behind that smile—even behind the slab of meat she had become—that Jack did not understand.

He had not seen Mandy for several months. She should be pleased to see him.

Then he noticed that the hands on his arms and legs were her own and her nails were digging in, promising never, ever to let him go, they were together now, it was safe here, safe . . .

"Jack!"

Still shaking, still slapped.

"Jack! For fuck's sake!"

Jack opened his eyes and Mandy disappeared. His dad was there instead, and for a split second Jack was confused. Mandy and his Dad looked so alike.

"Jackie, come with me," his dad said quietly. "Come on, we're leaving now."

"Is it morning?"

"Yes. Morning."

"Where's Mum?"

"Come on, son, we're going to go now. We're going to find Mandy."

Her name chilled him briefly, but then Jack remembered that even though she had been dead in his dream, still she'd been smiling. She had never hurt him, she *would* never hurt him. She would never hurt any of them.

"I need a pee."

"You can do that outside."

"What about food, Dad? We can't walk all that way without eating."

His dad turned his back and his voice sounded strange, as if forced through lips sewn shut. "I'll get some food together when we're downstairs, now come on."

"Mum!" Jack shouted.

"Jackie—"

"Mum! Is she awake yet, Dad?"

His father turned back to him, his eyes wide and wet and overflowing with grief and shock. Jack should have been shocked as well, but he was not, not really that shocked at all.

"Mum . . . " he whispered.

He darted past his father's outstretched hands and into the bedroom his parents had shared.

"Mum!" he said, relief sagging him against the wall. She was sitting up in bed, hands in her lap, staring at the doorway because she knew Jack would come running in as soon as he woke up. "I thought . . . Dad made me think . . . " *that you were dead.*

Nobody moved for what seemed like hours.

"She was cold when I woke up," his dad sobbed behind him. "Cold. So cold. And sitting like that. She hasn't moved, Jackie. Not even when I touched her. I felt for her pulse and she just looked at me . . . I felt for her heart, she just stared . . . she just keeps staring . . . "

"Mum," Jack gasped. Her expression did not change, because there was no expression. Her face was like a child's painting: two eyes, a nose, a mouth, no life there at all, no heart, no love or personality or soul. "Oh Mum . . . "

She was looking at him. Her eyes were dry so he could not see himself reflected there. Her breasts sagged in death, her open shoulder was a pale bloodless mass, like over-cooked meat. Her hands were crossed, and the finger she had pricked so that he could study her swarming blood under his microscope was pasty gray.

"We'll take her," Jack said. "When we get to Tewton they'll have a cure, we'll take her and—"

"Jack!" His father grabbed him under the arms and hauled him back towards the stairs. Jack began to kick and shout, trying to give life to his mother by pleading with her to help him, promising they would save her. "Jack, we're leaving now because Mum's dead. And Mandy is all we have left, Jackie. Listen to me!"

Jack continued to scream and his father dragged him downstairs, through the hallway and into the kitchen. He shouted and struggled, even though he knew his dad was right. They had to go on, they couldn't take his dead Mum with them, they had to go on. They'd seen dead people yesterday, and the results of dead people eating living people. He knew his dad was right but he was only a terrified boy, verging on his teens, full of fight and power and rage. The doors in his mind were as wide as they'd ever been, but grief makes so many unconscious choices that control becomes an unknown quantity.

Jack sat at the kitchen table and cried as his father filled a bag with food and bread. He wanted comfort, he wanted a cuddle, but he watched his dad work and saw the tears on his face too. He looked a hundred years old.

At last Jack looked up at the ceiling—he thought he'd heard movement from up there, bedsprings flexing and settling—and he told his dad he was sorry.

"Jack, you and Mandy . . . I have to help you. We've got to get to Mandy, you see that? All the silly stuff, all that shit that happened . . . if only we knew how petty it all was. Oh God, if only I could un-say so much, son. Now, with all this . . . Mandy and Mum can never make up now." Bitter tears were pouring from his eyes, no matter how much he tried to keep them in. "But Mandy and I can. Come on, it's time to go."

"Is there any news, Dad?" Jack wanted him to say yes, to hear they'd found a cure.

His dad shrugged. "TV's the same this morning. Just like that 'Be back soon' sign."

"You checked it already?"

"And the phone, and the radio. All the same. When I found your Mum, I thought . . . I wanted help."

They opened the front door together. Jack went first and as he turned to watch the door close, he was sure he saw his mother's feet appear at the top of the stairs. Ready to follow them out.

It was only as they came to the edge of the grotesquely cheerful garden that Jack saw just how much things had changed overnight.

Looking down the hillside he could recognize little. Yesterday had come along to kill everything, and last night had leeched any remnants of color or life from those sad corpses. Everything was dull. Branches dipped at the ground as if trying to find their way back to seed, grasses lay flat against the earth, hedgerows snaked blandly across the land, their dividing purpose now moot. Jack's eye was drawn to the occasional hints of color in clumps of trees or hedges, where a lone survivor stood proudly against the background of its dead cousins. A survivor much like them.

Nothing was moving. The sky was devoid of birds, and for as far as they could see the landscape was utterly still.

"Through the woods. Back of the house. Come on son, one hour and we'll be there." Jack thought it would be more like two hours, maybe three, but he was grateful for his dad's efforts on his behalf.

They skirted the garden. Jack tried desperately not to look at the cottage in case he saw a familiar face pressed against a window.

Ten minutes later they were deep in the woods, still heading generally upward towards the summit of the hill. The ground was coated with dead leaves—autumn in spring—and in places they were knee-deep. Jack had used to enjoy kicking through dried leaves piled along pavements in the autumn, his mother told him it was an indication of the rebirth soon to come, but today he did not enjoy it. His mum was not here to talk to him . . . and he was unsure of what sort of rebirth could ever come of this. He saw a squirrel at the base of one tree, grayer than gray, stiff in death but its limbs still twitching intermittently. It was like a wind-up toy whose key was on its final revolution. Some branches were lined with dead birds, and only a few of them were moving. There was an occasional rustle of leaves as something fell to the ground.

Grief was blurring Jack's vision, but even without tears the unreality of what was on view would have done the same. Where trees dipped down and tapped him on the shoulder, he thought they were skeletal fingers reaching from above. Where dead things lay twitching, he thought he could see some hidden hand moving them. There had to be something hidden, Jack thought, something causing and controlling all of this, otherwise what was the point? He believed strongly in reasons, cause and effect. Coincidence and randomness were just too terrifyingly cold to even consider. Without reason, his mum's death was pointless.

His dad kept reaching out to touch him on the head, or the shoulder, or the arm, perhaps to make sure he was still there, or maybe simply to ensure that he was real. Occasionally he would mumble incoherently, but mostly he was silent. The only other sound was the swish of dead leaves, and the intermittent impact of things hitting the ground for the final time.

Jack looked back once. After thinking of doing so, it took him several minutes to work up the courage. They had found an old track that led deep into the woods, always erring upwards, and they were following that path now, the going easier than plowing across the forest floor. He knew that if he turned he would see his mother following them, a gray echo of the wonderful woman she had been yesterday, her blood dried black on her clothes, smile caused by stretched skin rather than love. She had pricked her finger for him that Christmas, and to the young boy he'd been then, that was the ultimate sign of love—the willingness to inflict pain upon herself for him. But now, now that she was gone, Jack knew that his mother's true love was something else entirely. It was the proud smile every time she saw him go out to explore and experience. It was the hint of sadness in that smile, because *every single time* she said goodbye, somewhere deep inside she knew it could be the last. And it was the hug and kiss at the end of the day, when once again he came home safe and sound.

So Jack turned around, knowing he would see this false shadow of all the wonderful things his mother had been.

There was nothing following them, no one, and Jack was pleased. But still fresh tears came.

They paused and tried to eat, but neither was hungry. Jack sat on a fallen tree and put his face in his hands.

"Be brave, Jack." His dad sat next to him and hugged him close. "Be brave. Your mum would want that, wouldn't she?"

"But what about you, Dad?" Jack asked helplessly. "Won't you be lonely?"

His dad lowered his head and Jack saw the diamond rain of tears. "Of course I will, son. But I've got you, and I've got Mandy. And your mum would want me to be brave as well, don't you think?"

Jack nodded and they sat that way for a while, alternately crying and smiling into the trees when unbidden memories came. Jack did not want to relive good memories, not now, because here they would be polluted by all the dead things around them. But they came anyway and he guessed they always would, and at the most unexpected and surprising times. They were sad but comforting. He could not bear to drive them away.

They started walking again. Here and there were signs of life, but they were few and far between: a bluebell still bright amongst its million dead cousins; a woodpecker burrowing into rotting wood; a squirrel, jumping from tree to tree as if following them, then disappearing altogether.

Jack began to wonder how long the survivors would survive. How long would it be before whatever had killed everything else killed them, like it had his mum? He was going to ask his dad, but decided against it. He must be thinking the same thing.

In Tewton it would be safe. Mandy had said so, Mandy was there, and now she and Dad could make up for good. At least then, there would still be something of a family about them.

They walked through the woods and nothing changed. Jack's dad held the shotgun in both hands but he had no cause to use it. Things were grayer today, blander, slower. It seemed also that things were deader. They found three dead people beneath a tree, not one of them showing any signs of movement. They looked as though they had been dead for weeks, but they still had blood on their chins. Their stomachs were bloated and torn open.

Just before midday they emerged suddenly from the woods and found themselves at the top of the hill, looking down into a wide, gentle valley. The colors here had gone as well; it looked like a fine film of ash had smothered everything in sight, from the nearest tree to the farthest hillside. In the distance, hunkered down behind a roll in the land as if hiding itself away, they could just make out the uppermost spires and roofs of Tewton. From this far away it was difficult to see whether there were any signs of life. Jack thought not, but he tried not to look too hard in case he was right.

"Let's take a rest here, Jackie," his dad said. "Let's sit and look." Jack's mum had once used that saying when they were on holiday, the atmosphere and excitement driving Jack and Mandy into a frenzy, his dad eager to find a pub, an eternity of footpaths and sight-seeing stretched out before them. *Let's just sit and look*, she had said, and they had heeded her words and simply enjoyed the views and surroundings for what they were. Here and now there was nothing he wanted to sit and look at. The place smelled bad, there were no sounds other than their own labored breathing, the landscape was a corpse laid out on a slab, perhaps awaiting identification, begging burial. There was nothing here he wanted to see.

But they sat and looked, and when Jack's heartbeat settled back to normal, he realized that he could no longer hear his father's breathing.

He held his breath. Stared down at the ground between his legs, saw the scattered dead beetles and ants, and the ladybirds without any flame in their wings. He had never experienced such stillness, such silence. He did not want to look up, did not want events to move on to whatever he would find next. *Dad dead*, he named. *Me on my own. Me, burying Dad.*

Slowly, he raised his head.

His father was asleep. His breathing was long and slow and shallow, a contented slumber or the first signs of his body running down, following his wife to that strange place which had recently become even stranger. He remained sitting upright and his hands still clasped the gun, but his chin was resting on his chest, his shoulders rising and falling, rising and falling, so slightly that Jack had to watch for a couple of minutes to make sure.

He could not bear to think of his father not waking up. He went to touch him on the shoulder, but wondered what the shock would do.

They had to get to Tewton. They were here—hell, he could even *see* it—but still they found no safety. If there was help to be had, it must be where Mandy had said it would be.

Jack stood, stepped from foot to foot, looked around as if expecting help to come galloping across the funereal landscape on a white charger. Then he gently lifted the binoculars from his dad's neck, negotiated the strap under his arms, and set off along the hillside. Ten minutes, he figured, if he walked for ten minutes he would be able to see what was happening down in Tewton. See the hundreds of people rushing hither and tither, helping the folks who had come in from the dead countryside, providing food and shelter and some scrap of normality amongst the insanity. There would be soldiers there, and doctors, and tents in the streets because there were too many survivors to house in the buildings. There would be food as well, tons of it ferried in by helicopter, blankets and medicines . . . maybe a vaccine . . . or a cure.

But there were no helicopters. And there were no sounds of life.

He saw more dead things on the way, but he had nothing to fear from them. Yesterday dead had been dangerous, an insane, impossible threat; now it was simply no more. Today, the living were unique.

Jack looked down on the edge of the town. A scattering of houses and garages and gardens spewed out into the landscape from between the low hills. There was a church there as well, and a row of shops with smashed windows, and several cars parked badly along the two streets he could see.

He lowered the binoculars and oriented himself from a distance, then looked again. A road wound into town from this side, trailing back along the floor of the valley before splitting in two, one of these arteries climbing towards the woods he and his father had just exited. Jack frowned, moved back to where the road passed between two rows of houses into the town, the blurred vision setting him swaying like a sunflower in the breeze.

He was shaking. The vibration knocked him out of focus. There was a cool hand twisting his insides and drawing him back the way he had come, not only to his father, but to his dead mother as well. It was as if she were calling him across the empty miles that now separated them, pleading that he not leave her alone in that strange color-splashed cottage, singing her love to tunes of guilt and with a chorus of childlike desperation so strong that it made him feel sick. However grown up Jack liked to think he was, all he wanted at that moment was his mother. And in a way he *was* older than his years, because he knew he would feel like that whatever his age.

Tears gave him a fluid outlook. He wiped his eyes roughly with his sleeve and looked again, breathing in deeply and letting his breath out in a long, slow sigh.

There were people down there. A barricade of some sort had been thrown across the road just where houses gave way to countryside—there was a car, and some furniture, and what looked like fridges and cookers—and behind this obstruction heads bobbed, shapes moved. Jack gasped and smiled and began to shake again, this time with excitement.

Mandy must be down there somewhere, waiting for them to come in. When she saw it was just Jack and his dad she would know the truth, they would not need to tell her, but as a family they could surely pull through, help each other and hold each other and love each other as they always should have.

Jack began to run back to his dad. He would wake him and together they would go the final mile.

The binoculars banged against his hip and he fell, crunching dry grass, skidding down the slope and coming to rest against a hedge. A shower of dead things pattered down on his face, leaves and twigs and petrified insects. His mum would wipe them away. She would spit on her handkerchief and dab at the cuts on his face, scold him for running when he should walk, tell him to read a book instead of watching the television.

He stood and started off again, but then he heard a voice.

"Jack."

It came from afar, faint, androgynous with distance and panic. He could hear that well enough; he could hear the panic.

"Jack."

He looked uphill towards the forest, expecting to see the limp figure of his mother edge out from beneath the trees' shadows, coming at him from the woods.

"Jack!"

The voice was louder now and accompanied by something else—the rhythmic *slap slap slap* of running feet.

Jack looked down the hill and made out something behind a hedge denuded of leaves. Lifting the binoculars he saw his father running along the road, hands pumping at the air, feet kicking up dust.

"Dad!" he called, but his father obviously did not hear. He disappeared behind a line of brown evergreens.

Jack tracked the road through the binoculars, all the way to Tewton. His dad must have woken up, found him missing and assumed he'd already made his way to the town, eager to see Mandy, or just too grief-stricken to wait any longer. Now he was on his way into town on his own, and when he arrived he would find Jack absent. He would panic. He would think himself alone, alone but for Mandy. How would two losses in one day affect him?

His dad emerged farther down the hillside, little more than a smudge against the landscape now, still running and still calling.

Jack ran as well. He figured if he moved as the crow flies they would reach the barricade at the same time. Panic over. Then they would find Mandy.

He tripped again, cursed, hauled the binoculars from his shoulder and threw them away. As he stood and ran on down the hill, he wondered whether they would ever be found. He guessed not. He guessed they'd stay here forever, and one day they would be a fossil. There were lots of future fossils being made today.

He could no longer see his dad, but he could see the hedgerow hiding the road that led into Tewton. His feet were carrying him away, moving too fast, and at some point Jack lost control. He was no longer running, he was falling, plummeting down the hillside in a reckless dash that would doubtless result in a broken leg—at least—should he lose his footing again. He concentrated on the ground just ahead of him, tempted to look down the hillside at the road but knowing he should not, he should watch out for himself, if he broke a limb now and there were no doctors in Tewton . . .

As the slope of the hill lessened so he brought his dash under control. His lungs were burning with exertion and he craved a drink. He did not stop running, though, because the hedge was close now, a tangled, bramble-infested maze of dead twigs and crumbling branches.

Tewton was close too. He could see rooftops to his right, but little else. He'd be at the barricade in a matter of minutes.

He hoped, how he hoped that Mandy was there to greet them. She and their father would have made up already, arms around each other, smiling sad smiles. *I've named my fears,* Jack would tell her, and though their father would not understand they would smile at each other and hug, and he would tell her how what she had told him had saved him from going mad.

He reached the hedge and ran along it until he found a gate. His knees were flaring with pain, his chest tight and fit to burst, but he could see the road. He climbed the gate—there was a dead badger on the other side; not roadkill, just dead, and thankfully unmoving—and jumped into the lane.

It headed around a bend, and he was sure he heard pounding footsteps for a few seconds. It may have been his heart; it was thumping at his chest, urging him on, encouraging him to safety. He listened to it and hurried along the lane, moving at a shuffle now, more than a run.

As he rounded the bend everything came into view.

The people first of all, a couple of them still dragging themselves from the drainage reens either side of the road, several more converging on his father. He stood several steps from the barricade, glancing frantically around, obviously searching for Jack but seeing only dead people circling him, staring at him.

"Dad!" Jack shouted, at least he tried to. It came out as a gasp, fear and dread and defeat all rolled into one exhalation. Tewton . . . hope . . . .help, all given way to these dead things. For a fleeting instant he thought the barricade was a dividing line behind which hope may still exist, but then he saw that it wasn't really a barricade at all. It may have been once, maybe only hours ago, but now it was broken down and breached. Little more than another pile of rubbish that would never be cleared.

"Dad!" This time it *was* a shout. His dad spun around, and it almost broke Jack's heart to see the relief on his face. But then fear regained its hold and his dad began to shout.

"Jack, stay away, they're here, look! Stay away, Jack!"

"But Dad—"

His father fired the shotgun and one of the dead people hit the road. It—Jack could not even discern its sex—squirmed and slithered, unable to regain its feet.

Mandy, he thought, *where's Mandy, what of Mandy?*

Mandy dead, Mandy gone, only me and Dad left—

But the naming of his fears did him no good, because he was right to be afraid. He knew that when he heard the sounds behind him. He knew it when he turned and saw Mandy scrabbling out from the ditch, her long black hair clotted with dried leaves, her grace hobbled by death.

"Mandy," he whispered, and he thought she paused.

There was another gunshot behind him and the sound of metal hitting something soft. Then running feet coming his way. He hoped they were his father's. He remembered the dead people in the field yesterday, how fast they had moved, how quickly they had charged.

Mandy was gray and pale and thin. Her eyes showed none of his sister, her expression was not there, he could not *sense* her at all. Her silver rings rattled loose on long stick fingers. She was walking towards him.

"Mandy, Mandy, it's me, Jack—"

"Jack! Move!" His father's words were slurred because he was running, it *was* his footsteps Jack could hear. And then he heard a shout, a curse.

He risked a glance over his shoulder. His father had tripped and slid across the lane on his hands and knees, the shotgun clattering into the ditch, three of the dead folk closing on him from behind. "Dad, behind you!" Jack shouted.

His father looked up at Jack, his eyes widened, his mouth hung open, his hands bled. "Behind you!" he shouted back.

A weight struck Jack and he went sprawling. He half turned as he fell so that he landed on his side, and he looked up and back in time to see Mandy toppling over on top of him. The wind was knocked from him and for a few seconds his chest felt tight, useless, dead.

Perhaps this is what it's like, he thought. *To be like them.*

At last he drew a shuddering breath, and the stench of Mandy hit him at the same time. The worst thing . . . the worst thing of all . . . was that he could detect a subtle hint of *Obsession* beneath the dead animal smell of her. His mum and dad always bought *Obsession* for Mandy at the airport when they went on holiday, and Jack had had a big box of jelly-fruits.

He felt her hands clawing at him, fingers seeking his throat, bony knees jarring into his stomach, his crotch. He screamed and struggled but could not move, Mandy had always beaten him at wrestling, she was just so strong—

"Get off!" his dad shouted. Jack could not see what was happening—he had landed so that he looked along the lane away from Tewton—but he could hear. "Get the fuck off, get away!" A thump as something soft hit the ground, then other sounds less easily identifiable, like an apple being stepped on or a leg torn from a cooked chicken. Then the unmistakable metallic snap of the shotgun being broken, reloaded, closed.

Two shots in rapid succession.

"Oh God, oh God, oh . . . Jack, it's not Mandy, Jack, you know that don't you!"

Jack struggled onto his back and looked up at the thing atop him.

You can name your fears, Mandy had said, and Jack could not bear to look, this bastard thing resembling his beautiful sister was a travesty, a crime against everything natural and everything right.

Jack closed his eyes. "I still love you, Mandy," he said, but he was not talking to the thing on top of him now.

There was another blast from the shotgun. A weight landed on his chest, something sprinkled down across his face. He kept his eyes closed. The weight twisted for a while, squirmed and scratched at Jack with nails and something else, exposed bones perhaps—

A hand closed around his upper arm and pulled.

Jack screamed, shouted until his throat hurt. Maybe he could scare it off.

"It's all right, Jackie," a voice whispered into his ear. Mandy had never called him Jackie, so why now, why when—

Then he realized it was his father's voice. Jack opened his eyes as he stood and looked straight into his dad's face. They stared at each other because they both knew to stare elsewhere—to stare *down*—would invite images they could never, ever live with.

They held hands as they ran along the lane, away from Tewton. For a while there were sounds of possible pursuit behind them, but they came from a distance and Jack simply could not bring himself to look.

They ran for a very long time. For a while Jack felt like he was going mad, or perhaps it was clarity in a world gone mad itself. In his mind's eye he saw the dead people of Tewton waiting in their little town, waiting for the survivors to flee there from the countryside, slaughtering and eating them, taking feeble strength from cooling blood and giving themselves a few more hours before true death took them at last. The image gave him a strange sense of hope because he saw it could not go on forever. Hope in the death of the dead. A strange place to take comfort.

At last they could run no more. They found a petrol station and collapsed in the little shop, drinking warm cola because the electricity was off, eating chocolate and crisps. They rested until mid-afternoon. Then, because they did not know what else to do, they moved on once more.

Jack held his father's hand. They walked along a main road, but there was no traffic. At one junction they saw a person nailed high up on an old telegraph pole. Jack began to wonder why but then gave in, because he knew he would never know.

The countryside began to flatten out. A few miles from where they were was the coast, an aim as good as any now, a place where help may have landed.

"You okay to keep going, son?"

Jack nodded. He squeezed his dad's hand as well. But he could not bring himself to speak. He had said nothing since they'd left the petrol station. He could not. He was too busy trying to remember what Mandy looked like, imprint her features on his mind so that he would never, ever forget.

There were shapes wandering the fields of dead crops. Jack and his dad increased their pace but the dead people were hardly moving, and they seemed to pose no threat. He kept glancing back as they fell behind. It looked like they were harvesting what they had sown.

As the sun hit the hillsides behind them they saw something startling in the distance. It looked like a flash of green, small but so out of place amongst this blandness that it stood out like an emerald in ash. They could not run because they were exhausted, but they increased their pace until they drew level with the field.

In the centre of the field stood a scarecrow, very lifelike, straw hands hidden by gloves and face painted with a soppy sideways grin. Spread out around its stand was an uneven circle of green shoots. The green was surrounded by the rest of the dead crop, but it was alive, it had survived.

"Something in the soil, maybe?" Jack said.

"Farming chemicals?"

Jack shrugged. "Maybe we could go and see."

"Look," his dad said, pointing out towards the scarecrow.

Jack frowned, saw what his dad had seen, then saw the trail leading to it. It headed from the road, a path of crushed shoots aiming directly out towards the scarecrow. It did not quite reach it, however, and at the end of the trail something was slumped down in the mud, just at the boundary of living and dead crop. Jack thought he saw hair shifting in the breeze, the hem of a jacket lifting, dropping, lifting again, as if waving.

They decided not to investigate.

They passed several more bodies over the next couple of hours, all of them still, all of them lying in grotesque contortions in the road or the ditches.

Their hands were clawed, as if they'd been trying to grasp a hold of something before coming to rest.

Father and son still held hands, and as the sun began to bleed across the hillsides they squeezed every now and then to reassure each other that they were all right. As all right as they could be, anyhow.

Jack closed his eyes every now and then to remember what Mandy and his mum had looked like. Each time he opened them again, a tear or two escaped.

He thought he knew what they would find when they reached the coast. He squeezed his father's hand once more, but he did not tell him. Best to wait until they arrived.

For now, it would remain his secret.

***

Tim Lebbon *is a* New York Times-*bestselling writer from South Wales. He's had twenty novels published to date including* The Island, The Map of Moments *(with Christopher Golden),* Bar None, Fallen, Hellboy: The Fire Wolves, Dusk, *and* Berserk, *as well as hundreds of novellas and short stories. He has won four British Fantasy Awards, a Bram Stoker Award, and a Scribe Award, and has been a finalist for International Horror Guild and World Fantasy Awards. Forthcoming books include* The Secret Journeys of Jack London: The Wild *for HarperCollins (co-authored with Christopher Golden),* Echo City *for Bantam in the U.S. and Orbit in the U.K.,* Coldbrook *for Corsair in the U.K., and the massive short story collection* Ghosts and Bleeding Things *from PS Publishing (U.K.). Fox 2000 recently acquired film rights to* The Secret Journeys of Jack London, *and Lebbon is writing the screenplay with Christopher Golden. His story* Pay the Ghost *is in pre-production with Sidney Kimmel Entertainment, and several more of his novels and novellas are currently in development. Find out more at www.timlebbon.net.*

***

Lebbon juxtaposes the hope and optimism of a twelve-year-old boy against complete and utter death. As Jack makes his journey he discovers that not only humans, but animals, insects, plants, even color have died and been monstrously transformed. Jack's faith in his family and ability to name his fears propels both character and reader through the nightmare of what the world has become. Both hope and fears dwindle, but the reader remains transfixed.

Jack and his father reverse roles as the story develops. By the end, it is the child who is protecting the adult from what he suspects is the truth.

There's another possible "reversal" in the novella as well—a hint that the zombies, for all their menace and danger, seem to be weakening and dying off. They see bodies after they leave Mandy and continue to the coast, but no more fast-moving zombies attack them. We are left with a faint glimmer of positivity, if we wish to accept it: whatever has happened is over and done, it is no longer spreading, the zombies are dying off. If so, are there others somewhere in the world who have avoided it?

Dating Secrets of the Dead

David Prill

Hey Jerry, there's that new girl.
Oh yes. Her name's Caroline May Ames. She's a swell kid.
Why? Do you know her?
Not very well, Bud. I wish I did.
I don't know what it is, but there's something about her you like.
Well, she always looks nice for one thing.
They all look nice, at first . . .

Jerry hadn't had a date in an eternity. He didn't know why. They had dressed him so stylishly. His black dress shoes had such a sheen to them. His wispy brown hair was trimmed and combed. His cheeks had a ruddy, outdoorsy hue. His fingernails had once been nicely manicured—now they had grown long. Too long. Maybe that was it. Maybe his uncut fingernails were turning off the girls.

No, it had to be more than that.

All in all, I look pretty sharp, he thought.

Then maybe it's my personality or personal habits.

I'm soft-spoken—my breath would hardly fog a mirror.

Polite. To a fault.

Interesting experiences to share. Absolutely. My life review was a gripping melodrama.

Jerry didn't want to face rejection again, but he did like that new girl, Caroline May Ames. They had exchanged small talk once before, the day she arrived. They were in the same row, after all. She was so pretty. Her white dress had ivory beads and lace. Her blond hair cascaded comfortably over her shoulders. She had such a peaceful look on her face.

He called for her.

Hi, Caroline. This is Jerry.

Oh hi, Jerry.

I was wondering, Caroline, if you want to go out with me tonight?

Tonight? I'm sorry, I can't, Jerry. I already have a date for tonight. Why don't you call some other time?

Oh, okay. Thanks anyway, Caroline. Bye.

Goodbye, Jerry.

Strike out, Jerry thought, feeling dejected. Didn't she like him? She acted like she did. Then why didn't she want to go out with him?

He decided to ask Bud about it. Bud had been around longer than Jerry, and always seemed to have good advice to share.

. . . so I don't know what happened. I asked Caroline for a date, and she turned me down flat.

How long did the conversation last?

Not long. A minute or so.

That's good. Your call shouldn't go on for hours. That's a pretty sensible attitude. When did you ask her to go out with you?

Tonight.

There's your problem. Be sure not to wait until the last minute to ask a girl for a date. It's no compliment to any girl to call her so late that she thinks she's the last resort.

I never thought of that. Thanks a lot, Bud.

Glad to help, fella.

Jerry tried again the next day.

Hi, Caroline, this is Jerry.

Hi, Jerry.

Caroline, uh, I don't suppose you'd want to go out with me sometime?

Oh, I suppose we could. Call me sometime.

That was better. A real step in the right direction.

He told Bud about his success.

That's great, Jerry. When are you two going out, then?

Uh, we didn't exactly set a day.

How did you ask her?

Jerry told him.

Don't ask a girl out in a backhanded way that makes her feel uncomfortable. It's a mark of your insecurity, too. And one other tip: Don't ask a girl if she is busy on a certain night. That puts her on the spot.

Boy, this is more complicated than I thought, Jerry mused. *So how should I ask her then?*

Think of something to do that she might like. Don't leave it entirely up to her. Suggest two or three activities, and see how she responds. Perhaps go out with a group of friends.

There's a skating party on Friday. Maybe Caroline would want to do that.

Now you've got the hang of it.

He called for Caroline again.

Hi, Jerry.

Hi, Caroline. Say, the gang is going to a skating party on Friday. I was wondering if you'd want to go with me. We'd have to leave early, but we'd get back by eleven. Or else we could spend the evening watching the flesh rot off our bones. We'd get back later if we did that.

Gee, Jerry, the skating party sounds like loads of fun. I'd love to go.

Great. I'll come for you around six.

Jerry was smart. He kept a date calendar, and checked it before asking Caroline to the party. Not a bad idea.

Good boy! Bud congratulated Jerry when told of his success with Caroline. *I wish I could go to the skating party but I told my folks I'd spend the evening with them. They don't get out much anymore.*

I really appreciate your help, said Jerry. *I just wish I could take you with me!*

Jerry was joshing Bud, but it was true. His friend knew the proper habit patterns, and what it took to be popular.

The days leading up to his date with Caroline seemed to crawl and creep. Throughout the week Jerry quizzed Bud on how he should behave on his date, what to say, what a girl expects. Finally, the weekend rolled in, and Jerry grew stiff with anticipation.

Wardrobe. Jerry decided to wear what he had on. His dark suit. It made him look more mature. A few holes, hardly noticeable, some mild staining in the crotch area, but Caroline would understand. She was that kind of girl.

A few minutes before six Jerry showed up where Caroline lived. He didn't need Bud to tell him the importance of promptness. He wanted to make a good impression on her folks, too.

Her parents were side by side when he arrived.

Good evening, Mr. and Mrs. Ames. I'm Jerry Weathers, Caroline's friend.

Even though they were Midwestern stoic, Jerry felt at ease with her mom and dad. There wasn't enough left of them to make trouble.

Jerry, how nice to see you.

Caroline.

She looked wonderful. White dress. Beads. Blond hair. Shoulders. A portrayal of peace on her face.

Hi, Caroline. You look so natural.

Thanks. How nice of you to notice. She addressed her parents. *We should be back from the skating party by eleven.*

There is no magic formula about when to come home from a date. The hour Jerry and Caroline would return was decided by where they were going on their date, whether tomorrow is a school day, how many dates she has had recently, and so forth.

I'll take good care of her, Mr. and Mrs. Ames, said Jerry. *Good night.*

'Night, Mom and Dad. Don't wait up for us.

The skating party. It seemed unreal, that's how entranced he was with Caroline.

He felt light on his feet, Dead Astaire, his skate blades cutting into the dark sheet on the pond. They skated in a long loop, hand in hand. Caroline's hand was colder than Hell. He tried warming it up with his own, but it didn't seem to help much.

As they skated beneath the festering full moon, they seemed to get into a rhythm with each other, carried away with the dance. Jerry would release Caroline, just the tips of their fingers touching, then he would draw her back in, and they would spin around, laughing inside, and skate on down the ice. Caroline seemed to be enjoying herself a lot. She was a good kid.

Jerry had been concentrating on Caroline so much that he was surprised when he looked away and saw that the whole gang was watching them waltz across the pond.

We're a big hit, he said, nodding to the onlookers.

When Caroline realized they had an audience, she self-consciously tried to stop, her blade catching a ridge on the ice. She lost her balance, and they fell in time, too.

The gang rushed over.

Are you guys all right?

I think so, said Jerry. *Caroline, are you hurt?*

I'm fine. Just a little bump.

We should probably sit and watch the others skate for awhile.

No, don't stop, the gang said. *You two were skating so beautifully.*

Yes, how long have you been skating together?

Well, actually this is our first date, Jerry explained.

You're kidding! Wow. Talk about a perfect match.

Caroline got a blushing expression on her face, although no blood filled her cheeks. It was pretty cold out there on the pond.

I think we'll catch our breaths, Jerry said, helping Caroline back up onto her feet.

They skated carefully over to the edge of the pond, stepping through the snowbank to a concrete bench. A weather-worn angel watched over them, a dollop of snow on her nose.

Jerry tried to call up the advice Bud has passed on to him. What did he say to talk about? A popular movie, friends they have in common, anything that is of mutual interest.

Movies were out. He hadn't seen one in ages. Friends? She was new in his neighborhood. Anything they were both interested in. That was the solution, but what did they share other than their place of residence? He didn't know.

Say something . . .

Uh, Caroline . . .

Yes, Jerry?

That's a lovely dress you're wearing.

Why, thank you. You look very nice, too.

Do I really? I mean, it's my only suit . . .

It looks fine.

And my skin. The flaking . . . the bugs . . .

She took both of his hands in hers. *Jerry, I like you. For yourself. I don't care about the bugs. Forget about the bugs. You'd have to be looking for them to see them. You have a good heart. I'm glad you asked me out. I'm having a fun time. I really am.*

Gosh, Caroline, you're really a neat person.

Silence, and then Jerry began to feel awkward. Think of something.

Then it struck him. How could I have missed it? The perfect topic for first date small talk. He knew Bud would be proud.

I like the smell of . . . dirt. Do you?

I didn't at first. But I think I'm getting used to it.

Me, too. I mean, I didn't like it at first either. But after awhile, it kind of, you know, gets under your skin.

Yes, I suppose it does.

In the springtime, they bring flowers.

I love flowers.

Sometimes, you can smell the rain.

I always liked rain. Rain makes the whole world fresh and new.

Sometimes, there are leaks.

I suppose so.

They chatted for awhile longer, swapping death stories—she and her folks expiring in a car wreck on an ice-coated highway, he succumbing to an inoperable brain tumor—then returned to the pond. The skating party broke up as the moon went down. Things were going so well with Caroline that he didn't want to break the spell.

Caroline's mom and dad were inert when they got back. It was only a quarter to eleven.

I had a swell time tonight, said Caroline.

I'm glad you enjoyed the skating, Jerry said. *I'm glad you weren't hurt when you fell on the ice.*

I was more surprised than anything. All those people staring at us. It was like a dream.

They were having a good time together. But all good things, like life itself, must eventually come to an end.

Thank you for our date, Jerry said. *I had fun, too. I hope we can see each other again.*

So do I, Caroline said. *Please call for me anytime.*

In many communities, a good night kiss is expected as the customary way of ending a date. It can mean any number of things. A token of friendship, a simple way of saying thank you for the evening, a sign of affection. What it means depends on the two people and their definition of their relationship and themselves.

Jerry took the safe route. When Caroline rose, he squeezed her hand and searched for a smile.

The look on her face said she had a smile inside her, too.

And the date was over.

The next day, he told Bud about his evening with Caroline. Not in too much detail, because he didn't want to be one of those boys who doesn't respect a girl's privacy and reputation, and most importantly her personal feelings.

Your advice really helped me a lot, he told Bud.

Glad to be of service, guy.

I'm not sure what to do next. Should I wait a few days before calling her again? I don't feel like waiting. But I don't want her to think I'm too pushy either.

There's no perfect answer to your question. It depends on the two people and their definition of their relationship and themselves.

Gosh, I don't know, Bud. It all sounds pretty complicated.

It's the easiest thing in the world. You could call her today just to thank her for going with you to the skating party. That's a common courtesy. A girl would appreciate the gesture. Remember, though, to have a sensible attitude. Your call shouldn't go on for hours.

Should I ask her out again when I call?

After your courtesy call, I would wait a couple of days. By then it will be mid-week, and it will still give her several days notice . Remember, though, not to call her so late that she thinks she's the last resort.

So Jerry did call Caroline later that day, and handled it just the way Bud suggested. Although he yearned to talk to Caroline for hours, he kept it short. She seemed to genuinely appreciate his thoughtfulness.

Her receptive attitude toward him made his next call easy.

Hi Caroline, it's Jerry.

Hi, Jerry. How are you?

I'm doing very well, thank you. And yourself?

Just fine, thanks.

I was wondering, Caroline if you would like to go on a hay ride this Saturday? The whole gang is going.

Oh, I'd love to, Jerry.

Great. I'll come for you around six, if that's okay.

That would be perfect. I'll see you then, Jerry.

Thank you, Caroline. Goodbye.

Jerry passed the week in a daze. A wonderful new world was opening up for him. He thought about Caroline constantly, and eagerly anticipated their next engagement. A hay ride would be the ideal second date. You don't ask just anyone to go on a hayride. Skating is something you do separately, but a hayride is something you do . . . together. There could be several opportunities for floating his arm around her shoulder. Sweet. Bud strongly approved, too. Everything was going to be a shining golden sky.

And then disaster turned his social life on its ear.

Actually, more toward the front of his head.

One moment his left eyeball was tucked snugly into its socket where it belonged, the next moment it had migrated down his cheek, like a mouse peeking out of its hole.

The rotting must have progressed further than he realized. Jerry knew it was inevitable, although he hadn't cared to dwell on it, but why did it have to happen now? This week? So close to the hayride?

He tried to look on the bright side. The eye was still attached. That was worth something. Jerry tried to recall anatomy. Was it the optic nerve that secured the eyeball to the socket? And when that disintegrated . . .

What a fix.

Jerry immediately sought out Bud. He had to help. He just had to. Both of his eyes had long since vacated the premises. He must know what to do.

After hearing his dilemma, Bud said, *Well heck, I'd lend you mine, if I still had any.*

Can't we just pop it back in?

Afraid not. The normal rotting of tissue, plus the bugs, plus . . .

Okay, okay. So what am I going to do? I have a date with Caroline on Saturday. We're going on a hayride. I can't let her see me like this.

Don't call attention to it and she'll hardly notice.

How could she not notice? My eye is hanging halfway down my face for gosh sake.

Try to keep her on the side of your good eye.

I don't think that's going to solve much.

Listen, Jerry. This is just in the nature of things. You can't stop it. I can't stop it. We just do the best we can with what we have left of ourselves. Death goes on.

But Caroline . . .

You think she really likes you?

Yes. I do.

Then it won't matter. Consider this: if one of her eyes fell out of her head, would you stop seeing her?

Well, no . . .

There, you see? She probably feels exactly the same way.

But she's so pretty.

They're always pretty, in the beginning.

But what should I say to her?

Be straightforward. Girls appreciate that. There's no need to get graphic, of course. Avoid the temptation to seek sympathy. Have a positive, accepting attitude. You still have one good eye, don't you?

Well, yes . . .

If you let her know you're disturbed by it, then you'll just end up making her feel uncomfortable. She'll be glad to follow your lead. Once you explain the situation, don't bring it up again. Soon, you won't even remember that your eye is out of its socket, dangling there.

I don't know, Bud . . .

It will work, Jerry. Trust me. I haven't steered you wrong so far, have I?

Bud was right. His advice had been invaluable. He had common sense in bushels.

Jerry didn't want to spring any surprises on Caroline, so on Saturday morning he called for her.

Hi, Caroline. This is Jerry.

Well hi, Jerry. How are you?

I'm fine, Caroline. And yourself?

Fine, thank you. We're still on for tonight, aren't we?

Yes, of course. But, uh, there's a little problem.

A problem?

I'm just having some trouble with my eye.

Nothing too serious, I hope.

Oh, no, no. . . . It's just, well, not exactly in the socket anymore. It's sort of . . . hanging down.

My goodness.

I mean, it's still attached. No doubt about that.

Yes, of course.

Silence.

I'm sorry, Jerry said.

It's okay. I understand, I really do.

You do?

I sure do. You still have one good eye, don't you?

Yes.

Well there you go.

You mean you don't mind, Caroline? You'll still go on the hayride with me?

Yes, I'll still go on the hayride with you, silly. You're still the same person I went skating with, aren't you?

Gosh, Caroline, you're really a swell girl.

So I'll see you this evening and I don't want to hear another word about it.

So long, Caroline. And thank you.

Jerry put the eye out of his mind.

A few minutes before six he came to Caroline. It's wise to leave a little early for a date. That way, there's no need to rush when you arrive at your date's residence. Makes for a more relaxed and enjoyable experience for everyone.

Hi, Jerry.

Hi, Caroline. Good evening, Mr. and Mrs. Ames.

He felt a warm greeting. Apparently he met with their approval.

Caroline looked beautiful. White dress, beads, peace, etc.

You look just like yourself, said Jerry.

Thank you, Jerry. That's sweet of you to say.

Are you all ready then? Jerry asked.

All set. 'Night mom and dad. We'll be back by ten-thirty.

Good night, Mr. and Mrs. Ames. Don't worry, I'll take good care of Caroline.

When they arrived at the hayride, the gang was already piling into the rotting hay wagon. Jerry had a few kernels of uneasiness as they approached the wagon. Someone was hooking a chestnut mare horse into its bridle. Large chunks of flesh were missing from the horse's flanks. Much of its head was eaten away, a part of the jawbone showing. Nobody was making fuss about it. Jerry felt his self-confidence soar.

When they reached the business end of the wagon, Jerry stepped up first, and offered Caroline a hand. She took it and he pulled her up.

Hi gang, Jerry said.

Hi Jerry, the gang replied. *Nice to see you, Caroline.*

Hi everybody! Caroline said.

Jerry found a spot for them in the hay. He positioned himself so that Caroline had to sit on the side of his good eye. No sense drawing attention to the flaw if it could be easily avoided.

In a short time the driver hopped up on the front of the wagon, and gently shook the frayed reins. The skeletal horse broke into a trot, its sleigh bells sounding like a death rattle, the wagon rocking forward with the motion.

The driver guided the horse along the narrow trail that wound around the frozen pond and through the snowy field. Pines trees, statuary and ornate white buildings passed by.

What a wonderful idea this was, Caroline said. *This is really fun.*

I'm glad you came along.

Caroline patted Jerry on the forearm, then her fingers began to slide down toward his wrist, a clear sign that she was interested in holding hands.

Fortunately, Jerry first glanced down at her hand, then saw his own . . .

Immediately, he brought his arm across his chest and thrust his hand into the hay. Then, he reached across with his left hand and took hers.

I think I got a sliver, he explained.

Oh, let me see. I can take it out.

Well, it's in pretty deep. I'll remove it later. It doesn't hurt much at all, really.

This seemed to satisfy her.

Her fingers were cold, and his were gone.

Not all of them, perhaps two, possibly three. All he saw were black, rotted stumps. The digits must have fallen off after he hoisted her up onto the wagon. He didn't even feel their departure. Were they in the wagon? He scanned the bed in the vicinity of where he had been standing, but he couldn't spot them amid the hay and snow. They must have fallen into the snow back on the trail. He'd never find them. And even if he did, what good would they do him now?

Caroline must not have noticed. Otherwise, she wouldn't have tried to hold that hand.

The rest of the hayride Jerry spent in nervous preoccupation with his missing appendages. The eye was bad enough. He didn't want Caroline to think he was coming apart on her.

Why now? Why all of a sudden? It was almost like the more he tried to have a social life, the more his body rebelled.

When the hay wagon returned to their point of departure, the horse collapsing into dust, Jerry helped Caroline down to the ground with his left hand, keeping his right tucked into the pocket of his best suit. He didn't dare search the vicinity for his fingers now.

The gang hung out afterwards, gossiping and cracking wise like dead teenagers do. Jerry struggled to keep in good spirits. When they got back to her place, it was later than he expected.

Say, look at the time, said Jerry. *I told your folks I'd get you home by ten-thirty and here it is, almost eleven.*

I'm sure they'd understand. We aren't very late at all. There was nothing we could do about it, really.

I don't want your parents to think I'm taking advantage of you.

They won't think that. You can stay for awhile. I mean it.

Thank you for the offer, Caroline. I would just feel better if I took a rain check. You understand, don't you?

Oh, of course. You're such a gentleman, Jerry. Next time, I won't let you off the hook so easily.

Good night, Caroline.

Good night, Jerry. She leaned over and kissed him on the cheek, deftly avoiding his droopy eye. Her lips were still chilly from the hayride.

Jerry told Bud the rotten news when he returned to his plot.

Fingers rotting away, eh? Join the club.

But what can I do about it? I can't keep company with Caroline like this. She was okay with my eye, but I can't expect her to pretend forever. How are we supposed to hold hands?

Do it spiritually. Girls like a boy who has a kind heart. It makes them feel special.

I want to feel Caroline, touch her.

Use your other hand.

I did, but how long will that last? I'm surprised it's still attached.

There's no turning back, Jerry. There's an old saying around here: If you don't rest in peace, you'll come apart in pieces.

Look, my prospects aren't too good anyway. I appreciate your willingness to help me, Bud. I'll think of something. Maybe if we can keep going on group dates I can hide it from her.

And then what?

I don't know. I don't know. I'll come up with something.

Jerry knew he had to apologize to Caroline, after his behavior on the hayride.

The next day he called for her, trying to inject sunshine into his voice. He remembered sunshine, wistfully.

Hi Caroline, this is Jerry.

Hello, Jerry. How are you?

Very well, thanks.

That's good. I had a really fun time on the hayride, Jerry. Thank you for taking me.

I enjoyed it, too. That's why I was calling, Caroline. I wanted to apologize for my behavior at your place. I shouldn't have run off like that. You said it was okay if I hung around, and I should have trusted you.

Oh gosh, Jerry, there's no need to apologize. I understand. You were just trying to be sweet.

You're not mad at me then?

Of course not.

Wow, that's great to hear, Caroline. I wasn't sure. I mean, I didn't know. My eye . . .

You're fine, Jerry.

How about if I make it up to you anyway? The gang is going sledding this afternoon. Do you want to go?

Well, to be honest, Jerry, I was hoping we could do something by ourselves once.

Oh no . . .

Uh, what did you have in mind?

Why don't we just go for a walk? What do you say?

Jerry knew what he had to say.

Sure, Caroline, that sounds swell. What time do you want me to come over?

How about three?

Three it is.

Terrific. I'll see you then.

Goodbye, Caroline.

Jerry spent the rest of the day wringing his hand.

He couldn't keep his problem in his pocket all afternoon. He had to be honest with Caroline. If only they had given me gloves, he thought with high melancholy.

Three o'clock came like it couldn't wait to see him humiliated.

Jerry hated the fact that he felt trepidation about seeing Caroline. He wanted to feel excitement, anticipation, affection. Not this squeamish, nervous feeling.

On the way over to Caroline's, Jerry felt an odd sensation and it had nothing to do with his interior life. Something in the region of his feet. Suddenly he had trouble walking. And he didn't have to look to know that his toes had been eaten away by time or worms or some burrowing creature.

Jerry didn't get upset, just philosophical. He had hit some kind of plateau, gone from a being with one foot in this world and the other foot in the next, to both feet on the verge of rotting off his legs.

When his deterioration had been easy to hide, it had been possible to keep up appearances, pass as something he was not.

But now, with a dangling eye, stumps instead of fingers, a lot of extra space down at the end of his polished black shoes, there was only one path to take.

Jerry presented himself to Caroline as he was, a young man on the downside of his death. He hobbled the rest of the way to her place.

She was waiting for him, smelling the plastic flowers. A ice-crusted bouquet of pale purples, reds, and yellows.

Hi, Caroline.

Oh hi, Jerry. I didn't hear you coming. She looked at him with concern. *Are you okay? You're walking so strangely.*

This was it.

Well, Caroline, you see, my feet are rotting away. And my hand. He displayed it for her. And tried to force a smile on his natural and peaceful face. *I'm a real mess, aren't I?*

Maybe we should just stay here today. We could talk or something.

I want to walk, said Jerry. *Please walk with me, Caroline.*

Sure, Jerry. I'll walk with you.

They slowly strolled among the monuments and trees, stark oaks coated with ice, evergreens hanging heavy with snow. The moon was circled by a pale orange halo.

Why is it happening now, so fast? Caroline gently asked him. *Just the other day you were fine.*

Bud says it's because I won't rest in peace.

Have I met Bud?

I'm not sure. Bud Pollard. 1959-1976. Loving son devoted student friend of the community.

Oh, yes, I remember seeing him.

He's a good guy. He's always given me helpful advice.

I'm so sorry, Jerry. What are you going to do?

They had reached a bench sheltered by a hedge planted in an arc. With every step it seemed harder for Jerry to walk properly. His gait was a rolling, teetering travesty.

Let's sit down, Jerry said, and she helped him do that.

She was seated on his left, so he was able to hold her hand properly.

Caroline put her head on his shoulder. The decay hadn't hit there yet.

We need to have a talk, Jerry said.

Okay.

They looked at each other, his dangling eye trying to get into the act, too.

You know, Caroline, you're the first girl I've kept company with since I came here. And even if I would have known that dating you would make me decompose to beat the band, I wouldn't have changed a thing, that's how much I've treasured our time together.

I feel the same way. Listen, Jerry, pretty soon what's happening to you will overtake me, too. My eyeballs will go pop, toes and fingers fall off, bits and pieces eaten away. And the bugs . . .

We have this time together. We have the present, before all that happens.

Yes, isn't it wonderful?

Yes, but I'm withering away so quickly, said Jerry. *I don't know how long I've got before I won't be able to go for walks, or ice skating, or anything.*

Your suit still looks sharp.

I don't want to rush us, Caroline, but those are the facts. If we let the days go by thinking things will always be the way they are now, one day we'll wake up and I'll just be a pile of sludge you used to call a friend.

Oh, Jerry, please, don't talk like that.

We have to face it, Caroline. We can't deny this. He reached out for her with his rotting stump. She drew her hand away.

He gazed grimly at her. *This is our future, Caroline. In a few days you're going to be afraid to even look at me.*

A few remnant tears squeezed themselves from her barren ducts. *I won't be afraid, Jerry. I promise.*

Jerry hesitated for a moment. *What I'm saying, Caroline, is that if you want us to have any sort of . . . physical relationship, we can't wait.*

Caroline's peaceful, natural face was clouded with sadness.

I'm sorry it has to be like this, said Jerry. *I know this isn't considered good dating etiquette. It's not proper to pressure a girl into intimate relations. If there was another way . . .*

No, you're right, she said. *We have to face this. I don't want death to be denial, too.*

They sat in quiet spaces for a time, holding hands. A nuthatch lit on an evergreen branch, then flew off when it realized it wasn't alone. Its weight disturbed the branch, sending a dusting of snow down upon the heads of the dead.

So, Caroline, Jerry said shyly, *do you want to go back to my place?*

Jerry's place was in bad need of a dusting.

It's not much, he said, *but it's home.*

I like it. It's cozy.

Are you comfortable? he asked her.

I'm just fine. It's nice to be so close to you.

Don't worry about hurting me.

I won't. Can we do something about that eye? It's sort of in the way.

Oh, sure. Hang on . . . got it. Is that better?

Much better. Now I can touch your face, all over.

He began to touch her, too.

You don't think I'm easy, Jerry, do you?

No, of course not.

Have there been other girls . . . like me?

No, only the living.

That makes me feel good.

As they began to probe and pet, and then proceed to the most private of realms, Jerry began to feel parts of himself break away, disintegrate. His fine suit slowly collapsed in upon itself, soaking up what remained of his bodily fluids.

Jerry suddenly felt disgusted, even horrified and he didn't know why.

I have very strong feelings for you, Caroline whispered to him.

I feel the same about you.

What's wrong with me? he wondered. This should be the crowning moment of my death. Why do I feel so terrible, so guilt-wracked, so . . . wrong?

Caroline sensed it, too. *What's going on? Are you okay?*

I'm okay, he said. *I'm okay.*

But he wasn't. This felt so wrong, so . . . immoral.

At the very moment they consummated their deaths, as his body rotted away to utter uselessness, a shock of awareness hit him, as he understood what had disturbed him, why everything had felt so wrong.

And why now everything was feeling so right.

The final dating secret.

Jerry realized, as both of Caroline's eyes popped out upon her climax, and their precious ooze commingled, that if a living person has intimate relations with a dead body, it's called necrophilia.

If two dead bodies have intimate relations, it must be love.

David Prill *is the author of the cult novels* The Unnatural, Serial Killer Days, *and* Second Coming Attractions, *and the collection* Dating Secrets of the Dead. *"The Last Horror Show," from the* Dating Secrets *collection, was nominated for an International Horror Guild Award. His short fiction has appeared in* The Magazine of Fantasy & Science Fiction, Subterranean, Cemetery Dance, *and at Ellen Datlow's late, lamented* SciFiction *Web site. His story, "The Mask of '67," was published in the 2007 World Fantasy Award-winning anthology* Salon Fantastique, *edited by Ellen Datlow and Terri Windling. Another story, "Vivisepulture," can be found in* Logorrhea: Good Words Make Good Stories, *edited by John Klima. He lives in a small town in the Minnesota north woods.*

When the words "zombie romance" started being flung around a couple of years back, all I could think was: *A zom-rom-com classic was already published back in ought-two!* Okay, so maybe it's not sexy enough for today's market and the new-style zombie love is just *not* going to take decomposition into account. But Prill manages to pull off a combination of Booth Tarkington, those health class films and brochures that were out of date even when I was a teenager, laugh-aloud dark humor, adolescent psychology commentary, and a poignant story of first—albeit post-mortem—love. It even ends happily. I mean, as happily as it can . . . under the circumstances.

Lie Still, Sleep Becalmed

Steve Duffy

It was a night trip, and the thing to remember is: no one's looking for surprises on a night trip. You ride at anchor, out where it's nice and quiet; kick back, chill out, talk rubbish till sunup. No surprises.

Back when Danny had the *Katie Mae*, we often used to take her out of Beuno's Cove at ten, eleven PM, and head for the banks off Puffin Island, near the southeast tip of Anglesey; *we* being Danny, who owned the boat, Jack, who crewed on a regular basis, and me. Jack was a great big grinning party-monster who'd do anything for anyone; anything, that is, except resist temptation when it offered itself, as it seemed to on a regular basis. Any other owner but Danny would probably have sacked him, no matter how good he was with boats: the reason Danny didn't would never have been clear to an outsider, really. Claire, who was always quick to pick up on that sort of thing, reckoned that Jack—Mr. Happy-Go-Lucky—represented something that Danny—Mr. Plodder—had probably always dreamed of being himself, but had never quite worked up the nerve to go for. It was a classic case of vicarious wish-fulfilment, apparently.

"And I'll tell you something else about Danny," she'd added, "I bet once you get past that Big-I-Am act he puts on, it's Jack who does all the hard grafting—am I right? It's the same with you: if you didn't sort out all his tax returns and VAT for him, they'd probably have taken that boat off him by now. He likes to think he's running the show, but he'd be sunk without the pair of you. It's quite funny, really." I remember her whispering all this in my ear as we watched Jack and Danny playing pool in the basement bar of the Toad Hall, not long after we'd first started dating.

That was the summer of '95: on dry land it was banging, hammering heat wave all the way, long sun-drenched days and sticky muggy nighttimes. Out at sea, though, you got the breeze, cool and wonderful, and whenever the next day's bookings sheet was blank Danny needed little enough persuading to pick up a tray or two of Red Stripe and take the *Katie Mae* out for the night. Jack would turn up with a bag of Bangor hydroponic and we'd make the run out to the fishing banks west of the Conwy estuary; we'd lie out on the deck drinking, smoking, chatting about nothing in particular, or maybe go below to pursue the Great and Never-Ending Backgammon Marathon, in which stupendous, entirely fictional sums of money would change hands over the course of a season's fishing. Good times; easy, untroubled. I look back now and think how sweet we had it then.

One night in early August Claire said she wanted to go out with us. I can't really say why I was resistant to the idea. Part of it, if I'm honest, was probably to do with keeping her well away from Jack until I was a bit more confident in the relationship. Remember I told you about Jack and temptation? Well, if I'd gone on to mention me and insecurity, that would've given you the whole of the picture. Over and above that . . . I honestly don't know. Nothing like a premonition, nothing that dramatic or well-defined. Just the feeling, somewhere under my scalp, that things might be on the cusp; might be changing, one way or another, and changing irrevocably. The fact was I always made an excuse, put her off; until that particular night when it had all the potential to turn into an argument, which would have been our first. Fine, I said, yeah, come along, no problem.

It had been another scorcher. Walking down the hill to the harbor you could feel the pavement underfoot giving out the last of the day's heat to the baking breathless night; under the cotton of her tee-shirt the small of Claire's back was slick with sweat where my hand rested. Danny was waiting for us on the *Katie Mae*, and Jack came by soon after; he'd been away for the weekend at a festival, got back only that morning, slept till nine PM, and now here he was ready for action again, invincible. It was just gone half-eleven when we fired up the engine and cast off; I remember Claire squeezed my hand in excitement.

The last of the sunset was gone out of the sky, and it was very dark, very quiet, a still, calm night with just a sliver of the waning moon swinging round behind the headland. The beacon winked one, two, three as we eased out beyond the end of the breakwater, Claire and I sitting out on the foredeck, Danny and Jack in the wheelhouse. As always when we were putting out on a night trip, I felt that little kick of expectation: I'd get it in the daytime, too, but at night particularly. There was a magic to it, some song of the sea, pitched between shanties and sirens. "It's the ocean, innit?" Jack once

said; "you never know what it's going to throw at you," and soon enough I
learned this to be true. Tongue in cheek, I told the same thing to Claire as we
rounded the Trwyn y Ddraig and pulled away from the coast.

"Listen, I don't care what it throws at me," she said, arching like a cat
in the first stirrings of a sea-breeze, "just so long as it's this temperature or
below. Oh, that's good. That's the coolest I've been all day." She stretched out
on the foredeck, head propped up in my lap as I sat cross-legged behind her,
absently ruffling her hair with my fingers.

At this stage you probably need to know a bit about the layout of the
boat. The *Katie Mae* was thirteen meters stem-to-stern, pretty roomy for a
standard fishing vessel, with reasonably poky diesels (in need of an overhaul,
but fine so long as you didn't try and race them straight from cold). The
wheelhouse was amidships, the centre of the boat; behind that, on the aft
deck, were the gear lockers, the bilge pump, the engine hatch. Up towards
the stem, there was the foredeck and the Samson post. In the wheelhouse
we had VHF ship-to-shore, GPS, radar, and also the "fish-finder," the sonar
that not only showed the sea-bottom but tracked the shoals. Down below,
bench seats followed the shape of the hull for'ard of the wheelhouse above,
curving with the prow around a drop-down table where we kept the beer and
the backgammon set. Hurricane lights hung from the bulkheads between
the portholes, posters of mermaids were tacked up on the ceiling: all snug
as a bug in a rug. And outside, where Claire and I were, you had the best
air-conditioning in all North Wales, entirely free and gratis.

Claire snuggled her head in my lap, enjoying the cool breeze of our
passage. "This is nice," she said, letting the last word stretch to its full extent.
"Just like you to keep it all to yourself—typical greedy pig bloke."

I dodged her playful backward punches, one for every slur. "Keep what to
myself? A bunch of sweaty geezers sitting round getting smashed and talking
garbage all night? You should've said—I'd have taken you down the rugby
club, back in town."

"Getting smashed and talking garbage? Is that all there is to it? It's got to
be a bit more cerebral than that, surely—big smart boys like you, university
types and all?"

"You'd think so, wouldn't you?" Danny had joined us on the foredeck.
"Well, you'd be wrong. No culture on this here tub."

"If it's culture you want," I pointed out, moving over to make room, "I
believe P&O do some very nice cruises this time of year."

"Do you want the guided tour then, Claire?" Danny settled himself alongside us. That's Llandudno—see the lights round the West Shore?—and that's the marina at Deganwy over there."

Not to be outdone, I chipped in my own bit of local color. "This stretch here is where the lost land of Helig used to be, before the sea came in and covered it all."

"Helig ap Glannog, aye," Danny amplified in his amusingly nit-picking way, at pains to remind Claire just who was the captain on this boat, and who was the guy who helped out now and then. Danny's dad had fished these waters since the 1940s; he'd been delighted when his eldest dropped out of Bangor Uni and picked up a charter boat of his own. Since then, Danny had been busy proving Jack's adage that you could take the boy out of university, but you couldn't take university out of the boy. It was just a way he had. You couldn't let it get to you.

"Helig ap what?" Claire seemed slightly amused herself—remember, I told you she'd already got Danny figured out.

"Way back," Danny explained, "sixth century AD. There was a curse on the family, and a big tide came and covered all their lands, and everybody died except for one harpist on the hill there crying woe is me, woe is me, some shit or other. And nowadays hardly anyone moors a boat out there—"

"Except for Danny," I chipped in, "because he's big and hard and don't take no shit from no one, innit, Danny lad?" He tried to punch me in a painful place, but I rolled over just in time. "Who's steering this tub, anyway?"

"Jack," said Danny, waiting till I'd resumed my former position before trying, and failing once more, to hit me where it hurt. "We'll keep going for a bit," he went on, ignoring my stifled laughter, "till we're out of everyone's way. Then we'll drop anchor and get down to business." He rubbed his hands together in anticipation of the night's entertainment. "So, do you play backgammon then, Claire?"

Claire smiled sweetly, her blond hair blowing back into my face. "Well, I know the rules," she said, and nudged me surreptitiously.

Several hours later, Claire owned, in theory at least, the *Katie Mae*, the papers on Danny's house and fifty percent of both Jack's and mine earnings through to the year 2015. Down below Danny and Jack were skinning up and arguing over who was most in debt to who; Claire and I were up in the wheelhouse, enjoying a little quality relationship time with the lights out.

"Mmmm," she said, into my left ear. "That was easy enough."

"What?" I said. "Me? I'm dead easy, me. You should know that by now."

"Oh, I do," she said, "I do. No—I meant those two downstairs."

"*Down below*," I reminded her, in Danny's pedantic voice. "What—you mean you get up to this sort of thing with those two as well? I'm crushed."

She chuckled, and moved her hand a little. "There—is that better? Didn't mean to crush you. Are they always that dozy?"

"Well, you had an unfair advantage."

"What?"

"You were distracting them all the time."

"Me? What was I doing?"

"Nothing," I said, burying my face in her neck. "You were just making the most of your natural advantages: this, and this, and this . . . "

"Mmmm . . . ooh. What's that?"

"You mean you don't know what *that* is? Here, let me show you—"

"Not that." Firmly, she brushed the possibility aside. "That thing behind you. It's beeping."

"Beeping . . . ?" I disengaged myself awkwardly and looked around. "Oh, that. That's the fish-finder. Didn't think it was me."

"The whatter?"

"Fish-finder: it's sonar, like in the movies, ping-ping, ping-ping? It shows you the sea-bed underneath the vessel—down here, look—and then where the shoals are. Look, there's something: that blob there, coming up now."

"So is that fish, then?" There was another ping. The target was rising, moving closer to the boat, so far as I could tell. Or it could have been the boat was sinking, I wasn't an expert.

"Must be, I suppose. Hang on, Jack knows this kit better than I do—Jack?"

Jack's grinning head popped up from below: the original Jack-in-the-box. "Aye, aye, mateys—here you go, I've done up a little dragon each for you, all classy-like." He swarmed up the short companionway to join us in the wheelhouse. "Hell's teeth, now, what's this?" He flipped a switch up and down on the fish-finder. "Have you been pressing buttons again, Billy-thick-lad? Bloody cabin boys, Claire, I tell you—"

I dug him in the ribs, and we wrestled amiably for a moment. "It's nothing to do with me, that—I never touched it. It just went off."

"I see. Big boy done it and ran off, is that it?" He smiled at Claire. "No, you're in the clear for once. I'll tell you who'll have left this on—bloody

Captain Birdseye down there. You can't trust him to do anything properly: That right, Will?"

From down below came a smothered counter-accusation: Jack showed it his middle finger and grinned again, even more roguishly. I put an arm around Claire, just so's Jack didn't get carried away. "Claire wants to know is that a shoal or what?"

"Let's have a butcher's . . . what, that there? No, that's not a shoal." He bent over the screen. In its faint green glow he looked a little perplexed. "Too small, see? And it's right up on the surface, practically—I don't know what that is. Sometimes you get seals round Puffin Island, off the Orme even . . . I dunno. It might be a seal, I suppose." He glanced up, through the cabin window. "There isn't any moon, worse luck, but if we look over, lemme see . . . *that* way—" he pointed out on the starboard side—"we might be able to see something, if we get out on deck and stay quiet-like."

Which we did, joined by Danny, who'd just appeared from below decks with more beer; and perhaps I should mention at this point that Claire and I had only had a couple of cans each by that time. I'd been hitting on the majority of the joints as they went round, Claire hadn't, but we were both completely on the case so far as our shared perceptions went. Given what happened over the next hour or so, it's important you know that.

Out on the aft deck, Jack explained to Danny what we'd seen on the fish-finder. We were all of us whispering, in case we scared the seal; we were still expecting seals at this point. Danny nodded, and pottered over behind the wheelhouse on the port side. Claire cupped her hand around my ear and whispered, "What's he up to?" At that time I didn't know. Soon enough it would become clear.

The three of us on the aft deck—Jack, Claire and I—gazed out over the waves. It was difficult to make much out on the surface, even with the light in the wheelhouse switched off and our eyes accustomed to the darkness. Away off in the far distance was a glitter of shore-lights: Anglesey to the north-west, Penhirion and the mainland south-west. Between the lights on land and where we lay at anchor was mile after mile of still dark ocean. The green navigation light danced on the tops of the soft sluicing wavelets near the hull; all the rest was a vast murky undulation, slop and ebb, slop and ebb, featureless, unknowable.

Suddenly light sprang out from the *Katie Mae*, swinging through the darkness, settling on the waves in a rough rippling ellipse. I jumped a little, tightened my grip on Claire, looked round: there was Danny, all but invisible behind the spotlight on the wheelhouse roof, directing the strong beam through and beyond us to light up the slow dark waves. "Shit," swore Jack under his breath, then, louder, hissing: "Turn it off, man, you'll frighten it away! Bastard's left his nav-lights on as it is," he added *sotto voce*.

"I thought you wanted to see!" Danny sounded a bit smashed already. Claire looked at me, and I read the same judgement in her eyes. The harsh light from the *Katie Mae*'s spot made her look even paler than usual; almost translucent.

"We *do*, but we're not gonna see anythin' if you frighten it away, you knob! Turn it off and come back here—no—wait a minute . . . " Jack's voice trailed off, and I turned back to the water, trying to see what he'd seen. If anything, the spotlight made it harder; it was total illumination or total blackout, vivid purple afterimages blooming on your retinas whenever you looked outside its magic circle. I squinted, tried to shield my eyes. Beside me Jack was doing the same thing. "Hold it steady, over there—look—what's that?"

A slumped low shape in the black water. Dull and dark, the waves washing over it as it dipped and rose on a tranquil tide; then Claire gasped and dug her fingers into my arm as a slight swell lifted it far enough out of the water for us to see a gleam of white. A face, all tangled round with lank dark strands like seaweed.

Jack had seen it too. "Christ almighty," he breathed; then to Danny: "Hold it! Hold it there!"

"What?" shouted Danny.

"Look where you're pointing it, man! Forget about the bloody seal— there's someone in the water!" Abruptly Jack was gone from beside me, over to the aft lockers, flinging them open one after another. His voice came back on the quiet night air as Claire and I clung to each other and watched the body floating towards us in the spotlight: ". . . find anything on this *bastard* boat . . . " Then he was back, a long boathook under his arm like a jousting lance. "Right." He called to Danny: "Listen up. Claire's gonna come up and get that light, okay?" He glanced at Claire; she nodded. He smiled briefly at her and resumed: "You get down here and give Will a hand. I'm gonna hook him when he gets close enough in, then you two'll have to pull him up."

And we did just that: Danny and I knelt down in the scuppers, braced against the capstans while Jack leaned perilously far out from the side, one hand grasping the side of the boat, the other waving the boathook back and forth till the waterlogged shape drifted within reach. All the way in, until it was so close to the boat the spotlight wouldn't go far enough down on its mount, Claire never wavered: she knelt on the wheelhouse roof and trained the light dead straight on the bobbing body in the waves. Danny had got a torch from somewhere, and that gave us light enough for the last part of the job.

Jack's hook snagged in the clothing of the body; he hauled it in like a fish on a gaff, and Danny and I managed to get a grasp underneath its arms. Together we dragged it out of the water and up on to deck, where it plopped down as if on a fishmonger's slab, a cold dead weight of waterlogged clothing and wrinkled flesh.

I think we all thought at that time it was a dead man. It had been lying, after all, face down in the water; it was clammy cold to the touch; and we hadn't felt anything like a heartbeat as we heaved it aboard. The three of us stood around it as the saltwater drained off into the scuppers; no one quite knew what to say, or do. A hand touched my shoulder, and I nearly jumped off the side.

Claire had come down from the roof of the wheelhouse and was standing behind me. "Jesus," I muttered fretfully, and she squeezed my arm remorsefully, peering around me at the body on the deck. "Sorry," she whispered; then, quite unexpectedly, she buried her face in my shoulder. "Has anyone looked to see . . . " she began, and couldn't finish. Danny just looked at me, his tanned, weather-roughened face as pale as Claire's. It was left to Jack, as ever, to take care of the practicalities. "She's right," he said, grimacing; "suppose we'd better have a look who he is and that. Do us a favor, Danny boy; get that torch down here, will you?"

He knelt on the deck, and gently turned the body over by its shoulders. What we'd thought was seaweed around the head we could see now were long, damp locks of hair. Danny brushed them away from the face, a thing I doubt I could have done myself right then. He wiped his hand several times on the leg of his jeans, and straightened up a little. We could all see the face now: it was a man in his early twenties, unshaven, startlingly pallid. "Shit," Danny said, and the torch he was holding wobbled for a moment. "Just look at his face a minute, Jack . . . "

"I'm *looking* at his face." Jack sounded stressed. "What the fuck d'you think I'm *doing* down here—" and then he drew in his breath sharply.

"It's him, isn't it?" Like the torchbeam, Danny's voice was wavering slightly. "That lad we were talking to in the Liverpool Arms on Regatta Day that time, what's his name . . . "

"Andy." There was a slight roughness, a catch, to Jack's voice. "Andy something or other; crews on that boat out of Bangor these days, doesn't he? Andy, Andy . . . Christ, I must be going senile in my old age." He slapped the side of his head, and Claire jumped a little at the sudden noise in the midst of all that illimitable stillness. "Andy Farlowe, that's it. His old feller used to have a fishing boat in Conwy harbor; he's retired now, lives up Gyffin somewhere. Christ. I'll have to go round, I suppose, tell him what's happened—"

"*Wait.*" Claire's nails dug into my arm. "Wait. Look at him, Will."

"What?" I looked at her instead; she was staring fixedly at the body, her mouth slightly open. "*What?*" I asked her again, and she whispered it, no more, so quiet you would have missed it in the normal run of things: "He's *moving* . . . "

I was going to say, impossible, you're imagining it; but now as I looked I could see the limbs twitch, just a little. The hands clenched, unclenched, the head moved ever so slightly from side to side. It—he—gulped a little, and his jaw sagged open. A little trickle of seawater came out in a splutter. All at once his eyelids opened, and the eyes rolled back from up inside his head. He blinked once or twice, and seemed to be trying to speak.

Jack was down with him in a shot, finger probing the airway for obstructions, ear pressed to his mouth to gauge the breathing. "Fuck," he said, looking up as if unable to believe what he was seeing or feeling: "he's still alive, you know."

Not only that: within a few minutes he was conscious, talking, the lot. With Jack and Danny helping him we got him on his feet and down below decks, where Danny had the best part of a bottle of rum held against emergencies, like when we ran out of lager. He coughed and spluttered a bit, but it seemed to do the trick; he looked round at us, shook his head and cleared his throat. "Who are you lot, then?" he croaked. We all burst out laughing, I think from sheer relief as much as anything.

He couldn't say how long he'd been in the water: "I must've been spark out of it," was all he could manage. "You were that," said Jack, one arm round his shoulders in a bracing grapple. His attitude to the younger man seemed almost fatherly, most un-Jacklike: it was altogether more responsibility than I could remember him showing towards anything or anyone before.

"How about the boat?" asked Danny, and it suddenly occurred to all of us: how had he got out there in the first place? We looked at him: he closed his eyes briefly, as if trying to remember. "We gone out . . . " he began, and paused. Jack nodded encouragingly. "We gone out in the evening . . . in the straits past Beaumaris . . . " Every word seemed to be an effort; not so much physically, though he still looked very weak, but an effort of remembrance. It was like watching someone being asked to remember what he did on his birthday when he was seven.

"What happened, Andy? Did you fall overboard, or did the boat go down?" Danny seemed anxious to clear up the technicalities of it all.

"I was out on deck," Andy said slowly. He pushed his lank black mane of hair back, looked round helplessly for words. "It was . . . it was cold." Jack nodded, as if Andy had just given him the temperature down to the nearest degree centigrade; Andy hardly noticed. "In the water. It was cold." He shivered a little, and Claire said, "Have you got any spare clothes on board? We should get him out of those; he'll be freezing. He's probably in shock already: we should get him warm. Get some blankets round him as well if you've got them."

Jack sprang to it. "Shit, why didn't I think of that—see that locker under the seats there, Claire? You have a look in there; that's blankets. I think I've got a few things, jumpers and such, in there too, haven't I?"

Claire rummaged down in the locker, came up with a thick fisherman's sweater and a couple of blankets. "Right, mate," Jack rapped out a little paradiddle on the table-top. "Get you into these, shall we? Danny—let's have the engines on and home James, what about it?"

"Yeah . . . " Danny was a little slower to react; he was staring at Andy as if he was having trouble taking it all in. At first I put it down to him still being a bit smashed; I'd have thought what had happened in the last ten minutes would have sobered anyone up, but it all depended on what sort of state he'd been in in the first place—he was always a pig when it came to spliff. "Yeah: you come up too, Will. Get on the ship-to-shore, just in case, let them know there might be a problem with the . . . with the . . . what is it, Jack?"

"Wanderley." This over his shoulder as he turned the balled-up sweater right way out. "Better get on to them; nice one, Danny boy."

"The Wanderley, out of Bangor. Okay?" With one long last look at Andy, he turned and went up the companionway to the wheelhouse. I went to follow him; stopped, and said irresolutely, "Claire?" She looked up at me, reached instinctively for my hand.

"Never mind Claire—it's crowded enough in here." This from up in the wheelhouse. "Get up here, Will, I need you."

"You can give us a hand, Claire," said Jack, "give our boy here the once-over." He nudged Andy. "How about that for luck, eh, Andy lad? Floating in the water all night, and the first boat to come along's got a posh lady doctor on it!"

"I'm not a doctor, Jack," Claire told him patiently, correcting this mistake for no more than the third or fourth time that night. "I work at the hospital; I'm a junior pharmacist."

"Well, it's all the same, innit?" Jack wasn't listening. He smoothed the last of the folds out of the sweater, turned to face us with a determinedly bright smile. "You've done all the first aid and that, haven't you?"

"I might not have been paying attention, though," Claire said, in an uncharacteristically small girly-voice; but she knew she was beaten. Better women than her had been powerless in the grip of a full-on Jack attack. I squeezed her hand and turned to go up the companionway. She held on to it for a moment longer than I thought she would; I glanced back, and she was looking at me, her violet eyes dark and smudgy-looking in the lamplight. I raised an eyebrow, *what*? She bit at her lower lip, shook her head slightly, *nothing*, and gave my hand one last squeeze. I squeezed back, and smiled encouragingly. "See you later," I said, and Jack, overhearing me, said "yeah, yeah, get up there Will man."

Beside him on the bench, Andy looked up, silhouetted in the lantern light, running a hand through his sopping merman's mane. He did seem to be in some sort of shock; bewildered by it all, withdrawn almost, as if part of him was still floating out in the water, in the long night reaches where no boats came. He tried to smile; I smiled back, then trotted up the short companionway to join Danny in the wheelhouse.

"About time, Will." He sounded edgy, about half a beat off a full-scale Danny fluster. "Ship-to-shore, there: get a move on."

There was a limit to how much I could stand of Danny playing Captain Bligh, but this was not the time to bring it up. I said nothing, and flipped the switch on the radio. Nothing. I tried again: still nothing. "VHF's down," I said in a neutral tone, hoping Danny wouldn't take it the wrong way.

He did, of course. "*Down*? It can't be *down*, no way, I had it up and running this afternoon. Here—" He pushed past me in the constricted space. "It's simple, look. On, off . . . " He did exactly what I'd done: joggled the switch a few times. No gray-yellow glow on the LED frequency readout; no power-up, no nothing. Danny swore, and tried the other great standby of the non-technical layman, slapping the top of the set. The handset fell off its rest and dangled on its cord; besides that, nothing. That was Danny finished, then. "Bollocks," he muttered under his breath. "Bollocks, bollocks, bollocks . . ." He seemed disproportionately panicky, I thought. After all, it wasn't the first thing that had ever gone wrong on his old tub of a charter boat: most of the equipment was second-hand or obsolete, or both, and something or other was always conking out on us. So how come he was so hyper now? He shouted down the companionway: "Jack?"

"What?"

"Ship-to-shore's out."

"Out? What you mean, out? Channel eight for comms, channel sixteen for emergencies. Have I got to do everything on this poxy boat?"

"It's not coming on." Panic rose in Danny's voice, sending it high and querulous.

Silence for a second down below decks. Then, Jack's exasperated head thrust up the companionway: "Is it the batteries?"

Quickly I tried all the rest of the gear. The fish-finder, our newest piece of kit, ran off its own nickel-cadmiums, but everything else came off the main batteries, and it was all down, no power on board the whole of the *Katie Mae*. "Oh, brilliant," I said under my breath.

"There's no juice," Danny told Jack, who had watched me all the way round the wheelhouse and didn't need telling.

"What you think I am, Blind Pew? I can bloody see there's no juice—get your arse down that engine hatch and find out *why* there's no juice, Danny. Make yourself useful for once, 'stead of standing round giving other people orders."

That last bit didn't go down too well, but Jack had already vanished back below. Danny stood a moment by the wheel, breathing heavily, then barged past me out on deck. The engine hatch was in the stern: I could hear Danny swearing as he banged it open and clattered down the short ladder. A few seconds later, Jack came swarming up the companionway and out on to the aft deck. "Bloody typical," I heard him mutter, before he let himself down through the hatch to see what he could do.

I stood in the dark wheelhouse and tried to work out our options in this, our newly powerless state. Down below decks there were the hurricane lamps, and right now they were the only light we had, apart from Danny's torch. I looked at the inert console: without electricity, the head-up radar wouldn't work, and more to the point, neither would the ship-to-shore VHF

radio. Most worryingly of all, we could forget about the electric starter motor
for the diesels; and without the diesels, we were going nowhere in a hurry.
True, we might be able to start them using the auxiliary power supply, but
we'd had trouble with that before when the main batteries had run down
flat—which they had a habit of doing. It had been one of the things Danny
had been meaning to get around to, for which read: one of the things he was
going to get Jack to do for him.

At least there was the fish-finder, I thought sarcastically. That was still
doing a grand job there on the side of the console, beeping away occasionally,
mapping out the gently shelving bottom below the boat. Here and there on
the display stray sonar returns stirred lethargically; if we'd been on a charter
the punters would have been wetting themselves in anticipation of a big
haul. My attention was distracted from the slow drifts and patterns on the
electronic screen by Claire coming up the companionway.

"All right?" I smiled, to show her that everything was okay, just a few
minor hiccups here, absolutely no-problemo. The dauntless crew of the *Katie
Mae* coping with an emergency, just watch 'em go. "How's Andy?"

She didn't answer me straightaway. "Danny's gone to sort the batteries
out," I explained, assuming she was worried about the power being out;
then I looked at her more closely, and realized it was something more than
that. She was shaking from head to toe—quite literally shaking, gooseflesh
standing out on her bare skin.

I was ashamed of myself. It had been a long fifteen minutes or so since
we'd first had an inkling of something floating out there in the water: we'd
all been through the mill a bit, emotionally speaking. No wonder Claire was
still a bit freaked. I put my arms around her, but she didn't stop shivering.
"What's the matter?" I muttered into her soft-smelling hair. "No need to
worry now. It's all right."

She put her hands on my biceps and held me slightly away from her. "No
it's not, Will," she whispered urgently. "It's not all right—you don't know
the half of it."

"What is it?" I could tell it was bad from the intensity of her response.
"Why are you shaking like that?"

A huge reflexive tremor shook her all over. "It's down there." She indicated
the short companionway with a glance. "It's . . . it's *cold*. Don't you feel it?"

Now she mentioned it, I did. It was pleasantly cool in the wheelhouse, but
standing at the top of the companionway was like being in front of an open

walk-in fridge. "It's water-level down there," I explained, less than sure of my own explanation. "The water's always a few degrees colder than the ambient air temperature."

"It's not that." Claire shook her head vehemently, lips pursed. I had the feeling she knew very well what she wanted to say, but couldn't quite bring herself to say it: it was like watching someone with a stutter trying to spit it out. "It's . . . " she glanced back down the steps, "it's *him*." She hissed the last word, lips almost touching my ear.

"What do you mean?" I was whispering too.

Again she glanced down below; shook her head. "Not here," she said, and practically manhandled me backwards out of the wheelhouse: I had to brace my foot against the gutters to avoid going overboard. From aft came the clashing sounds of metal on metal, and of Jack and Danny arguing down the engine hatch. Claire and I went and knelt down on the foredeck, face-on to each other, knees touching.

"Should we be out here?" I wanted to know. "I don't think we ought to leave Andy on his own."

Claire took a deep breath. "Listen," she said, "that's the trouble. I've been down there with him just now, and there's something not right."

And here we were with the radio down, I thought. Brilliant. "How do you mean? Is he injured? Has he gone into shock or something?"

"Worse than that," she said, and my heart sank. "Didn't you feel anything down there?"

I looked at her, trying to work out what she was getting at. "Feel anything? Like what? I don't know: I was still a bit hyper from getting him out of the water and all that, you know?"

Claire frowned. "You were sat the other side of the table from him, weren't you?" I nodded. "So you couldn't—" A seagull swooped low over the boat sounding its harsh staccato alarm cry, a flash in the darkness over our heads. Claire jumped; if I hadn't been holding on to her she'd have probably gone over the side. She held on to me for a moment or two, then tried to tell it another way. "Listen. When you and Danny went up Jack was fussing round him like an old mother hen. He got him to take his clothes off and put dry ones on, towel himself off and what have you. I picked up the wet clothes; I was going to put them in one of the lockers, but I didn't like to—the touch of them . . . " She paused, controlled herself and carried on. "They were coming apart, Will; they were rotting away."

I didn't know what to say. "We were grabbing on to his clothes when we were trying to fish him out. I think we tore a few of the seams . . . "

"I didn't say *torn*," she said; "they were rotten, Will. Like they'd been in the water . . . I don't know. A long time."

"How long?" The voice behind me made me flinch. Danny had crept up on me again. I wished people would stop doing that; it had been a long night already, and I was getting edgy. Claire looked up. I could see the whites of her wide round eyes.

"The fabric was . . . disintegrating," she said. "A long time." Danny nodded. He seemed to be about to say something, but Claire went on:

"And that's not all. Jack got me to look him over, see if he was injured at all." Again the full-body reflex tremble. "It was like touching dead meat: he didn't have any warmth in him whatsoever. What his core temperature would have been . . . I was shivering just touching him, *but he wasn't*." She glanced between the two of us, to make sure we registered her emphasis. "He wasn't shivering, the way you would be if you'd been hauled out of the water in the middle of the night. He never shivered, not once. He was just sitting on the bench, looking at us . . . " She started to shake again, and I tightened the grip of my arm around her. She squeezed it gratefully, and continued:

"Then Jack followed you up into the cabin thing, and I was left down there with him." She clutched at both her shoulders, arms crossed tightly across her chest. "He hadn't put the dry clothes on or anything; he was just looking around, as if—as if he'd never seen anything quite like that before, you know? As if there was something he couldn't get his head around; like when you're in a dream, and the details are just, I don't know, *out* . . . wrong somehow. And everything's slowed down, and your reactions are like, you're trying to move, but everything's going like *this*—" She mimicked slow-motion, moving her head laboriously from side to side.

Yes, I thought, that was it; Claire had put her finger on it. I could see it now, the way he'd looked with a stupefied sort of incomprehension from one to the other of us as we'd gathered round him down below; the way he'd gazed at the lanterns hanging from the bulkheads, at the pictures of mermaids on the ceiling up above. Beside us on the deck Danny was nodding; he'd recognized it too.

"So, "Claire resumed: "I said to him, come on, better get these dry clothes on, or you'll catch your death. And he just; he looked round at me, and he nodded, but it was as if he couldn't really work out what I was asking him to do. I thought he might've taken a knock to the head or something, maybe he was still concussed, so I said, here, I'll help you, and I went over to him and sort of got his arms up above his head, you know, like when you're trying to put a jumper on a little kid?

"I was trying not to touch him too much, 'cos—" she looked at me, and I nodded *yeah, go on*—"and I got the dry jumper and slipped it over his head, and then . . . " She started shivering again, her voice suddenly tremulous. "And then I felt the back of his head, and there was all his hair, you know, all long and wet, and underneath it—" the words came out all in a rush "—underneath it there was this big dent in the back of his head, it was huge, like the size of my fist, and it was like the whole back of his head had been caved in, and you could feel the edges of the bones grinding together." She wrung at my arm, as if to make my own bones grind. "And I snatched my hand away, and I thought there'd be blood, but there wasn't any blood, and he just kept on looking at me, like he didn't understand . . . " She was crying by now, and I hugged her, as much to stop myself from shaking as to stop her.

Danny was still nodding his head. "I was trying to tell Jack down the engine hatch just now," he said slowly, and if he'd been drunk or stoned before, he sounded dead straight now. Scared out of his wits, but straight. "I heard something about a lad going missing off one of the Bangor boats—I couldn't think of the name, though. It might have been the Wanderley." He stopped.

"When did you hear that?" It didn't sound like my voice; it sounded like the voice of someone much younger and much, much more nervous.

" . . . Two or three days back," said Danny miserably, and none of us said anything for a minute or two there on the foredeck. Eventually I broke the silence.

"He can't . . . that can't be him. No way."

"You didn't touch his skin," said Claire stubbornly. "I did. He's been out the water fifteen minutes now, and he still hasn't got *any* body heat. That's not natural. Even in the middle of winter that wouldn't be natural. It's summer, a hot summer night. And he's freezing."

"You saw him," was all Danny said to me. "You saw what he was like."

"So he's still cold—so he's a bit out of it still—so what?" I was only resisting for fear of what might follow, because even to admit the possibility of what Claire and Danny were suggesting would be to kiss goodbye to anything resembling sanity, or safety. "He can't get warm. It doesn't make him a fucking zombie." Well, the word was out now.

Danny was shaking his head. "You don't last three days in the water, Will. If he went off that boat Saturday night, he'd 've been dead for Sunday. Sunday at the latest—and even then he still wouldn't 've been lying round waiting for us to come by. The coast guards would've been crawling all over this stretch, and the choppers from RAF Valley: they'd have got him if he'd been floating on top of the water, man . . . what is it?"

My mouth must have been open; it's a bad habit I have. I was thinking about back before in the wheelhouse, when Claire and I had been necking, and she'd asked me what was that thing going beep. The fish-finder, I'd said; and now I remembered it, that large echo we'd all thought was a seal. By the time we asked Jack, it was already up on the surface; but before that—I swallowed. Before that, it had been rising, slowly, from off the sea-bed. That's what corpses do, after a day or so. The gases balance out the dead weight, and they rise . . .

"*What*?" We were all extremely nervous now, Danny as much as anyone. "Spit it out, for Christ's sake."

"This is the Llys Helig stretch, isn't it?" My voice was steady, just. "We were talking about it, just before. What was it your dad used to say about this stretch?"

Danny was nodding before I'd finished. Clearly he'd been thinking along the same lines. "It was all along the banks here." He gestured out across the waves. "All the old fishermen; they said the sea was twitchy from here out to Puffin Island." Twitchy; that had been it. Strange word to use. "They said . . . they said it would spit out its drowned." He glanced back towards the wheelhouse unhappily.

"Yeah," I said, looking straight at Claire. I was going to tell her she was right, if I could find the bottle to come out with it, but in the end I just nodded. She didn't say anything; but she put a hand to my face and I held it, very tight.

"What are we gonna *do*—" began Danny, but then Jack shouted from down the engine hatch, "Oy! Knobber! *Hand* down here? Jesus . . . "

"Okay," I said, deciding I'd be the grown-up on this boat. "Look, whatever we do, we've got to get moving again. You go and get those diesels started up, Danny."

He was half-way over to the hatch before he remembered who was supposed to be playing captain. "What about you two? What are you going to do?"

"We're going to take care of the other thing," I said. In all my years on boats I'd never been seasick; but I came close to it then, thinking about what the two of us would have to do next.

Claire and I talked it over for five minutes or so. It wasn't that we disagreed on the crux of it—I think part of her had sensed the truth about Andy almost from the start, and I was all the way convinced by now—but she wasn't happy with what I proposed doing about it.

"It's murder," she said, and I said, "How can it be? He's dead already." Saying it like that was awful; as bad as touching him would have been, knowing what we knew now, as bad as the thought that what you'd touch was . . . not alive, not in any way that you could recognize. But something in her balked at doing the necessary thing. I tried to argue my case, to convince her, but the trouble was, what I wanted to do had nothing with reason or logic. It was as instinctive as treading in something and wiping your foot clean; as brushing a fly off your food.

But she knew that as well, every bit as much as I did. More so, because she'd been down in the cabin with him, had laid hands on his bare skin and felt . . . what she'd felt. I think those scruples we were both wrestling with were actually something more like nostalgia, a longing for the last few remnants of the everyday shape of things. Maybe in situations like that, you'll hang on to anything that says, this isn't happening, everything is perfectly normal, you can't seriously be going to do this . . .

But we were going to do it, because it had to be done. We couldn't have taken *that* back to harbor with us—we couldn't have walked him off the boat, taken him back to his dad in Conwy and said, look, here he is, here's your lad Andy back safe and sound. That would have been a hundred times crueler than what we were about to do now. So yes, I felt bad; but it was the lesser of two evils. I was completely sure of that, just as sure as I was that come the daylight, I would probably feel like the shittiest, most cowardly assassin in all creation. But it was hours yet till the daylight, and below decks we had a dead man who didn't know he was dead yet. So I went into the wheelhouse, stood at the top of the companionway and called "Andy?" The first time it got swallowed up in a sort of gag reflex; I gulped, and called out again, "Andy?"

No answer from below decks; just the slow pinging of the fish-finder. This was what I'd been afraid of. Gingerly, I grabbed the woodwork of the companionway hatch, and lowered myself into the space below decks. I was ready to spring back if anything happened; what, I didn't know. But I knew that I didn't want to do this; didn't want to look now into the lantern light and see—

He was sitting just as we'd left him. The jumper Claire had tried to put on him was ruched up around his chest; he had one arm still caught in the arm-hole, and I think it was that—something as banal and stupid as that— that finally convinced me, if I'd really needed convincing. A child could have poked his arm through that sleeve—*would* have done it, out of pure reflex; but Andy hadn't.

I stepped down, till there was just the table between us. "Andy?" I said again, and he looked up. I was already making to look away, but I couldn't help it, our eyes met. His eyes were so black, so empty; how could I have looked into them and thought him alive?

I'd meant to say something else, but what came out was, "You all right?" It was crazy enough on the face of it, but what would have been normal? He nodded; I could see him nodding, as I stared down at my feet. "Cold," he said; that was all. Then, out of nowhere, I found myself saying, "Come on: let's get your arm through there."

Considering what I had in mind, seemed like the height of hypocrisy; but I think it was a kinder instinct than I gave myself credit for at the time. Steeling myself, still not looking him straight in the face, I reached across and lifted the folding table up. I stretched out the wool of the jumper with one hand and slipped the other into the sleeve. Feeling around inside, my fingers touched his: he was making no attempt to reach through and hold on, which was probably just as well. Cold? More than cold; it was as if he'd never been warm, as if he'd lain on that ocean bed for as long as the sea had lain on the land. Fighting to keep my guts down, I dragged his arm through and let go the jumper. Released, his arm fell back down by his side; dead weight.

Doing that helped me with what came next, with the physical side of it at least. "Right," I said, in a ghastly pretence at practicality; "let's get you up on deck, shall we?" He looked up blankly. I had to look, had to make sure he was going to do it. Those eyes: I couldn't afford to look into them for too long. God knows what I would have seen in there; or what he might have seen in mine, perhaps. "Come on," I said, turned part-way away from him. "They're waiting for you up on deck."

In the end I had to help him to his feet. He was like a machine running down, almost; I hate to think what would have happened if we'd actually tried to take him back to dry land. Even through the layer of wool I could feel a dreadful pulpiness everywhere that wasn't bone. Again the gag came in my throat; I clamped my jaw shut and took him under one arm, and he came up unresisting, balanced precariously in his squelching shoes. A little puddle of rank seawater had collected around his feet. The smell—I was close enough to get the smell now, but I don't want to talk about it. I dream about it, sometimes, on bad sweating nights in the hot midsummer.

I motioned him ahead. Obediently, he stepped forward, and as he passed me I saw the horrible indentation in the back of his skull. The hair which had covered it before had flattened now, and the concave dent was all too clearly visible. No one could have taken a wound like that and survived. Just before I looked away, the bile rising in my throat, I thought I saw something in there; something white and wriggling. I came very near to losing it entirely in that moment.

If he'd needed help getting up the companionway, I would've had to have called Danny through—there was no way I could have touched him, not after seeing that wound in the back of his head. As it was, he put one foot on the steps, then, after what seemed ages, the next, and trudged up into the wheelhouse. I tried to focus on the normal things: on the feel of the wooden rail as I stepped up behind him into the wheelhouse; on the brass plaque that said *Katie Mae*, there beside the wheel; on the ping of the fish-finder in the silence. As Andy paused, silhouetted against the dim starlight of outside, waiting for me to tell him what to do next, I took several deep breaths. "Now?" I said, and waited for Claire's voice.

"Now," she said, a small voice from out of the darkness, and I ran forwards with both arms straight out in front of me. Andy was in the act of turning round, and I just glimpsed his eyes; there was a greenish phosphorescence to them in the dark, and Claire said later that I screamed out loud as my hands made contact with his shoulder-blades.

He was standing in the wheelhouse doorway. Ahead of him was just the narrow stretch of deck that linked fore and aft, and then the low side of the boat. Claire was crouching beneath the level of the wheelhouse door; on my signal she'd straightened up on to her hands and knees as I came up on Andy from behind. My push sent him careening forwards; he flipped straight over Claire's upthrust back and out over the side of the boat. There was a solid, crunching impact as he hit the water; Claire was up off her knees and into my arms as the cold spray drenched the pair of us.

"What the *fuck*?" It was Jack. He was standing in the engine hatch; clearly he couldn't believe what he'd just seen. "You stupid bloody—what the *fuck*, man?" He clambered up through the hatch and started towards us. Claire tried to get in his way, but he pushed her angrily to one side; she went sprawling into the wheelhouse. Jack squared up to me, fists clenched: no matter how smoothly it had gone with Andy, I saw I was in for at least one fight that evening. He swung away, cursing, and dropped to his knees; I realized he was scrabbling around down in the gutters for the boat-hook he'd used earlier, so that he could fish Andy out of the water a second time.

I was backing round on to the foredeck, trying to think what to do, how to explain it to him, when several things happened more or less simultaneously.

The spotlight on top of the wheelhouse glowed dully for a moment, then blinked sharply back into life; it caught Jack in the act of rising from his knees, boathook in one hand, the other shielding his squinting eyes as the beam shone full into his face. Danny's voice rose above the engine sound: "Got you, you bastard! Batteries up and *running*!" And in the wheelhouse, Claire was shouting: "Will? *Will!*"

Heedless of Jack, who by then was down on his knees plunging the boathook into the black water, I pushed past and into the wheelhouse. "What? What is it?"

Fist up to her mouth, Claire just stood there, unable to speak. Then she pointed at the console. The fish-finder was beeping still, more frequently than before, more insistently. I looked at the traces on screen and my mouth went dry.

Down underneath the *Katie Mae*, fathoms down in the dark and cold, big sluggish blips were rising; detaching themselves from the sea-bed, drifting up towards the surface. I didn't need Jack to interpret them for me this time; I recognized them all too well. Before, we'd thought they were seals. Now, we knew better.

" . . . Stay here," I managed to get out. Claire nodded, and I turned back to the doorway of the wheelhouse. There was Jack, bending over the side of the boat, his back to us. The stretch of water beyond him was brightly illuminated by our spotlight, still pointing where Claire had left it earlier. One look was all I needed. I grabbed Jack by the shoulder: he'd managed to hook a shapeless mass in the water, and was struggling to bring it in to the side of the boat. "Jack, Jack," I croaked in his ear; "wait, no, look out there . . . "

He pushed me away with a curse, went on trying to raise up the body in the water. I thumped his back, hard, and he swung round, ready to hit me. "Fucking *look*," I hissed, and almost despite himself he turned round.

There they were, caught by the spotlight on the still surface; bodies, rising up out of the sea. Five or six just in that bright ellipse of light; how many others, out there in the dark where we couldn't see? I'd counted at least a dozen on the fish-finder; there might be more by now. A low, unspeakably nasty sound came back to us over the waves, somewhere between a hiss and a gurgle. At the same time a stink hit us from off the water, like nothing I'd smelled before nor want to ever again. Jack turned back to me, round-eyed, horrified; opened his mouth to say something. Then it happened.

A hand came up and grasped the boathook. It nearly pulled Jack in; quickly he steadied himself, clutching at me and letting go his grip on the wooden shaft. The thing that had grabbed it—the thing Jack had thought was Andy—disappeared under the waves again, taking the boathook down with it, then bobbed back up to the surface. Whatever it was, it had been down there far longer than Andy had. Most of what had once made it human was rotted away; what was left was vile beyond my capacity to describe. It rested there on the swell awhile, goggling up at us as we stood petrified on the deck. Then, without warning, it swung the boathook up out of the water.

The metal hook ripped a long hole in Jack's T-shirt. Within seconds, the whole of his chest was slick with blood. He staggered back, and the hook caught on the belt of his jeans. It nearly dragged him into the water, but I grabbed him just in time. He was screaming, wordlessly, incoherently. So was I; but I held on tight, arms round his body, feet braced against the scuppers, straining backwards with all my might.

I managed to call out Danny's name. I felt him grab on to me from behind and yelled as loudly as I could, "Pull!" We both strained away, and then all of a sudden the pressure was off and we all three of us went sprawling backwards, me on top of Danny, Jack across both of us. We disentangled ourselves, and Jack pulled clear the boathook from his belt. Before he flung the whole thing as far away as he could, we had just enough time to see the hand and lower part of an arm that still clung to the other end.

Meanwhile Danny had seen what was happening out on the water, the bodies coming to the surface all around. From the look on his face I knew he was going to lose it unless I did something drastic, so without thinking I spun him round and practically threw him into the wheelhouse. "Get us out of here," I told him, and turned back to where Jack was kneeling on the deck. There was blood all over him, and over me too where I'd held on to him: I knelt down alongside him to see how badly he was hurt, but he pushed me away. I knew it was because of what Claire and I had done to Andy, but there was no time for that now. I looked round for something I could use to defend the boat with, yelling over my shoulder, "Danny! Move it!"

A throaty grumble came from aft as the diesels turned over, choked momentarily, then caught. "Get us out," I shouted, as there came a clang from the foredeck. I clambered up around the wheelhouse, spinning the spotlight around to face for'ard as I went. There was the boathook that Jack had thrown away, snagged this time on the prow. Something was using it to clamber up and over the rail: without thinking I ran towards it and kicked out hard. My foot sank part-way into a soft crunching mass; the momentum almost sent me spinning over, but I managed to steady myself on the Samson post as the thing splashed backwards into the water. There was something on my foot, some reeking slimy filth or other—I was scraping it frenziedly against one of the cleats, trying to get the worst of it off, when I became aware of Danny hammering the glass windscreen of the wheelhouse.

He was yelling something about "haul it in": I didn't understand what he was saying at first, but then I realized. We were still riding at anchor; Danny had revved the engines to loosen the anchor from its lodgement on the sea-bed, but before we could open up the throttle and head for clear water it needed to be winched all the way back in.

I edged back round the side of the wheelhouse, with no time to stop for Claire as she pressed her face to the glass, her lips forming words I couldn't hear. Below me, down in the water, things were moving up against the side of the boat. We had to get clear.

The capstan was on the starboard side, by the door to the wheelhouse. I gave a tug at the anchor-rope: it wouldn't shift. "Again," I called up to Danny in the wheelhouse; he engaged reverse thrust again, and the rope creaked, then gave a little as the anchor cleared the sea-bed. I threw the switch that turned on the electric motor of the capstan, but just at that moment there came a vicious tug on the rope. Sparks flashed beneath the motor housing, and an acrid gout of smoke rose from the capstan-head; I tried it again, and again, but the motor had burned out. Frantically, I tried to use the hand-bars to winch up the anchor, but the whole thing seemed to be fused solid.

"Jack," I shouted; he looked up from where he lay cradling his stomach, saw the problem, and struggled over to help.

Five fathoms, maybe six; that's thirty-six feet of rope first, then chain, and a heavy iron anchor at the end of it. It took Jack and I all the strength we could muster to raise it, arm over arm, winding the slack around the useless capstan-head. It wasn't the first time we'd had to haul up an anchor manually, but it seemed far heavier now than it ever had before, impossibly heavy, and when we'd got it almost all the way up, as far as the ten foot or so of chain before the anchor itself, I looked over the side to see if we were still snagged on anything.

Have patience with me now, because I have to tell this a certain way. In the village where I used to live as a child, near Diss in Norfolk, there was a pool out in the fields which was absolutely stiff with rudd, a freshwater fish related to the roach. We used to tie a piece of string around a fivepenny loaf and throw it in, and then we'd watch the water boil as we pulled on the string to bring the bread back up, the whole thing completely covered in a huge squirming feeding-cluster of rudd. That scene, that image, was what I thought of as I peered over the side of the *Katie Mae* and saw the anchor just below the surface.

Clustered round the anchor, hanging on to it in a crawling hideous mass, were maybe six or seven of the bodies; dragged up from the oozing deep, these, up from long years of slow decay down where the sun's warmth and light never penetrates, there on the chilly bottom. Green phosphorescent eyes stared back at me, and a billow of putrescence erupted in bubbles on to the surface. I dropped the anchor chain as if it had been electrified, and the gruesome mass sank back a foot or two into the water.

"Hang on!" Jack grabbed at the chain quickly before the lot went down again. "Keep it tight!" Out of his pocket he pulled a hunting-knife; I didn't get what he meant to do with it until he began to saw at the anchor-rope above the chain where it was wound round the capstan. Understanding at last, I pulled on the chain to keep the line taut. All the while, I was hearing things: sounds of splashing and gulping from over the side where the anchor was banging against the hull, and that awful gurgling hiss rising off the water again. Out of nowhere, words came into my head: *the voices of all the drowned . . .*

I didn't dare look down there; only when Jack sawed through the last strands of the rope and the freed chain rattled over the side did I risk one quick glance over, just in time to see the anchor with its cluster of bodies receding into the deep. Hands clutched vainly up towards the surface, and those greenish eyes blinked out into cold fathoms of blackness.

Sick to my stomach with fear and disgust, I turned away to where Jack was clambering to his feet. I tried to help him up, but he brushed my hand away and went foraging instead through the storage box where we'd formerly kept the anchor and its chain. He came up with an old length of chain about four feet long; he took a couple of turns around his fist, and swung the rest around. "You take the for'ard," he said, wincing as he held his wounded stomach; "I'll get the aft. Get something from in here—" he kicked the storage box—"and use the spotlight if you can, so's we can see what we're up against. *Danny!*" He roared the last word in the direction of the wheelhouse. "What's with the fucking hold-up? They're all around us, man: Will and me can't keep 'em off forever, you know!"

The boat was hardly moving in the water. From aft came the sound of spluttering, overstressed engines; Jack swore and looked at me narrowly. "You just keep your eyes peeled back here," was all he said; he tossed me the length of chain and stumbled off into the wheelhouse to get the *Katie Mae* moving again. Around us in the water, the shapes multiplied: there must have been twenty of them now, more maybe. Drawn by God knows what—the promise of dry land, perhaps, or some primal impulse more atavistic, more terrible than that—they were converging on the boat. And all I had was a four-foot length of chain to keep them off.

Maybe not all: suddenly there was the beam of the spotlight shining on to the aft deck, picking out the white painted railings, the glimmer of the sea beyond and below. I heard Claire's voice: "Over that way, Will;" the beam swung round, then steadied on a ghastly greenish arm slung over the port side.

I swung the chain at it. It cut a rent along the length of the arm, laid bare the glint of white bone, but the fingers didn't relinquish their grip. A head and shoulders hoisted up above the side of the boat. I gave it another swing of the chain, and this time the contact was good. It toppled upside-down, its head in the water, its feet caught up in the tyre buffers slung around the hull, and with a few more slashes I managed to dislodge it entirely. But by then Claire was screaming, "Behind you, behind you," and when I turned round another of the creatures was already halfway over the aft rail. Again I let fly, but not strongly or viciously enough. The chain only wrapped around its arm: it caught hold of the links, and began tugging me in towards it. Repulsed, I let go immediately; the thing teetered there a moment, then the engines kicked in at last. It was caught off balance and fell backwards: a horrible splintering noise and a shiver that went clean through the boat told me it had hit the propeller.

We began to pick up speed, pulling away from the writhing mass of bodies on the surface, but there were still a dozen or more of the things hanging on to the side of the boat, arms twined in the tyre buffers, hands clutching on to the railings, hammering at the clanging echoing hull. If we slowed down, they would try again to get up on board. We had to shift them somehow. I was leaning over the side, whacking away with a wrench from down the engine hatch, when Jack appeared at my side. The blood had dried black all down him, and he looked like he should have been in a hospital bed; instead, he was sloshing diesel oil from a big jerrycan over the side of the boat and on to the clinging bodies. "What you doing?" was all I could get out between panting.

"Kill or cure," he said grimly, edging all along the side of the boat emptying out the diesel on to the creatures that hung leechlike to the hull. In a minute he was back round to my other side. He dumped the jerrycan straight down onto the head of one of the things, sending it sinking beneath the waves, then reached in his pocket and brought out his cherished old brass Zippo with the engraved marijuana leaf. With just a trace of his usual flamboyance, he flicked open the top and ran the wheel quickly along the seam of his bloodied jeans, down, then up, like a gunslinger's quick-draw. The flint struck and the flame sparked bright, first time every time; Jack held it aloft for a second, then dropped it over the side.

I snapped my head back just in time, feeling my eyebrows singe and shrivel in the sudden blast of heat. Immediately, flames sprang up all along the waterline, lighting up the ocean all around us a vivid orange. For a little while we could see every detail of the things in the water; how they writhed and bubbled in the flame, how their mouths opened and closed, how they charred and blackened as the fire licked up the hull, blistering the paintwork, setting light to the tyre-buffers. I heard a hissing indrawn breath from Jack beside me, thought for a moment *oh no, he's fucked up, he's got it wrong with the diesel, the ship's going up*, and then I saw where he was looking down in the water. One of the burning bodies was Andy's: arm upraised, face still recognizable amidst the flames, it slowly rolled off the side and was lost in our wake, along with the rest of the corpses of the drowned.

It was already brightening in the east as we brought the *Katie Mae* back into harbor. All her sides were scorched and black and battered, and we—her crew—were similarly scarred, though in ways less obvious and maybe less repairable with a sanding-off and a fresh lick of paint. Jack had refused our help with his stomach wound on the way back; he'd sat out on the aft deck hugged into a fetal tuck, not talking to anyone, not looking anywhere except backwards at our lengthening wake. Claire and I sat squeezed up on the wheelhouse bench behind Danny, who stood at the wheel staring for'ard all the way home to Beuno's Cove. We didn't try talking to each other; really, what was there to say?

When we came alongside, Jack scrambled up on to the quayside to tie us up. He stood looking back at the boat for a second, silhouetted above us in the predawn light, then without saying anything he turned away. I glanced back at Danny and saw he was crying. Perhaps I should have done something, I don't know what, but Claire took my hand and more or less dragged me up on to the quay. We left him there on the deck; I wanted to say, are you going to be okay, but perhaps Claire was right. It was the last time I ever set foot on the *Katie Mae*.

Back home Claire ran straight upstairs and turned the shower on. I went up after about twenty minutes and she was squatting in a corner of the stall with the hot water running cold, arms wound about her knees, sobbing uncontrollably. What could I do? I got in there and fetched her out, got her dry, got her warm; but I couldn't stop her shivering, not until she finally fell asleep on the bed, hours later, after we'd tried and failed to talk through the events of the night just gone. We tried several times again, in the days and weeks that followed, but it never came to anything; we felt the way murderers must feel, and so, I suppose, did Jack, because not long after he moved away, and no one ever saw him again, not Claire or me, not even Danny.

Back to that first morning, though, the morning after. I stayed with Claire for a while till I was sure she was properly asleep, then I eased off the bed and went downstairs. There was a book I'd borrowed from Danny's old man, a collection of maritime myths and legends of North Wales: I went through it and found the entry for Llys Helig. A curse had been laid on Helig's family and their lands, vengeance for old wrongs, a whispering voice coming out of nowhere heard all around the great halls and gardens of Llys Helig prophesying doom on his grandsons and great-grandsons, and one day the floodwaters came and washed over everything. And ever since, said the legend, the drowned have never rested easy in that stretch. As if. I preferred Danny's dad's unvarnished version myself: that the sea was just twitchy out there, no more, no less. Nothing you could explain away with spells and whispers and fairy tales, a condition no story would cover; just a state of things, something you knew about and left well alone, if you knew what was good for you.

But there was something else; something that had been at the back of my mind ever since I'd first heard those hisses and gurgles out on the waves. I didn't have nearly as many books then as I have now, but it still took me the best part of half an hour to lay my hands on it: Dylan Thomas' *Selected Poems*. And I read there the poem, the one I'd half-remembered:

> *Under the mile off moon we trembled listening*
> *To the sea sound flowing like blood from the loud wound*
> *And when the salt sheet broke in a storm of singing*
> *The voices of all the drowned swam on the wind.*

Upstairs Claire moaned a little in her sleep. I got up, climbed the creaky stairs as quietly as I could, and eased myself on to the bed beside her. The curtains were pulled to, and the little bedroom under the eaves was getting stuffy in the full heat of the day. The paperback was still in my other hand, finger marking my place, and I read from it again:

> *We heard the sea sound sing, we saw the salt sheet tell*
> *Lie still, sleep becalmed, hide the mouth in the throat*
> *Or we shall obey, and ride with you through the drowned.*

I shivered, and beside me Claire shivered too, as if in unconscious sympathy. The sun was hot and strong through the bright yellow curtains, but I felt as if I'd never be warm again.

Steve Duffy's *stories have appeared in numerous magazines and anthologies in Europe and North America. His third collection of short supernatural fiction,* Tragic Life Stories *(Ash-Tree Press), was launched in Brighton, England, at the*

World Horror Convention 2010; his fourth, The Moment of Panic *is due to appear in 2011, and will include the International Horror Guild award-winning short story, "The Rag-and-Bone Men." Steve lives in North Wales. "Lie Still, Sleep Becalmed" was first published in 2007 in the Ash-Tree Press anthology* At Ease With The Dead. *It was nominated for that year's International Horror Guild Award for mid-length fiction, and seems to have tickled the fancy of quite a few readers and editors since then, which its author finds hugely gratifying. Thanks are due to Phil Wood, whose input into maritime goings-on was invaluable during the writing of the story, and whose friendship has been invaluable for much, much longer than that.*

And my thanks to Barbara Roden who reminded me of this chilling story from *At Ease with the Dead: New Tales of the Supernatural and Macabre* which she and her husband, Christopher edited a few years back.

Although we know the supernatural is at work here, I couldn't help but think about this story forensically, too, since some of our zombies display signs of being in the water longer than "Andy." Here are a few things I found out from *Forensic Taphonomy: The Postmortem Fate of Human Remains*, edited by by William D. Haglund and Marcella H. Sorg (CRC-Press, 1997): Bodies cool more rapidly in water than in air so decomposition, skeletonization, and disarticulation take longer; the colder the water, the slower the process. Thicker, nonorganic clothing can decelerate it somewhat, too, but marine scavengers chewing, biting, and tearing clothing can increase the surface area of the tissue resulting in faster microsavenger and bacterial activity. Crabs, by the way, like to attack facial flesh, eyes, and soft internal organs first. And wait till you get to the part about the role of sessile invertebrates . . .

The Great Wall:
A Story from the Zombie War

Max Brooks

The following interview was conducted by the author as part of his official duties with the United Nations Commission for postwar data collection. Although excerpts have appeared in official UN reports, the interview in its entirety was omitted from Brook's personal publication, now entitled *World War Z* due to bureaucratic mismanagement by UN archivists. The following is a first-hand account of a survivor of the great crisis many now refer to simply as "The Zombie War."

The Great Wall: Section 3947-11, Shaanxi, China

Liu Huafeng began her career as a sales girl at the Takashimaya department store in Taiyuan and now owns a small general store near the sight of its former location. This weekend, as with the first weekend of every month, is her reserve duty. Armed with a radio, a flare gun, binoculars, and a DaDao, a modernized version of the ancient Chinese broadsword, she patrols her five-kilometer stretch of the Great Wall with nothing but the "the wind and my memories" for company.

This section of the Wall, the section I worked on, stretches from Yulin to Shemnu. It had originally been built by the Xia Dynasty, constructed of compacted sand and reed-lined earth encased on both sides by a thick outer shell of fired mud brick. It never appeared on any tourist postcards. It could never have hoped to rival sections of the Ming-Era, iconic stone "dragon spine." It was dull and functional, and by the time we began the reconstruction, it had almost completely vanished.

Thousands years of erosion; storms and desertification, had taken a drastic toll. The effects of human "progress" had been equally destructive. Over the centuries, locals had used—looted—its bricks for building materials. Modern road construction had done its part, too, removing entire sections that interfered with "vital" overland traffic. And, of course, what nature and peacetime development had begun, the crisis, the infestation and the subsequent civil war finished within the course of several months. In some places, all that was left were crumbling hummocks of compact filler. In many places, there was nothing at all.

I didn't know about the new government's plan to restore the Great Wall for our national defense. At first, I didn't even know I was part of the effort. In those early days, there were so many different people, languages, local dialects that they could have been birdsong for all the sense it made to me. The night I arrived, all you could see were torches and headlights of a few broken-down cars. I had been walking for nine days by this point. I was tired, frightened. I didn't know what I had found at first, only that the scurrying shapes in front of me were human. I don't know how long I stood there, but someone on a work gang spotted me. He ran over and started to chatter excitedly. I tried to show him that I didn't understand. He became frustrated, pointing at what looked like a construction sight behind him, a mass of activity that stretched left and right out into the darkness. Again, I shook my head, gesturing to my ears and shrugging like a fool. He sighed angrily, then raised his hand toward me. I saw he was holding a brick. I thought he was going to hit me with so I started to back away. He then shoved the brick in my hands, motioned to the construction sight, and shoved me toward it.

I got within arm's length of the nearest worker before he snatched the brick away. This man was from Taiyuan. I understood him clearly. "Well, what the fuck are you waiting for?" He snarled at me, "We need more! Go! Go!" And that is how I was "recruited" to work on the new Great Wall of China.

[She gestures to the uniform concrete edifice.]

It didn't look at all like this that first frantic spring. What you are seeing are the subsequent renovations and reinforcements that adhere to late and postwar standards. We didn't have anything close to these materials back then. Most of our surviving infrastructure was trapped on the wrong side of the wall.

On the south side?

Yes, on the side that used to be safe, on the side that the Wall . . . that every Wall, from the Xia to the Ming was originally built to protect. The walls used to be a border between the haves and have-nots, between southern prosperity and northern barbarism. Even in modern times, certainly in this part of the country, most of our arable land, as well as our factories, our roads, rail lines and airstrips, almost everything we needed to undertake such a monumental task, was on the wrong side.

I've heard that some industrial machinery was transported north during the evacuation.

Only what could be carried on foot, and only what was in immediate proximity to the construction sight. Nothing farther than, say, twenty kilometers, nothing beyond the immediate battle lines or the isolated zones deep in infested territory.

The most valuable resource we could take from the nearby towns were the materials used to construct the towns themselves: wood, metal, cinder blocks, bricks—some of the very same bricks that had originally been pilfered from the wall. All of it went into the mad patchwork, mixed in with what could be manufactured quickly on sight. We used timber from the Great Green Wall[*] reforestation project, pieces of furniture and abandoned vehicles. Even the desert sand beneath our feet was mixed with rubble to form part of the core or else refined and heated for blocks of glass.

Glass?

Large, like so . . . *[she draws an imaginary shape in the air, roughly twenty centimeters in length, width and depth].* An engineer from Shijiazhuang had the idea. Before the war, he had owned a glass factory, and he realized that since this province's most abundant resources are coal and sand, why not use them both? A massive industry sprung up almost overnight, to manufacture thousands of these large, cloudy bricks. They were thick and heavy, impervious to a zombie's soft, naked fist. "Stronger than flesh" we used say, and, unfortunately for us, much sharper—sometimes the glazier's assistants would forget to sand down the edges before laying them out for transport.

[She pries her hand from the hilt of her sword. The fingers remain curled like a claw. A deep, white scar runs down the width of one palm.]

I didn't know to wrap my hands. It cut right through to the bone, severed the nerves. I don't know how I didn't die of infection; so many others did.

---

* The Great Green Wall: a prewar environmental restoration project intended to halt desertification.

It was a brutal, frenzied existence. We knew that every day brought the southern hordes closer, and that any second we delayed might doom the entire effort. We slept if we did sleep, where we worked. We ate where we worked, pissed and shit right where we worked. Children—the Night Soil Cubs—would hurry by with a bucket, wait while we did our business or else collect our previously discarded filth. We worked like animals, lived like animals. In my dreams I see a thousand faces, the people I worked with but never knew. There wasn't time for social interaction. We spoke mainly in hand gestures and grunts. In my dreams I try to find the time to speak to those alongside me, ask their names, their stories. I have heard that dreams are only in black and white. Perhaps that is true, perhaps I only remember the colors later, the light fringes of a girl whose hair had once been dyed green, or the soiled pink woman's bathrobe wrapped around a frail old man in tattered silken pajamas. I see their faces almost every night, only the faces of the fallen.

So many died. Someone working at your side would sit down for a moment, just a second to catch their breath, and never rise again. We had what could be described as a medical detail, orderlies with stretchers. There was nothing they could really do except try to get them to the aid station. Most of the time they didn't make it. I carry their suffering, and my shame with me each and every day.

Your shame?

As they sat, or lay at your feet . . . you knew you couldn't stop what you were doing, not even for a little compassion, a few kind words, at least make them comfortable enough to wait for the medics. You knew the one thing they wanted, what we all wanted, was water. Water was precious in this part of the province, and almost all we had was used for mixing ingredients into mortar. We were given less than half a cup a day. I carried mine around my neck in a recycled plastic soda bottle. We were under strict orders not to share our ration with the sick and injured. We needed it to keep ourselves working. I understand the logic, but to see someone's broken body curled up amongst the tools and rubble, knowing that the only mercy under heaven was just a little sip of water . . .

I feel guilty every time I think about it, every time I quench my thirst, especially because when it came my time to die, I happened, by sheer chance, to be near the aid station. I was on glass detail, part of the long, human conveyor to and from the kilns. I had been on the project for just under two months; I was starving, feverish, I weighed less than the bricks hanging from either side of my pole. As I turned to pass the bricks, I stumbled, landing on my face, I felt my two front teeth crack and tasted the blood. I closed my eyes and thought, *This is my time.* I was ready. I wanted it to end. If the orderlies hadn't been passing by, my wish would have been granted.

For three days, I lived in shame; resting, washing, drinking as much water as I wanted while others were suffering every second on the wall. The doctors told me that I should stay a few extra days, the bare minimum to allow my body to recuperate. I would have listened if I didn't hear the shouts from an orderly at the mouth of the cave,

"Red Flare!" he was calling. "Red Flare!"

Green flares meant an active assault, red meant overwhelming numbers. Reds had been uncommon, up until that point. I had only seen one, and that was far in the distance near the northern edge of Shemnu. Now they were coming at least once a week. I raced out of the cave, ran all the way back to my section, just in time to see rotting hands and heads begin to poke their way above the unfinished ramparts.

[We halt. She looks down at the stones beneath out feet.]

Here, right here. They were forming a ramp, using their trodden comrades for elevation. The workers were fending them off with whatever they could, tools and bricks, even bare fists and feet. I grabbed a rammer, an implement used for compacting earth. The rammer is an immense, unruly device, a meter-long metal shaft with horizontal handlebars on one end and a large, cylindrical, supremely heavy stone on the other. The rammer was reserved only for the largest and strongest men in our work gang. I don't know how I managed to lift, aim, and bring it crashing down, over and over, on the heads and faces of the zombies below me . . .

The military was supposed to be protecting us from overrun attacks like these, but there just weren't enough soldiers left by that time.

[She takes me to the edge of the battlements and points to something roughly a kilometer south of us.]

There.

[In the distance, I can just make out a stone obelisk rising from an earthen mound.]

Underneath that mound is one of our garrison's last main battle tanks. The crew had run out of fuel and was using it as a pillbox. When they ran out of ammunition, they sealed the hatches and prepared to trap themselves as bait. They held on long after their food ran out and their canteens ran dry. "Fight on!" they would cry over their hand-cranked radio, "Finish the wall! Protect our people! Finish the wall!" The last of them, the seventeen-year-old driver held out for thirty-one days. You couldn't even see the tank by then, buried under a small mountain of zombies that suddenly moved away as they sensed that boy's last breath.

By that time, we had almost finished our section of the Great Wall, but the isolated attacks were ending, and the massive, ceaseless, million-strong assault swarms began. If we had had to contend with those numbers in the beginning, if the heroes of the southern cities hadn't shed their blood to buy us time . . .

The new government knew it had to distance itself from the one it had just overthrown. It had to establish some kind of legitimacy with our people, and the only way to do that was to speak the truth. The isolated zones weren't "tricked" into becoming decoys like in so many other countries. They were asked, openly and honestly, to remain behind while others fled. It would be a personal choice, one that every citizen would have to make for themselves. My mother, she made it for me.

We had been hiding on the second floor of what used to be our five-bedroom house in what used to be one of Taiyuan's most exclusive suburban enclaves. My little brother was dying, bitten when my father had sent him out to look for food. He was lying in my parent's bed, shaking, unconscious. My father was sitting by his side, rocking slowly back and forth. Every few minutes he would call out to us. "He's getting better! See, feel his forehead. He's getting better!" The refugee train was passing right by our house. Civil Defense Deputies were checking each door to find out who was going and who was staying. My mother already had a small bag of my things packed; clothes, food, a good pair of walking shoes, my father's pistol with the last three bullets. She was combing my hair in the mirror, the way she used to do when I was a little girl. She told me to stop crying and that some day soon they would rejoin me up north. She had that smile, that frozen, lifeless smile she only showed for father and his friends. She had it for me now, as I lowered myself down our broken staircase.

[Liu pauses, takes a breath, and lets her claw rest on the hard stone.]

Three months, that is how long it took us to complete the entire Great Wall. From Jingtai in the western mountains to the Great Dragon head on the Shanhaiguan Sea. It was never breached, never overrun. It gave us the breathing space we needed to finally consolidate our population and construct a wartime economy. We were the last country to adopt the Redeker Plan, so long after the rest of the world, and just in time for the Honolulu Conference. So much time; so many lives, all wasted. If the Three Gorges Dam hadn't collapsed, if that other wall hadn't fallen, would we have resurrected this one? Who knows. Both are monuments to our shortsightedness, our arrogance, our disgrace.

They say that so many workers died building the original walls that a human life was lost for every mile. I don't know if that it was true of that time . . .

[Her claw pats the stone.]

But it is now.

—

Max Brooks *is the author of the two bestsellers* The Zombie Survival Guide *(2003) and* World War Z: An Oral History of the Zombie War *(2006) He has also written for* Saturday Night Live, *for which he won an Emmy. His graphic novel* The Zombie Survival Guide: Recorded Attacks *was published in 2009. A movie of* World War Z *is planned.*

—

Inspired by Romero zombies and Studs Turkel's oral history of World War II, Brooks stuck to the "laws" of his first book, *The Zombie Survival Guide*, in the writing of *World War Z*. Through a series of "interviews," Brooks provides a "history" of humanity's struggle against a worldwide outbreak of zombiism which, like a disease, mindlessly consumed, multiplied, and spread. Just as Romero used zombies for socio-political commentary pertinent to his era, so does Brooks. His zombie plague incorporates modern fears of terrorism, biological warfare, overwhelming natural catastrophes, climate change, and global disease. Since there are survivors left to be interviewed, humanity obviously triumphs, but the author's globally implemented solution can also be viewed as somewhat horrific.

First Kisses from Beyond the Grave

Nik Houser

My mother says I'm handsome. I believe her. It's something she's always said and it's always done me, more or less, the same amount of good.

"You're so lucky to be so smart and handsome!" she hollered from the porch as I waited for the bus to my new school. I remember the air was drastically cool for the tail end of summer, but I didn't want to go back in that house for a jacket and risk a second hug, a second kiss goodbye. I'd lost track of how many times Mom had said, "Don't worry, you'll make friends in no time!" but I could stand no more of those either. It was one of her favorite phrases, as though the clay of creation was mine to shape and mold into a brand-new clique of ostracized freaks with whom I had nothing in common save the fact that the social trapeze had snapped between our fingers somewhere between our eleventh and twelfth years.

So I stood at the curb, freezing like an idiot. I looked back at my mom standing in the open doorway, unwavering optimism painted over her face in great broad strokes. One of her legs hovered at a forty-five-degree angle from the other, so that Mouselini, our cat, wouldn't bolt out the door.

I smiled thinly, then looked back across the street where my best friend Art White snickered as he waited for our bus. At the sight of him, my head snapped back like a spider had swung in front of my face. I squished my eyes shut, then opened them, like a cartoon, which is what I must have looked like to the casual passerby, staring in astonishment as I was at the empty sidewalk across the street where my dead friend had stood only a moment before.

The morning after Art let all his blood run down the bathtub drain (rumor has it his mom kept running into the bathroom with cups, pitchers, and ice cube trays, trying to save some of it, some of him, before it all got away), the school bus stopped in front of his house. For years it had always stopped in front of his house and I'd always crossed the street to get on, just as I did that morning. Like always, I lurched to the back row of seats and propped myself against the window, reflexively leaving room for my pal, though I knew he would not be joining me.

The bus driver idled in front of Art's house. An uncomfortable silence fell over the crowded transport, something my English teacher Ms. Crane might refer to as a "pregnant pause." The driver was the only one on board who didn't already know. Everybody else had seen it on the news the previous night, had spread word via email and cell phones, text messages for the dead. Ask not for whom the cell tones, the cell tones for thee.

Gus the Bus looked up at me through the broad rearview mirror.

"I'm only waitin' another minute."

A month later, when I got the notice in the mail which informed me that I would be spending my latter three years of high school away from the boys and girls I had grown to love and loathe respectively, my mother was as positive as ever. It was June by then. School was out and Art was in the ground, missing his finals by a week.

"What a great opportunity!" Mom said when I was done reading the letter aloud at the dinner table. "You can meet new people and . . . " I glared at her across the table as she struggled to maintain her unwavering optimism . . . make new friends."

"You said the same thing to your cousin when he was sent to Riker's Island," Pop reminded her, looking over his glasses at the seven o'clock news on mute. My old man was nearsighted, but he loved the condescending erudition of looking over his tortoise-shell rims at whatever questionable piece of Creation happened to fall under his scrutiny.

"And he was so smart and handsome, too," Mom replied absently.

When the ghost of Art White had come and gone, I pulled the Notice of School District Transfer out of my pocket. It read like a draft notice, or one of those letters you get with a folded American flag to inform you that your child has been killed in action:

Dear Mr. Henry,

As superintendent of the Northside Public School District, it is my responsibility to inform you that as of September 1st, 2004, in an effort to further integrate our public schools, your street address will no longer be included in our district's educational zone roster and will henceforth be transferred to the Middle Plain School District. I apologize for any inconvenience this may cause.

Sincerely,

J.R. Sneider, Jr.

Superintendent, Northside Public School District

No sooner had I finished reading my own death sentence than the familiar, noisome expulsion of school bus air brakes sounded off at the far end of my street. I looked up for the bus, but saw nothing— only the familiar line of SUVs parked along the curbs and in driveways. A stiff breeze picked up and made me shiver with cold for the first time since last April when the previous winter exhaled its death rattle. Or maybe it was the sudden silence that ran that chill up my spine. The street was dead quiet, a far cry from the familiar din of leaf-blowers, garbage trucks, and protein shake blenders that usually accompanied Monday mornings on our fair boulev—

CREEEEEE-SWOOSH!

The door to the school bus swung open in front of me, coming within an inch of my face and exhaling a cloud of dusty, tomb-like air.

Startled by its sudden appearance, I backpedaled on the wet grass, tripped on a sprinkler, and fell flat on my back.

I lay there for a second, staring up at the overcast sky, trying to breathe. It had been a long time since I'd had the wind knocked out of me, and for a second I thought I was dying. At last the airlock in my chest opened up and I sat bolt upright, panting, and stared up at the great black school bus humming cantankerously in front of my house like a hearse built for group rates.

Where the fuck did that come from?

I looked up through the open door, at the driver staring ahead at the road, black jeans and a gray hooded sweatshirt draped over his wire-hanger frame. The sweatshirt's hood covered his eyes as he slowly turned his head toward me. The rest of his body remained frozen in place, both hands glued to the steering wheel.

I stood up, grabbed my sprinkler-soaked backpack, and looked back at my house, an are-you-seeing-what-I'm-seeing? face pointed at the empty doorway. Mom was gone. Only Mouselini stood on the front step, eyes wide and tail shocked-up, a tremulous rumble sounding from the depths of his twelve-year-old gut like a drawstring dolly that's been buried alive.

Behind me, the bus's engine revved, once. I turned and started up its steps, heard the door close behind me while the driver's hands remained on the wheel. At the top step I paused and stared down at my chauffeur, at the empty black space where the shade of his hood covered his eyes.

"Morning." I slipped on the thin, polite smile I saved for teachers, strangers, extended family.

I looked back at the empty bus. The seats and windows were in decent condition, but dusty and tired-looking, as though the great vehicle had only just been called back into service after decades of neglect.

"First to get on, last to get off, I guess." Again that thin smile, more for myself than the driver now.

The driver turned his pale, expressionless face back to the road as the houses, cars, and trees began to slip slowly past the windows. The bus betrayed no perceptible shudder or lurch when we pulled away from my home, as though we remained still while the stage set of the neighborhood was drawn back to the flies.

When I first received the notice of transfer, I thought my folks were responsible. I wasn't exactly inconsolable after Art leapfrogged over his elders into the Great Beyond, but I wasn't the same either. I lost weight, stopped sleeping, stopped jerking off. I think the fact that I put down my penis worried the 'rents more than putting down my fork. They'd read that loss of libido was a common part of the grieving process for any close friend or relative. But they also knew that he was my *only* close friend, and that I was dreading the fall. More than any summer before, the phonetics of the forthcoming season sounded to me, and to them, like some dramatic plunge I was about to take, a forty-foot dive into a glass of water.

Mom and Pop were both teachers at my school. Having them with me at home, with their lingering smells of chalk dust and textbooks, the tiny snowflakes of spiral-bound notebook paper torn from its binding caught unmelting in the hems of their clothes, was like bringing the funeral home with me. It was because of this that I started to wonder if maybe the transfer wouldn't be so bad.

Strangely enough, however, it was when I suggested this very notion, and the uncharacteristically positive outlook inherent therein, that my folks started worrying, in earnest, about my mental well-being.

As the bus drove on, the sky grew dark. My surroundings grew increasingly unfamiliar as we passed into a stretch of suburbs which had taken an early turn toward fall and even winter. On the street below, the bus's enormous tires scattered decay-colored leaves across sidewalks that crumbled into the road like rows of rotting teeth. It soon became apparent that we would be making no other stops.

Jesus Christ, I thought as we passed into the overcast farmlands beyond the city—a bleak stretch of wild, untended wheat interrupted only by the occasional skeleton of a burned-out barn, *I've been transferred to Deliverance High.* The sky was nearly black. The sight of it took me back to the tornado drills we practiced on days like this in the second grade, when we would duck under our desks with our thickest textbooks held tight over our heads, a mere three hundred pages of long division standing between us and total, whirling annihilation.

Eventually, the rolling fields gave way to a vast stretch of incinerated woodlands—black, emaciated cedars reaching out to the day-for-night sky like the arms of the damned on Judgment Day. I opened my mouth to holler down the row of seats, to casually inquire about the fire which had apparently torn through this area. But when I opened my mouth, the nervous vacuum inside me would let no words escape. I looked up at the mirror suspended above the driver, at the yawning sweatshirt hood which now absorbed his features entirely, then at the massive fog bank rushing toward us as we began to accelerate.

The landscape was quickly erased by the fog, as though we'd traveled beyond the borders of Nature's grand composition and were barreling toward the edge of God's very canvas. I closed my eyes, felt the bus shimmy and shake as it continued to accelerate. Every bump in the road felt like the one that would dislodge a wheel, every turn was the road ending at a thousand-foot cliff.

"Please, God," I muttered to myself, a knee-jerk theological reaction. "Please."

The word itself was the prayer, not so much asking for a safe arrival, but to simply let me *keep* everything that I had and was, to finish the things I'd planned to do. The bus shook and shivered, tires screaming against the road. All my blood pressed against the surface of my skin in a centrifuge of fear.

Everything that had ever happened to me: birth, laughter, friends, growing up, jerking off, Christmas, was boiled down to one word—

"PLEASE!" I screamed, my cry punctuated by the sound of the bus's door folding into itself as we came to a gentle stop. We were there.

I marched down the aisle on wobbly sea legs, bracing myself on the rubbery, crimson seatbacks. When I came to the driver I stopped to say something nasty, or sarcastic, or grateful, but when I saw his hands gripping the wheel, knuckles pressed against their gloved surfaces like only bone hid beneath, I thought better of it and climbed down the stairs to the curb.

"A fucking cemetery?" I asked myself aloud.

I surveyed the endless rows of tombstones to which I'd been delivered. No school. No students. Nothing but graves, trees, hills, fog.

I turned around to get back on the bus and ask the driver wh—

The bus was gone.

I looked down either side of the empty road, swallowed entirely by mist after ten yards in either direction. The driver had taken off as silently as he had arrived at my house that morning.

"Great. So what the fuck am I supposed to do now?"

As if in response, a lone crow cackled down at me from a nearby tree and took off over the stones. I watched him glide, then turn to croak at me again. A third time I watched him cruise out a dozen yards, double back, and let out another sonorous cackle.

"I'm already looking back at this and wondering what the fuck I was thinking," I said. I hopped the low wooden fence and followed the old black bird into the cemetery.

Most of the headstones were for people who'd died before I was born. Some dated within the year. Covered with moss and undergrowth, the sweat stains of finality and neglect, grave markers of every size and shape, from hand-carved mausoleums to wooden planks nailed together in cross formation, covered the surrounding hills in rows so crooked the caretaker had to be either cross-eyed, blind, or both.

When the old crow and I crested the last hill I looked back at the boneyard, at so many stones like goose bumps running up the spine of some tired leviathan.

I turned around to see where the crow had led me—a vista no less gloomy and depressing than the graveyard.

My new school was flat and broad and as featureless as it was silent. With a resigned sigh, I crossed a field of knee-high weeds, at either end of which stood a tall, crooked football goal, and hiked up the parking circle to the empty campus. The building itself was gray and unremarkable. The front door was unlocked. Inside, the lights were out. The only light came from the windows that lined a hallway to my right. The other side of the hall was lined with blue lockers, with the occasional break where a classroom door could be found. The tiled floor was white and clean. I started walking to see if anyone was home. All in all, it looked like your basic high school on a still, overcast Sunday afternoon. It was, however, Monday morning, and by now I was more annoyed than intimidated. I could be at my old school now, getting depressed, getting bored, getting horny. But instead I found myself wandering the empty halls of a forei—

What the fuck was that?

I whirled around, heart suddenly racing, more nervous than I'd let myself believe, and spied a tall locker door hanging halfway open a few yards away.

Whatever.

I turned back to where I was headed an—

"Who the fuck is there?!" I shouted, spinning around when the locker slammed shut behind me, its flat echo continuing past me down the hall.

"WHO—"

The locker creaked halfway open, slowly.

Someone's in there.

I took a step back with one foot, a step forward with the other, half brave and half smart. The front foot won. Slowly, I made my way toward the locker, sliding along the windows that lined the opposite wall to try and get a peek around the open door. The combination latch was missing. Only two rough screw holes remained where the lock had been torn off. I opened my mouth to say something to whoever was inside, some idle threat, but the vacuum inside my stomach had started up again, so that all I could manage was to slowly reach out, curl my fingers around the rusty locker door, and—

BA-RIIIING!!! went the homeroom bell. I jumped, slipped, cracked my head on the floor.

I stared up at the ceiling. The homeroom bell rang in my ears, bounced off the tile under my head. My first reaction was to panic that I was late, but once the combination of shock, terror, and pain had ebbed to a dull throb between my ears, I asked myself, "Late for what?" I didn't expect an answer.

Then the sounds came.

Something stirred outside.

I stood up and looked out the window at the hideous, skinless face staring in at me.

"Late," moaned the walking corpse on the opposite side of the glass. He looked about my age, his face puffed out in gaseous boils of decomposition. The flesh of his jaw hung loose, exposing a bloated green tongue laminated in pus and mud. He wore blue jeans and a varsity letterman's jacket. A backpack hung from his right shoulder. Dirt littered his unkempt hair, filled the spaces between his teeth.

I didn't even know I was screaming. The sound of my terror echoed down the hall, harmonizing with the great earthy rumble rising up from the ground outside as the tiled floor beneath my feet began to quake. Scared beyond coordination, I stumbled back on stilted legs and crashed into the wall of lockers behind me. My eyes stayed glued to the window, growing ever wider. Scores of rotten, worm-riddled bodies staggered from the cemetery beyond the football field, dusting the consecrated earth from their team jackets and cheerleader uniforms as they stalked en masse toward the school. No sooner had the first of the walking dead reached the parking lot than a ghostly white school bus pulled into the parking circle and expulsed a swarm of iridescent vapors who drifted toward the school dragging their souls and sack lunches behind them.

Thisisadreamthisisadreamthisisafuckingnightmare, I chanted in my head, pinching myself over and over until a trail of stinging, bloody fingernail marks lit up my arm like Christmas tree lights.

"You'll want to get those looked at." A voice from inside the locker behind me.

Again I shrieked, turned around, staggered into the middle of the hallway, surrounded by drifting, translucent ghouls from the white school bus. Twenty yards to my left, the front doors of the school opened, admitting the horde of teenage undead as they made their way inside like a river of coagulating blood. I looked back at the talking locker, which was now open. A tall, pale kid stepped out from within. He stretched out his folded arms and yawned, exposing two rows of healthy white razor-sharp teeth.

"Hey, watch it!" warned a female voice. The tall boy's clothes wavered in an unseen breeze.

"Fuckin' vapors." A second kid emerged from the next locker down, his face as gaunt and bloodless as his neighbor's. Beside him, one of the walking dead from outside bumped into a locker and fiddled clumsily with its combination.

"Next one down, you *moron!*" hollered a voice from inside the locker. The zombie moaned, lurched one step to the left, opened his locker, and pulled out a spiral notebook riddled with teeth marks.

"Hey!" yelled the voice from the locker. "That bonehead locked me in, you guys!"

The two boys in front of me snickered.

"You guys suck!" The voice banged on the inside of the locker.

"Yeah," the tall one chuckled. "That's kind of our thing."

The two vampiric jocks stalked down the hall, laughing wildly. By now the hall was swarming with rotten, lurching corpses, pale red-eyed kids staring ravenously at the cuts on my arms, and a gaggle of ghostly, transparent figures drifting over and through the meandering rabble. Wolf-men, swamp things, and hellhounds ambled to and fro, chatting briefly with each other as they parted ways to head to class.

"Come on, you guys!" pleaded the voice from inside the locker. "Lemme out!"

By the time the second bell rang, I was on my feet and the rest of the hall was empty. Well beyond shock, my heartbeat returned to normal. Calmly, I surveyed my surroundings. The occasional puddle of blood and ectoplasm notwithstanding, the loose bits of paper and scattered contraband cigarette butts at my feet gave the impression of a typical, harried Monday morning at Average Joe High School, USA.

"Hey," came the sad voice from the locker in front of me.

I turned to look at the three dark slats at the top of the locker door.

"Hey, new kid, lemme out or I'll suck the jelly from your eyeballs."

I stood there, staring blankly at the locker, slightly perplexed and, perhaps as a result of previous exposure to the relentless bullying I'd witnessed at my old high school, slightly amused. He clearly wasn't one of them. Just trying to fit in.

"Please?" the voice said, pitiful now, drained of all pretense of malice or ferocity.

I stepped up to the locker and tapped the combination lock. I always felt sorry for geeks and nerds, always helped them pick up their books while they dug wedgies out of their lower intestines.

"What's your combination?" I asked the locker.

"Six . . . six . . . five," the voice muttered hollowly.

At last the locker opened and out spilled the lanky, woe-begotten creature inside.

"You'd think with all the brains they ate, those fucking zombies would be like, geniuses, right?"

The kid bent down, dusted himself off. His voice sounded familiar. At first I was unsure. It sounded deeper and farther away than when I'd last heard it, a certain knowledge of things beyond haunting its cadence. But the sarcasm was unmistakable, and when he finally straightened himself up and showed me his bloodless, trademark smirk, all doubt vanished.

"Art?" I gasped, dropping my backpack into a splat of green, luminous jelly at my feet. I looked down at the long, deep canyons he'd cut into his arms only three months before. "Is that you?"

"Holy shit, man," my friend laughed, dead eyes wide with friendly astonishment. He leaned forward, pressed his cold, stiff chest against mine and hugged me. "Welcome to Purgatory High!"

"English, History, Health, Woodshop, Geometry, P.E.?"

Behind the registrar's desk, a skeleton in a moth-bitten sky blue pantsuit stared blankly up at me through a pair of faded pink reading glasses as I read my schedule aloud. Behind me, Art sat reading an old newspaper.

"Would you look at that," he muttered to himself. "Ollie North sold guns to Iran. Wait a minute . . . " He flipped over the newspaper, examined the date, then shrugged. "News to me," he obliged, and continued reading.

"Is that it?" I looked up from my schedule to the registrar, at the heavy layer of foundation mortared evenly across the surface of her skull, punctuated by two slashes of red-light-red lipstick, explosions of rouge, and neon-blue eye shadow, all watched over by a magnificent, Babel Tower beehive hairdo. A regular Bloomingdale's Day of the Dead Special.

"Is there a problem?" the secretary asked. Her rusty screen-door voice rose up from the center of her rib cage and escaped through two empty eye sockets adorned by a set of outrageously long false eyelashes.

"What do dead people need Geometry for?"

"You're not dead."

"I know. And yet I find myself asking the same question. I mean, come on, Health? You don't *have* health. You're dead!"

"This is Middle Plain High, young man. *Purgatory High*, if you will. *Good* little boys and girls, who die the *right* way, aren't sent here."

"Wait a minute. You mean I got transferred to like, Juvenile Hall for the Damned?" I threw up my hands. "That's great! Fantastic! Whatever. Doesn't matter." I leaned on the counter. "The point is I'm, you know, *alive*. Right? So obviously there's been a mistake. I shouldn't be here."

"That's what they all say."

By the time we got back to first period, Homeroom was over and English class had begun.

"Ah, Mr. Henry, welcome to our class." Mr. Marley stood in front of the blackboard, dressed in a turn-of-the-century waistcoat, dusty gray pantaloons and a powdered wig lying limp over his scalp, as though it had been ridiculed and debased by larger, more imposing wigs until all sense of pride or decorum had been wrung from its monochrome curls. Draped across the pedagogue's chest, over his arms, and around his legs was a seemingly endless length of rusty chains from which a series of padlocks and strong boxes rattled and clanged with his every movement.

I stood at the head of the class, staring at the erudite, emaciated apparition. He returned my gaze with polite impatience, no doubt accustomed to new students gawking at him.

"Chains you forged in life?" I asked casually.

He nodded like I'd asked if he'd gotten a haircut.

"Okey-dokey," I replied and turned to search for an empty seat.

As Mr. Marley began the lecture, I surveyed my classmates from the back row. I watched a gargoyle pass notes to a drowned drama queen covered over with seaweed and bright patches of dried brine. A studious nerd, the noose with which he'd hung himself still hanging around his neck, took notes while a bright red she-devil in a cheerleader's uniform giggled behind him.

Not much different than a regular high school, Art scribbled on a scrap of paper and passed to me. *Right?*

In the exact moment I finished reading the note, an anonymous spitball slammed into the five-inch-tall aborted fetus taking notes in front of me. He was dressed in a tiny basketball jersey and warm-up pants.

"What up, nigga'?!" the tiny voice hollered up at me, mistaking me for the perpetrator of the spitball. "You got a muthafuckin' problem!? You wanna piece a'this, son?!"

"No thanks," I said in the distracted fashion that warded off most every gangster and jock at my old school. I jotted down my response to Art's note: *Not as such.*

History class, as it turned out, was History of Everything. Purgatory High, apparently, had dug its foundations outside of the conventional space-time continuum, and could look at the history of the universe from a fairly objective vantage.

"Dude." Art put a hand on my shoulder, "I don't think it's a good idea for you to go in there."

"You mean about me gaining potentially hazardous foreknowledge of mankind's future which I could use to alter the course of human events?"

"Huh? No, I mean I got this joint from Lenny Baker and we should go smoke it."

"Nah, I'll pass, this whole day's been like one long, bad trip anyway."

"Suit yourself."

Over the next forty-five minutes I learned that (a) I would never be famous, (b) mankind would never be conquered by super-intelligent robots of our own design, and (c) ipso facto, my lifelong ambition of being the leader of the human resistance against their titanium-plated tyranny would never be fulfilled.

Such is life.

Next was Health Class.

On my way into the classroom, Missy Nefertiti, a hot little mummified number shrinkwrapped in a layer of Egyptian cotton no thicker than an anorexic neutrino, stumbled behind me in the hallway, spilling the contents of her purse at my feet.

"Thanks," she said absently as I knelt to help her.

I picked up a small, pearly jar which contained her brain, then another for her liver, and a third for her lungs.

"Where's the one for your heart?" I asked as we stood up together.

"No room," she replied. "I'd have to carry a bigger purse."

Five minutes into Health Class Ms. Tenenbaum-Forrester, a decomposing zombie, announced that this week would be Sexual Education and Awareness Week. It was at this point that I raised my hand, looked into my teacher's deflated, rotten-tomato eyes, and respectfully asked to be excused.

Lunch was no better.

"You gonna eat those brains?" Art asked from across our table. Roland, the gangster fetus from first period, sat to my left, poised on Missy Nefertiti's lap and free-styling to all who would listen, most notably, her big round gazungas.

"Ask George." I pointed to the towering zombie in a Middle Plain High basketball jersey sitting beside me. "They're his anyway."

Without a word, Art reached over the table and speared a forkful of gray matter from my tray.

"So what do you think so far, man?" He gestured at our surroundings with his fork.

I turned around, glanced back at the lunch line where a tall vampire dressed in fishnet tights and a Joy Division T-shirt leaned over the serving area and sank his teeth into the lunch lady's neck. I looked back at my friend sucking the dendrites from an oblongata kabob.

"I think you should chew with your mouth closed."

That afternoon, when the last horn of the apocalypse rang out the end of the school day, Art and I wandered back through the cemetery as our fellow students made their way to their graves, loaded up with that night's homework.

"Hey, Art," I said. "I've been meaning to—"

"Think fast!" interrupted a distant voice.

I turned around in time to throw up my hands and block a dive-bombing football before it spread my nose over my face like a warm pad of butter.

"Sorry about that, new guy!" From the direction of the dive-bombing pigskin, a burly, middle-aged man as wide as he was tall, dressed in a shimmering red leotard, hurdled a nearby tombstone and landed in front of us.

"You teach my gym class." I spoke to his huge, waxed handlebar mustache.

"That's right," the strong man agreed. "I was watching you today. You looked good. You've got good moves."

"I sat in a tree while everyone else ran around the track."

"Yeah, well, you've got to be in good shape to climb trees, right?"

"I was smoking two cigarettes at once."

"And *that's* the kind of go-getter attitude we need on our football roster, son! That little sneak attack earlier was my subtle way of testing potential new recruits!"

"There's a football team here?"

"Of course!"

"Do you get hoarse very often?"

"Excuse me?"

"Nothing. Besides, I didn't even catch the ball."

"But you managed to block it, which is better than most, let me tell you. So whad'ya say, son?"

"Um, no thanks. I'm not really what you'd call a team player."

There was a pause here, where I could almost hear the magnetic tape inside the coach's head reach the end of its reel and start rewinding itself for the next recruit.

"Well hey, no hard feelings!" he said and patted me on the back. He scanned the horizon and found his mark.

"Hey, DeMarco! Think fast!"

We turned and kept walking.

"Isn't Tim DeMarco deaf?" Art asked.

I shrugged, stared at my feet. We walked in silence for a time, weaving around the tombstones. Angels etched in granite stared up at us from stones marking the graves of children. Dead leaves pressed into the ground underfoot.

"I dunno," Art said at last.

"Huh?" I looked up at my friend.

"I don't know why I did it." My friend stared down at the dark little rivers running up the topography of his forearms, the barren, tilled flesh. "You know how, like, when you're trying to do something that takes a long time, like fixing something, or balancing something, and after a bunch of tries you finally just throw it at the wall because you're so frustrated? I don't know— that was how I felt about pretty much everything, I guess. I just sort of threw my life at the wall. I was tired of trying to fix it. Of course, it was only after I showed up here that I realized it wasn't *broken* to start with, just not *finished* yet. I dunno. That's what the school counselor told me. I guess that makes sense."

I didn't know what to say. It had been a long summer, during which I'd developed a staggering resentment for my best pal and his cowardly exit. I was angry at how selfish he could be, leaving me alone with this fucked-up world.

At last we came upon the road which had led me from my front door to

Death's door that morning. The sky was overcast and still, as it had been all day.

"I was pretty mad," I said at last, staring down at the uneven pavement.

Art let out a long breath, like he'd been holding it in for a while.

"I'm sorry, man," he said. He looked wistfully up at the treetops across the street. "If I could change anything . . . If I could go back and change *anything* I'd *ever* done, or left *undone* . . . I'd have felt up Suzie Newman at the Freshman Homecoming Dance."

I laughed and punched his shoulder as hard as I could, heard something crack under the putty-like flesh.

"Had I but known she'd become the biggest slut in our fucking class!" he entreated the clouds overhead, throwing his head back melodramatically and clenching his fists until the squeal of air brakes snatched the laughter out of our throats and tossed it on the ground like so much loaded dice.

We stood at the edge of the road, staring up at the hooded driver and his great black bus idling restlessly.

"Well, uh," Art backed away slowly. His eyes never left the driver. "I'll see you tomorrow man."

"Dude, wait!" I jogged a couple of steps to where my friend stood poised to sprint back through the boneyard. "You should come back with me," I whispered, and reached out for his shoulder. No sooner had my hand touched him then a bolt of lightning screamed out of the sky and seized my forearm in a cataclysmic Indian burn. The shock of the bolt knocked me back six feet through the dazzling, electrified air. I landed at the edge of the road, the wind knocked out of me, head buzzing like a pressure cooker full of hornets. I stood up slowly, gasping, reaching for the stars that swirled around my smoking head. By the time the Big Bang orbiting my head had dissipated in the encroaching dusk, my friend was gone.

I looked down at my arm, which was turning green, then up at the sky. Broad, rumbling thunderheads stared back at me like a reproachful parent. I remembered my uncle telling me about the time he was struck by lightning during his barnstorming days. He said it was like "God put a hand on my shoulder." He also said it "hurt like a motherfucker."

I craned my neck for a last glance at my friend, but there was no one, not even a crow.

"See you tomorrow," I said to cemetery, the vast stone harvest.

My only assignment that night was to memorize a poem of my choice, which I did, while nursing my fried appendage back to life and listening to my folks converse politely about their student, Ginger Banks, who had been brutally slain at school that afternoon. The cadence of John Donne bounced around my brain, playing tag with phrases like "teeth marks," "massive trauma," and "still at large."

Once my homework was done I could eat, as had been the rule of my family since my first day of kindergarten. The table was set with the summer dishes, though the brisk, teasing breath of fall could be felt in the breeze coming through the propped kitchen door. Autumn was my season—so haughty, yet sexy, it always reminded me of an aloof librarian with a brain full of Hawthorne and rabid, sexual fantasies.

Both my parents had a habit of reading at the table. You could always tell what kind of mood they were in by what they were reading. Grading papers meant they didn't want to talk. A newspaper meant they wanted to talk, but not about themselves, that the outside world would do just fine. A novel meant they were feeling romantic, while poetry meant I was going to sleep in the garage if I didn't want to lie awake to the sound of groans, spanking noises, and all manner of nauseating aural hullabaloo. Dr. Mengele, for all his crimes against nature and man, unknowingly left one form of torture untapped throughout his long years of evil: the sound of your own parents talking dirty to each other.

When I sat down at the table that night, I saw a folded *New York Times* beside my mother's plate, and a book of two thousand crossword puzzles adorning my father's place setting. I was safe. The table was set with two polite candles, three steaming chicken potpies, a bowl of green beans, and news of a bloodbath.

"I don't know what this world is coming to," my mother said, one hand on her paper, the other around her fork. "That poor girl."

"Didn't you used to have a crush on her, Zack?" My father glanced over the rim of his glasses at my blurred visage.

I shrugged and blew on a spoonful of thick, under-salted chowder. My mother was allergic to salt.

I thought about Ginger Banks, about her fiery red hair, and the first time I'd ever whacked off. She was the one I'd thought about on that distant autumn afternoon not so dissimilar from the evening we were presently enjoying. I'd always imagined her pubic hair as a tiny, quivering lick of flame where her warm, rosy thighs came together. I remember ejaculating far less than I thought I would.

"And in the women's lavatory of all places," my mother continued.

I held my spoon in front of my mouth, stared down at its congealing contents while my mother described the state in which Ginger Banks had been found—her head bashed in, with little bits of bone and brains scattered across the floor like the dashed dreams of every boy who'd ever dreamed of standing below her in a pep rally "cheeramid."

"Bruce Salinger is beside himself," my mother informed us. "I understand they had quite a thing."

"I thought she was dating George Dickson."

"Hmm, not sure. She could have been dating them both, for all I know, and for all either of them would care."

"She took quite a reputation with her when she went. Ms. Knotsworth was talking about it in the lounge."

"Speaking of the lounge, that new boy Pennybaum wandered in today while I was pouring myself a cup of java. What an odd young man, so pale and quiet. I think he was rather shaken up about what happened to poor Ginger. He was just wandering around in a daze. When I asked him what was the matter, all he could say was 'Brains.'"

"I think he's from Slovenia. Or is it Pennsylvania? Some vania or another. Which reminds me, your Aunt Ruth from Fairbanks called."

"Now why would Pennsylvania remind you of Fairbanks?"

"Oh, I don't know, it's just one of those things. Actually, I think I was at the supermarket today and I saw this can of tuna from Fairbanks right next to . . . "

Listening to my folks, I felt my appetite burn up and vanish, like my stomach was made of bright, flashing magnesium. I couldn't eat, but couldn't excuse myself from a full plate. So I sat there and watched my parents eat, in awe of these dull, lifeless creatures.

"I'm a nobody.
   Who are you?
   Are you a nobody too?"

"So let me get this straight," Art whispered from his desk. At the front of the class, Missy Nefertiti recited Emily Dickinson with all the passion and understanding of an empty Gucci shoebox. Tucked under her arm was a pearly, hand-carved jar adorned with the head of Anubis, in which she kept her brain. "You're saying that if *you* were the one that found Ginger Banks's corpse, you *wouldn't* sneak a peek before you called the cops? I'm sorry—which one of us is dead again?"

"All I'm saying is that it would depend on how gross she was," I hushed back. "I mean, her freakin' head was bashed in."

"So," Art replied. "You've *seen* her *head*."

Missy Nefertiti finished her poem and took her seat in front of Art.

"I heard she was already dead by the time they found her," Art informed me as I stood to walk to the front of the class, "before her last rites could be performed. Her soul's lost, dude! She's totally transferring here!"

I stood before my classmates, scanned their eyes, horns, and globules of protoplasm. I thought about Ginger Banks, and about her transferring to our school. I thought about cold pussy.

"Death be not proud," I began.

"Mr. Henry," the skeletal registrar addressed me as I waited to see Principal Grimm, "it appears that you were just dying to come back and see us."

"Was that supposed to be funny?" I asked from my chair.

"Do I look like I know funny?"

I glared at the tacky, painted skull glaring back at me with all the knowledge of the grave, then at the great wigwam of coiled, purple locks festooned on top of it.

"So, care to explain why you're here?"

I thought back to Mr. Marley interrupting my poem, waving his iron-clad arms in embarrassed indignation. As I'd gone back to my desk to collect my things, Roland the gangster fetus had offered me his condolences.

"Shit," he'd said, holding up a tiny fist for my fist to bump. "Grimm's secretary is scary, yo. They call 'er the muthafuckin' Clown of Dachau. Good luck."

At first I'd felt apprehensive about seeing the principal on my second day of school. But when an aborted fetus feels sorry for you, you have nowhere to go but up.

"So," I asked the neon skull to pass the time, "how did you die?"

There was a moment's pause, statistically long enough for someone to die in a car accident.

"A fanatical cultist blew himself up in the drive-thru where I worked. He was protesting the Korean War. He wasn't even Korean."

I paused a moment to reflect on the suddenness of it all, at having no time to say goodbye, to leave so many things left undone.

"Did you have to wear roller skates at work?"

"Yes."

"Mr. Henry, we have a problem."

Principal Grimm sat behind his tidy, faux-wood desk in a brown suit with a green tie. The pinstripes of his suit were the same width as the wood grain running along his desk. My first impression was that he was growing out of his furniture.

"You know, sir," I began casually, with just a hint of condescension. I've always found the best way to deal with authority figures is to talk to them like they're delivering your pizza. "I'm sorry if the poem offended anyone. I thought it was apropos."

Of course I knew perfectly well that my poem might offend the teacher. That was the point—the point of the poem and of high school in general, it seemed: Four years of sailing as fast as we could toward the edge of the earth to see if it was round.

"There's no need for an insincere apology, Mr. Henry. That's not what I need from you." Mr. Grimm gripped the surface of his desk and wheeled his rolling chair around to my side as all sense of subtle mockery was wrung from my guts like a sponge full of blood. I stared down his lower half, or lack thereof: His brown blazer ended in a bloody tangle of bone, sinew, and strips of torn flesh. Averting my gaze to let the nausea pass, I looked up at the surfboard mounted on the wall behind him. An elliptical path of two-hundred-some-odd teeth marks ran up the middle of the board where a massive chunk was missing. "You see, the same clerical error which was responsible for your transfer here, transferred one of our students to your old school, and apparently, there's been some sort of incident."

I recalled poor Ginger Banks and her bashed-in brains.

"Is she coming here?" I asked, perhaps a little too eagerly.

"Excuse me?"

"Ginger Banks. Is she transferring here, now that she's, you know, dead?"

Mr. Grimm's face looked somewhere far off, as though called by a bell only his ears could hear.

"I really couldn't say," he began tentatively. "What I can say is this: you can't go back to your old school while Mr. Pennybaum is enrolled there.

However, if he were to somehow meet an untimely *end* in your world, perhaps through the sudden rupture of his cranial cavity, you would be able to resume your place at your former alma mater."

"You're saying I have to kill this guy to go back to my old school?"

"Well, technically, he can't be *killed*, per se, because he already died. He's undead. A zombie, in the popular nomenclature."

"You want me to *kill* this guy?"

Mr. Grimm sighed and wiped a layer of ectoplasm from his perspiring brow.

"As of . . . " Mr. Grimm looked at his watch, held up an index finger. He opened his mouth, made ready to bring his hand down, then paused, and spoke quietly to his watch. *"What are you waiting fo*— NOW! Paul Pennybaum has killed three more of your former classmates."

"So you want me to stop him before he kills again."

"Mr. Henry, with deaths so sudden, the victims are bound to end up here. If this continues, our student-to-teacher ratio will be drastically upset. We're underfunded as it is. Lockers, desks, and food will start to run low."

I looked up at a corkboard mounted under the surfboard. This month's cafeteria menu was pinned to it by a single black thumbtack. I perused today's menu.

"So you want me to stop him before you run out of meatloaf?"

A long pause. Long enough for someone to realize that someone else has loved them all along.

"Yes," the principal nodded, rolled back behind his desk. His stomach rumbled. Behind the desk a dripping noise pricked the momentary silence. "That sounds about right."

When I left Mr. Grimm's office she was there, standing in profile, looking down at her new class schedule, just as I had done nearly twenty-four hours earlier, with equal amounts of disbelief and anger. I imagine it sucks finding out you're dead, especially when you were so popular. Ginger Banks was tiny, pale, her head shaved where they'd cleaned up the wound for her autopsy. She wore the cheerleader's uniform in which she'd died. Long, dark blood stains ran down the back of her white top.

I approached and opened my mouth to say something clever or sarcastic to the secretary to show Ginger how funny I was, how alive and breathing I was. But when I got close and felt all the boy in me flare up my front in a wave of campfire warmth, the speech centers of my brain stalled out. I tried to talk, to say something casual yet enigmatic. But I couldn't form a coherent sound, frozen in a mute, awkward panic, mouth open and eyes wide, like a wax museum dummy getting molested by a lonely security guard.

I came to my senses when she turned toward me and reflexively drew a wave of nonexistent hair behind her ear. She'd been crying. Watercolor veins of tear-diluted eye shadow ran down her cheeks. I closed my mouth, kept staring.

I love watching people cry. Maybe I shouldn't, but I do, and I've done nothing to change.

Still, I wanted to say something nice, something cool yet empathetic. But the problem was that I'm none of those things, really. Well, maybe I'm nice, but I'm too selfish to call myself a nice *person* and still be honest. Either way, I wanted to make her feel better about being dead. But how?

Say something, I thought to myself. *Make it good. Show some insight into the human condition that will lessen the blow of eternity rolling out before her.*

"Hey, at least now you can eat all you want and never get fat."

"Excuse me?" Ginger sniffed, wiped her nose on her bare forearm.

Oh God, just keep going you idiot. Don't stop till you can end on something good.

"Uh . . . you'll never get a pimple again?" *Never mind. Stop now.* "And you can smoke all you want."

"Who *are* you?" she asked.

"Plus, you died when you were still totally hot." *Please stop. For you own good.* "Just let that little nugget sink in."

For the love all that's holy . . . STOP!

She paused. Let it all sink in. More mad. Less sad. I have that effect on women.

"What are you, kidding?" she replied. "I'm freakin' *bald,* you moron!"

From behind the counter, Ms. Needlemeyer, the Clown of Dachau, cleared her throat.

"Mr. Henry—"

I held up a single index finger, finally feeling the residual ire of Principal Grimm's admission that my transfer here had been a clerical error.

"Can it. rollerball," I snapped, still locking eyes with Ginger, who flinched a little and smiled. Now that I'd made a complete fool of myself and had no chance of her being attracted to me, I could actually relax, be myself, and say something interesting. "Look Ginger, the most popular kid in school is an aborted fetus. I think bald's gonna work."

"Are you like, retarded or something?" Missy Nefertiti asked. Roland sat on her lap, leaning back against her tightly wrapped midriff. Missy took a jiggly bite of blood-flavored Jell-O.

"No doubt, son," Roland concurred. "You gotta be outta your goddamn mind."

"Whatever," I said absently. Across the cafeteria, Ginger ate alone at her table. "She looks alive."

"She dead, son," Roland said.

"So are you."

"But you're *not*," Art chimed in. "There are like, *laws* against that shit. Not like, *don't smoke pot laws*, but, you know, *real* ones."

I thought back to the previous day, to the lightning that had struck me when I suggested Art return with me to the land of the living. My arm was still a faded shade of aquamarine, and twitched when I tried to make a fist. What would become of my soul if I made it with Ginger Banks? Would it turn blue and feel fuzzy for a week? I could live with that.

"There's more than one high school for people like us, dude."

I glanced up at Art.

"What do you mean?"

"I mean stick around for the football game after school."

"Football game? Who the hell are we playing?"

Roland, Art, and Missy exchanged a look. Across the cafeteria, a pair of she-devils from the Spirit Squad sat down at Ginger's table and said something that made her smile.

"Why isn't anybody cheering?"

"What's the point?" Art asked. "It won't make any difference."

Even the cheerleaders sat on the sidelines watching the slaughter in total silence.

"The sun ain't even set yet, son."

I looked down at Roland sitting between me and Missy on the decrepit wooden bleacher. All around us the students and faculty made polite conversation in the packed stands, rarely watching the game as our hometown boys, the Middle Plain Lost Souls, were taken to school by the Inferno High Horsemen. Our players, a group of small, unassuming squirts with all the fighting spirit of a euthanized tree sloth were squaring off against the greatest generals of Satan's Legions. On the opposing sidelines, the Dark One himself sat in the bleachers, a great swirling mass of flame and agony contained in an old ratty letterman's jacket.

The grassy plain before us looked like a minefield in which every bomb had been detonated, so many times had our poor, brave lads been driven face-first into the sod. The score was thirty-six to zero. The opposing team had already rushed five hundred yards. A buzzer rang out to end the first quarter as the surrounding hills slurped down the last rays of sunlight. I edged my way to the stairs and stepped down to the sidelines where Ginger sat with the Spirit Squad.

"Hey, Zack!" She waved me over and scooched to make room for me on the bench. That one gesture made my heart beat so fast that every Christmas morning, every birthday I'd ever had, was instantly put to shame and forgotten. My whole life added up to that little space on the bench next to her teeny-tiny skirt.

"This is Misty and Twisty." Ginger waved to the two devils I'd seen in the cafeteria. The twins gave an upward half-nod that meant they'd seen me before, had scraped me off their shoe, and kept walking.

"Can you believe this game?" Ginger said.

"Yeah, I know. Why aren't you guys cheering?"

From the other side of the bench, Misty and Twisty sighed and rolled their eyes.

Ginger shrugged and bunched up her shoulders in a chilly gesture, leaning into me. She rubbed her hands up and down my bicep for warmth. Casually, I looked over my shoulder at Art, who studiously ignored me as the moon slowly hoisted itself over the field and the buzzer for the second quarter sounded.

"Come on, Ginger." Misty and Twisty stood with the rest of the squad and led Ginger before the crowd. I suddenly noticed that I was the only spectator still sitting. The entire crowd began to stamp and holler. The cheerleaders twirled and spun and ground their palms into their hips, spinning their heads around 360 degrees, whipping their hair in every direction. Too bad the crowd wasn't looking at them. All eyes were on the field as the home team broke their huddle, newly transformed into a raving band of howling wolflike demons. Matted black fur bristled through every seam in their uniforms. They howled up at the full moon blazing down on them.

The Middle Plain Lost Souls scored seven touchdowns in six minutes, plus seven two-point conversions, chewing their way through the opposing line until Inferno High didn't have enough players on the field to continue.

Ginger never stopped looking at me while she cheered. When it was all over I sought her out before the lightless vacuum of victory and popularity sucked her down for the rest of the evening. Misty and Twisty glared at me, my social ostracism forming a hideous, invisible hunch on my back which only they could see.

"Hey, can I walk you to your grave?"

Ginger stood at the stands, smiling broadly, out of breath. The air must have been gloriously thin at the top of a cheeramid. I imagined that when it dispersed and Ginger fell from the top and was caught, it must have been like the whole world was reaching out for you, wanting to make sure you're safe.

"Sure." Ginger's dead, glassy eyes caught the light of the full moon and swallowed it. Behind her, the other cheerleaders scratched behind the victorious players' ears. The crowd began to disperse.

As we left the field, Ginger put her arm around mine and put her head on my shoulder. I felt her cheek muscles tense with a smile.

"You're so warm," she said.

I looked back at the stands, at my friends studiously ignoring me, at Principal Grimm shaking his head. Across the field, someone else watched me. Though I didn't dare look back, I could feel a dark smile fix on me from the opposing sidelines, as the visiting team was carried off the field in defeat.

"I'm surprised you remember me, from when you were alive."

Ginger and I walked side by side through the rows of tombstones, fingers intertwined.

"Of course I remember you. Just 'cause you weren't popular doesn't mean you weren't cute." Ginger spoke to the moon, to the dead leaves at her feet.

"But I'm still not popular."

"So what?"

"So why do you like me?"

"Does it matter?"

"Not in the slightest. Just wondering why aren't you ignoring me now?"

"I don't know. Maybe vampires and ghosts don't have like, pheromones or something. And besides, you're *way* cuter than an aborted fetus."

"Awe shucks," I replied. "You're too good to me."

"You ain't seen nothin' yet, honey."

I could tell she'd said it before, with other guys, and that she recycled the phrase because she knew it was sexy. And it was sexy.

For a second, before her cold, dead tongue slid between my teeth, I thought, *maybe this isn't a good idea. What about the rules of Heaven and Earth?* But then my hand slid under her shirt, cupped her firm, icy breast, and I didn't care.

Let me tell you something you already know:

A polite girl or woman, with whom you've never spoken of sex, suddenly telling you where to go, grabbing your hand, and sliding it between her legs, admitting that she wants to feel good—in the years after that night, such a thing wouldn't seem like a big deal. Grown women can talk about what they want, what they need from you. But in high school, when girls are supposed to be ladies instead of human beings, hearing such things from a total hottie like Ginger Banks, when all I'd dared to dream of was first base and a decent view of second, was like looking for trace elements of fossilized bacteria on Mars and finding the Miss Hawaiian Tropic competition camped out at your landing site.

Her skin was achingly cold.

"You're freezing," I said.

"I get goose bumps all the time."

She stood there with her top off while we kissed. She kept her skirt on, her socks and shoes too. Half-dressed like that, that strange combination of nudity and modesty, was an intoxicating cocktail of dream life and daily life. I'd only ever seen one or the other. In movies, they always cut from the kissing to the sex montage. In pornos, "actors" peeled off their own clothes like layers of useless, dead skin. But when Ginger lay back on a patch of hallowed earth overrun with clover, grabbed my hips, and guided me into her hidden, frozen pussy, it was as though we'd fallen into the crack between fantasy and reality, into that twilight of sensuality which you can visit once, the first time, but only in dreams thereafter.

Plus, I'd always thought people called out each other's names when they did it. I've since learned that this is seldom the case. I've also learned that people seldom even think of each other when they're fucking each other. But back then, that night, I could only think of Ginger—and not even all of her, just her breasts, or her eyes, or how we tried to keep it in when we turned over so she could be on top. One thing at a time. I didn't even know my name.

She came when I came, *because* I came, I would later find out. Apparently, what I left in her was hot and anxious and she had only the chill of death to fill her insides the rest of the time. I haven't made many women cum since then.

"It's so weird just sitting here," she remarked afterwards, propped against the base of a towering, angelic grave marker. "I used to have to, you know, button up while my boyfriend defrosted the windshield so he could drop me off before curfew." She sighed. "It's so weird being dead. You know?"

"Not really."

"You will."

"Thanks."

She smiled at me, straightened her clothes, and reached back to try and tuck her buzzed-off hair behind her ears.

"I heard your hair keeps growing after you die," she said. "I hope it's true. You know—" She sounded serious all of a sudden (something else I would have to get used to, and dread—a woman getting a serious tone after a sound shag). "How do you know, for sure, that you shouldn't be here?"

"What do you mean?"

"I mean, think about it," she said.

But I didn't have to. Already my heart started rattling in my chest like a punching bag. She meant *how did I know I wasn't dead*. Did I know?

I started talking fast. More to myself than the dead girl scrutinizing my dazed expression.

"But I've gone home to my house and seen my parents and—"

"Did they talk to you? Did they acknowledge you?"

"No, but they usually don't. They—"

I stopped when I saw it. By the light of a lightning flash, I saw it staring back at me, unassuming, defiant, smug.

"Ohmigodimdead." I knelt in front of my grave, stared down at my name and the date underneath. July fourth. I died on Independence Day. I thought back to a firecracker nearly going off in my hand. It must have gone off too soon. I must have bled to death.

"I'm dead?" The world went quiet. Long enough for a light to turn red too soon.

The cool earth snuck up and cold-cocked me from behind. I was on the ground. Somewhere beneath me, I was *in* the ground. The transfer wasn't a mistake. I was supposed to be here in the land of the dead, haunting my parents at night, unable to let g—

"PSYYYYYYYYYCH!"

The call resounded through the boneyard. Disoriented from my fall, I tried to stand, tried to use my own tombstone for balance as it crumbled into a lumpy mass of gray, standard-issue, sophomore Art Class self-hardening clay and I fell into it on my way back to Earth.

From behind the nearest mausoleum, Art, Roland, and Missy Nefertiti leapt into the moonlight, the surprise causing my heart, my still-beating, magnificent, most all-important muscle to batter against its calcium housing, threatening to stop, but persevering nonetheless.

"Sha-ZAAM, son!" Roland called out, laughing hysterically before Missy nearly squashed him as she doubled over in hysterics.

"You guys are so fucking dead!" I swore to Art as he helped me to my feet. Had they been there listening to us the whole time? Did I care? No! I was alive! I was laid! It was funny, too—I'd equated those two states of being for so long, now that I got both at once, they seemed completely different.

I grinned at the smug bastard, punched him in the shoulder as hard as I could, which wasn't very hard. "You are so *fucking* DEAD!"

"I know."

Nobody parties like the dead. The damned have rhythm. The entire school celebrated our victory in the cemetery that night, stamping their feet, howling at the moon loud enough to wake the dead and serve them up a tall one from the keg.

Ginger stayed close to me, getting drunk and clingy as the night spiraled down into the rosy abyss of bad breath and good vibes. Living in Limbo, a place to which God apparently turned a blind eye, was like your folks going away for the weekend and leaving the keys in the ignition and the liquor cabinet unlocked. The idea of bashing Paul Pennybaum's skull in was as distant and meaningless as Monday morning seen from the observation deck of Friday night.

"Listen!" Ginger said to me over the music sometime after midnight. She was sweaty from dancing and talked right into my face with a boozy lack of depth perception. "I don't want you to think I'm a slut or anything because we fucked!"

"But *aren't* you kind of a slut?!" I howled and lit a cigarette.

"Well, yeah, but I don't want you to think of me that way!"

"I don't!"

"Good!" she proclaimed, then climbed on top of a broad, flat grave marker, took off her shirt, and started to dance. It was at that moment that I knew I was falling in love.

Just before dawn, things started to slow down, and my new girlfriend started to cry.

"I was sooooooo fucking popular!" she lamented, tears streaming down her face. The moon was down and all was dark. All around us, drunken kids and bilious abominations stumbled back to their graves. "I was about to get my *license!* And just 'cause that dumb-ass zombie ate my brains I wound up here. I should *totally* be in *Heaven!*"

"At least you didn't wind up in Hell."

"My cell phone doesn't get *any* reception here!" she shouted to the black sky. "I *am* in Hell!"

She sobbed. I held her close. Her nipples were hard under her shirt. Her tears were cold.

"What the fuck is a *last rite* anyway? Is that like, the directions to Heaven? They couldn't give me directions before I died, so I got lost and ended up here? I don't even believe in God!"

I struggled to find the right thing to say that would either make her feel better or at least make her stop crying.

"Yeah, but, you know, *He* believes in *you.*"

"Really?" she asked, teary-eyed and hopeful. "You think so?"

"Um . . . not really. Sorry. I just said that to make you feel better. I stopped believing in God before I stopped believing in Santa Claus."

In the next plot down, Brutus Forte, our school's star quarterback, slid down into his grave, drunk with victory, beer, adoration of the masses. Peering over the lip of his grave, I watched him fluff up the dirt where his head would rest, then reach up to the surface, and in a single, sweeping motion draw a pile of loose earth on top of him as he fell back, already sound asleep before his head touched the cool, wormy terra firma.

"Do you love me?"

"Huh?" I turned back to Ginger. She propped herself against a headstone, watching me like a mirror while she wiped away her smeared eye shadow. Dead leaves clung to her scalp and clothes. The last of the alcohol had left her body, leaving her more sober than she was before she started drinking, the way you get when you've stayed up late enough for the booze to find its way back out, temporarily flushing out the drunkenness of everyday self-denial.

"I know they want you to kill Paul Pennybaum," she continued. "If you do, you won't ever come back."

"Well, I could come back," I swallowed. "I mean . . . I'd have to do it like Art di—"

"But you wouldn't." She looked up at the moon, saw herself in it, pursed her lips, drew a finger around them to erase a smudge. "You're not that kind of person."

"What do you mean?"

"You're the kind of person that makes good decisions. That's why girls don't like you—as more than a friend I mean." She sighed, eyes focused on a leaf stuck in the front clasp of her bra. "You'll never break my heart," she said. She sounded a little surprised, and a little disappointed.

She looked up at me, caught my expression.

"I'm not stupid," she replied to my thoughts. "Girls understand boys. It's just that most of the time, we don't have to, or we don't want to."

"I don't wanna kill Paul. I want to keep coming to see you."

"Then *don't* kill him," she pleaded softly. "He'll probably get killed some other way, anyway. People die all the time. Look at *me*."

A cold wind rustled through the cemetery, a parent checking up on their child after lights-out. It found us and we huddled together. Ginger's skin made me even colder, but I didn't want to let go.

"I should get to bed," she said at last, and lowered herself into the empty grave beside us. Once in, she paused and peered up at me. Her head just barely came up above ground level. "Will you tuck me in?"

"Sure," I replied, and got down on my knees. As I worked the dirt into her grave, I thought about the times my father would wake me up and tell me I was having a nightmare. I never remembered having a bad dream, but I believed him and felt better with him there.

"When you're done," Ginger said before I covered her face, "you have to go."

"What do you mean?"

"You can't spend the night here, or you can never leave again."

"How do you know?"

"I don't know, I just know. It's just one of the rules. Your parents are probably worried sick."

"But I wan—"

"Nobody worries about me anymore," she interrupted.

She leaned forward, crawled her fingers through the hair on the back of my head, kissed me, then fell back to the dark earth, the dirt around her body caving in as she fell. Behind me, I could already hear the black bus idling at the side of the road.

"Where have you been?"

"Have you been drinking?"

"We've been so worried!"

"You have no idea!"

It's funny how quickly relief can turn to anger. It's like we keep both emotions spring-loaded inside the same little tin can inside our chests and when we let one feeling out, the other must inevitably follow.

"Did you drive drunk?" my father demanded to know, rubbing the sleep from his eyes. "Who have you been out with?"

"Zombies."

"Zombies? What is that, some kind of gang?" The old man inquired, exasperated from running every drug overdose and child-kidnapping scenario imaginable through his head while waiting to hear my key in the door. "Are you in a fucking gang now?"

My father rarely cussed at me. It was one of those rare glimpses I ever caught of his non-father personality. I rarely liked what I saw.

"Oh my God." My mother sat down at the table, her face in her hands. She looked up at her jailbird son. "Are you dealing drugs?"

I wanted to tell them to get real, to remember that the best lessons they ever learned was from the mistakes they made, that the first step in becoming your own person is to make a conscious decision *not* to become your parents.

But I didn't know how to say all that, to articulate what I would only learn years later when I yelled at my own kids, because the only way to grow old is to forget what it's like to be young. And besides, they didn't *deserve* a response, or so I believed. They'd never been this mad before, never talked to me like this. It made all their love, all their kind words and tender moments seem totally and unforgivably conditional.

"Yeah," I replied coldly. If they needed to blame everything on changes in the world outside, instead of changes in their son, I wouldn't stand in their way. "That's it." I started up to my room, spoke over my shoulder, let my words tumble down the stairs behind me. "The big bad wolf made me do it."

"That must be his supplier," I heard my father explain to my mother. "They all have nicknames. It's all—"

The door SLAMMED! on his words, caught them and held them like fingers in a car door.

I collapsed on my bed, listened to my parents fighting downstairs, turned on the ten o'clock news. Channel 4 was running an exposé on the deaths at my old high school. A young, statuesque, serious-minded telejournalist reported that students were living in a state of mourning, that grief had struck the school "like a brick through a stained-glass window." As she said this, a man with a clipboard stepped behind her, into frame, and waved off the mob of students mooning the camera and flashing middle fingers and gang signs.

"Excuse me, young man." The reporter snared a passerby and aimed the camera at him. It was Paul Pennybaum, lurching to class. Flies orbited his tilted head, alighting on his rotten fruit face and taking off again. His clothes were tattered and sullied from his time in the grave. His eyes looked at the world like a retarded monkey would look at a banana painted on a brick wall.

"Young man," the reporter began again, "how does it feel going to school under the shadow of Death?"

"Brains," Paul droned, with great effort, as he stared straight through the reporter.

"Yes," the reporter responded, "the victims have all suffered severe trauma to their craniums. How does that make you feel?"

"Feel . . . dead."

The reporter turned back to the camera.

"As you can see, some of the students here already consider themselves future victims. Back to you, Bob and Alice."

I changed the channel, tried to pick up some scrambled porn, but nothing was on. So I sat there in the dark, weighing the gravity of so much death against the weight of Ginger's body on top of mine. I supposed it was partially my fault. If I whacked Paul, got rid of him somehow, the killing would stop. But I would never see Ginger again. Thus, the combination of my lust for her and my loathing for my former classmates was enough to persuade me, before I whacked off and fell asleep, that most of them were better off dead anyway. Paul Pennybaum was by no means the only zombie at San Los Pleasovale High.

By the following Saturday, five more students and three teachers were dead at school. My parents spoke as though I was one of them. Good riddance. And don't give me that look, either. How many times have you looked around a room and, however fleetingly, wished half of them would just disappear?

At the table that morning, my father spoke of days gone by, when he and I would barbecue burgers in the backyard and play catch. My mother made no reply. Tears welled up in her eyes as she hid them behind that day's crossword. Sitting between them at the table, I wanted to remind my father that he was a vegetarian, and that we had played catch once. Neither of us liked it. We both hated sports. And while I couldn't claim to like the jocks at my school, I couldn't blame them for being what they were. After all, if I had the choice between being a moderately clever writer, amusing himself alone at his computer, or being a Neanderthal in a football jersey at a blowjob buffet (or so I have to imagine them), I'd have to think about it.

Leaning over his bowl of cereal, my father flipped to the business section, exposing the front page to the rest of the table. The headline read that both the FBI and the Centers for Disease Control and Prevention had been called in to investigate the series of deaths at my old high school.

I got up to leave when I heard my bus arrive to take me to the Homecoming pep rally and game. We'd been prepping for it all week—hanging streamers in the hallways at school, pinning up signs so parents and alums wouldn't get lost when they arrived for the game from their various planes of existence. I'd stayed late every day to help decorate and then fuck my girlfriend. Every day was Christmas. Then I would come home and see my parents asleep on the couch, in the armchair, at the kitchen table, dreaming in uncomfortable positions. First I'd be mad. Then I'd be sorry. Then I'd go to sleep feeling mad that they made me feel sorry.

I paused for a second at the door, looked back at my parents looking down at their papers and plates, not so much looking at these items of interest as not looking at me.

For all they know, I am in a gang. This could be the last time they see me, and they don't care. They wouldn't care if I was next.

Going out the door, I thought about what Ginger said every night when I tucked her into her grave and I always asked to stay a little longer. *If you stay,* she'd invariably warn me, *you can never go home.*

I thought about that as I got onto the bus, and about how little home felt like home anymore.

Well, maybe I will *be next.*

As we pulled away, I looked back at the house I'd grown up in. It felt like I hadn't been there in years, as though it had been sold long ago and that I'd only just returned for nostalgia's sake, but had changed my mind when I drew close, and decided to keep driving.

"Where are they?"

"They'll be here."

The air was cold and electrified, the sky black. It was two minutes till game time and the opposing team still had yet to show, as had their fans. The bleachers opposite ours were bare, the sidelines equally so.

"If they don't show, do they forfeit?"

"They'll show."

I sat in the top row of bleachers with Art and Roland.

"I need a smoke," Roland said. He and Art, along with the rest of the hushed crowd, watched the field intently. The players on our side had already made their big entrance and were sitting on their benches, waiting and watching the field. "Wish I could hold a cigarette."

That afternoon, the pep rally had proceeded as all such events do—cheering, clapping, yelling, clapping some more and yelling louder, followed by more cheering, and, time permitting, more yelling and clapping. All throughout, however, there had been something in the air between the fans and the players, something in their distant smiles that made our good wishes sound almost mournful—some unacknowledged dread, as though our boys were going off to war, that we might not ever see them again.

"But if they don't show up," I repeated.

"They'll show up."

My breath came out as a fog. Nobody else's did.

"But if they d—"

A sound rang out from On High—a lone trumpet echoing down from the cloud cover. I looked up at the sky, as did everyone, and felt fear choke my heart. The horn sounded once more, like a distant cavalry charge. As it did so, a solitary ray of golden light, no wider than a child's arm, pierced the clouds and focused on the fifty-yard line. A third time the trumpet sounded. My breath caught in my throat. I wanted to hide, to cover my face, so terrible was this sound that said *your dreams are over,* a sound that told you, convinced you, that *everything you thought you would become you will never become; all the plans you have laid for yourself, will never come to pass.* It was the bang of an unseen gun pointed at your heart. It was the sound of The End.

The fourth time the horn sounded it was joined by a chorus of bellicose brass, horns of war that wrung all will to resist from my body as the tiny spotlight that shone down on our home field widened suddenly, split the sky like a knife ripping open a wound, flooding the terrain with a rapturous, unflinching blaze as a host of seraphim in gold and white football jerseys poured down from the break in the clouds and stormed the field, a beautiful, thunderous stampede of infallible athletic ability with the greatest record of any school in the history of the universe. These were our opponents. This was Paradise High.

"We have to fight *Heaven* in our Homecoming Game?" I asked, totally flabbergasted. Across the field, a glowing body of halos and white robes filled the opposing stands.

"They've never been defeated," Art said and bit into a corndog.

"Why am I not surprised?"

"It ain't that bad, son," Roland offered. "It's like, this one doesn't count, you know?"

"Doesn't count?"

"Yeah, you know," Art said. "They can't be beat. Nobody's ever even scored on these guys. When God's sitting in the other team's bleachers, the bookies take the day off."

"Is that Genghis Khan looking through their playbook?"

"He's their head coach."

"But wasn't he, like, a bloodthirsty conqueror?"

"And a strategic genius."

"But wasn't he, like, a *bloodthirsty conqueror?*"

"Did the first-string linebackers at Harvard score 1600s on their SATs?" Roland asked.

I stared blankly down at the fetus.

"I don't *think* so," he answered as the whistle rang out for the kickoff.

I left when the scorekeeper lost count. The hometown crowd hadn't made a peep for the better part of three quarters. Whether we were too sorry to cheer for Middle Plain or too guilty to root against Heaven I couldn't say, but I supposed it didn't matter. My mind hadn't been on the game anyway.

I wandered back to the cemetery. Every grave was empty. Everyone had shown up to see their team get clobbered. I wondered why.

"You know, you're quite a unique young man."

I whirled around, surprised. I was going to school in the land of the dead, but a strange voice in the middle of a cemetery was still mildly alarming.

Ms. Needlemeyer, the Clown of Dachau, leaned against the wall of a mausoleum, trying to light a cigarette without the ability to inhale.

"Excuse me?" I asked.

"You're a very unique young man," she reiterated. "You are, after all, the only one who's ever been unhappy."

"Wha . . . huh? I don't get it."

"That's what you want to hear, isn't it?"

I stopped, looked at her with her painted skull and fallen stockings. She looked like a hooker who'd died propped against a lamppost and no one had noticed while she wasted away to nothing but bleached bones and a low-cut dress.

"No," I replied, softly.

"Here," she held out the as-yet unlit cigarette. "Little help?"

I plopped down on the tombstone beside her, lit her cigarette, handed it back.

"So what *do* you want to hear?"

I thought about that question, tried to look past the immediate thoughts of fame, money, sex. I thought about Ginger, and my 'rents. Most of all I thought about how everyone on the planet seemed to kind of suck, in a general way, while I, clearly the only one who didn't suck, seemed to be the only one that was unhappy.

"I want someone to tell me it's going to be all right."

A dry chuckle sounded in Ms. Needlemeyer's throat, the sound of drumsticks on a pelvic snare drum.

"What?" I asked.

"You, young man, are the only person that can honestly say that to yourself. That's what growing up is, hon." She held the cigarette between her bare teeth, let the smoke float up into her eye cavities in a dead French inhale. "Becoming that person."

Mercifully, across the churchyard and over the last hill, the final whistle of the game blew. We turned and watched the sky tear open behind the school. The angels flew home quickly, whooping and hollering and cheering like a parade.

"Everybody always wants to be somewhere else," Needlemeyer noted. "Always making plans to be somewhere they'd rather be. I don't imagine it's any different in Heaven. I'd just like to know where they'd rather be."

I looked at the painted bag of bones, at the dirt caked on my shoes.

I had to keep my distance from Ginger at the Homecoming Dance. No one but our inner circle of friends knew how serious things had gotten between us and no one else *could* know, or there would be hell to pay. Literally. So I stood against the wall with Art while Roland danced on Missy's outstretched palm and Ginger boogied beside them. After a few songs he came back to catch his breath. Missy went to the bathroom with Ginger.

"What the dilly, son?" Roland asked. He sounded like a winded rubber squeaker toy. "You upset about the game? Don't let it get to you, bro. We *always* lose Homecoming."

"Huh?" I looked up from my feet. "Oh. Nah, I don't care about that shit."

"Then what's up?" Art asked.

"Nothing."

"Yeah, right."

"You love her?" Roland asked.

On the dance floor, Misty and Twisty and everybody else danced. Everyone danced differently. I wondered what it had been like, years ago, when nobody danced alone. You found a partner or you waited for one, looking for someone to ask.

"I don't know," I replied.

"That means *no*, son. When it comes to love, anything but *yes* means *no*."

I watched Ginger and Missy come out of the bathroom. Ginger looked for me across the dance floor, found me. I met her gaze, held it as I walked out to the dance floor and took her hand for a slow song.

"What are you doing?" she asked.

I made no response. We fit our bodies together and started to move.

"I think I love you," Ginger said after the first refrain.

She said it the way everybody says it the first time, when what they really mean is *I think I want to tell you I love you*. She looked at me, wanting me to say it back. I wanted to say it back, but I couldn't speak. All the blood in my body reversed its flow. I felt like I did in the cemetery, when Art, Roland, and Missy had played the prank on me, convincing me that I'd been dead the whole time.

"Aren't you gonna say it too?"

There was a pause between songs, long enough for someone to bet it all and lose; long enough for a plane to make an emergency landing; long enough for the next song to load, and begin.

"I, I—"

"I mean, if this isn't love, what is?" she asked, needing me to have the answer.

Again I found no words. I couldn't speak to her. Couldn't look at her.

"What are you thinking about?" she pleaded softly. She pressed her head against my chest, let the familiar cold of her tears soak through my shirt.

"Nothing," I replied, the old conversational parachute that worked more like an anvil tied to a ripcord.

"Please tell me."

I looked down at her, and for the first and probably last time, spoke with absolute honesty to a woman who I cared about:

I'd been thinking about my mother, about a certain Christmas morning when I was seven years old. It was our hardest holiday together. My father had been laid off before the previous semester had begun and it had plunged him into a crisis of being from which it seemed he might never emerge. He slept most of the day and haunted our house at night while we slept. Once, when I couldn't sleep, I'd gone down for a drink of water and found the old man standing in front of the open refrigerator, talking to the appliance's innards like a door-to-door salesman might present his product on some anonymous stoop, trying his damnedest to get his foot in the door. He'd sold vacuums door-to-door one summer when he was nineteen to save for the down payment on a car. He was brushing up the old pitch. I didn't know this at the time.

Months later, when Christmas came, my mother picked out my presents, spent hours poring over the discount bins at Toys "R" Us and JCPenney's looking for toys I might like that wouldn't break the bank. When the morning of December twenty-fifth finally came around, I found her asleep on the couch. She'd waited until late to bring out the toys and had fallen asleep wrapping them. When I saw what Santa had brought, I cried. I said they were stupid. I said they were awful.

Like everyone, I've done some shitty things in my life. I've hurt good people, most of the time without meaning to. And I've forgiven myself for those misdeeds, because like everyone, I convince myself that the things I do, I do because I must. But I've never forgiven myself for what I said that morning.

My mother had tried to explain, rapidly wiping tears from her eyes before I could see them. She said that there must have been a mix-up. Santa, she explained, had confused our house with someone else's. She said she was surprised it didn't happen more often. But all I could do was cry and whine and complain about how good I'd been all year.

"I know, sweetie," she sniffed, comforting me, hugging me. "You've been so good. We'll write Santa a letter. We'll write him a letter and he'll clear everything up. You just have to give it a little time to get there."

By the following Christmas, I didn't believe in Santa Claus. Yet to this day, my mom still writes "From Santa" on a couple of presents every year.

"I don't get it," Ginger replied when I finished telling the story.

"That's what I think love is."

"But it's such a sad story," she explained. "What does that have to do with me?"

"I love you."

"I love you, too."

The second slow song ended. The DJ came on to announce that the next song would be the final slow number of the evening. I'd reason, years later, that neither of us really *loved* each other then. I'd also figure that it didn't really matter.

"I love this song," she said. It was a song about dreams, about having a nightmare that the singer's true love had died. "You know, I've never had a nightmare since I've been here. I don't think I've had a single dream."

I looked down at her, at the people staring at us with attraction and disgust.

"I love you," I said again, to the whiskers on her head.

"I love you too," she said as I pulled away, turned around, and began to run.

I found Paul in the gymnasium, trying to dribble a basketball and failing. As I approached, I watched him pick up a ball with both hands and drop it. He swatted at the bouncing thing and missed, waited for it to settle at his feet, then picked it up again. I looked at the floor around him, at the equipment he'd dragged from storage: dodge balls, footballs, soccer balls and nets, tennis rackets, swim caps, and racing hurdles. He was wearing a gym uniform. The shirt was inside-out. I picked up a metal baseball bat, felt the weight. I watched him pick up the basketball again. Outside, moonlight streamed in through the high windows. I held the bat over my shoulder, stood like a major leaguer. I thought about Ginger. I thought about Art's blood in his mom's ice cube trays. I thought about Christmas, and swung the bat.

They were asleep when I got home. The TV was on and the color bars watched over them silently. My father sat at the end of the couch with my mother sprawled out on the adjoining cushions, her head on Pop's lap. The old man's brow was creased, his throat moving and sounding, talking to someone in his dreams. His head ticked to the left and he spoke again, in his throat. His mouth opened suddenly, breathing in.

"Hey," I said quietly. I put a bloody hand on his twitching shoulder. "I'm home."

Nik Houser *was born in a small town which, when Nik was a boy, made the mistake of selling off the logging rights of a sacred forest which the local Cheyenne elders called Ta'ovo'omeno, or Pissed-Off Mountain The clear-cut trees were sold to a mill which supplied a variety of companies throughout the region. That Autumn, while writing a paper on Christopher Columbus, Nik's pencil, which had been made from Ta'ovo'omeno wood, came back to life and wrote a report of its own called "My Human Teacher is an Imperialist Butthead." Nik's teacher did not believe the boy's story about his pencil, though not for long. Undead paper products soon began to terrorize the town. Zombie books made from Ta'ovo'omeno paper would slam shut at the most suspenseful parts. Wooden chairs scooted away when someone tried to sit in them. Soon, the plague spread to anything made of wood: grocery sacks split, to-do lists wandered off, whole wood-frame houses began to creak and sway, ready to fall. One afternoon, Nik found a Post-It note (made from YOU-KNOW-WHAT) stuck to the fridge which read "Gone to find a better son, please die before we return." Nik and his family left town that very* *night. Recently, Mr. Houser tried to return to the town, only to discover that the covered bridge which lead to it had collapsed. There was no sign of the town beyond. Too many trees blocked the way. Please visit www.nikhouser.com*

———

Other than special thanks to Kit Reed who pointed me in the right direction to find Mr. Houser's story . . . really, what more can I say? Except, maybe, that if they do get that Zombie Channel going, I think this would make a keen basis for a series: *Gravestone High School.*

Zora and the Zombie

Andy Duncan

"What is the truth?" the houngan shouted over the drums. The mambo, in response, flung open her white dress. She was naked beneath. The drummers quickened their tempo as the mambo danced among the columns in a frenzy. Her loose clothing could not keep pace with her kicks, swings, and swivels. Her belt, shawl, kerchief, dress floated free. The mambo flung herself writhing onto the ground. The first man in line shuffled forward on his knees to kiss the truth that glistened between the mambo's thighs.

Zora's pencil point snapped. Ah, shit. Sweat-damp and jostled on all sides by the crowd, she fumbled for her penknife and burned with futility. Zora had learned just that morning that the Broadway hoofer and self-proclaimed anthropologist Katherine Dunham, on her Rosenwald fellowship to Haiti—the one that rightfully should have been Zora's—not only witnessed this very truth ceremony a year ago, but for good measure underwent the three-day initiation to become Mama Katherine, bride of the serpent god Damballa—the heifer!

Three nights later, another houngan knelt at another altar with a platter full of chicken. People in the back began to scream. A man with a terrible face flung himself through the crowd, careened against people, spread chaos. His eyes rolled. The tongue between his teeth drooled blood. "He is mounted!" the people cried. "A loa has made him his horse." The houngan began to turn. The horse crashed into him. The houngan and the horse fell together, limbs entwined. The chicken was mashed into the dirt. The people moaned and sobbed. Zora sighed. She had read this in Herskovitz, and in Johnson, too. Still, maybe poor fictional Tea Cake, rabid, would act like this. In the pandemonium she silently leafed to the novel section of her notebook. "Somethin' got after me in mah sleep, Janie," she had written. "Tried tuh choke me tuh death."

Another night, another compound, another pencil. The dead man sat up, head nodding forward, jaw slack, eyes bulging. Women and men shrieked. The dead man lay back down and was still. The mambo pulled the blanket back over him, tucked it in. Perhaps tomorrow, Zora thought, I will go to Pont Beudet, or to Ville Bonheur. Perhaps something new is happening there.

"Miss Hurston," a woman whispered, her heavy necklace clanking into Zora's shoulder. "Miss Hurston. Have they shared with you what was found a month ago? Walking by daylight in the Ennery road?"

Dr. Legros, chief of staff at the hospital at Gonaives, was a good-looking mulatto of middle years with pomaded hair and a thin mustache. His three-piece suit was all sharp creases and jutting angles, like that of a paper doll, and his handshake left Zora's palm powder dry. He poured her a belt of raw white clairin, minus the nutmeg and peppers that would make it palatable to Guede, the prancing black-clad loa of derision, but breathtaking nonetheless, and as they took dutiful medicinal sips his small talk was all big, all politics: whether Mr. Roosevelt would be true to his word that the Marines would never be back; whether Haiti's good friend Senator King of Utah had larger ambitions; whether America would support President Vincent if the grateful Haitians were to seek to extend his second term beyond the arbitrary date technically mandated by the Constitution. But his eyes—to Zora, who was older than she looked and much older than she claimed—posed an entirely different set of questions. He seemed to view Zora as a sort of plenipotentiary from Washington and only reluctantly allowed her to steer the conversation to the delicate subject of his unusual patient.

"It is important for your countrymen and your sponsors to understand, Miss Hurston, that the beliefs of which you speak are not the beliefs of civilized men, in Haiti or elsewhere. These are Negro beliefs, embarrassing to the rest of us, and confined to the canaille—to the, what is the phrase, the backwater areas, such as your American South. These beliefs belong to Haiti's past, not her future."

Zora mentally placed the good doctor waistcoat-deep in a backwater area of Eatonville, Florida, and set gators upon him. "I understand, Dr. Legros, but I assure you I'm here for the full picture of your country, not just the Broadway version, the tomtoms and the shouting. But in every ministry, veranda, and salon I visit, why, even in the office of the director-general of the Health Service, what is all educated Haiti talking about but your patient, this unfortunate woman Felicia Felix-Mentor? Would you stuff my ears, shelter me from the topic of the day?"

He laughed, his teeth white and perfect and artificial. Zora, self-conscious of her own teeth, smiled with her lips closed, chin down. This often passed for flirtation. Zora wondered what the bright-eyed Dr. Legros thought of the seductive man-eater Erzulie, the most "uncivilized" loa of all. As she slowly crossed her legs, she thought: Huh! What's Erzulie got on Zora, got on me?

"Well, you are right to be interested in the poor creature," the doctor said, pinching a fresh cigarette into his holder while looking neither at it nor at Zora's eyes. "I plan to write a monograph on the subject myself, when the press of duty allows me. Perhaps I should apply for my own Guggenheim, eh? Clement!" He clapped his hands. "Clement! More clairin for our guest, if you please, and mangoes when we return from the yard."

As the doctor led her down the central corridor of the gingerbread Victorian hospital, he steered her around patients in creeping wicker wheelchairs, spat volleys of French at cowed black women in white, and told her the story she already knew, raising his voice whenever passing a doorway through which moans were unusually loud.

"In 1907, a young wife and mother in Ennery town died after a brief illness. She had a Christian burial. Her widower and son grieved for a time, then moved on with their lives, as men must do. *Empty this basin immediately! Do you hear me, woman? This is a hospital, not a chickenhouse!* My pardon. Now we come to a month ago. The Haitian Guard received reports of a madwoman accosting travelers near Ennery. She made her way to a farm and refused to leave, became violently agitated by all attempts to dislodge her. The owner of this family farm was summoned. He took one look at this poor creature and said, 'My God, it is my sister, dead and buried nearly thirty years.' Watch your step, please."

He held open a French door and ushered her onto a flagstone veranda, out of the hot, close, blood-smelling hospital into the hot, close outdoors, scented with hibiscus, goats, charcoal, and tobacco in bloom. "And all the other family members, too, including her husband and son, have identified her. And so one mystery was solved, and in the process, another took its place."

In the far corner of the dusty, enclosed yard, in the sallow shade of an hourglass grove, a sexless figure in a white hospital gown stood huddled against the wall, shoulders hunched and back turned, like a child chosen It and counting.

"That's her," said the doctor.

As they approached, one of the hourglass fruits dropped onto the stony ground and burst with a report like a pistol firing, not three feet behind the huddled figure. She didn't budge.

"It is best not to surprise her," the doctor murmured, hot clairin breath in Zora's ear, hand in the small of her back. "Her movements are . . . unpredictable." As yours are not, Zora thought, stepping away.

The doctor began to hum a tune that sounded like

Mama don't want no peas no rice
She don't want no coconut oil
All she wants is brandy
Handy all the time

but wasn't. At the sound of his humming, the woman—for woman she was; Zora would resist labeling her as all Haiti had done—sprang forward into the wall with a fleshy smack, as if trying to fling herself face first through the stones, then sprang backward with a half-turn that set her arms to swinging without volition, like pendulums. Her eyes were beads of clouded glass. The broad lumpish face around them might have been attractive had its muscles displayed any of the tension common to animal life.

In her first brush with theater, years before, Zora had spent months scrubbing bustles and darning epaulets during a tour of that damned *Mikado*—may Gilbert and Sullivan both lose their heads—and there she learned that putty cheeks and false noses slide into grotesquerie by the final act. This woman's face likewise seemed to have been sweated beneath too long.

All this Zora registered in a second, as she would a face from an elevated train. The woman immediately turned away again, snatched down a slim hourglass branch and slashed the ground, back and forth, as a machete slashes through cane. The three attached fruits blew up, *bang bang bang*, seeds clouding outward, as she flailed the branch in the dirt.

"What is she doing?"

"She sweeps," the doctor said. "She fears being caught idle, for idle servants are beaten. In some quarters." He tried to reach around the suddenly nimble woman and take the branch.

"Nnnnn," she said, twisting away, still slashing the dirt.

"Behave yourself, Felicia. This visitor wants to speak with you."

"Please leave her be," Zora said, ashamed because the name Felicia jarred when applied to this wretch. "I didn't mean to disturb her."

Ignoring this, the doctor, eyes shining, stopped the slashing movements by seizing the woman's skinny wrist and holding it aloft. The patient froze, knees bent in a half-crouch, head averted as if awaiting a blow. With his free hand, the doctor, still humming, still watching the woman's face, pried her fingers from the branch one by one, then flung it aside, nearly swatting Zora. The patient continued saying "Nnnnn, nnnnn, nnnnn" at metronomic intervals. The sound lacked any note of panic or protest, any communicative tonality whatsoever, was instead a simple emission, like the whistle of a turpentine cooker.

"Felicia?" Zora asked.

"Nnnnn, nnnnn, nnnnn."

"My name is Zora, and I come from Florida, in the United States."

"Nnnnn, nnnnn, nnnnn."

"I have heard her make one other noise only," said the doctor, still holding up her arm as if she were Joe Louis, "and that is when she is bathed or touched with water—a sound like a mouse that is trod upon. I will demonstrate. Where is that hose?"

"No need for that!" Zora cried. "Release her, please."

The doctor did so. Felicia scuttled away, clutched and lifted the hem of her gown until her face was covered and her buttocks bared. Zora thought of her mother's wake, where her aunts and cousins had greeted each fresh burst of tears by flipping their aprons over their heads and rushing into the kitchen to mewl together like nestlings. Thank God for aprons, Zora thought. Felicia's legs, to Zora's surprise, were ropy with muscle.

"Such strength," the doctor murmured, "and so untamed. You realize, Miss Hurston, that when she was found squatting in the road, she was as naked as all mankind."

A horsefly droned past.

The doctor cleared his throat, clasped his hands behind his back, and began to orate, as if addressing a medical society at Columbia. "It is interesting to speculate on the drugs used to rob a sentient being of her reason, of her will. The ingredients, even the means of administration, are most jealously guarded secrets."

He paced toward the hospital, not looking at Zora, and did not raise his voice as he spoke of herbs and powders, salves and cucumbers, as if certain she walked alongside him, unbidden. Instead she stooped and hefted the branch Felicia had wielded. It was much heavier than she had assumed, so lightly had Felicia snatched it down. Zora tugged at one of its twigs and found the dense, rubbery wood quite resistant. Lucky for the doctor that anger seemed to be among the emotions cooked away. What emotions were left? Fear remained, certainly. And what else?

Zora dropped the branch next to a gouge in the dirt that, as she glanced at it, seemed to resolve itself into the letter M.

"Miss Hurston?" called the doctor from halfway across the yard. "I beg your pardon. You have seen enough, have you not?"

Zora knelt, her hands outstretched as if to encompass, to contain, the scratches that Felicia Felix-Mentor had slashed with the branch. Yes, that was definitely an M, and that vertical slash could be an I, and that next one—

MI HAUT MI BAS

Half high, half low?

Dr. Boas at Barnard liked to say that one began to understand a people only when one began to think in their language. Now, as she knelt in the hospital yard, staring at the words Felicia Felix-Mentor had left in the dirt, a phrase welled from her lips that she had heard often in Haiti but never felt before, a Creole phrase used to mean "So be it," to mean "Amen," to mean "There you have it," to mean whatever one chose it to mean but always conveying a more or less resigned acquiescence to the world and all its marvels.

"Ah bo bo," Zora said.

"Miss Hurston?" The doctor's dusty wingtips entered her vision, stood on the delicate pattern Zora had teased from the dirt, a pattern that began to disintegrate outward from the shoes, as if they produced a breeze or tidal eddy. "Are you suffering perhaps the digestion? Often the peasant spices can disrupt refined systems. Might I have Clement bring you a soda? Or"—and here his voice took on new excitement—"could this be perhaps a feminine complaint?"

"No, thank you, doctor," Zora said as she stood, ignoring his outstretched hand. "May I please, do you think, return tomorrow with my camera?"

She intended the request to sound casual but failed. Not in *Dumballa Calls*, not in *The White King of La Gonave*, not in *The Magic Island*, not in any best-seller ever served up to the Haiti-loving American public had anyone ever included a photograph of a Zombie.

As she held her breath, the doctor squinted and glanced from Zora to the patient and back, as if suspecting the two women of collusion. He loudly sucked a tooth. "It is impossible, madame," he said. "Tomorrow I must away to Port-de-Paix, leaving at dawn and not returning for—"

"It must be tomorrow!" Zora blurted, hastily adding, "because the next day I have an appointment in . . . Petionville." To obscure that slightest of pauses, she gushed, "Oh, Dr. Legros," and dimpled his tailored shoulder with her forefinger. "Until we have the pleasure of meeting again, surely you won't deny me this one small token of your regard?"

Since she was a sprat of thirteen sashaying around the gatepost in Eatonville, slowing Yankees aboil for Winter Park or Sunken Gardens or the Weeki Wachee with a wink and a wave, Zora had viewed sexuality, like other talents, as a bank of backstage switches to be flipped separately or together to achieve specific effects—a spotlight glare, a thunderstorm, the slow, seeping warmth of dawn. Few switches were needed for everyday use, and certainly not for Dr. Legros, who was the most everyday of men.

"But of course," the doctor said, his body ready and still. "Dr. Belfong will expect you, and I will ensure that he extend you every courtesy. And then, Miss Hurston, we will compare travel notes on another day, n'est-ce pas?"

As she stepped onto the veranda, Zora looked back. Felicia Felix-Mentor stood in the middle of the yard, arms wrapped across her torso as if chilled, rocking on the balls of her calloused feet. She was looking at Zora, if at anything. Behind her, a dusty flamingo high-stepped across the yard.

Zora found signboards in Haiti fairly easy to understand in French, but the English ones were a different story. As she wedged herself into a seat in the crowded tap-tap that rattled twice a day between Gonaives and Port-au-Prince, she found herself facing a stern injunction above the grimy, cracked windshield: "Passengers Are Not Permitted To Stand Forward While the Bus Is Either at a Standstill or Approaching in Motion."

As the bus lurched forward, tires spinning, gears grinding, the driver loudly recited: "Dear clients, let us pray to the Good God and to all the most merciful martyrs in heaven that we may be delivered safely unto our chosen destination. Amen."

Amen, Zora thought despite herself, already jotting in her notebook. The beautiful woman in the window seat beside her shifted sideways to give

Zora's elbow more room, and Zora absently flashed her a smile. At the top of the page she wrote, "Felicia Felix-Mentor," the hyphen jagging upward from a pothole. Then she added a question mark and tapped the pencil against her teeth.

Who had Felicia been, and what life had she led? Where was her family? Of these matters, Dr. Legros refused to speak. Maybe the family had abandoned its feeble relative, or worse. The poor woman may have been brutalized into her present state. Such things happened at the hands of family members, Zora knew.

Zora found herself doodling a shambling figure, arms outstretched. Nothing like Felicia, she conceded. More like Mr. Karloff's monster. Several years before, in New York to put together a Broadway production that came to nothing, Zora had wandered, depressed and whimsical, into a Times Square movie theater to see a foolish horror movie titled *White Zombie*. The swaying sugar cane on the poster ("She was not dead . . . She was not alive . . . WHAT WAS SHE?") suggested, however spuriously, Haiti, which even then Zora hoped to visit one day. Bela Lugosi in Mephistophelean whiskers proved about as Haitian as Fannie Hurst, and his Zombies, stalking bug-eyed and stiff-legged around the tatty sets, *all* looked white to Zora, so she couldn't grasp the urgency of the title, whatever Lugosi's designs on the heroine. Raising Zombies just to staff a sugar mill, moreover, struck her as wasted effort, since many a live Haitian (or Floridian) would work a full Depression day for as little pay as any Zombie and do a better job too. Still, she admired how the movie Zombies walked mindlessly to their doom off the parapet of Lugosi's castle, just as the fanatic soldiers of the mad Haitian King Henri Christophe were supposed to have done from the heights of the Citadel LaFerriere.

But suppose Felicia were a Zombie—in Haitian terms, anyway? Not a supernaturally revived corpse, but a sort of combined kidnap and poisoning victim, released or abandoned by her captor, her bocor, after three decades.

Supposedly, the bocor stole a victim's soul by mounting a horse backward, facing the tail, and riding by night to her house. There he knelt on the doorstep, pressed his face against the crack beneath the door, bared his teeth, and *sssssssst!* He inhaled the soul of the sleeping woman, breathed her right into his lungs. And then the bocor would have marched Felicia (so the tales went) past her house the next night, her first night as a Zombie, to prevent her ever recognizing it or seeking it again.

Yet Felicia *had* sought out the family farm, however late. Maybe something had gone wrong with the spell. Maybe someone had fed her salt—the hair-of-the-dog remedy for years-long Zombie hangovers. Where, then, was Felicia's bocor? Why hold her prisoner all this time, but no longer? Had he died, setting his charge free to wander? Had he other charges, other Zombies? How had Felicia become both victim and escapee?

"And how do you like your Zombie, Miss Hurston?"

Zora started. The beautiful passenger beside her had spoken.

"I beg your pardon!" Zora instinctively shut her notebook. "I do not believe we have met, Miss . . . ?"

The wide-mouthed stranger laughed merrily, her opalescent earrings shimmering on her high cheekbones. One ringlet of brown hair spilled onto her forehead from beneath her kerchief, which like her tight-fitting, high-necked dress was an ever-swirling riot of color. Her heavy gold necklace was nearly lost in it. Her skin was two parts cream to one part coffee. Antebellum New Orleans would have been at this woman's feet, in private, behind latched shutters.

"Ah, I knew you did not recognize me, Miss Hurston." Her accent made the first syllable of "Hurston" a prolonged purr. "We met in Archahaie, in the hounfort of Dieu Donnez St. Leger, during the rite of the fishhook of the dead." She bulged her eyes and sat forward slack-jawed, then fell back, clapping her hands with delight, ruby ring flashing, at her passable imitation of a dead man.

"You may call me Freida. It is I, Miss Hurston, who first told you of the Zombie Felix-Mentor."

Their exchange in the sweltering crowd had been brief and confused, but Zora could have sworn that her informant that night had been an older, plainer woman. Still, Zora probably hadn't looked her best, either. The deacons and mothers back home would deny it, but many a worshipper looked better outside church than in.

Zora apologized for her absentmindedness, thanked this—Freida?—for her tip, and told her some of her hospital visit. She left out the message in the dirt, if message it was, but mused aloud: "Today we lock the poor woman away, but who knows? Once she may have had a place of honor, as a messenger touched by the gods."

"No, no, no, no, no, no, no," said Freida in a forceful singsong. "No! The gods did not take her powers away." She leaned in, became conspiratorial. "Some *man*, and only a man, did that. You saw. You know."

Zora, teasing, said, "Ah, so you have experience with men."

"None more," Freida stated. Then she smiled. "Ah bo bo. That is night talk. Let us speak instead of daylight things."

The two women chatted happily for a bouncing half-hour, Freida questioning and Zora answering—talking about her Haiti book, the sights of New York, the smell of the turpentine harvest in the Florida pines. It was good to be questioned herself for a change, after collecting from others all the time. The tap-tap jolted along, ladling dust equally onto all who shared the road: mounted columns of Haitian Guards, shelf-hipped laundresses, half-dead donkeys laden with guinea-grass. The day's shadows lengthened.

"This is my stop," said Freida at length, though the tap-tap showed no signs of slowing, and no stop was visible through the windows, just dense palm groves to either side. Where a less graceful creature would merely have stood, Freida rose, then turned and edged toward the aisle, facing not the front but, oddly, the back of the bus. Zora swiveled in her seat to give her more room, but Freida pressed against her anyway, thrust her pelvis forward against the older woman's bosom. Zora felt Freida's heat through the thin material. Above, Freida flashed a smile, nipped her own lower lip, and chuckled as the pluck of skin fell back into place.

"I look forward to our next visit, Miss Hurston."

"And where might I call on you?" Zora asked, determined to follow the conventions.

Freida edged past and swayed down the aisle, not reaching for the handgrips. "You'll find me," she said, over her shoulder.

Zora opened her mouth to say something but forgot what. Directly in front of the bus, visible through the windshield past Freida's shoulder, a charcoal truck roared into the roadway at right angles. Zora braced herself for the crash. The tap-tap driver screamed with everyone else, stamped the brakes and spun the wheel. With a hellish screech, the bus slewed about in a cloud of dirt and dust that darkened the sunlight, crusted Zora's tongue, and hid the charcoal truck from view. For one long, delirious, nearly sexual moment, the bus tipped sideways. Then it righted itself with a tooth-loosening *slam* that shattered the windshield. In the silence, Zora heard someone sobbing, heard the engine's last faltering cough, heard the front door slide open with its usual clatter. She righted her hat in order to see. The tap-tap and the charcoal truck had come to rest a foot away from one another, side by side and facing opposite directions. Freida, smiling, unscathed, kerchief still angled just so, sauntered down the corridor between the vehicles, one finger trailing along the side of the truck, tracking the dust like a child. She passed Zora's window without looking up, and was gone.

"She pulled in her horizon like a great fish-net. Pulled it from around the waist of the world and draped it over her shoulder. So much of life in its meshes! She called in her soul to come and see."

Mouth dry, head aching from the heat and from the effort of reading her own chicken-scratch, Zora turned the last page of the manuscript, squared the stack and looked up at her audience. Felicia sat on an hourglass root, a baked yam in each hand, gnawing first one, then the other.

"That's the end," Zora said, in the same soft, non-threatening voice with which she had read her novel thus far. "I'm still unsure of the middle," she continued, setting down the manuscript and picking up the Brownie camera, "but I know this is the end, all right, and that's something."

As yam after yam disappeared, Felicia's eyes registered nothing. No matter. Zora always liked to read her work aloud as she was writing, and Felicia was as good an audience as anybody. She was, in fact, the first audience this particular book had had.

While Zora had no concerns whatsoever about sharing her novel with Felicia, she was uncomfortably aware of the narrow Victorian casements above, and felt the attentive eyes of the dying and the mad. On the veranda, a bent old man in a wheelchair mumbled to himself, half-watched by a nurse with a magazine.

In a spasm of experiment, Zora had salted the yams, to no visible effect. This Zombie took salt like an editor took whiskey.

"I'm not in your country to write a novel," Zora told her chewing companion. "Not officially. I'm being paid just to do folklore on this trip. Why, this novel isn't even set in Haiti, ha! So I can't tell the foundation about this quite yet. It's our secret, right, Felicia?"

The hospital matron had refused Zora any of her good china, grudgingly piling bribe-yams onto a scarred gourd-plate instead. Now, only two were left. The plate sat on the ground, just inside Felicia's reach. Chapter by chapter, yam by yam, Zora had been reaching out and dragging the plate just a bit nearer herself, a bit farther away from Felicia. So far, Felicia had not seemed to mind.

Now Zora moved the plate again, just as Felicia was licking the previous two yams off her fingers. Felicia reached for the plate, then froze, when she registered that it was out of reach. She sat there, arm suspended in the air.

"Nnnnn, nnnnn, nnnnn," she said.

Zora sat motionless, cradling her Brownie camera in her lap.

Felicia slid forward on her buttocks and snatched up two yams—choosing to eat them where she now sat, as Zora had hoped, rather than slide backward into the shade once more. Zora took several pictures in the sunlight, though none of them, she later realized, managed to penetrate the shadows beneath Felicia's furrowed brow, where the patient's sightless eyes lurked.

"Zombies!" came an unearthly cry. The old man on the veranda was having a spasm, legs kicking, arms flailing. The nurse moved quickly, propelled his wheelchair toward the hospital door. "I made them all Zombies! Zombies!"

"Observe my powers," said the mad Zombie-maker King Henri Christophe, twirling his stage mustache and leering down at the beautiful young(ish) anthropologist who squirmed against her snakeskin bonds. The mad king's broad white face and syrupy accent suggested Budapest. At his languid gesture, black-and-white legions of Zombies both black and white shuffled into view around the papier-mâché cliff and marched single file up the steps of the balsa parapet, and over. None cried out as he fell. Flipping through his captive's notebook, the king laughed maniacally and said, "I never knew you wrote this! Why, this is *good!*" As Zombies toppled behind him like ninepins, their German Expressionist shadows scudding across his face, the mad king began hammily to read aloud the opening passage of *Imitation of Life.*

Zora woke in a sweat.

The rain still sheeted down, a ceremonial drumming on the slate roof. Her manuscript, a white blob in the darkness, was moving sideways along the desktop. She watched as it went over the edge and dashed itself across the floor with a sound like a gust of wind. So the iguana had gotten in again. It loved messing with her manuscript. She should take the iguana to New York, get it a job at Lippincott's. She isolated the iguana's crouching, bowlegged shape in the drumming darkness and lay still, never sure whether iguanas jumped and how far and why.

Gradually she became aware of another sound nearer than the rain: someone crying.

Zora switched on the bedside lamp, found her slippers with her feet and reached for her robe. The top of her writing desk was empty. The manuscript must have been top-heavy, that's all. Shaking her head at her night fancies, cinching her belt, yawning, Zora walked into the corridor and nearly stepped on the damned iguana as it scuttled just ahead of her, claws clack-clack-clacking on the hardwood. Zora tugged off her left slipper and gripped it by the toe as an unlikely weapon as she followed the iguana into the great room. Her housekeeper, Lucille, lay on the sofa, crying two-handed into a handkerchief. The window above her was open, curtains billowing, and the iguana escaped as it had arrived, scrambling up the back of the sofa and out into the hissing rain. Lucille was oblivious until Zora closed the sash, when she sat up with a start.

"Oh, Miss! You frightened me! I thought the Sect Rouge had come."

Ah, yes, the Sect Rouge. That secret, invisible mountain-dwelling cannibal cult, their distant nocturnal drums audible only to the doomed, whose blood thirst made the Klan look like the Bethune-Cookman board of visitors, was Lucille's most cherished night terror. Zora had never had a housekeeper before, never wanted one, but Lucille "came with the house," as the agent had put it. It was all a package: mountainside view, Sect Rouge paranoia, hot and cold running iguanas.

"Lucille, darling, whatever is the matter? Why are you crying?"

A fresh burst of tears. "It is my faithless husband, madame! My Etienne. He has forsaken me . . . for Erzulie!" She fairly spat the name, as a wronged woman in Eatonville would have spat the infamous name of Miss Delpheeny.

Zora had laid eyes on Etienne only once, when he came flushed and hatless to the back door to show off his prize catch, grinning as widely as the dead caiman he held up by the tail. For his giggling wife's benefit, he had tied a pink ribbon around the creature's neck, and Zora had decided then that Lucille was as lucky a woman as any.

"There, there. Come to Zora. Here, blow your nose. That's better. You needn't tell me any more, if you don't want to. Who is this Erzulie?"

Zora had heard much about Erzulie in Haiti, always from other women, in tones of resentment and admiration, but she was keen for more.

"Oh, madame, she is a terrible woman! She has every man she wants, all the men, and . . . and some of the women, too!" This last said in a hush of reverence. "No home in Haiti is safe from her. First she came to my Etienne in his dreams, teasing and tormenting his sleep until he cried out and spent himself in the sheets. Then she troubled his waking life, too, with frets and ill fortune, so that he was angry with himself and with me all the time. Finally I sent him to the houngan, and the houngan said, 'Why do you ask me what this is? Any child could say to you the truth: You have been chosen as a consort of Erzulie.' And then he embraced my Etienne, and said: 'My son, your bed above all beds is now the one for all men to envy.' Ah, madame, religion is a hard thing for women!"

Even as she tried to console the weeping woman, Zora felt a pang of writerly conscience. On the one hand, she genuinely wanted to help; on the other hand, everything was material.

"Whenever Erzulie pleases, she takes the form that a man most desires, to ride him as dry as a bean husk, and to rob his woman of comfort. Oh, madame! My Etienne has not come to my bed in . . . in . . . *twelve days!*" She collapsed into the sofa in a fresh spasm of grief, buried her head beneath a cushion and began to hiccup. Twelve whole days, Zora thought, my my, as she did her own dispiriting math, but she said nothing, only patted Lucille's shoulder and cooed.

Later, while frying an egg for her dejected, red-eyed housekeeper, Zora sought to change the subject. "Lucille. Didn't I hear you say the other day, when the postman ran over the rooster, something like, 'Ah, the Zombies eat well tonight!'"

"Yes, madame, I think I did say this thing."

"And last week, when you spotted that big spider web just after putting the ladder away, you said, 'Ah bo bo, the Zombies make extra work for me today.' When you say such things, Lucille, what do you mean? To what Zombies do you refer?"

"Oh, madame, it is just a thing to say when small things go wrong. Oh, the milk is sour, the Zombies have put their feet in it, and so on. My mother always says it, and her mother too."

Soon Lucille was chatting merrily away about the little coffee girls and the ritual baths at Saut d'Eau, and Zora took notes and drank coffee, and all was well. Ah bo bo!

The sun was still hours from rising when Lucille's chatter shut off mid-sentence. Zora looked up to see Lucille frozen in terror, eyes wide, face ashen.

"Madame . . . Listen!"

"Lucille, I hear nothing but the rain on the roof."

"Madame," Lucille whispered, "the rain has stopped."

Zora set down her pencil and went to the window. Only a few drops pattered from the eaves and the trees. In the distance, far up the mountain, someone was beating the drums—ten drums, a hundred, who could say? The sound was like thunder sustained, never coming closer but never fading either.

Zora closed and latched the shutters and turned back to Lucille with a smile. "Honey, that's just man-noise in the night, like the big-mouthing on the porch at Joe Clarke's store. You mean I never told you about all the lying that men do back home? Break us another egg, Cille honey, and I'll tell *you* some things."

Box 128-B
Port-au-Prince, Haiti
November 20, 1936

Dr. Henry Allen Moe, Sec.
John Simon Guggenheim Memorial Foundation
551 Fifth Avenue
New York, N.Y.

Dear Dr. Moe,

I regret to report that for all my knocking and ringing and dust-raising, I have found no relatives of this unfortunate Felix-Mentor woman. She is both famous and unknown. All have heard of her and know, or think they know, the two-sentence outline of her "story," and have their own fantasies about her, but can go no further. She is the Garbo of Haiti. I would think her a made-up character had I not seen her myself, and taken her picture as . . . evidence? A photograph of the Empire State Building is evidence, too, but of what? That is for the viewer to say.

I am amused of course, as you were, to hear from some of our friends and colleagues on the Haiti beat their concerns that poor Zora has "gone native," has thrown away the WPA and Jesse Owens and the travel trailer and all the other achievements of the motherland to break chickens and become an initiate in the mysteries of the Sect Rouge. Lord knows, Dr. Moe, I spent twenty-plus years in the Southern U.S., beneath the constant gaze of every First Abyssinian Macedonian African Methodist Episcopal Presbyterian Pentecostal Free Will Baptist Assembly of God of Christ of Jesus with Signs Following minister, mother, and deacon, all so full of the spirit they look like death eating crackers, and in all that time I never once

came down with even a mild case of Christianity. I certainly won't catch
the local disease from only six months in Haiti . . .

Obligations, travel, and illness—"suffering perhaps the digestion," thank you, Dr. Legros—kept Zora away from the hospital at Gonaives for some weeks. When she finally did return, she walked onto the veranda to see Felicia, as before, standing all alone in the quiet yard, her face toward the high wall. Today Felicia had chosen to stand on the sole visible spot of green grass, a plot of soft imprisoned turf about the diameter of an Easter hat. Zora felt a deep satisfaction upon seeing her—this self-contained, fixed point in her traveler's life.

To reach the steps, she had to walk past the mad old man in the wheelchair, whose nurse was not in sight today. Despite his sunken cheeks, his matted eyelashes, his patchy tufts of white hair, Zora could see he must have been handsome in his day. She smiled as she approached.

He blinked and spoke in a thoughtful voice. "I will be a Zombie soon," he said.

That stopped her. "Excuse me?"

"Death came for me many years ago," said the old man, eyes bright, "and I said, No, not me, take my wife instead. And so I gave her up as a Zombie. That gained me five years, you see. A good bargain. And then, five years later, I gave our oldest son. Then our daughter. Then our youngest. And more loved ones, too, now all Zombies, all. There is no one left. No one but me." His hands plucked at the coverlet that draped his legs. He peered all around the yard. "I will be a Zombie soon," he said, and wept.

Shaking her head, Zora descended the steps. Approaching Felicia from behind, as Dr. Legros had said that first day, was always a delicate maneuver. One had to be loud enough to be heard but quiet enough not to panic her.

"Hello, Felicia," Zora said.

The huddled figure didn't turn, didn't budge, and Zora, emboldened by long absence, repeated the name, reached out, touched Felicia's shoulder with her fingertips. As she made contact, a tingling shiver ran up her arm and down her spine to her feet. Without turning, Felicia emerged from her crouch. She stood up straight, flexed her shoulders, stretched her neck, and spoke.

"Zora, my friend!"

Felicia turned and was not Felicia at all, but a tall, beautiful woman in a short white dress. Freida registered the look on Zora's face and laughed.

"Did I not tell you that you would find me? Do you not even know your friend Freida?"

Zora's breath returned. "I know you," she retorted, "and I know that was a cruel trick. Where is Felicia? What have you done with her?"

"Whatever do you mean? Felicia was not mine to give you, and she is not mine to take away. No one is owned by anyone."

"Why is Felicia not in the yard? Is she ill? And why are you here? Are you ill as well?"

Freida sighed. "So many questions. Is this how a book gets written? If Felicia were not ill, silly, she would not have been here in the first place. Besides." She squared her shoulders. "Why do you care so about this . . . powerless woman? This woman who let some man lead her soul astray, like a starving cat behind an eel-barrel?" She stepped close, the heat of the day coalescing around. "Tell a woman of power your book. Tell *me* your book," she murmured. "Tell *me* of the mule's funeral, and the rising waters, and the buzzing pear-tree, and young Janie's secret sigh."

Zora had two simultaneous thoughts, like a moan and a breath interlaced: *Get out of my book!* and *My God, she's jealous!*

"Why bother?" Zora bit off, flush with anger. "You think you know it by heart already. And besides," Zora continued, stepping forward, nose to nose, "there are powers other than yours."

Freida hissed, stepped back as if pattered with stove-grease.

Zora put her nose in the air and said, airily, "I'll have you know that Felicia is a writer, too."

Her mouth a thin line, Freida turned and strode toward the hospital, thighs long and taut beneath her gown. Without thought, Zora walked, too, and kept pace.

"If you must know," Freida said, "your writer friend is now in the care of her family. Her son came for her. Do you find this so remarkable? Perhaps the son should have notified you, hmm?" She winked at Zora. "He is quite a muscular young man, with a taste for older women. Much, *much* older women. I could show you where he lives. I have been there often. I have been there more than he knows."

"How dependent you are," Zora said, "on men."

As Freida stepped onto the veranda, the old man in the wheelchair cringed and moaned. "Hush, child," Freida said. She pulled a nurse's cap from her pocket and tugged it on over her chestnut hair.

"Don't let her take me!" the old man howled. "She'll make me a Zombie! She will! A Zombie!"

"Oh, pish," Freida said. She raised one bare foot and used it to push the wheelchair forward a foot or so, revealing a sensible pair of white shoes on the flagstones beneath. These she stepped into as she wheeled the chair around. "Here is your bocor, Miss Hurston. What use have I for a Zombie's cold hands? Au revoir, Miss Hurston. Zora. I hope you find much to write about in my country . . . however you limit your experiences."

Zora stood at the foot of the steps, watched her wheel the old man away over the uneven flagstones.

"Erzulie," Zora said.

The woman stopped. Without turning, she asked, "What name did you call me?"

"I called you a true name, and I'm telling you that if you don't leave Lucille's Etienne alone, so the two of them can go to hell in their own way, then I . . . well, then I will forget all about you, and you will never be in my book."

Freida pealed with laughter. The old man slumped in his chair. The laughter cut off like a radio, and Freida, suddenly grave, looked down. "They do not last any time, do they?" she murmured. With a forefinger, she poked the back of his head. "Poor pretty things." With a sigh, she faced Zora, gave her a look of frank appraisal, up and down. Then she shrugged. "You are mad," she said, "but you are fair." She backed into the door, shoved it open with her behind, and hauled the dead man in after her.

The tap-tap was running late as usual, so Zora, restless, started out on foot. As long as the road kept going downhill and the sun stayed over yonder, she reasoned, she was unlikely to get lost. As she walked through the countryside, she sang and picked flowers and worked on her book in the best way she knew to work on a book, in her own head, with no paper and indeed no words, not yet. She enjoyed the caution signs on each curve—"La Route Tue et Blesse," or, literally, "The Road Kills And Injures."

She wondered how it felt, to walk naked along a roadside like Felicia Felix-Mentor. She considered trying the experiment, when she realized that night had fallen. (And where was the tap-tap, and all the other traffic, and why was the road so narrow?) But once shed, her dress, her shift, her shoes would be a terrible armful. The only efficient way to carry clothes, really, was to wear them. So thinking, she plodded, footsore, around a sharp curve and nearly ran into several dozen hooded figures in red, proceeding in the opposite direction. Several carried torches, all carried drums, and one had a large, mean-looking dog on a rope.

"Who comes?" asked a deep male voice. Zora couldn't tell which of the hooded figures had spoken, if any.

"Who wants to know?" she asked.

The hoods looked at one another. Without speaking, several reached into their robes. One drew a sword. One drew a machete. The one with the dog drew a pistol, then knelt to murmur into the dog's ear. With one hand he scratched the dog between the shoulder blades, and with the other he gently stroked its head with the moon-gleaming barrel of the pistol. Zora could hear the thump and rustle of the dog's tail wagging in the leaves.

"Give us the words of passage," said the voice, presumably the sword-wielder's, as he was the one who pointed at Zora for emphasis. "Give them to us, woman, or you will die, and we will feast upon you."

"She cannot know the words," said a woman's voice, "unless she too has spoken with the dead. Let us eat her."

Suddenly, as well as she knew anything on the round old world, Zora knew exactly what the words of passage were. Felicia Felix-Mentor had given them to her. *Mi haut, mi bas.* Half high, half low. She could say them now. But she would not say them. She would believe in Zombies, a little, and in Erzulie, perhaps, a little more. But she would not believe in the Sect Rouge, in blood-oathed societies of men. She walked forward again, of her own free will, and the red-robed figures stood motionless as she passed among them. The dog whimpered. She walked down the hill, hearing nothing behind but a growing chorus of frogs. Around the next bend she saw the distant lights of Port-au-Prince and, much nearer, a tap-tap idling in front of a store. Zora laughed and hung her hat on a caution sign. Between her and the bus, the moonlit road was flecked with tiny frogs, distinguished from bits of gravel and bark only by their leaping, their errands of life. Ah bo bo! She called in her soul to come and see.

———

Andy Duncan's *stories have won two World Fantasy Awards and the Theodore Sturgeon Memorial Award and been nominated multiple times for the Hugo, Nebula, Stoker and Shirley Jackson awards. His latest novelettes are a* *supernatural romance set in Western Maryland,* The Night Cache *(PS Publishing, 2009); and "The Dragaman's Bride," a revisionist Appalachian folktale that concludes* The Dragon Book, *edited by Jack Dann and Gardner Dozois (Ace, 2009). His first collection is the award-winning* Beluthahatchie and Other Stories *(Golden Gryphon Press, 2000); a second,* The Pottawatomie Giant and Other Stories, *is forthcoming from PS Publishing. Recently published is a revised and expanded second edition of his non-fiction guidebook* Alabama Curiosities *(Globe Pequot, 2009). A graduate of the Clarion West writing workshop in Seattle, Duncan has taught at both the Clarion and Clarion West workshops; he also teaches interdisciplinary literary seminars on twenty-first-century science fiction and fantasy in the Honors College of the University of Alabama. He is a juror for the 2010 Philip K. Dick Award. Having taught undergraduates for seventeen years, Duncan lives in Frostburg, Maryland, where he is an assistant professor of English at Frostburg State University.*

Andy Duncan was fascinated with Zora Neale Hurston's description and photo of the "zombie" Felicia Felix-Mentor in her 1937 book, *Tell My Horse: Voodoo and Life in Haiti and Jamaica*. He based his fictional Zora on the real author but has noted the story is more about the U.S. pop cultural idea of the zombie from the 1930s and 40s than about Haitian zombies.

[You'll find another story in this volume, Neil Gaiman's *Bitter Grounds*, that references Hurston, too.]

As for the zombie herself, Louis P. Mars, M.D., a professor of psychiatry at the School of Medicine and of Social Psychology at the Institute of Ethnology, Port-au-Prince, in the Republic of Haiti, a Member of the Societe Medico-Psychologique of Paris, and a Haitian Public Health Officer wrote in *Man: A Record of Anthropological Science* (Vol. XLV, no. 22. pp. 38-40. March-April, 1945):

At first [the Mentors, who believed the woman to be a long-dead family member] had based their belief on the fact that the woman was lame. Before the real Felicia Felix Mentor died, she was lame as a result of a fracture of her left leg.

Her physical appearance and lameness in addition to the deep belief in the country that sometimes the dead come back to life, induced the

Mentors to believe that the strange woman was indeed their late sister Felicia.

I made an X-ray examination of both legs at the Central Hospital in Port-au-Prince. There was no evidence of a fracture and the lameness could therefore be attributed to muscular weakness due to undernourishment. This may be said to be the cause since, after she had a normal diet for two months, the lameness disappeared. She also gained weight.

This is evidently a case of schizophrenia and gives us an idea of how cases of similar nature are likely to arouse mass hysteria . . . The case under discussion was reported by Miss Zora Neale Hurston in her book *Tell My Horse*, in which she stated emphatically 'I know that there are Zombis in Haiti. People have been called back from the dead.' This American writer stated specifically that she came back from Haiti with no doubt in regard to popular belief of the Zombi pseudo-science.

Miss Hurston herself, unfortunately, did not go beyond the mass hysteria to verify her information, nor in any way attempt to make a scientific explanation of the case . . .

Dr. Mars doesn't mention it, but Hurston also offered a "scientific explanation" herself: "If science ever gets to the bottom of voodoo in Haiti and Africa, it will be found that some important medical secrets, still unknown to medical science, give it its power, rather than gestures of ceremony." [Hurston, Zora Neale. *Dust Tracks on a Road*. 2nd Ed. (1942: Urbana: University of Illinois Press, 1984, p. 205)]

Obsequy

David J. Schow

Doug Walcott's need for a change of perspective seemed simple: *Haul ass out of Triple Pines, pronto. Start the next chapter of my life. Before somebody else makes the decision for you, in spades.*

He grimly considered the shovel in his grasp, clotted with mulchy grave dirt. Spades, right. It was the moment Doug knew he could not go on digging up dead people, and it was only his first day on the job. Once he had been a teacher, with a teacher's penchant for seeing structure and symbols in everything. Fuck all that, he thought. Time to get out. Time to bail, now.

"I've got to go," he said, almost mumbling, his conviction still tentative.

Jacky Tynan had stepped down from his scoop-loader and ambled over, doffing his helmet and giving his brow a mop. Jacky was a simple, basically honest guy; a spear carrier in the lives of others with more personal color. Content with burgers and beer, satellite TV and dreams of a someday-girlfriend, Jacky was happy in Triple Pines.

"Yo, it's Douglas, right?" Jacky said. Everybody had been introduced shortly after sunrise. "What up?" He peeled his work gloves and rubbed his hands compulsively until tiny black sweatballs of grime dropped away like scattered grains of pepper.

"I've got to go," Doug repeated. "I think I just quit. I've got to tell Coggins I'm done. I've got to get out of here."

"Graves and stuff getting to ya, huh?" said Jacky. "You should give it another day, at least. It ain't so bad."

Doug did not meet Jacky's gaze. His evaluation of the younger man harshened, more in reaction against the locals, the natives, the people who fit into a white trash haven such as Triple Pines. They would hear the word "cemetery" and conclude "huge downer." They would wax prosaic about this job being perverse, therefore unhealthy. To them, digging up long-deceased residents would be that sick stuff. They all acted and reacted strictly according to the playbook of cliché. Their retinue of perception was so predictable that it was almost comically dull. Jacky's tone suggested that he was one of those people with an almost canine empathy to discord; he could smell when something had gone south.

Doug fought to frame some sort of answer. It was not the funereal atmosphere. The stone monuments, the graves, the loam were all exceptionally peaceful. Doug felt no connection to the dearly departed here . . . with one exception, and one was sufficient.

"It's not the work," Doug said. "It's me. I'm overdue to leave this place. The town, not the cemetery. And the money doesn't matter to me any more."

Jacky made a face as though he had whiffed a fart. "You don't want the money, man? Hell, this shit is easier than workin' the paper mill or doin' stamper time at the plant, dude." The Triple Pines aluminum plant had vanished into Chapter Eleven a decade ago, yet locals still talked about it as if it were still a functioning concern.

The people in Triple Pines never saw what was right in front of them. Or they refused to acknowledge anything strange. That was the reason Doug had to eject. He had to jump before he became one of them.

One of them . . .

A week ago, Doug had not been nearly so philosophical. Less than a week from now, and he would question his own sanity.

Craignotti, the job foreman, had seen Jacky and Doug not working-that is to say, not excavating-and already he was humping his trucker bulk over the hilltop to yell at them. Doug felt the urge to just pitch his tools and helmet and run, but his rational side admitted that there were protocols to be followed and channels to be taken. He would finish out his single day, then do some drinking with his workmates, then try to decide whether he could handle one more day. He was supposed to be a responsible adult, and responsible adults adhered to protocol and channels as a way of reinforcing the gentle myth of civilization.

Whoa, dude, piss on all that, Jacky might say. *Just run.* But Jacky rarely wrestled with such complexities. Doug turned to meet Craignotti with the fatalism of a man who has to process a large pile of tax paperwork.

A week ago, things had been different. Less than a week from now, these exhumations would collide with every one of them, in ways they could not possibly predict.

Frank Craignotti was one of those guys who loved their beer, Doug had observed. The man had a *relationship* with his Pilsner glass, and rituals to limn his interaction with it. Since Doug had started haunting Callahan's, he had seen Craignotti in there every night—same stool at the end of the bar, same three pitchers of tap beer, which he emptied down his neck in about an hour-and-a-half. Word was that Craignotti had been a long-haul big-rig driver for a major nationwide chain of discount stores, until the company pushed him to the sidelines on account of his disability. He had stepped down from the cab of his sixteen-wheeler on a winding mountain road outside of Triple Pines (for reasons never explained; probably to relieve himself among Nature's bounty) and had been sideswiped by a car that never saw him standing there in the rain. Presently he walked with a metal cane because after his surgery one leg had come up shorter than the other. There were vague noises of lawsuits and settlements. That had all happened before Doug wound up inside Callahan's as a regular, and so it maintained the tenuous validity of small-town gossip. It was as good a story as any.

Callahan's presented a nondescript face to the main street of Triple Pines, its stature noted solely by a blue neon sign that said BAR filling up most of a window whose sill probably had not been dusted since 1972. There was a roadhouse fifteen miles to the north, technically "out of town," but its weak diversions were not worth the effort. Callahan's flavor was mostly clover-colored Irish horse apples designed to appeal to all the usual expectations. Sutter, the current owner and the barman on most weeknights, had bought the place when the original founders had wised up and gotten the hell out of Triple Pines. Sutter was easy to make up a story about. To Doug he looked like a career criminal on the run who had found his perfect hide in Triple Pines. The scar bisecting his lower lip had probably come from a knife fight. His skin was like mushrooms in the fridge the day before you decide to throw them out. His eyes were set back in his skull, socketed deep in bruise-colored shadow.

Nobody in Triple Pines really knew anything bona fide about anybody else, Doug reflected.

Doug's first time into the bar as a drinker was his first willful act after quitting his teaching job at the junior high school that Triple Pines shared with three other communities. All pupils were bussed in from rural route pickups. A year previously, he had effortlessly scored an emergency credential and touched down as a replacement instructor for History and Geography, though he took no interest in politics unless they were safely in the past. It was a rote gig that mostly required him to ramrod disinterested kids through memorizing data that they forgot as soon as they puked it up on the next test. He had witnessed firsthand how the area, the towns, and the school system worked to crush initiative, abort insight, and nip talent. The model for the Triple Pines secondary educational system seemed to come from some early 1940s playbook, with no imperative to change anything. The kids here were all white and mostly poor to poverty level, disinterested and leavened to dullness. Helmets for the football team always superseded funds for updated texts. It was the usual, spirit-deflating story. Doug spent the term trying to kick against this corpse, hoping to provoke life signs. Past the semester break, he was just hanging on for the wage. Then, right as summer vacation loomed, Shiela Morgan had deposited herself in the teacher's lounge for a conference.

Doug had looked up from his newspaper. The local rag was called the *Pine Grove Messenger* (after the adjacent community). It came out three times weekly and was exactly four pages long. Today was Victoria Day in Canada. This week's Vocabulary Building Block was "ameliorate."

"Sheila," he said, acknowledging her, not really wanting to. She was one of the many hold-backs in his classes. Hell, many of Triple Pines' junior high schoolers already drove their own cars to battle against the citadel of learning.

"Don't call me that," Sheila said. "My name's *Brittany*."

Doug regarded her over the top of the paper. They were alone in the room. "Really."

"Totally," she said. "I can have my name legally changed. I looked it up. I'm gonna do it, too. I don't care what anybody says."

Pause, for bitter fulfillment: One of his charges had actually *looked something up*.

Further pause, for dismay: Sheila had presented herself to him wearing a shiny vinyl mini as tight as a surgeon's glove, big-heeled boots that laced to the knee, and a leopard top with some kind of boa-like fringe framing her breasts. There was a scatter of pimples between her collarbones. She had ratty black hair and too much eye kohl. Big lipstick that had tinted her teeth pink. She resembled a hillbilly's concept of a New York streetwalker, and she was all of fourteen-years-old.

Mara Corday, Doug thought. *She looks like a Goth-slut version of Mara Corday. I am a dead man.*

Chorus girl and pin-up turned B-movie *femme fatale*, Mara Corday had decorated some drive-in low-budgeters of the late 1950s. *Tarantula. The Giant Claw. The Black Scorpion.* She had been a Playboy Playmate and familiar of Clint Eastwood. Sultry and sex-kittenish, she had signed her first studio contract while still a teenager. She, too, had changed her name.

Sheila wanted to be looked at, and Doug avoided looking. At least her presentation was a relief from the third-hand, Sears & Roebuck interpretation of banger and skatepunk styles that prevailed among most of Triple Pines other adolescents. In that tilted moment, Doug realized what he disliked about the dunnage of rap and hip-hop: all those super-badasses looked like they were dressed in gigantic baby clothes. Sheila's ass was broader than the last time he had not-looked. Her thighs were chubbing. The trade-off was bigger tits. Doug's heartbeat began to accelerate.

Why am I looking?

"Sheila—"

"*Brittany.*" She threw him a pout, then softened it, to butter him up. "Lissen, I wanted to talk to you about that test, the one I missed? I wanna take it over. Like, not to cheat it or anything, but just to kinda . . . take it over, y'know? Pretend like that's the *first* time I took it?"

"None of the other students get that luxury, and you know that."

She fretted, shifting around in her seat, her skirt making squeaky noises against the school-issue plastic chair. "I know, I know, like, right? That's like, totally not usual, I know, so that's why I thought I'd ask you about it first?"

Sheila spent most of her schooling fighting to maintain a low C-average. She had won a few skirmishes, but the war was already a loss.

"I mean, like, you could totally do a new test, and I could like study for it, right?"

"You should have studied for the original test in the first place."

She wrung her hands. "I know, I know that, but . . . well let's just say it's a lot of bullshit, parents and home and alla that crap, right? I couldn't like do it then but I could now. My mom finds out I blew off the test, she'll beat the shit outta me."

"Shouldn't you be talking to a counselor?"

"Yeah, right? No thanks. I thought I'd like go right to the source, right? I mean, you like me and stuff, right?" She glanced toward the door, revving up for some kind of Big Moment that Doug already dreaded. "I mean, I'm flexible; I thought that, y'know, just this one time. I'd do anything. Really. To fix it. Anything."

She uncrossed her legs, from left on right to right on left, taking enough time to make sure Doug could see she had neglected to factor undergarments into her abbreviated ensemble. The move was so studied that Doug knew exactly which movie she had gotten it from.

There are isolated moments in time that expand to gift you with a glimpse of the future, and in that moment Doug saw his tenure at Triple Pines take a big centrifugal swirl down the cosmic toilet. The end of life as he knew it was embodied in the bit of anatomy that Sheila referred to as her "cunny."

"You can touch it if you want. I won't mind." She sounded as though she was talking about a bizarre pet on a leash.

Doug had hastily excused himself and raced to the bathroom, his four-page newspaper folded up to conceal the fact that he was strolling the hallowed halls of the school, semi-erect. He rinsed his face in a basin and regarded himself in a scabrous mirror. *Time to get out. Time to bail. Now.*

He flunked Sheila, and jettisoned himself during summer break, never quite making it to the part where he actually *left* Triple Pines. Later he heard Sheila's mom had gone ballistic and put her daughter in the emergency ward at the company clinic for the paper mill, where her father had worked since he was her age. Local residual scuttlebutt had it that Sheila had gotten out of the hospital and mated with the first guy she could find who owned a car. They blew town like fugitives and were arrested several days later. Ultimately, she used her pregnancy to force the guy to sell his car to pay for her train fare to some relative's house in the Dakotas, end of story.

Which, naturally, was mostly hearsay anyway. Bar talk. Doug had become a regular at Callahan's sometime in early July of that year, and by mid-August he looked at himself in another mirror and thought, *you bagged your job and now you have a drinking problem, buddy. You need to get out of this place.*

That was when Craignotti had eyeballed him. Slow consideration at reptile brain-speed. He bombed his glass at a gulp and rose; he was a man who always squared his shoulders when he stood up, to advise the talent of the room just how broad his chest was. He stumped over to Doug without his walking stick, to prove he didn't really need it. He signaled Sutter, the cadaverous bartender, to deliver his next pitcher of brew to the stool next to Doug's.

After some preliminary byplay and chitchat, Craignotti beered himself to within spitting distance of having a point. "So, you was a teacher at the junior high?"

"Ex-teacher. Nothing bad. I just decided I had to relocate."

"Ain't what I heard." Every time Craignotti drank, his swallows were half-glass capacity. One glassful, two swallows, rinse and repeat. "I heard you porked one of your students. That little slut Sheila Morgan."

"Not true."

Craignotti poured Doug a glass of beer to balance out the Black Jack he was consuming, one slow finger at a time. "Naah, it ain't what you think. I ain't like that. Those little fucking whores are outta control anyway. They're fucking in goddamned grade school, if they're not all crackheads by then."

"The benefits of our educational system." Doug toasted the air. If you drank enough, you could see lost dreams and hopes, swirling there before your nose, demanding sacrifice and tribute.

"Anyhow, point is that you're not working, am I right?"

"That is a true fact." Doug tasted the beer. It chased smooth.

"You know Coggins, the undertaker here?"

"Yeah." Doug had to summon the image. Bald guy, ran the Triple Pines funeral home and maintained the Hollymount Cemetery on the outskirts of town. Walked around with his hands in front of him like a preying mantis.

"Well, I know something a lotta people around here don't know yet. Have you heard of the Marlboro Reservoir?" It was the local project that would not die. It had last been mentioned in the *Pine Grove Messenger* over a year previously.

"I didn't think that plan ever cleared channels."

"Yeah, well, it ain't for you or me to know. But they're gonna build it. And there's gonna be a lotta work. Maybe bring this shithole town back to life."

"But I'm leaving this shithole town," said Doug. "Soon. So you're telling me this because—?"

"Because you look like a guy can keep his trap shut. Here's the deal: this guy Coggins comes over and asks me to be a foreman. For what, I say. And he says—now get this—in order to build the reservoir, for some reason I don't know about, they're gonna have to move the cemetery to the other side of Pine Grove—six fucking miles. So he needs guys to dig up all the folks buried in the cemetery, and catalogue 'em, and bury 'em again on the other side of the valley. Starts next Monday. The pay is pretty damned good for the work, and almost nobody needs to know about it. I ain't about to hire these fucking deadbeats around here, these dicks with the muscle cars, 'cept for Jacky Tynan, 'cos he's a good worker and don't ask questions. So I thought, I gotta find me a few more guys that are, like, responsible, and since you're leaving anyhow . . . "

Long story short, that's how Doug wound up manning a shovel. The money was decent and frankly, he needed the bank. "Answer me one question, though," he said to Craignotti. "Where did you get all that shit about Sheila Morgan, I mean, why did you use that to approach me?"

"Oh, that," said Craignotti. "She told me. Was trying to trade some tight little puddy for a ride outta town." Craignotti had actually said puddy, like Sylvester the Cat. *I tot I taw* . . . "I laughed in her face; I said, what, d'you think I'm some kinda baby-raper? I woulda split her in half. She threw a fit and went off and fucked a bunch of guys who were less discriminating. Typical small-time town-pump *scheiss*. She musta lost her cherry when she was twelve. So I figured you and me had something in common—we're probably the only two men in town who haven't plumbed *that* hole. Shit, we're so fucking honest, folks around here will think we're queer."

Honor and ethics, thought Doug. Wonderful concepts, those were.

There were more than a thousand graves in Hollymount Cemetery, dating back to the turn of the nineteenth century. Stones so old that names had weathered to vague indentations in granite. Plots with no markers. Minor vandalism. The erosion of time and climate. Coggins, the undertaker, had collated a master name sheet and stapled it to a gridded map of the cemetery, presenting the crew picked by Craignotti with a problem rather akin to solving a huge crossword puzzle made out of dead people. Doug paged through the list until he found Michelle Farrier's name. He had attended her funeral, and sure enough—she was still here.

After his divorce from Marianne (the inevitable ex-wife), he had taken to the road, but had read enough Kerouac to know that the road held nothing for him. A stint as a blackjack dealer in Vegas. A teaching credential from L.A.; he was able to put that in his pocket and take it anywhere. Four months after his arrival in Triple Pines, he attended the funeral of the only friend he had sought to develop locally—Michelle Farrier, a runner just like him.

In the afterblast of an abusive and ill-advised marriage, Michelle had come equipped with a six-year-old daughter named Rochelle. Doug could easily see the face of the mother in the child, the younger face that had taken risks and sought adventure and brightened at the prospect of sleeping with rogues. Michelle had touched down in Triple Pines two months away from learning she was terminally ill. Doug had met them during a seriocomic bout of bathroom-sharing at Mrs. Ives' rooming house, shortly before he had rented a two-bedroom that had come cheap because there were few people in town actively seeking better lodgings, and fewer who could afford to move up. Michelle remained game, as leery as Doug of getting involved, and their gradually kindling passion filled their evenings with a delicious promise. In her kiss lurked a hungry romantic on a short tether, and Doug was working up the nerve to invite her and Rochelle to share his new home when the first talk of doctor visits flattened all other concerns to secondary status. He watched her die. He tried his best to explain it to Rochelle. And Rochelle was removed, to grandparents somewhere in the Bay Area. She wept when she said goodbye to Doug. So had Michelle.

Any grave but that one, thought Doug. *Don't make me dig that one up. Make that someone else's task.*

He knew enough about mortuary tradition to know it was unusual for an undertaker like Coggins to also be in charge of the cemetery. However, small, remote towns tend not to view such a monopoly on the death industry as a negative thing. Coggins was a single stranger for the populace to trust, instead of several. Closer to civilization, the particulars of chemical supply, casket sales, and the mortician's craft congregated beneath the same few conglomerate umbrellas, bringing what had been correctly termed a "Tru-Value hardware" approach to what was being called the "death industry" by the early 1990s. Deceased Americans had become a cash crop at several billion dollars per annum . . . not counting the flower arrangements. Triple Pines still believed in the mom-and-pop market, the corner tavern, the one-trade-fits-all handyman.

Doug had been so appalled at Michelle's perfunctory service that he did a bit of investigative reading-up. He discovered that most of the traditional accoutrements of the modern funeral were aimed at one objective above all—keeping morticians and undertakers in business. Not, as most people supposed, because of obscure health imperatives, or a misplaced need for ceremony, or even that old favorite, religious ritual. It turned out to be one of the three or four most expensive costs a normal citizen could incur during the span of an average, conventional life—another reason weddings and funerals seemed bizarrely similar. It was amusing to think how simply the two could be confused. Michelle would have been amused, at least. She had rated one of each, neither very satisfying.

Doug would never forget Rochelle's face, either. He had gotten to play the role of father to her for about a week and change, and it had scarred him indelibly. Given time, her loss, too, was a strangely welcome kind of pain.

Legally, disinterment was a touchy process, since the casket containing the remains was supposed to be technically "undamaged" when removed from the earth. This meant Jacky and the other backhoe operators could only skim to a certain depth—the big scoops—before Doug or one of his co-workers had to jump in with a shovel. Some of the big concrete grave liners were stacked three deep to a plot; at least, Craignotti had said something about three being the limit. They looked like big, featureless refrigerators laid on end, and tended to crumble like plaster. Inside were the burial caskets. Funeral publicists had stopped calling them coffins about forty years ago. "Coffins" were boxes shaped to the human form, wide at the top, slim at the bottom, with the crown shaped like the top half of a hexagon. "Coffins" evoked morbid assumptions, and so were replaced in the vernacular with "caskets"—nice, straight angles, with no Dracula or Boot Hill associations. In much the same fashion, "cemeteries" had become "memorial parks." People did everything they could, it seemed, to deny the reality of death.

Which explained the grave liners. Interment in coffins, caskets, or anything else from a wax-coated cardboard box to a shroud generally left a concavity in the lawn, once the body began to decompose, and its container, to collapse. In the manner of a big, mass-produced, cheap sarcophagus, the concrete grave liners prevented the depressing sight of . . . er, depressions. Doug imagined them to be manufactured by the same place that turned out highway divider berms; the damned things weighed about the same.

Manning his shovel, Doug learned a few more firsthand things about graves. Like how it could take eight hours for a single digger, working alone, to excavate a plot to the proper dimensions. Which was why Craignotti had been forced to locate operators for no fewer than three backhoes on this job. Plus seven "scoopers" in Doug's range of ability. The first shift, they only cleared fifty final resting-places. From then on, they would aim for a hundred stiffs per working day.

Working. Stiffs. Rampant, were the opportunities for gallows humor.

Headstones were stacked as names were checked off the master list.

BEECHER, LEE, 1974-2002—HE PROTECTED AND SERVED. GUDGELL, CONROY, 1938-2003—DO NOT GO GENTLY. These were newer plots, more recent deaths. These were people who cared about things like national holidays or presidential elections, archetypal Americans from fly-over country. But in their midst, Doug was also a cliché—the drifter, the stranger. If the good folk of Triple Pines (the living ones, that is) sensed discord in their numbers, they would actively seek out mutants to scotch. Not One of Us.

He had to get out. Just this job, just a few days, and he could escape. It was better than being a mutant, and perhaps getting lynched. He moved on to STOWE, DORMAND R., 1940-1998—LOVING HUSBAND, CARING FATHER. Not so recent. Doug felt a little bit better.

They broke after sunset. That was when Doug back-checked the dig list and found a large, red X next to Michelle Farrier's name.

"This job ain't so damned secret," said Joe Hopkins, later, at Callahan's. Their after-work table was five: Joe, Jacky, Doug, and two more guys from the shift, Miguel Ayala and Boyd Cooper. Craignotti sat away from them, at his accustomed roost near the end of the bar. The men were working on their third pitcher. Doug found that no amount of beer could get the taste of grave dirt out of the back of his throat. Tomorrow, he'd wear a bandana. *Maybe.*

"You working tomorrow, or not, or what?" said Craignotti. Doug gave him an if-come answer, and mentioned the bandana. Craignotti had shrugged. In that moment, it all seemed pretty optional, so Doug concentrated on becoming mildly drunk with a few of the crew working the—heh—graveyard shift.

Joe was a musclebound ex-biker type who always wore a leather vest and was rarely seen without a toothpick jutting from one corner of his mouth. He had cultivated elaborate moustaches which he waxed. He was going gray at the temples. His eyes were dark, putting Doug in mind of a gypsy. He continued: "What I mean is, nobody's supposed to know about this little relocation. But they guys in here know, even if they don't talk about it. The guys who run the Triple Pines bank sure as shit know. It's a public secret. Nobody talks about it, is all."

"I bet the mayor's in on it, too," said Miguel. "All in, who cares? I mean, I had to pick mushrooms once for a buck a day. This sure beats the shit out of that."

"Doesn't bother you?" said Boyd Cooper, another of the backhoe jockeys.

Older, pattern baldness, big but not heavy. Bull neck and cleft chin. His hands had seen a lifetime of manual labor. It had been Boyd who showed them how to cable the lids off the heavy stone grave liners, instead of bringing in the crane rig used to emplace them originally. This group's unity as mutual outcasts gave them a basic common language, and Boyd always cut to the gristle. "Digging up dead people?"

"Nahh," said Jacky, tipping his beer. "We're doing them a favor. Just a kind of courtesy thing. Moving 'em so they won't be forgotten."

"I guess," said Joe, working his toothpick. He burnished his teeth a lot with it. Doug noticed one end was stained with a speck of blood, from his gums.

"You're the teacher," Boyd said to Doug. "You tell us. Good thing or bad thing?"

Doug did not want to play arbiter. "Just a job of work. Like re-sorting old files. You notice how virtually no one in Triple Pines got cremated? They were all buried. That's old-fashioned, but you have to respect the dead. Laws and traditions."

"And the point is . . . ?" Boyd was looking for validation.

"Well, not everybody is entitled to a piece of property when they die, six by three by seven. That's too much space. Eventually we're going to run out of room for all our dead people. Most plots in most cemeteries are rented, and there's a cap on the time limit, and if somebody doesn't pay up, they get mulched. End of story."

"Wow, is that true?" said Jacky. "I thought you got buried, it was like, forever."

"Stopped being that way about a hundred years ago," said Doug. "Land is worth too much. You don't process the dead and let them use up your real estate without turning a profit."

Miguel said, "That would be un-American." He tried for a chuckle but it died.

"Check it out if you don't believe me," said Doug. "Look it up. Behind all that patriotic rah-rah-rah about community brotherhood and peaceful gardens, it's all about capital gains. Most people don't like to think about funerals or cemeteries because, to them, it's morbid. That leaves funeral directors free to profiteer."

"You mean Coggins?" said Joe, giving himself a refill.

"Look, Coggins is a great example," said Doug. "In the outside world, big companies have incorporated most aspects of the funeral. Here, Coggins runs the mortuary, the cemetery, everything. He can charge whatever he wants, and people will pay for the privilege of shunting their grief and confusion onto him. You wouldn't believe the mark-up on some of this stuff. Caskets are three times wholesale. Even if they put you in a cardboard box—which is called an 'alternative container,' by the way—the charge is a couple of hundred bucks."

"Okay, that settles it," said Miguel. When he smiled big, you could see his gold tooth. "We all get to live forever, because we can't afford to die."

"There used to be a riddle," said Doug. "What is it: the man who made it didn't want it, the man who bought it had no use for it, and the man who used it didn't know it. What is it?"

Jacky just looked confused.

His head honeycombed with domestic beer, Doug tried not to lurch or slosh as he navigated his way out of Callahan's. The voice coming at him out of the fogbound darkness might well have been an aural hallucination. Or a wish fulfillment.

"Hey stranger," it said. "Walk a lady home?"

The night yielded her to him. She came not as he had fantasized, nor as he had seen her in dreams. She wore a long-sleeved, black, lacy thing with a neck-wrap collar, and her hair was up. She looked different but her definitive jawline and frank, gray gaze were unmistakable.

"That's not you," he said. "I'm a tiny bit intoxicated, but not enough to believe it's you." Yet. There was no one else on the street to confirm or deny; no validation from fellow inebriates or corroboration from independent bystanders. Just Doug, the swirling night, and a woman who could not be the late Michelle Farrier, whom he had loved. He had only accepted that he loved her after she died. It was more tragic that way, more delusionally romanticist. Potent enough to wallow in. A weeper, produced by his brain while it was buzzing with hops and alcohol.

She bore down on him, moving into focus, and that made his grief worse. "Sure it's me," she said. "Look at me. Take a little bit of time to get used to the idea."

He drank her in as though craving a narcotic. Her hair had always been long, burnished sienna, deftly razor-thinned to layers that framed her face. Now it was pinned back to exhibit her gracile neck and bold features. He remembered the contour of her ears. She smiled, and he remembered exactly how her teeth set. She brought with her the scent of night-blooming jasmine. If she was a revenant, she had come freighted with none of the corruption of the tomb. If she was a mirage, the light touch of her hand on his wrist should not have felt so corporeal.

Her touch was not cold.

"No," said Doug. "You died. You're gone."

"Sure, darling—I don't deny that. But now I'm back, and you should be glad."

He was still shaking his head. "I *saw* you die. I helped *bury* you."

"And today, you helped un-bury me. Well, your buddies did."

She had both hands on him, now. This was the monster movie moment when her human visage melted away to reveal the slavering ghoul who wanted to eat his brain and wash it down with a glass of his blood. Her sheer *presence* almost buckled his knees.

"How?"

"Beats me," she said. "We're coming back all over town. I don't know exactly how it all works, yet. But that stuff I was buried in—those *cerements*—were sort of depressing. I checked myself out while I was cleaning up. Everything seems to be n place. Everything works. Except for the tumor; that kind of withered away to an inert little knot, in the grave. I know this is tough for you to swallow, but I'm here, and goddammit, I missed you, and I thought you'd want to see me."

"I think about you every day," he said. It was still difficult to meet her gaze, or to speed-shift from using the accustomed past tense.

"Come on," she said, linking arms with him.

"Where?" Without delay his guts leaped at the thought that she wanted to take him back to the cemetery.

"Wherever. Listen, do you recall kissing me? See if you can remember how we did that."

She kissed him with all the passion of the long-lost, regained unexpectedly. It was Michelle, all right-alive, breathing, returned to him whole.

No one had seen them. No one had come out of the bar. No pedestrians. Triple Pines tended to roll up the sidewalks at 7:00 PM.

"This is . . . nuts," he said.

She chuckled. "As long as you don't say it's distasteful." She kissed him again. "And of course you remember that other thing we never got around to doing?"

"Antiquing that roll-top desk you liked, at the garage sale?" His humor was helping him balance. His mind still wanted to swoon, or explode.

"Ho, ho, very funny. I am so glad to see you right now that I'll spell it out for you, Doug." She drew a tiny breath of consideration, working up nerve, then puffed it out. "Okay: I want to hold your cock in my hand and feel you get hard, *for me*. That was the dream, right? That first attraction, where you always visualize the other person naked, fucking you, while your outer self pretends like none of that matters?"

"I didn't think that," Doug fibbed. Suddenly his breath would not draw.

"Yes you did," Michelle said. "I did, too. But I was too chicken to act. That's all in the past." She stopped and smacked him lightly on the arm. "Don't give me that lopsided look, like *I'm* the one that's crazy. Not now. Not after I died, thinking you were the best damned thing I'd found in a long time."

"Well, there was Rochelle," said Doug, remembering how cautiously they had behaved around her six-year-old daughter.

"My little darling is not here right now," she said. "I'd say it's time to fulfill the fantasy, Doug. Mine, if not yours. We've wasted enough life, and not everybody gets a bonus round."

"But—" Doug's words, his protests had bottlenecked between his lungs. (And for-crap-sake *why* did he feel the urge to *protest* this?)

"I know what you're trying to say. I died." Another impatient huff of breath—living breath. "I can't explain it. I don't know if it's temporary. But I'll tell you one thing I do know: All that shit about the 'peace' of the grave? It doesn't exist. It's not a release, and it's not oblivion. It's like a nightmare that doesn't conveniently end when you wake up, because you're not *supposed* to wake up, ever! And you know what else? When you're in the grave, you can hear every goddamned footfall of the living, above you. Trust me on that one."

"Jesus . . . " he said.

"Not Jesus. Neither Heaven nor Hell. Not God. Not Buddha, not Allah, not Yahweh. Nothing. That's what waits on the other side of that headstone. No pie in the sky by and by when you die. No Nirvana. No Valhalla. No Tetragrammaton. No Zeus or Jove or any of their buddies. Nothing. Maybe that's why we're coming back-there's nothing out there, beyond. Zero. Not even an echo. So kiss me again. I've been cold and I've been still, and I need to make love to you. Making love; that sounds like we're manufacturing something, doesn't it? Feel my hand. There's living blood in there. Feel my heart; it's pumping again. I've felt bad things moving around inside of me.

That happens when you're well and truly dead. Now I'm back. And I want to feel other things moving around inside of me. You."

Tomorrow, Doug would get fired as a no-show after only one day on the job. Craignotti would replace him with some guy named Dormand R. Stowe, rumored to be a loving husband and a caring father.

One of the most famous foreign pistols used during the Civil War was the Le Mat Revolver, a cap and ball weapon developed by a French-born New Orleans doctor, unique in that it had two barrels—a cylinder which held nine .40 caliber rounds fired through the upper barrel, and revolved around the lower, .63 caliber barrel, which held a charge of 18 or 20-gauge buckshot. With a flick of the thumb, the shooter could re-align the hammer to fall on the lower barrel, which was essentially a small shotgun, extremely deadly at close range, with a kick like an enraged mule. General J.E.B. Stuart had carried one. So had General P.G.T. Beauregard. As an antique firearm, such guns in good condition were highly prized. Conroy Gudgell cherished his; it was one of the stars of his modest home arsenal, which he always referred to as his "collection." His big mistake was showing his wife how to care for it. How to clean it. How to load it. How to fire it, you know, "just in case." No one was more surprised than Conroy when his loving wife, a respected first-grade teacher in Triple Pines, blew him straight down to Hell with his own collectible antique.

Ellen Gudgell became a widow at sixty-one years of age. She also became a Wiccan. She was naked, or "sky-clad," when she burned the braided horsehair whip in her fireplace after murdering Conroy. Firing the Le Mat had broken her right wrist; she'd had to make up a story about that. With her left hand she had poured herself a nice brandy, before working herself up into enough lather to phone the police, in tears, while most of Conroy's head and brains were cooling in various corners of his basement workshop. A terrible accident, oh my lord, it's horrible, please come. She kept all the stuff about Earth Mother religious revelations to herself.

She treated Constable Dickey (Triple Pines' head honcho of law enforcement) as she would one of her elementary school charges. Firm but fair. Matronly, but with just the right salting of manufactured hysteria. Conroy had been working with his gun collection in the basement when she heard a loud boom, she told the officer. She panicked and broke her wrist trying to move what was left of him, and now she did not know what to do, and she needed help.

And the local cops had quite neatly taken care of all the rest. Ellen never had to mention the beatings she had suffered under the now-incinerated whip, or that the last fifteen years of their sex life had consisted mostly of rape. When not teaching school, she used her free time—that is, her time free of Conroy's oppression—to study up on alternate philosophies, and when she found one that made sense to her, it wasn't long before she decided to assert her new self.

After that, the possibilities seemed endless. She felt as though she had shed a chrysalis and evolved to a form that made her happier with herself.

Therefore, no one was more surprised than Ellen when her husband Conroy thumped up the stairs, sundered head and all, to come a-calling more than a year after she thought she had definitively killed the rotten sonofabitch. His face looked exactly as it had when Coggins, the undertaker, had puttied and waxed it back into a semblance of human, dark sub-dermal lines inscribing puzzle pieces in rough assembly. The parts did not move in correct concert when Conroy spoke to her, however. His face was disjointed and broken, his eyes, oddly fixed.

"Time for some loving," is what Conroy said to her first.

Ellen ran for the gun cabinet, downstairs.

"Already thought of that," said Conroy, holding up the Le Mat.

He did not shoot her in the head.

Despite the fact that Lee Beecher's death had been inadvertent, one of those Act of God things, Constable Lon Dickey had always felt responsible. Lee had been a hometown boy, Dickey had liked him, and made him his deputy; ergo, Lee had been acting as a representative of the law on Dickey's behalf, moving a dead deer out of the middle of the road during a storm. Some local asshole had piled into the animal and left it for dead, which constituted Triple Pines' only known form of hit-and-run. If you'd had to guess the rest of the story, Dickey thought, you'd say *and another speeding nitwit had hit Lee*. Nope. Struck by lightning, for Christ's sake. Hit by a thunderbolt out of the ozone and killed deader than snakeshit on the spot, fried from the inside out, cooked and discarded out near the lumber yard which employed about a quarter of Triple Pines' blue-collar workforce.

Lee had been buried in his uniform. A go-getter, that kid. Good footballer. Instead of leaving Triple Pines in his rearward dust, as so many youngsters ached to do, Lee had stuck close to home, and enthusiastically sought his badge.

It was worth it to him to be called an "officer," like Dickey. Death in Triple Pines was nearly always accidental, or predictable—no mystery. This was not the place where murderers or psychos lived. In this neck of the woods, the worst an officer might have to face would be the usual rowdiness—teenagers, or drunks, or drunk teenagers—and the edict to act all authoritative if there was a fire or flood or something naturally disastrous.

Beecher's replacement was a guy named James Trainor, shit-hot out of the academy in Seattle and fulminating to enforce. Too stormtrooper for Triple Pines; too ready to pull his sidearm for a traffic stop. Dickey still had not warmed up to him, smelling the moral pollution of citified paranoia.

Feeling like a lazy lion surveying his domain, Dickey had sauntered the two blocks back to the station from the Ready-Set Dinette, following his usual cheeseburger late-lunch. (The food at Callahan's, a block further, was awful—the burgers as palatable as pucks sliced off a Duraflame log.) Time to trade some banter with RaeAnn, who ran the police station's desk, phones and radios. RaeAnn was a stocky chunk of bottle-blond business with multiple chins and an underbite, whose choice of corrective eyewear did not de-emphasize her Jimmy Durante nose. In no way was RaeAnn a temptation, and Dickey preferred that. Strictly business. RaeAnn was fast, efficient, and did not bring her problems to work. Right now she was leaning back at her station with her mouth wide open, which seemed strange. She resembled a gross caricature of one of those mail-order blowjob dolls.

Before he could ask what the hell, Dickey saw the bullet hole in the center of her forehead. Oh.

"Sorry I'm a little bit late, Chief," said Lee Beecher. He had grave dirt all over his moldy uniform, and his face was the same flash-fried nightmare that had caused Coggins to recommend a closed-casket service. Beecher had always called Dickey "Chief."

Deputy Trainor was sprawled behind Dickey's desk, his cap over his eyes, his tongue sticking out, and a circlet of five .357 caliber holes in his chest. Bloodsmear on the bulletin board illustrated how gracelessly he had fallen, hit so hard one of his boots had flown off. The late Lee Beecher had been reloading his revolver when Dickey walked in.

"I had to shoot RaeAnn, she was making too much bother," said Beecher. His voice was off, dry and croaky, buzzing like a reed.

Dickey tried to contain his slow awe by muttering the names of assorted deities. His hand wanted to feel the comfort of his own gun.

"How come you replaced me, Chief?" said the late Lee Beecher. "Man, I didn't quit or nothing. You replaced me with some city boy. That wasn't our deal. I thought you liked me."

"I—" Dickey stammered. "Lee, I . . . " He just could not force out words. This was too wrong.

"You just put me in the dirt." The late Lee Beecher shook his charred skull with something akin to sadness. He snapped home the cylinder on his pistol, bringing the hammer back to full cock in the same smooth move. "Now I'm gonna have to return the favor. Sorry, Chief."

Constable Dickey was still trying to form a whole sentence when the late Lee Beecher gave him all six rounds. Up at RaeAnn's desk, the radio crackled and the switchboard lit up with an influx of weird emergency calls, but there was no one to pay any attention, or care.

Doug's current home barely fit the definition. It had no more character than a British row flat or a post-war saltbox. It was one of the basic, ticky-tacky clapboard units thrown up by the Triple Pines aluminum plant back when they sponsored company housing, and abandoned to fall apart on its own across slow years once the plant folded. It had a roof and indoor plumbing, which was all Doug had ever required of a residence, because addresses were disposable. It had storm shutters and a rudimentary version of heat, against rain and winter, but remained drafty. Its interior walls were bare and still the same vague green Doug had always associated with academia. The bedroom was sort of blue, in the same mood.

He regretted his cheap sheets, his second-hand bed, his milk-crate night stand. He had strewn some candles around to soften the light, and fired up a portable, radiant oil heater. The heat and the light diffused the stark seediness of the room, just enough. They softened the harsh edges of reality.

There had been no seduction, no ritual libations, no teasing or flirting. Michelle had taken him the way the Allies took Normandy, and it was all he could muster to keep from gasping. His pelvis felt hammered and his legs seemed numb and far away. She was alive, with the warm, randy needs of the living, and she had plundered him with a greed that cleansed them both of any lingering recriminations.

No grave rot, no mummy dust. Was it still necrophilia when the dead person moved and talked back to you?

"I have another blanket," he said. His left leg was draped over her as their sweat cooled. He watched candle-shadows dance on the ceiling, making monster shapes.

"I'm fine," she said. "Really."

They bathed. Small bathtub, lime-encrusted shower-head. It permitted Doug to refamiliarize himself with the geometry of her body, from a perspective different than that of the bedroom. He felt he could never see or touch enough of her; it was a fascination for him.

There was nothing to eat in the kitchen, and simply clicking on the TV seemed faintly ridiculous. They slept, wrapped up in each other. The circumstance was still too fragile to detour into lengthy, dissipate conversations about need, so they slept, and in sleeping, found a fundamental innocence that was already beyond logic—a *feeling* thing. It seemed right and correct.

Doug awoke, his feet and fingertips frigid, in the predawn. He added his second blanket and snuggled back into Michelle. She slept with a nearly beatific expression, her breath—real, living—coming in slow tidal measures.

The next afternoon Doug sortied to the market to stock up on some basics and find some decent food that could be prepared in his minimal kitchen. In the market, he encountered Joe Hopkins, from the digging crew. Doug tried unsuccessfully to duck him. He wanted to do nothing to break the spell he was under.

But Joe wanted to talk, and cornered him. He was holding a fifth of bourbon like he intended to make serious use of it, in due course.

"There was apparently a lot of activity in the cemetery last night," he said, working his toothpick from one corner of his mouth to the other. Both ends were wet and frayed. "I mean, after we left. We went back this morning, things were moved around. Some graves were disrupted. Some were partially re-filled. It was a mess, like a storm had tossed everything. We had to spend two hours just to get back around to where we left off."

"You mean, like vandalism?" said Doug.

"Not exactly." Joe had another habit, that of continually smoothing his upper lip with his thumb and forefinger, as though to keep his moustache in line when he wasn't looking. To Doug, it signaled nervousness, agitation, and Joe was too brawny to be agitated about much for very long. "I tried to figure it, you know—what alla sudden makes the place not creepy, but threatening in a way it wasn't, yesterday. It's the feeling you'd have if you put on your clothes and alla sudden thought that, hey, somebody *else* has been wearing my clothes, right?"

Doug thought of what Michelle had said, about the dead hearing every footfall of the living above them.

"What I'm saying is, I don't blame you for quitting. After today, I'm thinking the same thing. Every instinct I have tells me to just jump on my bike and ride the fuck out of here as fast as I can go. And, something else? Jacky says he ran into a guy last night, a guy he went to high school with. They were on the football team together. Jacky says the guy died four years ago in a Jeep accident. But the he saw him, last night, right outside the bar after you left. Not a ghost. He wasn't that drunk. Then, this morning, Craignotti says something equally weird: That he saw a guy at the diner, you know the Ready-Set? Guy was a dead ringer for Aldus Champion, you know the mayor who died in 2003 and got replaced by that asshole selectman, whatsisname—?"

"Brad Ballinger," said Doug.

"Yeah. I been here long enough to remember that. But here's the thing: Craignotti checked, and today Ballinger was nowhere to be found, and he ain't on vacation or nothing. And Ballinger is in bed with Coggins, the undertaker, somehow. Notice how that whole Marlboro Reservoir thing went into a coma when Champion was mayor? For a minute I thought Ballinger had, you know, had him whacked or something. But now Champion's back in town-a guy Craignotti swears isn't a lookalike, but *the* guy. So now I think there was some heavy-duty money changing hands under a lot of tables, and the reservoir is a go, except nobody is supposed to talk about it, and now we're out there, digging up the whole history of Triple Pines as a result."

"What does this all come to?" Doug really wanted to get back to Michelle. She might evaporate or something if left alone too long.

"I don't know, that's the fucked up thing." Joe tried to shove his busy hands into his vest pockets, then gave up. "I'm not smart enough to figure it out, whatever it is . . . so I give it to you, see if any lightbulbs come on. I'll tell you one thing. This afternoon I felt scared, and I ain't felt that way since I was paddy humping."

"We're both outsiders, here," said Doug.

"Everybody on the dig posse in an outsider, man. Check *that* out."

"Not Jacky."

"Jacky don't pose any threat because he don't know any better. And even him, he's having fucking hallucinations about his old school buddies. Listen: I ain't got a phone at my place, but I got a mobile. Do me a favor—I mean, I know we don't know each other that well—but if you figure something out, give me a holler?"

"No problem." They traded phone numbers and Joe hurried to pay for his evening's sedation. As he went, he said, "Watch your ass, cowboy."

"You, too."

Doug and Michelle cooked collaboratively. They made love. They watched a movie together both had seen separately. They made more love. They watched the evening sky for several hours until chilly rain began to sheet down from above, then they repaired inside and continued to make love. The Peyton Place antics of the rest of the Triple Pines community, light years away from their safe, centered union, could not have mattered less.

The trick, as near as Billy Morrison could wrassle it, was to find somebody and pitch them into your hole as soon as you woke up. Came back. Revived. Whatever.

So he finished fucking Vanessa Billings. "Bill-ing" her, as his cohort Vance Thompson would crack, heh. Billy had stopped "billing" high school chicks three years ago, when he died. Now he was billing a Billings, wotta riot.

Billy, Vance, and Donna Christiansen had perished inside of Billy's Boss 302 rebuild, to the tune of Black Sabbath's "The Mob Rules" on CD. The car was about half gray primer and fender-fill, on its way back to glory. The CD was a compilation of metal moldies. No one ever figured out how the car had crashed, up near a trailer suburbia known as Rimrock, and no one in authority gave much of a turd, since Billy and his fellow losers hailed from "that side" of town, rubbing shoulders with an open-fire garbage dump, an auto wrecking yard, and (although Constable Dickey did not know it) a clandestine crack lab. The last sensation Billy experienced as a living human was the car sitting down hard on its left front as the wheel flew completely off. The speed was ticketable and the road, wet as usual, slick as mayonnaise. The car flipped and tumbled down an embankment. Billy dimly recalled seeing Donna snap in half and fly through the windshield before the steering column punched into his chest. The full tank ruptured and spewed a meandering piss-line of gasoline all the way down the hill. Vance's cigarette had probably touched it off, and the whole trash-compacted mess had burned for an hour before new rain finally doused it and a lumberyard worker spotted the smoke.

Their plan for the evening had been to destroy a bottle of vodka in the woods, then Billy and Vance would do Donna from both ends. Donna dug that sort of thing when she was sufficiently wasted. When they awoke several years later in their unearthed boxes, they renewed their pleasure as soon as they could scare up some more liquor. They wandered into a roadside outlet known as the 1-Stop Brew Shoppe and Vance broke bottles over the head of the proprietor until the guy stopping breathing. Then Donna lit out for the Yard, a quadrangle of trees und picnic benches near most of the churches in town. The Yard was Triple Pines' preferred salon for dropouts fond of cannabis, and Donna felt certain she could locate an old beau or two lingering among the waistoids there. Besides, she could bend in interesting new ways, now.

Billy had sought and duly targeted Vanessa Billings, one of those booster/cheerleader bitches who would never have anything to do with his like. She had graduated in '02 and was still—still!—living in her parents' house. It was a kick to see her jaw gape in astonishment at the sight of him. *Omigod, you like DIED!* It was even more of a kick to hold her by the throat and fuck her until she croaked, the stuck-up little cuntling. Getting Vanessa out of her parents' house caused a bit of ruckus, so Billy killed them, too.

Ultimately, the trio racked up so many new corpses to fill their vacant graves they needed to steal a pickup truck to ferry them all back to Hollymount. Their victims would all be back soon enough, and the fun could begin again.

None of them had a precise cognition of what they needed to do. It was more along the lines of an ingrained need—like a craving-to take the heat of the living to avoid reverting to the coldness of death. That, and the idea of refreshing their grave plots with new bodies. Billy had always had more cunning than intelligence, but the imperatives were not that daunting. Stupid dogs learned tricks in less time.

Best of all, after he finished billing Billings, Billy found he still had a boner. Death was apparently better than Viagara; he had an all-night hard-on. And since the night was still a toddler, he began to hunt for other chicks he could bill.

The sun came up. The sun went down. Billy thought of that rhyme about how the worms *play pinochle on your snout*. Fucking worms. How about the worms *eat your asshole inside-out*. For starters. Billy had been one super-sized organ smorgasbord, and had suffered every delicious bite. Now a whole fuckload of Triple Pines' good, upstanding citizens were going to pay, pay, pay.

As day and night blended and passed, Triple Pines continued to mutate.

Over at the Ready-Set Dinette, a pink neon sign continued to blink the word EAT, just as it had before things changed in Triple Pines.

Deputy Lee Beecher (the late) and RaeAnn (also the late) came in for lunch as usual. The next day, Constable Dickey (recently deceased) and the new deputy, James Trainor (ditto), joined them.

Vanessa Billings became Billy Morrison's main squeeze, and what with Vance and Donna's hangers-on, they had enough to form a new kind of gang. In the next few days, they would start breaking windows and setting fires.

Over at Callahan's, Craignotti continued to find fresh meat for the digging crew as the original members dropped out. Miguel Ayala had lasted three days before he claimed to have snagged a better job. Big Boyd Cooper stuck—he was a rationalist at heart, not predisposed to superstitious fears or anything else in the path of Getting the Job Done. Jacky Tynan had apparently taken sick.

Joe had packed his saddlebags and gunned his panhead straight out of town, without calling Doug, or anyone.

In the Gudgell household, every day, a pattern commenced. In the morning, Conroy Gudgell would horsewhip his treacherous wife's naked ass, and in the evening, Ellen Gudgell would murder her husband, again and again, over and over. The blood drenching the inside of their house was not ectoplasm. It continued to accrete, layer upon layer, as one day passed into another.

In the middle of the night, Doug felt askew on the inside, and made the mistake of taking his own temperature with a thermometer.

Eighty-seven-point-five degrees.

"Yeah, you'll run a little cold," said Michelle, from behind him. "I'm sorry about that. It's sort of a downside. Or maybe you caught something. Do you feel sick?"

"No, I—" Doug faltered. "I just feel shagged. Weak."

"You're not a weak man.'

"Stop it." He turned, confrontational. He did not want to do anything to alienate her. But. "This is serious. What if I start losing core heat? Four or five degrees is all it takes, then I'm as dead as a Healthy Choice entrée. What the hell is happening, Michelle? What haven't you told me?"

"I don't know," she said. Her eyes brightened with tears. "I'm not sure. I didn't come back with a goddamned manual. I'm afraid that if I go ahead and do the next thing, the thing I feel I'm supposed to do . . . that I'll lose you."

Panic cinched his heart. "What's the next thing?"

"I was avoiding it. I was afraid to bring it up. Maybe I was enjoying this too much, what we have right now, in this isolated bubble of time."

He held her. She wanted to reject simple comfort, but succumbed. "Just . . . tell me. Say it, whatever it is. Then it's out in the world and we can deal with it."

"It's about Rochelle."

Doug nodded, having prepared for this one. "You miss her. I know. But we can't do anything about it. There'd be no way to explain it."

"I want her back." Michelle's head was down, the tears coursing freely now.

"I know, baby, I know . . . I miss her, too. I wanted you guys to move in with me. Both of you. From here we could move anywhere, so long as it's out of this deathtrap of a town. Neither of us likes it here very much. I figured, in the course of time—"

She slumped on the bed, hands worrying each other atop her bare legs. "It was my dream, through all those hours, days, that things had happened differently, and we had hooked up, and we all got to escape. It would be great if you were just a means to an end; you know—just another male guy-person, to manipulate. Great if I didn't care about you; great if I didn't actually love you."

"I had to explain your death to Rochelle. There's no going back from that one. Look at it this way: she's with your mother, and she seemed like a nice lady."

When her gaze came up to meet his, her eyes were livid. "You don't know anything," she said, the words constricted and bitter. "Sweet, kindly old Grandma Farrier? She's a fucking sadist who has probably shot pornos with Rochelle by now."

"What?!" Doug's jaw unhinged.

"She is one sick piece of shit, and her mission was always to get Rochelle away from me, into her clutches. I ran away from home as soon as I could. And when I had Rochelle, I swore that bitch would never get her claws on my daughter. And you just . . . handed her over."

"Now, wait a minute, Michelle

She overrode him. "No—it's not your fault. She always presented one face to the world. Her fake face. Her human masque. Inside the family with the doors closed, it was different. You saw the masque. You dealt with the masque. So did Rochelle. Until Grandma could actually strap the collar on, she had to play it sneaky. Her real face is from a monster who needed to be inside a grave decades ago. I should know-she broke me in with a heated glass dildo when I was nine."

"Holy shit. Michelle, why didn't you tell me this before?"

"Which 'before'? Before now? Or before I died? Doug, I died not knowing you were as good as you are. I thought I could never make love to anybody, ever again. I concentrated on moving from place to place to keep Rochelle off the radar."

Doug toweled his hands, which were awash in nervous perspiration, yet irritatingly cold. Almost insensate. He needed to assuage her terror, to fix the problem, however improbable; like Boyd Cooper, to Get the Job Done. "Okay. Fine. I'll just go get her back. We'll figure something out."

"I can't ask you to do that."

"Better yet, how about we *both* go get her? Seeing you ought to make Grandma's brain hit the floor."

"That's the problem, Doug. It's been the problem all along. *I can't leave here.* None of us can. If we do . . . if any of us goes outside of Triple Pines . . . "

"You don't mean 'us' as in you-and-me. You're talking about us as in the former occupants of Hollymount Cemetery, right?"

She nodded, more tears spilling. "I need you to fuck me. And I need you to love me. And I was hoping that you could love me enough so that I didn't have to force you to take my place in that hole in the ground, like all the rest of the goddamned losers and dim bulbs and fly-over people in Triple Pines. I want you to go to San Francisco, and get my daughter back. But if you stay here if you go away and come back here—eventually I'll use you up anyway. I've been taking your heat, Doug, a degree at a time. And eventually you would die, and then resurrect, and then you would be stuck here too. An outsider, stuck here. And no matter what anyone's good intentions are, it would also happen to Rochelle. I can't kill my little girl. And I can't hurt you any more. It's killing me, but—what a joke—I can't die." She looked up, her face a raw, aching map of despair. "You see?"

Michelle had not, been a local, either. But she had died here, and become a permanent resident in the Triple Pines boneyard. The population of the town was slowly shifting balance. The dead of Triple Pines were pushing out the living, seeking that stasis of small town stability where once again, everyone would be the same. What happened in Triple Pines had to stay in Triple Pines, and the Marlboro Reservoir was no boon to the community. It was going to service coastal cities; Doug knew this in his gut, now. In all ways, for all concerned, Triple Pines was the *perfect* place for this kind of thing to transpire, because the outside world would never notice, or never care.

With one grating exception. Which suggested one frightening solution. *Time to get out. Time to bail, now.*

"Don't you see?" she said. "If you don't get out now, you'll never get out. Get out, Doug. Kiss me one last time and get out. Try to think of me fondly."

His heart smashed to pieces and burned to ashes, he kissed her. Her tears lingered on his lips, the utterly real *taste* of her. Without a word further, he made sure he had his wallet, got in his car, and drove. He could be in San Francisco in six hours, flat-out.

He could retrieve Rochelle, kidnap her if that was what was required. He could bring her back here to die, and be reunited with her mother. Then he could die, too. But at least he would be with them, in the end. Or he could put it behind him, and just keep on driving.

The further he got from Triple Pines, the warmer he felt.

David J. Schow *first wrote about zombies of a sort in the short story "Bunny Didn't Tell Us" in 1979 (not published until 1985). Then Book of the Dead shambled along and he became the only contributor with two stories in* Volume One: *the notorious "Jerry's Kids Meet Wormboy" and the opening story, "Blossom," written under the pseudonym "Chan McConnell." Chan reappeared in Volume Two with "DON't WALK," making Schow the only writer with three stories in the duology. Then Chan got gruesomely killed as part of the story "Dying Words," the whole Schow/McConnell chronology being explicated in the milestone collection* Zombie Jam *(2005), illustrated by zombie-meister Bernie Wrightson. With some bemusement, Schow watched as his tales of resurrected walkers—first called "geeks" in "Jerry's Kids," by the way—got strip-mined for assorted comic books and movie remakes. Under the present-day zombie boom, most of Schow's tales have been scooped up for reissue in a number of phonebook-sized anthologies about the living dead. He may yet have the last word. Until then he remains active in film/TV (most recent movie:* The Hills Run Red *[2009]) and publishing (with* Internecine, *a suspense novel;* Hunt Among The Killers of Men, *a pulp novel; and* The Art of Drew Struzan, *all 2010).*

As for commenting on "Obsequy," I'd like to quote some correspondence from Mr. Schow:

First we all said zombies would replace vampires in popular mass consciousness (ahead of our time as always). Now that it's happened, it seems like extreme overkill (if only they had listened to us earlier). While "Obsequy" self-consciously defies the trope of brain-gobbling, slavering reanimates, I think it still counts, or at least might be a tea break amidst the expected carnage.

One reason for all the current popularity of post-zombie-apocalypse fiction, I think, is that players need *no special qualifications* to participate. As long as you're alive, even a mook with a shotgun counts as human. It's also a kind of Wild West frontier wish-fulfillment (now we can kill anybody we want, but make sure you put them down permanently). A lot of people idealize this scenario as a terrific idea, a sort of post-apocalypse theme park in which they can now run amuck, unrestrained by the former niceties of society. The irony is that those who feel this would amount to some sort of big Doomsday rave would probably be the first victims of a world much harsher than their killing-spree dreams.

In a world that has marginalized, unmanned, and dis-employed most people, suddenly anybody who can draw a breath is *special* . . . for many, for the first time.

Oh yeah, I've mentioned the terms *ghoul* and *revenant*—both used in this story, elsewhere in story notes (for David Wellington and Kelly Link's stories, respectively). I think the undead in this story come close to the original meaning of *revenant*.

Deadman's Road

Joe R. Lansdale

The evening sun had rolled down and blown out in a bloody wad, and the white, full moon had rolled up like an enormous ball of tightly wrapped twine. As he rode, the Reverend Jebidiah Rains watched it glow above the tall pines. All about it stars were sprinkled white-hot in the dead-black heavens.

The trail he rode on was a thin one, and the trees on either side of it crept toward the path as if they might block the way, and close up behind him. The weary horse on which he was riding moved forward with its head down, and Jebidiah, too weak to fight it, let his mount droop and take its lead. Jebidiah was too tired to know much at that moment, but he knew one thing. He was a man of the Lord and he hated God, hated the sonofabitch with all his heart.

And he knew God knew and didn't care, because he knew Jebidiah was his messenger. Not one of the New Testament, but one of the Old Testament, harsh and mean and certain, vengeful and without compromise; a man who would have shot a leg out from under Moses and spat in the face of the Holy Ghost and scalped him, tossing his celestial hair to the wild four winds.

It was not a legacy Jebidiah would have preferred, being the bad man messenger of God, but it was his, and he had earned it through sin, and no matter how hard he tried to lay it down and leave it be, he could not. He knew that to give in and abandon his God-given curse, was to burn in hell forever, and to continue was to do as the Lord prescribed, no matter what his feelings toward his mean master might be. His Lord was not a forgiving Lord, nor was he one who cared for your love. All he cared for was obedience, servitude and humiliation. It was why God had invented the human race. Amusement.

As he thought on these matters, the trail turned and widened, and off to one side, amongst tree stumps, was a fairly large clearing, and in its center was a small log house, and out to the side a somewhat larger log barn. In the curtained window of the cabin was a light that burned orange behind the flour-sack curtains. Jebidiah, feeling tired and hungry and thirsty and weary of soul, made for it.

Stopping a short distance from the cabin, Jebidiah leaned forward on his horse and called out, "Hello, the cabin."

He waited for a time, called again, and was halfway through calling when the door opened, and a man about five-foot-two with a large droopy hat, holding a rifle, stuck himself part of the way out of the cabin, said, "Who is it calling? You got a voice like a bullfrog."

"Reverend Jebidiah Rains."

"You ain't come to preach none, have you?"

"No, sir. I find it does no good. I'm here to beg for a place in your barn, a night under its roof. Something for my horse, something for myself if it's available. Most anything, as long as water is involved."

"Well," said the man, "this seems to be the gathering place tonight. Done got two others, and we just sat asses down to eat. I got enough you want it, some hot beans and some old bread."

"I would be most obliged, sir," Jebidiah said.

"Oblige all you want. In the meantime, climb down from that nag, put it in the barn and come in and chow. They call me Old Timer, but I ain't that old. It's cause most of my teeth are gone and I'm crippled in a foot a horse stepped on. There's a lantern just inside the barn door. Light that up, and put it out when you finish, come on back to the house."

When Jebidiah finished grooming and feeding his horse with grain in the barn, watering him, he came into the cabin, made a show of pushing his long black coat back so that it revealed his ivory-handled .44 cartridge-converted revolvers. They were set so that they leaned forward in their holsters, strapped close to the hips, not draped low like punks wore them. Jebidiah liked to wear them close to the natural swing of his hands. When he pulled them it was a movement quick as the flick of a hummingbird's wings, the hammers clicking from the cock of his thumb, the guns barking, spewing lead with amazing accuracy. He had practiced enough to drive a cork into a bottle at about a hundred paces, and he could do it in bad light. He chose to reveal his guns that way to show he was ready for any attempted ambush. He reached up and pushed his wide-brimmed black hat back on his head, showing black hair gone gray-tipped. He thought having his hat tipped made him look casual. It did not. His eyes always seemed aflame in an angry face.

Inside, the cabin was bright with kerosene lamplight, and the kerosene smelled, and there were curls of black smoke twisting about, mixing with gray smoke from the pipe of Old Timer, and the cigarette of a young man with a badge pinned to his shirt. Beside him, sitting on a chopping log by the fireplace, which was too hot for the time of year, but was being used to heat up a pot of beans, was a middle-aged man with a slight paunch and a face that looked like it attracted thrown objects. He had his hat pushed up a bit, and a shock of wheat-colored, sweaty hair hung on his forehead. There was a cigarette in is mouth, half of it ash. He twisted on the chopping log, and Jebidiah saw that his hands were manacled together.

"I heard you say you was a preacher," said the manacled man, as he tossed the last of his smoke into the fireplace. "This here sure ain't God's country."

"Worse thing is," said Jebidiah, "it's exactly God's country."

The manacled man gave out with a snort, and grinned.

"Preacher," said the younger man, "my name is Jim Taylor. I'm a deputy for Sheriff Spradley, out of Nacogdoches. I'm taking this man there for a trial, and most likely a hanging. He killed a fella for a rifle and a horse. I see you tote guns, old style guns, but good ones. Way you tote them, I'm suspecting you know how to use them."

"I've been known to hit what I aim at," Jebidiah said, and sat in a rickety chair at an equally rickety table. Old Timer put some tin plates on the table, scratched his ass with a long wooden spoon, then grabbed a rag and used it as a potholder, lifted the hot bean pot to the table. He popped the lid of the pot, used the ass-scratching spoon to scoop a heap of beans onto plates. He brought over some wooden cups and poured them full from a pitcher of water.

"Thing is," the deputy said, "I could use some help. I don't know I can get back safe with this fella, havin' not slept good in a day or two. Was wondering, you and Old Timer here could watch my back till morning? Wouldn't even mind if you rode along with me tomorrow, as sort of a backup. I could use a gun hand. Sheriff might even give you a dollar for it."

Old Timer, as if this conversation had not been going on, brought over a bowl with some moldy biscuits in it, placed them on the table. "Made them a week ago. They've gotten a bit ripe, but you can scratch around the mold. I'll warn you though, they're tough enough you could toss one hard and kill a chicken on the run. So mind your teeth."

"That how you lost yours, Old Timer?" the manacled man said.

"Probably part of them," Old Timer said.

"What you say, preacher?" the deputy said. "You let me get some sleep?"

"My problem lies in the fact that I need sleep," Jebidiah said. "I've been busy, and I'm what could be referred to as tuckered."

"Guess I'm the only one that feels spry," said the manacled man.

"No," said, Old Timer. "I feel right fresh myself."

"Then it's you and me, Old Timer," the manacled man said, and grinned, as if this meant something.

"You give me cause, fella, I'll blow a hole in you and tell God you got in a nest of termites."

The manacled man gave his snort of a laugh again. He seemed to be having a good old time.

"Me and Old Timer can work shifts," Jebidiah said. "That okay with you, Old Timer?"

"Peachy," Old Timer said, and took another plate from the table and filled it with beans. He gave this one to the manacled man, who said, lifting his bound hands to take it, "What do I eat it with?"

"Your mouth. Ain't got no extra spoons. And I ain't giving you a knife."

The manacled man thought on this for a moment, grinned, lifted the plate and put his face close to the edge of it, sort of poured the beans toward his mouth. He lowered the plate and chewed. "Reckon they taste scorched with or without a spoon."

Jebidiah reached inside his coat, took out and opened up a pocket knife, used it to spear one of the biscuits, and to scrape the beans toward him.

"You come to the table, young fella," Old Timer said to the deputy. "I'll get my shotgun, he makes a move that ain't eatin', I'll blast him and the beans inside him into that fireplace there."

Old Timer sat with a double-barrel shotgun resting on his leg, pointed in the general direction of the manacled man. The deputy told all that his prisoner had done while he ate. Murdered women and children, shot a dog and a horse, and just for the hell of it, shot a cat off a fence, and set fire to an outhouse with a woman in it. He had also raped women, stuck a stick up a sheriff's ass, and killed him, and most likely shot other animals that might have been some good to somebody. Overall, he was tough on human beings, and equally as tough on livestock.

"I never did like animals," the manacled man said. "Carry fleas. And that woman in the outhouse stunk to high heaven. She ought to eat better. She needed burning."

"Shut up," the deputy said. "This fella," and he nodded toward the prisoner, "his name is Bill Barrett, and he's the worst of the worst. Thing is, well, I'm not just tired, I'm a little wounded. He and I had a tussle. I hadn't surprised him, wouldn't be here today. I got a bullet graze in my hip. We had quite a dust up. I finally got him down by putting a gun barrel to his noggin' half a dozen times or so. I'm not hurt so bad, but I lost blood for a couple days. Weakened me. You'd ride along with me Reverend, I'd appreciate it."

"I'll consider it," Jebidiah said. "But I'm about my business."

"Who you gonna preach to along here, 'sides us?" the deputy said.

"Don't even think about it," Old Timer said. "Just thinking about that Jesus foolishness makes my ass tired. Preaching makes me want to kill the preacher and cut my own throat. Being at a preachin' is like being tied down in a nest red bitin' ants."

"At this point in my life," Jebidiah said. "I agree."

There was a moment of silence in response to Jebidiah, then the deputy turned his attention to Old Timer. "What's the fastest route to Nacogdoches?"

"Well now," Old Timer said, "you can keep going like you been going, following the road out front. And in time you'll run into a road, say thirty miles from here, and it goes left. That should take you right near Nacogdoches, which is another ten miles, though you'll have to make a turn somewhere up in there near the end of the trip. Ain't exactly sure where unless I'm looking at it. Whole trip, traveling at an even pace ought to take you two day."

"You could go with us," the deputy said. "Make sure I find that road."

"Could," said Old Timer, "but I won't. I don't ride so good anymore. My balls ache I ride a horse for too long. Last time I rode a pretty good piece, I had to squat over a pan of warm water and salt, soak my taters for an hour or so just so they'd fit back in my pants. "

"My balls ache just listening to you," the prisoner said. "Thing is, though, them swollen up like that, was probably the first time in your life you had man-sized balls, you old fart. You should have left them swollen."

Old Timer cocked back the hammers on the double barrel. "This here could go off."

Bill just grinned, leaned his back against the fire-place, then jumped forward. For a moment, it looked as if Old Timer might cut him in half, but he realized what had happened.

"Oh yeah," Old Timer said. "That there's hot, stupid. Why they call it a fire place."

Bill readjusted himself, so that his back wasn't against the stones. He said, "I'm gonna cut this deputy's pecker off, come back here, make you fry it up and eat it."

"You're gonna shit and fall back in it," Old Timer said. "That's all you're gonna do."

When things had calmed down again, the deputy said to Old Timer, "There's no faster route?"

Old timer thought for a moment. "None you'd want to take."

"What's that mean?" the deputy said.

Old Timer slowly lowered the hammers on the shotgun, smiling at Bill all the while. When he had them lowered, he turned his head, looked at the deputy. "Well, there's Deadman's Road."

"What's wrong with that?" the deputy asked.

"All manner of things. Used to be called Cemetery Road. Couple years back that changed."

Jebidiah's interest was aroused. "Tell us about it, Old Timer."

"Now I ain't one to believe in hogwash, but there's a story about the road, and I got it from someone you might say was the horse's mouth."

"A ghost story, that's choice," said Bill.

"How much time would the road cut off going to Nacogdoches?" the deputy asked.

"Near a day," Old Timer said.

"Damn. Then that's the way I got to go," the deputy said.

"Turn off for it ain't far from here, but I wouldn't recommend it," Old Timer said. "I ain't much for Jesus, but I believe in haints, things like that. Living out here in this thicket, you see some strange things. There's gods ain't got nothing to do with Jesus or Moses, or any of that bunch. There's older gods than that. Indians talk about them."

"I'm not afraid of any Indian gods," the deputy said.

"Maybe not," Old Timer said, "but these gods, even the Indians ain't fond of them. They ain't their gods. These gods are older than the Indian folk their ownselfs. Indians try not to stir them up. They worship their own."

"And why would this road be different than any other?" Jebidiah asked. "What does it have to do with ancient gods?"

Old Timer grinned. "You're just wanting to challenge it, ain't you, Reverend? Prove how strong your god is. You weren't no preacher, you'd be a gunfighter, I reckon. Or, maybe you are just that. A gunfighter preacher."

"I'm not that fond of my god," Jebidiah said, "but I have been given a duty. Drive out evil. Evil as my god sees it. If these gods are evil, and they're in my path, then I have to confront them."

"They're evil, all right," Old Timer said.

"Tell us about them," Jebidiah said.

"Gil Gimet was a bee keeper," Old Timer said. "He raised honey, and lived off of Deadman's Road. Known then as Cemetery Road. That's 'cause there was a graveyard down there. It had some old Spanish graves in it, some said Conquistadores who tromped through here but didn't tromp out. I know there was some Indians buried there, early Christian Indians, I reckon. Certainly there were stones and crosses up and Indian names on the crosses. Maybe mixed breeds. Lots of intermarrying around here. Anyway, there were all manner people buried up there. The dead ground don't care what color you are when you go in, cause in the end, we're all gonna be the color of dirt."

"Hell, "Bill said. "You're already the color of dirt. And you smell like some pretty old dirt at that."

"You gonna keep on, mister," Old Timer said, "and you're gonna wind up having the undertaker wipe your ass." Old Timer cocked back the hammers on the shotgun again. "This here gun could go off accidently. Could happen, and who here is gonna argue it didn't?"

"Not me," the deputy said. "It would be easier on me you were dead, Bill."

Bill looked at the Reverend. "Yeah, but that wouldn't set right with the Reverend, would it Reverend?"

"Actually, I wouldn't care one way or another. I'm not a man of peace, and I'm not a forgiver, even if what you did wasn't done to me. I think we're all rich and deep in sin. Maybe none of us are worthy of forgiveness."

Bill sunk a little at his seat. No one was even remotely on his side. Old Timer continued with his story.

"This here bee keeper, Gimet, he wasn't known as much of a man. Mean-hearted is how he was thunk of. I knowed him, and I didn't like him. I seen him snatch up a little dog once and cut the tail off of it with his knife, just cause he thought it was funny. Boy who owned the dog tried to fight back, and Gimet, he cut the boy on the arm. No one did nothin' about it. Ain't no real law in these parts, you see, and wasn't nobody brave enough to do nothin'. Me included. And he did lots of other mean things, even killed a couple of men, and claimed self-defense. Might have been, but Gimet was always into something, and whatever he was into always turned out with someone dead, or hurt, or humiliated."

"Bill here sounds like he could be Gimet's brother," the deputy said.

"Oh, no," Old Timer said, shaking his head. "This here scum-licker ain't a bump on the mean old ass of Gimet. Gimet lived in a little shack off Cemetery Road. He raised bees, and brought in honey to sell at the community up the road. Guess you could even call it a town. Schow is the way the place is known, on account of a fella used to live up there was named Schow. He died and got ate up by pigs. Right there in his own pen, just keeled over slopping the hogs, and then they slopped him, all over that place. A store got built on top of where Schow got et up, and that's how the place come by the name. Gimet took his honey in there to the store and sold it, and even though he was a turd, he had some of the best honey you ever smacked your mouth around. Wish I had me some now. It was dark and rich, and sweeter than any sugar. Think that's one reason he got away with things. People don't like killing and such, but they damn sure like their honey."

"This story got a point?" Bill said.

"You don't like way I'm telling it," Old Timer said, "why don't you think about how that rope's gonna fit around your neck. That ought to keep your thoughts occupied, right smart."

Bill made a grunting noise, turned on his block of wood, as if to show he wasn't interested.

"Well, now, honey or not, sweet tooth, or not, everything has an end to it. And thing was he took to a little gal, Mary Lynn Twoshoe. She was a part Indian gal, a real looker, hair black as the bottom of a well, eyes the same color, and she was just as fine in the features as them pictures you see of them stage actresses. She wasn't five feet tall, and that hair of hers went all the way down her back. Her daddy was dead. The pox got him. And her mama wasn't too well off, being sickly, and all. She made brooms out of straw and branches she trimmed down. Sold a few of them, raised a little garden and a hog. When all this happened, Mary Lynn was probably thirteen, maybe fourteen. Wasn't no older than that."

"If you're gonna tell a tale," Bill said, "least don't wander all over the place."

"So, you're interested?" Old Timer said.

"What else I got to do?" Bill said.

"Go on," Jebidiah said. "Tell us about Mary Lynn."

Old Timer nodded. "Gimet took to her. Seen her around, bringing the brooms her mama made into the store. He waited on her, grabbed her, and just threw her across his saddle kickin' and screamin', like he'd bought a sack of flour and was ridin' it to the house. Mack Collins, store owner came out and tried to stop him. Well, he said something to him. About how he shouldn't do it, least that's the way I heard it. He didn't push much, and I can't blame him. Didn't do good to cross Gimet. Anyway, Gimet just said back to Mack, 'Give her mama a big jar of honey. Tell her that's for her daughter. I'll even make her another jar or two, if the meat here's as sweet as I'm expecting.'

"With that, he slapped Mary Lynn on the ass and rode off with her."

"Sounds like my kind of guy," Bill said.

"I have become irritated with you now," Jebidiah said. "Might I suggest you shut your mouth before I pistolwhip you."

Bill glared at Jebidiah, but the Reverend's gaze was as dead and menacing as the barrels of Old Timer's shotgun.

"Rest of the story is kind of grim," Old Timer said. "Gimet took her off to his house, and had his way with her. So many times he damn near killed her, and then he turned her lose, or got so drunk she was able to get loose. Time she walked down Cemetery Road, made it back to town, well, she was bleeding so bad from having been used so rough, she collapsed. She lived a day and died from loss of blood. Her mother, out of her sick bed, rode a mule out there to the cemetery on Cemetery Road. I told you she was Indian, and she knew some Indian ways, and she knew about them old gods that wasn't none of the gods of her people, but she still knew about them.

"She knew some signs to draw in cemetery dirt. I don't know the whole of it, but she did some things, and she did it on some old grave out there, and the last thing she did was she cut her own throat, died right there, her blood running on top of that grave and them pictures she drawed in the dirt."

"Don't see how that done her no good," the deputy said.

"Maybe it didn't, but folks think it did," Old Timer said. "Community that had been pushed around by Gimet, finally had enough, went out there in mass to hang his ass, shoot him, whatever it took. Got to his cabin they found Gimet dead outside his shack. His eyes had been torn out, or blown out is how they looked. Skin was peeled off his head, just leaving the skull and a few hairs. His chest was ripped open, and his insides was gone, exceptin' the bones in there. And them bees of his had nested in the hole in his chest, had done gone about making honey. Was buzzing out of that hole, his mouth, empty eyes, nose, or where his nose used to be. I figure they'd rolled him over, tore off his pants, they'd have been coming out of his asshole."

"How come you weren't out there with them?" Bill said. "How come this is all stuff you heard?"

"Because I was a coward when it come to Gimet," Old Timer said. "That's why. Told myself wouldn't never be a coward again, no matter what. I should have been with them. Didn't matter no how. He was done good and dead, them bees all in him. What was done then is the crowd got kind of loco, tore off his clothes, hooked his feet up to a horse and dragged him through a blackberry patch, them bees just burstin' out and hummin' all around him. All that ain't right, but I think I'd been with them, knowing who he was and all the things he'd done, I might have been loco too. They dumped him out on the cemetery to let him rot, took that girl's mother home to be buried some place better. Wasn't no more than a few nights later that folks started seeing Gimet. They said he walked at night, when the moon was at least half, or full, like it is now. Number of folks seen him, said he loped alongside the road, following their horses, grabbing hold of the tail if he could, trying to pull horse and rider down, or pull himself up on the back of their mounts. Said them bees was still in him. Bees black as flies, and angry whirling all about him, and coming from inside him. Worse, there was a larger number of folks took that road that wasn't never seen again. It was figured Gimet got them."

"Horse shit," the deputy said. "No disrespect, Old Timer. You've treated me all right, that's for sure. But a ghost chasing folks down. I don't buy that."

"Don't have to buy it," Old Timer said. "I ain't trying to sell it to you none. Don't have to believe it. And I don't think it's no ghost anyway. I think that girl's mother, she done something to let them old gods out for awhile, sicked them on that bastard, used her own life as a sacrifice, that's what I think. And them gods, them things from somewhere else, they ripped him up like that.

Them bees is part of that too. They ain't no regular honey bee. They're some other kind of bees. Some kind of fitting death for a bee raiser, is my guess."

"That's silly," the deputy said.

"I don't know," Jebidiah said. "The Indian woman may only have succeeded in killing him in this life. She may not have understood all that she did. Didn't know she was giving him an opportunity to live again . . . Or maybe that is the curse. Though there are plenty others have to suffer for it."

"Like the folks didn't do nothing when Gimet was alive," Old Time said. "Folks like me that let what went on go on."

Jebidiah nodded. "Maybe."

The deputy looked at Jebidiah. "Not you too, Reverend. You should know better than that. There ain't but one true god, and ain't none of that hoodoo business got a drop of truth to it."

"If there's one god," Jebidiah said, "there can be many. They are at war with one another, that's how it works, or so I think. I've seen some things that have shook my faith in the one true god, the one I'm servant to. And what is our god but hoodoo? It's all hoodoo, my friend."

"Okay. What things have you seen, Reverend?" the deputy asked.

"No use describing it to you, young man," Jebidiah said. "You wouldn't believe me. But I've recently come from Mud Creek. It had an infestation of a sort. That town burned down, and I had a hand in it."

"Mud Creek," Old Timer said. "I been there."

"Only thing there now," Jebidiah said, "is some charred wood."

"Ain't the first time it's burned down," Old Timer said. "Some fool always rebuilds it, and with it always comes some kind of ugliness. I'll tell you straight. I don't doubt your word at all, Reverend."

"Thing is," the deputy said, "I don't believe in no haints. That's the shortest road, and it's the road I'm gonna take."

"I wouldn't," Old Timer said.

"Thanks for the advice. But no one goes with me or does, that's the road I'm taking, provided it cuts a day off my trip."

"I'm going with you," Jebidiah said. "My job is striking at evil. Not to walk around it."

"I'd go during the day," Old Timer said. "Ain't no one seen Gimet in the day, or when the moon is thin or not at all. But way it is now, it's full, and will be again tomorrow night. I'd ride hard tomorrow, you're determined to go. Get there as soon as you can, before dark."

"I'm for getting there," the deputy said. "I'm for getting back to Nacogdoches, and getting this bastard in a cell."

"I'll go with you," Jebidiah said. "But I want to be there at night. I want to take Deadman's Road at that time. I want to see if Gimet is there. And if he is, send him to his final death. Defy those dark gods the girl's mother called up. Defy them and loose my god on him. What I'd suggest is you get some rest, deputy. Old Timer here can watch a bit, then I'll take over. That way we all get some rest. We can chain this fellow to a tree outside, we have to. We should both get slept up to the gills, then leave here mid-day, after a good dinner, head out for Deadman's Road. Long as we're there by nightfall."

"That ought to bring you right on it," Old Timer said. "You take Deadman's Road. When you get to the fork, where the road ends, you go right. Ain't no one ever seen Gimet beyond that spot, or in front of where the road begins. He's tied to that stretch, way I heard it."

"Good enough," the deputy said. "I find this all foolish, but if I can get some rest, and have you ride along with me, Reverend, then I'm game. And I'll be fine with getting there at night."

Next morning they slept late, and had an early lunch. Beans and hard biscuits again, a bit of stewed squirrel. Old Timer had shot the rodent that morning while Jebidiah watched Bill sit on his ass, his hands chained around a tree in the front yard. Inside the cabin, the deputy had continued to sleep.

But now they all sat outside eating, except for Bill.

"What about me?" Bill asked, tugging at his chained hands.

"When we finish," Old Timer said. "Don't know if any of the squirrel will be left, but we got them biscuits for you. I can promise you some of them. I might even let you rub one of them around in my plate, sop up some squirrel gravy."

"Those biscuits are awful," Bill said.

"Ain't they," Old Timer said.

Bill turned his attention to Jebidiah. "Preacher, you ought to just go on and leave me and the boy here alone. Ain't smart for you to ride along, 'cause I get loose, ain't just the deputy that's gonna pay. I'll put you on the list."

"After what I've seen in this life," Jebidiah said, "you are nothing to me. An insect . . . So, add me to your list."

"Let's feed him," the deputy said, nodding at Bill, "and get to moving. I'm feeling rested and want to get this ball started."

The moon had begun to rise when they rode in sight of Deadman's Road. The white cross road sign was sticking up beside the road. Trees and brush had grown up around it, and between the limbs and the shadows, the crudely painted words on the sign were halfway readable in the waning light. The wind had picked up and was grabbing at leaves, plucking them from the ground, tumbling them about, tearing them from trees and tossing them across the narrow, clay road with a sound like mice scuttling in straw.

"Fall always depresses me," the deputy said, halting his horse, taking a swig from his canteen.

"Life is a cycle," Jebidiah said. "You're born, you suffer, then you're punished."

The deputy turned in his saddle to look at Jebidiah. "You ain't much on that resurrection and reward, are you?"

"No, I'm not."

"I don't know about you," the deputy said, "but I wish we hadn't gotten here so late. I'd rather have gone through in the day."

"Thought you weren't a believer in spooks?" Bill said, and made with his now familiar snort. "You said it didn't matter to you."

The deputy didn't look at Bill when he spoke. "I wasn't here then. Place has a look I don't like. And I don't enjoy temptin' things. Even if I don't believe in them."

"That's the silliest thing I ever heard," Bill said.

"Wanted me with you," Jebidiah said. "You had to wait."

"You mean to see something, don't you, preacher?" Bill said.

"If there is something to see," Jebidiah said.

"You believe Old Timer's story?" the deputy said. "I mean, really?"

"Perhaps."

Jebidiah clucked to his horse and took the lead.

When they turned onto Deadman's Road, Jebidiah paused and removed a small, fat Bible from his saddlebag.

The deputy paused too, forcing Bill to pause as well. "You ain't as ornery as I thought," the deputy said. "You want the peace of the Bible just like anyone else."

"There is no peace in this book," Jebidiah said. "That's a real confusion. Bible isn't anything but a book of terror, and that's how God is: Terrible. But the book has power. And we might need it."

"I don't know what to think about you, Reverend," the deputy said.

"Ain't nothin' you can think about a man that's gone loco," Bill said. "I don't want to stay with no man that's loco."

"You get an idea to run, Bill, I can shoot you off your horse," the deputy said. "Close range with my revolver, far range with my rifle. You don't want to try it."

"It's still a long way to Nacogdoches," Bill said.

The road was narrow and of red clay. It stretched far ahead like a band of blood, turned sharply to the right around a wooded curve where it was a dark as the bottom of Jonah's whale. The blowing leaves seemed especially intense on the road, scrapping dryly about, winding in the air like giant hornets. The trees, which grew thick, bent in the wind, from right to left. This naturally led the trio to take to the left side of the road.

The farther they went down the road, the darker it became. By the time they got to the curve, the woods were so thick, and the thunderous skies had grown so dark, the moon was barely visible; its light was as weak as a sick baby's grip.

When they had traveled for some time, the deputy said, obviously feeling good about it, "There ain't nothing out here 'sides what you would expect. A possum maybe. The wind."

"Good for you, then," Jebidiah said. "Good for us all."

"You sound disappointed to me," the deputy said.

"My line of work isn't far from yours, Deputy. I look for bad guys of a sort, and try and send them to hell . . . Or in some cases, back to hell."

And then, almost simultaneous with a flash of lightning, something crossed the road not far in front of them.

"What the hell was that?" Bill said, coming out of what had been a near stupor.

"It looked like a man," the deputy said.

"Could have been," Jebidiah said. "Could have been."

"What do you think it was?"

"You don't want to know."

"I do."

"Gimet," Jebidiah said.

The sky let the moon loose for a moment, and its light spread through the trees and across the road. In the light there were insects, a large wad of them, buzzing about in the air.

"Bees," Bill said. "Damn if them ain't bees. And at night. That ain't right."

"You an expert on bees?" the deputy asked.

"He's right," Jebidiah said. "And look, they're gone now."

"Flew off," the deputy said.

"No . . . no they didn't," Bill said. "I was watching, and they didn't fly nowhere. They're just gone. One moment they were there, then they was gone, and that's all there is to it. They're like ghosts."

"You done gone crazy," the deputy said.

"They are not insects of this earth," Jebidiah said. "They are familiars."

"What," Bill said.

"They assist evil, or evil beings," Jebidiah said. "In this case, Gimet. They're like a witches black cat familiar. Familiars take on animal shapes, insects, that sort of thing."

"That's ridiculous," the deputy said. "That don't make no kind of sense at all."

"Whatever you say," Jebidiah said, "but I would keep my eyes alert, and my senses raw. Wouldn't hurt to keep your revolvers loose in their holsters. You could well need them. Though, come to think of it, your revolvers won't be much use."

"What the hell does that mean?" Bill said.

Jebidiah didn't answer. He continued to urge his horse on, something that was becoming a bit more difficult as they went. All of the horses snorted and turned their heads left and right, tugged at their bits; their ears went back and their eyes went wide.

"Holy hell," Bill said, "what's that?"

Jebidiah and the deputy turned to look at him. Bill was turned in the saddle, looking back. They looked too, just in time to see something that looked pale blue in the moonlight, dive into the brush on the other side of the road. Black dots followed, swarmed in the moonlight, then darted into the bushes behind the pale, blue thing like a load of buckshot.

"What was that?" the deputy said. His voice sounded as if it had been pistol whipped.

"Already told you," Jebidiah said.

"That couldn't have been nothing human," the deputy said.

"Don't you get it," Bill said, "that's what the preacher is trying to tell you. It's Gimet, and he ain't nowhere alive. His skin was blue. And he's all messed up. I seen more than you did. I got a good look. And them bees. We ought to break out and ride hard."

"Do as you choose," the Reverend said. "I don't intend to."

"And why not?" Bill said.

"That isn't my job."

"Well, I ain't got no job. Deputy, ain't you supposed to make sure I get to Nacogdoches to get hung? Ain't that your job?"

"It is."

"Then we ought to ride on, not bother with this fool. He wants to fight some grave crawler, then let him. Ain't nothing we ought to get into."

"We made a pact to ride together," the deputy said. "So we will."

"I didn't make no pact," Bill said.

"Your word, your needs, they're nothing to me," the deputy said.

At that moment, something began to move through the woods on their left. Something moving quick and heavy, not bothering with stealth. Jebidiah looked in the direction of the sounds, saw someone, or something, moving through the underbrush, snapping limbs aside like they were rotten sticks. He could hear the buzz of the bees, loud and angry. Without really meaning to, he urged the horse to a trot. The deputy and Bill joined in with their own mounts, keeping pace with the Reverend's horse.

They came to a place off the side of the road where the brush thinned, and out in the distance they could see what looked like bursting white waves, frozen against the dark. But they soon realized it was tombstones. And there were crosses. A graveyard. The graveyard Old Timer had told them about. The sky had cleared now, the wind had ceased to blow hard. They had a fine view of the cemetery, and as they watched, the thing that had been in the brush moved out of it and went up the little rise where the graves were, climbed up on one of the stones and sat. A black cloud formed around its head, and the sound of buzzing could be heard all the way out to the road. The thing sat there like a king on a throne. Even from that distance it was easy to see it was nude, and male, and his skin was gray—blue in the moonlight—and the head looked misshapen. Moon glow slipped through cracks in the back of the horror's head and poked out of fresh cracks at the front of its skull and speared out of the empty eye sockets. The bee's nest, visible through the wound in its chest, was nestled between the ribs. It pulsed with a yellow-honey glow. From time to time, little black dots moved around the glow and flew up and were temporarily pinned in the moonlight above the creature's head.

"Jesus," said the deputy.

"Jesus won't help a bit," Jebidiah said.

"It's Gimet, ain't it? He . . . it . . . really is dead," the deputy said.

"Undead," Jebidiah said. "I believe he's toying with us. Waiting for when he plans to strike."

"Strike?" Bill said. "Why?"

"Because that is his purpose," Jebidiah said, "as it is mine to strike back. Gird you loins men, you will soon be fighting for your life."

"How about we just ride like hell?" Bill said.

In that moment, Jebidiah's words became prophetic. The thing was gone from the grave stone. Shadows had gathered at the edge of the woods, balled up, become solid, and when the shadows leaped from the even darker shadows of the trees, it was the shape of the thing they had seen on the stone, cool blue in the moonlight, a disaster of a face, and the teeth . . . They were long and sharp. Gimet leaped in such a way that his back foot hit the rear of Jebidiah's animal, allowing him to spring over the deputy's horse, to land hard and heavy on Bill. Bill let out a howl and was knocked off his mount. When he hit the road, his hat flying, Gimet grabbed him by his bushy head of straw-colored hair and dragged him off as easily as if he were a kitten. Gimet went into the trees, tugging Bill after him. Gimet blended with the darkness there. The last of Bill was a scream, the raising of his cuffed hands, the cuffs catching the moonlight for a quick blink of silver, then there was a rustle of leaves and a slapping of branches, and Bill was gone.

"My God," the deputy said. "My God. Did you see that thing?"

Jebidiah dismounted, moved to the edge of the road, leading his horse, his gun drawn. The deputy did not dismount. He pulled his pistol and held it, his hands trembling. "Did you see that?" he said again, and again.

"My eyes are as good as your own," Jebidiah said. "I saw it. We'll have to go in and get him."

"Get him?" the deputy said. "Why in the name of everything that's holy would we do that? Why would we want to be near that thing? He's probably done what he's done already . . . Damn, Reverend. Bill, he's a killer. This is just as good as I might want. I say while the old boy is doing whatever he's doing to that bastard, we ride like the goddamn wind, get on out on the far end of this road where it forks. Gimet is supposed to be only able to go on this stretch, ain't he?"

"That's what Old Timer said. You do as you want. I'm going in after him."

"Why? You don't even know him."

"It's not about him," Jebidiah said.

"Ah, hell. I ain't gonna be shamed." The deputy swung down from his horse, pointed at the place where Gimet had disappeared with Bill. "Can we get the horses through there?"

"Think we will have to go around a bit. I discern a path over there."

"Discern?"

"Recognize. Come on, time is wasting."

They went back up the road a pace, found a trail that led through the trees. The moon was strong now as all the clouds that had covered it had rolled away like wind blown pollen. The air smelled fresh, but as they moved forward, that changed. There was a stench in the air, a putrid smell both sweet and sour, and it floated up and spoiled the freshness.

"Something dead," the deputy said.

"Something long dead," Jebidiah said.

Finally the brush grew so thick they had to tie the horses, leave them. They pushed their way through briars and limbs.

"There ain't no path," the deputy said. "You don't know he come through this way."

Jebidiah reached out and plucked a piece of cloth from a limb, held it up so that the moon dropped rays on it. "This is part of Bill's shirt. Am I right?"

The deputy nodded. "But how could Gimet get through here? How could he get Bill through here?"

"What we pursue has little interest in the things that bother man. Limbs, briars. It's nothing to the living dead."

They went on for a while. Vines got in their way. The vines were wet. They were long thick vines, and sticky, and finally they realized they were not vines at all, but guts, strewn about and draped like decorations.

"Fresh," the deputy said. "Bill, I reckon."

"You reckon right," Jebidiah said.

They pushed on a little farther, and the trail widened, making the going easier. They found more pieces of Bill as they went along. The stomach. Fingers. Pants with one leg in them. A heart, which looked as if it has been bitten into and sucked on. Jebidiah was curious enough to pick it up and examine it. Finished, he tossed it in the dirt, wiped his hands on Bill's pants, the one with the leg still in it, said, "Gimet just saved you a lot of bother and the State of Texas the trouble of a hanging."

"Heavens," the deputy said, watching Jebidiah wipe blood on the leg filled pants.

Jebidiah looked up at the deputy. "He won't mind I get blood on his pants," Jebidiah said. "He's got more important things to worry about, like dancing in the fires of hell. And by the way, yonder sports his head."

Jebidiah pointed. The deputy looked. Bill's head had been pushed onto a broken limb of a tree, the sharp end of the limb being forced through the rear of the skull and out the left eye. The spinal cord dangled from the back of the head like a bell rope.

The deputy puked in the bushes. "Oh, God. I don't want no more of this."

"Go back. I won't think the less of you, cause I don't think that much of you to begin with. Take his head for evidence and ride on, just leave me my horse."

The deputy adjusted his hat. "Don't need the head . . . And if it comes to it, you'll be glad I'm here. I ain't no weak sister."

"Don't talk me to death on the matter. Show me what you got, boy."

The trail was slick with Bill's blood. They went along it and up a rise, guns drawn. At the top of the hill they saw a field, grown up, and not far away, a sagging shack with a fallen down chimney.

They went that direction, came to the shack's door. Jebidiah kicked it with the toe of his boot and it sagged open. Once inside, Jebidiah struck a match and waved it about. Nothing but cobwebs and dust.

"Must have been Gimet's place," Jebidiah said. Jebidiah moved the match before him until he found a lantern full of coal oil. He lit it and placed the lantern on the table.

"Should we do that?" the deputy asked. "Have a light. Won't he find us?"

"In case you have forgotten, that's the idea."

Out the back window, which had long lost its grease paper covering, they could see tombstones and wooden crosses in the distance. "Another view of the graveyard," Jebidiah said. "That would be where the girl's mother killed herself."

No sooner had Jebidiah said that, then he saw a shadowy shape move on the hill, flitting between stones and crosses. The shape moved quickly and awkwardly.

"Move to the center of the room," Jebidiah said.

The deputy did as he was told, and Jebidiah moved the lamp there as well. He sat it in the center of the floor, found a bench and dragged it next to the lantern. Then he reached in his coat pocket and took out the bible. He dropped to one knee and held the bible close to the lantern light and tore out certain pages. He wadded them up, and began placing them all around the bench on the floor, placing the crumpled pages about six feet out from the bench and in a circle with each wad two feet apart.

The deputy said nothing. He sat on the bench and watched Jebidiah's curious work. Jebidiah sat on the bench beside the deputy, rested one of his pistols on his knee. "You got a .44, don't you?"

"Yeah. I got a converted cartridge pistol, just like you."

"Give me your revolver."

The deputy complied.

Jebidiah opened the cylinders and let the bullets fall out on the floor.

"What in hell are you doing?"

Jebidiah didn't answer. He dug into his gun belt and came up with six silver tipped bullets, loaded the weapon and gave it back to the deputy.

"Silver," Jebidiah said. "Sometimes it wards off evil."

"Sometimes?"

"Be quiet now. And wait."

"I feel like a staked goat," the deputy said.

After a while, Jebidiah rose from the bench and looked out the window. Then he sat down promptly and blew out the lantern.

Somewhere in the distance a night bird called. Crickets sawed and a large frog bleated. They sat there on the bench, near each other, facing in opposite directions, their silver loaded pistols on their knees. Neither spoke.

Suddenly the bird ceased to call and the crickets went silent, and no more was heard from the frog. Jebidiah whispered to the deputy.

"He comes."

The deputy shivered slightly, took a deep breath. Jebidiah realized he too was breathing deeply.

"Be silent, and be alert," Jebidiah said.

"All right," said the deputy, and he locked his eyes on the open window at the back of the shack. Jebidiah faced the door, which stood halfway open and sagging on its rusty hinges.

For a long time there was nothing. Not a sound. Then Jebidiah saw a shadow move at the doorway and heard the door creak slightly as it moved. He could see a hand on what appeared to be an impossibly long arm, reaching out to grab at the edge of the door. The hand clutched there for a long time, not moving. Then, it was gone, taking its shadow with it.

Time crawled by.

"It's at the window," the deputy said, and his voice was so soft it took Jebidiah a moment to decipher the words. Jebidiah turned carefully for a look.

It sat on the windowsill, crouched there like a bird of prey, a halo of bees circling around its head. The hive pulsed and glowed in its chest, and in that glow they could see more bees, so thick they appeared to be a sort of humming smoke. Gimet's head sprouted a few springs of hair, like withering grass fighting its way through stone. A slight turn of its head allowed the moon to flow through the back of its cracked skull and out of its empty eyes. Then the head turned and the face was full of shadows again. The room was silent except for the sound of buzzing bees.

"Courage," Jebidiah said, his mouth close to the deputy's ear. "Keep your place."

The thing climbed into the room quickly, like a spider dropping from a limb, and when it hit the floor, it stayed low, allowing the darkness to lay over it like a cloak.

Jebidiah had turned completely on the bench now, facing the window. He heard a scratching sound against the floor. He narrowed his eyes, saw what looked like a shadow, but was in fact the thing coming out from under the table.

Jebidiah felt the deputy move, perhaps to bolt. He grabbed his arm and held him.

"Courage," he said.

The thing kept crawling. It came within three feet of the circle made by the crumpled bible pages.

The way the moonlight spilled through the window and onto the floor near the circle Jebidiah had made, it gave Gimet a kind of eerie glow, his satellite bees circling his head. In that moment, every aspect of the thing locked itself in Jebidiah's mind. The empty eyes, the sharp, wet teeth, the long, cracked nails, blackened from grime, clacking against the wooden floor. As it moved to cross between two wads of scripture, the pages burst into flames and a line of crackling blue fulmination moved between the wadded pages and made the circle light up fully, all the way around, like Ezekiel's wheel.

Gimet gave out with a hoarse cry, scuttled back, clacking nails and knees against the floor. When he moved, he moved so quickly there seemed to be missing spaces between one moment and the next. The buzzing of Gimet's bees was ferocious.

Jebidiah grabbed the lantern, struck a match and lit it. Gimet was scuttling along the wall like a cockroach, racing to the edge of the window.

Jebidiah leaped forward, tossed the lit lantern, hit the beast full in the back as it fled through the window. The lantern burst into flames and soaked Gimlet's back, causing a wave of fire to climb from the thing's waist to the top of its head, scorching a horde of bees, dropping them from the sky like exhausted meteors.

Jebidiah drew his revolver, snapped off a shot. There was a howl of agony, and then the thing was gone.

Jebidiah raced out of the protective circle and the deputy followed. They stood at the open window, watched as Gimet, flame-wrapped, streaked through the night in the direction of the graveyard.

"I panicked a little," Jebidiah said. "I should have been more resolute. Now he's escaped."

"I never even got off a shot," the deputy said. "God, but you're fast. What a draw."

"Look, you stay here if you like. I'm going after him. But I tell you now, the circle of power has played out."

The deputy glanced back at it. The pages had burned out and there was nothing now but a black ring on the floor.

"What in hell caused them to catch fire in the first place?"

"Evil," Jebidiah said. "When he got close, the pages broke into flames. Gave us the protection of God. Unfortunately, as with most of God's blessings, it doesn't last long."

"I stay here, you'd have to put down more pages."

"I'll be taking the bible with me. I might need it."

"Then I guess I'll be sticking."

They climbed out the window and moved up the hill. They could smell the odor of fire and rotted flesh in the air. The night was as cool and silent as the graves on the hill.

Moments later they moved amongst the stones and wooden crosses, until they came to a long wide hole in the earth. Jebidiah could see that there was a burrow at one end of the grave that dipped down deeper into the ground.

Jebidiah paused there. "He's made this old grave his den. Dug it out and dug deeper."

"How do you know?" the deputy asked.

"Experience . . . And it smells of smoke and burned skin. He crawled down there to hide. I think we surprised him a little."

Jebidiah looked up at the sky. There was the faintest streak of pink on the horizon. "He's running out of daylight, and soon he'll be out of moon. For a while."

"He damn sure surprised me. Why don't we let him hide? You could come back when the moon isn't full, or even half full. Back in the daylight, get him then."

"I'm here now. And it's my job."

"That's one hell of a job you got, mister."

"I'm going to climb down for a better look."

"Help yourself."

Jebidiah struck a match and dropped himself into the grave, moved the match around at the mouth of the burrow, got down on his knees and stuck the match and his head into the opening.

"Very large," he said, pulling his head out. "I can smell him. I'm going to have to go in."

"What about me?"

"You keep guard at the lip of the grave," Jebidiah said, standing. "He may have another hole somewhere, he could come out behind you for all I know. He could come out of that hole even as we speak."

"That's wonderful."

Jebidiah dropped the now dead match on the ground. "I will tell you this. I can't guarantee success. I lose, he'll come for you, you can bet on that, and you better shoot those silvers as straight as William Tell's arrows."

"I'm not really that good a shot."

"I'm sorry," Jebidiah said, and struck another match along the length of his pants seam, then with his free hand, drew one of his revolvers. He got down on his hands and knees again, stuck the match in the hole and looked around. When the match was near done, he blew it out.

"Ain't you gonna need some light?" the deputy said. "A match ain't nothin',"

"I'll have it." Jebidiah removed the remains of the Bible from his pocket, tore it in half along the spine, pushed one half in his coat, pushed the other half before him, into the darkness of the burrow. The moment it entered the hole, it flamed.

"Ain't your pocket gonna catch inside that hole?" the deputy asked.

"As long as I hold it or it's on my person, it won't harm me. But the minute I let go of it, and the aura of evil touches it, it'll blaze. I got to hurry, boy."

With that, Jebidiah wiggled inside the burrow.

In the burrow, Jebidiah used the tip of his pistol to push the Bible pages forward. They glowed brightly, but Jebidiah knew the light would be brief. It would burn longer than writing paper, but still, it would not last long.

After a goodly distance, Jebidiah discovered the burrow dropped off. He found himself inside a fairly large cavern. He could hear the sound of bats, and smell bat guano, which in fact, greased his path as he slid along on his elbows until he could stand inside the higher cavern and look about. The last flames of the Bible burned itself out with a puff of blue light and a sound like an old man breathing his last.

Jebidiah listened in the dark for a long moment. He could hear the bats squeaking, moving about. The fact that they had given up the night sky, let Jebidiah know daylight was not far off.

Jebidiah's ears caught a sound, rocks shifting against the cave floor. Something was moving in the darkness, and he didn't think it was the bats. It scuttled, and Jebidiah felt certain it was close to the floor, and by the sound of it, moving his way at a creeping pace. The hair on the back of Jebidiah's neck bristled like porcupine quills. He felt his flesh bump up and crawl. The air became stiffer with the stench of burnt and rotting flesh. Jebidiah's knees trembled. He reached cautiously inside his coat pocket, produced a match, struck it on his pants leg, held it up.

At that very moment, the thing stood up and was brightly lit in the glow of the match, the bees circling its skin-stripped skull. It snarled and darted forward. Jebidiah felt its rotten claws on his shirt front as he fired the revolver. The blaze from the bullet gave a brief, bright flare and was gone. At the same time, the match was knocked out of his hand and Jebidiah was knocked backwards, onto his back, the thing's claws at his throat. The monster's bees stung him. The stings felt like red-hot pokers entering his flesh. He stuck the revolver into the creature's body and fired. Once. Twice. Three times. A fourth.

Then the hammer clicked empty. He realized he had already fired two other shots. Six dead silver soldiers were in his cylinders, and the thing still had hold of him.

He tried to draw his other gun, but before he could, the thing released him, and Jebidiah could hear it crawling away in the dark. The bats fluttered and screeched.

Confused, Jebidiah drew the pistol, managed to get to his feet. He waited, listening, his fresh revolver pointing into the darkness.

Jebidiah found another match, struck it.

The thing lay with its back draped over a rise of rock. Jebidiah eased toward it. The silver loads had torn into the hive. It oozed a dark, odiferous trail of death and decaying honey. Bees began to drop to the cavern floor. The hive in Gimet's chest sizzled and pulsed like a large, black knot. Gimet opened his mouth, snarled, but otherwise didn't move.

Couldn't move.

Jebidiah, guided by the last wisps of his match, raised the pistol, stuck it against the black knot, and pulled the trigger. The knot exploded. Gimet let out with a shriek so sharp and loud it startled the bats to flight, drove them out of the cave, through the burrow, out into the remains of the night.

Gimet's claw-like hands dug hard at the stones around him, then he was still and Jebidiah's match went out.

Jebidiah found the remains of the Bible in his pocket, and as he removed it, tossed it on the ground, it burst into flames. Using the two pistol barrels like large tweezers, he lifted the burning pages and dropped them into Gimet's open chest. The body caught on fire immediately, crackled and popped dryly, and was soon nothing more than a blaze. It lit the cavern up bright as day.

Jebidiah watched the corpse being consumed by the Biblical fire for a moment, then headed toward the burrow, bent down, squirmed through it, came up in the grave.

He looked for the deputy and didn't see him. He climbed out of the grave and looked around. Jebidiah smiled. If the deputy had lasted until the bats charged out, that was most likely the last straw, and he had bolted.

Jebidiah looked back at the open grave. Smoke wisped out of the hole and out of the grave and climbed up to the sky. The moon was fading and the pink on the horizon was widening.

Gimet was truly dead now. The road was safe. His job was done.

At least for one brief moment.

Jebidiah walked down the hill, found his horse tied in the brush near the road where he had left it. The deputy's horse was gone, of course, the deputy most likely having already finished out Deadman's Road at a high gallop, on his way to Nacogdoches, perhaps to have a long drink of whisky and turn in his badge.

Joe R. Lansdale *is the author of over thirty novels and numerous short stories. His novella,* Bubba Hotep, *was made into an award-winning film of the same name, as was* Incident On and Off a Mountain Road. *Both were directed by Don Coscarelli. His works have received numerous recognitions, including the Edgar, seven Bram Stoker awards, the Grinizani Prize for Literature, American Mystery Award, the International Horror Award, British Fantasy Award, and many others.*

I reckon this here story might've left y'all are hankering to hear more about The Reverend Jebidiah Mercer.

You are in luck as he appears in several of Joe. R. Lansdale's stories and the novel *Dead in the West*, a zombie western. The novel and four stories—one never before collected, one brand new—are being republished as *Deadman's Road* by Subterranean Press.

Bitter Grounds

Neil Gaiman

1
"Come Back Early or Never Come"

In every way that counted, I was dead. Inside somewhere maybe I was screaming and weeping and howling like an animal, but that was another person deep inside, another person who had no access to the face and lips and mouth and head, so on the surface I just shrugged and smiled and kept moving. If I could have physically passed away, just let it all go, like that, without doing anything, stepped out of life as easily as walking through a door, I would have. But I was going to sleep at night and waking in the morning, disappointed to be there and resigned to existence.

Sometimes I telephoned her. I let the phone ring once, maybe even twice before I hung up.

The me who was screaming was so far inside nobody knew he was even there at all. Even I forgot that he was there, until one day I got into the car—I had to go to the store, I had decided, to bring back some apples—and I went past the store that sold apples and I kept driving, and driving. I was going south, and west, because if I went north or east I would run out of world too soon.

A couple of hours down the highway my cell phone started to ring. I wound down the window and threw the cell phone out. I wondered who would find it, whether they would answer the phone and find themselves gifted with life.

When I stopped for gas I took all the cash I could on every card I had. I did the same for the next couple of days, ATM by ATM, until the cards stopped working.

The first two nights I slept in the car.

I was halfway through Tennessee when I realized I needed a bath badly enough to pay for it. I checked into a motel, stretched out in the bath, and slept in it until the water got cold and woke me. I shaved with a motel courtesy kit plastic razor and a sachet of foam. Then I stumbled to the bed, and I slept.

Awoke at 4:00 AM, and knew it was time to get back on the road.

I went down to the lobby.

There was a man standing at the front desk when I got there: silver-gray hair although I guessed he was still in his thirties, if only just, thin lips, good suit rumpled, saying, "I ordered that cab an hour ago. One hour ago." He tapped the desk with his wallet as he spoke, the beats emphasizing his words.

The night manager shrugged. "I'll call again," he said. "But if they don't have the car, they can't send it." He dialed a phone number, said, "This is the Night's Out Inn front desk . . . . Yeah, I told him . . . . Yeah, I told him."

"Hey," I said. "I'm not a cab, but I'm in no hurry. You need a ride somewhere?"

For a moment the man looked at me like I was crazy, and for a moment there was fear in his eyes. Then he looked at me like I'd been sent from Heaven. "You know, by God, I do," he said.

"You tell me where to go," I said. "I'll take you there. Like I said, I'm in no hurry"

"Give me that phone," said the silver-gray man to the night cle-rk. He took the handset and said, "You can *cancel* your cab, because God just sent me a Good Samaritan. People come into your life for a reason. That's right. And I want you to think about that."

He picked up his briefcase—like me he had no luggage—and together we went out to the parking lot.

We drove through the dark. He'd check a handdrawn map on his lap, with a flashlight attached to his key ring; then he'd say, "Left here," or "This way"

"It's good of you," he said.

"No problem. I have time."

"I appreciate it. You know, this has that pristine urban-legend quality, driving down country roads with a mysterious Samaritan. A Phantom Hitchhiker story. After I get to my destination, I'll describe you to a friend, and they'll tell me you died ten years ago, and still go round giving people rides."

"Be a good way to meet people."

He chuckled. "What do you do?"

"Guess you could say I'm between jobs," I said. "You?"

"I'm an anthropology professor." Pause. "I guess I should have introduced myself. Teach at a Christian college. People don't believe we teach anthropology at Christian colleges, but we do. Some of us."

"I believe you."

Another pause. "My car broke down. I got a ride to the motel from the highway patrol, as they said there was no tow truck going to be there until morning. Got two hours of sleep. Then the highway patrol called my hotel room. Tow truck's on the way. I got to be there when they arrive. Can you believe that? I'm not there, they won't touch it. Just drive away. Called a cab. Never came. Hope we get there before the tow truck."

"I'll do my best."

"I guess I should have taken a plane. It's not that I'm scared of flying. But I cashed in the ticket; I'm on my way to New Orleans. Hour's flight, four hundred-and-forty dollars. Day's drive, thirty dollars. That's four hundred-and-ten dollars spending money, and I don't have to account for it to anybody. Spent fifty dollars on the motel room, but that's just the way these things go. Academic conference. My first. Faculty doesn't believe in them. But things change. I'm looking forward to it. Anthropologists from all over the world." He named several, names that meant nothing to me. "I'm presenting a paper on the Haitian coffee girls."

"They grow it, or drink it?"

"Neither. They sold it, door to door in Port-au-Prince, early in the morning, in the early years of the century"

It was starting to get light, now.

"People thought they were zombies," he said. "You know. The walking dead. I think it's a right turn here."

"Were they? Zombies?"

He seemed very pleased to have been asked. "Well, anthropologically, there are several schools of thought about zombies. It's not as cut-and-dried as popularist works like *The Serpent and the Rainbow* would make it appear. First we have to define our terms: are we talking folk belief, or zombie dust, or the walking dead?"

"I don't know," I said. I was pretty sure *The Serpent and the Rainbow* was a horror movie.

"They were children, little girls, five to ten years old, who went door-to-door through Port-au-Prince selling the chicory coffee mixture. Just about this time of day, before the sun was up. They belonged to one old woman. Hang a left just before we go into the next turn. When she died, the girls vanished. That's what the books tell you."

"And what do you believe?" I asked.

"That's my car," he said, with relief in his voice. It was a red Honda Accord, on the side of the road. There was a tow truck beside it, lights flashing, a man beside the tow truck smoking a cigarette. We pulled up behind the tow truck.

The anthropologist had the door of the car opened before I'd stopped; he grabbed his briefcase and was out of the car.

"Was giving you another five minutes, then I was going to take off," said the tow-truck driver. He dropped his cigarette into a puddle on the tarmac. "Okay, I'll need your triple-A card, and a credit card."

The man reached for his wallet. He looked puzzled. He put his hands in his pockets. He said, "My wallet." He came back to my car, opened the passenger-side door and leaned back inside. I turned on the light. He patted the empty seat. "My wallet," he said again. His voice was plaintive and hurt.

"You had it back in the motel," I reminded him. "You were holding it. It was in your hand."

He said, "God damn it. God fucking damn it to hell."

"Everything okay there?" called the tow-truck driver.

"Okay," said the anthropologist to me, urgently. "This is what we'll do. You drive back to the motel. I must have left the wallet on the desk. Bring it back here. I'll keep him happy until then. Five minutes, it'll take you five minutes." He must have seen the expression on my face. He said, "Remember. People come into your life for a reason."

I shrugged, irritated to have been sucked into someone else's story.

Then he shut the car door and gave me a thumbs-up.

I wished I could just have driven away and abandoned him, but it was too late, I was driving to the hotel. The night clerk gave me the wallet, which he had noticed on the counter, he told me, moments after we left.

I opened the wallet. The credit cards were all in the name of Jackson Anderton.

It took me half an hour to find my way back, as the sky grayed into full dawn. The tow truck was gone. The rear window of the red Honda Accord was broken, and the driver's-side door hung open. I wondered if it was a different car, if I had driven the wrong way to the wrong place; but there were the tow truck driver's cigarette stubs, crushed on the road, and in the ditch nearby I found a gaping briefcase, empty, and beside it, a manila folder containing a fifteen-page typescript, a prepaid hotel reservation at a Marriott in New Orleans in the name of Jackson Anderton, and a packet of three condoms, ribbed for extra pleasure.

On the title page of the typescript was printed:

This was the way zombies are spoken of. They are the bodies without souls. The living dead. Once they were dead, and after that they were called back to life again.—Hurston, *Tell My Horse*

I took the manila folder, but left the briefcase where it was. I drove south under a pearl-colored sky.

People come into your life for a reason. Right.

I could not find a radio station that would hold its signal. Eventually I pressed the scan button on the radio and just left it on, left it scanning from channel to channel in a relentless quest for signal, scurrying from gospel to oldies to Bible talk to sex talk to country, three seconds a station with plenty of white noise in between .

. . . Lazarus, who was dead, you make no mistake about that, he was dead, and Jesus brought him back to show us—I say to show us . . .

. . . what I call a Chinese dragon. Can I say this on the air? Just as you, y'know get your rocks off, you whomp her round the backatha head, it all spurts outta her nose. I damn near laugh my ass off . . .

. . . If you come home tonight I'll be waiting in the darkness for my woman with my bottle and my gun . . .

. . . When Jesus says will you be there, will you be there? No man knows the day or the hour, so will you. be there . . .

. . . president unveiled an initiative today . . .

. . . fresh-brewed in the morning. For you, for me. For every day. Because every day is freshly ground . . .

Over and over. It washed over me, driving through the day, on the back roads. Just driving and driving.

They become more personable as you head south, the people. You sit in a diner, and along with your coffee and your food, they bring you comments, questions, smiles, and nods.

It was evening, and I was eating fried chicken and collard greens and hush puppies, and a waitress smiled at me. The food seemed tasteless, but I guessed that might have been my problem, not theirs.

I nodded at her politely, which she took as an invitation to come over and refill my coffee cup. The coffee was bitter, which I liked. At least it tasted of something.

"Looking at you," she said, "I would guess that you are a professional man. May I enquire as to your profession?" That was what she said, word for word.

"Indeed you may," I said, feeling almost possessed by something, and affably pompous, like W.C. Fields or the Nutty Professor (the fat one, not the Jerry Lewis one, although I am actually within pounds of the optimum weight for my height). "I happen to be . . . an anthropologist, on my way to a conference in New Orleans, where I shall confer, consult, and otherwise hobnob with my fellow anthropologists."

"I knew it," she said. "Just looking at you. I had you figured for a professor. Or a dentist, maybe."

She smiled at me one more time. I thought about stopping forever in that little town, eating in that diner every morning and every night. Drinking their bitter coffee and having her smile at me until I ran out of coffee and money and days.

Then I left her a good tip, and went south and west.

2
"Tongue Brought Me Here"

There were no hotel rooms in New Orleans, or anywhere in the New Orleans sprawl. A jazz festival had eaten them, everyone. It was too hot to sleep in my car, and even if I'd cranked a window and been prepared to suffer the heat, I felt unsafe. New Orleans is a real place, which is more than I can say about most of the cities I've lived in, but it's not a safe place, not a friendly one.

I stank, and itched. I wanted to bathe, and to sleep, and for the world to stop moving past me.

I drove from fleabag motel to fleabag motel, and then, at the last, as I had always known I would, I drove into the parking lot of the downtown Marriott on Canal Street. At least I knew they had one free room. I had a voucher for it in the manila folder.

"I need a room," I said to one of the women behind the counter.

She barely looked at me. "All rooms are taken," she said. "We won't have anything until Tuesday"

I needed to shave, and to shower, and to rest. What's the worst she can say? I thought. I'm sorry, you've already checked in?

"I have a room, prepaid by my university. The name's Anderton."

She nodded, tapped a keyboard, said "Jackson?" then gave me a key to my room, and I initialed the room rate. She pointed me to the elevators.

A short man with a ponytail, and a dark, hawkish face dusted with stubble, cleared his throat as we stood beside the elevators. "You're the Anderton from Hopewell," he said. "We were neighbors in the *Journal of Anthropological Heresies*." He wore a white T-shirt that said "Anthropologists Do It While Being Lied To."

"We were?"

"We were. I'm Campbell Lakh. University of Norwood and Streatham. Formerly North Croydon Polytechnic. England. I wrote the paper about Icelandic spirit walkers and fetches."

"Good to meet you," I said, and shook his hand. "You don't have a London accent."

"I'm a Brummie," he said. "From Birmingham," he added. "Never seen you at one of these things before."

"It's my first conference," I told him.

"Then you stick with me," he said. "I'll see you're all right. I remember my first one of these conferences, I was scared shitless I'd do something stupid the entire time. We'll stop on the mezzanine, get our stuff, then get cleaned up. There must have been a hundred babies on my plane over, IsweartoGod. They took it in shifts to scream, shit, and puke, though. Never fewer than ten of them screaming at a time."

We stopped on the mezzanine, collected our badges and programs. "Don't forget to sign up for the ghost walk," said the smiling woman behind the table. "Ghost walks of Old New Orleans each night, limited to fifteen people in each party, so sign up fast."

I bathed, and washed my clothes out in the basin, then hung them up in the bathroom to dry.

I sat naked on the bed, and examined the papers that had been in Anderton's briefcase. I skimmed through the paper he had intended to present, without taking in the content.

On the clean back of page five he had written, in a tight, mostly legible scrawl, *In a perfect perfect world you could fuck people without giving them a*

piece of your heart. And every glittering kiss and every touch of flesh is another
shard of heart you'll never see again. Until walking (waking? calling?) on your own
is unsupportable.

When my clothes were pretty much dry I put them back on and went down to the lobby bar. Campbell was already there. He was drinking a gin and tonic with a gin and tonic on the side.

He had out a copy of the conference program, and had circled each of the talks and papers he wanted to see. ("Rule one, if it's before midday, fuck it unless you're the one doing it," he explained.) He showed me my talk, circled in pencil.

"I've never done this before," I told him. "Presented a paper at a conference."

"It's a piece of piss, Jackson," he said. "Piece of piss. You know what I do?"

"No," I said.

"I just get up and read the paper. Then people ask questions, and I just bullshit," he said. "Actively bullshit, as opposed to passively. That's the best bit. Just bullshitting. Piece of utter piss."

"I'm not really good at, um, bullshitting," I said. "Too honest."

"Then nod, and tell them that that's a really perceptive question, and that it's addressed at length in the longer version of the paper, of which the one you are reading is an edited abstract. If you get some nut job giving you a really difficult time about something you got wrong, just get huffy and say that it's not about what's fashionable to believe, it's about the truth."

"Does that work?"

"Christ yes. I gave a paper a few years back about the origins of the Thuggee sects in Persian military troops. It's why you could get Hindus and Muslims equally becoming Thuggee, you see—the Kali worship was tacked on later. It would have begun as some sort of Manichaean secret society—"

"Still spouting that nonsense?" She was a tall, pale woman with a shock of white hair, wearing clothes that looked both aggressively, studiedly Bohemian and far too warm for the climate. I could imagine her riding a bicycle, the kind with a wicker basket in the front.

"Spouting it? I'm writing a fucking book about it," said the Englishman. "So, what I want to know is, who's coming with me to the French Quarter to taste all that New Orleans can offer?"

"I'll pass," said the woman, unsmiling. "Who's your friend?"

"This is Jackson Anderton, from Hopewell College."

"The Zombie Coffee Girls paper?" She smiled. "I saw it in the program. Quite fascinating. Yet another thing we owe Zora, eh?"

"Along with *The Great Gatsby*," I said.

"Hurston knew F. Scott Fitzgerald?" said the bicycle woman. "I did not know that. We forget how small the New York literary world was back then, and how the color bar was often lifted for a genius."

The Englishman snorted. "Lifted? Only under sufferance. The woman died in penury as a cleaner in Florida. Nobody knew she'd written any of the stuff she wrote, let alone that she'd worked with Fitzgerald on *The Great Gatsby*. It's pathetic, Margaret."

"Posterity has a way of taking these things into account," said the tall woman. She walked away.

Campbell stared after her. "When I grow up," he said, "I want to be her."

"Why?"

He looked at me. "Yeah, that's the attitude. You're right. Some of us write the bestsellers; some of us read them. Some of us get the prizes; some of us don't. What's important is being human, isn't it? It's how good a person you are. Being alive."

He patted me on the arm.

"Come on. Interesting anthropological phenomenon I've read about on the Internet I shall point out to you tonight, of the kind you probably don't see back in Dead Rat, Kentucky. Id est, women who would, under normal circumstances, not show their tits for a hundred quid, who will be only too pleased to get 'em out for the crowd for some cheap plastic beads."

"Universal trading medium," I said. "Beads."

"Fuck," he said. "There's a paper in that. Come on. You ever had a Jell-O shot, Jackson?"

"No."

"Me neither. Bet they'll be disgusting. Let's go and see."

We paid for our drinks. I had to remind him to tip.

"By the way," I said. "F. Scott Fitzgerald. What was his wife's name?"

"Zelda? What about her?"

"Nothing," I said.

Zelda. Zora. Whatever. We went out.

3
"Nothing Like Something Happens Anywhere"

Midnight, give or take. We were in a bar on Bourbon Street, me and the English anthropology prof, and he started buying drinks—real drinks, this place didn't do Jell-O shots—for a couple of dark-haired women at the bar. They looked so similar they might have been sisters. One wore a red ribbon in her hair; the other wore a white ribbon. Gauguin might have painted them, only he would have painted them bare-breasted, and without the silver mouse-skull earrings. They laughed a lot.

We had seen a small party of academics walk past the bar at one point, being led by a guide with a black umbrella. I pointed them out to Campbell.

The woman with the red ribbon raised an eyebrow. "They go on the Haunted History tours, looking for ghosts. You want to say, 'Dude, this is where the ghosts come; this is where the dead stay.' Easier to go looking for the living."

"You saying the tourists are alive?" said the other, mock concern on her face.

"When they get here," said the first, and they both laughed at that.

They laughed a lot.

The one with the white ribbon laughed at everything Campbell said. She would tell him, "Say 'fuck' again," and he would say it, and she would say "Fook! Fook!" trying to copy him. And he'd say, "It's not *fook,* it's *fuck,*" and she couldn't hear the difference, and would laugh some more.

After two drinks, maybe three, he took her by the hand and walked her into the back of the bar, where music was playing, and it was dark, and there were a couple of people already, if not dancing, then moving against each other.

I stayed where I was, beside the woman with the red ribbon in her hair.

She said, "So you're in the record company, too?"

I nodded. It was what Campbell had told them we did. "I hate telling people I'm a fucking academic," he had said reasonably, when they were in the ladies' room. Instead he had told them that he had discovered Oasis.

"How about you? What do you do in the world?"

She said, "I'm a priestess of Santeria. Me, I got it all in my blood; my papa was Brazilian, my momma was Irish-Cherokee. In Brazil, everybody makes love with everybody and they have the best little brown babies. Everybody got black slave blood; everybody got Indian blood; my papa even got some Japanese blood. His brother, my uncle, he looks Japanese. My papa, he just a good-looking man. People think it was my papa I got the Santeria from, but no, it was my grandmomma—said she was Cherokee, but I had her figgered for mostly high yaller when I saw the old photographs. When I was three I was talking to dead folks. When I was five I watched a huge black dog, size of a Harley-Davidson, walking behind a man in the street; no one could see it but me. When I told my mom, she told my grandmomma, they said, 'She's got to know; she's got to learn.' There was people to teach me, even as a little girl.

"I was never afraid of dead folk. You know that? They never hurt you. So many things in this town can hurt you, but the dead don't hurt you. Living people hurt you. They hurt you so bad."

I shrugged.

"This is a town where people sleep with each other, you know. We make love to each other. It's something we do to show we're still alive."

I wondered if this was a come-on. It did not seem to be.

She said, "You hungry?"

"A little," I said.

She said, "I know a place near here they got the best bowl of gumbo in New Orleans. Come on."

I said, "I hear it's a town where you're best off not walking on your own at night."

"That's right," she said. "But you'll have me with you. You're safe, with me with you."

Out on the street, college girls were flashing their breasts to the crowds on the balconies. For every glimpse of nipple the onlookers would cheer and throw plastic beads. I had known the red-ribbon woman's name earlier in the evening, but now it had evaporated.

"Used to be they only did this shit at Mardi Gras," she said. "Now the tourists expect it, so it's just tourists doing it for the tourists. The locals don't care. When you need to piss," she added, "you tell me."

"Okay. Why?"

"Because most tourists who get rolled, get rolled when they go into the alleys to relieve themselves. Wake up an hour later in Pirates' Alley with a sore head and an empty wallet."

"I'll bear that in mind."

She pointed to an alley as we passed it, foggy and deserted. "Don't go there," she said.

The place we wound up in was a bar with tables. A TV on above the bar showed *The Tonight Show* with the sound off and subtitles on, although the subtitles kept scrambling into numbers and fractions. We ordered the gumbo; a bowl each.

I was expecting more from the best gumbo in New Orleans. It was almost tasteless. Still, I spooned it down, knowing that I needed food, that I had nothing to eat that day.

Three men came into the bar. One sidled; one strutted; one shambled. The sidler was dressed like a Victorian undertaker, high top hat and all. His skin was fish-belly pale; his hair was long and stringy; his beard was long and threaded with silver beads. The strutter was dressed in a long black leather coat, dark clothes underneath. His skin was very black. The last one, the shambler, hung back, waiting by the door. I could not see much of his face, nor decode his race: what I could see of his skin was a dirty gray. His lank hair hung over his face. He made my skin crawl.

The first two men made straight to our table, and I was, momentarily, scared for my skin, but they paid no attention to me. They looked at the woman with the red ribbon, and both of the men kissed her on the cheek. They asked about friends they had not seen, about who did what to whom in which bar and why. They reminded me of the fox and the cat from *Pinocchio*.

"What happened to your pretty girlfriend?" the woman asked the black man.

He smiled, without humor. "She put a squirrel tail on my family tomb."

She pursed her lips. "Then you better off without her."

"That's what I say."

I glanced over at the one who gave me the creeps. He was a filthy thing, junkie thin, gray-lipped. His eyes were downcast. He barely moved. I wondered what the three men were doing together: the fox and the cat and the ghost.

Then the white man took the woman's hand and pressed it to his lips, bowed to her, raised a hand to me in a mock salute, and the three of them were gone.

"Friends of yours?"

"Bad people," she said. "Macumba. Not friends of anybody"

"What was up with the guy by the door? Is he sick?"

She hesitated; then she shook her head. "Not really. I'll tell you when you're ready"

"Tell me now"

On the TV Jay Leno was talking to a thin blond woman, IT&S NOT UST THE MOVIE, said the caption. SO H.VE SS YOU SEEN THE AC ION FIGURE? He picked up a small toy from his desk, pretended to check under its skirt to make sure it was anatomically correct, [LAUGHTER], said the caption.

She finished her bowl of gumbo, licked the spoon with a red, red tongue, and put it down in the bowl. "A lot of kids they come to New Orleans. Some of them read Anne Rice books and figure they learn about being vampires here. Some of them have abusive parents; some are just bored. Like stray kittens living in drains, they come here. They found a whole new breed of cat living in a drain in New Orleans, you know that?"

[SLAUGHTER s] said the caption, but Jay was still grinning, and *The Tonight Show* went to a car commercial.

"He was one of the street kids, only he had a place to crash at night. Good kid. Hitchhiked from L.A. to New Orleans. Wanted to be left alone to smoke a little weed, listen to his Doors cassettes, study up on chaos magick and read the complete works of Aleister Crowley. Also get his dick sucked. He wasn't particular about who did it. Bright eyes and bushy tail."

"Hey," I said. "That was Campbell. Going past. Out there."

"Campbell?"

"My friend."

"The record producer?" She smiled as she said it, and I thought, *She knows. She knows he was lying. She knows what he is.*

I put down a twenty and a ten on the table, and we went out onto the street, to find him, but he was already gone. "I thought he was with your sister," I told her.

"No sister," she said. "No sister. Only me. Only me."

We turned a corner and were engulfed by a crowd of noisy tourists, like a sudden breaker crashing onto the shore. Then, as fast as they had come, they were gone, leaving only a handful of people behind them. A teenaged girl was throwing up in a gutter, a young man nervously standing near her, holding her purse and a plastic cup half-full of booze.

The woman with the red ribbon in her hair was gone. I wished I had made a note of her name, or the name of the bar in which I'd met her.

I had intended to leave that night, to take the interstate west to Houston and from there to Mexico, but I was tired and two-thirds drunk, and instead I went back to my room. When the morning came I was still in the Marriott. Everything I had worn the night before smelled of perfume and rot.

I put on my T-shirt and pants, went down to the hotel gift shop, picked out a couple more T-shirts and a pair of shorts. The tall woman, the one without the bicycle, was in there, buying some Alka-Seltzer.

She said, "They've moved your presentation. It's now in the Audubon Room, in about twenty minutes. You might want to clean your teeth first. Your best friends won't tell you, but I hardly know you, Mister Anderton, so I don't mind telling you at all."

I added a traveling toothbrush and toothpaste to the stuff I was buying. Adding to my possessions, though, troubled me. I felt I should be shedding them. I needed to be transparent, to have nothing.

I went up to the room, cleaned my teeth, put on the jazz festival T-shirt. And then, because I had no choice in the matter; or because I was doomed to confer, consult, and otherwise hobnob; or because I was pretty certain Campbell would be in the audience and I wanted to say goodbye to him before I drove away, I picked up the typescript and went down to the Audubon Room, where fifteen people were waiting. Campbell was not one of them.

I was not scared. I said hello, and I looked at the top of page one.

It began with another quote from Zora Neale Hurston:

Big Zombies who come in the night to do malice are talked about. Also the little girl Zombies who are sent out by their owners in the dark dawn to sell little packets of roasted coffee. Before sun-up their cries of "Café grille" can be heard from dark places in the streets and one can only see them if one calls out for the seller to come with the goods. Then the little dead one makes herself visible and mounts the steps.

Anderton continued on from there, with quotations from Hurston's contemporaries and several extracts from old interviews with older Haitians, the man's paper leaping, as far as I was able to tell, from conclusion to conclusion, spinning fancies into guesses and suppositions and weaving those into fact.

Halfway through, Margaret, the tall woman without the bicycle, came in and simply stared at me. I thought, *She knows I'm not him. She knows.* I kept reading though. What else could I do? At the end, I asked for questions.

Somebody asked me about Zora Neale Hurston's research practices. I said that was a very good question, which was addressed at greater length in the finished paper, of which what I had read was essentially an edited abstract.

Someone else—a short, plump woman—stood up and announced that the zombie girls could not have existed: zombie drugs and powders numbed you, induced deathlike trances, but still worked fundamentally on belief-the belief that you were now one of the dead, and had no will of your own. How she asked, could a child of four or five be induced to believe such a thing? No. The coffee girls were, she said, one with the Indian rope trick, just another of the urban legends of the past.

Personally I agreed with her, but I nodded and said that her points were well made and well taken, and that from my perspective—which was, I hoped, genuinely anthropological perspective—what mattered was not whether it was easy to believe, but, much more importantly, if it was the truth.

They applauded, and afterward a man with a beard asked me whether I might be able to get a copy of the paper for a journal he edited. It occurred to me that it was a good thing that I had come to New Orleans, that Anderton's career would not be harmed by his absence from the conference.

The plump woman, whose badge said her name was Shanelle Gravely-Kin was waiting for me at the door. She said, "I really enjoyed that. I don't want you to think that I didn't."

Campbell didn't turn up for his presentation. Nobody ever saw him again.

Margaret introduced me to someone from New York and mentioned that Zora Neale Hurston had worked on *The Great Gatsby*. The man said yes, that was pretty common knowledge these days. I wondered if she had called the police, but she seemed friendly enough. I was starting to stress, I realized. I wished I had not thrown away my cell phone.

Shanelle Gravely-King and I had an early dinner in the hotel, at the beginning of which I said, "Oh, let's not talk shop." And she agreed that only the very dull talked shop at the table, so we talked about rock bands we had seen live, fictional methods of slowing the decomposition of a human body, and about her partner, who was a woman older than she was and who owned a restaurant, and then we went up to my room. She smelled of baby powder and jasmine, and her naked skin was clammy against mine.

Over the next couple of hours I used two of the three condoms. She was sleeping by the time I returned from the bathroom, and I climbed into the bed next to her. I thought about the words Anderton had written, hand-scrawled on the back of a page of the typescript, and I wanted to check them, but I fell asleep, a soft-fleshed jasmine-scented woman pressing close to me.

After midnight, I woke from a dream, and a woman's voice was whispering in the darkness.

She said, "So he came into town, with his Doors cassettes and his Crowley books, and his handwritten list of the secret URLs for chaos magick on the Web, and everything was good. He even got a few disciples, runaways like him, and he got his dick sucked whenever he wanted, and the world was good.

"And then he started to believe his own press. He thought he was the real thing. That he was the dude. He thought he was a big mean tiger-cat, not a little kitten. So he dug up . . . something . . . someone else wanted.

"He thought the something he dug up would look after him. Silly boy. And that night, he's sitting in Jackson Square, talking to the Tarot readers, telling them about Jim Morrison and the cabala, and someone taps him on the shoulder, and he turns, and someone blows powder into his face, and he breathes it in.

"Not all of it. And he is going to do something about it, when he realizes there's nothing to be done, because he's all paralyzed. There's fugu fish and toad skin and ground bone and everything else in that powder, and he's breathed it in.

"They take him down to emergency, where they don't do much for him, figuring him for a street rat with a drug problem, and by the next day he can move again, although it's two, three days until he can speak.

"Trouble is, he needs it. He wants it. He knows there's some big secret in the zombie powder, and he was almost there. Some people say they mixed heroin with it, some shit like that, but they didn't even need to do that. He wants it.

"And they told him they wouldn't sell it to him. But if he did jobs for them, they'd give him a little zombie powder, to smoke, to sniff, to rub on his gums, to swallow. Sometimes they'd give him nasty jobs to do no one else wanted. Sometimes they'd just humiliate him because they could—make him eat dog shit from the gutter, maybe. Kill for them, maybe. Anything but die. All skin and bones. He'd do anything for his zombie powder.

"And he still thinks, in the little bit of his head that's still him, that he's not a zombie. That he's not dead, that there's a threshold he hasn't stepped over. But he crossed it long time ago."

I reached out a hand, and touched her. Her body was hard, and slim, and lithe, and her breasts felt like breasts that Gauguin might have painted. Her mouth, in the darkness, was soft and warm against mine.

People come into your life for a reason.

4
"Those People Ought to Know Who We Are and Tell That We Are Here"

When I woke, it was still almost dark, and the room was silent. I turned on the light, looked on the pillow for a ribbon, white or red, or for a mouse-skull earring, but there was nothing to show that there had ever been anyone in the bed that night but me.

I got out of bed and pulled open the drapes, looked out of the window. The sky was graying in the east.

I thought about moving south, about continuing to run, continuing to pretend I was alive. But it was, I knew now, much too late for that. There are doors, after all, between the living and the dead, and they swing in both directions.

I had come as far as I could.

There was a faint tap-tapping on the hotel-room door. I pulled on my pants and the T-shirt I had set out in, and barefoot, I pulled the door open.

The coffee girl was waiting for me.

Everything beyond the door was touched with light, an open, wonderful predawn light, and I heard the sound of birds calling on the morning air. The street was on a hill, and the houses facing me were little more than shanties. There was mist in the air, low to the ground, curling like something from an old black-and-white film, but it would be gone by noon.

The girl was thin and small; she did not appear to be more than six years old. Her eyes were cobwebbed with what might have been cataracts; her skin was as gray as it had once been brown. She was holding a white hotel cup out to me, holding it carefully, with one small hand on the handle, one hand beneath the saucer. It was half filled with a steaming mud-colored liquid.

I bent to take it from her, and I sipped it. It was a very bitter drink, and it was hot, and it woke me the rest of the way.

I said, "Thank you."

Someone, somewhere, was calling my name. The girl waited, patiently, while I finished the coffee. I put the cup down on the carpet; then I put out my hand and touched her shoulder. She reached up her hand, spread her small gray fingers, and took hold of mine. She knew I was with her. Wherever we were headed now, we were going there together.

I remembered something somebody had once said to me. "It's okay. Every day is freshly ground," I told her.

The coffee girl's expression did not change, but she nodded, as if she had heard me, and gave my arm an impatient tug. She held my hand tight with her cold, cold fingers, and we walked, finally, side by side into the misty dawn.

⌐

Bestselling author **Neil Gaiman** *has long been one of the top writers in modern comics, as well as writing books for readers of all ages. He is listed in the* Dictionary of Literary Biography *as one of the top ten living post-modern writers, and is a prolific creator of works of prose, poetry, film, journalism, comics, song lyrics, and drama. Some of his notable works include* The Sandman *comic book series,* Stardust, American Gods, Coraline, *and* The Graveyard Book. *Gaiman's writing has won numerous awards, including World Fantasy, Hugo, Nebula, IHG, and Bram Stoker, as well as the 2009 Newbery Medal. Gaiman's official Web site, www.neilgaiman.com, now has more than one million unique visitors each month, and his online journal is syndicated to thousands of blog readers every day.*

⌐

A mysterious, melancholy, yet lovely story that mixes the metaphorical zombie (a person who feels dead inside) with the atmosphere of New Orleans, and Zora Neale Hurston's encounters with zombiism. (See the note with "Zora and the Zombie.") The girl with the red ribbon in her hair mentions Santeria. Santeria is the Spanish name for the Afro-Caribbean religion Lukumi. (The word translates as "the way of the saints" and is not accepted by its adherents.) A "cousin" of Voudou, it is associated primarily with Cuba. Since our fictional character is of mixed race and from Brazil—unless she's lying, you never can tell with these fictional characters—she might be familiar with Umbanda which is practiced in Rio de Janeiro, São Paulo, and southern Brazil. Yet another religion arising out of the African Diaspora it is also known, pejoratively, as Macumba (a word that commonly means "witchcraft.")

Beautiful White Bodies

Alice Sola Kim

The fall after Justine moved back home, the high school girls became beautiful. She saw it herself, from behind the counter of the coffee shop by her old high school. The beauty spread viciously: first to one girl, then two, then four, and now almost twenty.

Once it struck, the girls became impossibly beautiful in the space of days. Even if you could pay some super-surgeon-sculptor-sage (a three-way cross between Dr. 90210, Michelangelo, and Maimonides) to crack open your face like a watermelon and chisel away at it until your bones were fine and symmetrical, you still wouldn't look like these girls. Their necks were too long. And the whites of their eyes? Much too white!

Justine had moved back home after losing her job at a weekly paper in the city. She was now a twenty-seven-year-old who lived with her parents. Magazines like *Time* and *Newsweek* called it "boomeranging," as if vaudeville canes were emerging from the childhood homes of millions of young adults to yank them out of their lives as consultants and assistants and editors and back into their old bedrooms, where they would download music from the Internet and collect Cheeto dust in their emerging wrinkles.

So for now Justine was at the coffee shop—not belonging, not young but not old. She dealt with it. Many geniuses had sections in their biographies that could be described as "The Shitty Years" so perhaps all this was necessary. As long as it was temporary.

Pearl came into the coffee shop.

"Caffeine," said Pearl, "I need it." Lacking beauty, Pearl was one of those girls for whom style was a refuge. Today she was wearing a hound's-tooth coat, its tall funnel neck covering her up to the chin, like a mod ninja. Some sparkly lip gloss was smeared on the collar.

"Sure," Justine said. "But you need to pay this time."

Pearl moaned. "How about you put it on my tab?"

"Girl, if we did tabs here, it'd be about time for us to break your kneecaps for nonpayment."

Pearl pulled a cranky, ha-ha face. Justine poured her a mug anyway.

Pearl was Justine's friend, and yes, Pearl was in high school. Justine was as embarrassed as any normal person would be, but also she was charmed by funny, artsy Pearl, an obsessive shut-in who worshipped alt-weeklies, music festivals, zines, homemade screen-printed T-shirts, and boys with torsos like female runway models. Justine didn't have any siblings, and she justified her friendship with Pearl by telling herself that she'd always wanted a little sister, whether that was true or not.

"When are you off today?" said Pearl.

"Another hour. Then Greg takes over."

"Mmm, Greg taking over," said Pearl.

"He's not that great," Justine said. But if Greg wasn't that great, he was still pretty fucking good. He was one who had cast off the stupidity of his teenage years—had given away his bowling shirts and skater sneakers and shaved his floppy, trying-too-hard hair into an even quarter-inch all over his head—in order to become nothing. Nothing was good. Nothing was hot, actually. There wasn't anything bad you could say about nothing.

"You only say that because you can't have him, according to society's rules."

Pearl knew the rule for determining the youngest person you could date. Take your age, halve it, add seven. Greg was nineteen. Pearl was sixteen. Justine was at an age where nobody was the right age for her. It was the world she had stuck herself back into, all kids and parents. She had Rip Van Winkled herself in a backwards, sideways, mixed-up sort of way.

"Hon, he's a fetus," said Justine. "He's an egg."

Pearl shrugged and looked around the room. Justine thought maybe this big sisterly/old-school diner waitress "hon" thing wasn't working so well. Always, she had to recalibrate.

At a window table near the front door, a girl named Rebecca was laughing with a boy. She kept slapping the table and throwing her head back, her teeth glistening in her gaping mouth. Her face was careless and unarranged in the way of all beautiful girls who knew that, on them, ugly looked good. Rebecca used to be a plain, chunky girl who wore her hair in pomaded hanks over her face. Now she looked like something a talented goth high school student would draw in her notebook—a manga goddess with big-irised sepia eyes and witchy white skin and an upper lip with two fine, pointy peaks.

Justine glanced over at Pearl. Pearl was staring at Rebecca, her face too ravenous and obvious, beaming out painful *pick me pick me* rays.

"Check her out," said Pearl, subdued. "Miss Thang."

"He should have seen her two weeks ago," said Justine.

"Why her? No wait, why everyone but me?" Pearl said. She sounded five years old for a moment. "I have to show you something. It'll just take a minute." She scurried around the counter to stand next to Justine and set down her laptop.

"So, I started this blog last week," Pearl said. "As a record of all the weirdness going on here lately. You know." She scrolled halfway down the page, and found a post that had a YouTube video embedded, which she clicked on. "You are going to pee your pants when you see this," she said.

There were three girls in the video. They leaned in close to the webcam, their faces turned moony and wide by the slight fisheye effect of the lens, but no less lovely. They sat there, very still, just blinking and smiling. Justine could tell that Pearl thought they were perfect. It showed in the yearning stretch of her neck, the way she held her breath for the entire duration of the video.

But the girls, even though they were beautiful in their way, looked wrong. Justine thought she recognized the one on the left—but was that really Khadija? The face was morphed, skin faded to a pale glow, hair hanging down in sleek, heavy curtains, the same style as the others. She could be mistaken; the girls in the video all looked alike. All of them distinctly uncanny, with airbrushed skin and features with sizes and shapes that fell just a bit beyond the human norm. No one looked like that, except for video game characters.

Their staring grew intolerable. The video played for a minute and a half. Justine was relieved when it ended.

"Look, they've got a whole YouTube channel." Pearl clicked over to a screen with long columns of thumbnails. She snickered. "It's all the same thing, with different girls. Dumb hos."

Justine was chilled, but she tried to match Pearl's light tone. "High school kids," she said. "I don't understand you. They're not even doing anything. People used to have to do something to become Internet-famous."

"Don't act so old. I don't understand us either."

"God! What's the point? That's pornography that's non-pornographic. But still completely embarrassing to watch in public."

"I know," said Pearl. "That's why I made us hide behind the counter. It's skeevy. But you have to admit it's also super-interesting! That's what my blog is about, this whole phenomenon. I totally think it's a phenomenon. Someone needs to analyze it. Like, how do I have the stupid luck to live in a place where everyone is suddenly beautiful? God, it sucks. I wish I was dead."

Pearl was awkward-looking, with a pug nose and gappy teeth and tender, glowing cystic acne. She was so short and stocky that she appeared to be from a high-gravity planet. To top it off, she was Filipino-American in a town where most everyone had only recently made room in their worldview for Asians who were 1) Chinese and 2) Japanese people (not so much the people themselves, but the *idea* of them, at least). *So what the hell was Pearl, some like mutated Chinese chick? Or perhaps Mexican?* Probably things would have been easier for her if she were, like, Miss The Philippines 2009, some kind of pretty that was universal enough to play in all nations; but she wasn't. Still, Pearl was so clever, so curious, so fun, they should have given two shits about her no matter what, and then Justine remembered how she had hated her own high school, and she'd hated life too. She'd hated everything. She remembered what it was like to not so much wish you were dead, but to feel bad and lonely enough that you'd *tell* everyone you wished you were dead.

"This is wonderful, Pearl," said Justine, nodding at the blog page. "What a timely project. I can send it around to people I know, try to get you some more traffic."

Pearl's eyes widened. "That. Would be. So great!" She took her computer and sat down at a small table. Soon she was typing at a rapid clip.

Justine rested her elbows on the counter, sucking her cheeks in and out, in and out. All around her, beautiful girls were sitting at the tables and on the floors with their jackets and backpacks spread around them, as if they had parachuted in. Some of them were resting their heads on the table while their friends talked over them. Such tired, languid beauties. She was not afraid of them when they were at rest, when they didn't look up at her and creep her out with their impossible faces. When they left, they left plates of muffins, poked into infinity crumbs, and full drinks with only the foam licked off. That too was awful. What was with these girls? Were they are all on crash diets?

Pearl, friend to the arts, also wanted to be an actress. She was playing Tzeitel in the high school's production of *Fiddler on the Roof*.

Justine attended opening night by herself. Greg was sitting a few seats away. He had said hello to her when he sat down. To her horror, her hand had moved up to pat her hair, as if pulled by a fishing line.

The great thing about high school plays was that almost everyone was exactly physically wrong for their roles. Tevye, a tall boy with girlish wrists, had a fake belly that sagged in his shirt and sometimes swung in the opposite direction of his torso. Pearl played the oldest sister, but she was the smallest. Now Pearl and her two sisters stamped up to the front of the stage and started shrieking the lyrics to "Matchmaker."

Justine's stomach began to growl. There hadn't been time to eat dinner. *Fiddler on the Roof* had its moments of quiet (buried somewhere in the traditional musical Song Scene transitional-oho-we-just-said-the-first-few-words-of-the-next-song-I-think-it's-time-to-Sing Song structure) and during those moments, her stomach yowled and moaned.

"Father, I love him!" said one of the sisters.

Justine wrapped her arms around her waist. It didn't help. If anything it pushed the noises out of her stomach more hastily. *Baaaaaaarrrroooooool.* Greg made eye contact once. Then he was laughing, staring straight ahead with his lips clamped shut.

During intermission, Justine escaped. She walked down the hallway and out the front doors. Hunched over by the entrance, she dug through her bag for some Tums. Greg stepped out of the building.

"Are you okay?" he said.

"Just hungry. I guess that's obvious."

"Possibly a little." They smiled. "They're doing good so far," he said.

"Yeah. Pearl's really talented," she said. "Who are you here for?"

"My brother," said Greg. "It sucks. They didn't give him any lines. They made him play the violin, but he messed that up too. You saw. I don't know what they were thinking, it's not like playing the violin is easier than acting. Do you want to go get something to eat? I'm hungry too."

The auditorium was lit up. You could see down the length of the dark hallway right into the back rows of the auditorium, everything tiny and bright and precious, like a diorama. People were starting to file back in.

Justine said, "I don't know. Pearl, she has a few more scenes."

Greg didn't try to convince her. He just stood there, waiting. It seemed respectful of him, but who knew. He was thin. She couldn't see any of his body through his clothing, only his shoulders.

Glaaaauuwwwwhoaa, intoned her stomach.

"It's speaking German," said Greg. "Or Chinese."

Like Greg's appearance, his apartment gave away nothing of himself—all the things superficial that ended up being important. What kind of music do you like, are you a food snob, do you consider yourself well-traveled, how much disposable income do you have, do you care if people who are thirty feet away from you and will never meet you think kindly of you?

Greg's apartment was neat. He had no books, but there was a stack of DVDs rented from the library, on the coffee table by the couch. There was a gray kitten sleeping on a pet bed in the corner of the living room, curled up like a little slug. Justine admired the kitten as Greg told her darling facts about it, like its name and the fates of its siblings and which items it had destroyed, and then they were kissing and moving toward his bedroom in this clumsy backwards kissing tango. Justine hadn't had sex with that many people, but she was accustomed to guys who had specific tastes and would try to pretend that they had just thought up those ideas. (*Say, what if I were to come on your feet? Wouldn't that be fun? Cool and different, right?*). But Greg in bed was like his anonymous apartment and haircut, as forgettable as someone who might be a kindly serial killer.

Greg sat up afterward and asked Justine if she wanted to take a shower. "With me," he added.

She blinked and blinked as if it would make Greg disappear.

"Why are you laughing?" he said, laughing. "That's not weird."

"I'm not laughing," she said. "You go ahead. I'll be in."

"All right," he said. "But don't wait too long. The hot water runs out fast." He went into the bathroom. She heard the spiky hiss of the shower turning on, and pressed her palms into her stomach. She still had not eaten. Greg had forgotten to offer her food! She had slept with a nineteen-year-old, and forgotten to eat dinner. Now Justine felt the panicky regret that comes after you've fucked someone you didn't intend to fuck, so strong that you would gnaw off your leg to escape from the sex trap, in fact you would do anything to rewind the tape, dick goes out of vagina, THIS NEVER HAPPENED.

It would have been nice to shower with Greg, she knew. The slow, hot Laundromat press of their bodies. But she had already done one type of thing, and she could not allow herself to do the next. What would come after the shower—sitting around in bathrobes, all pruney and sleepy, trying to make conversation?

Oof. Now she was hungrier than ever. She grabbed her clothes, squirming a little when she pulled on her damp underwear, and went into the bathroom. Greg was rubbing soap under his arms. She tapped on the glass. He turned around, grinning, and then pressed his dick up to the glass until it looked like a flatworm, or half of a hot dog. He seemed to think it was pretty funny, and did a dance, squeegeeing his dick around on the shower door.

"Why'd you get dressed?" he said.

Justine began to feel a little bit damned. The bathroom was steamy from Greg's shower and her feet stuck to the floor, as if she was being pulled down into a sweltering, sweating Hell. "I don't have time." She stepped back. "I'm meeting up with Pearl. And getting dinner."

"Oh no! I forgot you were hungry!" Water ran into Greg's open mouth.

"No worries! Finish your shower. I'll see you at work tomorrow, and maybe we shouldn't mention this to anyone, I feel like they'd put me under arrest or something! Not that this was illegal, though, unless you were lying about your age, ha ha . . . " She paused. "*Sorry,*" she finally said, in a loud desperate honk, then escaped. The kitten was sitting on the coffee table licking its smoke-colored legs. It swiped at her with its claws as she went by.

It was fully night, and the streetlights had switched on. The sidewalk was dotted with bushes and sparse trees that, in the dark, seemed too full of intentions and possibilities, and Justine veered to avoid them. Hurrying down the block, Justine felt a wet hand on her shoulder. "Wait," Greg was saying. He was holding a towel around his waist with one hand and reaching out to her with the other, and then a girl came lurching around the corner, rattling the bushes and crashing into them.

Justine took the girl's arm and held her up. "Rebecca?" said Justine. Rebecca lifted her head, her mouth slack. Justine brushed Rebecca's hair off her face, away from her mouth, and said, "What's—" when Rebecca's body spasmed. She fell forward on her knees and threw up. There was blood in her vomit, big dark gleaming garnets of it. It pooled and spread over the sidewalk and dripped into the gutter. Justine and Greg both yelled. Greg ran back to his apartment to call 911, while Justine squatted there next to Rebecca, rubbing her quaking back, watching her puke and puke and puke until the ambulance came.

After asking Justine and Greg some questions, the paramedics took Rebecca away. The ambulance zoomed down the street, rattling and wailing, and the quiet pressed down on them. "Come back for that shower sometime," Greg said sadly, and left.

Safely nestled in her car, Justine drove to Burger King and bought two cheeseburgers and extra-large fries and tried not to think about puke as she ate the internally scalding fries by the handful. There was an ancient alchemical recipe for gold, which involved stirring melted lead without once thinking the word "hippopotamus." This was just like that: if she didn't think about puke or Rebecca or Greg or beauty or hot dogs, she would be fine.

Justine made another quick stop at the twenty-four-hour supermarket to buy flowers for Pearl. Tzeitel had been Pearl's biggest role yet. As she drove to Pearl's, feeling gross and grimy, she thought about her ex-boyfriend. He would be glad if he knew what she'd been up to tonight. He was the webmaster at the weekly paper where she had worked. He had broken up with her six months ago, but she knew that he still needed more reasons to not like her, so that he could check the breakup off firmly as a GOOD DECISION. The Greg thing would do it.

But he would never find out. The longer you lived, the more things you did that you could never tell anyone about. The embarrassing, horrible shit didn't end when you stopped being a teenager. Different people were marooned on different islands inside of you—one person held her breath when she walked past dead pigeons, crushed against the curb like dirty work gloves, and one person thought racist things about a waiter who screwed up her lunch order, and one person lost her job because (wait for it) she pushed her techie ex-boyfriend down five steps in the emergency stairwell of their office building, during an argument. This person did not think about how easily the ex-boyfriend could spin the story as her pushing him down the stairs—implying a whole flight of them—without even needing to lie, exactly, because five steps is still plural-stairs. And in the arena of Downsizing Weekly Paper, a battle between Webmaster and Really Only Semi-Talented Writer is easy to call.

Maybe Justine did wish there had been a whole flight of stairs stretching out behind her ex. But she didn't want to know about this person who crouched right underneath her surface, a fish under murky ice, frozen but still alive. Every day Justine worked hard to forget this person. She bit a ragged semi-circle from her cheeseburger and swallowed everything down.

Justine texted Pearl from the backyard. Pearl let her in. Justine didn't like sneaking in through the back door. It made her feel like a secret boyfriend, or even possibly a sex criminal, when all she was doing was visiting her friend. She never knew if she should take off her shoes or not.

"Where were you?" said Pearl.

"It's a long story," Justine mumbled. Pearl squinted at her. Time for the truth. "I was going to find something to eat during intermission but I met someone and went over to their place. I'm really, really sorry."

Pearl gawped. She played at being worldly, but secretly she couldn't yet believe that you could go home with someone, just like that . . . and *emerge unscathed*. She had seen too many slasher films and episodes of *Law & Order: Special Victims Unit* to not suspect that all unfamiliar men wanted to peel her skin off and wear it as a bathing suit. She had never dated anyone.

"You had sex!" said Pearl.

"I don't know."

"Greg! You had sex with Greg!"

Times like this, Justine wondered if the blood had rushed to her cheeks in tiny dots that spelled out cursive words; she was that easily read. "It was a horrible, awful mistake," she said. "Please don't be mad."

"What? It doesn't bother me. Greg's pretty, but he's too pretty to have a crush on. I don't need that kind of trouble."

They just sat there.

Then Pearl said, "You're, like, a sexy older woman. No reason he wouldn't go for that." She wiggled her butt in her papasan chair, like a furious bee inside of a peony, and crossed her arms. "It's kind of weird, but maybe it doesn't matter at your age. You don't seem that much older than him." Pearl was trying to be kind. Justine appreciated it.

"No. I do. At least to me," Justine said.

"I was amazing," Pearl suddenly announced. She was still wearing stage makeup. Up close, her rouge was bright and overwhelming and sick. It was how Justine had pictured scarlet fever might look.

Justine sighed. "I'm sorry. Here, I got you flowers. And a cheeseburger, if you want it."

Pearl smiled for a moment. "A cold cheeseburger, ew." But she rolled her eyes as she took the flowers. "Great, flowers. I already got some from my supportive parents! Oh wait, they didn't come to the fucking play. I got some from my boyfriend! Oh, wait, I don't have a boyfriend."

"Pearl, did something happen?"

"For college," said Pearl, "I am moving to a city where all the cute boys have Asian fetishes. For real." She sighed hopelessly.

"Come on, tell me what's wrong," said Justine. Pearl stared at the floor and started scratching the inside of her left elbow, where the skin was already hot pink. "Stop scratching," Justine said, and put out her hand. Pearl got in one more good scratch and then sat on her hand.

She said, "That's cool you got laid. I got totally freaking rejected. That's why I left the cast party early. What if you actually liked Greg, like you cared about him and wanted him to be your boyfriend instead of just using him to see if you could have sex with a teenager. . . ." Justine flinched. "But he didn't like you back because there were so many better-looking girls swarming around? And maybe he *would* have liked you if those girls weren't there? You're decent-looking, so maybe you don't know what I mean, and you're not a teenager anymore, so life doesn't suck as much. But it happens to me all the time. Because I'm ugly, and everyone else is turning beautiful."

There was no point in telling Pearl that everything would be fine.

"I think you're lovely," said Justine. "These boys just don't appreciate it yet. You're going to be glad that you didn't involve yourself with all these high school shitheads when you get to college. Your whole world's going to open up."

"*Glad*?" said Pearl.

"Bad word," said Justine quickly. "Sorry. I'll go to the play again tomorrow. I won't be a skank during intermission again. We can go get dinner after."

Pearl kicked the air. "Doesn't matter. The other performances have been cancelled. Everyone got sick at the cast party. Marla told me. People were throwing up in line for the bathroom. It sounded awful."

"You're kidding." Justine told Pearl about Rebecca. Pearl sat up so straight that her chair yawed and nearly toppled.

"I knew it!" she said. "It's the pretty girl anemia. I know this sounds sick, but I don't care—whatever they have, I want it. It's not just me. You should see what's going on at school. Everyone's trying to catch it. They're hanging out with the pretty girls, trying to touch them. I even saw—" Here Pearl lowered her voice. "Well, I didn't see it myself, but I heard that someone got someone's tampon out of that thing, the period box, from the bathroom stall, and they were going to do something with it." She shuddered.

"I wish you hadn't told me that," said Justine. The cheeseburger was trapped like a hairball somewhere between her chest and her stomach. It wasn't going anywhere.

"It might not be true. They were making fun of this one girl who was acting all desperate."

"It's sad," said Justine. "You know, people used to have parties where they'd deliberately catch smallpox from someone, like a mild case so they'd be immune after. But I don't know what those girls are doing."

"Maybe it's better than being ugly forever."

"Pearl—you're so young. Nothing is forever right now. I remember how it felt when I was in high school," said Justine. She tried not to pull out her high school mastery often, with Pearl.

Pearl rested her hand on her eyes, a snottily mature gesture. "No offense. But you're being close-minded and acting *so incredibly old*. I can't deal with this right now."

"Fine, I'll go," said Justine, standing. "I was only trying to help. Pearl . . ."

"You actually don't know anything," said Pearl.

When Justine left Pearl's house, she saw that Pearl had already turned off her lights. The whole house was dark now.

A question: was Justine beautiful? It was hard to say. She occupied a certain middle ground. She "cleaned up well," if "cleaning up" meant applying various paints and powders and unguents to her face until she looked like a high-contrast Photoshop job of herself. But she no longer knew what she looked like. Whenever she drifted while working and her laptop grayed out, she would see herself reflected in the dark LCD, and she could not tell if the screen distorted her face or if that was the face itself.

But there were people enough in the world to tell her what she looked like. Some days it seemed as though everyone in the whole world wanted her to know what she looked like—the way they shouted from cars, beamed her subliminal messages from TV screens and movie theaters and magazines. If only they would all shut the fuck up. If only she had been taught not to listen. It was too late to save herself; she wondered if it was too late to save Pearl.

The next day, Justine woke up late. Her mother had already gone to work, leaving a note on the fridge that read: *Tried to wake you up but you were completely dead. Sorry! Oatmeal on the stove. Love, Mom.*

The street by the coffee shop was blocked off. Justine parked as close as she could and walked over. Where the coffee shop had been, there was a huge, puffy white tent that wiggled in the breeze like a fat ghost, shuddering away from the metal spikes impaling each corner of it to the cement. Small crowds of people, some in neon yellow Hazmat suits, huddled near the entrance. Justine came closer. A person in a Hazmat suit emerged from the tent. Justine saw rows and rows of flaps inside, like fluttering laundry lines.

"Excuse me," said the Hazmat suit, in a sexless voice. "Sorry, Miss." The suit's mask was black, silvered with a reflective sheen. The suit put its big mitt of a hand up. "You can't come in."

"What's going on? I work here."

"You must return to your home and await further instructions. This town is under quarantine."

"Is this about Rebecca? She was sick. We called an ambulance for her last night."

"Oh, Rebecca," sighed the suit. "Rebecca Norbeck is dead. We are with the Centers for Disease Control and Prevention. You may have something very bad here. Four girls died in the night."

Justine shook her head. Rebecca might have been puking her guts out, but even so, she'd never looked better. She, above all, had been so pleased with her new beauty. She would come into the coffee shop and order big foofy drinks, sipping at them with a thrilled, almost cross-eyed screwball comedienne expression, except Justine knew that she was only pretending. Those drinks grew cold on the table, full to the brim. Nevertheless, in the last two weeks, Rebecca had acted like everything was delicious, especially the love-struck boys and girls who stood awkwardly at her table, trying to make conversation as she put away the vampire novels that she never finished reading anymore.

"No, I don't think so," said Justine. "I just saw her last night. She was sick, but not that bad."

"The virus works quickly. This coffee shop may be a vector. The high school is a vector. The body-piercing parlor is a vector. Anything the young people have touched is a vector. Please—go home, await further instructions. Although," and the suit cocked its head with a loud crinkle, "You may be too old to get it. We've been wondering about that."

"I feel fine," Justine said, distracted. "So how many girls have gotten sick?"

"Feeling fine is one thing. Do you feel pretty?"

"What?"

"Never mind. Just go home. If you have any little high school girlfriends, please tell them to stay in their homes and call this hotline number." The suit produced a card from its thigh pocket and handed it to Justine. "The rate of infection is growing. The virus grows ever more virulent. You must warn all of your unpopular friends as well. The beauty sickness is no longer co-morbid with popularity. It is trickling down."

The suit politely waved her away from the entrance. When Justine reached the roadblock, the suit was gone. In the crowds, she saw people she recognized. Lots of parental types, swarming around the tents and anyone with a clipboard. Justine turned away. She wanted to jump back in time, warn the girls as they chose door number two, the beauty prize—she would tell them that death was waiting there, *don't do it*, but maybe they wouldn't have listened. Justine called Pearl. Nobody answered. Her heart beat faster as she started her car.

Justine pulled up in front of the high school and saw Pearl's friend Marla standing at the curb by herself, crying. Crowds of people were working around the high school, blocking off the entrances and setting up tents around the many buildings.

When Marla saw Justine, she waved frantically, the too-long sleeves of her hoodie flapping.

Marla yanked the car door open and threw herself inside. "They kidnapped Pearl!" she told Justine. Some girls had followed them out of school. Marla and Pearl had waited at the front, too afraid to walk home. The girls surrounded them and dragged Pearl into their car.

"It's because of that blog," said Marla, sniffling. "They were pissed. They didn't like what Pearl said about them. I told her not to post that stuff, but she said if those bitches don't understand that YouTube videos are on the actual Internet for everyone to see, then it's their own fault. You have to find her."

"Oh boy," sighed Justine. "I will. Just . . . don't touch your face anymore. Don't touch anything. You don't want to get sick."

Marla shrugged. They were silent for a long time, while Justine drove to Marla's house. A few other buildings had been encircled by the white tents, and the CDC people walked in and out, their movements softened by their awkward suits so that they looked like astronauts, not even on Earth but already in space, drifting from station to station.

Marla burst into tears again. "I hate Pearl. I'm all alone now." Her face was blotchy, her eyes like slits in an overripe fruit. "I'm going to be the only one."

Justine didn't need to ask what she meant.

On the lawn in front of Pearl's house, six girls stood in a circle. Justine recognized some of them from the coffee shop and the YouTube video. Deanna and Katie were cheerleaders, and with them were Khadija and Nora, who were, respectively, president and activities coordinator of the school manga and anime interest club. The other two girls Justine didn't recognize.

The suit had said that beauty was no longer co-morbid with popularity. It was true. Weeks ago, these girls had started out in different social worlds, but you couldn't even tell by their clothes anymore. As they changed, they had all started wearing older-brother-style sweatshirts and gym shorts and huge flannel shirts and flip-flops, as if the normal world of normal-looking people had lost all interest to them. They had stopped grabbing at beauty; now they swam in it; they breathed it in and out.

Justine got out of her car. The girls, even the ones who'd been muscular or rounded or stocky, were now all equally spindly. She could take them. But as she walked past them to Pearl's front door, she was afraid. They looked as still and perfect as mannequins. It was scarier than dealing with something that seemed alive. They were like girl-shaped landmines.

She banged on the door and rang the doorbell. "Pearl," she shouted. "Pearl! Let me in!" No one answered. She turned around to face the girls.

"What did you do with her?" she said. Deanna shrugged. They all did, their lips curling up at the edges like burning paper.

"This is serious. People are dying. You're all in danger." As Justine spoke, she knew how weak and lame she sounded.

The girls shrugged again. Justine wanted to pull the sidewalk out from under them, to knock them over like bowling pins. Anything to plow through the total brick wall of teenage stoicism.

Justine said, "Where are her parents?"

"They're all at that big meeting for parents," said Nora. "It's too late, though."

"What's too late?"

"I don't know," said Nora. "Stuff."

They laughed. They glided closer, moving to surround Justine. She was nervous. They were so damn tall, and their faces blocked out the world around her in a circle of horrible loveliness, creating an alien ecosystem in which Justine—imperfect, spotted, human—could not breathe.

"Pearl doesn't want to talk to you," said Deanna. "She doesn't feel well."

"Don't lie to me. You're not her friends."

"Like you are. How old are you again? Fifty billion?"

"It's creepy you want to be Pearl's friend," said Khadija, in a lilting, lispy voice. *Iths creepy you wanna be Pearlth fren.*

"Fuck off," said Justine. "Get out of here, or I'm calling the police."

"Fine," one of them said. "Do it."

They stood there, pushing their sleeves up. Justine was afraid again— these girls didn't seem sick, no, they were fierce and wicked. She pushed Nora, but realized her mistake as soon as she felt Nora's shoulder, all tendon and bone like a pig knuckle. Nora fell onto Khadija, and Khadija stumbled into another girl. They screamed like normal girls. Nora stood up and pulled down the neck of her sweatshirt over her shoulder. She already had a bruise as big as an apple, a deep red one that seemed to pulse and grow more vivid as they looked.

"Look what you did!"

"Holy shit," gasped Justine. There was no way. She hadn't done anything. Perhaps something lurking beneath her surface was capable of punching a teenage girl, but she had only pushed a little. "It was an accident."

"We're calling the police on you," yelled Deanna.

"Nora, you need to go to the hospital," said Justine. "This isn't normal." Justine reached into her pockets to find the card that the suit had given her, but then the girls stepped even closer.

"You're not normal, bitch," said Nora.

Khadija lifted a fist, and her T-shirt sleeve shifted to reveal an evil bruise blossoming right where Nora had bumped into her.

Justine kept saying, "Sorry, I'm sorry," and ran to her car. She drove away in a panic, as the girls rubbed their wounds and screamed swear words at the retreating car.

Justine's mother was sitting on the couch. "Justine," she shouted, as if she was throwing a surprise party. She hugged her daughter so swiftly that Justine's teeth clacked together. "I was so worried about you." Her mother kept talking as she held her, her voice echoing against Justine's skull. She hadn't gone to work after all. The roads out of town were blocked. "They just told me about this disease that all the young girls were getting. I thought you had gotten sick, or you were trapped somewhere. . . ."

"I'm not young anymore, Mom."

"Things can still happen to you," her mother said. "Not young, my ass."

"I'm not in high school. I'll be fine." Justine tried to wiggle out of her grasp. Weren't mothers supposed to be the ones with motherly bosoms? But her mother was small and flat-chested, and also quite buff ever since she'd started taking Cardio Powerlifting at the local gym. You must have gotten your father's boobs, her mother would say, sometimes enviously, sometimes not.

Her mother brushed back Justine's hair. "You don't look any different," she said. Justine felt disappointed in a small and distant way. "Thank god for that. Be quiet. I'm allowed to worry. When you're a million years old, I'll still be a million-and-thirty-three."

"Dang."

"I know." Her mother stepped back. "I should go wash my hands now."

"Mom! Are you serious? I'm not sick." Then she remembered her fight with the girls, and how easily Nora had folded under her hands. "I guess you should."

"I wish we at least had those masks," her mother fretted. "Those SARS masks."

"Sit down, Mom," said Justine. "Relax. I'll start dinner."

"Dinner? Sure you're feeling well?" Her mother didn't smile. She snapped the living room window curtains shut before sitting down again. "Poor girls," she said. "It seems so much worse that they get beautiful before it happens."

The next day, Justine's mother went out to attend some community meetings. Justine stayed home, doing research without knowing what she was looking for or why, except for the fear that Pearl too might be in trouble. Her mother had been relieved. "Good idea," she said. "Stay inside. Forever if you can."

Pearl's blog was still up, but all the old posts had been deleted. The only thing left on the page was a video, embedded without commentary. Justine clicked on it. The video was an edited clip of an old movie from 1933, *Footlight Parade*. James Cagney's character raced around town, trying to think up a concept for his new theatrical extravaganza. Suddenly he stopped, struck by the sight of some black kids playing in the street around a gushing fire hydrant, and grew excited, ecstatic. "Look at that!" he shouted. "*That's* what the prologue needs—a mountain waterfall splashing on beautiful white bodies!" From there, the scene cut straight to the big Busby Berkeley number: rows of scantily clad young women sliding down an artificial waterfall, bodies gleaming white in stark contrast against the pitch-dark water. The women wore rubber caps molded into the shapes of hairstyles. They writhed in synchronized frenzy, grinning through wet lipstick. Then they joined arms in two long lines, and interwove their legs to form the shape of a zipper, which opened and closed itself up again in the path of a single swimmer traveling up and down the line of interlocking leg-teeth.

Justine had to stop watching. She hit pause and took a few breaths. Then she clicked through to YouTube and searched for the videos of the local girls. Once again, she looked at the girls looking at her. The low-quality resolution washed them out, simplifying and deepening their features until they looked less like girls and more like drawings of girls. She couldn't stop watching them. Neither could everyone else. The view count was up to twenty million.

Modeling agencies were sending representatives to her town. Justine scrolled through pages and pages of "I wish it were me" and "Lucky girls" and "Put that in a syringe and stick it into me!" from all varieties of girls and women and boys and men. Others wanted in, too: movie directors, talent agents, pharmaceutical giants, fundamentalists, cosmetics companies, Disney, journalists, perverts. There was some big-ass money at stake here. If only there were a way to prevent the dying.

Though even with the dying, surely they could work something out.

Outside the living room window, Justine saw that a few other houses on the street had been covered with bloated white tents, houses like spongy funguses, puffballs growing into the shapes of houses. These were houses that girls had lived in.

Pearl had texted her once during those two days.

The text read: *still ugly*.

Justine texted her back immediately but got no response.

She went online again, and saw that people were comparing the situation to a video game, a movie, a comic, a TV show, and, much less frequently, a book.

On the night of the third day, Justine received another text from Pearl. It read: *come over*. A few seconds later, her phone beeped again. The next text read: *at gregs apt. will explain*.

This didn't upset Justine. At least not in the way she thought it would. Greg was not hers and she did not want him.

Only, she did begin to feel worried for him. She refused to think any more about this.

Her mother was asleep. Justine shut the door carefully behind her. She wore a pair of knit wool gloves, to put some kind of barrier between her and the rest of the world. Now she wished that they did have SARS masks. For one wild moment, she thought about wrapping a long piece of toilet paper around her face.

She decided to walk to Greg's apartment to avoid being stopped by officials. Without the thin hard shell of her car, she felt like a kind of forest creature darting around in the woods, the billowing white tents like fairy tale houses, filled with the same ominous promises.

She felt fifteen again, and it wasn't just because she didn't have a car.

One of the tents had a long, jagged rip down the front. Justine saw it out of the corner of her eye, and automatically sped up her steps. By the time she got to Greg's apartment, she was almost running. Her feet hurt. Someone buzzed her into the building and she took the stairs two at a time. About to knock on Greg's door, she got a funny feeling, a sense of unutterable wrongness. Her armpits went damp. She tried the doorknob instead. The door opened.

Pearl was slumped at the kitchen table, facedown, her head resting on her arms. She was very still.

"Hello," said Justine.

Pearl lifted her head. She was wearing a fake nose attached to a mustache, bushy eyebrows, and black-framed eyeglasses, a Groucho Marx-type thing.

"Yo," she said.

Justine sat down at the table across from her. "Why aren't you at home?"

"I ran away. I didn't want the disease nerds to bother me."

"They could have helped you."

"Doubt it." Pearl sat up and stared at Justine. There was something different about Pearl. Pearl was taller. Something had taken her neck and waist and gently yanked them longer. And her boobs, her *boobs* . . . . "Stop looking at me," Pearl said. "I think you should know—I'm not *doing* Greg or anything. He's just letting me stay here."

"It's fine with me if you're *doing* Greg."

"He's still obsessed with you. All he does is ask about you."

"Don't tell me that. We're not together. It doesn't matter. How are you?"

"Me? I'm beautiful now." Pearl adjusted her eyeglasses with a poke of her finger.

"Can I see?"

"No, you can't see. I'm turning into a fucking white girl. It's annoying. It's like, even this stupid disease has Western-influenced ideas of beauty. Big eyes, pale skin, whatever. I grew six inches. Look, my nose bridge got taller too! I could never wear glasses before, they were always slipping off my face. It's bullshit. But I am hot stuff." Pearl reached across the table and tapped Justine on the arm in a friendly, off-hand way. "How are you feeling? You look like you feel like shit."

"I'm fine. I'm always fine. I've been telling everyone that I'm fine. Ask me a new fucking question," said Justine. "It's you I'm worried about."

"Hmm. Are you acting like a major bitch right now?"

Justine relaxed a bit. "Sure," she said. "Nice to see you too."

They both smiled. It was the best they could do.

"Justine, please don't worry," Pearl said. "Check out my new rack! It's okay, you can look. I'm great. I've never been better."

"Except you're turning into a white girl," said Justine.

"See, that's why I had to run away," said Pearl. "What if my parents checked up on me? They pull back the covers on my bed only to find this bee-*yoo*-tiful white child!" Pearl started laughing. "You know what's fucked? They'd like me better this way. I bet Sarah Anderson's parents loved it when she caught the disease and went all double-lidded and six feet tall, like them. From now on they'll never have to admit she's adopted!" Laughing, laughing.

"Stop," Justine said, but Pearl kept chortling, her mouth frozen into a rectangle of wet white teeth. Underneath her disguise, Pearl was flushed pink and plush and spotless. Justine went around the table and pulled off her gloves. She bent to touch Pearl's forehead. It was freezing cold. She drew her hand back. "Oh," she said.

"Do I have a fever?" said Pearl plaintively.

"No. Not really."

"I feel really bad." Pearl closed her eyes. "I'm hungry."

"Oh, Pearl," said Justine. "Just eat something." She went into the kitchen and looked through the shelves. "Look, there's tons of food."

Pearl shook her head until her disguise almost fell off. "That's why the other girls died. They couldn't eat food. Something in them ate them up from the inside." She started to cry. "I know what to do to feel better. I bet they knew too. But I don't want to do it. I don't think I *can*." This last word she wailed.

Do . . . *what, exactly*? Justine didn't want to ask. Right now, she needed to keep herself stupid, frozen. She knew she was going to find out sooner or later. The later the better. "Don't cry," she said. "It'll be okay. I'm here for you." She went to Pearl, putting her hands on Pearl's shoulders and gripping them gently, remembering Nora. "Pearl?" she said.

Pearl stopped crying. There was a blankness in her eyes, behind the glasses, and Justine was close enough to see it. Pearl's face shone with tears, but now the tears looked fake, as if they had just appeared there under her eyes without a history, without reason.

Then Pearl grabbed Justine's arm with both hands and held it to her mouth.

She swiftly bit down on Justine's fleshy forearm without breaking the skin. Justine was afraid to move, to do anything that would bring her nearer to those teeth. Pearl's head jerked up, Justine's arm still in her mouth. They looked at each other.

Pearl spit out Justine's arm; the suction made a quiet popping sound. "Just kidding," she said. She leaned back in her chair.

Justine wiped her arm on her jeans. There was no spit on it. She said, "Where's Greg?"

"He's out." Pearl put her head down on the table again.

"Is that the truth?" Justine said carefully.

She watched Pearl's head nod. "But," Pearl said into the table, "he'll probably come back again. It's his apartment. Nice furniture, nice cat, comfortable bed . . . "

"You are doing Greg." Justine tried to say these words without making them mean anything.

"Maybe," said Pearl. "For the same reason you did it. You wanted to see if you could. Being beautiful is great." She made a weird noise, a sigh that went from high-pitched to low and back again. "But it's tiring."

Justine moved to touch Pearl on the back of her head, but thought better of it. "You scare me," she said, and swallowed. "Why don't we get out of here? We'll sneak out of town."

Pearl lifted her head and smiled.

"Fuck you, I'm serious."

"Why?" said Pearl. "No, wait. That's a nice idea. I wish we could do that. But I'm past that point." She lifted her slender hands, and Justine could see that she no longer had lines on her palms.

Pearl said, "I hate to tell you, but this thing's going to catch on. I can feel it."

They fell silent. Justine wondered where the kitten was.

Eventually, Justine said, "Do what you need to do." She was probably not supposed to say that. "Or, I don't know. Good luck, Pearl."

Pearl laughed. Then she stopped short, as if a switch was flicked inside her throat. "Thank you, Justine," she said very seriously. "You realize we can't be friends anymore."

"Yes," Justine said. "It makes me sad."

"Me too," said Pearl.

Sadness rose up inside them like a plasma, plugging up their throats, pushing their eyeballs out, hurting their chests. Justine wanted to hug Pearl and take her out for dinner at their favorite diner, where they would talk all night and draw on the table with the condensation from their sodas. On nights like those, Justine didn't feel as young as Pearl, exactly, but she felt as if they had the same amount of future stretching out ahead of them. They would both go home before dawn, and the sun would rise on a normal morning of a normal day. No one would have turned beautiful, and that would be just fine.

"Can you open the window for me?" said Pearl. "It's hot."

It wasn't, but Justine went and opened the window. Pearl came and stood next to her.

"Listen," Pearl said. "It's my friends. My other friends are coming over."

If Justine tried hard enough, she could make out girls' voices as they shuffled through town in one big laughing group.

"Maybe I should get going," she said.

"Yeah, dude. You might even want to run."

"That bad?" Justine said lightly. It was very important to be calm now. It was very important that she keep all her limbs to herself, as if she was on some junky, deadly amusement park ride.

"I kinda want a hug," said Pearl, "but I guess that's a bad idea." Her disguise began to slip, but this time she didn't try to stop the slow elevator slide of the glasses down her nose. Justine knew that she had until when the disguise fell off to leave the apartment. *Thank you, Pearl, for this mercy*, she thought, and then turned and ran.

At the threshold to the apartment building, Justine stopped and inhaled, letting the icy air clear away the grime from her brain. There were things she needed to be thinking about. Her life had been yanked out of her hands, remolded, and returned to her twisted and unrecognizable. Now she would have to make something out of it. Down the block, some of the streetlights were broken or burned out. The way home was obvious; what might happen to her in those dark spaces in-between was not.

She knew her final role in this now: she was going to become the latest in a long, proud line of girls who ran. She would be one of those girls who ran to save their mothers, girls who knew how to cobble together weapons out of household items, girls who could kill without crying, girls who grew up to be women with weathered creases down their cheeks and mysterious, hard-earned eyepatches. Women with pasts, women who could admit everything: *That was me. I was there. I did that.* Justine got tired just thinking about it.

Pearl's role would be entirely different. It struck Justine that Pearl would have been applying to colleges soon. It was all so ridiculous. Pearl had really only wanted to get out of town. Now she didn't need college anymore; a girl like her could and would go everywhere without it.

Good luck, Pearl, Justine whispered. *Good luck, everyone else in the world.*

She prepared herself. Her leg muscles twitched. She would leap over the sidewalk cracks, ignore the white tents and the rustling bushes full of insects and animals and other things. She would not look for Greg. There would be no hesitation in her body.

In this way, she might make it home.

Now Justine really could hear the girls coming. Someone muttering, low and sarcastic, followed by a high-pitched giggle. She couldn't hear shoes. Maybe they weren't wearing shoes. Oh fuck, where were their shoes?

Every molecule in her body fired a starting shot, quick and hot and electric, and then she was off.

Alice Sola Kim is currently a student in the MFA Writing Program at Washington University in St. Louis. Her short fiction has appeared or is forthcoming in Asimov's Science Fiction, Lightspeed, Strange Horizons, *and* Lady Churchill's Rosebud Wristlet. *"Beautiful White Bodies" was honor-listed for the 2009 James Tiptree, Jr. Award.*

Zombies are an empty canvas, unmolded clay, a blank screen you can project anything onto. You can accept a disease that turns the dead into walking corpses who want only to devour the living? It's even easier to believe in zombie virus that turns teenage girls into the societal ideal of the desirable female. Oh yeah, you get pretty—then you die. You think the consequence of death would stop most people from wanting to "catch" beauty?

Glorietta

Gary A. Braunbeck

"Pining to live, I was constrained to die,
Here, then, am I . . .

"Poor soul; he suffered. But, at end, no child
Ever more gently fell asleep.
He smiled.
As if all contraries were reconciled."
—Walter de la Mare, "Epilogue"

The first questions are always the same, as are the responses:
    Mom? Dad? Sis? Do you recognize me this year?

• • •

Do you like the Christmas tree? Remember when I made this decoration in kindergarten? You liked it so much, Dad. Remember? See, I even strung popcorn.

• • •

Yet another Christmas spent both above-ground and alive. You can't understand why you still bother, why it is you hang on to a pitiful, even pathetic, shred of hope. Some nights, watching the lights as they blink on the tree and the Christmas music fills the empty rooms of the family home, you can almost—*almost*—pretend that everything is fine, you're still ten years old and that this year you *will* stay awake long enough to catch Santa slipping down the chimney, even if there is a banked fire blazing.

• • •

You'll listen, as always, and hope for something; a sound, a whisper, a spark of recognition in the eyes. Listen and hope, but all the while know what you'll get.

...

Still, even their silence is a sort-of gift, isn't it? Because at least they remember enough about their previous lives to come home for Christmas. They remember the house. They remember in which rooms they spent the most time during the holidays. They remember where everyone sits around the tree and how to turn off the lights so only the glow of the tree and tinsel and the fire provide illumination. They remember all of this, all three of them.

...

They just don't remember you.

...

At age forty-eight you have learned a new, albeit nearly useless, lesson: something about your disease repels the living dead. The first time you realized this, in the days and weeks following the awakenings, was when you had no choice but to leave the house and go in search of food and medicine. There was still power then, and the unlooted grocery stores and pharmacies still had plenty of supplies, much to your astonishment. You were in the pharmacy, gathering up the boxes of hypodermics, the vials of Dilauded, and the steroids you'd need to keep yourself alive and pain-free. You were almost finished when you decided, what the hell, grab some Percocet and Demerol, as well, because sometimes the Dilauded made you far too weak and woozy. Six large shopping bags you had, filled with enough prescription medicine to keep you going for a couple of years, even if you took more than the prescribed dosage. You were on your way out when you walked right into a group of five of the living dead, gathered around your car in the parking lot. You thought, *This is it*, as they began stumbling toward you, but as soon as the first one was close enough to touch you, something like a shadow crossed its decomposed features and it pulled away its hand, and then simply stood there *staring* at you. The rest did the same. After what seemed an hour but was in fact only a minute or two, the five of them turned away from you and shambled on.

You used to keep a gun, but that's long been thrown out. They want nothing to do with you. You spent months afterward in search of others who were sick—cancer, AIDS, leukemia—something, *anything* that marked them as *persona non grata* to the living dead. You did find a few people, but they were so far gone that there was no community made with them; you even helped a few to end their suffering, and then used their guns to pulp their brains so they wouldn't come back. The eleven-year-old boy with leukemia thanked you as you sank the plunger, sighing into sleep, dressed in his Spider-Man pajamas. You hated shooting him, but you'd promised, and he'd kissed your cheek before falling asleep for the very last time. You sat there, holding his hand until you were certain he was gone. Then did what had to be done.

You no longer search out the marked ones. Though you know what you do—what you *did*—was the right thing, it still hurt too much, caused too many sleepless nights, gave you too many bad dreams and sick-making memories. It's better this way. You keep telling yourself that. Maybe one of these days you'll even start to believe it in your heart of hearts.

And then came that first Christmas after Mom, Dad, and Jenny died in the automobile accident when Dad had swerved to avoid hitting a cat that had frozen in fear. You handled all the arrangements, set up viewing hours, sent notices to the paper. The day before the funeral all of the dead opened their eyes, stood up, and began walking around. You did not see the mangled remains of your family until Christmas Eve, when you awoke from a nap to find all three of them sitting in the living room, staring at the spot where the Christmas tree was usually displayed. So you did what a good son and older brother would do under the circumstances; you went to the basement and dug out the tree and all of the decorations and began setting up everything. A few minutes into your project, your family began removing decorations from the boxes and hung everything exactly, precisely where the traditional decorations always went. Your little sister even arranged the Nativity set on the fireplace mantle.

But not a one of them looked at you with anything like recognition.

Still, it was better than being alone. It is always better than being alone—another thing you tell yourself constantly in the hopes that you will one day believe it.

Merry Christmas, everyone, you say to them every year.

• • •

Merry Christmas.

• • •

This year will be no different. Oh, some of the accoutrements will change—you taught yourself how to make turducken, and your recipe is pretty good, if you do say so yourself, and you'll set four places at the dinner table, knowing that you'll be the only one eating. The menthol cream you rub under your nose kills most of your family's stench, so you at least can keep an appetite, providing you don't look at them for too long, or too often.

• • •

In the years since the awakenings, you have become a good carpenter, a decent-enough electrician, an excellent plumber, an all-around first-rate handyman. The gas-powered generators keep the electricity flowing into the house, though you're careful not to waste power. You use only the downstairs, having boarded up and sealed the entrance to the upper floors after removing everything you might need or want.

You stand in the kitchen watching them decorate the tree, arrange the Nativity set, string the popcorn. *It's a Wonderful Life* is playing on DVD in high-definition Blu-Ray, Jimmy Stewart's face filling the 65-inch flat-screen plasma television you took from an electronics store last year. A digital home theater system guarantees exquisite sound. You couldn't give less of a damn about any of it right now—although you find that you've come to appreciate the middle of the movie much more, the part where it's all dark and hopeless. You recognize that look of terror and grief and helplessness that is a permanent fixture on Stewart's face in these sequences. You see something like it every time you glance at your reflection in a mirror. You laugh at the heavy-handed melodrama of that thought. It's an odd sound, hearing your own laughter at Christmas time. It's almost like the old days, the good days, the happy-enough days.

They've rotted away so much, you wonder how it is they manage to move around at all, but somehow they manage. They drip, they leak, sometimes sections of flesh or a digit falls off, a tooth drops to the floor, yet they keep going. You wonder if there is something still *them* in there, some small part of their consciousness that remembers who and what they once were, and is trying to recapture some essence of that former life. *Do they dream?* you wonder.

So you ask.

• • •

Do you dream?

• • •

Cornbread or rolls?

• • •

Red wine okay with everyone?

• • •

Did I ever mean anything to any of you?

• • •

No need to get all sugary on me, folks, just a simple yes or no.

• • •

I still love you guys, you know that?

• • •

You move into the living room, stepping around the Christmas paraphernalia, and turn off the sound on the DVD player. It's time for Christmas music. This year, you stole a multi-disc player, one that reads MP3s, and you've set up the discs so that you will have twenty-four hours of continuous Christmas music. Dad used to love to sit in the kitchen with the lights turned down and listen to Christmas music while he had a beer or two. You've got several cases of his favorite beer. One bottle sets open next to his favorite mug. For a moment earlier, he stared at it as a shadow crossed his face, as if he knew this were something he ought to remember. Mug and bottle are still on the table.

How do you like the new refrigerator? I got it a couple of weeks ago. Moved it all by myself. Damn thing can hold a ton of food. Do you like it, Mom?

• • •

Hey, why do you suppose doctors never use the word consumption anymore? No, now it's TB. I think consumption's a fine word, you know?

• • •

I found the old photo albums. They're right there on the coffee table. Maybe you want to look through them later? That might be fun, don't you think? All of us flipping through the images, the years, the memories. Been a while since I took a trip down Amnesia Lane. Sound good?

• • •

Sorry, I didn't quite catch that.

• • •

That's okay, you can tell me later.

You turn around and damn near drop the salad bowl because your little sister is standing right there in front of you, just . . . staring.

Jenny?

• • •

Jenny, is there something you want?

• • •

What is it, Sis?

• • •

Please say . . . *something*. Grunt. Sigh, snort, *anything*.

• • •

You close your eyes and swallow back the feelings that are trying to come to the surface. You knew this year would be no different. Christ only knows what Jen wants in here, what she remembers. You just know it's got nothing to do with you. You step around her and put the salad bowl on the table. Jen does not move. The oven timer sounds: the turducken is ready to go.

Dinner's ready!

• • •

You sit. They sit. You eat. They don't. On the disc, Greg Lake is singing about how he believed in Father Christmas. This is your favorite Christmas song, even though if you think about it, it's a damned depressing one—but then so is Elvis's "Blue Christmas," so why overthink it?

The turducken is delicious. The mashed potatoes are just right. The rolls are great. And the homemade pecan pie is the perfect way to end the meal.

You go to your usual place on the far right-hand side of the sofa and watch the tree lights blink, watch the banked fire blaze, watch Jimmy Stewart run through dark streets. You pick up one of the photo albums and open to a random page. That was you, once. That was your family, once.

The pain is getting pretty bad. You've been sticking with the Demerol for the last couple of days because you wanted to be lucid enough in case something happened—a word, a gesture, a touch, something, anything.

The rest of the family take their traditional places. You look out the window and see that it's begun to snow. Good God, could there ever be a more perfect Norman Rockwell-type of Christmas scene?

You make yourself an eggnog and Pepsi. Everyone used to say how disgusting that sounded, so when you'd make the drink for your friends and family when all were still alive, you'd never tell them what it was until after they'd tasted it. Once tasted, everyone loved it. Your legacy. Could do worse.

Afraid I'm not feeling too well, folks. Haven't been taking my meds like I should.

• • •

Isn't anyone going to scold me for that?

• • •

You stare at the unopened Christmas presents under the tree. It's been so long since you've wrapped them you've forgotten what's in any of the boxes, only that they were gifts you gave a lot of thought to, hoping that they'd make everyone smile.

You go into the kitchen and remove several 4 mg vials of Dilauded from the refrigerator, make yourself another eggnog and Pepsi, and grab the bottles of Percocet and Demerol.

Back in the living room, in your traditional place, you lay out everything, then discard the Percocet and Demerol because they seem like overkill. Overkill. Funny-sounding word, that. Considering.

You draw the vials of Dilauded into the syringe until it is full. You almost tap it to clear any air bubbles, then realize what a silly thing that would be.

This has been a nice Christmas, hasn't it?

• • •

It really means a lot to me, that you still come here and help with all the decorating.

• • •

You look at the television. Jimmy Stewart is now back in the real world, and everyone in town is dumping money on his table. Donna Reed smiles that incredibly gorgeous smile that no other actress has ever managed to match.

Bach's "Sheep May Safely Graze" begins to play. The perfect song to end the day. To end on. To end. You slip the needle into your arm but do not yet sink the plunger. There is a passing moment of brief regret that you threw out the gun, because you know what that's going to mean. But maybe you won't remember, and, in not remembering, there will be no caring, no hurt, no regret or loneliness.

You look at each of your family members one more time. None return your gaze. They look either at the tree or the fire or at the snow outside.

Merry Christmas, everyone, you say.

• • •

You slowly sink the plunger. If your research has been correct, once the syringe has been emptied, you will have at best ninety seconds of consciousness remaining, but you can already feel yourself slipping down toward darkness before the plunger has hit bottom. But that's all right.

You have enough time to pull the needle from your arm and lay back your head.

Bach fades away, and is followed by "Let There Be Peace on Earth." You're surprised to feel a single tear forming in your right eye.

Do you like . . . like the music, Dad?

• • •

Shadows cross your face, obscuring the lights of the tree. You blink, still slipping downward, and see that your family is surrounding you. Looking at you. At *you*.

You reach out one of your hands. It takes everything that remains of you to do this.

. . . , you say.

. . . , they reply.

And your family, with the light of recognition in their eyes, as if they have missed their son and brother for all of these years, takes hold of you, enfolding you in their arms, and the best Christmas you've ever known is completed.

Gary A. Braunbeck *is the author of the acclaimed Cedar Hill series of stories and novels, which includes* In Silent Graves, Coffin County, Far Dark Fields, *and the forthcoming* A Cracked and Broken Path. *His work had garnered five Bram Stoker Awards, as well as an International Horror Guild Award. He lives in Worthington, Ohio with his wife, author Lucy A. Snyder, and five cats that don't hesitate to draw blood if he fails to feed them in time. He has been rumored to sing along with Broadway show tunes, but no recorded evidence of this exists or has yet to be found.*

Although Braunbeck hints there are dangers to humans from zombies—his protagonist's disease makes him immune to the "awakening" and unpalatable to zombies—it appears "offstage." And, despite the zombie family's apparent lack of recognition of their still-human relation, *something* draws them back, year after year, to their home. He leaves it to the reader to decide what.

Farewell, My Zombie

Francesca Lia Block

They call a male P.I. a private Dick. So what would they call me? Not the C word or the V word, that would be much too offensive. There are plenty of Dicks but no Vaginas walking around. That just wouldn't be right, now would it? Maybe my title would be Jane. Private Jane. Dick and Jane. Makes you wonder why Jane hasn't been used as a nickname for female genitalia before. Better than a lot of them. Men have a nicer selection.

It was one of those warm L.A. autumn days when you felt guilty if you were at the beach while other people were working or freezing their asses off somewhere, and even more guilty if you were sitting in an office letting your life slip away. That's what I was doing. Sitting in my office with my black-booted feet up on the table (even though it was too hot for boots), staring at the window, wondering why I wasn't at the beach. But I knew why. The beach made me think of Max.

I tried to distract myself by poking around some paranormal activity Web sites on the iMac. There was an extended family in the Midwest who ghost hunted together. They had a disclaimer on their site that they could turn down any job that felt too dangerous. The woman kept spelling the word "were" like "where" and "You're" like "your." That happened so much online I wondered if someone had officially changed it and not told me.

That was when I got the call.

"Merritt," I said.

"Jane Merritt?" the caller asked.

"Speaking."

"Sorry, I . . . I need some help."

"That's what we're here for. You'll just need to come in and fill out some forms."

There was a silence on the line and for a second I thought the call had dropped.

"Hello?"

"Uh, yeah. Thanks. Sorry"

"So when would you like to come in? Everything perfectly confidential, of course."

"Thanks. Sorry. It's about my father."

"I see. Yes."

"He's a monster."

I waited for the giggling on the other end. She was obviously very young. I got calls like this all the time. Curious teens with too much time on their hands.

No giggling.

"I mean really," she said. "A real monster."

Then she hung up.

No one else called that day. Business had been slow. I left the office early and stopped at the West L.A. Trader Joe's for a few groceries. Bagels, cream cheese, apples, celery, the cheapest Pinot Noir I could find, and a tub of cat cookies, plus a can of food for David. I wanted to buy myself flowers because that's what all the women's magazines tell you to do when you haven't been fucked in too long, but I decided not to waste the money.

There was big bouquet of fourteen white roses with a pink cast. They looked pretty good but I knew they'd blow up in a few days in this weather, petals loosening from their cluster and drifting to the floor. Besides, roses were another thing that reminded me of Max.

I went home and watched CNN while David and I ate dinner. Bad news as usual. The economy, disasters, war. Not to mention global warming and assorted acts of violence. It was like a horror movie, really. I drank the whole bottle of wine. Then I took a bath and went to bed. I had really weird dreams about letting Max go by himself on a train at night and then realizing what I had done and not being able to get anyone to understand why I was so upset when he didn't come home. Dreams are cruel; they won't let you forget.

Coco Hart came to see me about a week later. She was a beautiful girl in a private school uniform skirt and blouse and a ratty sweatshirt that was too hot for the weather. Her long hair up in a ponytail and makeup so lightly and carefully applied that only the most discerning eyes would notice it. She looked perfectly well adjusted but her fingernails were bitten down so far that it hurt to look at them.

"I called you," she said after she'd introduced herself. Her eyes darted around the room trying to find clues. I don't have any in this tiny, dingy office. Not even a photo of Max. I had to hide it in a drawer.

"About your father?"

She nodded.

"Is he hurting you?"

"No," she said. "Sorry. It's not that."

"You can tell me. I'm here to help."

"Thank you. You were the only woman I could find. Well except that one who tries to entrap the guys by wearing wigs in their favorite color."

People always mention her when they come to see me. I'm nothing like that Amazon. Just cause we are both Janes.

"So why not her?"

"I heard that interview with you."

There's only been one. It was in conjunction with the new *X-Files* movie. The local news compared me to Fox Mulder because of my interest in the paranormal. I expected business to boom after that but it didn't. In L.A. you have to look like a movie star with big tits or be a guy to make it big in this business. I'm neither.

In the interview I talked a little about some weird, dark stuff, the kind of thing teenagers and *X-Files* fans eat up. But most teens aren't going around hiring a P.I. and the *X-Files* fans would rather watch David Duchovny reruns. Like the famous female P.I. who wears the wigs he has a lot more sex appeal than I do.

Coco put her hand to her mouth as if she were about to chew on what was left of her nails, then thought better of it and folded her hands tightly in her plaid-skirted lap. She looked out at the sunny fall day. The leaves of the tree outside my window looked like they were on fire. I didn't know what kind of tree it was. I wondered why Coco was here and not at some mall with her friends or something.

She took some crumpled bills out of her sweatshirt pocket and put them on the table.

"That's all I have," she said. "But I'll get more."

"And you want me to do what exactly?"

"Oh. Uh. Sorry." She hesitated. "Do you believe in zombies?" she said, finally.

Fuck.

Sorry but I am not going to pretend to you that I am normal. I am not normal in any way. Yes I shop at Trader Joe's and watch CNN, get my hair cut on a regular basis, shower, and use deodorant. I wear my dark hair scraped back in a tight bun like I did on the force, and dress in flat-front black trousers and white-stretch button down shirts from the Limited and black heels or flats or boots from Macy's and lightweight trench coats. But that's the only normal stuff.

First of all I am a female P.I. Second of all I live in a silver Airstream trailer in my ex-husband's backyard in Mar Vista. I walk or bike everywhere because I'm afraid that even driving a little will make more holes in the ozone. I wear black Converse and keep my heels in my backpack. I smoke cigarettes even though I know they are bad for me but I take vitamins and won't eat anything with hydrogenated oils or wash my hair with shampoo that has sodium laurel sulfate because I heard it is a carcinogen. I don't know why I really care; it must be left over from being a mom and the thing that happened—although I don't believe that was really the cause.

I have a dog named David who is like my son. When spell check tells me to write "that" instead of "who" while referring to my dog I get angry. He is a mutt and he likes to roam the neighborhood and bring back presents. Sometimes he brings me pigeons and I thank him but then I scold him. Once on Easter he came to the door of the trailer holding a fully cooked ham proudly in his jaws. I didn't scold him for that although some nice family must have had a gaping hole in their dinner menu. David likes me to hold him like a baby with his round tummy sticking out and his front paws draped over my arm like little hands. Sometimes I forget that he is a dog.

I had a real son once. His name was Max. Now he's gone but I don't want to talk about it. I was a cop and I got kicked off the force after what happened. I had what they call a breakdown and Max's dad who is also a cop divorced me and married a kickboxing instructor named Kimmy. When I got out of the hospital they let me live in the trailer in the backyard of what used to be my home. I can see my old house through the trailer window. It is a long, low structure painted avocado green. My ex and I were always planning on repainting it but we never got around to that. Then Kimmy came and picked the green. It looks nasty, even monstrous in certain lights. I planted the roses in the garden but I've stopped trying to take care of them. Once Kimmy came out while I was watering and weeding. I said, "Sorry," and scuttled back into my trailer. The roses remind me.

At night I stay up watching the windows of my old bedroom until the lights go out.

I went into this work because I didn't know what else to do. I thought it would help me forget to get up every day and go to my little office on Washington. It helps me forget that I was ever Max's mom but it makes me remember the hospital and the doctor's face, as I sit here waiting for someone who really needs me to come in.

I mostly just follow cheating husbands and wives. Once I followed a woman who was engaged to two men at the same time. The guy who hired me was so upset he started crying in my office. Then he wanted me to dress up like her and fuck him. That was the most eventful case I'd handled so far. But the thing that happened with Max made me open to the possibility of stuff that wasn't so easy to understand.

Coco told me that her father had been behaving very strangely. She'd seen him eating flesh in big, gross, salivating bites and it didn't look like cow, pig, goat, lamb, chicken, or turkey. Let's just say that. And he never spoke anymore. After his stroke he shambled around the house with these heavy steps just staring at the floor. He grumbled and grimaced and that was all. His skin was a weird shade of greenish white and once when he was asleep she'd felt for a pulse and there wasn't one there. He smelled bad, too.

I said, "Sorry but I have to ask you something. What makes you think he's one of the undead though? I mean, how do you think this could have happened?"

Coco's father was a car salesman in Van Nuys. He'd done pretty well for himself selling SUVs until people stopped being able to afford gas at almost five dollars a gallon. The stress was too much for him. While waiting for the electric car to return he'd had a stroke and almost died. Well, according to Coco there was no "almost" involved.

"When he came back from the hospital," Coco said. "He just wasn't the same."

"What was he like before?" I asked.

"Well, kind of like now. Except I recognized the meat he ate and he had better skin tone and a pulse. And . . . sorry, but . . . he didn't smell so bad."

I tried not to say, "Ouch. Harsh." I was trying to behave with some decorum.

"You sound very angry at your father," I said, recalling a psych class I'd taken in junior college.

"Sorry. My father is all right. Well, he was. Before he turned into a monster. I mean, he's a Republican. He voted for George W. And he's against women's right to choose. He still supports the war. But he'd never lay a hand on me, you know. But I'm worried about what he's doing to other people. Where he like, gets his dinner and that kind of thing."

"Why didn't you go to the police?" I asked."

"Um, I think you know why. Sorry . . ."

"So you came to me."

"Well," she said, "Not everyone's kid gets stolen by zombies. I mean, I saw it on YouTube."

Okay, sorry it's true. The thing I'm known for is about Max and the zombies. I wasn't really interviewed by the local news. I made a video for YouTube and posted it talking about what happened. That's how Coco had found me. Not the guy whose fiancée was cheating on him; he got my name out of the phone book.

See, people think my kid got sick and died but I know better. No one wants to talk about it because they're afraid everyone will think they are crazy. Or maybe because they're afraid of even worse consequences.

"What do you want me to do?" I asked Coco.

"Would you please pretend you're a customer and check him out?" she asked. "They have really good deals on Escalades now," she added.

"I ride a bike."

I borrowed Daniel's car and went to the car dealership where Coco's dad worked. They hired him back part time after the stroke. It was night and the cars glowed surreally in the fluorescent lights. The air smelled obscenely of flowers and motor oil.

Mr. Hart lumbered out toward me, tucking his shirt into his pants. He had a large belly and stiff legs and arms. His skin did have an unhealthy sheen to it.

"How can I help you, young lady?" he groaned. A foul, sulfur smell emitted itself from his body. "We have some great deals on SUVs tonight. What are you driving?"

"A bike," I said.

He looked at me dully. "Thinking of upgrading then?"

"You don't sell any electric cars?" I asked.

"No. Why? You do a lot of driving?"

"Not so much. I'm concerned about the environment."

"Global warming? Sweetheart, that's a myth they created to scare you, believe me. No such thing. God knows what He's doing."

I smoothed back my hair. It was unnaturally hot for an October evening. There was something hellish about that kind of heat this time of year. I thought of the ice floes melting at the North pole and the polar bears dying. I was sweating uncomfortably and I was afraid I might be staining my white blouse. I used deodorant but I had stopped wearing antiperspirant because of the link between aluminum and Alzheimer's. Not that I cared. Alzheimer's might actually be all right. You stagger around in a state of detachment and forgetting.

There are certain things I can't forget, no matter how hard I try. No matter how many photographs I hide or how much zombie research I do. They pop into my mind when I least expect them.

Max used to ask me, "Mommy, when is the Earth going to explode? When is the sun going to burn us up?" Once he said, "Mommy will you hold me from the time the Earth was made until it ends?"

"Yes, honey," I said. "I will hold you forever."

He curled up into my arms, his delicately boned, dusty brown feet tucked up on my lap. His eyes were big and brown with eyelashes that all the nurses in the hospital said they wanted.

"It's not fair," they cooed.

Of course, it was more than fair. The other stuff was what wasn't fair.

"How about a Prius?" I asked Mr. Hart.

"How about a Hummer? Owned by a little old lady from Pasadena. Almost no mileage."

"I'll think about it," I said. "Sorry," I said. And left.

There is a proliferation of zombies around lately, let me tell you.

My ex Daniel's girlfriend Kimmy is not behaving at all normally, even for a stressed out, middle-aged, hyperactive kickboxing instructor dame. She drones on and on about herself and is unable to ask anyone questions about how they are doing. She wears the same rapacious grin frozen on her face at all times, even when she is angry. She talks loudly and proudly at all social gatherings about how she had tumors in her uterus and can no longer have any more children. (I know Daniel finds this perversely comforting; no chance of any more children means no chance of any more tragedies for him). She never lets anyone see her eat, not even Daniel. (He told me this; I think even he is worried). While she cooks his dinner she tells him she caught a bite at the gym and that she doesn't digest food well after four PM. She walks with jerky movements and snaps her gum spastically and calls everyone "dude." Do you see?

In addition there is that presidential candidate and his running mate. I believe they have been bitten. Look at their glassy eyes. Listen to their hollow voices—hers more shrill but hollow still. Read about their policies to destroy nature and take away women's rights, gay rights. I can just imagine them hunting people out of helicopters and gnawing on someone's thighbone with gristle between their teeth.

I remember that doctor at the hospital where Max was. He strolled out into the waiting room and tried to take my hand but I wouldn't let him touch me. His skin was greenish white under the fluorescence and his legs and arms were stiff.

When I saw him I knew. I thought it was going to be like on TV where they say, "I'm sorry."

I didn't want to hear those words from him. So I said them first.

"I'm sorry!" I screamed. I fell to my knees. "I'm so so sorry."

Zombies are reanimated corpses. I looked it up online. It said that if there is an invasion find a shopping mall or grocery store and barricade yourself inside. Then you will have plenty of supplies until you can come up with a plan.

I called Coco.

"Yes, I think you're right."

"What?"

"He seems to be what you say he is."

"Thanks for . . . Sorry . . . Um. What should we do about it?"

"Come meet me," I said. "But try not to say 'sorry' so much."

"Sorry. I mean . . . "

"It's okay. I do it too. You're very polite. Most people in L.A. don't say 'thank you' so much either."

"Oh. Sorry. We're from Florida."

I should be the one saying "sorry."

Okay, so I'm not a legitimate P.I. My ex, Daniel, rented this office for me. It's on Washington next to a store that sells knives and other exotic weaponry. The rent was cheap. Daniel thought it might help me after what happened with Max. He thought it would be good for me to have some place to go to every day, something to get dressed for. Kind of like playing office when you're a kid. Okay, so I hadn't really had any clients except for Coco, but hell, at least I had her. The guy with the cheating fiancée—I made him up. But not Coco. Not the zombie father. I would never lie to you about zombies.

Coco came in wearing a pair of skinny jeans, black-and-white checked Van's slip-on sneakers and the same oversized sweatshirt with the sleeves pulled down over her hands. She looked like a typical teenager except that her face had a very serious expression. She kept the sleeves of her sweatshirt bunched in her hand while she gnawed on her fingers. She wasn't even pretending that she didn't bite her nails this time.

"Thank you for looking into this."

"You're welcome."

"What are we going to do?" she asked me. "What did you do before?"

"You can't panic," I said. "But at the same time you must be vigilant not to get bitten."

She nodded. "He hasn't tried that."

"What precautionary actions are you taking?" I asked her.

"I have a secret hideaway stashed with water and food supplies," she told me.

"That's good."

"And I sleep with my door locked."

"Good."

Then she said, "Can I ask you something?"

I knew what was coming.

"Would you write on my arm?" She shoved up her sweatshirt sleeve and stuck out her bare forearm. There were raised white scars running horizontally just above her wrists.

I was wrong. I hadn't expected that question nor had I expected the scars. It took me a moment to talk. "What do you mean? I asked.

"With a Sharpie. I think it will help me to be brave. If you write a message."

I had no idea what to write but I took the Sharpie she handed me and opened it. It smelled like chemicals. It smelled like back-to-school and summer sports camp when I had to write Max's name on his baseball hat and backpack and lunch box. A bunch of lunchboxes were recalled because of lead content. I wondered what other dangerous substances lurked in products for children. There were carcinogens in things that seemed perfectly innocuous, like bubble bath and hot dogs.

"I don't think Sharpie is good for your skin," I told Coco. "It doesn't say non-toxic. It's permanent."

"Exactly."

She was still holding her arm out so I wrote, "Farewell, My Zombie," She smiled with satisfaction and pulled her sleeve down over it.

"Don't let your father see," I said.

She nodded.

"What happened? To your wrist."

"When I was a baby I got really sick," she said. "I'm better now. But I had to take all this medication and get all these treatments that really fucked me up. Sorry. Messed me up. I'd survived all that but I my life at home sucked and I didn't want to live anymore."

I suddenly wished I'd insisted on using non-toxic marker on her arm. "I understand," I said. "But you can't give up now. I mean, really. You can't."

She looked at me blankly.

"Okay?"

"Okay," she said. Then: "Can I ask you something else?"

Here it was.

"What really happened with your son?" she said, just as I thought she would.

I hadn't talked about it in so long.

"Everyone thought he had a brain tumor," I said. "But it wasn't like that. It wasn't like that at all. They wanted him and they got him. So that's why I'm here. In case I can help anyone else."

Coco reached out and gently touched my hand. "Sorry but . . . do you think, maybe, you just might not want to look at what really happened?"

I jumped as if she'd slapped me. "Get out please," I said.

"Oh! Sorry! I'm so sorry, Miss Merritt. I didn't mean to upset you."

The thing is, maybe Coco's right. Maybe Max really did have cancer. Maybe Coco had cancer and recovered and then wished she hadn't. Maybe her father isn't a zombie but maybe he did lay a hand on her. Maybe there's no such thing as global warming and it's okay to drive an Escalade but I don't think so. Maybe people are just out there trying to scare us. Hmmm. Maybe the presidential candidate and his running mate are not trying to eat us up. Maybe I'm crazy; maybe I'm perfectly sane. Who knows?

Well, baby, I know this. Today I am going to shut the office and ride my bike (because who wants to take a chance on making that hole in the ozone bigger just in case) down Washington to the beach. I am going to take off my shoes and walk on the wet sand. I am going to eat my cheese sandwich and watch the sun set like a beautiful apocalypse. Maybe I'll even build a sandcastle. Those are the things you and I used to do. That is why I haven't been to the beach in all these years. But today at sunset I am going to close my eyes and I am going to remember every little thing I can about you. From your eyelashes clumped with salt water, to the sand under your fingernails, to the little curled shells of your toes. I am going to remember all our days at the beach and the way you used to burrow into my arms when you were cold and the way, when you were a little older you used to pick roses from the garden for me, in spite of the thorns. I miss you, baby. I am going to apologize to Coco and when she comes back but I am not going to apologize to any more zombies. I am going to find out some more details and if a zombie or cancer whatever you want to call it threatens Coco Hart or any kids I know I am going to kick that motherfucker zombie's ass. I miss you, baby. But it is better than forgetting.

⌒

Francesca Lia Block *is the award-winning, bestselling author of numerous books. Her work has been translated into many languages. She has received numerous honors, including the Margaret A. Edwards Lifetime Achievement Award and the Phoenix Award, as well as citations from the American Library*

*Association, The New York Times Book Review, and the School Library Journal.
Born in Los Angeles, where she still lives, Block's writing is often informed and
inspired by the city's sprawling subculture.*

Block's title is, of course, a parody of Raymond Chandler's *Farewell, My
Lovely*, the second novel he wrote featuring hard-boiled Los Angeles private
eye Philip Marlowe. One of the themes of Chandler's novel is obsession. The
zombie, these days, can be used as a metaphor for many things. Block leaves
us wondering if zombies are real in the world she has devised or a metaphor
or simply part of Jane's obsession.

Trinkets

Tobias S. Buckell

George Petros walked down the waterfront, the tails of his coat slapping the back of his knees. An occasional gust of wind would tug at his tri-cornered hat, threatening to snatch it away. But by leaning his head into the wind slightly, George was able to manage a sort of balancing act between the impetuous gusts of wind and civilization's preference for a covered head.

The cobblestones made for wobbly walking, and George had just bought new shoes. He hadn't broken them in yet. But the luxury of new shoes bought the fleeting edges of a self-satisfied smile. The soles of his new shoes made a metronomic tick-tick-tick sound as he hurried towards his destination, only slowing down when he walked around piles of unloaded cargo.

Men of all sorts, shapes, and sizes bustled around in the snappy, cold weather. Their breath steamed as they used long hooks to snatch the cargo up and unload it. George walked straight past them. He did not put on airs or anything of the sort, but he hardly made eye contact with the grunting dockworkers.

His destination was the *Toussaint*. George could tell he was getting closer, the quiet suffering of the New England dockworkers yielded to a more buoyant singing.

George detoured around one last stack of crates, the live chickens inside putting up a cacophony of squawks and complaint, and saw the *Toussaint*. The ship was hardly remarkable; it looked like any other docked merchantmen. What *did* give people a reason to pause were the people around the ship: they were Negroes. Of all shades of colors, George noticed.

Free Negroes were around the North. But to see this many in one area, carrying guns, talking, chatting, flying their own flag. It made people nervous. Ever since the island of Haiti drove the French from its shores for its independence, their ships had been ranging up and down the American coast. George knew it made American politicians wonder if the Negroes of the South would gain any inspiration from the Haitians visible freedom.

The crew stood around the ship, unloaded the cargo, and conducted business for supplies with some of the New England shopkeepers. George himself was a shopkeeper, though of jewels and not staples of any sort. He nodded, seeing some familiar faces from his street: Bruce, Thomas. No doubt they would think he was here for some deal with the Haitians.

The smell of salt and sweat wafted across the docks as George nodded to some of the dockworkers, then passed through them to the gangplank of the ship. One of the Haitians stopped him. George looked down and noticed the pistol stuck in a white sash.

"What do you need?" He spoke with traces of what could have been a French accent, or something else. It took a second for George to work through the words.

"I'm here for a package," George said. "Mother Jacqueline . . . "

The man smiled.

"Ah, you're that George?"

"Yes."

George stood at the end of the plank as the Haitian walked back onto the ship. He was back in a few minutes, and handed George a brown, carefully wrapped, parcel. Nothing shifted when George shook it.

He stood there for a second, searching for something to say, but then he suddenly realized that the tables had been turned, and now *he* was the one who wasn't wanted here. He left, shoes clicking across the cobblestones.

In the room over his shop George opened the parcel by the window. Below in the street horses' feet kicked up a fine scattering of snow. When it settled by the gutters, it was stained brown and muddy with dung.

The desk in front of him was covered in occasional strands of his hair. He had a small shelf with papers stacked on it, but more importantly, he had his shiny coins and pieces of metal laid out in neat, tiny little rows. George smiled when the light caught their edges and winked at him. Some of the coins had engravings on them, gifts between lovers long passed away. Others had other arcane pieces of attachment to their former owners. Each one told George a little story. The jewelry he sold downstairs meant nothing. Each of the pieces here represented a step closer to a sense of completion.

He cut the string on the package and pulled the paper away from a warm mahogany box lid. The brass hinges squeaked when he opened it.

Inside was a letter. The wax seal on it caught George's full attention; he sat for a moment entranced by it. The faint smell of something vinegary kicked faint memories back from their resting places, and Mama Jaqi's distant whisper spoke to him from the seal.

"Hear me, obey me . . . "

George sucked in his breath and opened the seal to read his directions. *There is a man*, the letter read, *right now sitting in a tavern fifteen or so miles south of you. You should go and listen to his story . . .*

There was a name. And the address of the tavern.

Who is Louis Povaught? George wondered. But he didn't question the implicit order given. Layers of cold ran down his back, making him shiver. Automatically, without realizing it, he pulled something out and put it in his pocket, then shut the box. As he donned his coat and walked out of the shop to find a carriage he told Ryan, the shop's assistant, that he would be back "later," and he should close the shop himself.

Hours later, the sky darkening, George's cab stopped in front of "The Hawser." A quick wind batted the wooden sign over the door around. George paid and walked through door. It was like any other tavern: dim, and it smelled of stale beer and piss. He looked around and fastened his eyes on a Frenchman at the edge of the counter.

Frenchman, Negro, Northerner, Southerner, English . . . to George, all humanity seemed more or less the same after he met Mama Jaqi. Yet even now he could feel that he was being nudged towards the Frenchman. This is the man he was supposed to meet, as irrational as it may have seemed. George carefully stamped his new shoes clean, leaned over to brush them off with a handkerchief he kept for exactly that purpose, then crossed the tavern to sit by the Frenchman.

The Frenchman—who would be Louis Povaught, George assumed—sat slouched over. He hardly stirred when George sat next to him. The barkeep caught George's eye, and George shook his head. When he turned back to look at Louis, the man was already looking back at him.

Louis, unfortunately, hadn't spent much time keeping up his appearances. A long russet-colored beard, patchy in some places, grew haphazardly from his cheeks. His bloodshot eyes contained just a hint of green, lost to the steady strain of enthusiastic drinking.

"I think, not many people walk in here who do not order drink," he declared. "No?"

George pulled out his purse and caught the eye of the barkeep. "He'll have another," George told the barkeep. George looked down and pulled out paper money, leaving the shiny coins inside.

"And you," Louis said. "Why no drink?"

"It no longer does anything for me," George explained. He reached his hand into the pocket of his undercoat. Something was there. Like something standing just at the edge of his vision, he could remember picking it up.

Now George pulled it out. It was a silver chain with a plain cross on the end. He held it between the fingers of his hand and let the cross rest against the countertop.

"I have something for you, Louis," George heard himself saying. "Something very important."

Louis turned his tangled hair and scraggly beard towards George. The chain seductively winked; George locked his eyes with the entwined chains and followed them down to the rough countertop. Such beautiful things human hands made.

Louis' gasp took George's attention back to the world around the necklace.

"Is this what I think it is?" Louis asked, reaching tentatively for it. His wrinkled hands shook as they brushed the chain. George did not look down for fear of being entranced again. He did not feel the slightest brush of Louis' fingernail against his knuckle.

"What do you think it is?" George asked.

Louis turned back to the counter.

"My brother Jean's necklace," Louis said. "On the back of this, it should have engrave . . . " Louis waved his hand about, "J.P. It is there, no?"

George still didn't look down.

"I imagine so."

Louis leaned back and laughed.

"*Merde.* So far away, so damn far away, and that bitch Jacqueline still has talons. Unlucky? Ha," he spat. "Do you know my story?"

"No," George said. "I do not."

The barkeep finally delivered a mug of beer, the dirty amber fluid spilling over the sides and onto the bar top where it would soak into the wood and add to the dank and musky air. Louis took it with a firm grasp and tipped it back. It took only seconds before the mug contained nothing but slick wetness at the bottom.

Louis smacked the mug down. "Buy me another, damn you," he ordered. George tapped the counter, looked at the barkeep, and nodded.

Stories, George thought, could sometimes be as interesting as something shiny and new. He would indulge Louis, yes, and himself. He handed Louis the necklace.

"Jean was much the better brother," Louis said. "I think it broke my father's heart to hear he died in Haiti. My father locked himself in his study for three days. Did not eat, did not drink. And when he came back out, he put his hand on my shoulder, like this—" Louis draped a heavy arm over George and leaned closer. His breath reeked of beer. "—and he tells me, he tells me, 'Louis, you must go and take over where you brother has left off.' That is all he tells me. I never see him again."

Louis pulled back away. "And Katrina, my wife, she is very, *very* sad to see me go away to this island. But I tell her it is good that I take over the business Jean created. I will make for her a better husband. My brother has left me a good legacy. Hmmm. I did good business. I made them all proud. Proud! And you know what," Louis said, looking down at the necklace, "it was all great until Jean walked into my office three month later. It was unnatural . . . I'd seen his grave! There were witnesses . . . "

"Business was good?" George interrupted Louis. "What did you do?"

Louis ran a thumb around the rim of his glass.

"It didn't cost much. A boat. Provisions. We bought our cargo for guns . . . and necklaces, or whatever: beads and scrap." He opened a weathered palm. There was nothing in it.

"What cargo?" George interrupted. This was the point. It was why Mama Jaqi had sent him.

"Slaves," Louis said. "Lots of slaves."

"Ah, yes," George said. Mama Jaqi had been a slave.

"I made money," Louis said. "For the first time I wasn't some peasant in Provencal. I had a house with gardens." Louis looked at George. "I did good! I gave money to charity. I was a good citizen. I was a good *businessman.*"

"I am sure you were," George said. He felt nothing against Louis. In another life, he would maybe have sympathized with Louis' arguments. He remembered using some of them once, a long time ago. A brief flash of a memory occurred to him. George had desperately blabbered some of the same things, trying to defend himself to the incensed Mama Jaqi.

George shook away the ghostlike feel of passion to prod Louis' story along.

"But what a shock seeing your brother must have been." George was here for the story. He wanted it over quickly. Time was getting on, and George had to open the shop tomorrow. He would have to finish Mama Jaqi's deed soon.

"I thought some horrible trick had been played on me," Louis said. "I had so many questions about what had happened. And all Jean would do was tell me I had to leave. Leave the business. Leave the island. I refused." Louis made a motion at the bartender for more beer. "I was still in Haiti when it all began. Toussaint . . . the independence. I lost it all when the blacks ran us all off the island. I slipped away on a small boat to America with nothing. Nothing." Louis looked at George, and George saw a world of misery swimming in the man's eyes. "In France, they hear I am dead. I can only think of Katrina remarrying." He stopped and looked down at George's arm.

"What is it?" George asked.

Louis reached a finger out and pulled back the cuff of George's sleeve. Underneath, a faint series of scars marked George's wrist.

"Jean had those," Louis said. The barkeep set another mug in front of Louis, and left after George paid for it. "Do me a favor," Louis said, letting go of George's sleeve. "One last favor."

"If I can," George said.

"Let me do this properly, like a real man. Eh? Would you do that?"

"Yes," George said.

Louis took his last long gulp from the mug, then stood up.

"I will be out in the alley."

George watched him stagger out the tavern.

After several minutes George got up and walked out. The distant cold hit him square in the face when he opened the door, and several men around the tables yelled at him to hurry and get out and shut the door.

In the alley by the tavern, George paused. Louis stepped out of the darkness holding a knife in his left hand, swaying slightly in the wind.

Neither of them said anything. They circled each other for a few seconds, then Louis stumbled forward and tried to slash at George's stomach. George stepped away from the crude attempt and grabbed the Frenchman's wrist. It was his intent to take the knife away, but Louis slipped and fell onto the stones. He fell on his arm, knocking his own knife away, then cracked his head against the corner of a stone.

Louis didn't move anymore. He still breathed, though: a slight heaving and the air steaming out from his mouth.

George crouched and put a knee to Louis' throat. The steaming breath stopped, leaving the air still and quiet. A long minute passed, then Louis opened an eye. He struggled, kicking a small pool of half-melted snow with his tattered boots. George kept his knee in place.

When Louis stopped moving George relaxed, but kept the knee in place for another minute.

The door to the tavern opened, voices carried into the alley. Someone hailed for a cab and the clip-clop of hooves quickened by the tavern. George kept still in the alley's shadows. When the voices trailed off into the distance George moved again. He checked Louis' pockets until he found what he wanted: the necklace. He put it back into his own pocket. Then he stood up and walked out of the alley to hail his own cab.

The snow got worse towards the harbor and his shop. The horses pulling the cab snorted and slowed down, and the whole vehicle would shift and slide with wind gusts. George sat looking out at the barren, wintry landscape. It was cold and distant, like his own mechanical feelings. He could hear occasional snatches of the driver whistling *Amazing Grace* to himself and the horses.

Mama Jaqi had done well. George felt nothing but a compulsion for her bidding. *Obey* . . . no horror about what he had just done. Just a dry, crusty satisfaction.

When he got out George paid the driver. He took the creaky back steps up. He lit several candles and sat in his study for a while, still fully dressed. Eventually he put his fingers to the candle in front of him and watched the edges turn from white, to red, to brown, and then to a blistered black. The burnt flesh smelled more like incense than cooked flesh.

He pulled them away.

Tomorrow they would be whole again.

George pulled the silver necklace out with his good hand. He set it on the shelf, next to all the other pieces of flashy trinkets. Another story ended, another decoration on his shelf.

How many more would it take, George wondered, before Mama Jaqi freed him? How many lives did she deem a worthy trade for the long suffering she knew as her life? Or for the horrors of George's own terrible past? George didn't know. She'd taken that ability away from him. In this distant reincarnation of himself, George knew that any human, passionate response he could muster would be wrong.

Even his old feelings would have been wrong.

Long after the candles burned out George sat, waiting.

Tobias S. Buckell *is a Caribbean-born writer who grew up in Grenada, the British Virgin Islands, and the U.S. Virgin Islands. He has published stories in various magazines and anthologies. His three Caribbean SF novels,* Crystal Rain, Ragamuffin, *and* Sly Mongoose *were published by Tor Books, as well as the* New York Times *bestselling novel* Halo: The Cole Protocol. *He is currently working on his next book.*

Buckell's subtle story is yet another interpretation of what a zombie could be. Here, George Petros, an early nineteenth-century New England jeweler, is obviously Mama Jaqi's zombie—but he is an emotionless "distant re-incarnation of himself" with the appearance and demeanor of a normal man and superhuman powers of regeneration. But, as with many zombie stories, the author uses fiction to make a social comment: Mama Jaqi, a slave recently freed in the Haitian Revolution, is taking revenge on slavetraders. George's last name is of interest, too. In Haitian Voudou, there are two primary types of spirits (loa): *Rada* and *Petwo* (or *Petro, Pethro,* etc.). The Petwo are "hotter" loas than the Rada, and less compromising. They are also associated with the brutal experience of slavery and consequent uprisings against it. In Greek *petros* means "a piece of rock; a stone."

Dead Man's Land

David Wellington

The dead man couldn't get away, no matter how hard he struggled. Barbed wire wreathed the outer perimeter of the WalMart parking lot, long droopy coils of it that bounced every time he tried to convulse his way to freedom. The blotchy skin of his neck tore open and a little dried blood sifted out. He pulled again, his arm held motionless by the wire and then stopped again, confused, lacking the brainpower to unsnag himself, lacking the energy to panic.

The girl—Winona—threw a rock that bounced off his skull but didn't crack the bone. She had blond hair pulled back in a braid curled and oiled until it looked like metal and eyes the color of old glass bottles. We stood on the loading dock of the superstore a hundred yards from the dead man. My hair and clothes still smelled like the cookfires burning inside. I couldn't wait to get out there, onto the road again. My cargo had already thrown one tantrum that morning, demanding she be allowed to stay. Too bad for her.

"Is this enough?" her father asked. He wore a bright orange vest and a baseball hat crowned with a ring of bird skulls. He was an Assistant Manager for WalMart and a man of some importance. He held out to me an orange plastic pill bottle. The label had been worn off long ago and the contents were a mixed assortment of colorful capsules and tablets, some of them crumbled near to dust, all of them decades past their expiration date. I nodded to the manager and grabbed the girl's hand. "Now you're mine," I told her, "and you'll behave, or else." Her father pursed his lips but I don't make my living coddling the civilized folk of the stores. I pointed at the dead man in the wire. "That's just what we call a slack. Too dumb and too far gone to hunt us, sure. You make too much racket throwing stones, though, and you'll attract his friends, and they *bite*."

She merely stared at me, those green eyes wide and vacant. A look she'd practiced, sure. She didn't care, wasn't going to care unless I gave her a reason. I pulled her along behind me as I stormed down the ramp to the parking lot. In my other arm I cradled my spring-lance, the one thing in the world I couldn't afford to lose.

"If any harm comes to her—" the manager shouted at my back.

I finished the thought for him. "Then you won't see me again." It wasn't what he wanted to hear. Screw him.

There was no gate or door in the barbed wire for us to pass through. Instead a couple of boys who were watching the captive slack dragged out a sheet of plywood and leaned it up against the barrier, making a ramp for us. The girl refused to climb the ramp. Maybe she thought she'd get splinters. "My name is Cher," I told her. "I'm what your dad calls a Roadie. You know what that means?"

"Half human being, half wild folk," Winona said, watching the boys instead of me. "You travel between the Stores. You cross Dead Man's Land, to conduct our trade. That makes you our servant. Do you know what I am? I'm the daughter of a Manager and you've been hired to protect me."

"I suppose that's so, on this side," I said. I picked her up by the back of her pants and threw her over the wire. Behind me on the loading dock I heard someone gasp and someone else yell. I ran over the ramp and kicked it back, cutting off the only way in, getting shut of the place. I grabbed her yellow hair and stared into those green, green eyes. I showed her my spring-lance, a coffee can on the end of a wooden pole. The can concealed a spring-loaded steel spike long enough to skewer most heads. "Now we're in my world, little girl. Now you're nothing but ghoulbait. Understand?"

Why was I so hard on her? She needed to behave, of course, or she could get us killed. But there was more, a special reason to hate her, and it could be summed up in two words: Full up.

That was what they told my grandfather when he went to the great stores along the New Jersey Turnpike with me in his arms, back when the highways were still crowded with the fleeing going north and going south. "Full up," they said at Barnes and Noble. Full up at CostCo and TJ Maxx. No room for us who waited too long.

So he took me into the wilds, which at that time were lush and green but no higher than your ankle. The mowed lawns, the abandoned houses of suburbia. We hid where we could and moved on every morning. We lived on canned food and we listened to the radio in the dark, listened to static when that was all there was, hoping to hear of shelter somewhere, real shelter.

Full up. They were all full up before we arrived. Not enough food to go around, not any more room, they told him. He died in the wild and I could have joined a tribe in Montclair, they would have taken me in but instead I crushed his head with a rock before I'd even begun to weep. I would not be a wild woman, a friend to the dead. I would not be a savage.

I didn't go hungry for long. The Stores needed me and my kind. We meant communication and trade and that meant survival. They let me sleep on their floors. They paid what I asked. And every time I looked one in the eyes I saw those words again, and I hated them all over again. There was no room in my heart for this girl. I was full up, too.

We couldn't make the thirty miles to Home Depot in one day but I wanted us as far from the WalMart as possible before nightfall. The commotion our leaving made would draw too much attention—probably for days to come Winona's father would be watching ghouls circle his perimeter, looking for the source of all that noise. He would lock his big loading gates and pray for them to leave him in peace, for his fence to hold them back.

We didn't have that option. I pushed us hard. I led Winona through a drainage ditch behind the store, through reeds taller than me and water scummed with mosquito larvae. On the far side we had to cross an old asphalt access road, a broken field of smooth black fragments with bright green weeds sticking up in unnatural rectilinear patterns. It took us most of an hour to get to the far side and over the sway-backed fencing there. It would have taken me a quarter of that time, alone. They don't need proper shoes in the Stores and what she had were old passed-down sneakers so well-used the laces were crusted in place.

Beyond the road the woods began, the real dead man's land. I saw the signs of ghouls everywhere, on every scraped tree trunk, on every broken branch. I was looking for one thing, to convince myself I wasn't just being paranoid. When I finally found it I felt almost relieved.

In a clearing in the shadow of a creaking utility pylon where the high grass grew yellow and thin I saw a splash of red. I pushed through the sighing vegetation to get closer and bent to touch the ground. A broad swath of grass had been bent back, crushed by the weight of a human being. Blood soaked the ground and turned the long stalks red. I dug around amidst the roots for a moment and came up with a broken leg bone—too long and thin to be human. Probably white-tailed deer. The femur had been cracked open so the marrow could be sucked out.

I squatted and ran a few blades of the grass through my fingers, letting the dried blood powder away like rust. Winona stared at the discarded bone as if it might come back to life at any moment. She'd probably never seen a meat bone before that wasn't in the bottom of a stew pot.

"There's one nearby," I told her, whispering. The dead don't linger when they've eaten and there was nearly no chance of the ghoul still being within earshot. Still I don't make a habit of raising my voice out in the woods. "He ate recently so he'll be strong and fast."

"But so he's full, then, and he won't attack us," she said, her fingers brushing the fibrous surface of the femur. She wasn't scared. The little idiot.

"A living thing, an animal might not but this is a dead man. If he can't find human he'll eat deer or rabbits or mice. If he can't find meat he'll chew the bark off of trees and stuff himself full of grass. He doesn't care if he eats so much he pops, he'll still want more, even if it just slides down his gullet and out the hole in his belly. The more he eats the hungrier he gets."

She shrugged and laid back in the grass, probably exhausted after her long hike. I could see it in her eyes. She didn't need to worry, she thought. I would protect her.

So I did just that: I yanked her up to her feet and got us moving again, despite her exhaustion.

You smell them first, long before you see them. It's a mixed blessing—scent is a fickle sense to have to rely on. The stink of decaying meat keeps you on your toes but you can't tell what direction it's coming from. You could walk right into the ghoul and not know it. They don't make much noise. They never talk or cough or sneeze.

I had him in my nose for most of the afternoon, on and off. Once I thought I saw him but it was only slacks, a whole line of them on the crest of a hill. They walked in single file, the one in front missing most of the flesh from his skull. Just red-shot eyes rolling in a blank skull. Their clothes, filthy and torn, still kept the colors of the old time. Some of those colors never fade. In red and blue and purple T-shirts and dresses they looked almost merry up there, silhouetted against the setting sun. They walked without looking to the side, without knowing where they headed. This is their world now and they're safe within it as long as the don't get too close to the Stores.

I kept the girl down, hidden under a berry bush until they were gone just to take care.

In the middle of an overgrown housing development I hauled Winona over the splintered remains of a picket fence and into a house that had only been partly burned down, most of its roof missing but the walls solid as when they were put up. The stink of the ghoul was everywhere—he couldn't be more than a quarter mile away, even if he was upwind. Inside I held the door closed by shoving furniture up against it. It was the best I could do short of boarding us in and that's never a good idea. I let the girl collapse on an old water-stained sofa and searched the place. Green saplings grew through the floorboards of the living room while old pictures, still bright and fresh, lined the stairway to the upstairs. Smiling people out in the sunshine, boats on clean water. The frames of the pictures were riddled with wormcast and some had rotted away altogether.

Night came down, early as it does in October. The girl refused to sleep on any of the house's beds they were so infested with bugs. Instead she wanted to stay up and talk. I sat in one corner of an upstairs room under a hole in the roof, the spring-lance across my knees and listened, too tired to shut her up properly.

"My children will be managers," she told me, at some length. "Great men, great warriors and they will finally rid the land of the monsters. That is the destiny of my line. The story was told often around our fires."

I shifted slightly—the carpet under me was damp. "Is that why you're going so far away? To have babies?"

She nodded readily and gave me a smile that could have sold toothpaste in the old time. "To be wed to the General Manager of Home Depot and to bear his heirs."

"The big man's tired of fucking his first cousins," I guessed. "Makes sense. They've got bad skin out that way 'cause it's too close to the old chemical plants. Me, I never gave much thought to a baby. Just one more corpse to walk the earth in the end."

"That's doom talk, and it's not allowed at WalMart," she scolded me. She played with a DVD case she'd found in the entertainment center, the card insert showing a man dressed like a bat. She opened and closed the plastic with a snap, over and over again, snap snap, snap snap. A good sound of well-made pieces fitting together perfectly. Everything sounded like that in the old time. "It's not just about babies, anyway. This will be a strategic alliance, uniting two Exits and drawing borders for future conquests to come. I imagine you have no use for politics—"

"Shush," I told her. I'd heard something downstairs. She kept prattling on for a minute till she saw that I meant it. The sound came again. Wood screeching on wood. Furniture scraping on a hardwood floor. The ghoul was testing my barricade.

They can smell you, just like you can smell them, and they don't need to rest. You can't hide for long.

A chest of drawers squealed and crashed as it fell over. A chair tumbled away from the door. I lifted the windowsill as quietly as I could and gestured for Winona to go on, out onto the roof. The second-floor window let out onto a slope of rotten shingles that skidded out from under her and she wouldn't let go of the sill.

I crawled over her and carefully slipped my way down to the gutter so I could look over the edge. The ghoul looked up at the same time and we made eye contact. He had on the loose gray pants of a wild man, stained now with deer blood. Most of his hair had fallen out and something had eaten his lips, leaving ragged skin that failed to cover his crooked teeth. His eyelids were gone too, giving him the look of a bloody death's head.

I skittered back onto the roof. Below I heard him redouble his efforts, slamming a bookshelf to the side. He would be through the door soon. Winona started screaming. "Kill it! It's right there! Just kill it!"

It was an eight foot drop to the ground. There were some scraggly bushes down there to break my fall but I landed badly and lost a fraction of a second jumping back up to my feet. By that time the ghoul had turned to face me, slaver running out of the hole in his face. I could see the blotchy sores on his gray skin, I could hear his teeth grinding together in anticipation.

"Do your job!" Winona howled. Her fingers couldn't hold her on the slope of the roof and suddenly she was sliding, falling on the loose shingles. I had been one step ahead of her—bringing the spring-lance around to line up my shot I was a breath's span away from firing when she called me. I managed to ignore the distraction of her falling off the roof. The dead man didn't—he swung his head up and to the side, looking for the source of the noise.

The spring-lance connected with his head, but not in the right place. The coffee can slid back, triggering a latch, and the lethal spike clanged out of the sheath and into his flesh. His jawbone exploded inside his fragile skin, yellow teeth flying from his mouth to clatter on the ground. The blow knocked him backward and off his feet but it had failed to penetrate his brain.

I jumped back and looked up at the roof. Winona had fallen into the gutter, which had bent but not broken. I only caught half a glimpse of her—a pale shape hanging in the darkness. Meanwhile the ghoul was recovering from my attack. The spring-lance was useless until I could crank back the spring.

He stood up, clutching at the place where his jawbone had been. His eyes focused on me with horrible slowness.

"Winona!" I shouted. "You stay there and be quiet!"

The ghoul started in to charge me, his head down, his broken fingernails stretched out to grab and tear my clothes and my skin. I turned around and headed into the woods, running as fast as my legs could carry me.

The dead are slow. You can outrun them, for a while.

"Come on, girl! Winona! Show yourself!"

She wasn't there when I got back. Which was the bad news. I couldn't find any blood or torn clothes, either, meaning the ghoul didn't get her. That could be very bad news. It could mean she'd run off on her own. I doubted it.

It took me most of the night to outrun the ghoul. He was a tough character, real strong, but none of them are ever as fast as a living person. If you don't exhaust yourself with sprinting, if you don't trip on an old curb and break your leg, you can escape them. It's how I've stayed alive so long.

I lead him in a wide loop through the subdivision, up cracked streets and through backyards full of play sets rusted down to twisted scrap. I could hear him behind me, smell him too, but I kept my eyes on my feet. I could step on an abandoned toy or even an old lawnmower lost in the high grass and it would be over. I could trip over an exposed cable or pipe. I could run right into a tree and give myself a concussion.

You have to not panic, is all. I kept my heading and I kept moving. Well before dawn his stench was just a memory in my nose, a last whiff of corruption that lingered on me well past the time I'd lost him. I circled back, made a wide circuit around the row houses in case he caught smell of me again. Eventually I wound up right where I started, ready to resume my travels.

Except Winona was gone. I tore the house apart looking for her, turned over every decaying mattress, broke open every closet and scared a few mice for my trouble. I looked all around the yard, constantly aware that the ghoul was still nearby. I searched the nearby houses.

Three doors down I found the remains of a campfire on what had been somebody's front lawn, a time ago. I found some old cans, emptied and licked clean. I found flat places in the grass where wild folk had laid out in the night.

I felt the ashes of the fire and they were still warm. I still had a chance, then. At least as long as the General Manager of the Home Depot didn't mind receiving my cargo slightly used.

It's not hard to find the villages of the wild folk on a calm day, even though they move from time to time, even though they are little more than tent towns and colorless and small. You look for smoke, is all, and it's something my grandfather taught me. You get to a high place, say the top of an old commercial building or you climb on top of a bent old power pylon and you look across the land. If you don't squint too hard you'll see them, the columns of smoke. Thin gray pencil lines rising in the air.

I tracked them down through a low defile that ran parallel to an old state highway. I moved quietly but I didn't waste time. I could hear them before long but I trailed behind, keeping my distance. I waited for them to camp and then I waited for the sun to sink over the hills. Only then did I move in.

There were maybe seventy of them, a fair-sized encampment and far more than I could take on with just my two arms. There were children with them, some as young as five. The wild folk have their babies in the woods and raise them where they can. Very few survive to puberty. It's why they keep their women pregnant at all times, and why they're constantly looking for new breeding stock.

I saw them like pinkish ghosts in the falling light, their undyed clothing and their pale skin moving between the trees like inverted shadows. I saw their fires and their animal-hide tents stretched over battered old aluminum poles. I saw their pet slack.

Every band of wild folk has one. A dead man, usually an ancestor, who they keep and feed. Some are simple totems, rallying points for the tribe. Some are valued because they can do tricks. I watched this one work his single gimmick over and over. The wild folk would bring him scraps of paper, bits and ends they had found in the old houses. The slack had a plastic pen wired to his hand. A girl of maybe ten years would fill it with ink from time to time as the slack signed his name, over and over. Who could say what dim chunk of his rotting brain, what curl of gray matter was left to him, that let him do that. He looked quite happy to sign and sign away, his fleshless face turned upward in a pure and innocent smile, his tattered body jiggling with the joy of it.

Every time he finished a signature the wild folk would laugh and cheer. It was something of the old world, something they might remember doing themselves. It was a thing of power, every name an incantation. I don't suppose it matters why. It was a good trick, for a slack, and entertainment is what you make of it out on the road.

I gave them an hour of darkness—just long enough to have their dinner ready—and then I stepped out of the shadows and into the light. I made myself known with a loud, warbling screech and threw my lance down before me.

Every eye in the encampment turned my way. Every hand reached for a weapon. Yet my intentions could not be more clear. I had dealings with the wild folk before, many a time, whether or not I knew any of this band. Their lives are unlike the life of the Stores. They don't hold to so many rules. But they still have a few, and I knew them, and how to make them work for me.

"I want some dinner, and I want some information," I said. I held my arms outstretched the way a ghoul might. In this case I was showing them I was unarmed.

The leader of the band came to me then. He was nearly my age—ripe, for a wild man—and some kind of fungal infection lined his cheeks and forehead with angry ridges. Muscles crawled across his chest and shoulders like vines pulled taut. He wore drawstring pants and shoes of fine deer hide. The top of a human skull, sawed away just above the eye sockets, perched atop his unwashed hair.

"You come to join us, Roadie? You come to be a friend to the dead?" he asked. He didn't look happy but he didn't look like he wanted to kill me, either.

"Not hardly. I've come for dinner, like I said."

He nodded. He'd be willing to feed me, in exchange for my leaving them alone.

I went on. "And I've come to be told where the girl is. The girl with hair like gold and eyes like old glass bottles. I'll be taking her with me."

His eyes narrowed. He moved sideways, scuttling around me, looking me over. He wanted to know if I had any real weapons on me. Say a pistol, or even a zip gun. Say a knife in a hidden sheath. He glanced at the spring-lance at my feet but it was well out of my reach.

"Finder's, keepers," he said, finally, when he was sure I was defenseless. He had a hatchet in his own hand, a steel thing at least half made of rust. It wouldn't keep an edge any more but it would do just fine for bashing in my face. "She's weak, but she can birth some babies for us. We won't be giving her up." He looked me up and down again but this time it was my breasts and my crotch he sized up. "Maybe you want to make a trade? Maybe you want to come be our babymaker?"

"Not hardly," I said again.

His brothers, his cousins, his uncles came out of the tents then or stepped up from their campfires or ghosted in out of the woods. They had spears and knives in their hands. Some of them wore leather thongs around their throats, tight as chokers, with finger bones dangling from them. That marked them as killers, as those who had fought before. They came close, close enough to strike me, but not close enough that I could touch them. They knew this kind of entertainment all too well. There was no chance of me taking them. I was a tough thing, all muscle and sinew, and stronger by far than any wild folk, fed up better on Store food, trained by hard life on the road. Against their leader, maybe, or maybe even him and his best two champions, maybe. But there were just too many of them.

"Roadies are too smart for this kind of aggro," the leader said. "Too smart to come in here and start something they can't finish." He was figuring out my game, and far too soon. "You playing at something, Roadie?"

I shrugged my shoulders elaborately. "You won't give her back, then. All right." I took my water bottle from my belt and showed it to him. He turned away and spat. He wouldn't drink my water. It might be poisoned.

I shrugged again. I had to draw this out a little longer. Slowly, as if to assure them of my good intentions, I unscrewed the cap from my water bottle. Slowly I lifted the bottle, as if to drink.

Then the wind changed and a familiar smell lit up my nose and I smiled. I turned over the bottle and rabbit's blood spilled out on the ground.

Behind me, come looming out of the shadows, the ghoul appeared, his broken mouth black and wide as a cave as if he would swallow the wild folk whole. I'd been teasing and taunting and coaxing him along all day and finally he had caught up. He smelled the blood and the hunger in him must have spiked. He came shambling for me—for the leader—for anything warm.

In the confusion I grabbed up my lance and slipped past their leader. I dodged around a cook fire and tore open the flap of the first tent I found. Inside a huddle of children looked up at me, terrified.

I'd brought death down on them, maybe. I didn't waste time on guilt. The next three tents I found were empty. Behind me the leader and his extended family were whooping with fear and running every way, their weapons up, their hands raised. The ghoul would lunge at one of them, then another. They would dance away from him, yelping like dogs. He stumbled like a drunkard from one body to the next.

I tripped over the slack in the middle of the encampment. He looked up at me and raised his pen hand, perhaps wanting another piece of paper. Endless copies of his signature littered the ground about his feet. My skin rumpled, my stomach flipped at the nearness of him, this harmless dead man. Reflexively I raised the spring-lance. But no. If I took the girl and ran this band of wild folk might forget me, after a time of seeking revenge. If I did in their pet slack, however, they would chase me like furies. I pushed past him and headed for the next tent.

Winona stepped out of it before I even arrived. Her hair hung loose around her face, piled in careless hummocks like the yellow grass revealed by the melting snows of spring. Her eyes saw me and I saw in them a hurt that went beyond blame. A hurt that needed healing of a kind I could not offer. She was stark naked, her little body smeared with dirt and ash and paint. I knew what that meant.

They had tied her feet and hands together with leather cord. She could shuffle forward but not walk with any speed. I didn't have the time to free her so I grabbed her up over my shoulder and I ran into the darkness, leaving the camp in chaos behind.

We hid in a tree, our exhausted bodies draped over the branches, and spent the night not sleeping, but listening for any sound, and smelling, our noses twitched, even as we dozed.

The next day I brought her back toward the Turnpike. We passed through the overgrown asphalt of an old school parking lot, climbing over places where the pavement had cracked like the top of a loaf of bread. The brick building loomed over us in silent decay, its windows broken, its doors standing open to let us look in on empty rooms full of dirt and dead leaves.

"They kept a dead man among them," Winona said to me as we climbed an endless on-ramp to the Pike. "They kept him like a milking cow, like a treasure."

It was the first thing she'd said to me since I left her in the abandoned house. I considered what to say long and hard. "They are the friends of the dead. It's why you call them wild."

"This much I knew, yes. That when one of them dies, they are left uncleansed. No relative will strike the sacred blow."

Which is what they call it in the Stores. The Final Duty of Kinship. The Sacred Blow. Which amounts to taking a sledgehammer to the brains of your loved ones when they pass. It's a necessary thing. I did for my grandfather, didn't I? I'm no wild folk savage. Still. I never saw it like some holy thing, as Winona's people did. I saw it as a sadness, a sharp sadness on the world.

"They have avowed never to strike a dead thing. They make a pact with their ancestors, you see. They will not harm the dead, which is sin, and in exchange, the dead will let them survive."

"The dead know nothing of treaties and compacts," Winona said, a little of her old uppity pride glowing behind her eyes. I guess maybe she was going to be all right. "Such foolishness. Such evil."

Now a Roadie may never judge those she trades with. So I kept my peace.

The ghoul found us again the next evening, just as the sky started turning orange. Maybe he got a meal out of the wild folk. Maybe they outran him. It didn't matter. He had my smell in his dead nose and he couldn't not come for me. He was a thing of nature, as pure, if not as innocent, as the smile on the face of the paper-signing slack.

For days he tracked me. For days I tried to give him the slip. It was for naught. We were like two arrows launched in the air at the same target. At some point our paths would cross. Smart as I am, I decided I would choose when it might happen.

I smelled him and then I heard him. I readied myself for him. I put Winona in an old storm cellar and locked the door behind me. Then I walked out into the middle of a suburban street with my spring-lance loose in my hands. I spread my legs a little, kept my knees unlocked. I tried to sense where he was, what direction he might be coming from.

He surprised me, as they do. He came from behind and I barely had time to pivot on my left foot, my right foot high to kick out at him. I caught him in the stomach and knocked him backwards. It gave me a splinter of a moment to bring the lance around.

His hands came for me, his broken jaws, his whole body swimming through the air as time slowed to a near standstill. My eyes focused on his head until every little detail stood out. The dark veins beneath his cheek. The ragged hole in the side of his head where my spring-lance had caught him before, like a second, rotten ear.

His fingers caught at my belt, wove themselves through the cord to anchor himself to me. The next blow would tear my flesh open and make me bleed.

At least it might have, if I'd been a trace slower. I pressed the end of the coffee can against his forehead. It was a centered strike, a perfect placement. His own momentum pressed his face against my spring-loaded weapon. The coffee can slid backward and released the hidden latch. The spike jumped forward, its glinting point emerging from the back of his skull and catching the moonlight.

He fell on me, all spark of animation fleeing, and I might have been pinned by a collapsing chimney. His body sputtered out its last spastic movement and then stopped.

I rolled out from under him and lay looking up at purple clouds that stretched in thick bands across the whole of the sky. I waited a while, to catch my breath, before I stood again.

Atop three flagpoles in the Home Depot's parking lot long Mylar banners snapped in the air, welcoming us to our destination. At the loading dock a party of warriors in orange smocks waited to receive us. They wore circlets carved of rosewood on their temples and had gold and silver chains wrapping their forearms like vambraces. The General Manager himself stood silhouetted in the doorway, a fire behind him throwing long shadows down toward us. He was a gray-haired old man with a white scar running across the full length of his chest. He wore nothing but a pair of tight-fitting elastic shorts, black and satiny with gold piping. Beads and bones and jewels were woven in his long hair. He smiled to see Winona, and he gestured to her to come into his arms, to come to his bed, perhaps.

"He doesn't waste his time," I said. We were still out of earshot. I'd planned on giving the girl a final lecture in what a beastly little hardship she'd been. Instead I wondered if maybe I shouldn't turn around and get back on the road with her.

"It is a grand destiny, to make the heirs who will rid the world of the monsters," Winona announced. She looked a bit scared, but not of the bulge in the General Manager's underwear. Something else had her in its teeth.

She turned to look at me with those eyes the color of old glass bottles. "He'll know," she said. "He'll know I'm not intact." Her voice was very small.

I stared at her. I stared and stared. I didn't like her. I never would. But I knew what they would do to her if they found out she'd been had by the wild folk. It was none of her fault but that wouldn't enter their calculations. They would be Full Up, if they found out.

We were women, both of us. Women of the world now. I sighed and took my water bottle from my pack. It was gummy inside with rabbit's blood. I filled it a little way up with good water and swirled it around, then pushed it into the girl's hand.

I hissed instructions at her. "You ask him to undress in private, and maybe he'll let you. You make it sound like you're shy, like you're just a little girl. Some men like that. When he's gone, you spill this out on the sheets and lie in it." I stared right into her eyes, for the last time. "Do it right, do it secretive and he'll never know."

She held my gaze and she nodded and then she looked away. Step by step she walked away from me, and toward her destiny.

The people of Home Depot owed me dinner at the very least but I didn't bother taking it. I was back in Dead Man's Land before I knew it, and glad to be there.

David Wellington is the author of seven novels. His zombie novels Monster Island, Monster Nation, *and* Monster Planet *(Thunder's Mouth Press) form a complete trilogy. He has also written a series of vampire novels including (so far)* Thirteen Bullets, Ninety-Nine Coffins, Vampire Zero, *and* Twenty-Three Hours. *He began a werewolf series (with Three Rivers Press), starting with* Frostbite *(2009) and continuing with* Overwinter *(2010). Wellington began his publishing career by serializing his horror fiction online, posting short chapters of a novel three times a week on a friend's blog. Response to the project was so great that in 2004 Thunder's Mouth Press contracted to publish* Monster Island *and its sequels in print. His novels have been featured in* Rue Morgue, Fangoria, *and the* New York Times. *For more information please visit www.davidwellington.net.*

Post-apocalyptic fiction often posits humanity returning to a primal society. That often bodes poorly for most female characters, but Wellington balances the powerless "girl as commodity" image nicely with a strong woman "Roadie" who negotiates a life for herself by strength, cunning, and a distrust of the living as well as the dead.

In "Dead Man's Land," Wellington also applies the world "ghoul" to the walking dead—which gives me a chance to mention something about ghouls.

In the original *Night of the Living Dead*, the titular creatures are never referred to as zombies, but they are called ghouls as part of a news report on television. Others have used "ghoul" and "zombie" interchangeably as well, but the two are not traditionally synonymous.

Ahmed K. Al-Rawi ("The Arabic Ghoul and its Western Transformation" *Folklore*, Vol. 120, Issue 3. December 2009) describes the original idea of a ghoul as:

> . . . a kind of devilish genie . . . part of beliefs held by Arabs long before the advent of Islam and was a perceived reality for most people living in Arabia . . . Throughout different historical and religious periods, the character of the ghoul remained the same, being represented as an ugly human-like monster that dwelt in the desert and secluded locations, in order to delude travellers by lighting a fire and thus leading them astray. In some cases, this creature was said to have killed travellers. However, when Antoine Galland translated the Arabian Nights into French in the eighteenth century, some features were added to the ghoul in order to intensify its fearful characteristics. For example, Galland emphasised that the ghoul used to dig graves and eat corpses if it needed food, an idea that was never mentioned in any of the Arabic sources. Accordingly, numerous English writers followed Galland's description and further fantasised in their works about the viciousness of this creature.

The "further fantasizing" resulted in several variants from human grave robbers to humans who are morbidly fascinated with death or the dead to supernatural creatures that lurk in graveyards to feed on or defile mortal remains. Occasionally, ghouls appear in horror literature as beings who devour the living. Modern variants include humans who come back from the dead but do not eat human flesh and are distinct creatures unlike any form of zombie. Chelsea Quinn Yarbro's legendary vampire Saint-Germain has a ghoul servant, Roger. Roger is an undead immortal who prefers his meat raw, but otherwise appears to be human.

Brian McNaughton, in his 1997 collection *The Throne of Bones*, created a unique world of ghoulery. His creatures shared many traits one usually associates with vampires, but they also ate humans. If these ghouls managed to devour enough of a victim's brain, they acquired his or her memories and could even assume the physical appearance of whomever they digested.

Ghouls seem, no matter the variety, seem to me to be a different breed of beastie than the zombie.

Disarmed and Dangerous

Tim Waggoner

Gleaming steel talons came streaking toward my face, and though my reflexes aren't what they used to be, I managed to dodge to the right in time to keep from losing anything more than my left ear. I wasn't particularly concerned. An ear's not all that important, and I could always get it reattached later. Assuming that the demon on the other end of those talons didn't turn me into shredded zombie flakes first.

The steel talons—possibly a surgical augmentation since the rest of the creature appeared organic—sank into the alley wall, neatly pinning my ear to the brick in the process. The alley walls were covered with leech-vine, but luckily for the demon, its talons had sunk into a patch of brick where the vine was thin. Even luckier, the inorganic substance of its talons didn't prod the vine into attacking. The demon grunted in frustration and the scale-covered muscles on its arm tightened as it fought to pull its hand free. This would have been an excellent time for me to turn and run like hell—or in my case, do a shuffling half-walk, half-run—away from the demon. But I had unfinished business with the damned thing. Besides, it had my ear.

A variety of specialized weaponry comes in handy in my line of work, and I reached into the outer pocket of my suit jacket and withdrew one of my most useful tools.

With a final yank the demon managed to pull its hand loose, and it turned to face me, shark teeth bared in a savage snarl, my bloodless ear still stuck to one of its talons. When it saw the weapon I held aimed at the corrugated hide directly between its eyes, the snarl became a chuckle.

"A squirt gun?" Its voice sounded like ground glass being shaken in a coffee can. "Are you insane? *Real* bullets wouldn't do much more than tickle me!"

"I know." I tightened my finger on the plastic trigger and began pumping streams of holy water into the demon's face.

The creature howled in pain as its facial scales began to sizzle and smoke. The demon threw up its hands to protect itself, the motion dislodging my ear and sending it flying. I didn't see where it landed; I was a bit busy. I'd look for it later—assuming I survived. I kept firing, if that's the right term to use when your ammo is liquid, hoping to at least disable the demon, if not kill it. Unfortunately, the demon had other ideas.

Bellowing in agony, eyes squeezed shut and weeping blood, the creature lashed out and fastened its thick fingers around the wrist of my gun hand. Before I could react, the demon yanked, and my right arm came out of the socket as easily as a greasy wing parting from an overcooked chicken. I had only a single thought.

Not again!

"I have to warn you, Matt. This isn't the prettiest work I've ever done. I'm a houngan, not a surgeon."

"Don't worry about it. I got over being vain about my appearance about the same time I stopped breathing. Look at it this way: you have an important advantage over a medical doctor. You don't have to worry about your patient dying if you screw up."

It was late afternoon, and my confrontation with the demon lay several hours in the future. I was sitting on a stool in Papa Chatha's workshop, shirt off, holding my right arm in place with my left hand while Papa, seated next to me, played seamstress. His brow was furrowed in concentration, and small beads of sweat had gathered on the mahogany skin of his smoothly shaven head. His white pullover shirt and pants were splotched with stains that looked too much like blood. None of if was mine, though. I hadn't bled for a long time. One of the advantages to being a zombie.

Another benefit was that I felt no pain as Papa sank the bone needle into the gray-tinged flesh of my shoulder. I could feel pressure as the pointed tip emerged from the ragged skin of my left arm, felt the tug as Papa pulled the thread through, but that was all. I looked away, but not because I found it uncomfortable to watch someone reattaching a limb that had once been part of my body. I've gotten banged up quite a few times since I came to Nekropolis, and Papa's usually the one who gets stuck trying to put the pieces back together. I didn't want to watch because seeing Papa at work reminded me that not only couldn't I experience pain, I couldn't experience pleasure, either. Not physically, at any rate.

I scanned the shelves in Papa's workroom, taking in the multitude of materials that a professional voodoo practitioner needs to perform his art: wax-sealed vials filled with ground herbs and dried chemicals, jars containing desiccated bits of animals—rooster claws, lizard tails, raven wings—books and scrolls piled on tabletops next to rattles and tambourines of various sizes, along with pouches of tobacco, chocolate bars, and bottles of rum. Papa said he used the latter three substances to make offerings to the Loa, the voodoo spirits, and while I had no reason to doubt him, over the years I've noticed that he tends to run out of rum before anything else.

"There." Papa broke off the thread with his ivory-white teeth then tied the end into a knot. I turned back and examined the result. The stitching looked tight enough, but the pattern was uneven, to put it kindly. Papa hadn't been kidding about the aesthetic qualities of his sewing. You'd think a guy who makes as many voodoo dolls as he does would be a better seamstress.

"Give it a try," Papa said.

I made a fist with my right hand and flexed the arm. It moved stiffly, but that had nothing to do with Papa's repair job and everything to do with the fact that I was dead.

I lowered my arm. "Feels good. Thanks." I rose from the stool and went over to the chair where I'd draped my shirt, suit jacket, and tie. Most zombies wear whatever rags they died in, but I'm not your run-of-the-mill walking dead man. I'm still self-aware and possess free will. Before I came to this dimension, back when I was alive, I worked as a homicide detective in Cleveland. I wore a suit on the job then, and I still wear one now. Makes me feel more human, I guess.

Papa continued sitting on his stool while I got dressed. "Sorry I couldn't do more for the skin, but the spells I used to fuse the bone and muscle back together should last for about a month before they need to be reapplied," he said. "That is, assuming you don't irritate any more cyclops." He frowned. "Cyclopses? Cyclopsi?" He shrugged. "Whatever."

I finished with my tie and slid on my jacket. "You know Troilus. Always trying one scam or another to make easy money. This time it was a protection racket." I lowered my voice to a bass monotone in what I thought was a passable imitation of the cyclops. "'Pay me a hundred darkgems a week or you might end up taking a bath in Phlegethon.'"

Phlegethon is the river of green fire that surrounds Nekropolis and separates the city's five sections. It's a cold fire that burns the spirit instead of the flesh, but its waters are home to giant serpents called Lesk who are only too eager to use their sharp teeth to take care of what the flames can't.

Papa grinned. "I assume you were hired to encourage Troilus to pursue alternative methods of securing an income. Your employer anyone I know?"

"A vampire named Kyra who has a tattoo parlor on the other side of the Sprawl, not far from the Bridge of Forgotten Pleasures. She uses living ink, and the tattoos she creates move through their wearer's skin. It's a striking effect."

Papa nodded. "This is the first time I've heard her name, but I've seen her work before. So what did you do?"

"I decided on the subtle approach. I tracked down Troilus and told him that if he didn't stop threatening people, I'd poke his eye out."

Papa laughed. "*Very* subtle! Let me guess: in response, Troilus yanked your arm out of the socket."

"That's right. But I'm nothing if not professional. Instead of getting angry, I calmly asked Troilus to give me my arm back. People like him are used to getting what they want through violence, and he was so surprised by my lack of reaction that he just looked at me with that basketball-sized eye of his for a moment before doing as I asked."

"And what did you do after that?"

"Undead or not, I'm a man of my word. An arm doesn't have to be attached to be useful, you know." I looked at the fingers on my right hand and frowned. "I think there's still some vitreous fluid under my nails."

Papa grinned and shook his head. "One of these days, Matt, you're going to get yourself torn into so many bits that not even Father Dis will be able to put you back together."

"Let's hope that day's a long time coming." I reached into the inner pocket of my suit jacket and took out a handful of darkgems. My fee for helping Kyra. I hadn't charged her much, but even though I was dead and no longer needed food or drink, I still needed money to cover the rent on my apartment and to pay Papa Chatha for his services. Not only for today's repair, but for the regular application of the preservative spells that keep me from rotting and smelling like Lake Erie at low tide.

I held them out to Papa Chatha. "I know it's not enough, but I'll get you the rest when I can."

He took the gems and tucked them into a pocket of his white shirt. "Tell you what, I'll call it even if you stick around and play a few games of rattlebones with me."

I hesitated before replying. Not long, but long enough for Papa to notice.

"I'd love to, but I've got an appointment to see another client."

Papa could've asked me to call and reschedule. We do have cell phones in Nekropolis, along with our own Aethernet, too. But he just smiled—a touch sadly, I thought—and nodded his understanding. I mumbled a quick goodbye and departed Papa's workshop. I was lying. I didn't have any appointment scheduled, but I'd never been much for socializing, even when I was alive. Besides, I needed to scrounge up some more work if I was going to pay Papa the rest of what I owed him. Even houngans have expenses. It's not like dried raven wings come free, you know.

And I stunk at rattlebones anyway.

Monsters are real. So are witches and ghosts and just about any other thing you can think of that goes bump in the night. They co-existed alongside humanity for thousands of years, peacefully enough for the most part. But several centuries ago Father Dis—who supposedly was worshipped as a god of death by the Romans—decided that humans were becoming too numerous and more importantly too dangerous to share the planet with. Dis met with five other powerful supernatural beings called Darklords to decide what should be done. Several of the Lords wanted to enslave humanity or simply exterminate the pests altogether, but in the end it was decided that the Darkfolk, as supernaturals call themselves, would relocate to another dimension, a realm of darkness called the Null Plains, and there they would create their own home, a vast city to rival any that had ever existed on Earth.

Nekropolis.

The Darklords didn't completely sever their ties to Earth, though. After all, not only was it their original home, the Darkfolk had all sorts of uses for humanity's technology—not to mention humans themselves. Five mystic portals between Earth and Nekropolis were created, each one controlled by a different Darklord. I came through one of those portals as a living man, chasing a suspect in a series of ritualistic murders that had happened in Cleveland. By the time I'd finished with, as Elvis used to say, TCB, the suspect was dead and I was too. Except I didn't stay that way. I couldn't return home as a zombie—without Papa Chatha's preservation spells I'd eventually rot away to nothing—so I had no choice but to remain in Nekropolis and try to make a new life for myself here. It was easier than you'd think. I didn't have any family or friends to speak of back home, and Darkfolk aren't all that different than humans, not deep down. They have needs and desires, and while most try to fulfill them lawfully, many don't. Too many.

Since I was a cop on Earth, I use those same skills to pay the bills here. But Nekropolis doesn't have an organized police force. Each of the five Darklords sees to justice in his or her domain, while Father Dis—with the aid of his squadron of golem-like Sentinels—oversees the entire city, including the Darklords. But just like back home, justice isn't always applied fairly and consistently in Nekropolis, and that's when people turn to me, Matthew Richter, zombie PI.

Papa Chatha's workshop was located in the Sprawl, a riotous maze of streets and buildings ruled over by Lady Varvara, the Demon Queen. Although *ruled* is too strong a word. The Sprawl is a combination of Times Square on New Year's Eve, Mardi Gras, and Carnivale in Rio—a never-ending party with Varvara serving as eternal hostess. I make my home here, not because I'm especially fond of the chaotic anything-goes atmosphere, but because I've had a few run-ins with the other Darklords, and I'm not exactly welcome in their domains. Besides, this is where all the work is.

Case in point: only a few moments after I left Papa's, a woman came hurrying up to me. I'd never seen her before; if I had, I'd have remembered. She was beautiful, with long blond hair that fell halfway down her back, and she was tall, well over six foot, with a trim, well-toned body. The state of her physical fitness was easy to assess because she wasn't wearing any clothing. Not that she was naked, exactly. From the neck up, her skin was a creamy ivory, but from the neck down—excluding her hands—it was black. Not African-American black, but black-black. Obsidian. The color created the illusion that she was wearing a black skin-tight body suit, especially in the shadowy half-light provided by Umbriel, the dark sun which shrouds Nekropolis in perpetual dusk.

"Excuse me—are you the dead guy who helped out Kyra, the tattoo artist?"

She stopped as she reached me, out of breath, and I wondered how far she'd run to find me. All the way from the other side of the Sprawl, I guessed, given her mention of Kyra. That meant whatever her problem was, it was urgent. At least to her.

"That's me. Matthew Richter." I offered my right hand for her to shake. My arm movement felt a little loose and wobbly, and I wondered if Papa's repair job was already starting to go bad. It's not like him to do shoddy work, but then again, reattaching entire limbs isn't normally part of a houngan's repertoire.

The woman eyed my hand for a moment before giving it a perfunctory shake. Citizens of Nekropolis are generally tolerant of racial and species differences, but even here, few people are thrilled to touch a zombie's flesh.

"My name's Maera." She looked as if she wanted to wipe her hand off, but since she wasn't wearing any clothes, she didn't have anything to wipe it off onto other than her own body. As she struggled with this dilemma, I took the opportunity to examine her more closely.

She was strikingly beautiful, especially given her wardrobe choice, so much so that I wondered when someone would finally get around to inventing Viagra for zombies. But if I had any doubt about Maera's beauty, I had only to look around at our fellow pedestrians. All the men on the street, and more than a few women, gazed at Maera with intense interest. Some seemed to merely appreciate the aesthetics of her appearance, while others—most notably the vampires, ghouls, and lycanthropes in the crowd—clearly hungered for her, and not just sexually. I wasn't certain what race she was at first. Back on Earth, racial distinctions mattered only in a social sense, and even then they were only part of an individual's background, not a defining quality. Individuality is just as important a factor in Nekropolis, but racial qualities carry more weight here. When dealing with someone on these streets, it's important to know if in the back of their minds they're considering eating you, drinking your blood, possessing your body, devouring your soul, or any combination thereof.

Maera's teeth were blunt, and she had no excess body hair or feral gleam in her eyes. So she wasn't one of the Bloodborn or a lyke, and she was far too attractive to be a ghoul. She wasn't a ghost or a revenant. Her handshake had been too solid and firm. I thought for a moment that she might be human, perhaps one of the witchfolk known as the Arcane, but then I noticed multicolored flecks in her eyes rotating slowly, like small organic kaleidoscopes.

"You're a demon," I said.

She nodded. "How could you tell?"

"I'm a detective. It's my job." Clients expect you to say stuff like that. It's all part of the package they're buying.

I didn't add that she was extremely beautiful for a demon. They come in all shapes and sizes, and some of them can change their form as easily as you or I change clothes. But no matter what body they appear in, they can't disguise their eyes.

Maera continued. "Kyra's the one who did my . . . outfit." She gave me a tentative, almost shy smile. "I saw her today, and she told me how you helped her with the cyclops, and I thought . . ." Her fragile smile fell away and she looked as if she might cry.

"You're in trouble, and you need help." I didn't need to be a detective to figure this part out.

Maera nodded.

"Tell me about it."

She drew in a trembling breath and started talking.

"They're holding him on the second floor," Maera whispered.

We were standing close together in an alley across the street from the building in question. So close that, if I hadn't been dead, I could've felt Maera's breath in my ear as she whispered. I was disappointed I couldn't. There are a lot of things about being alive that I miss, and you can probably imagine most of them, but it's the small, unexpected things I miss the most. Like a woman's breath on my skin.

This was one of the seamier neighborhoods in the Sprawl, and that's saying something. The sidewalks were cracked—when they were paved at all—and the buildings looked like they were made out of crumbling sandstone instead of brick. The windows were boarded or barred, and probably protected by cheap wardspells that were just as likely to backfire and injure the residents as repel intruders. Leech-vine covered walls and roofs, and rat-like vermen skulked through the shadows, fighting over whatever rancid treasures they came across. The few pedestrians that were either brave or foolish enough to walk the street moved with quick, determined strides, expressions coldly neutral, gazes alert for any challenge or threat. None of them appeared to be armed, but I knew they were, some of them heavily so. No one came here without a means of protecting themselves, myself included.

The building Maera had pointed out looked no different than any of the others on the street, but then, if what she'd told me was true, it was important the occupants didn't draw attention to themselves.

"How many?" I asked.

"I only saw two. The rest of the building was deserted."

Appeared deserted, I amended mentally. "How long ago was that?"

"It was early, before noon. I was too upset to notice the exact time, though."

According to Maera's story, this morning she and her lover—a male demon named Finn—had been on their way to the Six-Legged Café, one of Nekropolis' more specialized eateries, for a breakfast of live cockroaches and blood-fattened tics. But before they could reach the restaurant, a pair of men approached them and drew obsidian daggers with intricate runes carved into the blades. The instant nausea that surged through Maera's gut told her the weapons were Dire Blades, knives created specifically to slay supernatural creatures of all kinds. Of course, as sharp as the daggers were, they were quite capable of killing non-supernatural beings as well. Dire Blades were so lethal to supernaturals that it hurt just to hold them, and there was only one group in the city tough enough to wield them: the Dominari, Nekropolis' version of the Mafia

The two mobsters—a werewolf with cybernetic implants and a creature that resembled a bipedal lobster with opposable thumbs on its claws—told the demon lovers that they had come to collect the darkgems Finn owed them. Maera had known Finn loved to gamble—after all, they'd met at a tangleclaw table—but she hadn't known that her boyfriend had been dumb enough to borrow money from a Dominari loan shark to finance his hobby. A hobby, as it turned out, that he was spectacularly bad at. Finn had been sure he'd win enough to pay back the darkgems he owed along with the steep interest the Dominari toughs wanted. But Finn had hard luck and even less skill, and he didn't have a single gem to his name, and Maera didn't have much more than what it would take to pay for their buggy breakfast.

The Dominari sharks were less than pleased, but when they saw how beautiful Maera was, not to mention the striking way she "clothed" herself, they decided to cut Finn a break. They wouldn't kill him on the spot . . . *if* his gorgeous girlfriend used her unnatural assets to earn the money Finn owed them. Maera started to tell Techwolf and Lobster-Head that she had no intention of prostituting herself for them, but before she could get more than a couple words out, the lycanthrope pricked Finn on the back of the hand with his Dire Blade. That brief touch was enough to cause the demon to scream in agony, and Maera, tears streaming from her kaleidoscope eyes, told them she'd do anything they wanted, just as long as they didn't hurt Finn anymore.

After that, the two Dominari toughs escorted the demon lovers to this blighted neighborhood and marched them into the abandoned building across the street. Inside, in one of the upper rooms, they shoved Finn onto the floor and bound him in manacles made from the same enchanted obsidian as their Dire Blades, rendering him helpless. Then Maera received her instructions on just how much money she had to make and how fast she had to make it in order to pay back the debt Finn owed the Dominari and save his life. And she was warned that if she so much as looked in a Sentinel's direction, let alone told her tale of woe to one of the golems, Finn would die for certain, and she'd be next.

Filled with despair but seeing no other choice, Maera returned to her usual stomping grounds in the Sprawl, picked out a street corner to conduct business on, and prepared to do what she had to do. But before she could attract her first customer, Kyra saw her and came over to talk, specifically, to tell her about what this zombie PI she'd hired had done to a certain greedy cyclops earlier. Maera realized then that she *did* have another choice, and after asking Kyra where I could be found, the demoness abandoned her street corner and hurried off to search for me.

At least, that's the story Maera told. But she *was* a demon, and her kind had been known to tell a fib now and again. I was withholding judgment on her tale until I'd had a chance to check it out more thoroughly.

"You stay here and keep out of sight," I told her. "I'll go see how the land lays."

Without waiting for her to reply, I left the alley and started across the street. Instead of walking, though, I shuffled, dragging my left leg and allowing my arms to dangle loosely at my sides. I canted my head to the left and let my mouth gape open. If I'd been able to produce any saliva, I'd have drooled. There aren't many benefits to being a zombie, but instant camouflage was one of them. Walking—or rather shuffling—dead are common in Nekropolis, so much so that people pay them little attention. As long as I don't moan *"Braaaaaaaiiiinsssss . . ."* and try to take a bite out of someone's skull, once I go into my act, I might as well be invisible.

I made it to the sidewalk in front of the Dominari sharks' hideout without drawing any undue attention to myself. I doubted I'd done so unobserved, though. The sharks would either have sentry wards on the building to warn them of anyone's approach, or if they were too cheap to pay for the spellwork, one of them would be keeping watch on the street through a window, mostly likely one of the two on the second story facing the street. I couldn't simply look up and check without risking blowing my disguise. Regular zombies aren't bright enough to recognize a building for what it is, let alone understand what windows are. But there was a way to make that work for me.

I continued shuffling toward the building and bumped into the wall, like a goldfish bopping its nose against the glass of its bowl. I was careful to avoid the leech-vine clinging to the front of the building. It couldn't do much to me since I was already dead, but it would snag hold of me nevertheless, and I couldn't fight my way free without ruining my act. I stumbled back from the wall, waving my arms erratically and looking around in confusion: right, left, down, and then up. If anyone was watching, all they would see is another brain-dead zombie perplexed by the seemingly magical appearance of a large solid object in his path. And when that zombie looked up, he saw a dingy, tattered curtain drawn away from the right second-floor window, and then a second later, he saw it fall back into place. I didn't get a look at whoever had been standing at the window. Considering the dark light cast by Umbriel, everyone in Nekropolis is usually standing in shadow of one sort or another. But the movement of the curtain was enough to let me know that someone was indeed on the second floor of the building, and that whoever it was knew a zombie had come calling. I just hoped they bought my act and decided I was a harmless nuisance to be ignored.

I stumbled around for a moment as if unsure what to do next before finally heading down the sidewalk toward the alley at the side of the building. I was tempted to look back across the street to see if Maera had done as I'd told her, but I didn't want to give her away in case I was still being observed. I shuffled into the alley, did my bump-into-the-wall bit again, and looked up. Leech-vine completely covered this side of the building, so thick that I couldn't tell if there were windows here or not. I decided to take a chance that if there were, the vines would block any view of the alley, and I hurried to the other end at my usual less-than-breakneck-but-faster-than-a-shuffle speed. I knew the longer I took to reconnoiter the place, the more time whoever was inside would have to get suspicious.

Behind the building was a cross alley that provided a lovely view of the backsides of another row of vine-covered hovels. Detritus filled the alley, along with rats, cats, dogs, vermen, and other less-identifiable scavengers, all sifting through the open landfill for whatever they could find to eat, including each other. But I hadn't come here to observe the local fauna in action. I'd come in search of a back door, and I'd found one. The problem was, it was wide open and someone was standing in the doorway grinning at me—someone who now possessed a fancy new ocular implant in place of the eye I'd poked out earlier.

"Hello, Troilus. Whoever your cyber-doc is, he, she, or it did a decent job." In some ways, the technology in Nekropolis is more advanced than Earth's. The physiognomy of supernatural creatures—given their overall strength and healing capacity—lends itself far more easily to biomechanical and genetic enhancement than humans. Troilus' eye implant was a little crooked, it wept pus, and from the way the skin around it had blistered, I knew the machinery was running hot. The image resolution was probably substandard too, but all in all, not bad for what had surely been a rush job completed by a street surgeon.

The cyclops was bald, though he had a curly black beard. He was heavily muscled, and wore a white tunic, black belt, and sandals. The front of the tunic was stained reddish brown, and it took me a moment to realize that Troilus hadn't changed it since this morning. He'd either been in one hell of a hurry for revenge, or he was a mega slob. Probably both, I decided.

"I think I actually did you a favor," I said. "Your cyber-eye makes you look twice as intimidating as you did before. Of course, it also makes you look twice as ugly too, and I didn't think that was possible."

Troilus' large hands curled into equally large fists. "If you got any more jokes, you better tell them fast," he growled. "Because when I get hold of you, the first thing I'm going to do is rip out your tongue so I don't have to listen to you yammer on anymore."

I contemplated a witty rejoinder, trying to decide between *I don't give tongue on the second date* and *Go to hell, asshole*, when I heard trash rustle behind me. "Hello, Maera. I was wondering when you were going to show up."

I turned around and, sure enough, there she was, looking beautiful as ever, kaleidoscope eyes glittering, lips stretched into a cold, cruel smile.

"There's no Finn and no Dominari loan sharks," I said. "Just a pissed-off cyclops and his demon friend."

"Business associate," Maera corrected. "You didn't think Troilus planned to go into the protection racket by himself, did you?"

"I suppose he's the brawn and you're the brains."

Her smile widened, pliable demon flesh stretching farther than a human's could without tearing. I'd seen similar effects before, but it was still disturbing to watch. "Actually, we're both brawn."

Maera's attention-getting form blurred and shifted, and when she'd finished rearranging herself, instead of a beautiful naked woman with a black body-suit tattoo, standing before me was a hulking reptilian demon with steel talons jutting forth from its thick scaly fingers.

"This your real shape?" I asked.

Maera shrugged her massive shoulders. "I'm whatever I choose to be." Her voice had become high-pitched, brittle, and grating, like metal fragments and glass shards rubbing together.

"That's true of everyone, one way or another," I countered.

A heavy hand gripped my shoulder, and Troilus turned me back around to face him. "Spare us the philosophy," he said. "I got enough of that from the damned Greeks."

"Tell me one thing before you start dismembering me." Before Troilus could deny me, I hurried on. "You could've jumped me anytime. Why bring me here, and using such an elaborate cover story to boot?"

It's hard to read the expression of someone whose only eye looks like a large camera lens, but a smug tone crept into the cyclops' voice. "To humiliate you, of course. You think you're so smart, so tough . . ." He sneered. "How does it feel to know that you've been outsmarted by a pair of street crooks?"

"If it ever happens, I'll let you know." While Troilus had been talking, I'd reached into my pants pocket and pulled out a handful of narrow white plastic pouches. I took one between my thumb and forefinger, aimed it at Troilus' new eye, and squeezed. The packet burst under the pressure and thick red liquid splattered his lens. Before he could react, I took hold of the remaining packets, squeezed them in my fist, and smeared the gooey red results onto the cyclops' tunic to join the stains already present.

"What the—what is this gunk?" Troilus reached toward his ocular implant to clear his lens, but all he succeeded in doing was smearing it around more.

Maera laughed. "It's ketchup, you moron!" The demon looked at me. "Is this your idea of a secret weapon?"

"That's right." I grabbed hold of Troilus' arm, spun him around once, kicked him in the kneecap to knock him off balance, and then shoved. I'm not any stronger than I was when alive, but I had the advantage of surprise. The cyclops went stumbling backward and landed on his mythological ass in a pile of trash.

Maera laughed even harder, but the demon's laughter quickly died away as the first of the alley's hungry scavengers—attracted by the smell of the ketchup—began to swarm over Troilus, Mostly bugs at first, but larger creatures swiftly followed. Within seconds, Troilus was screaming and thrashing about, trying to shake off his attackers. But his exertions lessened, his screams diminished, and soon he lay still and quiet, and the scavengers were able to continue feeding in peace.

Maera gaped as she watched her partner's remains being swiftly and efficiently disposed of.

"Everything tastes better with ketchup," I said.

Maera turned to me, her kaleidoscope eyes flashing with fury, and thrust her steel talons toward my face.

"I already had that arm reattached once today, and I still haven't paid for it!"

Maera grinned as she tossed the limb in question aside. Her scaly hide was dotted with charred, smoking patches where the holy water had struck, but the wounds weren't enough to incapacitate her.

"Forget the arm," she said. "You're not going to need it anymore. As a matter of fact, when I'm through, you're not going to need your body at all."

The demon continued grinning as she came toward me. I'd dropped the squirt gun when she tore my arm off, and the weapon lay on the ground. I could operate it with my left hand well enough if I could get hold of it, but there was no way I could get past Maera now. I stepped back as Maera advanced, and I felt myself bump into the alley wall. Coils of thirsty leech-vine wrapped around my body, barbs penetrating my clothing and sinking deep into my flesh, pinning me in place.

"Perfect!" Maera said in delight. She stopped in front of me, close enough to reach me but not so close that she was in danger of being attacked by leech-vine. "The way I figure it, you're already dead, so the leech-vine won't hurt you. It'll probably let go of you in a minute once it realizes there's nothing inside your veins for it to feed on. But it should hold you still long enough for me to tear your head off. If you're dead, you can't be killed, and that means you'll stay conscious even after you're decapitated." She leaned in closer, and her grin widened. "I'm going to take you home and make you my pet. I might get a birdcage for you, or maybe I'll just keep you in a box. Who knows? I might start a whole new trend: pet zombie heads!"

She reached out with her steel-taloned hands, but before she could take hold of my head, I spoke.

"You're right: leech-vine can't hurt me, and I can continue to survive as just a head. But you forgot something."

Maera's thick brow wrinkled in a frown. "What?"

"My arm." I nodded toward the ground.

Maera looked down just time to see my arm—which had crawled over to us in the time it had taken the demon to advance—snatch hold of a leech-vine tendril and jam it against it her reptilian foot. The vine, realizing it had something alive to feed on, released me and whipped a dozen tendrils toward Maera. She screamed as the leech-vine covered her body and pulled her tight against the alley wall. The air was filled with soft slurping sounds as the vine began to drain the demon's blood, but I didn't look. Maybe Maera, like Troilus, had deserved what she got, but that didn't mean I had to gloat about it. I understand death better than most, and I know it's never something to celebrate.

With a sigh, I bent down to retrieve my arm for the second time that day. I tucked the limb under my remaining arm and walked out of the alley, headed back to Papa's.

"So when did you first become suspicious of Maera?" Papa asked. For the second time that day, the voodoo priest worked on reattaching my arm, but with one difference: instead of using a needle and thread to hold the skin together, he employed a hot soldering gun. I wondered what burning zombie flesh smelled like, and I was glad my nose was as dead as the rest of me.

"When Maera first approached me, she told me she was a customer of Kyra's. But Kyra specializes in living, animated tattoos that move across the wearer's skin—Maera's full-body tattoo didn't move. That didn't mean that Kyra *couldn't* have done the work, but it started me thinking."

Papa squinted one eye shut as he worked, and while the smell didn't seem to affect him, I noticed he made sure to breathe through his mouth. "And where did those thoughts lead?" he asked.

"Maera's story sounded good on the surface, and it's exactly the sort of thing the Dominari does, but that was the problem: it sounded *too* good. Why would Techwolf and Lobster-Head take both Finn *and* Maera to their hideout? They could've given her their instructions when they first accosted the two demons on the street. Why waste time forcing Maera to accompany them to their pesthole of a neighborhood? The faster she started turning tricks, the faster the Dominari would get their money back."

"Maybe the loan sharks didn't want to conduct their business in the public eye." He gave me an embarrassed smile. "If they'd been real, I mean."

"I'll admit Maera's story wasn't completely out of the realm of possibility. The loan sharks *might've* wanted to make their demands on her in private, and they *might've* wanted her to see Finn in manacles, just to drive home the point that they were deadly serious. And despite their warning not to seek help from the Sentinels, Maera *might've* decided to take a chance on the zombie detective that had helped out her friend Kyra. But that was one too many *might'ves* for me. I decided her story was bogus, and after that, it was just a matter of playing along until I could figure out what her game was."

"And you nearly ended up as a talking head in a birdcage for your troubles," Papa said. He touched the hot metal tip of the soldering gun to my shoulder one last time, and then leaned back. "Finished. Try to take it easy on the arm for the next few days so the spells have a chance to take hold fully, all right? Same with the ear."

"Sure thing." I reached up with left hand and touched the ear Papa had also reattached. The arm worked and the ear didn't fall off, so all was right with the underworld—at least for the time being. I got up from the stool and slipped on the pullover shirt that Papa had loaned me. My suit jacket and shirt were riddled with holes from where the leech-vine had grabbed me, and while Papa had used his soldering gun to seal the punctures on my dead flesh, he drew the line at tailoring. Considering how bad his sewing was, I didn't mind.

Papa rose from his stool, turned off the soldering gun, and placed it on his workbench to cool.

"There's one last thing," I said. "Since Maera's story was a lie—"

"She didn't pay you," Papa finished. "Which means that not only don't you have the darkgems to cover the balance on your last repair, you can't pay for this one either."

"Afraid not."

Papa grinned. "No worries. You'll pay when you can. You always do." He stuck out his hand and we shook.

I'd told a small lie of my own to Papa just then. There was something more about Maera, something that I'd learned from her and Troilus. Solitude can be all well and good, but sometimes it's nice to have a friend.

"If you have the time, I'm up for a game of rattlebones," I said, then added, "If the offer's still good."

Papa looked at me, and for a moment I thought he might comment on my change of heart, but instead he grinned even wider and clapped me on the back gently, careful not to ruin his latest repair.

"Always, my friend. Always."

⎯

Tim Waggoner's *most current novels are the* Nekropolis *series of urban fantasies and the* Lady Ruin *series for Wizards of the Coast. In total, he's published over twenty novels and two short story collections, and his articles on writing have appeared in* Writer's Digest *and* Writers' Journal, *among others. He teaches creative writing at Sinclair Community College and in Seton Hill University's Master of Fine Arts in Writing Popular Fiction program. Visit him at www. timwagonner.com and and www.nekropoliscity.com.*

⎯

As Waggoner explains in his story—but is able to expand on more fully in *Nekropolis*, the novel for which this story serves as a "prequel"—his supernatural creations exist in another dimension that interacts with the mundane world and its humans. His hard-boiled zombie private investigator works in a world of demons, werewolves, magic, and other supernaturals— often technologically enhanced. But, don't worry, purists, the brainless-walking-dead brand of zombies still shamble about in his world, too.

Like more and more speculative fiction authors these days, Waggoner crosses so many genres you can't keep count. Readers seem to love the imaginative results writers are coming up with. Critics who love to devise definitions and marketers who feel books belong in slots, however, aren't always in step with the writers or readers. That—even though it is a topic pertinent to zombies—is, however, another subject.

The Zombie Prince

Kit Reed

What do you know, fool, all you know is what you see in the movies: clashing jaws and bloody teeth; raw hunger lurching in to eat you, thud thud thud.

We are nothing like you think.

The zombie that comes for you is indifferent to flesh. What it takes from you is tasteless, odorless, colorless and huge. You have a lot to lose.

The incursion is gradual. It does not count the hours or months it may spend circling the bedroom where you sleep. For the zombie, there is no anxiety and no waiting. We walk in a zone that transcends disorders like human emotion. In the cosmos of the undead there is only being and un-being, without reference to time.

Therefore your zombie keeps its distance, fixed on the patch of warmth that represents you, the unseemly racket you make, breathing. Does your heart have to make all that noise, does your chest have to keep going in and out with that irritating rasp? The organs of the undead are sublimely still. Anything else is an abomination.

Then you cough in your sleep. It is like an invitation.

We are at your bedroom window. The thing we need is laid open for us to devour.

For no reason you sit up in bed with your heart jumping and your jaw ajar: What?

Nothing, *you tell yourself, because you have to if you're going to make it through the night.* Just something I ate.

Hush, if you enjoy living. Be still. Try to be as still as me. Whatever you do, don't go to the window! Your future crouches below, my perfect body cold and dense as marble, the eyes devoid of light. If you expect to go on being yourself tomorrow when the sun comes up, stay awake! Do it! This is the only warning you'll get.

One woman alone, naturally you are uneasy, but you think you're safe. Didn't you lock the windows when you went to bed last night, didn't you lock your doors and slip the dead bolt? Nice house, gated community with Security patrolling, what could go wrong? You don't know that while you sleep the zombie seeks entry. This won't be anything like you think.

Therefore you stumble to the bathroom and pad back to your bedroom in the dark. You drop on the bed like a felled cedar, courting sleep. It's as close as you can get to being one of us. Go ahead, then. Sleep like a stone and if tonight the zombie who ha come for you slips in and takes what it needs from you, tomorrow you will not wake up, exactly.

You will get up. Changed.

When death comes for you, you don't expect it to be tall and gorgeous. You won't even know the name of the disaster that overtakes you until it's too late.

Last night Dana Graver wished she could just bury herself in bed and never have to wake up. She'd rather die than go on feeling the way she does.

She wanted to die the way women do when the man they love ends it with no apologies and no explanation. "I'd understand," she cried, "if this was about another girl." And Bill Wylie, the man she thought she loved—that she thought loved her!—Bill gave her that bland, sad look and said unhelpfully, "I'm sorry, I just can't do this any more."

Her misery is like a bouquet of broken glass flowers, every petal a jagged edge tearing her up inside. She would do any thing to make it stop. She'd never put herself out—no pills, no razor blades for Dana Graver, no blackened corpse for Bill to find, although he deserves an ugly shock.

She'd never consciously hurt herself but if she lies on her back in the dark and *wills* herself to die it might just accidentally happen, would that be so bad? Let the heartless bastard come in and find his sad, rejected love perfectly composed, lovely in black with her white hands folded gracefully and her dark hair flowing, a reproach that would haunt him for the rest of his life. *Look what you did to me.* Doesn't he deserve to know what it sounds like to hear your own heart break?

Composed for death, Dana dozes instead. She drops into sleep like an ocean, wishing she could submerge and please God, never have to come back up. She . . .

She jerks awake. *Oh God, I didn't mean it!*

There is something in the room.

With her heart hammering she sits up, trembling. Switches on the light.

The silent figure standing by the dresser looks nothing like the deaths a single woman envisions. No ski mask, so this is no home invasion; no burglar's tools. It isn't emblematic, either, there's no grim reaper's robe, no apocalyptic scythe. This isn't SARS coming for her and it isn't the Red Death. The intruder is tall and composed. Extremely handsome. Impeccable in white. The only hint of difference is the crescents of black underneath the pale, finely buffed fingernails.

She shrieks.

In ordinary incursions the victim's scream prompts action: threats or gunshots or knife attack, the marauder's lunge. This person does nothing. If it is a person. The shape of the head is too perfect. There is something sublime in its unwavering scrutiny. Chilled, Dana scrambles backward until she is clinging to the bed stead. She throws the lamp at it, screaming. "Get out!"

It doesn't move. It doesn't speak.

There is only the crash as the glass lamp-base shatters against the wall behind the huge head. The light itself survives, casting ragged shadows on the ceiling. The silence spins out for as long as Dana can stand it. They are in stasis here.

When she can speak, she says, "What are you doing here?"

Is it possible to talk without moving your lips? The stranger in her room doesn't speak. Instead, Dana knows. Uncanny. she *knows*.

—**Good evening. Isn't that what you people say?**

She does what you do. She opens her throat and screams to wake the dead.

—**Don't do that**.

"I can't help it!"

—**I'm sorry. I'm new at this**.

"Who are you?"

—**You mean the name I used to have? No idea. It left me when I died** . . .

"Died!"

The intruder continues —**and I would have to die again to get it back, and you know what death brings. Dissolution and decay. Sorrow.**

"*What* are you?"

—For the purposes of this conversation, you can call me X. Every one of us is known as X.

"Oh my God. Oh, my God!"

The great head lifts. —**Who?**

"Get out." Higher. Dana sends her voice high enough to clear the room and raise the neighborhood. "Get out!" When she uncovers her face the intruder hasn't advanced and it hasn't run away.

It hasn't moved. It is watching her, graceful and self-contained. As if her screams are nothing to it. —**No.**

"Get out or I'll . . . " Groping for the empty pistol she keeps under the pillow she threatens wildly. "I'll shoot!"

—**Go ahead.** So calm. Too calm! —**It won't change anything.**

"Oh." Noting the fixed, crystalline eyes she understands that this is true. "Oh my *God*."

The bedroom is unnaturally still. So is the intruder. Except for the trembling Dana can't control, except for her light, irregular breathing, she too manages to stay quiet. The figure in white stands without moving, a monument to patience. There is a fixed beauty to the eyes, a terrifying lack of expression. They are empty and too perfect, like doll's eyes: too pale to be real, blue as blown flowers with stars for pupils. —**Don't be afraid. That won't change anything either**.

Dana isn't afraid, exactly, she is too badly hurt by the breakup with Bill to think much about anything else, and this? What's happening here in her bedroom is too strange to be real. It's as though she is floating far above it. Not an out-of-body experience, exactly, but one in which everything changes.

The intruder is impeccable in a white suit, black shirt, bright circle of silver about one wrist—silver wire braided, she notes in the kind of mad attention to detail that crisis sparks in some people. The rapt gaze. Like an underground prince ravished by its first look at the sun. The attention leaves her more puzzled than frightened. Flattered, really, by that gaze fixed on her as if she really matters. As if this strange figure has come to break her out of the jail that is her life. Bill's betrayal changed her. She was almost destroyed but even that is changing.

She can't forgive Bill but with this magnetic presence in her room, for seconds at a time she almost forgets about Bill.

The dark hair, the eyebrows like single brush strokes, the pallor are eerie and sinister and glamorous. She doesn't know whether to flirt or threaten. Better the former, she thinks. *Let Bill come in and finds us, that will show him.* Unless she's stalling until her fingers can find bullets and load the gun. As if she could make a dent in that lustrous skin. "What is this?" she asks, overtaken. "Why are you here?"

The answer takes too long coming. It is not that the stranger has stopped to choose its words. It exists without reference to time. When the answer comes, it isn't exactly an answer. —**You are my first**.

"First what?" First what, she wonders. First love? First kill? The stranger is so gorgeous standing there. So courteous and so still. Impervious. None of her fears fit the template. If Dana's clock is still running, she can't read the face. Unnerved by the absence of sound—this intruder doesn't shift on its feet, it doesn't cough or clear its throat; she doesn't hear it breathing!—she whispers, "What are you?"

—**Does the word *undead* mean anything to you?**

"No!" It doesn't. Nice suit, cultivated manner, he's a bit of a mystery, but the handsome face, the strange, cool eyes lift him so far out of the ordinary that the rules don't pertain here. He's here because he's attracted to her. "You don't look like a . . . "

—**Zombie?**

Then it does! Images flood the room, blinding her to everything but the terror. Dana flies out of bed, rushing the door, ricocheting off the stranger's alabaster facade with her hands flying here, there. Screaming, she hurls herself at the sealed bedroom window, battering on the glass.

—**Or walking dead.**

"No!" A zombie.

—**If you prefer.**

This is a zombie. "No, no! Oh my God, don't touch me!"

—**Hold still.** It has an eerie dignity. —**I'm not going to eat you.**

Idiot human. If you're afraid of getting your face gnawed off or your arm ripped out of its socket and devoured, you've seen too many movies. Your body is of no interest to us, not me, not any. We don't hunt in packs nor do we come in pairs. The zombie travels alone and the zombie takes what it needs without your knowing it. What I take can be extracted through the slightest opening; a keyhole, the crack under your bedroom door. Like a rich man the morning after a robbery, you may not even know what is missing.

"Don't." Sobbing, Dana retreats to the bed, pulling the covers up in a knot. All her flailing, her failed attempts to escape, all that screaming and the intruder hasn't advanced a fraction of an inch. So calm and so very beautiful. In a way it's everything she wants, she thinks, or everything she wants to be. Unless it's everything she's afraid of. She is a tangled mass of conflicting emotions—grief and terror and something as powerful as it is elusive. "What do you want?"

—Zombies do not want. They need.

"You're not going to . . . " She locks her arms across her front with an inadvertent shudder.

—Do you really believe I want to chew your arm off?

"I don't know what I believe!" This is not exactly true. In spite of what it says, Dana is afraid it's here to devour her. *Doesn't have to be me,* she thinks cleverly. Odd what rejection does to you; her heart congeals like a pond in a flash freeze. Why not pull a switch and buy her safety with a substitute? In a vision of the fitness of things she sees Bill broken in two for his sins; she hears Bill howling in pain as the zombie's pale, strong hands plunge into his open chest, and when this happens? Maybe she and her elegant zombie will make love while Bill dies and that'll show him, that will damn well show him. "If you want to eat," she says in a low voice, "I can feed you."

—If that was what I came for you'd be bare bones by now.

She does what you do in ambiguous situations. She asks a polite question. "How . . . How did you get this way?"

—No idea. Zombies do not remember.

This brings Dana's head up fast. "You don't remember anything?"

—No.

Thoughtfully, she says, "So you don't remember how it happened."

—No. Nothing from before. The silence is suddenly empty, as though the thing in her bedroom has just walked out and closed the door on itself.

Nothing, it is the nature of our condition. There was a name on my headstone when I got up and walked, but I had no interest in reading it. There was this silver bracelet on my wrist that must have meant something to me once. Engraving inside, perhaps, but I don't need to read it. Who gave it, and what did I feel for her back when I was human? Human I'm not. There is no grief in the zone where I walk, There is no loss and no pain, and yet . . .

I came out of the grave wiped clean. I came out strong and powerful and insentient. Yet there is this great sucking hole at my center. It burns. I need. I need . . .

What?

"But all this time you've been dead. I mean, undead. You must be starved." Clever Dana's fingers creep toward the phone. She can't imagine what she needs to say to please him. "I can get you somebody. Somebody big. Practically twice my size."

—**No thank you.**

"Really." All she has to do is tell the bastard she's OD'd on sleeping pills. Guilt will have him here in a flash. "Tall. Overweight." Fat, she thinks, Bill is fat and now that she thinks about it, probably unfaithful. "Fleshy. Just let me make this call."

—**You don't understand.** Terrifying but beautiful, in a way, the flat blue gaze. That grave shake of the head. —**Flesh is anathema to us**.

Idiot woman, do you imagine I came here to feed? Flesh-eating monsters may exist, botched lab experiments or mindless aberrations raised from the grave by toxic spills, but they are only things *with no awareness of outcomes and this is the difference between them and us.*

When you have been dead and buried, outcomes are everything to you.

Eat and the outcome is inevitable. Gorge on flesh—take even one bite!—and it all comes back: life, memory and regret, rapid, inexorable decay and with it, an insatiable desire for the fires of home.

Gnawing anxiously at her lower lip, Dana is too distracted to feel her teeth break the skin. She sees the intruder's eyes shift slightly. They are fixed not on her throat, but on her mouth. She shakes her head, puzzled. "You're really not hungry?"

—**When you have been dead and buried, mortal concerns are nothing to you**.

"So you really don't have to eat."

—**If we do we lose everything.**

"But when you die you lose everything," she says, shivering.

—**If you mean little things like pain and memory, yes.**

This brings Dana's head up. "Nothing hurts?"

—**Nothing like that. No.**

"Wait," she says carefully. "You don't feel anything?"

—**We are above human flaws like feeling . . .**

"And you don't remember anything. Oh. Oh!" The truth comes in like a highway robber approaching in stages. She says in a low voice, I can't imagine what that's like."

— **. . . and mortality.**

Her breath catches and her heart shudders at the discovery. Her hand flies to cover it. "Oh," she cries. "Oh!"

Easy. This is easy. Greedy, vulnerable girl. I knew you before you saw this coming. Who wouldn't want to forget and who doesn't love oblivion? Who would risk all that for a scrap of meat, the taste of blood? Knowing flesh can destroy us.

Topple and your former self comes back to you. All the love and pain and terror and excitement and grief and intolerable suspense that come with mortality. All you want to do is go home. You want to go home!

Aroused and terrified, you set out. With your restarted heart thudding, you approach the house. You are burning to rejoin the family. Walk into the circle: am I late? *as though nothing's happened. Do not expect to find them as you left them. You have changed too. Are changing as your body begins to decay—too fast, all that lost time to make up for.*

It will be harsh.

Do not imagine that—wherever you come from, no matter how sorely you are missed—they will be glad to see you. Didn't they drop dirt and roses on your coffin a dozen years ago when they put you away? They sobbed when you slipped into a coma and fell dead, no cause the doctors could find, so sad. They loved you and begged God to bring you back to them, but they didn't mean it.

Not like this.

Your body is no longer in stasis. You are in a footrace with decay. The changes begin the minute your heart resumes beating so hurry, you are on fire. If only you can see them again! Hurry. Try to make it home while they can still recognize you! You will decompose fast because, face it, you died a long time ago. You've been around too long. In the end, you'll die again, and the family? Look at them sitting around the supper table in the yellow light, photo of you on the mantel, pot roast again. God in His Heaven and everything in its place. Do you really want to blunder in and interrupt that?

You should hang back, but now that you remember, now that you feel, *you are excited to see them, you can't wait! Be warned, nothing is as you remember.*

Not any more. With your arms spread wide in hopes you will come surging out of the darkness, incandescing with love, but do not be surprised when they run screaming. Your loving face is a terror, your gestures are nightmarish, they are horrified by the sounds you make, your heartfelt cries that they can't quite decipher bubbling out of your rotting face.

Pray to God that your home is so far away that you won't make it even though you are doomed to keep going. Sobbing, you will forge ahead on bloody stumps, heading home until the bones that hold you up splinter and you drop. Now hope to God that what's left of you decomposes in a woods somewhere, unseen by the loved ones you're trying so desperately to reach. You need to see them just once more and you need it terribly, but be grateful that they are spared this final horror. You will die in the agony of complete memory, and you will die weeping for everything you've lost.

Time passes. The silence is profound. It is as though they are sharing the same long dream. Certain things are understood without having to be spoken. At last Dana snaps to attention. Like a refrigerator light set to go on when the door opens, the handsome figure in her bedroom remains motionless, with its great hands relaxed at its sides and crystal eyes looking into something she can only guess at. Alert now, excited by the possibilities, Dana tilts her head, regarding him. Carefully, she resumes the catechism. "You really don't feel anything?"

—**No**.

Dana studies the beautiful face, the graceful stance. Absolute composure, like a gift. She says dreamily, "That must be wonderful." Some time during the long silence that has linked them, she stopped thinking of the zombie who has come for her as an it. This is a man, living or dead or undead, a beautiful man in her room and he is here for her. Without speaking he tells her, —**When you have been dead and buried there is no wonderful . . .**

"I see." Not sure where this is going, Dana touches her Speed Dial. On her cell phone, Bill has always been number One. Her zombie notes this but nothing in his face changes. If he hears the little concatenation of beeps and the phone's ringing and ringing cut short by Bill's tiny, angry "What!" it makes no difference to him. When she's sure Bill is wide awake and listening Dana opens her arms to the intruder, saying in a new voice, "But we can still . . . "

— **. . . and no desire . . .**

"But you're so beautiful." She expects him to say, *So are you.*

— . . . **looks are nothing to you . . .**

"That's so sad!" The phone is alive with Bill's angry squawking.

—**because you never change**.

"Oh!" This makes her stop and think. "You mean you never get old?"

—**No.**

For Bill's benefit she continues on that same sexy note. Oddly, it seems to fit the story that's unfolding. "And nothing hurts . . . "

—**No, nothing hurts.**

Far out of reach, Bill shouts into the phone. "Dana . . . "

As Dana purrs like a tiger licking velvet. "But everybody wants."

—**Zombies don't want. They need.**

She is drawn into the rhythm of the exchange, the metronomic back and forth. God he is handsome, she would like to run her hands along that perfect jaw, down the neck and inside the shirt collar to that perfect throat. "And you need . . . "

Without moving he is suddenly too close. She sees green veins lacing the pale skin.

—**Something elusive. Infinitesimal. You won't even miss it. And when it's gone . . .**

"Dammit, Dana!"

"But when it's gone . . . "

—**You will be changed.**

"Changed," she says dreamily, "and nothing will hurt any more."

—**When you have been dead and buried pain is nothing to you.**

"Will I be like you?"

—**In a way.**

She says into the growing hush, "So I'll be immortal."

—**In a way.**

There is an intolerable pause. Why doesn't he touch her? She doesn't know. He is close enough for her to see the detail on the silver bracelet; he's next to the bed, he is right *here* and yet he hasn't reached out. Unaccountably chilled as she is right now—something in the air, she supposes—Dana is drawn. Whatever he is, she wants. She has to have it! Her voice comes from somewhere deep inside. "What do you want me to do?"

His cold, cold hand rises to her cheek but does not touch it. —**Nothing.**

"Are we going to, ah . . . " Dana's tone says, *make love.* She is distantly aware of Bill Wylie still on the phone, trying to get her attention.

"Dana, do you hear me?"

"Shut up, Bill. Don't bother me." She wants to taunt him with the mystery. She doesn't understand it herself. She wants to make love with this magnetic, unassailable stranger; she wants to *be* him. She wants him to love her as Bill never did, really, and she wants Bill to hear everything that happens between them. She wants Bill Wylie to lie there in his outsized bachelor's bed listening as his seduction unfolds, far out of sight and beyond his control—Bill, who until last night she expected to marry and live with forever. Let this night sit in Bill's imagination and fester there and torture him for the rest of his life. Whatever she does with this breathtaking stranger will free her forever, and Bill? It will serve him right. "Come take what you want."

"Damn it to hell, Dana, I'm coming over!"

—When you have been dead and buried you do not know desire.

Yet there is a charge in the air between them.

The mind forgets but the body remembers. Bracelet glinting on my arm. What's the matter with me? Zombies know, insofar as they know anything, that you extract the soul from a distance. Through a keyhole, through a crack in a bedroom window. Always from a distance. This is essential. This knowledge is embedded: get too close and you get sucked in. And yet, and yet! It is as though the bracelet links X to the past it has no memory of. Interesting failure here, perhaps because this is its first assault on the precincts of the living. Zombies come out of the grave knowing certain things, but this one is distracted by unbidden reminders of the flesh, the circle of bright silver around the bone like a link to the forgotten.

"Then what," Dana cries as destiny closes in on her; she is laughing, crying, singing in a long, ecstatic giggle that stops suddenly as all the breath in her lungs—her *soul*—rushes out of her body and into his, along with the salty blood from her cut lip, the hanging shred of skin. "What will you take?"

—Everything.

Dana . . . can't breathe . . . she doesn't have to breathe, she . . . Lifeless, she slips from his arms as her inadvertent lover— if he is a lover—staggers and cries out, jittering with fear and excitement as emotion and memory rush into him. Shuddering back to life, he will not know which of them performed the seduction.

"Oh my God," he shouts, horrified by the sound of his own voice. "Oh my *God*."

That which used to be Dana Graver does not speak. It doesn't have to. The word is just out there, shared, like the air Dana is no longer breathing. —**Who?**

My God, my God *I am Remy L'Hereux and I miss my wife so much! For my sins, I was separated from my soul and with it, everything I care about. For my sins I was put in the grave and for my sins, my empty body was raised up, and what I did that was so terrible? I ran away with the* houngan's *daughter. We met at Tulane, we fell in love and believe me, I was warned! My Sallie's father was Hector Bonfort, they said, a doctor they said, very powerful. A doctor, yes, I said, but a doctor of what? And without being told I knew, because this was the one question none of them would answer. I should have been afraid, but I loved Sallie too much. I went to her house. I told him Sallie and I were in love. Hector said we were too young, fathers always do. I said we were in love and he said I would never be good enough for her, so we ran away. I laughed in his face and took her out of his house one night while he was away at a conference.*

MY Sallie left him a note: Don't look for us, *she wrote.* We'll be back when you accept Remy as your own son. *The priest we asked to marry us begged us to reconsider; he warned us.* "You have made a very grave enemy, and I . . . " *He was afraid. We went to City Hall and the registrar of voters married us instead. Silver bracelet for my darling instead of a ring. Hector did not swear vengeance that I heard, but I knew he was powerful. Nobody ever spelled out what he was. I knew, but I pretended not to know. Sallie and I were so much in love that I took her knowing he would come for me. God, we were happy. God, we were in love.*

Sallie, so bright and so pretty with her whole heart and soul showing in her face, we were so happy! But we should have known it was not for long. When Jamie came he was the image of both of us. Our little boy! The three of us were never happier than we were in New York, as far away from New Orleans as we could go. I couldn't stay at Tulane, not with Hector's heart turned against me. In New York, we thought we could be safe. There are always flaws in plans cobbled out of love. Hector found out. Then he, it. Something came for me. I got sick. I fell into a coma, unless it was a trance. I didn't know what was happening, but Sallie did. She prayed by my bedside. She cried.

We were torn apart by my death, I could hear her sobbing over my bed in the days, the weeks after I fell unconscious but I couldn't reach out and I couldn't talk to her. I heard her sobbing in the room, I heard her sobbing on the telephone, I heard her begging her father the houngan *to come and release me from the trance. I tried to warn her but I couldn't speak.* Whatever you do, don't tell him where we are. *Then I felt Hector in the city. On our street. In my house.*

Deep inside my body where what was left of me was hiding. I felt the intrusion, and that before he ever came into my room. It was only a matter of time before his hand parted me down to the center, and I was lost. I was buried too deep to talk but I begged Sallie: Don't leave me alone! *Then Hector was in the room and in the seconds when Sallie had to leave us alone—our son was crying, Jamie needed her, she'd never have left me like that if it hadn't been for him—when Sally left I felt Hector approaching—not physically, but from somewhere much closer, searching, probing deep. Reaching into the arena of the uncreated.*

Sallie came in and caught him. "Father. Don't!"

"I wasn't doing anything."

"I know what you were doing. Bring him back!"

"I'm trying," he said. It was a lie.

Then he put his ear to my mouth, his ear *and my God with the sound of velvet tearing, my soul rushed out of me.* "Father," *Sallie cried and he thumped my chest with his big fist: CPR. Then he turned to her.*

"Too late," he said. "When I came into the house Remy was already dying."

She rushed at him and shoved him aside. Before he could stop her she slipped her silver bracelet on my wrist. I was almost gone but I heard her sobbing, "Promise to come back."

The grief was crushing. It was almost a relief to descend into the grave with my sweetheart's tears still drying on my face and the bracelet that bound us rattling on my wrist, forgotten. Until now. My God, until now!

What have I done?

I was better off when I was no more than a thing, *like that beautiful, cold woman rising from the bed but it's too late to go back. Where I felt no pain and no desire, desire is reawakened.*

I want to go home!

I have go. Go home to Sallie, the love of my soul, and I want to see Jamie, our son. I miss them so much, but I can't! I have been dead and buried and I don't know how long it's been. I would give anything to see them but for their protection, I have to stay back. Sallie wants to see me again, but not like this. The hand I bring up to my face is redolent of the grave and when I open my mouth I taste the sweet rot rising inside of me.

I can't go back to them, not the way I am,

I won't.

I have to. I can't not *go because with the return of life comes the awful, inexorable compulsion. Better I throw myself in front of a train or into a furnace than do this to the woman I love. I know what's happening, the rushing decay because to live again means you're going to die, and when you have been dead and buried, death comes fast. I have to stop. I have to stop myself. I . . .*

The creature on the bed does not speak. It doesn't have to. —**Have to go home.**

I have to go home. In a return of everything that made him human—love, regret and a terrible foreboding and before any of these, compulsion—in full knowledge of what he has been and what he is becoming, Remy L'Hereux turns his back on the undead thing on the bed, barely noting the fraught, anxious arrival of Billy Wylie, who has no idea what he's walking into.

That which had been Dana Graver sits up, its eyes burning with a new green light and its pale skin shimmering against the black nightgown.—**Then go.**

I'm going now.

Kit Reed *has stories appearing in* Postscripts, Asimov's, Kenyon Review, *and several invited anthologies this year. A collection from PS Publishing is scheduled for 2011.* Publishers Weekly *praised* Enclave *(2009) as "a gripping dystopian thriller." Other novels include* The Baby Merchant, J. Eden, *and* Thinner Than Thou, *which won an ALA Alex award. Often anthologized, her stories appear in venues ranging from* The Magazine of Fantasy and Science Fiction, Asimov's SF, *and* Omni *to* The Yale Review, The Kenyon Review *and* The Norton Anthology of American Literature. *Her collections include* Thief of Lives, Dogs of Truth, *and* Weird Women, Wired Women, *which, along with the short novel* Little Sisters of the Apocalypse, *was a finalist for the Tiptree Prize. A Guggenheim fellow and the first American recipient of a five-year literary grant from the Abraham Woursell Foundation, she is Resident Writer at Wesleyan University.*

Booklist's review of Reed's collection *Dogs of Truth* had this to say about "The Zombie Prince": "There's even a story, the almost-sweet creepy . . . in which zombies get to be something other than moaning hulks out to eat brains . . . " True enough.

There's also, to me, something particularly disturbing about the human in this tale, Dana.

Selected Scenes from the End of the World: Three Stories from the Universe of *The Rising*

Brian Keene

I: Family Reunion

"Where are they?" Stephen Smeltzer yawned.

"Maybe they got delayed," Carl suggested. "Traffic could be bad."

"No." Stephen shook his head. "They would have called."

"This is your family we're talking about," Carl grunted. "Do you really expect your mom or stepfather to pick up the phone and let you know they're running late? That would indicate common courtesy on their parts."

"What are you saying?"

"I mean your mom was mentally abusive to you all these years, and your stepfather used to beat the shit out of you both. Why would they feel the need to call and let us know they're late?"

"Okay," Stephen replied. "But they're still my family, and I do love them, despite everything. My step-dad; he's been trying to make up for all of that ever since he got diagnosed with prostrate cancer. And Mom has mellowed with age."

"They'll have to prove it to me. We've been together eighteen years, Stephen, and I've seen just what your family is capable of. I hate the way they treat you, sometimes. Just because your step-dad has suddenly been humbled by his own mortality, doesn't excuse the fact that he's a bully."

Stephen watched the pier through the rain, looking for his mother and stepfather's car, or his sister's van.

"Besides," Carl continued, "if your mom is as psychic as she claims, wouldn't she have seen whatever delayed them in advance?"

"Cheri would call at least. She's got Dad with her."

Stephen's real father had his leg amputated the year before, and now spent his time in a wheelchair, popping pain pills and drinking himself into oblivion. He was coming to the reunion with Stephen's sister, Cheri.

The raindrops whispered against the boat's deck, and plunked into the waters of Lake Vermilion. In the distance, they could see the town. Stephen's family was supposed to arrive around dawn, after driving all night, for the annual family reunion. The gathering was held each year at Stephen and Carl's place on Ghost Island. The lakeside dwelling was accessible from the mainland only by boat.

Carl reached out and squeezed his hand. "The weather probably slowed them down. That's all. Everything will be fine."

Stephen smiled at him, and tried to relax. That was easy to do with Carl at his side. They'd met when Stephen was nineteen and Carl was thirty-two, and Stephen still thanked God every day for putting Carl in his life.

The boat rocked slightly as Carl walked over to the radio and turned it on. Stephen watched him as he moved past—the Richard Gere type, with thick, gray hair and a solid, healthy build. The past eighteen years together had been wonderful, and Stephen looked forward to many, many more. Carl had helped him get over so much; so many shadows from his past.

Were it not for Carl, he'd never be able to host these annual reunions. Some things never stayed buried.

His past—his family—was one of those things.

Carl turned the dial, searching the airwaves. Curiously, there was no music, no traffic reports, no zany morning show antics. Each station featured announcers talking in the same grim, somber tones.

Federal authorities were not commenting on why a government research center in Hellertown, Pennsylvania had been shut down overnight. The Director of Homeland Security assured the reporters that the situation was under control, and that there was no danger to the public, but due to national security concerns, they couldn't say more at this time. Terrorism was not suspected.

In Escanaba, Michigan, over twenty people had been killed, and dozens more injured, when an apparent riot erupted during a rock concert.

Stranger still, some form of mass hysteria seemed to be springing up at random across the country and, according to some reports, throughout the world. The reports didn't make a whole lot of sense, and it was apparent that some of the newscasters were skeptical as they read them.

Stories of the dead coming back to life—in morgues and at funerals and in the back of ambulances and on the battlefield.

"Sounds like those movies you always watch, and the stuff you read and write," Carl laughed. "Where the corpses run around and eat people?"

"Yeah," Stephen replied, shivering. "Weird, huh?"

Headlights pierced the early morning gloom, and a moment later, his sister's van pulled up, followed by his mother's car.

Stephen took a deep breath. Goosebumps dotted his arms, and he wondered why. He chalked it up to the dampness in the air.

Carl led him across the deck. "Come on. Brave face. It's only one weekend."

They climbed onto the dock and slowly walked towards the parking lot. Nobody got out of the vehicles. As they got closer, Stephen grew alarmed. There was a jagged, splintered hole in the car's windshield, and the van's front grille was crumpled. A splash of red covered the white hood.

Stephen broke into a run. "Oh God! There's been an accident!"

He could see his sister's silhouette behind the rain-streaked van windshield, but couldn't tell if she was hurt or not. As he dashed around to the driver's-side door, Carl opened the sliding door on the side.

Stephen's father rolled out on top of him, and sank his teeth into Carl's ear.

Cheri burst from the vehicle, slamming the door into Stephen's legs. He collapsed to the ground, skinning his palms on the wet asphalt. Cheri giggled. Somewhere out of sight, his parent's car doors creaked open.

"Sorry we're late, Stephen," Cheri croaked. *"There was a major fender bender in Duluth, and then we stopped for a bite."*

His sister was a grisly sight. Her nose was a swollen, broken bulb, and a portion of her scalp had peeled back, revealing the pink meet between it and her skull. She reached for him, and Stephen gaped in horror. His sister's hand was broken at the wrist, and twisted into a deformed claw.

"Cheri," he gasped. "You're hurt!"

Carl shrieked.

"Wow," Cheri snickered, *"I haven't seen Dad this active in awhile."*

Stephen stared in horror at Carl's ear dangling from his father's clenched teeth.

His mother, stepfather, and sister advanced on him. His mother's right arm was missing from the elbow down, and his stepfather's face was split in two.

Stephen cast one last, shocked glance at Carl. His father had his face buried in Carl's neck, burrowing into the flesh.

Then Stephen fled. Eighteen years of comfort and bliss were forgotten, overridden by blind panic. Carl's agonized final screams echoed in his ears. Stephen jumped onboard the boat, started the engine, and sped away across the water.

Back at the house, the radio and television talked about the chaos spreading across the world—worsening by the hour.

Later that day, Carl and the others arrived on the island, dripping wet from their long walk along the bottom of the lake.

And then they had a family reunion.

II: The Ties That Bind

"I wonder what time it is."

"Time for you to die."

"Stop that." Philip got up from his bedside chair. The alarm clock in the bedroom broke during the struggle. The power was still on—although sporadic. He walked into the kitchen, glanced at the microwave clock, and saw that it was after midnight. Outside, the distant sound of far-away thunder rolled across the sky.

Champ brushed up against his leg. Philip bent down and scratched the dog's back end. Champ wagged his tail in delight. Then Philip readjusted the wet handkerchief tied around his face. It helped block out the smell.

He sighed. "It's very late."

"It is indeed," Denise cackled from the bedroom. *"Too late for you all! Humanity's numbers are dwindling while ours grow. We are more than the stars. More than infinity."*

Philip rubbed his tired eyes. They were out of coffee and tea—almost out of food. He was physically and mentally exhausted, but he couldn't sleep. The couch hurt his back, and the bed—the bed they'd slept in—was out of the question. Denise had been tied to it for almost a week now, and she was leaking.

Slowly, he walked back into the bedroom. Champ trotted after him, stopping at the bedroom door. He refused to enter the room. Instead, he stood at the door and growled.

Denise was strapped spread-eagled to the bed frame with bungee and extension cords. More cords bound her torso to the mattress. There was a horrible bite mark on her arm. It was black around the edges, and oozed a stinking, yellowish-brown fluid. The bite was what had killed her—one of the neighborhood kids, dead but hungry. Philip had destroyed the zombie with a garden hoe to the back of its head, but that changed nothing. Infection set in. Within days, Denise was dead, as well.

"Getting a good look?" the zombie rasped.

Philip stared at her. Denise's bathrobe was stained and crusty. Her abdomen had distended and then burst, and her bowels had evacuated. Her white cheeks were sunken, and her eyes looked hollow.

Despite all of this, she was still the most beautiful woman he'd ever seen.

"Why did this have to happen?" he asked. "Why to us? We were happy, weren't we?"

The zombie groaned. *"I've told you. I have your wife's memories and your wife's body, but I am* not *your wife."*

"No," Philip shook his head. "You are. To me you still are. If Denise's memories of us together still exist, then she still exists. What are we, if not memories? You are my wife, Denise, and I still love you."

A worm wriggled out of the corner of Denise's left eye. Philip tried to ignore it.

"You know what I miss the most? The little things. Watching a movie together or taking a walk. Talking—not like we're doing now, but really talking to each other. You know? Holding your hand. Watching you while you sleep."

He leaned forward.

"What are you doing?" Denise snarled.

"Holding your hand, the way I used to."

Her left hand fluttered against the bedpost, tied right at the wrist and again at the elbow. He took her hand in his. The skin was cold and clammy, but still felt like Denise. If he closed his eyes, he could picture them walking around the lake together, hand in hand, just like this.

He squeezed.

Denise squeezed back. Hard. Philip's knuckles popped. Her laughter sounded like rustling leaves. Champ howled.

Philip gasped. "You're hurting me."

414   **Brian Keene**

Denise began to sing. *"I wanna hold your haaand. I wanna hold your hand."*

"Stop it!" Philip yanked his hand free and backed away from the bed.

"Come on, darling," Denise tittered. *"You remember the words, don't you?"*

Philip rubbed his fingers. They felt greasy. His pulse was racing, and he fought to keep his emotions in check. A tear rolled down his face.

"Why are you doing this? Tell me, Denise. Why? Can't things be the way they were?"

"Why are you holding me like this," the zombie countered. *"Keeping me here? Why not just let me go?"*

"Because we made a promise," he whispered. "Till death do us part? That was our vow. But not even death kept us apart. You died—when that kid bit you on the arm, you got sick and you died. But you came back. You're still here. You're still with me. Till death do us part."

He went to the kitchen and selected the biggest knife in the drawer. Then he fed Champ for the last time, a mixture of dog food and rat poison. Champ gulped it down, wagging his tail. Philip returned to the bedroom and sat down in the chair again. He ran the blade across his wrists, and then slashed his own throat.

Philip died with their wedding vow on his lips.

His soul departed—

—and something else took its place.

The thing inside Philip sat up, examined his body, and then looked at Denise. It freed her corpse, and they began to hunt, free, unchained, and together in death—never to part.

III: The Viking Plays Patty Cake

The air burned their lungs, thick with smoke from the fires—and the stench of the dead.

Chino pushed a branch out of the way and peered through the bushes. "What's wrong with him?"

"Don't know." King shrugged. "He ain't a zombie. Looks more like a Viking."

They studied the giant on the park bench. He was impressive; early forties but in good shape, well over six feet tall, decked out in tattoos and earrings.

His hands clutched an M-1 Garand, the barrel still smoking from the round he'd just drilled into a zombie. The creature sprawled on the ground ten feet away—minus its head. The grass and pavement were littered with more bodies. An assortment of weapons lay scattered on the bench; two more rifles, four grenades, a dozen handguns, and boxes of ammunition for each. Next to those was a large backpack, filled with bottled water and food.

The Viking sat like a statue, his eyes roving and watchful. Another zombie closed in on him from the right. The rifle roared and the creature's head exploded.

The Viking never left the bench. He brought down three more before the rest of the creatures fell back. From their vantage point, Chino and King heard one of the monsters ordering others to find guns. Several of them raced off.

The Viking began muttering to himself. "Patty cake, patty cake . . . "

Chino crouched back down. "The fuck is wrong with him? Why don't he hide?"

"I don't know," King said. "Maybe he's crazy."

"Got an awful lot of firepower," Chino observed. "We could use that shit."

"Word."

The Viking fired another shot. From far away, deep inside the city, more gunfire echoed.

Chino's fingers tightened around his .357. "That the Army guys shooting?"

"Maybe," King said. "They've been trying to take the city back. Held it up to the railroad tracks down on Eight Mile, but then they got overrun by them things."

Chino shook his head. "Why bother. Ain't nobody in charge anymore. Why don't they just bail?"

King peeked again. The zombies still kept their distance from the man with the guns, but more were coming; dead humans, dogs, cats, squirrels. The Viking calmly reloaded, still mumbling under his breath.

"Patty cake, patty cake, baker's man . . . "

"What's he doing?" Chino whispered.

"Playing patty cake."

Chino grunted. "Whole world's gone crazy."

"There're still people in charge. You know Tito and his crew?"

"The ones holed up inside the public works building?"

King nodded. "I was talking to him three days ago. Went out there and traded six cases of beer for some gasoline. They got a ham radio."

"How they working it? Power been out for a week."

"Generator," King said. "They heard some military general got parts of California under control. And there's a National Guard unit in Pennsylvania that's taken back Gettysburg. Could happen here, too."

Chino frowned. "That would suck. I like the way things is. Do what we want, when we want. We got the guns."

"Not as many as that guy." King nodded at the Viking.

Both men peeked out of the bushes again. The zombies inched closer, circling the park bench. Some now carried rifles as well. The Viking put down the Garand, and picked up a grenade. His eyes were steel.

"Open fire," one of the zombies commanded. *"He is just one human."*

With one fluid movement, the Viking pulled the pin and tossed the grenade toward the undead. There was a deafening explosion. Dirt and body parts splattered onto the grass. The Viking threw a second grenade, but one of the creatures snatched it up and flung it back. The explosive soared towards the bushes—the bushes concealing Chino and King.

"Shit . . . " King shoved Chino forward. "Move your ass!"

The grenade failed to detonate, but neither man noticed. They were too busy dashing from the shrubbery—and directly, they realized too late, into the firefight. The M-1 Garand roared, and the zombies returned fire.

"Motherfucker," Chino shouted. "We done it now!"

Bullets plowed through the dirt at their feet and whizzed by their heads. Chino and King opened fire, helping the Viking mow down the remaining zombies. Within seconds, all of the dead were dead again.

The Viking turned his weapon on the men.

"Whoa!' King held up his hands. "We're alive, yo. Don't shoot!"

The Viking didn't respond.

"Chino," King whispered. "Put your gun down."

"Fuck that." Chino spat in the grass. "Tell that puta to put his down first."

King smiled at the Viking. "We don't mean no harm. Hell, we just helped you."

"Why?"

King blinked. "Because you were in trouble, man. Why you sitting out here in the open like that, Mister . . . ?"

"Beauchamp." The Viking's shoulders sagged, and he put the rifle down. "Mark Beauchamp."

Chino lowered his weapon, wondering what King was up to.

"Why you out here on this bench, Mr. Beauchamp?" King's eyes flicked over the stranger's arsenal. He licked his lips. "Wouldn't it be safer trying to find some shelter? Come wit' us, we can hide you."

"No." The Viking shook his head. "I don't think so. I'm waiting."

"Waiting? For what?"

The Viking's eyes turned glassy, and King realized the man was fighting back tears.

"I had a job at the Ford stamping plant, just south of the city. Wasn't what I wanted to do with my life, but it was okay. Fed my family. Had a wife, Paula, and four kids. My son's twenty-one. My daughters are fifteen, fourteen, and five months."

The Viking paused, and despite the tears welling up in his eyes, he smiled.

"I think raising my boy was easier than the girls."

King nodded.

Chino shifted from foot to foot, his finger flexing around the trigger. Was King just going to talk the guy to death?

"I was at work when it happened. I heard it all started in Escanaba, but it spread to Detroit fast. By the time I got home, Paula and the kids were gone. No note. Nothing. The evacuation order didn't go out until a day later, so I don't know what happened."

His face darkened, and then he continued.

"There was blood in our kitchen—a lot of blood. I don't know whose it was. And one of the windows was broken. But that's all."

"Sorry to hear that," King said.

"I spent the first twelve days looking for them. But then I got an idea. We used to come here. I'd sit on this bench with my daughter, Erin, and we'd play patty cake. So I'm waiting, see? They'll come back. Paula wouldn't just leave like that. She knows how worried I'd be. I'm waiting for my family. I miss my kids."

"And just shooting zombies?"

"Yeah. I've become a pretty good shot. Used to have a kick-ass pellet gun."

"What about the birds, man? How you gonna shoot them?"

"Haven't bothered me yet. And my family will be here before the birds show up. You'll see."

King glanced at Chino, then back at the Viking. He tried swallowing the lump in his throat.

"Sure you won't come with us?"

The Viking shook his head.

King slowly approached the bench. Chino tensed. Here it came. King had the guy off guard. Now he'd pop him, they'd grab the shit, and get the hell gone before more zombies came back. But King didn't waste the guy. Instead, he shook his hand.

"Good luck."

"Thanks."

King turned back to Chino. "Come on. Let the man wait in peace."

Chino's eyes nearly popped out of his head. "Say what?"

"You heard me," King growled. "Let him be."

King trudged across the grass, and Chino ran to catch up with him. He grabbed King's arm and spun him around.

"The fuck was that all about? We could have smoked him."

"No," King said, his voice thick with emotion. "We ain't touching him."

"Why not?"

"Because," King sighed, "I miss my kids, too."

An artillery shell whistled over the city. The explosion rumbled through the streets.

Beneath it all, they heard the Viking playing patty cake.

Brian Keene *is the author of over twenty books, including* Darkness on the Edge of Town, Urban Gothic, Castaways, *and many more. He also writes comic books such as* The Last Zombie *and* Dead of Night: Devil Slayer. *His work has been translated into German, Spanish, Polish, Italian, French, and Taiwanese. Several of his novels and stories have been optioned for film, one of which,* The Ties That Bind, *premiered on DVD in 2009 as a critically-acclaimed independent short. Keene's work has been praised in such diverse places as the* New York Times, The History Channel, The Howard Stern Show, CNN.com, Publishers Weekly, Fangoria Magazine, *and* Rue Morgue Magazine. *Keene lives in Central Pennsylvania. You can find him online at www.briankeene.com.*

Keene's zombies are as gruesome and horrific as any you'll encounter and, scarier still, they can think. Instead of mindless wandering flesh-and/or braineaters, his world is suddenly full of aggressive, weapon-wielding monsters. The genesis of these zombies is explained in novels *The Rising* and *City of the Dead*. Keene's zombies are not the result of a vague virus, alien infestation, or unexplained plague, they are actually demon-possessed and form an undead army with a leader who has an agenda that includes not only destroying Earth, but assaulting Heaven itself.

The Hortlak

Kelly Link

Eric was night, and Batu was day. The girl, Charley, was the moon. Every night, she drove past the All-Night in her long, noisy, green Chevy, a dog hanging out the passenger window. It wasn't ever the same dog, although they all had the same blissful expression. They were doomed, but they didn't know it.

> *Bız buradan çok hoslandık.*
> We like it here very much.

The All-Night Convenience was a fully stocked, self-sufficient organism, like the *Starship Enterprise*, or the *Kon-Tiki*. Batu went on and on about this. They didn't work retail anymore. They were on a voyage of discovery, one in which they had no need to leave the All-Night, not even to do laundry. Batu washed his pajamas and the extra uniforms in the sink in the back. He even washed Eric's clothes. That was the kind of friend Batu was.

> *Burada tatil için mi bulunuyorsunuz?*
> Are you here on holiday?

All during his shift, Eric listened for Charley's car. First she went by on her way to the shelter and then, during her shift, she took the dogs out driving, past the store first in one direction and then back again, two or three times in one night, the lights of her headlights picking out the long, black gap of the Ausible Chasm, a bright slap across the windows of the All-Night. Eric's heart lifted whenever a car went past.

The zombies came in, and he was polite to them, and failed to understand what they wanted, and sometimes real people came in and bought candy or cigarettes or beer. The zombies were never around when the real people were around, and Charley never showed up when the zombies were there.

Charley looked like someone from a Greek play, Electra, or Cassandra. She looked like someone had just set her favorite city on fire. Eric had thought that, even before he knew about the dogs.

Sometimes, when she didn't have a dog in the Chevy, Charley came into the All-Night Convenience to buy a Mountain Dew, and then she and Batu would go outside to sit on the curb. Batu was teaching her Turkish. Sometimes Eric went outside as well, to smoke a cigarette. He didn't really smoke, but it meant he got to look at Charley, the way the moonlight sat on her like a hand. Sometimes she looked back. Wind would rise up, out of the Ausible Chasm, across Ausible Chasm Road, into the parking lot of the All-Night, tugging at Batu's pajama bottoms, pulling away the cigarette smoke that hung out of Eric's mouth. Charley's bangs would float up off her forehead, until she clamped them down with her fingers.

Batu said he was not flirting. He didn't have a thing for Charley. He was interested in her because Eric was interested. Batu wanted to know what Charley's story was: he said he needed to know if she was good enough for Eric, for the All-Night Convenience. There was a lot at stake.

What Eric wanted to know was, why did Batu have so many pajamas? But Eric didn't want to seem nosy. There wasn't a lot of space in the All-Night. If Batu wanted Eric to know about the pajamas, then one day he'd tell him. It was as simple as that.

Erkek arkadaşınız varmı?
Do you have a boyfriend?

Recently Batu had evolved past the need for more than two or three hours' sleep, which was good in some ways and bad in others. Eric had a suspicion he might figure out how to talk to Charley if Batu were tucked away, back in the storage closet, dreaming his own sweet dreams, and not scheming schemes, doing all the flirting on Eric's behalf, so that Eric never had to say a thing.

Eric had even rehearsed the start of a conversation. Charley would say, "Where's Batu?" and Eric would say, "Asleep." Or even, "Sleeping in the closet."

Charley's story: she worked night shifts at the animal shelter. Every night, when Charley got to work, she checked the list to see which dogs were on the schedule. She took the dogs—any that weren't too ill, or too mean—out for one last drive around town. Then she drove them back and she put them to sleep. She did this with an injection. She sat on the floor and petted them until they weren't breathing anymore.

When she was telling Batu this, Batu sitting far too close to her, Eric not close enough, Eric had this thought, which was what it would be like to lie down and put his head on Charley's leg. But the longest conversation that he'd ever managed with Charley was with Charley on one side of the counter, him on the other, when he'd explained that they weren't taking money anymore, at least not unless people wanted to give them money.

"I want a Mountain Dew," Charley had said, making sure Eric understood that part.

"I know," Eric said. He tried to show with his eyes how much he knew, and how much he didn't know, but wanted to know.

"But you don't want me to pay you for it."

"I'm supposed to give you what you want," Eric said, "and then you give me what you want to give me. It doesn't have to be about money. It doesn't even have to be something, you know, tangible. Sometimes people tell Batu their dreams if they don't have anything interesting in their wallets."

"All I want is a Mountain Dew," Charley said. But she must have seen the panic on Eric's face, and she dug in her pocket. Instead of change, she pulled out a set of dog tags and plunked it down on the counter.

"This dog is no longer alive," she said. "It wasn't a very big dog, and I think it was part Chihuahua and part collie, and how pitiful is that. You should have seen it. Its owner brought it in because it would jump up on her bed in the morning, lick her face, and get so excited that it would pee. I don't know, maybe she thought someone else would want to adopt an ugly little bedwetting dog, but nobody did, and so now it's not alive anymore. I killed it."

"I'm sorry," Eric said. Charley leaned her elbows against the counter. She was so close, he could smell her smell: chemical, burnt, doggy. There were dog hairs on her clothes.

"I killed it," Charley said. She sounded angry at him. "Not you."

When Eric looked at her, he saw that that city was still on fire. It was still burning down, and Charley was watching it burn. She was still holding the dog tags. She let go and they lay there on the counter until Eric picked them up and put them in the register.

"This is all Batu's idea," Charley said. "Right?" She went outside and sat on the curb, and in a while Batu came out of the storage closet and went outside as well. Batu's pajama bottoms were silk. There were smiling hydrocephalic cartoon cats on them, and the cats carried children in their mouths. Either the children were mouse-sized, or the cats were bear-sized. The children were either screaming or laughing. Batu's pajama top was red flannel, faded, with guillotines, and heads in baskets.

Eric stayed inside. He leaned his face against the window every once in a while, as if he could hear what they were saying. But even if he could have heard them, he guessed he wouldn't have understood. The shapes their mouths made were shaped like Turkish words. Eric hoped they were talking about retail.

Kar yağacak.
It's going to snow.

The way the All-Night worked at the moment was Batu's idea. They sized up the customers before they got to the counter—that had always been part of retail. If the customer was the right sort, then Batu or Eric gave the customer what they said they needed, and the customer paid with money sometimes, and sometimes with other things: pot, books on tape, souvenir maple syrup tins. They were near the border. They got a lot of Canadians. Eric suspected someone, maybe a traveling Canadian pajama salesman, was supplying Batu with novelty pajamas.

Siz de mi bekliyorsunuz?
Are you waiting too?

What Batu thought Eric should say to Charley, if he really liked her: "Come live with me. Come live at the All-Night."

What Eric thought about saying to Charley: "If you're going away, take me with you. I'm about to be twenty years old, and I've never been to college. I sleep days in a storage closet, wearing someone else's pajamas. I've worked retail jobs since I was sixteen. I know people are hateful. If you need to bite someone, you can bite me."

Başka bir yere gidelim mi?
Shall we go somewhere else?

Charley drives by. There is a little black dog in the passenger window, leaning out to swallow the fast air. There is a yellow dog. An Irish setter. A Doberman.

Akitas. Charley has rolled the window so far down that these dogs could jump out, if they wanted, when she stops the car at a light. But the dogs don't jump. So Charley drives them back again.

Batu said it was clear Charley had a great capacity for hating, and also a great capacity for love. Charley's hatred was seasonal: in the months after Christmas, Christmas puppies started growing up. People got tired of trying to house-train them. All February, all March, Charley hated people. She hated people in December too, just for practice.

Being in love, Batu said, like working retail, meant that you had to settle for being hated, at least part of the year. That was what the months after Christmas were all about. Neither system—not love, not retail—was perfect. When you looked at dogs, you saw this, that love didn't work.

Batu said it was likely that Charley, both her person and her Chevy, were infested with dog ghosts. These ghosts were different from the zombies. Nonhuman ghosts, he said, were the most difficult of all ghosts to dislodge, and dogs were worst of all. There is nothing as persistent, as loyal, as *clingy* as a dog.

"So can you see these ghosts?" Eric said.

"Don't be ridiculous," Batu said. "You can't see that kind of ghost. You smell them."

Civarda turistik yerler var mı, acaba?

Are there any tourist attractions around here, I wonder?

Eric woke up and found it was dark. It was always dark when he woke up, and this was always a surprise. There was a little window on the back wall of the storage closet, that framed the dark like a picture. You could feel the cold night air propping up the walls of the All-Night, thick and wet as glue.

Batu had let him sleep in. Batu was considerate of other people's sleep.

All day long, in Eric's dreams, store managers had arrived, one after another, announced themselves, expressed dismay at the way Batu had reinvented— *compromised*—convenience retail. In Eric's dream, Batu had put his large, handsome arm over the shoulder of the store managers, promised to explain everything in a satisfactory manner, if they would only come and see. The store managers had all gone, in a docile, trusting way, trotting after Batu, across the road, looking both ways, to the edge of the Ausible Chasm. They stood there, in Eric's dream, peering down into the Chasm, and then Batu had given them a little push, a small push, and that was the end of that store manager, and Batu walked back across the road to wait for the next store manager.

Eric bathed standing up at the sink and put on his uniform. He brushed his teeth. The closet smelled like sleep.

It was the middle of February, and there was snow in the All-Night parking lot. Batu was clearing the parking lot, carrying shovelfuls of snow across the road, dumping the snow into the Ausible Chasm. Eric went outside for a smoke and watched. He didn't offer to help. He was still upset about the way Batu had behaved in his dream.

There was no moon, but the snow was lit by its own whiteness. There was the shadowy figure of Batu, carrying in front of him the shadowy scoop of the shovel, full of snow, like an enormous spoon full of falling light, which was still falling all around them. The snow came down, and Eric's smoke went up and up.

He walked across the road to where Batu stood, peering down into the Ausible Chasm. Down in the Chasm, it was no darker than the kind of dark the rest of the world, including Eric, especially Eric, was used to. Snow fell into the Chasm, the way snow fell on the rest of the world. And yet there was a wind coming out of the Chasm that worried Eric.

"What do you think is down there?" Batu said.

"Zombie Land," Eric said. He could almost taste it. "Zomburbia. They have everything down there. There's even supposed to be a drive-in movie theater down there, somewhere, that shows old black-and-white horror movies, all night long. Zombie churches with AA meetings for zombies, down in the basements, every Thursday night."

"Yeah?" Batu said. "Zombie bars too? Where they serve zombies Zombies?"

Eric said, "My friend Dave went down once, when we were in high school, on a dare. He used to tell us all kinds of stories."

"You ever go?" Batu said, pointing with his empty shovel at the narrow, crumbly path that went down into the Chasm.

"I never went to college. I've never even been to Canada," Eric said. "Not even when I was in high school, to buy beer."

All night the zombies came out of the Chasm, holding handfuls of snow. They carried the snow across the road, and into the parking lot, and left it there. Batu was back in the closet, sending off faxes, and Eric was glad about this, that Batu couldn't see what the zombies were up to.

Zombies came into the store, tracking in salt and melting snow. Eric hated mopping up after the zombies.

He sat on the counter, facing the road, hoping Charley would drive by soon. Two weeks ago, Charley had bitten a man who'd brought his dog to the animal shelter to be put down.

The man was bringing his dog because it had bit him, he said, but Charley said you knew when you saw this guy, and when you saw the dog, that the dog had had a very good reason.

This man had a tattoo of a mermaid coiled around his meaty forearm, and even this mermaid had an unpleasant look to her: scaly, corseted bottom; tiny black dot eyes; a sour, fangy smile. Charley said it was as if even the mermaid were telling her to bite the arm, and so she did. When she did, the dog went nuts. The guy dropped its leash. He was trying to get Charley off his arm. The dog, misunderstanding the situation, or rather, understanding the situation, but not the larger situation, had grabbed Charley by her leg, sticking its teeth into her calf.

Both Charley and the dog's owner had needed stitches. But it was the dog who was doomed. Nothing had changed that.

Charley's boss at the shelter was going to fire her, anytime soon—in fact, he had fired her. But they hadn't found someone to take her shift yet, and so she was working there, for a few more days, under a different name. Everyone at the shelter understood why she'd had to bite the man.

Charley said she was going to drive all the way across Canada. Maybe keep on going, up into Alaska. Go watch bears pick through garbage.

"When a bear hibernates," she told Batu and Eric, "it sleeps all winter and never goes to the bathroom. So when she wakes up in spring, she's really constipated. The first thing she does is take this really painful shit. And then she goes and jumps in a river. She's really pissed off now, about everything. When she comes out of the river, she's covered in ice. It's like armor. She goes on a rampage and she's wearing armor. Isn't that great? That bear can take a bite out of anything it wants."

Uykum geldi.
My sleep has come.

The snow kept falling. Sometimes it stopped. Charley came by. Eric had bad dreams. Batu did not go to bed. When the zombies came in, he followed them around the store, taking notes. The zombies didn't care at all. They were done with all that.

Batu was wearing Eric's favorite pajamas. These were blue, and had towering Hokusai-style white-blue waves, and up on the waves, there were boats with owls looking owlish. If you looked closely, you could see that the owls were gripping newspapers in their wings, and if you looked even closer, you could read the date and the headline:

"Tsunami Tsweeps Pussy

Overboard, All is Lots."

Batu had spent a lot of time reorganizing the candy aisle according to chewiness and meltness. The week before, he had arranged it so that if you took the first letter of every candy, reading across from left to right, and then down, it had spelled out the first sentence of *To Kill a Mockingbird*, and then also a line of Turkish poetry. Something about the moon.

The zombies came and went, and Batu put his notebook away. He said, "I'm going to go ahead and put jerky with Sugar Daddies. It's almost a candy. It's very chewy. About as chewy as you can get. Chewy Meat gum."

"Frothy Meat Drink," Eric said automatically. They were always thinking of products that no one would ever want to buy, and that no one would ever try to sell.

"Squeezable Pork. *It's on your mind, it's in your mouth, it's pork.* Remember that ad campaign? She can come live with us," Batu said. It was the same old speech, only a little more urgent each time he gave it. "The All-Night needs women, especially women like Charley. She falls in love with you, I don't mind one bit."

"What about you?" Eric said.

"What about me?" Batu said. "Charley and I have the Turkish language. That's enough. Tell me something I need. I don't even need sleep!"

"What are you talking about?" Eric said. He hated when Batu talked about Charley, except that he loved hearing her name.

Batu said, "The All-Night is a great place to raise a family. Everything you need, right here. Diapers, Vienna sausages, grape-scented Magic Markers, Moon Pies—kids like Moon Pies—and then one day, when they're tall enough, we teach them how to operate the register."

"There are laws against that," Eric said. "Mars needs women. Not the All-Night. And we're running out of Moon Pies." He turned his back on Batu.

Some of Batu's pajamas worry Eric. He won't wear these, although Batu has told him that he may wear any pajamas he likes.

For example, ocean liners navigating icebergs on a pair of pajama bottoms. A man with an enormous pair of scissors, running after women whose long hair whips out behind them like red and yellow flags, they are moving so fast. Spiderwebs with houses stuck to them.

A few nights ago, about two or three in the morning, a woman came into the store. Batu was over by the magazines, and the woman went and stood next to Batu.

Batu's eyes were closed, although that doesn't necessarily mean he was asleep. The woman stood and flicked through magazines, and then at some point she realized that the man standing there with his eyes closed was wearing pajamas. She stopped reading through *People* magazine and started reading Batu's pajamas instead. Then she gasped, and poked Batu with a skinny finger.

"Where did you get those?" she said. "How on earth did you get those?"

Batu opened his eyes. "Excuse me," he said. "May I help you find something?"

"You're wearing my diary," the woman said. Her voice went up and up in a wail. "That's my handwriting! That's the diary that I kept when I was fourteen! But it had a lock on it, and I hid it under my mattress, and I never let anyone read it. Nobody ever read it!"

Batu held out his arm. "That's not true," he said. "I've read it. You have very nice handwriting. Very distinctive. My favorite part is when—"

The woman screamed. She put her hands over her ears and walked backwards, down the aisle, and still screaming, turned around and ran out of the store.

"What was that about?" Eric said. "What was up with her?"

"I don't know," Batu said. "The thing is, I thought she looked familiar! And I was right. Hah! What are the odds, you think, the woman who kept that diary coming in the store like that?"

"Maybe you shouldn't wear those anymore," Eric said. "Just in case she comes back."

Gelebilirmiyim?
Can I come?

Batu had originally worked Tuesday through Saturday, second shift. Now he was all day, every day. Eric worked all night, all nights. They didn't need anyone else, except maybe Charley.

What had happened was this. One of the managers had left, supposedly to have a baby, although she had not looked in the least bit pregnant, Batu said, and besides, it was clearly not Batu's kid, because of the vasectomy. Then, shortly after the incident with the man in the trench coat, the other manager had quit, claiming to be sick of that kind of shit. No one was sent to replace him, so Batu had stepped in.

The door rang and a customer came into the store. Canadian. Not a zombie. Eric turned around in time to see Batu duck down, slipping around the corner of the candy aisle, and heading towards the storage closet.

The customer bought a Mountain Dew, Eric too disheartened to explain that cash was no longer necessary. He could feel Batu, fretting, in the storage closet, listening to this old-style retail transaction. When the customer was gone, Batu came out again.

"Do you ever wonder," Eric said, "if the company will ever send another manager?" He saw again the dream-Batu, the dream-managers, the cartoonish, unbridgeable gape of the Ausible Chasm.

"They won't," Batu said.

"They might," Eric said.

"They won't," Batu said.

"How do you know for sure?" Eric said. "What if they do?"

"It was a bad idea in the first place," Batu said. He gestured towards the parking lot and the Ausible Chasm. "Not enough steady business."

"So why do we stay here?" Eric said. "How do we change the face of retail if nobody ever comes in here except joggers and truckers and zombies and Canadians? I mean, I tried to explain about how new-style retail worked, the other night—to this woman—and she told me to fuck off. She acted like I was insane."

"The customer isn't always right. Sometimes the customer is an asshole. That's the first rule of retail," Batu said. "But it's not like anywhere else is better. I used to work for the CIA. Believe me, this is better."

"Were you really in the CIA?" Eric said.

"We used to go to this bar, sometimes, me and the people I worked with," Batu said. "Only we have to pretend that we don't know each other. No fraternizing. So we all sit there, along the bar, and don't say a word to each other. All these guys, all of us, we could speak maybe five hundred languages, dialects, whatever, between us. But we don't talk in this bar. Just sit and drink and sit and drink. Used to drive the bartender crazy. We used to leave nice tips. Didn't matter to him."

"So did you ever kill people?" Eric said. He never knew whether or not Batu was joking about the CIA thing.

"Do I look like a killer?" Batu said, standing there in his pajamas, rumpled and red-eyed. When Eric burst out laughing, he smiled and yawned and scratched his head.

When other employees had quit the All-Night, for various reasons of their own, Batu had not replaced them.

Around this same time, Batu's girlfriend had kicked him out, and with Eric's permission, he had moved into the storage closet. That had been just *before* Christmas, and it was a few days *after* Christmas when Eric's mother lost her job as a security guard at the mall and decided she was going to go find Eric's father. She'd gone hunting online, and made a list of names she thought he might be going under. She had addresses as well.

Eric wasn't sure what she was going to do if she found his father, and he didn't think she knew, either. She said she just wanted to talk, but Eric knew she kept a gun in the glove compartment of her car. Before she left, Eric had copied down her list of names and addresses, and sent out Christmas cards to all of them. It was the first time he'd ever had a reason to send out Christmas cards, and it had been difficult, finding the right things to say in them, especially since they probably weren't his father, no matter what his mother thought. Not all of them, anyway.

Before she left, Eric's mother had put most of the furniture in storage. She'd sold everything else, including Eric's guitar and his books, at a yard sale one Saturday morning while Eric was working an extra shift at the All-Night.

The rent was still paid through the end of January, but after his mother left, Eric had worked longer and longer hours at the store, and then, one morning, he didn't bother going home. The All-Night, and Batu, they needed him. Batu said this attitude showed Eric was destined for great things at the All-Night.

Every night Batu sent off faxes to the *World Weekly News,* and to the *National Enquirer,* and to the *New York Times.* These faxes concerned the Ausible Chasm and the zombies. Someday someone would send reporters. It was all part of the plan, which was going to change the way retail worked. It was going to be a whole different world, and Eric and Batu were going to be right there at the beginning. They were going to be famous heroes. Revolutionaries. Heroes of the revolution. Batu said that Eric didn't need to understand that part of the plan yet. It was essential to the plan that Eric didn't ask questions.

Ne zaman geri geleceksiniz?
When will you come back?

The zombies were like Canadians, in that they looked enough like real people at first, to fool you. But when you looked closer, you saw they were from some other place, where things were different: where even the same things, the things that went on everywhere, were just a little bit different.

The zombies didn't talk at all, or they said things that didn't make sense. "Wooden hat," one zombie said to Eric, "Glass leg. Drove around all day in my wife. Did you ever hear me on the radio?" They tried to pay Eric for things that the All-Night didn't sell.

Real people, the ones who weren't heading towards Canada or away from Canada, mostly had better things to do than drive out to the All-Night at 3 AM. So real people, in a way, were even weirder, when they came in. Eric kept a close eye on the real people. Once a guy had pulled a gun on him—there was no way to understand that, but, on the other hand, you knew exactly what was going on. With the zombies, who knew?

Not even Batu knew what the zombies were up to. Sometimes he said that they were just another thing you had to deal with in retail. They were the kind of customer that you couldn't ever satisfy, the kind of customer who wanted something you couldn't give them, who had no other currency, except currency that was sinister, unwholesome, confusing, and probably dangerous.

Meanwhile, the things that the zombies tried to purchase were plainly things that they had brought with them into the store—things that had fallen, or been thrown into the Ausible Chasm, like pieces of safety glass. Rocks from the bottom of Ausible Chasm. Beetles. The zombies liked shiny things, broken things, trash like empty soda bottles, handfuls of leaves, sticky dirt, dirty sticks.

Eric thought maybe Batu had it wrong. Maybe it wasn't supposed to be a transaction. Maybe the zombies just wanted to give Eric something. But what was he going to do with their leaves? Why him? What was he supposed to give them in return?

Eventually, when it was clear Eric didn't understand, the zombies drifted off, away from the counter and around the aisles again, or out the doors, making their way like raccoons, scuttling back across the road, still clutching their leaves. Batu would put away his notebook, go into the storage closet, and send off his faxes.

The zombie customers made Eric feel guilty. He hadn't been trying hard enough. The zombies were never rude, or impatient, or tried to shoplift things. He hoped that they found what they were looking for. After all, he would be dead someday too, and on the other side of the counter.

Maybe his friend Dave had been telling the truth and there was a country down there that you could visit, just like Canada. Maybe when the zombies got all the way to the bottom, they got into zippy zombie cars and drove off to their zombie jobs, or back home again, to their sexy zombie wives, or maybe they went off to the zombie bank to make their deposits of stones, leaves, linty, birdsnesty tangles, all the other debris real people didn't know the value of.

It wasn't just the zombies. Weird stuff happened in the middle of the day too. When there were still managers and other employers, once, on Batu's shift, a guy had come in wearing a trench coat and a hat. Outside, it must have been ninety degrees, and Batu admitted he had felt a little spooked about the trench coat thing, but there was another customer, a jogger, poking at the bottled waters to see which were coldest. Trench-coat guy walked around the store, putting candy bars and safety razors in his pockets, like he was getting ready for Halloween. Batu had thought about punching the alarm. "Sir?" he said. "Excuse me, sir?"

The man walked up and stood in front of the counter. Batu couldn't take his eyes off the trench coat. It was like the guy was wearing an electric fan strapped to his chest, under the trench coat, and the fan was blowing things around underneath. You could hear the fan buzzing. It made sense, Batu had thought: this guy had his own air-conditioning unit under there. Pretty neat, although you still wouldn't want to go trick-or-treating at this guy's house.

"Hot enough for you?" the man said, and Batu saw that this guy was sweating. He twitched, and a bee flew out of the gray trench coat sleeve. Batu and the man both watched it fly away. Then the man opened his trench coat, flapped his arms, gently, gently, and the bees inside his trench coat began to leave the man in long, clotted, furious trails, until the whole store was vibrating with clouds of bees. Batu ducked under the counter. Trench-coat man, bee guy, reached over the counter, dinged the register in a calm and experienced way so that the drawer popped open, and scooped all the bills out of the till.

Then he walked back out again and left all his bees. He got in his car and drove away. That's the way that all All-Night stories end, with someone driving away.

But they had to get a beekeeper to come in, to smoke the bees out. Batu got stung three times, once on the lip, once on his stomach, and once when he put his hand into the register and found no money, only a bee. The jogger sued the All-Night parent company for a lot of money, and Batu and Eric didn't know what had happened with that.

Karanlık ne zaman basar?
When does it get dark?

Eric has been having this dream recently. In the dream, he's up behind the counter in the All-Night, and then his father is walking down the aisle of the All-Night, past the racks of magazines and towards the counter, his father's hands full of stones from the Ausible Chasm. Which is ridiculous: his father is alive, and not only that, but living in another state, maybe in a different time zone, probably under a different name.

When he told Batu about it, Batu said, "Oh, that dream. I've had it too."

"About your father?" Eric said.

"About your father," Batu said. "Who do you think I meant, *my* father?"

"You haven't ever met my father," Eric said.

"I'm sorry if it upsets you, but it was definitely your father," Batu said. "You look just like him. If I dream about him again, what do you want me to do? Ignore him? Pretend he isn't there?"

Eric never knew when Batu was pulling his leg. Dreams could be a touchy subject. Eric thought maybe Batu was nostalgic about sleeping, maybe Batu collected pajamas in the way that people nostalgic about their childhoods collected toys.

Another dream, one that Eric hasn't told Batu about. In this dream, Charley comes in. She wants to buy a Mountain Dew, but then Eric realizes that all the Mountain Dews have little drowned dogs floating in them. You can win a prize if you drink one of the dog sodas. When Charley gets up to the counter with an armful of doggy Mountain Dews, Eric realizes that he's got one of Batu's pajama tops on, one of the inside-out ones. Things are rubbing against his arms, his back, his stomach, transferring themselves like tattoos to his skin.

And he hasn't got any pants on.

Batık gemilerle ilgileniyorum.
I'm interested in sunken ships.

"You need to make your move," Batu said. He said it over and over, day after day, until Eric was sick of hearing it. "Any day now, the shelter is going to find someone to replace her, and Charley will split. Tell you what you should do, you tell her you want to adopt a dog. Give it a home. We've got room here. Dogs are good practice for when you and Charley are parents."

"How do you know?" Eric said. He knew he sounded exasperated. He couldn't help it. "That makes no sense at all. If dogs are good practice, then what kind of mother is Charley going to be? What are you saying? So say Charley has a kid, you're saying she's going to put it down if it cries at night or wets the bed?"

"That's not what I'm saying at all," Batu said. "The only thing I'm worried about, Eric, really, is whether or not Charley may be too old. It takes longer to have kids when you're her age. Things can go wrong."

"What are you talking about?" Eric said. "Charley's not old."

"How old do you think she is?" Batu said. "So what do you think? Should the toothpaste and the condiments go next to the Elmer's glue and the hair gel and lubricants? Make a shelf of sticky things? Or should I put it with the chewing tobacco and the mouthwash, and make a little display of things that you spit?"

"Sure," Eric said. "Make a little display. I don't know how old Charley is, maybe she's my age? Nineteen? A little older?"

Batu laughed. "A little older? So how old do you think I am?"

"I don't know," Eric said. He squinted at Batu. "Thirty-five? Forty?"

Batu looked pleased. "You know, since I started sleeping less, I think I've stopped getting older. I may be getting younger. You keep on getting a good night's sleep, and we're going to be the same age pretty soon. Come take a look at this and tell me what you think."

"Not bad," Eric said. "We could put watermelons with this stuff too, if we had watermelons. The kind with seeds. What's the point of seedless watermelons?"

"It's not such a big deal," Batu said. He knelt down in the aisle, marking off inventory on his clipboard. "No big thing if Charley's older than you think. Nothing wrong with older women. And it's good you're not bothered about the ghost dogs or the biting thing. Everyone's got problems. The only real concern I have is about her car."

"What about her car?" Eric said.

"Well," Batu said. "It isn't a problem if she's going to live here. She can park it here for as long as she wants. That's what the parking lot is for. But whatever you do: if she invites you to go for a ride, don't go for a ride."

"Why not?" Eric said. "What are you talking about?"

"Think about it," Batu said. "All those dog ghosts." He scooted down the aisle on his butt. Eric followed. "Every time she drives by here with some poor dog, that dog is doomed. That car is bad luck. The passenger side especially. You want to stay out of that car. I'd rather climb down into the Ausible Chasm."

Something cleared its throat; a zombie had come into the store. It stood behind Batu, looking down at him. Batu looked up. Eric retreated down the aisle, towards the counter.

"Stay out of her car," Batu said, ignoring the zombie.

"And who will be fired out of the cannon?" the zombie said. It was wearing a suit and tie. "My brother will be fired out of the cannon."

"Why can't you talk like sensible people?" Batu said, turning around and looking up. Sitting on the floor, he sounded as if he were about to cry. He swatted at the zombie.

The zombie coughed again, yawning. It grimaced at them. Something was snagged on its gray lips now, and the zombie put up its hand. It tugged, dragging at the thing in its mouth, coughing out a black, glistening, wadded rope. The zombie's mouth stayed open, as if to show that there was nothing else in there, even as it held the wet black rope out to Batu. The wet thing hung down from its hands and became pajamas. Batu looked back at Eric. "I don't want them," he said. He looked shy.

"What should I do?" Eric said. He hovered by the magazines. Charlize Theron was grinning at him, as if she knew something he didn't.

"You shouldn't be here." It wasn't clear to Eric whether Batu was speaking to the zombie. "I have all the pajamas I need."

The zombie said nothing. It dropped the pajamas into Batu's lap.

"Stay out of Charley's car!" Batu said to Eric. He closed his eyes and began to snore.

"Shit," Eric said to the zombie. "How did you do that?"

There was another zombie in the store now. The first zombie took Batu's arms and the second zombie took Batu's feet. They dragged him down the aisle and toward the storage closet. Eric came out from behind the counter.

"What are you doing?" he said. "You're not going to eat him, are you?"

But the zombies had Batu in the closet. They put the black pajamas on him, yanking them over the other pair of pajamas. They lifted Batu up onto the mattress, and pulled the blanket over him, up to his chin.

Eric followed the zombies out of the storage closet. He shut the door behind him. "So I guess he's going to sleep for a while," he said. "That's a good thing, right? He needed to get some sleep. So how did you do that with the pajamas? Is there some kind of freaky pajama factory down there?" The zombies ignored Eric. They held hands and went down the aisles, stopping to consider candy bars and Tampax and toilet paper and all the things that you spit. They wouldn't buy anything. They never did.

Eric went back to the counter. He wished, very badly, that his mother still lived in their apartment. He would have liked to call someone. He sat behind the register for a while, looking through the phone book, just in case he came across someone's name and it seemed like a good idea to call them. Then he went back to the storage closet and looked at Batu. Batu was snoring. His eyelids twitched, and there was a tiny, knowing smile on his face, as if he were dreaming, and everything was being explained to him, at last, in this dream. It was hard to feel worried about someone who looked like that. Eric would have been jealous, except he knew that no one ever managed to hold on to those explanations, once you woke up. Not even Batu.

Hangi yol daha kısa?
Which is the shorter route?

Hangi yol daha kolay?
Which is the easier route?

Charley came by at the beginning of her shift. She didn't come inside the All-Night. Instead she stood out in the parking lot, beside her car, looking out across the road, at the Ausible Chasm. The car hung low to the ground, as if the trunk were full of things. When Eric went outside, he saw that there was a suitcase in the backseat. If there were ghost dogs, Eric couldn't see them, but there were doggy smudges on the windows.

"Where's Batu?" Charley said.

"Asleep," Eric said. He realized that he'd never figured out how the conversation would go, after that.

He said, "Are you going someplace?"

"I'm going to work," Charley said. "Like normal."

"Good," Eric said. "Normal is good." He stood and looked at his feet. A zombie wandered into the parking lot. It nodded at them, and went into the All-Night.

"Aren't you going to go back inside?" Charley said.

"In a bit," Eric said. "It's not like they ever buy anything." But he kept an eye on the All-Night, and the zombie, in case it headed towards the storage closet.

"So how old are you?" Eric said. "I mean, can I ask you that? How old you are?"

"How old are you?" Charley said right back.

"I'm almost twenty," Eric said. "I know I look older."

"No you don't," Charley said. "You look exactly like you're almost twenty."

"So how old are you?" Eric said again.

"How old do you think I am?" Charley said.

"About my age?" Eric said.

"Are you flirting with me?" Charley said. "Yes? No? How about in dog years? How old would you say I am in dog years?"

The zombie finished looking for whatever it was looking for inside the All-Night. It came outside and nodded to Charley and Eric. "Beautiful people," it said. "Why won't you ever visit my hand?"

"I'm sorry," Eric said.

The zombie turned its back on them. It tottered across the road, looking neither to the left, nor to the right, and went down the footpath into the Ausible Chasm.

"Have you?" Charley said. She pointed at the path.

"No," Eric said. "I mean, someday I will, I guess."

"Do you think they have pets down there? Dogs?" Charley said.

"I don't know," Eric said. "Regular dogs?"

"The thing I think about sometimes," Charley said, "is whether or not they have animal shelters, and if someone has to look after the dogs. If someone has to have a job where they put down dogs down there. And if you do put dogs to sleep, down there, then where do they wake up?"

"Batu says that if you need another job, you can come live with us at the All-Night," Eric said. His lips felt so cold that it was hard to talk.

"Is *that* what Batu says?" Charley said. She started to laugh.

"Batu likes you," Eric said.

"I like him too," Charley said. "But I don't want to live in a convenience store. No offense. I'm sure it's nice."

"It's okay," Eric said. "I don't want to work retail my whole life."

"There are worse jobs," Charley said. She leaned against her Chevy. "Maybe I'll stop by later tonight. We could always go for a long ride, go somewhere else, and talk about retail."

"Like where? Where are you going?" Eric said. "Are you thinking about going to Turkey? Is that why Batu is teaching you Turkish?" He wanted to stand there and ask Charley questions all night long.

"I want to learn Turkish so that when I go somewhere else I can pretend to be Turkish. I can pretend I *only* speak Turkish. That way no one will bother me," Charley said.

"Oh," Eric said. "Good plan. We could always go somewhere and not talk, if you want to practice. Or I could talk to you, and you could pretend you don't understand what I'm saying. We don't have to go for a ride. We could just go across the road, go down into the Chasm. I've never been down there."

"It's not a big deal," Charley said. "We can do it some other time." Suddenly she looked much older.

"No, wait," Eric said. "I do want to come with you. We can go for a ride. It's just that Batu's asleep. Someone has to look after him. Someone has to be awake to sell stuff."

"So are you going to work there your whole life?" Charley said. "Take care of Batu? Figure out how to rip off dead people?"

"What do you mean?" Eric said.

"Batu says the All-Night is thinking about opening up another store, down there," Charley said, waving across the road. "You and he are this big experiment in retail, according to him. Once the All-Night figures out what dead people want to buy, it's going to be like the discovery of America all over again."

"It's not like that," Eric said. He could feel his voice going up at the end, as if it were a question. He could almost smell what Batu meant about Charley's car. The ghosts, those dogs, were getting impatient. You could tell that. They were tired of the parking lot, they wanted to be going for a ride. "You don't understand. I don't think you understand?"

"Batu said that you have a real way with dead people," Charley said. "Most retail clerks flip out. Of course, you're from around here. Plus you're young. You probably don't even understand about death yet. You're just like my dogs."

"I don't know what they want," Eric said. "The zombies."

"Nobody ever really knows what they want," Charley said. "Why should that change after you die?"

"Good point," Eric said.

"You shouldn't let Batu mess you around so much," Charley said. "I shouldn't be saying all this, I know. Batu and I are friends. But we could be friends too, you and me. You're sweet. It's okay that you don't talk much, although this is okay too, us talking. Why don't you come for a drive with me?" If there had been dogs inside her car, or the ghosts of dogs, then Eric would have heard them howling. Eric heard them howling. The dogs were telling him to get lost. They were telling him to fuck off. Charley belonged to them. She was *their* murderer.

"I can't," Eric said, longing for Charley to ask again. "Not right now."

"Well, that's okay. I'll stop by later," Charley said. She smiled at him and for a moment he was standing in that city where no one ever figured out how to put out that fire, and all the dead dogs howled again, and scratched at the smeary windows. "For a Mountain Dew. So you can think about it for a while."

She reached out and took Eric's hand in her hand. "Your hands are cold," she said. Her hands were hot. "You should go back inside."

Rengi begenmiyorum.
I don't like the color.

It was already 4 AM and there still wasn't any sign of Charley when Batu came out of the back room. He was rubbing his eyes. The black pajamas were gone. Now Batu was wearing pajama bottoms with foxes running across a field towards a tree with a circle of foxes sitting on their haunches around it. The outstretched tails of the running foxes were fat as zeppelins, with commas of flame hovering over them. Each little flame had a Hindenburg inside it, with a second littler flame above it, and so on. Some fires you just can't put out.

The pajama top was a color that Eric could not name. Dreary, creeping shapes lay upon it. Eric had read Lovecraft. He felt queasy when he looked at the pajama top.

"I just had the best dream," Batu said.

"You've been asleep for almost six hours," Eric said. When Charley came, he would go with her. He would stay with Batu. Batu needed him. He would go with Charley. He would go and come back. He wouldn't ever come back. He would send Batu postcards with bears on them. "So what was all that about? With the zombies."

"I don't know what you're talking about," Batu said. He took an apple from the fruit display and polished it on his non-Euclidean pajama top. The apple took on a horrid, whispery sheen. "Has Charley come by?"

"Yeah," Eric said. He and Charley would go to Las Vegas. They would buy Batu gold lamé pajamas. "I think you're right. I think she's about to leave town."

"Well, she can't!" Batu said. "That's not the plan. Here, I tell you what we'll do. You go outside and wait for her. Make sure she doesn't get away."

"She's not wanted by the police, Batu," Eric said. "She doesn't belong to us. She can leave town if she wants to."

"And you're okay with that?" Batu said. He yawned ferociously, and yawned again, and stretched, so that the pajama top heaved up in an eldritch manner. Eric closed his eyes.

"Not really," Eric said. He had already picked out a toothbrush, some toothpaste, and some novelty teeth, left over from Halloween, which he could give to Charley, maybe. "Are you okay? Are you going to fall asleep again? Can I ask you some questions?"

"What kind of questions?" Batu said, lowering his eyelids in a way that seemed both sleepy and cunning.

"Questions about our mission," Eric said. "About the All-Night and what we're doing here next to the Ausible Chasm. I need to understand what just happened with the zombies and the pajamas, and whether or not what happened is part of the plan, and whether or not the plan belongs to us, or whether the plan was planned by someone else, and we're just somebody else's big experiment in retail. Are we brand-new, or are we just the same old thing?"

"This isn't a good time for questions," Batu said. "In all the time that we've worked here, have I lied to you? Have I led you astray?"

"Well," Eric said. "That's what I need to know."

"Perhaps I haven't told you everything," Batu said. "But that's part of the plan. When I said that we were going to make everything new again, that we were going to reinvent retail, I was telling the truth. The plan is still the plan, and you are still part of that plan, and so is Charley."

"What about the pajamas?" Eric said. "What about the Canadians and the maple syrup and the people who come in to buy Mountain Dew?"

"You need to know this?" Batu said.

"Yes," Eric said. "Absolutely."

"Okay, then. My pajamas are *experimental CIA pajamas*," Batu said. "Like batteries. You've been charging them for me when you sleep. That's all I can say right now. Forget about the Canadians. These pajamas the zombies just gave me—do you have any idea what this means?"

Eric shook his head no.

Batu said, "Never mind. Do you know what we need now?"

"What do we need?" Eric said.

"We need you to go outside and wait for Charley," Batu said. "We don't have time for this. It's getting early. Charley gets off work any time now."

"Explain all of that again," Eric said. "What you just said. Explain the plan to me one more time."

"Look," Batu said. "Listen. Everybody is alive at first, right?"

"Right," Eric said.

"And everybody dies," Batu said. "Right?"

"Right," Eric said. A car drove by, but it still wasn't Charley.

"So everybody starts here," Batu said. "Not here, in the All-Night, but somewhere *here*, where we are. Where we live now. Where we live is here. The world. Right?"

"Right," Eric said. "Okay."

"And where we go is there," Batu said, flicking a finger towards the road. "Out there, down into the Ausible Chasm. Everybody goes there. And here we are, *here*, the All-Night, which is on the way to *there*."

"Right," Eric said.

"So it's like the Canadians," Batu said. "People are going someplace, and if they need something, they can stop here, to get it. But we need to know what they need. This is a whole new unexplored demographic. So they stuck the All-Night right here, lit it up like a Christmas tree, and waited to see who stopped in and what they bought. I shouldn't be telling you this. This is all need-to-know information only."

"You mean the All-Night or the CIA or whoever needs us to figure out how to sell things to zombies," Eric said.

"Forget about the CIA," Batu said. "Now will you go outside?"

"But is it our plan? Or are we just following someone else's plan?"

"Why does that matter to you?" Batu said. He put his hands on his head and tugged at his hair until it stood straight up, but Eric refused to be intimidated.

"I thought we were on a mission," Eric said, "to help mankind. Womankind too. Like the *Starship Enterprise*. But how are we helping anybody? What's new-style retail about this?"

"*Eric,*" Batu said. "Did you see those pajamas? Look. On second thought, forget about the pajamas. You never saw them. Like I said, this is bigger than the All-Night. There are bigger fish that are fishing, if you know what I mean."

"No," Eric said. "I don't."

"Excellent," Batu said. His experimental CIA pajama top writhed and boiled. "Your job is to be helpful and polite. Be patient. Be *careful*. Wait for the zombies to make the next move. I send off some faxes. Meanwhile, we still need Charley. Charley is a natural-born saleswoman. She's been selling death for years. And she's got a real gift for languages—she'll be speaking zombie in no time. Think what kind of work she could do here! Go outside. When she drives by, you flag her down. Talk to her. Explain why she needs to come live here. But whatever you do, don't get in the car with her. That car is full of ghosts. The wrong kind of ghosts. The kind who are never going to understand the least little thing about meaningful transactions."

"I know," Eric said. "I could smell them."

"So are we clear on all this?" Batu said. "Or maybe you think I'm still lying to you?"

"I don't think you'd lie to me, exactly," Eric said. He put on his jacket.

"You better put on a hat too," Batu said. "It's cold out there. You know you're like a son to me, which is why I tell you to put on your hat. And if I lied to you, it would be for your own good, because I love you like a son. One day, Eric, all of this will be yours. Just trust me and do what I tell you. Trust the plan."

Eric said nothing. Batu patted him on the shoulder, pulled an All-Night shirt over his pajama top, and grabbed a banana and a Snapple. He settled in behind the counter. His hair was still standing straight up, but at 4 AM, who was going to complain? Not Eric, not the zombies. Eric put on his hat, gave a little wave to Batu, which was either, Glad we cleared all *that* up at last, or else, So long!, he wasn't sure which, and walked out of the All-Night. This is the last time, he thought, I will ever walk through this door. He didn't know how he felt about that.

Eric stood outside in the parking lot for a long time. Out in the bushes, on the other side of the road, he could hear the zombies hunting for the things that were valuable to other zombies.

Some woman, a real person, but not Charley, drove into the parking lot. She went inside, and Eric thought he knew what Batu would say to her when she went to the counter. Batu would explain when she tried to make her purchase that he didn't want money. That wasn't what retail was really about. What Batu would want to know was what this woman really wanted. It was that simple, that complicated. Batu might try to recruit this woman, if she didn't seem litigious, and maybe that was a good thing. Maybe the All-Night really did need women.

Eric walked backwards, away and then even farther away from the All-Night. The farther he got, the more beautiful he saw it all was—it was all lit up like the moon. Was this what the zombies saw? What Charley saw, when she drove by? He couldn't imagine how anyone could leave it behind and never come back.

Maybe Batu had a pair of pajamas in his collection with All-Night Convenience Stores and light spilling out; the Ausible Chasm; a road with zombies, and Charleys in Chevys, a different dog hanging out of every passenger window, driving down that road. Down on one leg of those pajamas, down the road a long ways, there would be bears dressed up in ice; Canadians; CIA operatives and tabloid reporters and All-Night executives. Las Vegas showgirls. G-men and bee men in trench coats. His mother's car, always getting farther and farther away. He wondered if zombies wore zombie pajamas, or if they'd just invented them for Batu. He tried to picture Charley wearing silk pajamas and a flannel bathrobe, but she didn't look comfortable in them. She still looked miserable and angry and hopeless, much older than Eric had ever realized.

He jumped up and down in the parking lot, trying to keep warm. The woman, when she came out of the store, gave him a funny look. He couldn't see Batu behind the counter. Maybe he'd fallen asleep again, or maybe he was sending off more faxes. But Eric didn't go back inside the store. He was afraid of Batu's pajamas.

He was afraid of Batu.

He stayed outside, waiting for Charley.

But a few hours later, when Charley drove by—he was standing on the curb, keeping an eye out for her, she wasn't going to just slip away, he was determined to see her, not to miss her, to make sure that she saw him, to make her take him with her, wherever she was going—there was a Labrador in the passenger seat. The backseat of her car was full of dogs, real dogs and ghost dogs, and all of the dogs poking their doggy noses out of the windows at him. There wouldn't have been room for him, even if he'd been able to make her stop. But he ran out in the road anyway, like a damn dog, chasing after her car for as long as he could.

Kelly Link (kellylink.net) is the author of three collections of short stories, Stranger Things Happen, Magic for Beginners, *and* Pretty Monsters. *Her short stories have won three Nebulas, a Hugo, and a World Fantasy Award. Link and her family live in Northampton, Massachusetts, where she and her husband, Gavin J. Grant, run Small Beer Press (smallbeerpress.com), and play ping-pong. In 1996 they started the occasional zine* Lady Churchill's Rosebud Wristlet *(smallbeerpress.com/lcrw).*

"The Hortlak," according to critic Laura Miller, is like "a Raymond Carver story on mescaline." Can't say I disagree, but Link's story also reminds me of a surrealistic take on Dennis Etchison's classic story "The Late Shift."

As for the zombies, they are somewhat mysterious, but seem benign—but they *do* force unwanted pajamas on Batu.

The Turkish word "hortlak" is usually translated as "ghost," "spook" (I don't think they mean the CIA type, but Link might), "ghoul" (which I mentioned in connection with David Wellington's story), or "revenant."

Although it has been used in various ways in literature (and elsewhere) a revenant (*revenant* means "returning" in French) was originally a corporeal ghost or someone returned from the dead to terrorize the living, usually for a specific reason or to seek revenge. Eric Draven in James O'Barr's *The Crow*, for instance, might be considered a revenant.

Dead to the World

Gary McMahon

I stand at the topmost window of our fortified house, looking out at the dead. They are clearly defined in the moonlight; clumsy figures draped in rags and peeling tatters of skin. They are the first ones I have seen in quite some time, but their appearance was always inevitable.

They will never leave us alone.

We have been in the old farmhouse for two weeks, now—enough time for Coral to have recovered from the badly twisted ankle she sustained when we were running from an infested warehouse district, and to finish what little food we found in the place when we arrived.

Coral is downstairs now, packing. We travel light; everything we once owned has now been abandoned, other than crucial items like water bottles, a tin opener, knives and the gun.

I watch the dead as they stumble around amongst the trees, sniffing us out. It was quiet here when we first arrived, with no traces of anyone in the immediate vicinity, but now they have discovered us. I wonder if they can smell our living flesh, or perhaps the blood in our veins? They must have developed some kind of hunting instinct over the past ten years since the term "dead" began to mean something different from simply an end to walking about. They always find us, no matter how far and how fast we run.

We were both active political campaigners back then, before things changed. We attended rallies and marches for world peace and hunger; worked with charities to help Third World countries with massive debts, unstable regimes, and little hope of helping themselves. In short, and to borrow a phrase from an old song, we cared a lot.

That term, the Third World, has been outdated since the Cold War ended in the early 1990s. During that unique state of drama and conflict after World War II, when it seemed that the opposing blocs of the Soviets and the Western World were destined to blow us all to hell, the Third World countries watched and starved and wondered just who might help them.

Now, I know what that really means—to watch helplessly as forces beyond your control reshape and destroy everything you have ever known and believed in.

I think of all this now, as I watch the scattered dead walk through the darkened tree line and approach the fence that borders the farmhouse property. It occurs to me that what we have now is a kind of Fourth World—a group of (dead) people aligned with no political viewpoint or ideology, and whose needs have been honed down to the basic drive to feed. To feed on the rest of us . . . to feed on the living.

I turn away from the window—from the moonlight and the dark ground and the stumbling, staggering corpses—and walk out of the room, shutting the door quietly behind me as I head for the stairs. I am afraid to make a sound. The next sound I hear might be that of my own mind snapping.

"Have you checked all the rooms up there?" Coral looks up from fastening the rucksacks as I enter the downstairs living room. Her face is too pale, too thin. We haven't eaten in three days and her hunger has now become a visible thing, a terrifying luminescence that shines from beneath her sallow skin.

I nod. "There's nothing left up there. We have everything. Where's the gun? I saw a few of them out there, coming out of the woods."

She points towards the corner of the room, where the rifle is propped up against cushions on a dusty armchair. We do not have much ammunition left, and I doubt that we will be lucky enough to stumble on any before what we do have runs out completely. This is rural England not downtown Los Angeles. The best we can hope for is to find some old farmer's shotgun in another of the abandoned properties we continually hop between like frogs on lily pads.

I cross the room and pick up the rifle. Ten years ago I had never held a gun, would not have known how to fire one. These days I am an efficient marksman. I have to be, to save on bullets. "Won't be long," I say, leaving the room and going back up the stairs.

Back at the window I see that the dead have already come closer to the fence. One of them is even attempting to climb, but having only one arm seems a hindrance to his progress. There are four of them in total—the one trying to climb over the fence and three others who stand watching him, their bodies limp and ragged.

I raise the rifle and take aim, enjoying its heft at my shoulder. The sight line is perfect; an unrestricted view from the high window. I caress the trigger, waiting until the right moment, when my heart seems to stop beating for a second to allow me to take the shot. I pull the trigger. The tallest one—who is wearing some kind of dark overalls—twitches backwards as the side of his head explodes in a shock of dark matter. He takes three tiny backward steps before hitting the ground.

The other two do not even glance in his direction. I take them down with a shot each, heads going up like watermelons stuffed with cherry bombs.

Then I shoot the one on the fence. He hangs there, trapped in the razor wire, what is left of his brains leaking out of the large wound in what remains of his forehead.

I pull the gun back inside and secure the window, pulling the shutters tight and testing that they are solid. Then I go back downstairs to my wife.

Coral is sitting in the same dusty armchair where previously she'd put the gun. She is weeping quietly, her narrow shoulders hitching. "We can't keep doing this," she says, between almost silent sobs. "We can't go on."

I go to her but am unable to offer the comfort she needs. We are beyond all that—the world has gone past such small intimacies, tiny shows of affection. Instead I kneel down in front of her, placing my hands on her thighs. "We *have* to go on. There's nothing else to do. We've run out of food here, now. The choice is simple—we either stay here and die, or we move and put off dying for a few more weeks or months."

The silence in the room feels like an invasion of some kind: it robs us of our ability to communicate at any effective level. We have become strangers, travelling companions, little more than a couple of empty shells shuffling along in search of something that no longer exists.

"I miss the baby," she says, finally looking me in the eye. Her cheeks are wet. Her lips quiver. She has not mentioned the baby since she miscarried, and I was forced to lay the squawking undead thing to rest. I had hoped that she might have pushed all thoughts of the baby—no name, just "the baby"—from her mind to focus on the immediate business of survival. But no, if I am honest I have known all along that she could never forget what happened. I have watched her mind slowly crumple, like a deflating balloon, for months now, since it happened.

"We . . . we can't talk about that. Things are different now. There was no baby." I stand up and back away, appalled by my own lack of humanity, my utter inability to even discuss that terrible evening. "I'll get the other water bottles."

I leave her there in the darkness, clasping at her face with hands that have become talons. In the kitchen I pick up the two plastic bottles of well water and stuff them into the third small rucksack. Then I walk back through the house to the living room, where Coral is now standing in the shadows by the big boarded-up window, staring at the drapes.

"We need to go now," I say, not without compassion.

She turns to face me. Her tears have all dried up. She walks to my side, her face taut and filled with hate. We walk together to the front door, where I tug loose the timbers and open the door. I go first, scanning the area outside, and Coral follows me in silence, her eyes burning holes into my back.

We walk to the edge of the property, open the gate, and take the small road through the trees, passing within a few yards of the dead folk I shot earlier. A large crow is perched on the chest of one of the fallen corpses. It looks up as we pass by, and then lowers its beak into the mass of decayed flesh and bone to continue its scant meal.

Coral walks at my side, a constant companion through the darkness. She says nothing and I am glad of the breakdown in communication. There is no longer room for sentiment in this world. We must all be hard as stone, cold as a rifle barrel.

I hear no sounds of life as we continue along the road, the trees on either side of us stirring in a slight breeze. Dark clusters of leaves wave in the night, branches heave and creak, and somewhere deep inside the wood a bough breaks, falling to the ground with a soft thud.

The only light out here is that of the moon and the stars. The electricity supply failed years ago, and the only sources of power that remain now are from privately-operated generators. Soon there will be no one left to run them; the dead already outnumber the living, and it cannot be long until they dominate the planet.

I think again of those developing countries all those years ago, and the committees I sat on, the fund-raisers I organized to help them—starving people living in tumble-down shacks, entire families surviving for days on a handful of rice.

What of this Fourth World nation? What will happen when *their* food runs out, when there is nobody left alive for them to kill and eat? Will they simply rot down to nothing, the process accelerated because they have nothing to consume? What will the world be like when there are no living people left on its surface, when the only feet who tread this land are those of the long dead?

I glance again at Coral, but she is staring straight ahead, her eyes narrowed and her mouth a grim line in her face. Her hair is long and greasy, her teeth rotten and her breath stale. If I did not know her and simply caught sight of her out here, I would assume that she was one of them—one of the dead. Is this how I look as well?

When I think of what we have now become, I am filled with a sense of depression that seems almost pleasurable. At least it is some kind of emotional response. Previously I had thought myself incapable of even this small thing.

Coral takes a folded map from her back pocket and lifts it up to her face, where she can study its lines and symbols. Her pace slows while she examines the map, and I watch the trees for movement. I am uneasy that we have not yet encountered any of the dead. The fact that four of them were hanging around at the fence must mean that there are more nearby.

"There's a small community of some sort about three miles down the road. There might be some canned stuff in a cupboard someone forgot, or a stash in one of the houses." Her voice is hard, like stones rubbing up against each another in a shallow ditch.

"It's worth a try. If we don't find food soon, we're going to die."

"Is that all you care about? Survival at any cost?" The tone of her voice does not change—the question is asked in the same way she spoke about the town or village. "Existing no matter how much of you has already died?"

"To be honest, I don't even care about that anymore. It's just something to do, a target to aim for. We have two options . . . die now or die later. As soon as I stop seeing the point of dying later, I'll sit down on the ground and swallow a bullet from this rifle." I say all this without feeling. It is simply how it is, the way we have to be now. It is what we are.

She says no more on the subject. I can tell that she is angry but does not have the energy to rage against me and my stupid, ill-thought-out philosophy.

The trees are like dark shapes cut out of night by a child. They make a jagged black outline across the slightly lighter sky. The stars are tiny splatters against this backdrop, spilled paint from the same child's art box. At one time

I would have thought the sight beautiful, but now it is just another thing that I can see. None of these sights makes any kind of genuine impression upon me. I watch them without truly seeing them.

The road is long and straight. We might reach the end or we might not, it matters little in the scheme of things. But we must continue. Forward motion is all we have, all we live for. There is nothing else. I do not even care about the community Coral saw on the map. We will either get there or we won't, and there will be a forgotten few cans of food or there won't.

It matters not.

I see them as we approach a rusted, abandoned flatbed truck lying in a ditch. There are four or five of them, milling about in the middle of the road, walking in small circles like bored shoppers waiting at the back of a lengthy queue. We keep walking. There is no point in running. The only way is forward. I feel Coral tense at my side and hear the sharp intake of breath as she counts them. I unsling the rifle from my shoulder with practiced ease—an almost graceful movement that probably makes me look like I have handled firearms my entire life.

"This could get messy," she says, slipping the baseball bat from her pack. She picked it up in a sports shop in an out-of-town shopping center almost two months ago. It is already stained dark with blood.

I think what hurts Coral most is going against her natural instincts. She is a giver, a helper, and this new selfish mode of existence is something she finds it impossible to reconcile with her old identity as someone who could never stop giving. Back before the world began to die, it was she who convinced me to give my time to charitable causes, to find ways to help my fellow man—serving in late-night soup kitchens, advising in cramped offices for poorly funded causes. She won me over with her caring manner, and all the love she had to give scared the hell out of me and made me feel small in a world grown so large with troubles.

If she could, I think Coral would set up a charity for the dead. Bring-and-buy sales, sit-ins at the local council offices—equal rights for the undead. Instead, she is forced to bring the ones she meets to extinction with her baseball bat, or with the gun that I now bring around and point at the group in the road. Coral loathes herself for having become such a proficient assassin.

"Try not to let them suffer," she whispers, as she always does. Part of her problem is that she still sees them as human. She cannot divorce the living from the dead, and this, I fear, will be her undoing. It might also be mine.

As soon as they see us, the dead people begin to move in our direction.

None of them are too fresh, so their progress is slow and bewildered, like the movements of a group of ailing senior citizens in line for a free dinner. One of them, I notice, is sitting on the ground, and when he fails to stand I realize why. He has no legs, just a torso, and he pulls himself along on his hands, mouth open in a hungry leer.

I shoot him first, for purely aesthetic reasons. Then, striding forward like a gunslinger from some old Western movie, I begin to take the rest of them down, shot after shot after shot . . . They make strange sounds in their throats, as if they are attempting to speak—half-words, near-sentences that might in fact be nothing of the kind. I aim for the heads—nobody knows why the brains are the only sure targets—and watch as shattered bone dances white in the air, mixed with a red so dark it is almost black.

A female is the last of the bunch, looming towards us with skeletal arms outstretched and claw-like hands clutching. Slow-moving, yet lethal if she is allowed within touching distance, the female opens her mouth and hisses like a snake. Her face is mostly mottled skull, with barely any flesh left to cling to its sharp angles. Coral steps in and swings the bat, almost taking off the female's head with a single blow. The skull leans so far sideways on the decayed strings of neck muscle that one cheek touches an exposed shoulder blade. Coral swings again, this time completing the job. The skull parts with the ropy gristle, tumbling to the ground where the female's left foot, in mid-step, kicks it like a football. The body takes one more stride before going down like a sack of dried offal.

Coral is crying. She always cries when she kills. It is her charitable nature, the part of her old self that she is unwilling to lose. Unlike me, she prefers to remain human, and sees these tears as purification, a cleansing of her soul after committing such indecent acts to prolong our tedious survival.

"Come on," I say, worried that there are more of them lurking in the trees. They are mostly slow and very dumb—dim-witted and not even possessing enough intelligence to carry out a coordinated attack. But in enough numbers they can be dangerous. If enough of them attack at once, it is easy to be overpowered, and they will take you down and eat you. If they leave enough of you to get back up and walk, you will become one of them.

We reach the village at sunset. A small group of cottages lining one side of the road, with a post office and a corner shop flanked by concrete posts. It is barely large enough to be called a village at all, and there are no signs of life. The shop has already been looted, while the post office is a blackened heap of bricks and charred timbers. Whoever did this is long gone, and probably dead by now. I cannot recall the last time we saw a living person. There must be so few of us left.

Again I wonder what will happen when there are none, and if in fact Coral and I might be the last living people in the country, or perhaps in the world. The thought, rather than terrifying, is strangely comforting. When at last we are gone, I imagine the whole planet becoming that mythical Fourth World I considered earlier—filled with rotting corpses with nothing to eat. Unable to help themselves, their bodies falling apart and filling the earth with dust. Valleys of dust. Rivers of dust. Dust that will remain undisturbed for all eternity.

"It's the same as everywhere else. Nothing. No food. No people. Just . . . fucking . . . nothing . . . " Coral falls to her knees, dropping her bag, and pummels the ground with her fists, drawing blood. I watch in silence, unable to help her and unwilling to even try. She sprawls on her belly and wails, a verbalization of her inadequacy, her inability to help herself and anyone else. But can't she see that there is no one left to help?

I walk over to the little grocery shop and step through the shattered doorway. The shelves are empty, the counter smashed beyond repair. Refrigerators are overturned. A microwave lies disemboweled on the floor next to a pile of empty snack wrappers. The shop has been thoroughly cleaned-out of all supplies but for a single dented can of garden peas, which sits on a shelf like a bad joke. I imagine someone laughing as they placed it there, impressed by their own vicious humor.

I reach out and pick up the can. It is better than nothing, but only just. I stuff the can into my pack and leave the shop, wishing that I could remember how to cry. I am thinking of the baby—the stillborn whose eyes turned upon me and whose mouth opened to snap with toothless gums at my shaking fingers—and even then I am unable to connect with my emotions. Coral, however, is still on the ground, still weeping, her hands still bloodied and ragged. "I'll get some plasters," I say, reaching into my pack.

"Bastard!" she snarls, and I can only agree with her assessment.

Later that night, after a meal of cold peas and bitter memories, I awake in the darkness and the mattress beside me is cold and empty. I close my eyes and try to get back to sleep, but something whispers for my attention—a gentle breeze, perhaps through an open window, or a door that has not been shut when someone went outside.

I lift myself from the bed and put on my clothes—no rush, no hurry. Whatever has happened has happened. Whatever will be will be. There is no room now for sentimental thoughts and actions, for love and tenderness. These are the times of the closed hand, the hard fist, and each decision is tougher than the last. This is the Fourth World.

I pick up the gun and drift through the room like a ghost, slipping through the doorway to the upstairs landing of the small house at the end of the row—beyond the burned-out post office and the shop with its empty shelves and scattered furnishings. Standing at the top of the stairs, I can see that the front door is open. Pale moonlight spills across the welcome mat. That slight breezes trickles in through the gap.

I step gently down the stairs, through the doorway, and out into the night. The air is fresh and smells so very clean, like a promise of salvation. But I know not to trust such positive thoughts, and cast them gladly from my mind.

I walk along the narrow street—the houses and cottages to my left—my bare feet soundless on the cold, dense tarmac, the rifle held at port arms. There is sweat on my back, stones in my heart, and death is perched like a big black bird upon my shoulder.

She is there, in the darkness and moonlight, kneeling down in the middle of the road. Coral, my wife—a woman I can no longer allow myself to know and to love. Beyond the road, where she is kneeling, is a dark grove of trees. She is staring at the trees, at the blackness between their broad trunks, her arms held out as if in supplication, or welcome.

I move slowly, afraid to confront the moment, but realizing deep down that I cannot turn away. All I have is forward motion, momentum. When this ceases to be enough, I will slip the rifle barrel into my mouth and taste the darkness for one final time.

A dark bird plummets from the sky and perches on a nearby rock—it is a crow, possibly even the same one we saw yesterday, at the farm. Yesterday now seems so far away. For ten years we have kept up the charade, this pretence of life, and now it is all coming apart. The center is unable to hold. Ten years of shambling forward, never looking back, becoming even more dead than the dead things we are trying to outrun.

I continue walking towards the spot where my wife is on her knees, committing some self-created act of atonement. Darkness blooms around her, like a black mist, and I walk into it—a willing witness to whatever scene she has chosen to perform.

I can now see that Coral's body is shaking, as if she is having some kind of fit. But still her hands are raised, lifted to the heavens. As I get closer I see the figures—two of them, with more standing behind. Thin and wiry, shrouded in the darkness of the grove of trees. The one at the front is leaning down in front of my wife, his withered white hands buried in her stomach up to the wasted wrists to access the charity she is willingly giving. He pulls the moist red offerings from the cavity of her gut, lifting them to his lips and rubbing them across his chin as he begins to feast.

I raise the rifle and move in a tight curve, coming towards the scene from the side. It is this positioning that enables me to see that Coral is still alive and that she is weeping . . . and beneath the tears is a calm, beatific smile.

The worst thing, in Coral's case, was the fact that she had to turn against her true nature and become utterly selfish. But she could not do that—she was unable to put herself first. Always one for compassion, at the very last she is still giving of herself. My charitable wife . . . my little bleeding heart—the very organ which, even now, is being removed from her chest by dead hands and brought up to a grinning dead mouth.

Perhaps the baby was the final straw? Maybe my own failure to be there for her, putting my own survival first instead, was the final blow to her already weakened defenses?

And even now, right at the end, I continue to fail her. I fail her yet again.

Quickly I lift the rifle and take aim, then fire a single bullet into the back of her head. There will be no solidarity here, no politic with the dead. The back of her skull comes apart and her blood anoints those she wished to help, bathing them in her desire to share. For even at the moment of her death, Coral just can't stop giving.

I remain in the house for days afterwards, becoming gradually weaker with hunger. A sense of sorrow trickles slowly into me like water spilled on porous stone. At last there is a semblance of emotion. I miss Coral—her constant presence at my side—even though at the end she hated me.

I stay beneath the bedclothes after the second day, not even going downstairs to use the toilet. The bed begins to smell and the sheets are soaking wet, but I am long past caring. The sun rises and sets, the window lightens and darkens, my mind wanders. I remember green fields and children playing, couples walking hand-in-hand and the promise of a future that was not dead . . .

I lose count of the days, slipping between sleeping and wakefulness as easily as closing my eyes. The room is a mirage and the walls seem to shimmer. When I hear the noise downstairs—a crashing splintering sound—I suspect that it is the dead breaking in to finish me off. At last they have found me. I hope they choke on my gristle and that my bones shatter and stab them in the brain.

Footsteps on the stairs—slow, uneven, stumbling. The door opens . . . the room goes dark.

When I open my eyes again I am no longer alone. There is a man standing by the bed. He is not dead. His hair is brown and clean, and the overalls he wears are freshly washed. I can tell by the overpowering smell of soap that he has been well looked after. I stare at him, waiting for something to happen.

"How do you feel?"

I can barely answer. "Bad."

"I'm sorry that we couldn't come sooner. We've been watching you for days, weighing up the situation and waiting for the area to clear. To be safe." His face barely moves as he speaks. There is a name-tag on his chest pocket, but I am too tired to read what it says.

"Who are you?" I whisper.

"I'm part of a collective. We have been hiding out for years, stockpiling supplies. Everything we have is shared equally between the members of the group." His eyes blink.

"What do you want?"

"We can offer you food and shelter . . . a life, of sorts. All you need to do is work with us, become *one of us*." His hands clench at his sides. "Help us to re-build something good."

"How long have you been watching us?"

"A few days. We had to be sure . . . be safe."

"Did you see what happened to my wife?"

He pauses before answering. "I'm sorry. I wish we could've come earlier, but it wasn't safe. I'm sorry."

Sorry. I have never met anyone so sorry in my whole life.

"Not. Safe." I stare at him, knowing that this has all come much too late to mean anything. "And you have food and shelter?"

"Yes. We have those things, and much more." He lifts his left hand, which clasps a small sack that I had not noticed before. Cans and bottles rattle and sing as he shakes it at arm's length, almost teasing me.

My response surprises me almost as much as him.

"I don't want your . . . fucking . . . *charity.*" I pull down the bedclothes and use the rifle hidden beneath the stained sheets to shoot him in the head. I smile as the blood sprays and his knees buckle, toppling him to the floor. The sack rolls from his lifeless fingers, spilling its precious contents across the floorboards.

After a long time I finally get out of bed and cross the room. There is food and water and, even better, medicine. It is no longer charity—now that he is unable to offer these things freely, it is simply so much found goods. Now they are mine.

Days later, after the food and the water and the drugs, I am feeling much better. My mind is clear and my body has regained some strength. I still cannot think of a good enough reason to swallow a bullet, so instead I will go looking for the man's comrades. And when I find them, I will show them what it means to be sorry.

Only then can I rest—when the world truly belongs to the dead.

Gary McMahon's fiction has appeared in magazines and anthologies in the U.K. and U.S and has been reprinted in both The Mammoth Book of Best New Horror *and* Year's Best Horror and Fantasy. *He is the British-Fantasy-Award-nominated author of* Rough Cut, All Your Gods Are Dead, Dirty Prayers, How to Make Monsters, Rain Dogs, Different Skins, Pieces of Midnight, Hungry Hearts, *and has edited anthology* We Fade to Grey. *Forthcoming are several reprints in "Best of" anthologies, a story in the mass market anthology* The End of the Line, *novels* Pretty Little Dead Things *and* Dead Bad Things *from Angry Robot, and* The Concrete Grove *trilogy from Solaris. His Web site: www.garymcmahon.com/.*

McMahon's story brings up the question of just who the monsters are.

Douglas E. Winters once said: "A deft morality play for television, Rod Serling's "The Monsters Are Due on Maple Street," warned of the dangers of seeking the monstrous in skin other than our own. Just as Jane Austen's *Northanger Abbey* (1818) signaled the certain sunset of the gothic by critiquing its preoccupation with the external, Serling's simple scenario, in which everyday people hasten with McCarthyite fervor to condemn each other as monsters, underscored the fragile reign of the creature . . . Now that we have seen the monsters—now that they have arrived on Maple Street—we have learned that certain truth: They are us."

The Last Supper

Scott Edelman

Walter's mind was at one time rich with emotions other than hunger, but those feelings had long since fallen away. They'd dropped from his being like the flesh, now absent, which had once kept the wind from whistling through his cheeks.

Gone was happiness. Gone greed. Gone anger and love and joy.

Now there was but hunger, and hunger only.

As Walter, his joints as stiff as his brain, staggered through the deserted streets of what had until recently been one of the most heavily populated cities in the world, that hunger burned through him, becoming his entire reason for being.

Hunger had not been an issue for him at first. During the early weeks of his rebirth, there had been enough food for all. The streets had teemed with meat. The survivors hadn't all evacuated at once. There were always plenty of the foolish lingering, which meant that he had little competition for the hunt. Those initial weeks of his renewed time on Earth had been about as easy as that of a bear smacking salmon skyward from a boiling river during spawning season.

Those days were gone. Now there was not even a faint whiff of food left to tease him from a distance. The streets were filled with an army of the hungry above, devourers who no longer had objects of desire upon which to fulfill their single purpose. For weeks, or maybe months, or perhaps even years—for his sense of time had been burned away along with most of his sense of self—walking the streets was akin to wandering through a maze of mirrors and seeing reflected back nothing more than duplicates of who he was, of what he had become—a bag of soiled clothing and shredded flesh, animated by a dead, dead soul.

Staggering through a deserted square that lay in the former heart of the city, stumbling by shattered storefronts and overturned buses, he sought out flesh with a hunger grown so strong that it was less a conscious thought than a tropism born out of whatever affliction had brought him and the rest of the human race to this state. His senses, torn and ragged though they were, radiated out in search of fresh meat, as they had every day since he had been reborn.

Nothing.

No scent filled his sunken nose, no sound his remaining ear. Yet he kept surging forward, sweeping the city, borne fruitlessly ahead out of a bloodlust beyond thought. Until this day, when what was left of his tongue began to salivate.

Blood. Somewhere out there was blood. Something with a pulse still radiated life nearby.

Whatever called to him was barely alive itself, and hidden, and quiet, but from its refuge its essence rang like a shout. Drawn by the vibrations of its life force, he turned from the square onto a broad avenue and then onto a narrow side street, knocking aside any barriers blocking the path to his blood—*his* blood now. He righted an overturned trashcan (but his promised meal was not hidden there), kicked up soot as he walked through the remnants of an ancient bonfire (but no, nothing there, either), and kept moving forward until he arrived at a large black car flipped over on one side against a light pole, its roof split open.

He pushed his way through a carpet of broken glass and peered down into what remained of the driver's side door. He touched the steering wheel and a charge of energizing bloodlust coursed through him. Though the wheel's leather skin had long ago been peeled away, he could feel the blood that had blossomed there right after impact, still feel the throbbing of its vanished presence. But he knew, if he could be said to know anything, that ghostly blood could not alone have been the call that he had heard, for after all the carnal scavenging that had occurred, no remnants of the accident could possibly still exist. The tug on his attention had to be more than that. Something was here, waiting for him.

Or hiding from him.

In the back of the tilted car, a rustling came from under shredded remnants of seat stuffing. From beneath the mound of makeshift bedding, confused eyes peered out at him. Walter filled with a surge of lust, and dropped atop the creature. A dog yelped—only a dog, and not a man, a man whose scream would strengthen him—and exploded into frantic wriggling, but there was no way the animal could get away from the steel cage of Walter's hands. Seeing the nature of his victim's species, the lust was gone. There was no longer anything appealing about this prey.

But his hunger remained.

The dog whimpered as Walter shifted his fingers to surround its neck and cradle its head in his hands. Its bright eyes pleaded and teased, but Walter had learned that the promise of satiation there was pointless. He slowly tightened his grip anyway, and the animal split in two, its head popping off to drop at his feet. He held the oozing neck up to his lips, and drank.

The blood was warm. The blood was salty.

The blood was useless.

His hunger still raged, his needs unsatisfied. What he required could only be provided by the blood of human, and not animal, intelligence. He let the dog fall, where it was immediately forgotten. There had to be something more still left on the face of the Earth. He moved on, clumsy but determined, his hunger once more an all-consuming creature. It wasn't that he needed that flesh to live. Its presence in his leaky stomach was never what powered him. The strength of his desire was unrelated to any practical end.

He hungered, and so he needed to hunt. That was what he did. That was what he was.

He returned to endless days and nights spent walking the length and breadth of his island, but his prowling proved useless. Though he sniffed out the useless life of other dogs, and rats, and the last few surviving animals who had somehow not starved to death unfed at the zoo, nothing human called to him. The city was empty.

One day, much later, he paused in the harbor, and looked west toward the rest of his country, a nation that he had never seen in life. He listened for the call of something faint and distant, waited as the evidence of his senses washed over him. In an earlier time, he would have closed his eyes to focus, but his eyes no longer had lids to close.

The static of the city's life, quivering nearby, no longer rose up to distract him. There was no close cacophony muffling him from the rest of the continent, just a few remaining notes vibrating out from points west. He began to walk toward them, pulled by the memory of flesh.

He dragged his creaking body along the shoreline until he came to a bridge, and then he crossed it, picking his way past snapped cables, overturned cars, and rifts through which could be seen the raging river below. He had no map, and needed none, any more than a baby needed a map to her mother's breast, or a flower needed a map to the sun.

Concrete canyons gave way to ones born of rock, and time passed, light and dark dancing to change places as they had since the beginning of time, though he did not number the days they marked. The count did not matter. What mattered was that the sounds he heard, the stray pulsings in the distance, increased in volume as he moved.

His trek was not an easy one. He was used to concrete jungles, not the forest primeval, and yet that is where he was forced to travel, for life, if it wanted to stay alive, stayed far from highways as well. As he slipped on wet leaves and tumbled over fallen logs, he could feel an occasional beacon of information snuffed out, as another life was silenced, another slab of meat digested. Walter was not the only one on the prowl, and somehow he knew that if he did not hurry, the hunt would soon be over for him forever. As weeks passed, he could hear what had once been a constant chorus diminish into a plaintive solo. As Walter could pick out no other competing chorus, perhaps it was the final solo.

Its pull grew yet stronger, and as the flames of its sensations flickered higher, rubbing his desire raw, he moved even more quickly, stumbling lamely through a hilly forest.

Until one stumble became more than just a stumble. His ankle caught on an exposed root, and he then felt himself falling. He fell against what appeared to be a carpet of leaves, which exploded and scattered when he hit them, allowing him to fall some more.

From the bottom of a well twice his height, he looked up to a small patch of sky, and saw the first face in an eternity that was, amazingly, not like looking in a mirror. The flesh of the man's face was pink and red, and as he breathed, puffs of steam came from his lips.

Then those lips, surrounded by a beard, moved, and a rough voice, grown unused to forming the sounds of human speech, said wearily, "Hello."

Walter had not heard another's voice in a long while, and that last time it had been molded in a scream.

Seeing the man up there, looking smug and seeming to feel himself safe, filled Walter with rage—the first time in ages anything but pure hunger filled him. He slammed his fists wildly against the muddy walls of his hole, unconsciously seeking a handhold that could bring him to the waiting feast above, but there was nothing he could grasp. As he struggled to beat out grips with which to climb, his flesh grew flayed against sharp stones and splintered roots, yet he did not tire. He would have gone on forever like that, a furious engine of need, had not the man above begun dropping further words to him down below. They were not frightened words or angry words or begging words, the only sort that Walter was lately used to hearing, so their tone confused him. He wasn't sure what kind of words they were, and so he paused in his fury to listen.

"I've been waiting for you," said the man, his head and shoulders taunting Walter in the slice of sky above. "We have a lot to talk about, you and I. Well . . . actually . . . *I* have a lot to talk about. All you have to do is listen. Which is good, because I have learned from others of your kind that all you are capable of doing is listening, and barely that."

The man extended his arm over the hole. He rolled up his left sleeve, and then used his right hand to remove a large knife from a scabbard strapped to one thigh.

"This should help you to listen," he said.

Walter could understand none of the words. But even he understood what happened next. The blade sliced the flesh of the man's inner forearm, and bright blood flowed across his skin, spilled into the crook of his elbow, and then dripped in freefall. At the bottom of the pit, Walter tilted his head back like a man celebrating a spring rain, the stiff muscles in his neck creaking from the effort. He caught the short stream of drops on the back of his shredded throat.

"That's all I can spare you for now," the man said, pressing gauze against his voluntary wound and rolling his sleeve back down. "But then, you don't like to hear that, do you?"

Walter had no idea what he liked or didn't like to hear. All he knew was the hunger. That brief taste had caused it to surge, multiplying the pain and power of his desire. He roared, flailing wildly at the walls of his prison.

"If you can only shut up," said the man, "you'll get more. We need to come to an agreement, and then, only then, there'll be more. Can you understand that?"

Walter responded by throwing himself against the earthen walls of his narrow prison, but his response gained him nothing. As he battered his fists against the side of the pit, three of his fingers snapped off and dropped to the uneven floor. As he struggled more franticly, those body parts were ground beneath his feet like fat worms.

"This isn't going to work," muttered the man above, who began to weep. "I must have gone mad."

He crumpled back out of Walter's field of vision. Though he could still sense the brimming bag of meat above, its disappearance from his line of sight lowered Walter's rage, and he subsided slightly. His hunger still overwhelmed him, but he was no longer overtaken by the mindless urge to flail. He howled without ceasing at the changing clouds above, at the sun, and at the moon, until his captor reappeared, suddenly to him, and sat on the lip of the hole. The man let his feet dangle over the edge. Walter leapt as high as his dusty muscles would let him, and tried to snatch the man's heels, but he could not reach them. He tried once again, still falling short. The man snorted. Or laughed. Or cried. Walter couldn't quite tell which.

"You can't kill me," the man said, peering down through his knees. "Well, you *can*, but you shouldn't. Because once you kill me, it might be all over. Can you understand that? It's been years since I saw another human being. Do you realize that? I may be it."

Walter growled in response, and continued to batter against the sides of his prison.

"Damn," moaned the man. "What do I have to do to get your attention?"

Walter saw him bring out the knife again. The man looked at the line on his arm which had now become a long, thin scab, and then down below, where Walter's shed fingers were being crushed. The man shook his head, and then pulled his upper body back so that all Walter could see were dangling feet.

"This time," the man said, "I've got to do whatever it takes."

Then Walter heard a dull thud, one accompanied by a sharp intake of breath and a visible jerking of the man's legs. When the man leaned forward again, a handkerchief was wrapped around one hand. He used his good hand to dangle a bloody finger out over the pit.

"Listen to me now," the man said. Walter, frozen, stared at the offered digit. "I may be your last meal for the rest of your eternal life. I may be the last human left on earth. Try to get that through your undead head."

Then the man let the finger drop.

Walter leapt and caught it in midair. He had it in his mouth before his feet hit the ground. He chewed so fiercely that he ate his lips away, and many of his teeth popped from their sockets. If the man were continuing to speak, Walter would never have known it, as the sounds of his feasting as he attacked his small snack echoed deafeningly. Silence did not return until after the digit was devoured, and only then did Walter look skyward again.

"I want to live," said the man. "I don't want this to be the end of the human race. We have to make some sort of peace, you and I. We have to reach some sort of an agreement. That's why I moved out here and filled these hills with pits like this one. I knew that your kind would eventually sweep out from the cities and find me even here in the middle of nowhere, and I wanted to be ready for you.

"You have to tell the others. You have to let them know. Know that I'm the last. That if you just pluck me off the face of the earth, there will be nothing left, only eternal hunger. Is that something you can understand? Is that something you can communicate to the others? If so, that way they'll let me live. They'll let the human race live."

What the man said was meaningless, as Walter was for the most part beyond words. He knew the word hunger, though, plucking it from the forest of words that were being dropped on him. But that was about it. He could not perceive the man's message, could not possibly pass it on to others, for as far as his consciousness allowed, even if it were capable of containing such a message, there *were* no others. There was only Walter, Walter below and his food above—and the food was not getting any closer.

The man pulled his legs up from the hole, and for a moment it looked to Walter as if he was leaving, but instead, there was another thud. Then the man poked his head over the lip, even closer this time, for instead of sitting on the lip, the man was peering down while lying on his stomach. Then the man brought his hands around to show another dangling finger to Walter. Walter leapt unsuccessfully as he waited for the flesh to be dropped.

"I can see that this is the only thing you will understand. Do you see now? If you eat me, then it will all be over. Eternal hunger, with nothing more ever waiting at the other end to quench it. But if we can make a deal, I can help you feed for a long while. I can give you blood, and even some flesh from time to time."

The man dropped his finger, and this time, Walter caught it directly in his mouth. His teeth began crunching on it immediately, but unlike before, he did not take his eyes off his captor. Walter looked up at the blood soaking through the handkerchief in the man's other hand. The man noticed Walter's gaze, and loosened the cloth. He dangled his damaged hand down into the pit, and shook it. The handkerchief unwrapped slowly and dropped softly down. Walter caught it and tossed it into his mouth. He sucked on the blooming stain, the corners of the handkerchief hanging out of his mouth and down his chin.

"Do we have a deal?" asked the man. His eyes were wide, and he was so caught up in his hope that he did not immediately pull back his extended hand. Filled with lust at the sight of the wet wounds inflicted there, Walter ran to the wall and leapt up toward them, wedging his feet in the damp mud of the pit wall before the man could yank himself back. Walter's remaining fingers locked around the man's remaining finger, and with his dead weight, Walter started pulling the man, sliding him forward so that more of his body hung over the edge.

"No!" shouted the man. "I'm the last man on Earth! You can't do this! Without me, you'll have nothing! Don't you understand?"

But Walter did not understand, not really, and his screaming and scrambling did little to slow his descent into the hole. Walter pulled him down mercilessly—for he had no mercy, only hunger—and at last, after far too long, the hunger was allowed to run free. Walter began with the man's lips, silencing the urgent pleas, and then he gnawed his way deep into the man's chest, cracking his ribs and burrowing into his heart. Walter's face grew slick with blood as he gorged himself. It had been far too long since he had fed this well, and even though he remained trapped at the bottom of a pit, he had no space for tomorrow, no thought of saving anything aside for a future day. He savored the flesh and sucked the bones, and then . . . then it was all gone much too soon.

Momentarily sated, Walter looked up at clouds, sniffing out the universe. He listened for the pulse of the planet, and discovered in that instant that his jailor had been correct, though as Walter had not understood the meaning of what the man had been babbling to him, he did not in fact realize that was what he was doing. But indeed, there was no other movement of blood in the world. No others were left.

All that existed for Walter now was a few square feet of ground, his dirt wall, and the sky above. Time passed. Walter could not say whether it passed quickly or slowly, as he had no true conception of time, just the fact that the opening above regularly darkened and lightened again. During the days, his view was occasionally altered by a bird flitting by, and at night there was the occasional flash of a falling star. Hunger returned and was his constant companion, but there was no longer any point in raging.

Mud and leaves and the detritus of time slowly filled the spot on where he stood. As he paced from side to side, he rose a little each day, so gradual as to be almost imperceptible. He did not realize what was happening until enough time had passed that he was finally high enough to peer over each the lip. He pulled himself up to the surface and stood seeing the whole world again for the first time in ages, rather than just a tunnel-vision picture of the sky . . . and the difference didn't really matter to him. For whether he was trapped in a hole or free on land again, nothing had changed. His only companion for now and forever more was his hunger, and since he could no longer smell anything out there with which to quench it, since the world was now a dead beast inhabited only by others of his kind, it mattered little where he spent the rest of eternity.

Strangely, the sky seemed filled with falling stars. And yet, they did not behave the way such things were meant to behave. Instead of vanishing out quickly as had the living human race, the bright spots cross-crossed the sky like embers that refused to die. During the day, the stars still shone, another anomaly he no longer had the brain power to consider. Walter moved on without a destination.

He wandered the world aimlessly, but only until he noticed that the stars themselves were no longer moving aimlessly. The stars were on the move in a purposeful manner, and as he gazed into the sky, he knew where they were heading. With the memory of the last man on Earth forever branded on his lips, he followed the path they made, moving back east across a country that was continuing to crumble, that was transforming from civilization into debris.

The bridge into the city, when he saw it again after what had been hundreds of years, had collapsed into the river. He had to pick his way over floating rubble, still bound together by cables, to move from shore to shore. He walked the city streets once more, continuing to watch the sky. When so many stars filled the sky that it seemed impossible to fit any more, their trajectories shifted. When night fell this time, Walter could make out more clearly that they were carving concentric circles in the sky. He walked beneath the heart of them, his hunger positioning him there. Others of his kind joined him.

As he watched, a single star began to drop, pulling itself away from the carefully choreographed dance in the sky, becoming more than just a speck, gaining dimension as it fell. By the time it reached the buckled pavement on which Walter stood, it had grown into a globe several stories high. The fact that it floated there, sprouting legs on which it came to rest, had no affect on Walter. He sensed only dead machinery, and felt nothing, not even curiosity.

When the outlines of a door appeared and then opened, that all changed. As a walkway eased its way out from the opening to touch the ground, Walter could feel again that old familiar tingling which had been missing for so long.

A tall, attenuated creature walked down the ramp, followed by a hovering cylindrical machine half again as tall. The visitor, its two arms and two legs garbed in a soft silver, stepped off the ramp into what for it was a new world, and then walked toward Walter and his brethren. Walter, agitated by a humanoid form stinking of the raw stuff of life, rushed forward, only to thud against an invisible wall that surrounded the giant globe. Flesh was close, so close, and Walter was enraged. He could not comprehend why this thing was not already being torn apart by his remaining teeth.

Walter roared, and his deafening anger was soon joined by the keening of the other zombies who ringed the ship. The being removed a helmet, revealing a face which, though off in its proportions, contained all the right elements—eyes, nose, mouth and so on—that signified humanity. This only served to fill Walter with a further fury. The alien surveyed the crowd, looking at the crescent of the undead with all-too-human eyes. He then held a slender hand out toward Walter, who suddenly found himself able to surge forward ahead of the others. Arms outstretched, he raced toward the flesh—his flesh—but stopped short in front of his meal, frozen as if encased in metal bands. Walter struggled to close that final gap, but could not.

Suddenly, Walter was floating a few feet off the rubble. He tilted back, both alien and globe vanishing from his field of vision to be replaced by the sky. He could see the moving stars pause in their flight. The alien stepped closer, and Walter was overcome by the need to open his mouth, to gnaw, to rend, but his body no longer followed the command of those needs. The metal cylinder, which had trailed closely behind the visitor, tilted on its side and floated to Walter's feet. It slid over Walter, engulfing him, encasing him from head to what remained of his toes. He was trapped once more. This time, whether or not his actions would have been as futile as before, he was unable to even bang against the sides of his prison.

The patch of metal before Walter's face cleared to transparency.

"Hello," the alien said, in a voice unused to forming the sounds of human speech. It leaned in close to Walter. "We have traveled a long way in search of our ancient cousins."

It waved its thin hands over the exterior of the cylinder, and sequential lights flashed, a rainbow coursing over Walter's mottled skin. He struggled to escape their glow, but regardless of his rage, he moved in his mind only. When the colors ceased, his rage continued on.

"How sad," said the alien. "Our cousins are still here, and yet . . . they are gone. They are all gone."

The words were meaningless to Walter, barely even heard over the angry voices in his head which called him to feed. Then the cylinder pulled away, and Walter found himself upright again, his muscles once more his own. He started to leap forward, but as he was in midair, the strange creature waved its arms, and Walter was back with the others. His momentum there still carried him to complete his trajectory, and he slammed against the invisible shield.

The visitor walked back up the ramp, the cylinder floating by its side, their metal path retracting back into the ship. The creature paused in the doorway and turned. It was still looking toward Walter as the door closed and the force field died. Walter rushed the craft, but it rose effortlessly back into the sky before he could beat himself against its glittering sides.

The bright stars which had up until then formed circles in the sky vanished, but Walter barely noticed the emptiness above. So great was his lust for flesh that he was driven to return immediately to his hungry wandering, where he found nothing but that his hunger increased. His hunt through the rubble of humanity would prove fruitless, for his senses never again tingled to tease his immortal desire.

The sun and the moon continued to trade places, but no stars ever returned to move through the sky, and Walter's hunger, which left no room for any other emotions, never faded—

—at least not until, eons later, Earth's close and constant star expanded to fill his world with fire and erase his hunger forever.

Scott Edelman *has published more than seventy-five short stories in anthologies such as* The Solaris Book of New Science Fiction, Crossroads: Tales of the Southern Literary Fantastic, MetaHorror, Moon Shots, Mars Probes, *and* Forbidden Planets, *and in magazines such as* Postscripts, The Twilight Zone, Absolute Magnitude, Science Fiction Review, *and* Fantasy Book. *His first short story collection,* These Words Are Haunted, *appeared in 2001. What*

Will Come After, a complete collection of his zombie fiction, was released May 2010 by PS Publishing. He has been a Stoker Award finalist five times, in the categories of both Short Story and Long Fiction. Additionally, Edelman currently works for the Syfy Channel as the Editor of Blastr *(formerly known as* SCI FI Wire). *He was the founding editor of* Science Fiction Age, *which he edited during its entire eight-year run. He has been a four-time Hugo Award finalist for Best Editor.*

As you can probably guess from the existence of a collection of them, Edelman has written quite a few zombie stories. This one particularly appealed because it comes close to being a parable of sorts—or several. To quote an ecclesiastical source:

> The word *parable* (Hebrew *mashal*; Syrian *mathla*, Greek *parabole*) signifies in general a comparison, or a parallel, by which one thing is used to illustrate another. It is a likeness taken from the sphere of real, or sensible, or earthly incidents, in order to convey an ideal, or spiritual, or heavenly meaning. As uttering one thing and signifying something else, it is in the nature of a riddle (Hebrew *khidah*, Gr. *ainigma* or *problema*) and has therefore a light and a dark side ("dark sayings," Wisdom 8:8; Sirach 39:3), it is intended to stir curiosity and calls for intelligence in the listener . . . [Barry, William. "Parables." *The Catholic Encyclopedia*. Vol. 11. New York: Robert Appleton Company, 1911.]

Parable or not, Edelman's "last supper" is, indeed, our final taste of zombie fiction. Hope you've enjoyed the meal!

Publication History

Francesca Lia Block, "Farewell, My Zombie" © 2009. First publication: *Black Clock 10*, Spring/Summer 2009. Reprinted by permission of the author.

Gary A. Braunbeck, "Glorietta" © 2008. First Publication: *The World is Dead*, ed. Kim Paffenroth (Permuted Press, 2008). Reprinted by permission of the author.

Max Brooks, "The Great Wall: A Story from the Zombie War" © 2007. First Publication: *Dark Delicacies II: Fear: More Original Tales of Terror and the Macabre by the World's Greatest Horror Writers,* eds. Del Howison and Jeff Gelb (Running Press, 2007). Reprinted by permission of the author.

Tobias Buckell, "Trinkets" © 2001. First Publication: *The Book of All Flesh*, ed. James Lowder (Eden Studios, 2001). Reprinted by permission of the author.

Steve Duffy, "Lie Still, Sleep Becalmed" © 2007. First Publication: *At Ease with the Dead: New Tales of the Supernatural and Macabre,* eds. Barbara and Christopher Roden (Ash-Tree Press, 2007). Reprinted by permission of the author.

Andy Duncan, "Zora and the Zombie" © 2004. First Publication: *Scifi.com,* February 2004. Reprinted by permission of the author.

Scott Edelman, "The Last Supper" © 2003. First Publication: *The Book of Final Flesh*, ed. James Lowder (Eden Studios, 2003). Reprinted by permission of the author.

Neil Gaiman, "Bitter Grounds" © 2003. First Publication: *Mojo: Conjure Stories*, ed. Nalo Hopkinson (Mysterious Press, 2003). Reprinted by permission of the author.

Nik Houser, "First Kisses From Beyond the Grave" © 2006. First Publication: *Gargoyle Magazine #51*, 2006. Reprinted by permission of the author.

Brian Keene, "Three Scenes from the End of the World" © 2010. Originally published as three separate stories as "The Ties That Bind" in *Unhappy Endings* (Delirium Press, 2009), "The Viking Plays Patty Cake," and "Family Reunion" in *The Rising: Selected Scenes From the End of the World* (Delirium Press, 2008). Reprinted by permission of the author.

Alice Sola Kim, "Beautiful White Bodies" © 2009. First Publication: *Strange Horizons*, Part One: December 7, 2009; Part Two: December 14, 2009. Reprinted by permission of the author.

Joe R. Lansdale, "Deadman's Road" © 2007. First Publication: *Subterranean*, Spring 2007. Reprinted by permission of the author.

Kelly Link, "The Hortlak" © 2003. *The Dark: New Ghost Stories,* ed. Ellen Datlow (Tor, 2003). Reprinted by permission of the author.

Tim Lebbon, *Naming of Parts* © 2000. First Publication: *Naming of Parts* (PS Publishing, U.K., 2000). Reprinted by permission of the author.

Gary McMahon, "Dead to the World" © 2009. First Publication: *The Dead That Walk*, ed. Stephen Jones (Ulysses Press, 2009). Reprinted by permission of the author.

David Prill, "Dating Secrets of the Dead" © 2002. First Publication: *The Magazine of Fantasy & Science Fiction,* June 2002. Reprinted by permission of the author.

Kit Reed, "The Zombie Prince" © 2004. First Publication: *The Magazine of Fantasy & Science Fiction,* June 2004. Reprinted by permission of the author.

David J. Schow, "Obsequy" © 2006. *Subterranean #3*, 2006. Reprinted by permission of the author.

David J. Schow, "Introduction" © 2010. Originally published as the "Introduction" and "Afterword" of *Zombie Jam* (Subterranean Press, 2003). Reprinted by permission of the author.

Michael Marshall Smith, "The Things He Said" © 2007. First Publication: *Travellers in Darkness: The Souvenir Book of the World Horror Convention 2007*. Reprinted by permission of the author.

Kevin Veale, "Twisted" © 2009. First Publication: *Weird Tales #354*, Fall 2009. Reprinted by permission of the author.

Tim Waggoner, "Disarmed and Dangerous" © 2009. First Publication: *Spells of the City*, eds. Jean Rabe and Martin H. Greenberg (DAW, 2009).

David Wellington, "Dead Man's Land" © 2009. First Publication: *The World is Dead*, ed. Kim Paffenroth (Permuted Press, 2008). Reprinted by permission of the author.

About the Editor

Paula Guran is the editor of Pocket Book's Juno fantasy imprint and nonfiction editor for *Weird Tales* magazine. In an earlier life she produced weekly e-mail newsletter *DarkEcho* (winning two Bram Stoker Awards, an International Horror Guild Award award, and a World Fantasy Award nomination), edited *Horror Garage* magazine (earning another IHG and a second World Fantasy nomination), and has contributed reviews, interviews, and articles to numerous professional publications. She's also done a great deal of other various and sundry work in sf/f/h publishing. Earlier anthologies Guran has edited include *Embraces, Best New Paranormal Romance*, and *Best New Romantic Fantasy 2*. In addition to this anthology, she recently edited the first of the new *Year's Best Dark Fantasy and Horror* anthology series for Prime Books. Forthcoming anthologies for Prime include *Vampires: The Recent Undead* and *Halloween!* By the end of 2010 she will also have edited four dozen published novels and three collections.